CW00557201

The Edgar Wallace
Super Pack

Hardcover ISBN 13: 978-1-5154-4244-8
Trade Paperback ISBN 13: 978-1-5154-4245-5

The Edgar Wallace Super Pack

by Edgar Wallace

The Dark Eyes of London
The Vampire of Wembley:
and Other Tales of Murder, Mystery, and Mayhem
The Face in the Night
The Worst Man in the World

The Dark Eyes of London

Contents

Larry Holt in Paris

LARRY HOLT sat before the Café de la Paix, watching the stream of life flow east and west along the Boulevard des Italiens. The breath of spring was in the air; the trees were bursting into buds of vivid green; the cloud-flecked skies were blue; and a flood of golden sunshine brought out the colours of the kiosks, and gave an artistic value even to the flaring advertisements. Crowded motor-buses rumbled by, little taxis dashed wildly in and out of the traffic, to the mortal peril of unsuspecting pedestrians.

A gendarme, with cloak over his shoulder, stood in a conventional attitude on the kerb, his hand behind him, staring at nothing, and along the sidewalk there were hurrying bareheaded girls, slow-moving old men, and marching poilus. Itinerant vendors of wares loafed past the tables of the café, dusky-faced Arabs with their carpets on their arms, seedy-looking men who hawked bundles of picture post cards and would produce, at the slightest encouragement, cards which were not for the public gaze. All these things and people were a delight to Larry Holt, who had just returned from Berlin after four years' strenuous work in France and Germany, and felt in that holiday spirit to which even the mind of a detective will ascend.

The position occupied by Larry Holt was something of a mystery to the officials of Scotland Yard. His rank was Inspector, his work was the administrative work of a Commissioner; and it was generally understood that he was in the line for the first vacant assistant commissionership that came along. The question of his rank, of his prospects, did not trouble Larry at that particular moment. He sat there, absorbing the sweetness of spring with every breath he drew. His good-looking face was lit up with the sheer joy of living, and there was in his heart a relief, a sense of rest, which he had not experienced for many a long day.

He revealed himself a fairly tall man when he rose, after paying the waiter, and strolled round the corner to his hotel. It was a slow progress he made, his hands in his pockets, his soft felt hat at the back of his head, a half-smile on his parted lips as he gripped a long black cigarette holder between his white teeth.

He came into the busy vestibule of the hotel, the one spot in Paris where people hustle and rush, where bell-boys really run, and even the phlegmatic Briton seems in a frantic hurry, and he was walking towards the elevator, when, through the glass door leading to the palm court, he saw a man in an attitude of elegant repose, leaning back in a big chair and puffing at a cigar.

Larry grinned and hesitated. He knew this lean-faced man, so radiantly attired, his fingers and cravat flashing with diamonds, and in a spirit of mischief he passed through the swing doors and came up to the lounger.

"If it isn't my dear old friend Fred!" he said softly.

Flash Fred, Continental crook and gambler, leapt to his feet with a look of alarm at the sight of this unexpected visitation.

"Hullo, Mr. Holt!" he stammered. "You're the last person in the world I expected to see——"

"Or wanted to see," said Larry, shaking his head reproachfully. "What prosperity! Why, Fred, you're all dressed up like a Christmas tree."

Flash Fred grinned uncomfortably, but made a brave show of indifference.

"I'm going straight now, Mr. Holt," he said.

"Liar you are, and liar you will always be," said Larry without heat.

"I swear to you on the Book——" began Fred vigorously.

"If," said Larry without resentment, "you stood between your dead aunt and your failing uncle, and took an oath on Foxe's Book of Martyrs, I wouldn't believe you."

He gazed admiringly at Fred's many adornments, at the big pin in his tie, at the triple chain of gold across his neatly tailored waistcoat, at his white spats and patent shoes, and then brought his eyes back to the perfectly brushed hair.

"You look sweet," he said. "What is the game? Not," he added, "that I expect you to tell me, but it must be a pretty prosperous game, Fred."

The man licked his dry lips.

"I'm in business," he said.

"Whose business are you in now?" asked Larry, interested. "And how did you get in? With a jemmy or a stick of dynamite? That's a new line for you,

Fred. As a rule, you confine yourself strictly to picking crumbs of gold off the unwary youth of the land—and," he added significantly, "in picking the pockets of the recently deceased."

The man's face went red.

"You don't think I had anything to do with that murder in Montpellier?" he protested heatedly.

"I don't think you shot the unfortunate young man," admitted Larry, "but you were certainly seen bending over his body and searching his clothes."

"For identification," said Fred virtuously. "I wanted to find out who did it."

"You were also seen talking to the man who did it," said Larry remorsefully. "An old lady, a Madame Prideaux, looking out of her bedroom window, saw you holding him and then saw you let him go. I presume he 'dropped.'?"

Fred said nothing at first. He hated a pretended gentleman who descended to the vulgarity of employing the word "drop" for "bribe."

"That's two years ago, Mr. Holt," he said. "I don't see why you should rake that thing up against me. The examining magistrate gave me a clean bill."

Larry laughed and dropped his hand on the man's shoulder.

"Anyway, I'm off duty now, Fred. I'm going away to enjoy myself."

"You ain't coming to London, I suppose?" asked the man, looking at him quickly.

"No," said Larry, and thought he saw signs of relief.

"I'm going over to-day," said Fred, in a conversational tone. "I was hoping we'd be fellow-passengers."

"I'm grieved to shatter your hopes," said Larry, "but I'm going in the other direction. So long."

"Good luck!" said Fred, and looked after him with a face which did not indicate any desire for Larry Holt's fortune.

Larry went up to his room and found his man brushing his clothes and laying them out on his bed. Patrick Sunny, the valet he had endured for two years, was a serious young man with staring eyes and a round face, and he grew suddenly energetic on Larry's appearance. He brushed and he hissed, for he had been in a cavalry regiment.

Larry strolled to the window and looked down on the Place de l'Opéra at the busy scene.

"Sunny," he said, "you needn't brush those dress things of mine. Pack 'em."

"Yes, sir," said Sunny.

"I'm going to Monte Carlo by the night train."

"Indeed, sir?" said Sunny, who would have said exactly the same if Larry had expressed his intention of going to the Sahara or the North Pole.

"To Monte Carlo, Sunny!" chortled Larry. "For six bright, happy, expensive weeks—start packing at once."

He picked up the telephone from the writing-table and called the Travel Bureau.

"I want a sleeper and a first-class reservation for Monte Carlo by to-night's train," he said. "Monte Carlo," he repeated louder. "No, not Calais. I have not the slightest intention of going to Calais—thanks." He hung up the receiver and stood looking at his servitor. "I hate talking to you, Sunny," he said, "but I must talk to somebody, and I hate your name. Who gave you that horrible name?"

"My forefathers," said Sunny primly, continuing his brushing without looking up.

"They rather missed the 'bus, didn't they?" asked Larry. "For if there is anything less like a bright spring day than you, I should like to avoid it. But we're southward bound, Sunny, to this Côte d'Azur, to the land of flowers and folly, to the orange-groves—do you like oranges, Sunny?"

"I prefer walnuts, sir," said Sunny, "but fruit of any kind means nothing to me."

Larry chuckled and sat on the edge of the bed.

"We're going to be criminals and take people's money from them," he said, "instead of nosing about the criminal practices of others. No more robberies, defalcations, forgeries and murders, Sunny. Six weeks of dolce far niente."

"I don't play that game myself, sir," said Sunny. "I prefer cribbage."

Larry picked up the afternoon paper and had turned its columns. There were quite a few items of news to remind him of his profession and its calls. There was a big bank robbery at Lyons, a mail coach had been held up in Belgium by armed robbers; and then he came to a paragraph.

"The body of a man picked up on the steps leading down from the Thames Embankment has been identified as Mr. Gordon Stuart, a rich Canadian. It is believed to be a case of suicide. Mr. Stuart had been spending the evening with some friends at the theatre, and disappeared between the acts, and was not seen again until his body was discovered. A coroner's inquest will be held in due course."

He read the paragraph twice, and frowned.

"A man doesn't usually go out between the acts of a play and commit suicide—unless the play is very bad," he said, and the obedient Sunny said, "No, sir."

He threw the newspaper down.

"Sunny, I'm getting into bad habits. I'm taking an interest in lunacy, and for that same reason I notice that you've folded my trousers so that the crease comes down the side. Unfold 'em, you lazy devil!"

He spent the afternoon making preparations for his journey, and at half-past six, with his trunks in the hands of the porters and Sunny carrying his overcoat, he was settling his bill at the cashier's desk, had folded up the receipt and was putting it in his pocket when a bell-boy came to him.

"Monsieur Holt?" he asked.

"That's my name," said Larry, and looked suspiciously at the thing in the boy's hand. "A telegram?" he said. "I don't want to see it."

Nevertheless, he took it in his hand and opened the blue paper with a disapproving grimace and read:

"Very urgent, on special police service. Clear the line. Larry Holt, Grand Hotel, Paris.

"Very worried about Stuart drowning stop case presents unusual features stop would be personally grateful if you would come over at once and conduct investigation."

It was signed by the Chief Commissioner, who was not only his superior but his personal friend, and Larry put the telegram in his pocket with a groan.

"What time do we arrive in Monte Carlo, sir?" asked Sunny when he joined him.

"About this day twelvemonth," said Larry.

"Indeed, sir?" said Sunny, politely interested. "It must be a very long way."

Sir John Hason

FLASH FRED, whose other name was Grogan, had a genuine grievance; for, after he had been solemnly assured by a reputable officer of the law that he intended going to Monte Carlo, he had found him on the Paris boat train, and though he carefully avoided him he knew that Larry was well aware that they were fellow-passengers.

At Victoria Fred made a rapid exit from the station, not being perfectly satisfied in his mind that Larry's business in London was altogether unconnected with Fred's own activities. Larry saw the disappearing back of the crook, and smiled for the first time since he had left Paris.

"Take my things to the flat," he said to Sunny. "I'm going to Scotland Yard. I may be home to-night, I may not be home until to-morrow night."

"Shall I put out your dress things?" said Sunny. All that concerned him was the gentlemanly appearance of his employer. To Sunny the day was divided into three parts—tweed, broadcloth and pyjamas.

"No—yes—anything you like," said his master.

"Yes, sir," responded the obliging Sunny.

Larry drove straight to the Yard, and had some difficulty in making an entry, because he was unknown to the local officials; but presently he was ushered into the big room where Sir John Hason rose from his desk and came across to meet him with outstretched hand.

"My dear Larry," he said, "it is awfully good of you to forgo your holiday. You are a brick! Of course I knew you would come, and I've given you room forty-seven and the smartest secretary I have seen in Scotland Yard for many a day."

They were old friends and old school-mates, John Hason and Larry Holt, and between the two men there was an affection and a confidence which is rarely found between men in the same profession.

"I don't know forty-seven," said Larry, taking off his overcoat with a smile, "but I'll be happy to know the smartest secretary in Scotland Yard. What's his name?"

"It isn't a he, it's a she," smiled Hason. "Miss Diana Ward, who's been with me for about six months and is really the smartest and most reliable girl I've ever had working with me."

"Oh, a female secretary!" said Larry gloomily, then brightened. "What you say goes, John; and even this paragon of virtue doesn't worry me. I suppose she's got a voice like a file and chews gum?"

"She is rather unprepossessing, but looks aren't everything," said Sir John dryly. "Now sit down, old man; I want to talk to you. It is about this Stuart case," he began, offering his cigarette box to the other. "We only discovered yesterday that Stuart was a very rich man. He has been living in this country for nine months at a boarding-house in Nottingham Place, Marylebone. He was a mysterious individual, who went nowhere, had very few friends, and was extraordinarily reticent. It was known, of course, that he had money, and his bankers in London, who revealed his identity when they discovered he was dead, were in his secret; that is to say, his secret so far as his identity is concerned."

"When you say he went nowhere, what do you mean? Did he stay in the boarding-house all the time?"

"I'm coming to that," said Sir John. "He did go somewhere, but why, nobody knows. Every afternoon it was his practice to take a motor drive, and invariably he went to the same place—to a little village in Kent, about twenty-five miles out. He left the motor-car at one end of the village, walked through the place, and was gone for a couple of hours. We have made inquiries and we have discovered this, that he spent quite a lot of time in the church, an old Saxon edifice the foundations of which were laid a thousand years ago. Regularly as the clock he'd return after two hours' absence, get into the car, which was hired, and be driven back to Nottingham Place."

"What was the name of the village?"

"Beverley Manor," said the Chief Commissioner. "Well, to resume. On Wednesday night, departing from his usual practice, he accepted the invitation of a Dr. Stephen Judd to go to the first night of a new show at the Macready Theatre. Dr. Stephen Judd is the managing director of the Greenwich Insurance Company, a small affair and quite a family concern, but having a pretty good name in the City. Mr. Judd is a genial person who dabbles in art and has a very beautiful house at Chelsea. Judd had a box for the first night of the show—which is a perfectly rotten one, judging by the newspaper notices—Box A. Stuart came, and, according to Judd, was very restless. In the interval between the second and third acts he slipped out of the theatre, unobserved, and did not come back, and was not seen again until we found his body on the Thames Embankment."

"What sort of a night was it?" asked Larry.

"Bright in the early part, but rather misty and inclined to be foggy later," said Sir John. "In fact, the constable who was patrolling that particular beat where the body was found reported that it was very thick between half-past three and half-past four."

Larry nodded. "Is there any possibility of his having mistaken his way in the fog and fallen into the water?" he asked.

"None whatever," replied Sir John emphatically. "Between the hour he disappeared and half-past two in the morning the Embankment was entirely clear of fog, and he was not seen. It was a very bright night until that hour."

"And here is another curious circumstance," the Commissioner went on. "When he was discovered, he was lying on the steps with his legs in the water, his body being clear—and," he added slowly, "the tide was still rising."

Larry looked at him in astonishment.

"Do you mean to say that he hadn't been deposited there by the falling tide?" he asked incredulously. "How could he be there, with his legs in the water, when the tide was low, as it must have been, when he came upon the steps?"

"That is my contention," nodded Sir John. "Unless he was drowned immediately he left the theatre when the tide was high and was falling, it seems almost impossible that he could have been left on the steps at daybreak, when the tide was rising."

Larry rubbed his chin.

"That's queer," he said. "There's no doubt about his being drowned?"

"None whatever," replied the Commissioner, and pulled open a drawer, lifting out a little tray on which were a number of articles. "These were the only things found in his pockets," he said. "A watch and chain, a cigar-case, and this roll of brown paper."

Larry took up the latter object. It was about an inch in length, and was still sodden with water.

"There is no writing on it," said Sir John. "I opened it when it first came in, but thought it better to roll it back and leave it as it was for another inspection when it dried."

Larry was looking at the watch, which was an ordinary gold half-hunter.

"Nothing there," he said, snapping back the case, "except that it stopped at twenty past twelve—presumably the hour of his death."

Sir John nodded.

"The chain is gold and platinum," mused Larry, "and at the end is a—what?"

There was a little cylinder of gold about an inch and a half long.

"A gold pencil fitted in here," said Larry. "Have they found the pencil?"

Sir John shook his head.

"No, that is all we discovered. Apparently Stuart was not in the habit of wearing rings. I'll have these sent to your office. Now will you take on the case?"

"But what is the case?" asked Larry slowly. "Do you suspect foul play?"

The Commissioner was silent.

"I do and I don't," he said. "I merely say that here are the elements of a terrible crime. But for the fact that he has been found on the steps with the tide still rising, and it was obviously low when he died, I should have thought it was an ordinary case of drowning, and I should not have opposed a verdict of accidental death if the jury reached that conclusion."

Larry looked at the watch again.

"It's strange," he said, speaking half to himself, and then: "I'll take these things into my room, if I may."

"I expected you would want them," said the Commissioner. "Now will you see the body?"

Larry hesitated.

"I'll see Doctor Judd first," he said. "Can you give me his address?"

Sir John looked up at the clock over his mantelpiece.

"He will be at his office. He's one of those indefatigable persons who work late. Number 17 Bloomsbury Pavement; you can't miss the building."

Larry gathered up the tray and moved to the door.

"Now for the unattractive secretary," he said, and Sir John smiled.

The Secretary

ROOM NO. 47 was on the floor above that where the Commissioner's office was situated. It lay at the end of a long corridor, facing the detective. He carried the tray in one hand and opened the door with the other, walking into a comfortable little bureau.

"Hallo!" he said in surprise. "Am I in the wrong office?"

The girl, who had risen from her desk, was young and extremely pretty. A mass of dull gold hair, dressed low over her broad forehead, gave an added emphasis to clear grey eyes that were regarding him with surprise. She was neat and slim of figure, and when she smiled Larry thought he had hardly ever seen so gracious and pleasant a lady.

"This is Inspector Holt's office," she said.

"Good Lord!" said Larry, coming slowly into the room and shutting the door behind him. He went to the other desk and put down the tray, and the girl looked puzzled.

"This is Inspector Holt's office," she repeated. "Are those things for him?"

Larry nodded, looking at the girl in wonder.

"What is that?" he asked suddenly, pointing to a glass and a jug on a side table which was covered with a small white cloth.

"Oh, that is for Inspector Holt," she said.

Larry looked into the jug.

"Milk?" he said in wonder.

"Yes," said the girl. "Inspector Holt is rather old, you know, and when I asked the Commissioner if he would like something after his journey, the Commissioner suggested invalid's food and milk; but I can't make invalid's food here, and—"

His shriek of merriment stopped her, and she stared at him.

"I am Inspector Holt," he said, drying his eyes.

"You?" she gasped.

"I'm the lad," said he complacently. "John, the Commissioner, has played a joke on you, miss—I don't know your name. Now, would you be good enough to ask the aged Miss Ward to step in?"

A smile twitched her lips.

"I am Miss Ward," she said, and it was Larry's turn to stare. Then he put out his hand with a smile.

"Miss Ward," he said, "we're companions in misfortune. Each has been equally a victim of a perfidious police commissioner. I'm extremely glad to meet you—and relieved."

"I'm a little relieved," laughed the girl as she went to her desk, and Larry, watching every movement, thought she floated rather than walked.

"Sir John said you were sixty and asthmatic, and told me to be careful that no draughts should come into the office. I've had a draught excluder specially fitted this afternoon."

Larry thought a moment.

"Perhaps it's as well I didn't go to Monte Carlo," he said, and sat down at his desk. "Now let us start, shall we?"

She opened her book and took up a pencil, whilst Larry examined the trinkets that lay on the tray.

"Take this down, please," he said. "Watch made Gildman of Toronto, half-hunter, jewel-balanced; No. A778432. No scratches on the inside." He opened the case and snapped it again, then tried the stem winder. "Wound less than six hours before death took place."

She looked up.

"Is this the Stuart case?" she asked.

"Yes," said Larry. "Do you know anything about it?"

"Only what the Commissioner's told me," she replied. "Poor man! But I'm getting so used to horrors now that I'm almost hardened. I suppose one feels that way if one's a medical student. I was a nurse for two years in a blind asylum," she added, "and that helps to toughen you, doesn't it?" She smiled.

"I suppose it does," said Larry thoughtfully, and wondered how young she had been when she started to work for her living. He put her at twenty-one and thought that was a fairly generous estimate of her age. "Do you like this work?" he asked.

She nodded.

"I love it," she said. "Sir John says that one of these days he's going to make me a—" She hesitated for a word.

"A sleuth? Don't say you're going to be a sleuth," begged Larry. "I thought we had this business to ourselves. Female competition to-day—"

She shook her head.

"You're neglecting your work, Mr. Holt," she said. "I've got as far as the watch."

He chuckled a little and resumed his inspection.

"Chain made of platinum and gold, length twelve inches, swivel at end, and container of a gold pencil—at least, I presume it was gold," he dictated. "The pencil wasn't found?"

"No," she said. "I particularly asked the sergeant who brought the goods whether the pencil had been found."

Larry looked at her in surprise.

"Did you notice that?"

"Oh yes, I noticed that too," said Marjorie calmly. "The knife has gone too."

He looked across at her in genuine amazement.

"What knife?" he asked.

"I guessed it was a knife," said she. "The swivel is too large to be attached to a pencil only. If you look you will see a little ring—it has probably got entangled with the ring holding the pencil. It was broken when it came in, but I pressed it together. It looked as if somebody had wrenched it off. I guessed the knife," she said, "because men so often carry a little gold penknife there."

"Or a cigar-cutter?" suggested Larry.

"I thought of that," she said, nodding, "but they'd hardly have taken the trouble to nip off a cigar-cutter."

"They?" he asked.

"Whoever killed Stuart," she said quietly, "would have removed all weapons from his possession."

He looked at the chain again and saw the other ring, and wondered why he had not noticed it before.

"I think you're right," he said after a further examination. "The ring is much larger—it had slid up the chain, by the way—and there are distinct scratches where the knife was wrenched off. Hm!" He put down the object on the table, and looked at his own watch. "Have you seen the rest of the things?" he asked.

She shook her head.

"I've only examined the watch."

He looked around for some receptacle, and saw a cupboard in the wall.

"Is this empty?" he asked, and she nodded. "Then we'll leave the examination of these until I come back. I have to see somebody."

He slipped the tray into the closet and locked the door, handing the key to the girl. He was half-way to the door when he remembered.

"You won't be here when I come back? I suppose you have some sort of office hours?"

"I make it a practice never to stay after two o'clock in the morning," she said gravely.

19

She met the frank admiration in his eyes without embarrassment.

"I don't think I have ever met a girl like you," he said slowly, and as though he were speaking his thoughts aloud.

She flushed and dropped her gaze. Then she laughed and looked at him again, and he thought that her eyes were like stars.

"It may be that we have never met anybody like each other," she said.

And Larry Holt left Scotland Yard, conscious that a new and a very potent interest had come into his life.

Flash Fred Sees a Client

FLASH FRED had seen Larry Holt off the premises of the railway terminus; for, though he had left the station building first, he had waited until Larry's taxi had gone.

He had a particular desire that he should not be shadowed that evening, and to this was engrafted a wholesome respect for the perspicacity and genius of Larry Holt. On the Continent of Europe, whereever crook met crook, it was generally and unanimously agreed that the first person they wished to meet on the other side of the Styx was Larry Holt. Only they did not say "on the other side of the Styx"; they said, simply and crudely, "in hell." The ruthlessness of this man, once he got his nose on to the trail, was a tradition and a legend; and Fred, more than any other man, had reason to fear him.

He gave Holt ten minutes' start and then doubled back to the station, left his suit-case at the cloak room and came out at one of the side entrances where the cabs were ranked, and, choosing the first of these, he gave an address. Ten minutes later he was set down in a quiet Bloomsbury square, devoted in the main to lawyers' offices. There was an exception to these. The building at which he alighted was a narrow and tall erection of red brick, and though no light showed in the lower office, there was a subdued gleam in the windows of the upper floor. A commissionaire on duty in the hall looked at Fred askance.

"The office has been closed for hours, sir," he said, shaking his head. "We open at nine in the morning."

"Is Dr. Judd on the premises?" asked Flash Fred, shifting his cigar from one corner of his mouth to the other.

The commissionaire hesitated.

"Mr. Judd is still busy, sir, and I don't think he wants to see anybody."

"Oh, you don't, don't you?" sneered Fred. "Now, you go upstairs to the governor and tell him that Mr. Walter Smith wants to see him. Don't forget the name—it's an unusual one," he added humorously.

The commissionaire looked dubiously at the visitor.

"I shall only get into trouble," he grumbled, as he stepped into one of the two small elevators and, pressing the automatic knob, he went quickly up out of view.

Apparently Mr. Judd's office was situated on the top floor, for it was some time before the whine of the motor ceased. After a while it began again, and the commissionaire descended.

"He'll see you, sir," he said. "Will you step this way?"

"You ought to know me by now, sergeant," said Fred as he walked into the lift. "I've been here pretty regularly the past few years."

"Maybe I wasn't on duty," said the commissionaire as the lift slowly ascended. "There are two of us here, you know. Were you a friend of Mr. David's, sir?"

Fred did not chuckle, he did not even smile.

"No, no," he said airily, "I don't know Mr. David."

"Ah, very sad, very sad!" said the commissionaire. "He died suddenly four years ago, you know, sir."

Fred did know, but he did not confess the fact. The death of Mr. David had robbed him of a possible source of income by right, whereas now he only had that income by favour, and might at any time lose that and gain a term of imprisonment if the jovial Dr. Judd grew tired of paying blackmail.

The lift stopped and he stepped out and followed the commissionaire to a door, at which the uniformed man knocked. A loud voice bade them come in, and Flash Fred swaggered into the handsome apartment with a cool nod to its occupant.

Dr. Judd had risen to meet him.

"All right, sergeant," he said to the commissionaire, and flicked a silver coin across the room, which the man caught deftly.

"Get me some cigarettes," he said. And when the door had closed: "Sit down, you rascal," said Dr. Judd good-humouredly. "I suppose you've come to get your pound of flesh."

He was a tall, stout man, florid of face and heavy of build. His forehead was bald, his eyes were deep-set and wide apart; he had about him an air of comfort and boisterous good humour. Fred, in no wise abashed, sat down on the edge of a chair.

"Well, doctor," he said, "I'm back."

Dr Judd shook his head and searched his pockets for a cigarette.

"What do you want—a cigarette?" said Fred, reaching for his case, but the doctor shook his head and his smile was broad, good-humoured but significant.

"No, thank you, Mr. Grogan," he said with a chuckle. "I don't smoke cigarettes that are presented to me by gentlemen of your profession."

"What is my profession?" growled Flash Fred. "You don't think I was trying to dope you, do you?"

"I was expecting you," said the other, without answering the question, and seated himself. "If I remember rightly, you have a strong objection to taking cheques."

Flash Fred grinned.

"Quite right, governor," he said. "That is still my weakness."

The doctor took a bunch of keys from his pocket, walked to the safe, snapped back the lock, and then, looking over his shoulder:

"You needn't watch this too closely, my friend; except when I have to pay blackmailers, I never keep money in this safe."

Fred made a little grimace.

"Hard words never killed anybody," he said sententiously.

The doctor took out a packet, slammed the door and turned the key, came slowly back to the desk and threw down a fat envelope. Then he consulted a little book which he took from a drawer.

"You're three days ahead of your time," he said, and Fred nodded admiringly.

"What a brain you've got for figures, doctor!" he said. "Yes, I'm three days ahead of my time, but it's because I've got to get out of England pretty quick to meet a friend of mine in Nice."

The doctor threw the packet across to him, and he caught it clumsily.

"There are twelve hundred pounds in that envelope. You needn't count them, because they're all there," said Dr. Judd, and leaning back in his chair, he took out a golden toothpick, eyeing the other straightly and thoughtfully. "Of course I am the biggest fool in the world," he said, "or I would never submit to this iniquitous blackmail. It is only because I want to keep the memory of my dead brother free from calumny that I do this."

"If your brother goes shooting up people in Montpellier and I happen to be on the spot," said Flash Fred unctuously, "and help him to escape—as I did, and I can prove it—I think I'm entitled to a little compensation."

"You're an unutterable scoundrel," said the other in his pleasant way, and smiled. "And you amuse me. Suppose, instead of being what I am, I were a bad-minded man? Suppose that I was desperate and couldn't find the money? Why, I might—do anything!"

He guffawed at the thought of doing anything very terrible.

"It wouldn't make any difference to me," said Fred. "But it wouldn't make any difference to you, either. I've got all the facts written down about that shooting—how I helped the man escape and recognized him in London as Mr. David Judd when I came back—and my mouthpiece has got it."

"Your lawyer?"

"Sure, my lawyer," said Fred, nodding. He leaned forward. "You know, I didn't believe your brother had died. I thought it was a fake to get me out of the way, and I shouldn't have believed it if I hadn't seen it in the papers and been to the funeral."

Dr. Judd rose and replaced his toothpick.

"That a man like you could besmirch a name like his!" he said. All the good humour had gone out of his voice, and he trembled with indignation and passion.

He had passed to the other side of the table and stood glowering down at Flash Fred, and Fred, who was used to such scenes—for this was not his first blackmailing case—merely smiled.

"He was the best man that ever lived, the cleverest, the most wonderful," said Dr. Judd, and his face was white. "The greatest man perhaps that this world has seen." His voice shook with the intensity of his emotion. "And for you——" He reached down, and before Fred knew what had happened, the big hand had gripped him by the collar and jerked him to his feet.

"Here, none of that!" cried Fred, and strove to break loose.

"The money I do not mind paying," Judd went on. "It is not that which maddens me. It is the knowledge that you have it in your power to throw mud at a man——" Here his voice broke, and the other hand came up.

With a cry like a wild beast, Fred flung himself back with all his might and broke the grip of his adversary. Suddenly, as if by magic, there appeared in his hand a revolver.

"Put 'em up and keep 'em up, damn you!"

And then a voice, the gentlest voice in the world, asked:

"Can I be of any assistance?"

Fred turned with a start. Larry Holt was standing in the doorway, an engaging smile upon his face.

The Will

FLASH FRED looked upon the intruder, a picture of comical amazement.

"You don't lose no time, do you?" The protest was forced from him, and Larry laughed softly.

"For carrying concealed weapons, you're pinched, Fred."

"It's no crime in this country," growled the other, putting up his gun.

By this time Dr. Judd had recovered himself.

"You know our friend, Mr. Grogan," he said easily. "He's a member of our amateur dramatic society, and we were practising a scene from the Corsican

Brothers. I suppose it looked rather alarming."

"Thought it was Julius Cæsar," said Larry dryly. "The scene between Cassius and Brutus, though I don't remember the gun play."

The doctor looked at Flash Fred and then at Larry.

"I'm afraid I don't know you," he said. He was still rather white, but his tone had recovered its good nature.

"I am Inspector Larry Holt from Scotland Yard," said Larry. "Now seriously, Dr. Judd, are you charging this man with anything?"

"No, no, no," said Judd with a laugh. "Honestly, we were only doing a little harmless fooling."

Larry looked from one to the other. The managing director of an insurance company, even a small company, does not fool with a known criminal.

"You know this man, I suppose?"

"I've met him several times," said Judd easily.

"You know also that he's a member of the criminal classes, and that he is in fact 'Flash Fred,' who has served penal servitude in this country and a term of imprisonment in France?"

The doctor said nothing for a while.

"I'm afraid I guessed that too," he said in a low voice, "and in consequence my association with the man must seem rather curious to you—but I cannot explain."

Larry nodded. The one perturbed person in the room was Flash Fred. He was in an agony of apprehension lest Dr. Judd told his secret and the reason for his visit. But Judd had no such intention.

"You can go now," he said curtly, and Fred, trying to summon up some of his old swagger, lit a cigar with a hand that trembled, and Larry watched the operation.

"You want 'Nervine for the Nerves,' Fred," he said. "I saw a chemist's shop open at the corner of the street when I came along."

Fred walked out with a pitiable attempt at indifference, and Larry watched him go. Then he turned to the doctor.

"I'm sorry I came in at such an inconvenient moment," he said, "though

I don't think you were in any danger. Fred gets all his fine dramatic effects by pulling, not by shooting."

"I don't think so either," said the doctor with a laugh. "Sit down, Mr. Holt. I certainly didn't expect to see you. I work rather late here at nights."

"There was nobody down below when I came," said Larry, "and that is my excuse for coming up unannounced."

The doctor nodded.

"I sent the commissionaire out to buy me some cigarettes, and here he is."

There was a tap at the door and the commissionaire came in and laid a packet on the table in confirmation.

"Now what can I do for you?" asked Judd, as he took a cigarette from the packet and lit it. "I suppose it is the Stuart case? I've seen one of your men to-day."

Larry nodded.

"It is the Stuart case," he said. "I wanted a few additional details. I've only just taken charge of the business, and interrupted my investigation of the—remains, in order to see you before you left the office."

"I know very little," said the doctor, smoking comfortably. "He came with me to the theatre the night before last. A queer, quiet, reticent man, I met him quite by accident. As a matter of fact, I was in a car that collided with his taxicab and I was slightly injured; he called upon me, and that is how the friendship began—if you can call it a friendship."

"Tell me about the night before last," asked Larry, and the doctor looked up at the ceiling.

"Now let me think. I can give you the exact time almost, for I am a somewhat methodical person. I met him at the entrance to the theatre at seven-forty-five, and we both went into Box A. That is the last box on the left, or O.P. side. The box is on a level with the street, the stalls and pit being below the level. We sat there through two acts, and then, just before the curtain came down on the second act, he made an excuse and went out of the box, and he was never seen again."

"None of the attendants saw him?"

"No," said the doctor, "but that, I think, is easily explained. It was a first night, and, as you know, the attendants are very interested in the action of a play, and fill the doorways and the entrances to gangways, looking at the stage, when of course they should be attending to their business."

"Did you know he was Stuart, a semi-millionaire?" asked Larry.

"I hadn't the slightest idea," said the doctor truthfully. "I knew nothing whatever about his past life except that he had come from Canada."

Larry was disappointed.

"I hoped I was going to get a lot of information from you," he said. "Nobody seems to have known Stuart, and naturally I thought that you would have been in his confidence."

"Neither I nor his bank manager was in his confidence," said the doctor. "It was only this morning that I heard from the manager of the London and Chatham that he was a client of theirs. We knew absolutely nothing of him except that he had plenty of money."

A few minutes later Larry was walking down Bloomsbury Pavement, and he was a very thoughtful man. What had Flash Fred been doing in that office? What was the significance of that flashing of the revolver and the white face of Dr. Judd? It was another little mystery, into which he had not time to investigate, and any way it was no concern of his. Ahead of him, his iron-shod stick tapping the pavement, was a man who walked slowly and deliberately. Larry passed him, and, waiting for a cab which he had signalled, saw him again.

"Blind," he noted casually, not interrupting his thought of Fred and the doctor.

But he had no time for side trails and side issues, and, entering the cab, he drove to Westminster.

He was not going back to the Yard immediately. First he had a gruesome little duty to perform. At the Westminster mortuary, whither the cab had taken him, he found two Scotland Yard officers awaiting him.

The examination of the body was a brief one. The only mark was an abrasion of the left ankle, and then Larry began an inspection of the clothing, which had been placed in an adjoining room.

"There is the shirt, sir," pointing to a garment which had been roughly folded. "I can't understand those blue marks on the breast."

Larry carried the garment under a light. It was a dress shirt, rough dried, and the purple specks on the breast were clearly visible.

"Made by an indelible pencil," said Larry, and in a flash remembered the missing pencil-case. But what meant those specks, which formed three rough lines of indecipherable pothooks and hangers?

And then the solution came to Larry, and quickly he turned the dress front inside out and uttered an exclamation. Written on the inside were three lines, and it was the indelible pencil markings which had soaked through that had caused the speckly appearance of the front of the shirt.

The water had made the purple pencil markings run, but the words were distinct.

"In the fear of death I, Gordon Stuart, of Merryhill Ranch, Calgary, leave all my possessions to my daughter, Clarissa, and I pray the courts to accept this as my last will and testament.–Gordon Stuart."

Underneath was written:

"It is now clear to me that I have been betrayed by——"

There followed a letter which looked like an "O," but at this point the writing abruptly terminated.

Larry raised his eyes and met those of his subordinate.

"Here is the strangest will that has ever been made," he said in a hushed voice.

He put down the shirt and walked back to the mortuary chamber, and again examined the body. One hand was clenched, and evidently this fact had been overlooked by the doctors. Using all his strength, he forced the fingers apart, and something fell with a tinkle to the stone floor. He stooped and picked it up. It was a broken sleeve-link of a peculiar pattern. The centre was of black enamel, the rim was of tiny diamonds. He made a further inspection, without discovering anything new.

Then he looked at his companion, and his forehead was wrinkled. What did this mean? What association had all these circumstances with each other? They could be connected, he felt sure of that—the strange encounter between Flash Fred and Dr. Judd, the will on the shirt, and now this new clue. An atmosphere of impenetrable mystery enveloped this case like a fog behind which strange and inhuman shapes were moving, dimly glimpsed and as dimly suspected.

Murder!

He knew it, he felt it—every shadowy shape he passed on his way to his office whispered the word "Murder!"

The Writing in Braille

THE GIRL was making tea on an electric stove when he came in.

"Hallo!" he said with a start. "I had forgotten you," and she smiled.

"Tell me," he asked quickly, "did Stuart have any cuff-links?"

She nodded and took a small packet from her table.

"The Commissioner forgot to send these on; they came in just after you left," she said.

He opened the paper. The links were of plain gold, without crest or monogram.

He took the enamel and diamond half-link from his pocket and inspected it.

"What is that?" she asked. "Did you find it in—" She hesitated.

He nodded.

"I found it in his hand," he said quietly.

"Then it is murder, you think?"

"I'm certain," said he. "It will be most difficult to prove, and unless a miracle happens, the villain who committed this crime will go free."

He opened the cupboard and took out the tray, adding to the collection the two gold links and the half-link he had found in the dead man's hand.

"Nothing at all," he said, shaking his head. Then he remembered he had not examined the little roll of brown paper. "I don't know what this is; it was found in his pocket."

He flattened it out on the table, and the girl came to the opposite side and bent over, looking at the paper as he smoothed it out. It was a strip about four inches long and two wide.

"Nothing written here," he said, and turned it over. "Nor here. I'll have it photographed to-morrow."

"One moment," she said quickly, and took the paper from his hand, passing the tips of her delicate fingers over its surface.

He saw her face go white.

"I thought so," she whispered. "I was almost sure of that when I saw the embossing."

"What is it?" he asked quickly.

"There are some words here written in Braille—the language of the blind," she said, and again her fingers went over the surface, pausing now and again with a puzzled frown on her face.

"Braille?" he repeated in amazement, and she nodded.

"I used to read it when I was in the Institute," she said, "but some of these words have been damaged, probably by the water. Some are distinct. Will you write them down as I spell them?"

He snatched up a pen, pulled a piece of paper from the rack, and waited. Even in that moment he thought how curiously the positions had been reversed, and how he had become the secretary and she the detective.

"The first word is 'murdered,'?" she said. "And then there is a space, and then the word 'dear'; then there's another gap, and the word 'sea' occurs, and that is all."

With this weird message between them they stared at one another. What blind man, amidst those blind shades which had mouthed and gibbered to him in the fog, had sent this message?

What was there behind the ragged scroll of soaked paper? Whose link did the dead man hold in his stiffened hand? Why was he murdered? There had been money in his pocket, his possessions were untouched. It was not for robbery that he had been struck down. Not for vengeance, for he was a stranger.

One fact stood out, one tangible point from whence Larry knew his future movements would radiate.

"Murder!" he said softly, "and I'll find the man who did it, if he hides himself in hell!"

A Telegram from Calgary

DIANA WARD was looking at her chief with a new interest in her fine eyes.

"Braille," he said in a low voice. "That is the written language of the blind, isn't it?"

She nodded.

"Yes, there are books and newspapers printed in that type," she said. "It is a sort of embossed character made of a number of small dots, the relation of one with the other producing the letter."

She took up the paper again.

"When blind people write, they use a small instrument and a guide, but this has been written in a hurry by somebody who worked without any guide. I can feel how irregularly it is done, and the illegibility of the words which I cannot read is due almost as much to bad writing as to the action of the water."

He took this curious clue into his hands and examined it.

"Could Stuart have done it with his pencil?"

She shook her head, and then asked quickly:

"Have you found the pencil?"

"No," said Larry grimly, "but I've found what the pencil was used for."

He opened the parcel he had brought in and showed the shirt and its tragic message written inside the front.

"Why inside?" he said thoughtfully. "It's written on the left too."

Diana understood.

"It would necessarily be written on the left side if he used his right hand," she said.

"But why on the inside?"

She shook her head.

"I don't know. It would have been much simpler to——"

"I have it!" cried Larry triumphantly. "He wrote this will where it would not be seen by somebody or other. If it had been written outside, it would have been seen, and probably destroyed."

She shivered a little.

"I'm not quite hardened yet," she said with a smile. "There is something terrible about this, isn't there? I think you are right; and if we go on that assumption, that he wrote this will in such a manner in order to keep it from the eyes of a third person, we must suppose that that third person existed. In other words, there was somebody of whom he was afraid—or, if you like, at whose hands he feared death—and the murder was premeditated, for he must have been in the custody of that somebody for some time before he met his dreadful end."

She stopped suddenly, for Larry's eyes were fixed on her, and she dropped her own and flushed.

"You're rather wonderful," he said softly; "and if I'm not jolly careful I'm going to lose my job."

He saw a look of doubt in her eyes and laughed.

"Now, Miss Ward," he said banteringly, "we are going to start fair, and you must acquit me of any professional jealousy."

"Jealousy!" she scoffed. "That would be absurd."

"Not so absurd," said Larry. "I've known men to be jealous of women for less reason. And now"—he glanced at his watch—"I think you had better go home. I'll get a taxi. Have you far to go?"

"Only to the Charing Cross Road," she said.

"Then I'll take you home," said Larry. "It's nearly one o'clock."

She had already started putting on her coat and her hat.

"Thank you, I'll go alone," she said. "It isn't far. Really, Mr. Holt, I don't want you to get into the habit of taking me home every time I'm late. I'm quite used to being out by myself, and I won't have a taxi."

"We'll see about that," said Larry. He was writing rapidly on a cable form.

"If I can get this cable through in time, it ought to reach the Chief of Police in Calgary by tea-time yesterday!"

"Yesterday?" she said in surprise. "Oh, of course; they are nine hours late on Greenwich time," and Larry groaned.

"I'll have to try some new ones on you," he said.

They walked home together, but as it happened, the girl's tiny apartment lay in the direction that he had to take. Larry reached Regent's Park, where his own flat was situated, and found the patient Sunny laying out his pyjamas.

"Sunny," said Larry, as, clad in these garments and his flowered dressing-gown, he sipped a cup of chocolate, "somewhere in this city is a very unpleasant gentleman, name unknown."

"I expect there are many like that, sir," said Sunny.

"And somewhere in England is a man who is known as the Public Executioner, and it's my job in life to bring them together!"

He was at Scotland Yard at half-past eight the following morning, and to his surprise the girl was before him, and the departmental memoranda and the various documents which come to every head of Scotland Yard were neatly arranged on his blotting-pad.

"A cablegram has just come in," said the girl. "I didn't open it. You must tell me what you want done about cables and telegrams."

"Open 'em all," said Larry. "I have no private business—and the only scented notes which come to me can be read without bringing a blush to the youngest cheek."

She came across the room with the cablegram in her hand, and he took it.

"Calgary," he said, looking at the address. "That's pretty quick work." And then his mouth opened in amazement, for the telegram read:

"Stuart had no child. He was not married."

He looked at the girl.

"Check Number One," he said.

She took the telegram from him and examined the hour at which it was dispatched.

"This is a common-knowledge telegram," she said.

"What do you mean by common knowledge?" asked Larry good-humouredly.

"Well, it must have been answered just as soon as it arrived, and the man who sent this wrote from what is common knowledge. In other words, he didn't attempt to make any investigations, but took the fact for granted; probably he asked somebody in the office, 'Is Stuart married or a bachelor?' and when they said he was a bachelor, he dispatched the reply."

Larry folded the wire and put it away in his desk.

"If it is common knowledge that Stuart was not married, it merely complicates a situation which is not exactly clear. Here is a man who dies and is obviously murdered, and in a few moments preceding his death writes his will secretly on the inside of his shirt. It is possible, by the way, that he may have done this in the presence of his murderers without their being aware of the fact, and I should think that is most likely."

"I thought that," she agreed.

"He was murdered, and writes his will on the stiff breast of his shirt, leaving the whole of his property to his daughter. Now, a sane man—and there is no reason to suppose that he was anything but sane—does not invent a daughter on the spur of the moment; so it is obvious that the Chief of the Calgary Police is wrong."

"It is equally certain that if he was married it was not in Calgary or even in Canada, where the fact would be known," said the girl. "Secret marriages are possible in a great city, but in small places, amongst very prominent people—and apparently he lived not in a town but on a ranch—the fact that he was married could not escape knowledge."

On the way home the previous evening Larry had told the girl almost all that the Commissioner had told him. It was not usual for him to make confidantes so quickly, but there was something very appealing about Diana Ward, and his confidence, usually a matter of slow growth, had come to maturity in a flash.

The girl was looking thoughtfully down at her desk.

"If he was married secretly," she said slowly, "would it not be—in——"

"In London, of course," said Larry, nodding. "Send a cable to the Chief of the Calgary Police, asking him particulars about Stuart's known movements, when he was in London last before his present visit."

The Memorial Stone

SHE NODDED, took out a telegram form from her rack, and began writing. Larry glanced through the reports mechanically, initialed one, and put the others aside. Then he opened the cupboard and, taking out the tray, carried it to the table. He examined the watch again in the light of day, the swivel ring, the cigar-case, and lastly the roll of paper. By daylight the embossed characters were visible, and he put his finger-tips over them very gingerly. He was not, however, accustomed to reading Braille, and he realized that his hand was a heavy one compared with the delicate touch of his secretary. She had finished her writing, had rung a bell and handed the telegram to him to read.

"That's all right," said Larry, and, when the uniformed messenger had come and taken the telegram away: "Do you notice anything peculiar about this piece of paper?" he asked, pointing to the Braille message.

"Yes," she said. "I was looking at it before you came. You don't mind?" she asked quickly, and Larry laughed.

"You can examine anything except my conscience," he said. "Did you notice"—he turned his attention to the paper again—"that one end of this paper is less discoloured than the other?"

"I noticed that one end was drier than the other last night," she said, "and that of course is the reason. It was on the dry end that we got our best results. For instance, the word 'murderer' was almost untouched by the water; it was damp but not moist."

He nodded, and she opened a drawer of her desk and took out a sheet of brown paper.

"I brought this with me," she said. "It is a sheet from a Braille book, and I was trying experiments with strips I had torn from the book, soaking them

35

in my wash-basin. Here is the result." She took out a little roll of shapeless pulp, which skinned when she attempted to unwind it.

"Humph!" said Larry. They had both reached the same conclusion, but by different processes—she by actual experiment, he by deduction; and the conclusion they had come to was that the roll of paper had been placed in Gordon Stuart's pocket after the body had left the water.

"There would be enough moisture in the clothes to saturate it through," said Larry. "This paper is very absorbent, almost as much so as blotting paper. So we have come to this—that Gordon Stuart was drowned, and after he was drowned his body was handled by some person or persons, one of whom slipped this message into his pocket, and that person was either a blind man or one who believed——" He stared at her. "By Jove!" he said, as a thought struck him.

"What were you going to say?" she asked.

"Is it possible——" He frowned. It was an absurd idea. The man or woman who left this message on the body expected that Diana Ward would read it.

She held no official position, and the fact that she was Larry Holt's secretary was a purely fortuitous circumstance, which could not have been anticipated by any outside person. Yet a hasty telephone call to the Chief of Internal Intelligence revealed the fact that there was no Braille expert at Scotland Yard, the only man who knew the system being at that time on sick leave for six months.

"I think you can dismiss the idea that the message was intended for me," said the girl with a smile. "No, it was written by a blind man, or it would have been written better. A person with the use of his eyes, or——"

"Suppose he were writing in the dark?" asked Larry. He put the tray away and locked the cupboard.

The girl shook her head.

"If he were not blind, he would not be in possession of the instrument to make these markings," she said, and Larry felt that was true.

He spent two hours dictating letters to various authorities, and at eleven o'clock he rose and put on his coat and hat.

"We're going for a joy ride," he said.

"We?" she repeated in surprise.

"I want you to come along," said Larry, and this time his tone was authoritative, and the girl meekly obeyed.

There was a car waiting for them at the entrance to the Yard, and the driver evidently had already received his instructions.

"We're going to Beverley Manor, the village which Stuart was so fond of visiting," he said. "I particularly want to discover what attractions the old Saxon church had for this unhappy man. He doesn't seem to have been an archæologist, so the fact that the foundations were a thousand years old would not interest him."

It was a glorious spring day, with just a sufficient nip in the air to bring the colour to young and healthy cheeks. The hedgerows were bursting into vivid green, and the grassy banks were yellow with primroses. They sat silent, this man and woman whom fate had thrown together in such strange circumstances, enjoying the golden day and thankful of heart to be alive in that season of renewal. All the world was living. The air was lively with hurrying birds, going about their business of nest-making. They saw strange furtive shapes creeping across the road from burrow to burrow; and in one sheltered old-world garden which they passed white lilacs were blooming.

Beverley Manor was a straggling village at the foot of the Kentish Rag. Beyond its church it had few attractions for visitors, for it lay off the main Kentish road, a tiny backwater of rural England, where life ran a smooth unruffled course.

They pulled up at the inn, where Larry ordered lunch, and then they set forth on foot to the church, which lay a quarter of a mile away along a white and pleasant road. It was not a pretty church; its square tower was squat and unlovely, and successive generations, endeavouring to improve its once simple lines, had produced a medley of architecture in which Romanesque, Gothic and Norman struggled for recognition.

"It rather swears, doesn't it?" said Larry irreverently as they passed through the old lych-gate into the churchyard.

The door of the church was open, and the edifice was empty. However disturbing its outside might be, there was serenity and peace and simplicity in the calm interior.

Larry had hoped to find memorial tablets placed in the wall of the church which would give him some clue to Stuart's movements. But beyond a brass testifying to the virtues of a former vicar, and the tomb of an ancient Bishop of Rochester, the church was innocent of memorials. Larry then began a systematic inspection of the graves. Most of them were very old, and their inscriptions indecipherable.

He came at last to the far end of the cemetery, where half a dozen workmen were carrying a new stone wrapped in canvas, and he and the girl stood side by side watching them in silence as they deposited their load by a well-kept grave.

"I'm afraid we've had our journey for nothing," said Larry. "We'll make a few inquiries in the village, and then we'll go back to London."

He was turning to go, when one of the men stripped the canvas covering from the headstone.

"We might as well know who this is," said Larry, and stepped forward to look.

The men stood on one side to give him a better view, and he read; and, reading, gasped.

To the Memory of
Margaret Stuart,
Wife of
Gordon Stuart
(of Calgary, Can.).
Died May 4th, 1899.
Also His Only Daughter
Jeane,
Born 10th June, 1898.
Died 1st May, 1899.

The girl had joined him now, and together they stood staring down at the headstone.

"His only daughter!" said Larry in a tone of bewilderment. "His only daughter! Then who is Clarissa?"

The Man Who Lost a Finger

AN EXAMINATION of local records produced no satisfactory result. Margaret Stuart had died at a farm three miles out of Beverley Manor, and the farm had changed hands twice since the date of her death.

"Twenty years ago?" said the farmer whom Larry interviewed. "Why, twenty years ago this place was a sort of nursing home. It was run by a woman who took in invalids."

Where the woman is, he could not say. She was not a local woman. He thought he had heard she was dead.

"I've been racking my brains to recall her name," said the farmer. "I told the gentleman yesterday that he'd best go to Somerset House——"

"A gentleman here yesterday?" said Larry quickly. "Was there somebody inquiring yesterday?"

"Yes, sir, a man from London," said the farmer. "He came down in a car and offered me fifty pounds if I could tell him the name of the woman who kept this place as a home, and a hundred pounds if I could give him any information about a lady that died here twenty-two years ago. A lady named Stuart."

"Oh, indeed?" said Larry, alert now. Nobody from Scotland Yard had made the inquiries he was well aware. "What was this gentleman like who called yesterday?" he asked.

"Rather a tall man," said the farmer. "I didn't see his face properly because he had his overcoat buttoned up to his chin. But I did notice that he'd lost the little finger on his left hand."

On their way back to London both Larry and Diana Ward were absorbed in their own thoughts. The car was threading through the traffic of Westminster Bridge Road before Larry made any reference to their visit.

"Who is in such a frantic hurry to discover all about the Stuarts," he asked, "and will give fifty pounds for information? And who is his daughter Clarissa, and how can he have a daughter Clarissa, when his only daughter lies at Beverley Manor?"

"You inquired at the stonemason's when we came through Beverley. Didn't they tell you anything?" asked the girl.

He nodded.

"The stone was put up by order of Mr. Stuart, who was in the habit of coming to the churchyard every day to sit beside the grave. The memorial was ordered two months ago, and the stone was seen and approved by Gordon Stuart only last week."

He bit his lip thoughtfully.

"Between last week and the night of his murder, Stuart must have discovered that he had another child." He shook his head. "That sort of thing doesn't happen," he said decisively, "not in real life anyway."

He spent ten minutes with the Commissioner, and afterwards went into the city, and the girl did not see him till seven o'clock that night. She had had instructions from him that she was not to wait, as it was a Saturday and her office hours ended at one. But she was sitting at her desk, reading, when he came in, and he was so elated that he did not reprove her.

"I've got it!" he said exultantly.

"The murderer?" she asked with a start.

"No, no, the story of Stuart. Has there been any reply to my cablegram?"

Diana shook her head.

"It doesn't matter very much," he said briskly as he paced the office. "I've secured the registration of the marriage. It occurred in the Diamond Jubilee year, in August, 1897, and was celebrated at a church in Highgate. Don't you see what happened?"

"I don't quite see," she said slowly.

"Well, I'll tell you. Gordon Stuart, a young man at the time, was on a visit to this country. I have found that he stayed at the Cecil Hotel from June to August, 1897. He married the girl, whose name was Margaret Wilson, and returned to the Cecil Hotel alone in March, '98. There is a record there that he left for Canada two days after he came back to the hotel. They keep a book in which they write down the addresses to which letters should be forwarded, and there was no difficulty whatever in tracing his movements so far. Then I went to see the vicar of the church where he was married; and here I had a great find."

He paused, rumpled his hair and frowned.

"I really should like to know who is that tall man who has lost the little finger of his left hand," he said irritably.

"Why?" she asked in surprise.

"He had been there a day before me," said Larry, and then, shaking off his annoyance: "Here is the story—the story told by Stuart to the vicar, whom he met in the Strand on the day before he sailed for Canada, never to return until he came back eight or nine months ago.

"The vicar married him, and remembered the circumstances very well. He said Stuart was a very nervous and somewhat conceited man, who lived in terror of his father, a rich landowner in Canada. Stuart confessed to him, over a cup of tea which they had together at the Cecil, that he was leaving his wife and going back to Canada to break the news of his marriage to his father. He was in considerable doubt as to what his father would say, or, to be more exact, he had no doubt whatever that the old man would kick up a shine. The impression left on the vicar's mind was that the old man would disinherit him. To cut a long story short, he said he was leaving London the next day, and at the first opportunity he should tell his father, and then he would return for his wife.

"There's no doubt in my mind," Larry went on, "that Stuart did not tell his father, that he kept the secret of his marriage carefully hidden, and in a panic at being found out, he broke off all communication with his wife."

The girl shook her head.

"One doesn't want to judge the dead too harshly," she said, "but it was not a manly thing to do."

"I agree," said Larry. "It wasn't sporting. He must have left his wife a considerable sum of money. At any rate, when the vicar saw her she was in comfortable circumstances and gave him that impression. Stuart left in March. In June, 1898, three months later, his child was born—the child he never saw, and about whom in all probability he never heard until years of remorse worked upon him and he came back to England to find his wife and establish her in the position to which she was entitled.

"He must have employed an inquiry agent. And the end of his quest was a discovery in the churchyard of Beverley Manor—the grave of his wife and his only child."

"What about Clarissa?" asked the girl, and Larry shrugged.

"That is Mystery No. 2 which has got to be cleared up."

She was silent, this thoughtful girl, and her pretty brows were wrinkled in perplexity. Presently she put down the pen she had been so assiduously biting, and looked across at him with a slow, triumphant smile, a smile which found a ready response in his face.

"You've solved it?" he asked eagerly, and she nodded. "You've solved the mystery of Clarissa?"

"I think it's one of the easiest of the problems to solve," she said calmly, "and I must have been silly not to have thought of it before. Have you the registration of birth?"

"I haven't got that; we're making a search for it to-morrow," said Larry.

"I can save you the trouble," replied Diana Ward. "Clarissa is the other twin daughter."

"Twins!" gasped Larry, and the girl nodded, her eyes dancing with merriment at his surprise.

"Obviously," she said. "Poor Mrs. Stuart had twin daughters. One of them died; the other is Clarissa, of whom Stuart learnt, perhaps, in the last few hours of his life."

Larry looked at her in awe.

"When you are Chief Commissioneress of the Metropolitan Police," he said, "I shall be very obliged to you if you make me your secretary. I feel I have a lot to learn."

Edgar Wallace

Mr. Strauss "Drops"

FLASH FRED had not left London: he had no intention of leaving London, if the truth be told. He had certain doubts in his mind which he had determined to set at rest, certain obscurities on his horizon which he desired should be dispersed. Flash Fred was a clever man. If he had not been clever, he would not have lived in the excellent style he adopted, nor possessed chambers in Jermyn Street and a motor-brougham to take him to the theatre at night. His working expenses were heavy, but his profits were vast. He had many irons in the fire and burnt himself with none of them—which is the art of success in all walks of life.

On the evening of the day that Larry had made his discovery Flash Fred, in the seclusion and solitude of his ornate sitting-room, had elaborated a theory which had followed very close upon a discovery he had made that morning. Men of his temperament and uncertain prospects suffer from a chronic dissatisfaction. This dissatisfaction is half the cause of their departure from the straight and narrow path, and is wholly responsible for their undoing. A hundred pounds a month, payable yearly, is a handsome income; but the underworld abhor anything that savours of steadiness, regularity and system—three qualities which are so associated with prison life that they carry with them a kind of taint particularly distressing to the lag-who-was.

Twelve hundred pounds a year for five years is six thousand pounds, or twenty-four thousand dollars at the present rate of exchange—a respectable sum; but five years represents a big slice taken out of the hectic life of men like Flash Fred. Twelve hundred pounds at best represents only two coups at trente et quarante, and can be lost in three minutes.

Dr. Judd was a collector. It had been reported to Fred that Dr. Judd's residence at Chelsea was a veritable treasure-house of paintings and antique jewellery. Fred had read a newspaper paragraph that Dr. Judd was the possessor of historical gems worth fifty thousand pounds. Though Fred had no passion for history, he had an eye to the value of precious stones. And the theory he had evolved was in the main arithmetical. If he could get away with ten thousand pounds' worth of property in twenty-four hours, he would not

43

only have anticipated his income for eight or nine years, but he would be saved the fag of coming to London every twelve months to collect it. Much might happen in twelve months. It might not always be possible for him to make the journey, since prison authorities are notoriously difficult to persuade. Or he might be dead.

To get that movable property would be difficult, because the doctor was hardly the kind of man to leave his property unguarded. Indeed, the ordinary methods of effecting an entrance were repugnant to Fred's professional feelings. For he gained his livelihood by the cleverness of his tongue and the lightning adjustment of certain brain cells to meet emergencies, and to him a jemmy was an instrument of terror, since it implied work. But there was another method—and once he had made his get-away, would the doctor dare prosecute?

That afternoon, sauntering aimlessly through Piccadilly Circus at the midday hour, he had come face to face with a tall, stoutish man, who, after one glance at him, had attempted to avoid a meeting; but Fred had caught him by the arm and swung him round.

"Why," he said, "if it isn't old No. 278! How are you, Strauss?"

Mr. Strauss's face twitched nervously.

"I think you've made a mistake, sir," he said.

"Come off it," demanded Fred vulgarly, and, taking him by the arm, led him down Lower Regent Street.

"Excuse my not recognizing you," said Mr. Strauss nervously, "but I thought at first you were a bull—split we call them in this country."

"Well, I'm not," said Flash Fred. "And how has the old world been treating you, hey? Do you remember G Gallery at Portland, in B Block?"

The face of the stout man twitched again. He did not like being reminded of his prison experience, though in truth he had little against the prisoner who had occupied the adjoining cell.

"How are you getting on?" he asked. And it happened that that morning Flash Fred had gone out without any visible diamonds—he carried them in his hip pocket, for he trusted nobody.

"Bad," said Fred, which was a lie, but no good crook admits that he is prosperous. Then suddenly: "Why did you think I was a split, Strauss?"

Strauss looked uncomfortable.

"Oh, I just thought so," he said awkwardly.

"Are you at the old game?"

Fred looked at the other steadily and saw his eyes shift.

"No, I'm going straight now," he said.

"A liar you are, and a liar you will always be," said Fred, quoting Larry Holt. "I'll bet you're on the way to 'fence' something."

Again the man looked round as though seeking a way of escape; and Fred, who never despised an opportunity, however small, held out a suggestive palm and said laconically, "Drop!"

"Only a few things," said Mr. Strauss hurriedly. "Thing that were given to me or wouldn't be missed—just odds and ends like. A couple of salt-spoons . . ." He enumerated his loot.

"Drop!" said Fred again. "I'm hard up and want the money. I'll take a share and you shall have the money back—one of these days."

Mr. Strauss dropped, with a curse.

"Come and have a drink," said Fred briskly, when the transaction had been completed to his satisfaction.

"You've left me with about three pounds' worth," grumbled the man. "Really, Mr. Grogan, I don't think you're fair," and he looked at the other suspiciously. "And you don't look as if you're hard up either."

"Appearances are deceptive," said the cheerful Fred, and led the way into a private bar. "What are you now—valet or butler?"

"Butler," replied Strauss, tossing down a dram. "It's not a bad place, Mr. Grogan."

"Call me Fred," begged Flash Fred.

"It seems a liberty," said Strauss, and meant it. "I've got a butler's job with a very nice gentleman," he said.

"Rich?"

Mr. Strauss nodded.

"Yards of it," he said briefly. "But what's the good? He knows I'm a lag, and he's very decent to me."

Fred was eyeing him narrowly.

"You still dope, I see?" he said, and the man flushed.

"Yes," he said gruffly, "I take a little stimulant now and again."

"Well," said Fred, "who is your boss?"

"You wouldn't know him." Mr. Strauss shook his head. "He's a City gentleman, head of an insurance office."

"Dr.–Judd?" asked Flash Fred quickly.

"Why, yes," said the other in surprise. "How did you know?"

They parted soon after, and Flash Fred was a thoughtful man for the rest of the day, and his plans began to take shape towards the evening.

He dressed himself with care after dark, and strolled Strandwards, for he numbered amongst his other accomplishments that of an experienced squire of dames. He had a ready smile for the solitary girl hurrying homewards, and though the rebuffs were many, such conquests as he had to his credit added to the pleasures of memory. Between St. Martin's Church and the corner of the Strand he drew blank, for such girls as he saw were unattractive or were escorted. Opposite Morley's Hotel he saw a peach.

He caught one glimpse of her under a light-standard and was transfixed by the rare beauty of her face. She was alone, and Fred swung round and in two strides had overtaken her.

"Haven't we met before?" he asked, raising his hat, but asked no more. Somebody caught him by the collar and jerked him back.

"Fred, I shall really have to be severe with you," said the hated voice of Larry Holt, and Fred developed an instant grievance.

"Haven't you got a home to go to?" he wailed, and continued his journey to the Strand in a bitter mood, for the romance had been shaken out of him, and he could still feel the knuckles of the shaker at the back of his neck.

*

The girl passed on, unconscious of the fact that Larry Holt had been behind her. It was not an unusual experience to be spoken to in the street, and she had grown hardened to that also.

She lived above a tobacconist's shop in the Charing Cross Road, and Larry saw her open the side door and go into the dark passage; he waited for a few minutes, then continued his walk.

This girl had made an extraordinary impression upon him. He told himself that it was not her delicate beauty, or anything about her that was feminine, but that it was her genius, her extraordinary reasoning faculties which attracted him; and, to do him justice, he believed this. He was not a susceptible man. Beautiful women he had known, on both sides of the border line which separates the good from the bad, the honest from the criminal. He had had minor affairs in his youth, but had come through those fiery dreams unscorched and unmarked by his experiences.

So he told himself. It was extraordinary that it was necessary to tell himself anything; but there was the indisputable fact that he spent a great deal of his spare time in arguing out his attitude of mind toward Diana Ward. And he had known her something over twenty-four hours!

Diana Ward was not thinking of Larry as she went into her flat. Her mind was wholly occupied by the problems which the Stuart case presented. She felt that, if the missing Clarissa were found, they would be on the high road to discovering the cause of Stuart's death and the reason for this hideous crime.

She slammed the door and went up the dark and narrow stairs slowly. The upper part of the tobacconist's was let off in three flats, and she occupied the highest and the cheapest. The tenants of the other two were, she knew, spending the week-end in the country. The first floor was occupied by a bachelor Civil Servant, a hearty man whose parties occasionally kept her awake at night; the second floor by a newspaper artist and his wife; and she had no reason to complain of her neighbours.

She had reached the second landing, her foot was on the stairs of the final two flights, when she stopped. She thought she had heard a noise, the faint creak of a sound which she had felt rather than heard. She waited a second, and then smiled at her nervousness. She had heard these creaks and whispers before on the dark stairs, but had overcome her timidity to discover that they were purely imaginary. Nevertheless, she walked up a little more slowly and reached the landing from whence rose a short flight of stairs to her own apartments. The landing was a broad one, and as she turned, with one hand on the banisters, she put out the other in a spirit of bravado as though she groped for some hidden intruder.

And then her blood turned to water, for her hand had touched the coat of a man! She screamed, but instantly a hand, a big unwholesome hand, covered her face, and she was drawn slowly backward. She fought and struggled with all her might, but the man who held her had almost superhuman strength, and the arm about her was like a vice. Then, suddenly, she went limp, and momentarily the arm that held her relaxed.

"Fainted, have ye?" said a harsh voice, and as a hand came feeling down for her face, the other arm relaxed a little more.

With a sudden dart the girl broke free, ran up the remaining stairs and opened and slammed the door. There was a key on the inside and this she turned with a heart full of gratitude that she had never locked her bedroom door from the outside. She flew across the room, stopping only to switch on the lights, pulled out a drawer and took from its depths a small revolver. Diana Ward came from a stock which was not easily scared, and, though her heart was pounding painfully, she ran back at the door and flung it open.

She stood for the space of a few seconds. She heard a stealthy footstep on the stairs and fired. There was a roar of fear and a blunder of feet down the stairs. Only for a moment did she hesitate, and then raced down the stairway in pursuit. She heard the thump of feet on the landing lower down, heard the rattle of the door, and came down the last flight to find it open and nobody in sight.

Concealing the revolver in a fold of her dress, she stepped out into the Charing Cross Road. At this hour there were few pedestrians, and she looked round for some sign of her assailant. A light motor-van was driving away, and the only person she saw near at hand was an old blind man. The iron ferrule of his stick came "tap-tap-tap," as he stumbled painfully along.

"Pity the blind," he wailed; "pity the poor blind!"

Burglars at the Yard

SUNNY," said Larry to his servitor, "London is a terrible city."

"Indeed it is, sir," said Mr. Patrick Sunny.

"But it has one bright, radiant feature which redeems it from utter desolation and abomination."

"I think you're right, sir," said Sunny. "I've often noticed that myself, sir. I'm very fond of the picture houses myself."

"I'm not talking about the picture houses," snapped Larry. "Nothing is further from my thoughts than the cinema houses. I am talking of something different, something spiritual."

"Would you like a whisky and soda, sir?" asked Sunny, at last securing a tangible line.

"Get out!" roared Larry, bubbling with laughter. "Get out, you horrible materialist! Go to the pictures."

"Yes, sir," said Sunny, "but it's rather late."

"Then go to bed," said Larry. "Stop a bit. Bring me my writing-case."

He was wearing his favourite indoor kit, a dressing-gown, a pair of old cricketing trousers and a soft shirt, and now he filled his polished brier with a sense of physical well-being.

"Believe me, Sunny," said Larry Holt impressively, "there are many worse places than London on a bright spring day, when your heart——"

There was a faint rat-tat-tat on the other door. "A visitor at this time of night!" said Larry in surprise. It could not be from Scotland Yard, because Scotland Yard use the telephone freely, a little too freely sometimes.

"I think there's somebody at the door, sir," said Sunny.

"That's a fine bit of reasoning on your part," said Larry. "Open it."

He waited and heard a brief exchange of questions. The visitor was a woman; and before he could guess who it was, the door opened and Diana Ward came in. He saw by her face that something had happened, and went to meet her.

"What is the matter?" he asked quickly. "That man didn't follow you?"

"What man?" she demanded in surprise.

"Flash Fred."

She shook her head.

"I don't know whether it was Flash Fred," she said grimly, "but if he is somebody particularly unpleasant, it was probably he."

"Sit down. Would you like some coffee? I'm just going to have a cup. Sunny, get two coffees."

"Yes, sir," said Sunny, and then, significantly, "Do you want me to go out to the pictures, sir?"

Larry blushed angrily.

"Get some coffee, you—you—you——" he spluttered. "Now, what is it?"

The girl told the story of her adventure without preliminary. Larry listened with a serious face.

"You say he was big? That rules out Flash Fred," he said. "Do you think it was a burglar—somebody who had broken in and whom your arrival interrupted?"

"I don't think so," she shook her head. "In fact, I know that it was a much more serious attack. When I got back to my flat, I went through all the rooms. In the dining-room, the room to which I would have gone first in ordinary circumstances, I found a long laundry basket."

"A laundry basket?" he repeated in surprise.

She nodded.

"It was lined with a sort of quilting, very thick, and the lid was padded in the same way. Inside of it was this."

She laid down the object she had been carrying. It looked like an airman's cap, except that there was no opening for the mouth.

He took it up and sniffed, though, there was no need for this, for he had noticed the sweet scent when she had come into the room.

"It is saturated in chloroform," he said. "Of course, this would not make you entirely insensible, but it would have quietened you."

He paced the room, his hands in his pockets, his chin on his chest.

"Did you find anything else?"

"When I got out into the street," she said, "a laundry van was just moving off. I noticed it particularly, because I thought at the time that the word 'laundry'—and that was all the inscription the van bore—had been written by an amateur, and very badly done."

"I can't understand it," said Larry, bewildered. "The brute couldn't have got you away. He must have had some assistants in the house."

"I don't agree with you," she said quietly. "This man was terribly strong. I felt like an infant in his arms, and it would have been a very simple matter for him to have slid the basket down the stairs and carried it out across the pavement with the help of the man who was driving the van."

"But why you?" he asked, bewildered. "Why should they bother about you?"

She did not reply immediately.

"I am wondering," she said at last, "whether I have by accident stumbled upon some clue which incriminates the Stuart murderers. Perhaps, without knowing that I have such a clue, I am in possession of information which they wish to suppress."

Larry was very thoughtful.

"Just wait here a little while and I'll change," he said, and disappeared from the room.

The girl looked round the cosy flat appreciatively and Sunny came in, bearing a tray, first stopping outside the door to cough loudly, to the intense annoyance of Larry, who heard him from the other room.

"Will you have sugar, miss?" asked Sunny solemnly, and when she nodded: "Some ladies don't like sugar. It makes them fat."

"I'm not very much afraid of getting fat," she smiled.

"No, ma'am, you wouldn't be," said Sunny agreeably.

On the way to the flat she asked Larry laughingly if Sunny agreed with everything he said.

"With everything I've ever said," said Larry. "He drives me to despair sometimes. I have yet to find the subject upon which Sunny has an independent, definite opinion."

Later he was to discover there was at least one matter in which Sunny had a mind of his own, but that time was distant.

They came to the apartment in Charing Cross Road, and Larry began his search. He had brought a flash lamp with him, and inspected every stair, without, however, coming upon a single clue that would identify the mysterious assailant.

"Now we'll have a look at your room."

He examined the laundry basket, which the girl had exactly described.

"Nothing new here," he said. "See if anything is missing."

She made an independent search and came back to him in the sitting-room with a puzzled face.

"My green coat, an overcoat I wear, and a hat have disappeared."

"A distinctive hat?" he asked quickly.

"What do you mean by a distinctive hat?" she asked in surprise.

"Is it rather striking?"

"It is rather," she smiled. "It is a golden yellow hat which I wear with my green coat."

He nodded.

"Have you worn it to the Yard?" he asked.

"Often," she replied in surprise.

"Then that's it," said he. "Come down with me. I don't want to leave you alone."

She followed him into the street, and he went into the nearest telephone booth and rang up Scotland Yard and got the officer on duty at the door.

"Has Miss Ward been in to-night? It is Inspector Holt speaking," he asked.

"Yes, sir," was the reply. "She's just gone out."

Larry groaned.

"But I haven't been to Scotland Yard," she said in surprise.

"Somebody has impersonated you!" he said shortly.

They were in the grim building on the Thames Embankment within a few minutes, and the door of 47 was apparently untampered with. He opened the door and switched on the lights.

"Oh, yes," he said softly, for the doors of the cupboard wherein he had kept the clues concerning the death of Stuart hung broken upon their hinges.

He pulled out the tray and gave a rapid glance at its contents.

The Braille writing had disappeared!

Fanny Weldon Tells the Truth

HE LIFTED the telephone, and presently:

"Send the first two officers in the building," he said, "and a messenger, quick!"

The girl was watching interestedly. Now she saw the real Larry Holt, the man of whom it is said by the Commissioner that "he slept trailing." At his request, she stood outside the open door whilst he conducted an investigation. The light jemmy which the intruder had used he had not troubled to take away. It lay on the floor, and he picked it up with a piece of paper and carried it to the light.

A short thread of cotton adhered to its rough end, which meant that its user had worn cotton gloves to avoid finger-prints. His only hope was the tray. It was a flat glass tray with wicker sides and handles, and he knew that if the gloves came off anywhere it would be here; for a person unaccustomed to working in gloves would remove them to examine the smaller objects. And his surmise was right. When he breathed on the polished back of the gold watch, a distinct thumb-print was visible.

By this time two officers had arrived.

"Is there a man on duty in the print department?" asked Larry.

"Yes, sir," replied the officer.

"Take this watch down. Hold it by the stem. If he cannot bring up the print by powder I want it photographed and verified within the next hour."

The burglar had made another faux pas. Larry had pulled out the waste-paper basket without disturbing its contents and had taken out three screwed-up pieces of paper, two of which proved to be nothing more important than memoranda in Diana's writing. The third, however, was a plan of the room, drawn in ink by a skilful hand, the cupboard being marked and the positions of the desks shown.

"They thought there were three cupboards here," said Larry, pointing. "There is one supposed to be on the left of the fireplace," he looked up and raised his eyebrows. "By Jingo, they're right!" he said. "And another behind the door," he looked and nodded. "They know this room much better than I do, Miss Ward," he said, and looked at the paper again. "The man who drew this has a knowledge of architectural drawing," said he. "I think we'd better have a safe and a bodyguard," he added bitterly.

Somebody appeared in the doorway. It was Sir John Hason, who sometimes returned to his office at night to take advantage of the quiet and freedom from interruption which the evening hours afforded.

"What has happened, Larry?" he asked.

"Oh, nothing," said Larry airily, "only a burglar has broken into Scotland Yard! Don't you think we ought to send for the police?" he asked sardonically and Sir John grinned. But the smile came off his face instantly.

"They haven't taken the Stuart clues, have they?"

"The only clue that matters," replied Larry. "It would be a good idea if we brought some Boy Scouts into this building to look after our movable property!"

"I like you when you're funny," said the Commissioner, but he was serious. "We'll have the doorkeeper up."

The doorkeeper, when he came, could give no satisfactory explanation, except that he had thought it was Miss Ward who had passed. It was the practice to call the number of the room when its occupants came in for duty, and this was also the custom after office hours. The visitor had said "47," and had been allowed to pass unchallenged.

"There have been no strangers here, have there?" asked Larry.

"No," said the girl, and then: "There was a blind man here this afternoon: you remember, you wanted to see the instruments these poor people use, and I asked the little old man who sells matches on the Embankment to come up."

Larry remembered.

"At any rate, he couldn't have made a plan of the room," he said.

"The system seems to be a little bit groggy," said Sir John when the doorkeeper had gone. "We can't really blame this man. It is our own fault."

"There's hardly enough light in the main hall to read a newspaper placard," complained Larry. "Here is the finger-print gentleman."

The officer who came up had a broad smile: the smile of a man who had justified his hobby.

"Got it first time, sir," he said. "Fanny Weldon, 280 Coram Street. Here's her record." He handed the card to Larry.

"Twice gaoled for impersonation," he read. "That's the woman. But how did she come into this game?"

The officer who had taken the watch away, and who now restored it, supplied the information.

"Fanny's a queer woman, sir," he said. "She hasn't a spark of originality, and she's had all her trouble through helping other people in their schemes. Big Joe Jaket employed her to impersonate Miss Lottie Home, the actress, about two years ago; and then she was employed by somebody else to impersonate a barmaid whilst the landlord was away, when the Mannic gang cleared out three thousand from the Hotel Victor Hugo."

Larry was sitting at the table, his chin in his palm, thinking.

"That is what has happened," he said. "These people have got track of all the crooks in London, and it's just as likely they've employed Fanny. 280 Coram Street, I think you said? We'll see what Fanny has to say for herself."

He did not see Fanny until daylight. 280 Coram Street was a corner house, apparently rented out in rooms. Soon after daybreak a cab drew up to the kerb outside the door and a woman stepped out and paid the driver. As she walked to the door, Larry came behind her and took her arm. She turned round with an exclamation of fright. She was a pretty woman with a shrewish mouth.

"Here, what are you doing?" she asked in alarm.

"You're coming for a little walk with me," said Larry.

"Is it a cop?" she asked, going pale.

"A fair cop," said Larry, and, still holding her elbow, led her to the nearest police station, where Diana and his officers were waiting.

On the way to the station she bewailed her fate.

"This comes of being obliging," she said bitterly. "What's the charge?"

"Sacrilege," said Larry solemnly, and she was astonished.

"Sacrilege? What do you mean? Breaking into a church or something?"

"Breaking into Scotland Yard," said Larry.

She drew a long breath.

"Then it is a cop!" she said.

"You've said it," replied her captor.

They put her in the steel pen, but not before she had been searched by one of the woman attendants. The search produced £150 in bank-notes, which Fanny, who had now recovered her good spirits, insisted should be counted.

"I've lost things in police stations before," she said significantly.

She was not taken to the cells, but in a little waiting-room Larry and Diana interviewed her. And the presence of Diana was a source of great interest to the prisoner.

"You've brought your young lady along, I see?" she said flippantly. She was gamin right through, despite her smart clothes and her elaborate jewellery. "Is this the lady I 'took off'?"

"She's the identical lady," said Larry. "Now, Fanny, I'm going to talk to you like a father."

"Go ahead and don't mind me," said Fanny recklessly. "But I can tell you that I've been going straight for months," and Larry grinned.

"I should like to draw a line alongside that straight course of yours," he said. "It'd be a bit bumpy. Fanny, I'm going to give you a chance. And I shall be perfectly frank with you. Scotland Yard doesn't want the world to know that a female hook has broken in under its nose and pinched certain articles of value."

The woman laughed softly, and, catching Diana's eye, winked.

"It takes a woman to do that sort of thing, eh, dearie?" she asked. "Proceed with your story, Mr. Busy Fellow. But if you think I'm going to give anybody away, why, you're making a mistake."

"You will give away just what I want you to give away," said Larry sharply. "You are going to tell me who employed you to do this job."

She shook her head.

"You will also tell me who was the man to whom you handed the stuff, and where."

Again she shook her head, but she was in a good humour.

"There is no use in asking me questions," she said. "I'm not going to answer. You can put me into the cell just as soon as you like, and save yourself a lot of trouble."

"I'll put you into the cell after I've charged you," said Larry quietly, and the woman looked up sharply.

"You have charged me with breaking and entering," she said.

"That is not the crime which I shall bring against you," said Larry. "If I get no satisfaction from you now I shall take you back to the pen and charge you with being an accessory to the murder of Gordon Stuart on the night of the twenty-third of April."

She looked at him, speechless.

"Murder?" she repeated. "Good Gawd! You don't mean that I'm in—"

"You're in bad," said Larry. "You're assisting murderers to escape the processes of justice. You were employed to steal a very important clue which the police held, and which might have led to the conviction of the murderer—and that is sufficient offence to bring you under the gravest suspicion."

She was serious now.

"Do you mean that?" she asked.

"I do indeed," said Larry earnestly. "See here, Fanny, I don't want you to think I'm kidding you. I'm giving it you as straight as it's possible for one human being to give a thing to another. You went out to steal the clue which might have led to the arrest of the murderers."

"What is your name?" she asked.

"I am Inspector Larry Holt," and she gasped.

"Suffering Moses! Then I am in bad!" she said. "I thought you were abroad. Now, Mr. Holt, I'll tell you. I've heard a lot about you, and I'm told that you always play straight with a hook. I knew nothing about this job until yesterday afternoon, and then I had a telephone call asking me to meet Big Jake, or Blind Jake as they call him."

"Blind Jake?" repeated Larry, to whom the name was new, and then he recalled the blind match-seller on the Embankment who had come to his office—but it could not be he. Diana had said he was a small man.

"Your men know all about him, Mr. Holt," Fanny hesitated. "He's a wicked man. Now, that sounds funny coming from me; but if you know what I mean, he's just wicked. I'm scared to death of Blind Jake, and there isn't a hook in London who isn't. He's been inside twice: once for unlawfully wounding and once for being in possession of property. There used to be three of 'em, all hooks together, and all blind! We used to call 'em the blind eyes of London, because they could get about quicker than you, and in a fog they'd beat the best detectives that ever lived, because fog never means anything to them. Blind Jake used to be the boss of the three, and then one of 'em disappeared and I heard he was dead. We never heard much about them for twelve months, and then Blind Jake turned up again with yards of money. I believe he is working for a big boss."

"Well, you met Blind Jake?"

"Yes," she nodded. "He gave me the plan—"

"Not his own—he couldn't draw," interrupted Larry.

"Not him," said the woman contemptuously. "No, he brought the plan with him. I've got it somewhere. Maybe it's in the bag you've taken."

"Don't worry about the plan," said Larry. "I found that in the office."

"Well, Blind Jake told me how to go about it, said he would give me a coat and a hat that this young lady always wore when she went to the Yard, and I got instructions that I was to say '47' when I went into the room, and run upstairs quick."

"What were you told to get?"

"A little roll of brown paper," said the woman. "They told me where it was and almost how it was placed in the tray." She shrugged her shoulders. "I can't guess how they knew."

"I can," said Larry and turned to the girl. "The little old match-seller recovered his sight! Where can I find Blind Jake?" he asked the woman.

"You won't find him," she said, shaking her head. "He never comes out by day—at least, very seldom."

"What is he like in appearance?"

"Very big and as strong as an ox."

Diana uttered an exclamation.

"Has he a beard?" she asked.

"Yes, miss," said the woman. "A little greyish kind of beard."

"It was the man on the stairs," said Diana, "I am certain of it."

Larry nodded.

"Well," he said, addressing the woman, "when did you hand over the stuff?"

"About two o'clock this morning. That was the time he said I was to meet him at the lower end of Arundel Street in the Strand, near the Embankment. And a pretty fine temper he was in, too."

"Do you know where he lives?" asked Larry.

She shook her head.

"Years ago they used to live in Todd's Home," she said. "That's an institute in Lissom Lane, Paddington, where they used to look after the blind hawkers. But I don't think he's there now."

Larry took the woman back to the charge room.

"You can release her on my recognisance," he said. "Fanny, you will report to me to-morrow morning at Scotland Yard at ten o'clock."

"Yes, sir," said Fanny. "What about my money?"

Larry thought a moment.

"You can take that," he said.

"If anybody tells me," said Fanny, as she collected and counted her notes with offensive care, "that the police are dishonest, I shall have something to say."

Todd's Home

MY DEAR," said Larry gently, "you really must go home and go to bed."
Diana shook her head laughingly.

"I really am not tired, Mr. Holt," she said. "Won't you let me go along with
you? You know, you promised to keep me in this case."

"I didn't promise to keep you up all night," he said good-humouredly, "and
you're looking a wreck. I don't think I shall do anything much more this
morning—except sleep," said he. "Now, off you go. There's a providential taxi
crawling this way," he said, and whistled.

She was feeling desperately tired, and she knew his words were the words
of wisdom. But she made one last ineffectual protest. Larry was adamant. The
cab drew up and he opened the door for her.

"Sergeant Harvey will go home with you," he said, and drew Harvey aside.
"Go upstairs to Miss Ward's room, search it thoroughly, and remain on duty
on the lower landing until you're relieved."

He watched the cab out of sight, then turned to the second officer who had
accompanied him.

"Now, sergeant," he said, "I think we will investigate Todd's Home."

It was some time before they found another taxi, and Larry had a
constitutional objection to walking. Six o'clock was booming out from the
church towers when the cab put them down before Todd's Home. It was a
bleak, unlovely house, the windows covered with blue-wash. A long black
board, covering the width of the house, was inscribed in faded gold letters:
"Todd's Home for the Indigent Blind."

Larry expected he would have some difficulty in making the inmates hear,
but he was mistaken; for, hardly had he knocked when the door was opened
by a little man.

"That's not Toby and not Harry and not Old Joe," he said loudly. "Who
is it?"

Larry saw that he was blind.

"I want to see the superintendent," he said.

"Yes, sir," said the man in a tone of respect. "Just wait here, will you?"

He went down a long passage full of turns and angles, so that he disappeared from sight, and presently they heard him shuffling back in his slippered feet, and behind him walked a tall man wearing a white clerical collar. His eyes were covered with dark blue glasses, and he too felt his way along the passage.

"Won't you please come in?" he said in an educated voice. He was a man of powerful build, and his clean-shaven face denoted a strength of character out of the ordinary. "I am John Dearborn—the Rev. John Dearborn," he explained as he led the way. "We have few visitors here, alas! I'm afraid Todd's Home is not very popular."

He did not speak resentfully but cheerfully, and as one who had a great spirit. Nor did he make allusion to the early hour they had chosen.

"It is a little farther along, gentlemen," he said. "I know there are two of you because I can hear your footsteps. Mind the step—this way."

He pushed open a door and they went in. The room was cosily furnished, and the first thing that Larry noticed was the bare condition of the walls; and then he remembered, with a little pang, that the blind have no need for pictures.

A curious little instrument stood by the side of the table, which was the principal article of furniture in the room, and a tiny wheel was spinning as they came in. The superintendent walked unerringly to the machine. There was the snap of a button and the wheel ceased to revolve.

"This is my dictating machine," he explained, turning to them with a smile. "I am engaged in literary work, and I can dictate to this cylinder, which is then transferred to an operator who types from my voice."

Larry expressed polite interest.

"Now, gentlemen," said the Rev. John Dearborn as he seated himself, "to what am I indebted for the honour of this visit?"

"I am an officer from Scotland Yard," said Larry, "and my name is Holt." The other inclined his head.

"I hope none of my unfortunate men have been getting into trouble?" he asked.

"I don't exactly know yet," said Larry. "At present I am searching for a man called Blind Jake."

"Blind Jake?" repeated the other slowly. "I don't think we have had such a name in the Home since I have been in charge. I've been here for four years," he explained. "It used to be run, and very badly run, by a man who got together quite the worst type of blind men in London. You know that the blind are wonderful and heroic, and the majority of them are positively an inspiration to those who have sight. But there are a class of men so afflicted who are the scum of the earth. You have probably heard of the Dark Eyes?"

"Not until this morning," said Larry, and the other nodded.

"We have got rid of those people, and we have now very respectable old hawkers who come here, where everything is done for them. You would like to see the home?"

"You don't know Blind Jake?"

"I have never heard of him," said the Rev. John Dearborn, "but if you will come with me, we will make inquiries."

The Home consisted of four dormitories and a common room; and in this latter, reeking with tobacco smoke, sat the inmates of the Home. Larry looked round and could scarcely repress a shiver.

"Just one moment," said Mr. Dearborn, when he had ushered the two men into the passage. He returned shortly, shaking his head.

"Nobody there knows Blind Jake, though one has heard of him."

They ascended to the first dormitory.

"I don't suppose you want to see any more," said Mr. Dearborn.

Larry raised his head.

"I thought I heard somebody groaning."

"Yes, yes, a sad case," said the superintendent. "There are cubicles upstairs for those men who can afford to pay a little more than their fellows. In one of them we have a man who, I fear, is going out of his mind. I have had to report the case to the local authorities."

"May we go upstairs?" asked Larry.

"With pleasure," said the Rev. Dearborn, after a moment's hesitation. "The only thing I am afraid of," he said as he led the way, "is that the language of this man will distress you."

In a little cubicle lay a wizened man of sixty, who tossed desperately to and fro in his bed, and all the time he was talking, talking to some invisible person. And Larry, watching him, wondered.

"Brute! Coward!" muttered the man on the bed. "You'll swing for it, mark my words! You'll swing for it!"

"It is very terrible," said the Rev. John Dearborn, turning away and shaking his head. "This way, gentlemen."

But Larry did not move.

"All right, Jake, you'll suffer too! Mark my words, you'll suffer! Let them do their dirty work! I didn't put the paper in his pocket, I tell you."

Larry took a step into the cubicle, and, bending over, shook the man.

"Let go my arm, you're hurting it," said the man on the bed, and Larry released his hold.

"Wake up," he said, "I want to speak to you."

But the man went talking on, and Larry shook him again.

"Leave me alone," growled the old man. "I don't want to have any more trouble."

"What is your name?" asked Larry.

"I don't want any more trouble," said the man.

"He's quite delirious," said John Dearborn. "He is under the impression that he's accused of a practical joke on one of his friends down stairs."

"But he said 'Jake,'?" said Larry.

"There is a Jake below—Jake Horley. Would you like to see him? He's a little fellow and rather amusing."

Disappointed, Larry walked down the stairs and took farewell of his conductor.

"I am very glad to have had a visit from the police," said John Dearborn. "I only wish that we could persuade other people to come to us. You have seem some of our work and some of the difficulties with which we are faced. Before you go," he added, "perhaps you will tell me why you are seeking

Blind Jake? The men will be consumed with curiosity to know the reason for this police visit."

"That is easy to satisfy," smiled Larry. "There is a charge against him made by a woman to the effect that she was employed by him to commit a felony."

The police officer who was with him gasped, for it is not the practice of the police to give away their informants.

Larry opened the door himself and paused with his hand upon the handle.

"Pardon my asking what may be a very painful question, Mr. Dearborn," he said gently. "Are you afflicted——?"

"Oh, yes," said the other cheerfully, "I am quite blind. I wear these glasses from sheer vanity. I think they improve my appearance." He laughed softly.

"Good-bye," said Larry, shaking his disengaged hand, and then he pulled the door open and came face to face with Flash Fred.

Flash Fred was dumbfounded, and he walked backwards down the few steps at some peril to himself. Larry surveyed him, his head on one side, like an inquisitive hen.

"Are you following me or am I following you?" he asked gently. "And why this early rising, Fred? Have you been out all night at your—business?"

For once Fred had no words. He had walked all the way from Jermyn Street to Paddington, and had been very careful to see that he had not been followed. At last he found his voice.

"So it was a trap, was it?" he said bitterly. "I might have guessed it. But you've got nothing on me, Mr. Holt."

"I have several things on you," said Larry pleasantly. He had unconsciously closed the door of the Home behind him. "I don't like your face, I don't like your jewels, I positively loathe your record. What is the idea, Fred? Have you called to deliver a contribution? Is your conscience pricking you?"

"Stow that stuff, Mr. Holt," growled Fred, and to Larry's surprise began walking away with him.

"Aren't you going to the Home?" he asked.

"No, I'm not," snapped Fred.

They walked on in silence, Fred between the two police officers, and his thoughts were very busy. They had reached the broad thoroughfare of Edgware Road before he had completed his mental exoneration.

"I don't know what you've got me for. You can't pinch me for ancient 'istory."

In moments of perturbation Fred suffered certain lapses of style.

"History," corrected Larry. "For the matter of that, I don't know why you're with us. But since you've forced yourself upon us, and since there's nobody to see the disgraceful company I keep, I will endure you."

Fred stopped short.

"Do you mean to tell me that I'm not pinched?" he asked incredulously.

"So far as I am concerned you are not," said Larry, "unless Sergeant Reed has a private engagement with you."

"Not me, sir," smiled Sergeant Reed. "Who told you you were pinched, Fred?"

"Well, that beats it," said Fred, aghast. "What was the game?"

"Don't you know somebody at the Home?"

"I don't know it from a cowshed," said Fred. "I had to inquire my way of a milkman."

"You should have asked a policeman," murmured Larry. "There are plenty about."

"There are too many about for me," replied Flash Fred vindictively. "Here, Mr. Holt," he said with sudden seriousness, "you're a gentleman, and I know you wouldn't put me wrong."

Larry passed the compliment without comment.

"Well?" he said, and Fred dived into his inner pocket and produced a letter.

"What do you make of this, sir?" he asked.

Larry opened the letter, which was addressed to Fred Grogan, and began:

"They are going to arrest you to-morrow. Larry Holt has the warrant for execution. Come to Todd's Home in Lissom Lane at half-past six in the morning and ask to see 'Lew,' and he will give you information that will help you to make a get-away. Don't allow yourself to be shadowed, or tell anybody where you are going."

It was unsigned, and Larry folded the letter and was about to give it to Fred.

"Do you mind if I keep this?" he asked.

"No sir, I don't mind. But, Mr. Holt, will you tell me," he demanded nervously, "is there any truth in that yarn of my being pinched?"

Larry shook his head.

"So far as I know you are not on the list, and certainly I have no warrant for you, Fred," he said. "In fact, you have such a good record just now that if you ran straight you could pretty well live without fear of the police."

"Sounds damned uninteresting to me," said Flash Fred as he slouched off, and Larry let him go.

Fanny Has a Visitor

NO. 280 CORAM STREET was an apartment house, and Mrs. Fanny Weldon occupied two rooms, one facing Coram Street and one a side turning. She lived well and she paid well, gave little or no trouble, and the breath of scandal did not touch her name. Not noticeably. She was in truth the star boarder, and her landlady would have gone very far to oblige Fanny, always providing that the fair name of 280 was not assailed.

This woman crook had spent a busy night, yet sleep refused to come to her in the day, and she rose at three in the afternoon and busied herself with those occupations which women of all kinds find interesting. She had a hat to trim, some dainty silk to iron, a little mending and a little darning.

"You were up late last night, Mrs. Weldon?" said the landlady, bringing her tea with her own hands.

Fanny nodded.

"To be exact, I wasn't in bed all night," she said, "I went to a dance. What time is it?"

"Six o'clock. I thought you were sleeping, and as you didn't ring, I didn't disturb you."

"I'm going to bed early to-night," said Fanny, yawning. "Is there anything fresh?"

"No, my dear," said the landlady, professionally maternal. "We've got a new young gentleman in the opposite room," she jerked her thumb at the door. "A gentleman from Manchester, and very quiet. Mrs. Hooper made some trouble about the dinner." She retailed grisly gossip of the boarding-house.

"Send me up something cold on a tray," said Fanny. "I am going to bed early. I have a very important appointment to-morrow."

She was looking forward to her appointment with Larry Holt in no great spirit of enthusiasm.

It was half-past seven when the woman undressed slowly and went to bed. She was deadly tired, and she fell asleep almost before her head touched the pillow. The dreams of evil-doers are no more unsound as a rule than the dreams of the pure and virtuous. But Fanny was over-tired and dreamt badly—ghastly dreams of monstrous shapes; of high buildings on the parapet of which she was poised, ready to fall; of men who chased her armed with long bright knives—and she turned and twisted in her bed restlessly. Then she dreamt she had committed a murder: she had murdered Gordon Stuart. She had never heard of Gordon Stuart until Larry had mentioned his name, but she pictured him as a weak youth.

And now the day of doom had come, she dreamt, and they brought her from the cell with her hands strapped behind her, and she paced slowly by the side of a white-robed clergyman into a little shed. And then a man, an executioner, had stepped out, and he had the mocking face of Blind Jake. She felt the rope about her neck, and tried to scream, but it was choking her, choking her. She woke up.

Two hands were about her throat, and in the reflected light from a street lamp outside, she looked up into the sightless face of Blind Jake. It was no dream, it was reality! She tried to move, but he held her so that she was powerless. One of his knees pressed on her and he was talking softly, a sibilant whisper, meant only for her ear.

"Fanny, you gave me away," he whispered. "You gave me away, you devil! Poor old Blind Jake! You tried to put him into jug, you did! I know all about it. I've got a little pal at Todd's who told me. And now you're going out, d'ye hear?"

She was choking, choking; she could not articulate, she felt her face going purple and the cruel hands tightening. And then the light switched on, and the "man from Manchester" who had occupied the bedroom on the opposite side of the landing, and who had waited throughout the night listening for the stealthy tread of Blind Jake, knowing that he would come after he had learnt he was betrayed—Larry Holt, a long Browning in his hand, covered the strangler.

"Put up your hands, Jake," he said, and Blind Jake turned round with a low growl like the snarl of a tiger at bay.

The Fight in the Dark

FOR a moment they stood thus, neither man moving, then Jake put up his hands slowly.

"Got a little gun, have ye?" he growled. "You're not going to hurt a poor old man, Mr. Holt?"

"Come forward steadily," said Larry, "and don't try any tricks or you'll be sorry for yourself."

"Sorry enough now, Mr. Holt," grumbled the man.

It was wonderful to watch him. He moved as lightly as a girl, and his extraordinary sixth sense enabled him to avoid every obstacle which stood in his way.

Larry was in a dilemma. The man's advance toward him brought the half-fainting woman on the bed in the line of fire. But for that he undoubtedly intended to shoot if the man showed fight, but it was impossible to fire now, even to save his life, without risking the life of Fanny Weldon. And yet it would have been unfair and asking the impossible to expect the man to advance by any other way, the furniture in the room being disposed as it was. But the real danger to Larry he never saw until it was upon him.

The big man came forward, his hands in the air, and one of them touched awkwardly the hanging electric light. And then before Larry knew or guessed what was happening, the big man's hand closed round the bulb, there was a deafening explosion as it burst under the pressure, and the room was in darkness.

To fire now would have been madness, and Larry put one foot back and braced himself to meet the shock of the body which he knew was hurtling towards him. And then he found himself in the hands of Blind Jake. Diana had not exaggerated his strength. It was terrific, and though Larry was a strong man he felt himself going under. What might have been the result of that struggle, Larry Holt has never speculated upon in cold blood. But there came an interruption, the sound of an opening door on the landing above and a man's voice, and then Blind Jake lifted the detective as though he had been a bundle of rags, and flung him to the other end of the room, where he lay gasping and breathless.

A second later the door had opened and Blind Jake was going down the carpeted stairs faster than any man with eyesight would have dared.

Larry struggled to his feet, took his flash lamp from the floor and found his revolver where it had dropped. He picked it up and, running to the window, flung it open and peered out. But Blind Jake had already gone round the corner.

Somebody brought another globe, and Larry went to look after the girl. She was still unconscious, the purple marks about her throat testifying to the character of Blind Jake's grip.

"You had better get a doctor," he said to the landlady, who was the third person in the room, and she looked at him with suspicion and distrust.

"What were you doing in this room?" she asked accusingly. "I am going to send for a policeman."

"Send for two," said Larry, "and get a doctor."

Fortunately the police station was near at hand, and the divisional surgeon had been called to examine a doubtful case of drunkenness, and he was on the spot within a few minutes.

By this time the woman had come back to life, but had subsided into a condition of hysteria, painful to witness.

"You had better get her into an infirmary or a hospital, I think, doctor," said Holt, and the surgeon agreed.

He was looking at the marks about her throat with a puzzled expression.

"No man could have done this," he said, "he must have used an instrument of some kind."

Larry laughed. It was a very rueful laugh.

"If you think that, doctor," he said, "you'd better have a look at my throat," and he showed the red weal where Blind Jake's thumb and finger had gripped.

"Do you mean to say that he did that to you?" asked the doctor incredulously.

"I do not mean to say very much about it," said Larry, "because it is not an adventure of which I am inordinately proud, but he picked me up like a tennis ball and chucked me amongst the crockery-ware under the window."

The doctor whistled. By this time the landlady had been assured of Larry's bona fides and was at once apologetic and tearful at the indignity which had been offered to her house by the presence, even for one night, of a detective officer.

Larry went out into the street to breathe the night air. He was dizzy and shaky and sore. The fact that he, Larry Holt, who had pretensions to winning the middle-weight amateur championship, had been treated like a punch-ball did not distress him. What made him grave was the knowledge that there was loose in the world, and in the city of London, a man of the criminal classes more dangerous than a tiger, with the strength of a bear and an intelligence which was little better than a monkey's.

"And that exhausts the whole Zoological Gardens," said Larry after he had enumerated the unpleasant qualities of his assailant.

Half an hour afterwards every police station received an all-stations message, and the hunt for Big Jake had begun.

Larry reached his flat at three o'clock, and Sunny was dozing peacefully in a chair. He aroused his servant with a gentle tap.

"Sunny," said he, "I have had the experience of a lifetime."

"I suppose you have, sir," said Sunny, blinking himself awake. "Will you have some coffee too, sir?"

Larry was thinking, thinking, thinking. He stood with his hands in his pockets and his legs wide apart, gazing down at the hearthrug.

"He took me by the scruff of the neck, Sunny," he said softly, "and he threw me to the other side of the room."

"He would, sir," said Sunny. "What time would you like your tea in the morning?"

Weary and sick as he was, Larry had to laugh.

"If I were brought home with my neck broken, Sunny," he demanded irritably, "what would you do?"

"I should stop the morning papers, sir," said Sunny without hesitation. "I think I should be doing right, sir."

"Haven't you got a heart?" snarled Larry.

"No, sir," was the surprising reply. "The doctor says it's indigestion, sir."

Larry made a gesture of despair, kicked off his boots, slipped off his coat and vest, followed that with his collar and tie, and loosening his braces, he lay down on the bed and pulled the eiderdown over him. He did this partly because he was very tired and partly because he knew that it would annoy Sunny.

Mr. Grogan Meets a Lady

THERE was a fashionable wedding on the Monday at St. George's, Hanover Square. A queue of motor-cars and broughams stretched in all directions and lined both sides of the streets and partly filled Hanover Square.

Amongst those present, as they say, was Mr. Frederick Grogan. Flash Fred had not been invited, for two reasons. In the first place the friends of bride and bridegroom did not know him, and in the second place he would not have been invited if they had. But a little thing like an invitation did not worry Fred. He knew that when the family of the bride and the bridegroom were meeting for the first time and were regarding one another with mutual suspicion and deprecation, and when all sorts of obscure cousins emerged from the oblivion which happily covered them and were not even recognizable to the principal actors in the great drama, that a face such as his, and a smartly tailored figure such as he possessed, would pass muster and gain for him a prominent seat. So he arrived at St. George's in a glossy silk hat, white kid gloves, and perfectly pressed trousers, and made his way up the aisle, where he was mistaken for the bridegroom.

He had not come because he wished to break into society, but because it was a new fashion for women to wear their precious jewels in the early hours of the morning at such functions as these. He had no particular piece of villainy in view. He was merely surveying the land as a good general might survey a possible battlefield.

Marriages did not interest him. He regarded them as superfluous ceremonies indulged in by the idle rich and the hopeless bourgeoisie. The ceremony, which was long, bored him to extinction, and he heartily regretted having taken so prominent a place and being prevented, in consequence, from stealing gently out, or from watching the people who were in his rear. At last the service ended, the organ pealed a triumphant note, and the bride and bridegroom, looking extremely ashamed of themselves, processed solemnly down the aisle, and Fred fell in, in the ranks of the near and dear, and came out on to the steps.

He was wondering whether it would be politic or advisable to go on to the reception, having discovered where that reception would be held, when somebody touched his arm, and he turned quickly.

"Hallo, Dr. Judd!" he said, relieved. "I thought it was that fellow Holt. He follows me about until he's got on my nerves."

Dr. Judd, a fine figure of a man in his morning dress, was eyeing him sternly.

"You told me you were going to Nice," he said.

"I missed the train," replied Fred glibly, "and my pal went on without me. I'm staying over for a few days and then I hope to get away."

Dr. Judd was thoughtful.

"Walk a little way along with me," he said. "I want to talk to you."

They walked without speaking a word to one another into Hanover Square, and turned towards Bond Street.

"You are getting on my nerves, Mr. Grogan," said Dr. Judd. "At least I thought I had the satisfaction of knowing that you were taking abnormal risks on the continent of Europe. Instead I find you living a fashionable life in Jermyn Street."

"I thought you said you didn't know I was still here?" asked Fred quickly.

"I said nothing of the sort," replied the calm doctor. "I merely remarked that I thought you had said you were going to Nice."

"Oh, you knew I was here, then," said Fred.

"I had heard you were here," said Dr. Judd. "Now, Mr. Grogan, don't you think you and I should effect some sort of compromise?"

Fred was all ears.

"In what way?" he asked cautiously.

"Suppose," said Dr. Judd, "I gave you a lump sum down on condition that you did not bother me again?"

Nothing better suited Fred's plans. Supposing the sum were a reasonable one, he would be saved the bother and anxiety of a burglary. Or he might even add that relaxation to swell his profits.

"I'm agreeable," he said, after a reasonable pause, and Dr. Judd eyed him seriously.

"You will have to keep faith with me," he said. "I do not intend parting with £12,000—"

"£12,000!" said Fred quickly. "Yes, that seems a nice tidy sum."

"I repeat," said the doctor, "I do not intend parting with that sum unless I have a guarantee that you will not molest me again. Will you dine with me at my house in Chelsea to-morrow night at eight o'clock?"

Fred nodded.

"There will be a few people to dinner," said the doctor, "but nobody who knows you, and I must ask as a personal favour that you will not endeavour to follow up any acquaintance you make to-morrow night."

"Don't you think I am too much of a gentleman to do that sort of thing?" asked Fred, virtuously indignant.

"I don't," said the doctor shortly, and parted from him at the corner of Bond Street.

Twelve thousand pounds! That was a most admirable arrangement, and Fred, whose funds were getting low, trod on air as he strolled down Old Bond Street toward Piccadilly.

In his exaltation, when his generous soul had swollen, and his whole mental system was experiencing the sensation of largeness, he saw a girl on the opposite side of the road. Hers was not a face to be forgotten. He had seen it once under an electric light between St. Martin's and the Strand, and he increased his pace, crossing the road and following behind her, not, however, without an anxious glance behind him. For once Larry Holt was invisible.

"It could not have happened better," said Fred, for he was sensible of his fine appearance.

He overtook her at the corner of Piccadilly and raised his hat with a smile, and for a moment Diana was under the impression that she knew this stranger and her hand was half-way up when he made the mistake of repeating that fashionable formula:

"Haven't you and I met before somewhere?"

She drew her hand back.

"My dear," said Fred, "you're the most wonderful thing in the world, and I simply want to know you!"

This, too, was part of the formula and had been effective on many occasions.

"Then you had better call on me," she said, and Flash Fred scarcely believed his good fortune.

She opened the little leather bag she carried and took out a card, scribbling a number.

"A million thanks!" said Fred elegantly as he took the card. "I'll give you mine in a minute. Now what about a little dinner——" He lifted the card and read: "Miss Diana Ward—a beautiful name," he said. "Diana! Room 47," and then his face underwent a change. "Scotland Yard!" he said hollowly.

"Yes, I am with Mr. Larry Holt," she said sweetly, and Fred swallowed something.

"If he ain't here you're here, and if you're not here he's here," he said savagely. "Why can't you leave a gentleman alone?"

The Insurance Money

THAT afternoon Diana made a request of her employer which disappointed him a little.

"Certainly," he said, "I shan't want you this evening. Going to a dance, do you say?"

She nodded.

"That's fine," he said heartily. "I hope you enjoy yourself."

It chilled him a little, for he was so completely absorbed by the game that he could not understand that what was fun to him was work to her. She must have read his thoughts, for she said, with a little jerk of her chin which was characteristic of her:

"I am merely going on duty, Mr. Holt. I should not have thought of going to the dance, but the man who asked me is a young underwriter to whom I was secretary for about six months," she said.

"You seem to have started work at a very early age," he smiled. "Did you go to a public school?"

"I went to a council school," she replied quietly. "My aunt who brought me up was very poor."

"You didn't know your father and mother?"

She shook her head.

"I hope you're not going to associate me with the missing Clarissa," she smiled. "I am afraid my origin is a little less romantic. I am always expecting to find my father figuring in the records of Scotland Yard, if he is alive, for Mrs. Ward never spoke of him except in uncomplimentary terms. Yes, I did begin work rather young."

"You say you are going on duty," he interrupted her. "What do you mean?"

She went to her desk and took up her handbag, opened it and produced a letter.

"It will interest you to know," she smiled, "that Mr. Gray's wife will be there to chaperon me and joins in the invitation."

It did interest Larry very much indeed. He did not say so because he thought it might be indiscreet, and he was not quite sure of how he would express the pleasure that news brought to him.

"Here is the paragraph that made me decide to go," said the girl, and read:

"We have had a pretty bad time lately. The loss of a ship in the Baltic hit my partner rather hard, and I have had to pay out a very considerable sum of money over the death of a man named Stuart."

"Stuart?" said Larry quickly. "That can't be our Stuart. By the way, the jury have just returned a verdict of 'Found drowned' in that case. We did not care to oppose the verdict, or offer any evidence which might put the murderers on their guard. Stuart, eh?" he nodded to himself several times. "I owe you an apology, Diana," he said, using her name for the first time. "I thought you were going to frivol, and I was hoping that you were sufficiently interested in this case to give your whole mind to it."

She looked at him with kindling eyes, and her face was flushed pink.

"I am giving all my mind to it," she said in a low voice. "It is lovely working with you," and then, to change the subject, she told him of her adventure with Fred.

"Poor old Fred," chuckled Larry. "You have the satisfaction of knowing that he will avoid you like the plague for the future. What time will you come back?" he asked.

"Why?" She was surprised.

"I was wondering whether you could come here, or whether I'd be waiting on the door-mat for you in Charing Cross Road. I want to know what you have discovered."

She nibbled her finger thoughtfully.

"I will come to the Yard," she said. "I'll be here soon after eleven."

She looked with narrowed eyes at the mark on his throat.

"Does that feel awfully sore?" she asked sympathetically.

"Not so bad," said Larry. "Injury to vanity doing very badly. It will take some time before that heals."

"He must be terribly strong," she said with a shudder. "I shall never forget that night on the stairs. I suppose there is no news of him?"

"None whatever," said Larry. "He's gone to ground."

"Are you watching the Home?"

"The Home?" he said in surprise. "No, I don't think that is necessary. The superintendent seems a very decent sort of man. I saw the local police inspector and he told me that every man in the Home is an honest character, and he can vouch for all of them except the fellow they call 'Lew.' He was the man I saw upstairs who seemed to be half-demented."

"I want to ask you a favour," she said. "Will you take me to-morrow to the Home?"

"Ye-es," he hesitated, "but——"

"But will you?"

"Surely if you wish to go, but I don't think you'll find any clue there to bring us nearer to the gentleman who murdered Stuart."

"I wonder?" she said thoughtfully.

She permitted him to lunch with her that day: it was a joyous meal for Larry and he was unusually incoherent. The afternoon was a more serious time for him, for his search for documentary proof that Diana's theory was correct and that Mrs. Stuart had had twin daughters had been unavailing. There was no record of the children's births, though the files at Somerset House had been diligently examined.

"Check Number Two," said Larry.

"Which will be overcome," replied the girl, "though it is curious that a woman of Mrs. Stuart's position should have neglected to register her children."

She said this and smiled, and Larry asked her why.

"Mrs. Ward had views on that subject. My aunt, whose name I bear," she said. "She hated vaccination, registration, and education!"

"What happened to your aunt? Did she die?" asked Larry.

The girl was silent.

"No—she didn't die."

She said this so strangely that Larry looked at her and the girl went crimson.

"I oughtn't to talk about her if I'm not prepared to go on," she said quietly. "I—I come from a very bad stock, Mr. Holt. My aunt stole from her employer, and I rather think she made a practice of doing so. At any rate, when I was twelve, she went away for quite a long time and I never saw her again."

Larry crossed the room and laid his hand on the girl's shoulder.

"My dear," he said, "you have succeeded in shaking loose and establishing yourself in a truly marvellous way. I am very proud of you."

When she looked up her eyes were filled with tears.

"I think she drank: I'm not quite sure. She was very good to me when I needed her most," she said. "I would like to know what has happened to her, but I simply dare not ask."

"She went to prison?"

The girl shook her head.

"I think it was an inebriates' home," she said. "Now, what are you doing this afternoon?" she demanded briskly, and Larry laid down his programme, dictated a letter or two and went out leaving her to finish them.

With every step he took, the Stuart mystery grew more and more of a tangle. Dead ends and culs-de-sac met him at every turn, and even the fact that Stuart had been murdered was no fact, but a theory based upon the eccentricity of the tide which had left his body on the steps of the Embankment, and a piece of paper, now stolen, embossed with Braille characters.

He stopped in his walk when he was half-way up Northumberland Avenue, and took out his pocket-book.

"Murdered . . . dear . . . sea . . ." he read, and shook his head.

"Why the 'dear'?" he wondered. The man who attempted to betray the murderers would not go to the trouble of writing 'dear sir,' and, anyway, it occurred in the wrong place. For the girl had pointed out the characters at the end of the second line.

"Dear, dear, dear," he repeated as he strolled along, and then, for no reason at all, a name came into his mind. Dearborn! He laughed quietly. That good soul of a clergyman, labouring amongst the men who lived in everlasting darkness! He shook his head again. It is a fact which all people can verify that if you see an unusual name for the first time you meet with it again in the course of twenty-four hours. His walk carried him beyond Shaftesbury Avenue, and in passing a theatre the name caught his eye. He checked himself and stooped down to read the play-bill of a theatre.

"John Dearborn," he read.

Dearborn was apparently the author of the play which was being performed here. What was the theatre? He stepped back in the roadway and looked up at the name in coloured glass on the edge of the awning. The Macready! It was from the Macready Theatre that Gordon Stuart disappeared!

Without hesitation he walked into the vestibule to the booking-office and his quick eyes fell upon the plan which the office keeper had before him. There were precious few blue marks, indicating that seats had been taken.

"Can you tell me where I can find Mr. John Dearborn?" he asked.

The office keeper looked at him with an air of pained resignation.

"You're not a friend of the management's, are you?"

"No," admitted Larry, "I am not."

"You're not a friend of Mr. Dearborn's, by any chance, are you?" asked the clerk carelessly, and Larry shook his head. "Well," said the man, "I'll speak my mind. I didn't want to hurt your feelings. I don't know where to find Mr. Dearborn, and I wish the management didn't know where to find him either! I'm leaving this week," he said, "so it doesn't matter very much what I say. He's about the rottenest playwright that the world has ever seen. I'm not choking you off buying a seat, am I?" he asked good-humouredly.

"No, no," said Larry with a smile.

"Well, I won't persuade you to buy one," said the box-office keeper. "I haven't any grudge against you, anyway! We had six people in at the Saturday matinee, and we look like having three to-night. The only people who take any interest in this play are the Commissioners in Lunacy, who come along and watch the audience, and whenever a lunatic breaks out of Hanwell they send the keepers here to search the house."

"You haven't answered my question. Do you know where I can find the author of this unfortunate play?"

The clerk shrugged his shoulders.

"He runs a mission for something or other in the West End. Poor chap, he's blind and maybe I oughtn't to slate him. But he writes rotten plays."

"Is he continuously writing plays?" asked Larry in surprise.

"Continuously," said the other glumly. "I think he writes them in his sleep."

"And they're all produced?"

The man nodded.

"And they're all failures?"

Again the man nodded.

"But why? Surely the management would not produce successive failures from the same pen?"

"They do," said the clerk in despair, "and that is why the Macready is a byword—"

"How long has John Dearborn been writing?" asked Larry.

"Oh, about ten years. Mind you, it's not bad stuff in parts. It's more mad than bad."

"Does he ever come here?"

"Never," said the man, shaking his head. "I don't know why, but he doesn't, not even to rehearsals."

"One more question. To whom does the theatre belong?"

"To a syndicate," said the clerk, who was now growing restive under the questions. "May I ask why you're making all these inquiries?"

"I'm just asking," said Larry with a smile, and seeing that no more information could be got, he went out.

It was rather an amazing situation, he thought. But to connect that one word "dear" with the author of bad plays, or give to Mr. Dearborn, an obvious philanthropist, any evil significance, was absurd. He was outside the theatre when he suddenly remembered and went back.

"As a great personal favour," he said, "could I see the house?"

The clerk demurred at first, but eventually summoned an attendant.

"You'll find it pretty dark," he said. "The house lights are not on."

Larry followed the attendant into the dress-circle and surveyed the little theatre. It was in gloom. The curtain was down, and the seats were sheeted in holland.

"Which is Box A?" asked Larry, for that was what he came to see.

The man led him along a passage through a heavy curtain and down a narrower passage which ran at the back of the boxes, and at the end he stopped and opened a door on his right. Larry stepped in. The box was in darkness, and he lit a match.

There was nothing peculiar about Box A, except that the carpet on the floor was thick and rich and the three chairs which formed its furniture were beautifully designed.

"Are all the boxes furnished like this?" asked Larry.

"No, sir," said the man, "only Box A."

Larry came out and examined the passage. Opposite the door of Box A, a thick red curtain was draped on the wall. He drew it aside and found an iron door on which in red letters were the words, "Exit in case of fire."

"Where does this lead to?" he asked.

"To a side street, sir," said the man. "To Cowley Street. It is not really a street, but a passage which is the property of this theatre and is blocked up at one end."

Larry tipped the man and went out. He was nearer to the solution of Gordon Stuart's disappearance and murder at that moment than he had ever been before. And he knew it.

He was in his office at half-past ten that night, waiting impatiently for the arrival of the girl, and endeavouring by self-analysis to discover whether his eagerness to see her was due to his professional zeal or to his personal interest in the girl herself.

She came at ten minutes to eleven, and he, who had never seen her before save in her working dress, was stricken dumb at the sight of this radiant beauty. He could not know that the black tulle dress she wore cost her something less than £5, or that the bandeau of black leaves about her golden hair cost something short of ten shillings. To him she was magnificently arrayed, and a creature so divine and ethereal that he hardly dared speak to her.

"Come in," he said; "you're making the furniture look shabby."

She laughed, dropped her cloak on her chair, and Larry forgot the official and important side of her visit and would have continued in oblivion if she had not brought him to earth with a triumphant:

"I've got it!"

"Got it?" he stammered. "Oh, yes, you saw your underwriting friend."

She opened a little satin bag and took out a piece of paper.

"I've made some notes," she said. "My friend was very hard hit by Stuart's death, and it is this Stuart."

Larry whistled.

"How did it happen?" he asked.

"My friend is an underwriter. He's in the insurance business," she explained. "When a man has his life insured for a very large sum, as you probably know, the company that issues the policy does not retain all the risk. It sends round to other offices and to various underwriters offering each underwriter some of the responsibility. It appears that my friend, the underwriter, underwrote three thousand pounds' worth of the reinsurance."

"Three thousand pounds' worth?" said Larry in astonishment. "Then, in the name of Heaven, for how much was Stuart insured?"

"I asked that," she nodded and lifted her paper. "On the policy which was endorsed by Mr. Gray the sum of £50,000 was mentioned, but Mr. Gray says that there was another policy for a similar amount."

Larry sat down, his eyes gleaming.

"So that was the business end of Stuart's death, was it? Insured for £100,000! Did your friend pay?"

"Naturally he paid," said the girl, "the moment the company which had accepted the insurance had sent in its claim. He had nothing else to do but to find the money."

"What is the name of the company?"

She paused and looked at him.

"The Greenwich Insurance Company," she replied slowly, and he jumped to his feet.

"Dr. Judd," he said softly.

At the Pawnbroker's

HE ESCORTED the girl downstairs, and they stood talking in the hall. There was a car at the door, a luxury which she easily explained.

She was using the Gray's car, which was to go back and pick up the underwriter and his wife at two o'clock.

"I hate declining your invitation," said Larry, "but I am hanging on to the end of a wire. I sent Harvey on a tour of investigation to-day, and he promised to 'phone me round about midnight."

She was looking at him in some concern.

"Aren't you rather overdoing it?" she said. "You don't get any sleep?"

He laughed.

"I am one of those fortunate people who can do without sleep," he said boastfully, and then an official came out of one of the ground-floor rooms.

"There is a call through for you, sir," he said.

"Come along," said Larry. "I may get this business off and then I shall be able to revel in that millionaire feeling."

He went back to his room and the girl followed. It was not Sergeant Harvey who had called him, but the inspector in charge of the Oxford Lane police station.

"Is that Inspector Holt?" he asked.

"That's me," said Larry ungrammatically.

"You circulated a description of a sleeve-link of black enamel and diamonds."

"Yes," said Larry quickly.

"Well," said the man, "Mr. Emden, of Emden and Smith, pawnbrokers, brought a pair of links exactly tallying with the description published in the Hue and Cry."

"Have you got them there?" asked Larry eagerly.

"No, sir," said the inspector. "But Mr. Emden is here, if you would like to interview him. He can get the links in the morning. He happened to be reading the Hue and Cry to-night after dinner and he came upon the description, and immediately walked over to the station. He lives close by."

"I'll come down," said Larry.

"What is it?" asked the girl. "Have they found the links?"

Larry shook his head.

"They've found a pair of links exactly like the one which was found in Gordon Stuart's hand," he said, a little puzzled. "I can't understand that. If it had been half a link, or a link and a half, that would have been clearly a clue."

He looked dubiously at the switchboard and the operator.

"If Sergeant Harvey comes through," he said, "tell him to ring me again, or if he is in reach of the office to come back and wait for me. I am going to the Oxford Lane police station. Incidentally," he said to the girl as they came out, "I will accept a lift in your palatial conveyance."

He dropped her at her flat. There was a lounger outside who saluted Larry.

"You are not putting a guard on me?" said the girl in surprise. "I think that's unnecessary, Mr. Holt."

"My own experience tells me that it is very necessary," said Larry grimly. "The gentleman who tossed me about as though I were a feather is not wanting in courage. There is no other way into the house except by this front door, is there?" he asked the detective on duty.

"No, sir, I have had a good look round, and I've also been into the lady's rooms."

She gasped.

"How?" she asked.

"I had a duplicate key made from yours," said Larry. "I hope you don't mind. And talking of keys," he added, "the appearance of Blind Jake in Fanny Weldon's room is now no mystery at all. She had given him a key of the house in case she missed him with the swag on Saturday night. He was to come up and take it from her. She was in such terror of him that she did not dare refuse the key, but she must have forgotten she had loaned it, for she would never have slept."

He said good night to her and went on to Oxford Lane, on foot.

Mr. Emden proved to be a mild little man in pince-nez.

"I happened to be running through the list of properties stolen," he said, "and I came upon this description of yours, Mr. Holt."

He showed a fold of the paper on which a drawing of the link, whose fellow was sought, appeared.

"You say you have a pair?"

"Yes, sir," said the man. "It was pledged with me this morning. As a matter of fact, it happened to be me who took the pledge. I don't as a rule work behind the counter, but one of my clerks had gone on a message, and when the man came in I took the links and gave the pledger £4 for them."

"They are not of a usual pattern, are they?" asked Larry, and Mr. Emden shook his head.

"They are very unusual," he said. "I don't remember having seen a pair exactly like those before. I think they must be of a French make. They were slightly damaged. Three of the diamonds on the rim were missing or I should have given him a great deal more."

"Do you know the man who pledged them?"

"No, sir. He was a smart-looking fellow who told me he'd got tired of them. My impression was——" He hesitated.

"Well?" said Larry.

"Well, I thought, in spite of his good appearance, that he looked like one of these smart thieves that abound in the West End, and I had an idea that he was pledging them, not so much because he wanted the money, but because he wanted to put them in a safe place. A thief will often do that and take the chance of the pawnbroker discovering that the property is missing or wanted by the police."

Larry nodded.

"Smartly dressed," he said thoughtfully, and then quickly: "Did he wear any diamonds?"

"Yes, sir," said the pawnbroker, "that is why I thought he was planting the stuff. Four pounds isn't much to advance on property of that value, but he didn't make any fuss."

"What name?" asked Larry.

"He gave the name of Mr. Frederick, and I think an accommodation address."

"Flash Fred!" said Larry. "Is Jermyn Street in your district?" he asked the inspector.

"Yes, sir," said the officer.

"Send a couple of men out and pull in Flash Fred. Bring him here first, and afterwards, if it is necessary, I'll take him to Cannon Row."

"Is it an arrest?" asked the inspector.

"A detention merely. He may be able to explain, but I think he'll have to be clever if he gets out of this. Now, Mr. Emden," he said, turning to the pawnbroker, "I'm afraid I can't wait until the morning and I must ask you to accompany me to your shop and let me have the actual links."

"With pleasure, sir," said the pawnbroker. "I expected something like that and I brought my keys over. My shop is only about five minutes' walk away."

Accompanied by a plain-clothes officer they went to the shop and Mr. Emden fitted the key in the side door, but as he pressed the key into the keyhole the door gave.

"Why, the door's open," he said in surprise, and went quickly down the side passage. He tried another door, but there was no need even to go through the formality of putting a key in the lock. The door was ajar and

Larry's pocket lamp revealed the mark of the jemmy that had opened it. The pawnbroker hurried into his main premises and switched on the light.

A book lay on the counter, open at the page of that day's transactions.

"Where did you put these links?" asked Larry quickly.

"In the safe, in my private office," said the man. "Look," he turned to the book, "there is the number."

"Also the word 'safe,'?" said Larry, "and somehow I don't think you'll see your safe intact."

And his words proved prophetic. The big "burglar-proof" safe presented a somewhat untidy appearance, for a hole had been burnt in the steel and the lock had disappeared. Articles of value there were none. Every package had been cleared out.

"I think they have got those links," said Larry grimly.

In Flash Fred's Flat

AFTER the discovery in the pawnbroker's shop Larry went back to the police station to make yet another discovery. Flash Fred was not in his lodgings.

"I wish you would come down and see his flat, sir," said the officer who had gone to make the arrest. "I think that something queer has happened."

"If there has been anything in this case which has not been queer," said Larry with asperity, "I should like to hear about it!"

Flash Fred lived in Modley House, Jermyn Street, a block of service flats, and the porter had a strange story to tell.

"Mr. Grogan came in at about eleven o'clock to-night," he said, "and went up to his flat. I took him a syphon of soda he ordered, and said good night to him.

"Afterwards I went round seeing that the service doors were shut and that the lights had been out in the kitchen, then came to my cubby-hole to have my supper and read the evening newspaper."

The "cubby-hole" was a space under the stairway which had been converted into a little office where the tenants left their keys.

"At about half-past twelve I thought I heard a sound like a shot and a man's voice shout something and I came out into the passage and listened. There was still a sort of disturbance going on, so I went up to the second floor where the sound came from and listened again. There was a light in Mr. Grogan's flat. I could see that through the transom. It was the only light visible. I knocked at the door and after a while Mr. Grogan came to the door, and I tell you he was a most terrifying sight. He had a big knife in his hand and his clothes were smothered with blood.

'Oh, it's you, is it?' he said. 'Come in.'

"I went into the sitting-room and a pretty sight it was! Chairs thrown over, the table upside down, and glasses and bottles scattered over the floor. Outside Mr. Grogan's window are the stairs of the fire-escape, and the window was open.

'What's wrong, sir?' I asked.

'Nothing particular,' he said, 'only a burglar broke in. That's all. Give me a whisky-and-soda.'

"He was trembling from head to foot and was very excited. He kept muttering to himself, but I didn't hear what he said. When I came back with the whisky-and-soda he had cleaned the knife and was more calm. I found him standing at the open window, looking down into the yard, where the fire-escape leads, and then I noticed that one of the pictures hanging on the wall was smashed by a bullet. I knew it was a bullet because I was in the Metropolitan Police for some years, and I've seen a similar mark. I told him there would be serious trouble over this disturbance because the other tenants would complain, but he asked me not to worry about that, and gave me £50 to pay his rent and any expenses that we had been put to, and asked me to keep the flat until he returned. He said he was going abroad."

"What happened then?" asked Larry when the man paused.

"Well, sir, he came out with a bag, got into a cab and drove off, and that's the last I saw of him."

Larry made an examination of the room and he found that the porter's description had been a faithful one. The room was illuminated by a cluster of three lights hanging from the ceiling and covered by a shade. One of the globes was smashed, and Larry drew the attention of the porter to this.

"Yes, sir, these lights work on two circuits: one switch turns on one and the other switch turns on two. As a rule Mr. Grogan only has the single light on."

Larry nodded.

"I pretty well know what happened," he said.

He could picture the scene in the room: the intruder coming through the window, Flash Fred covering him with his revolver, and the big man advancing with upraised hands until he could reach the globe and crush it in his powerful paw. And then Fred had fired and the man was on him, but Fred was too slippery. Fred had been cleverer than he. These continental crooks who take enormous risks do not depend so much upon their guns as upon their knives, and to Blind Jake's surprise—for Blind Jake it must have been—Grogan had met the onrush and the suffocating hug of this animal-man with a steel blade, and, releasing his hold, Blind Jake must have made his escape through the open window. But where was Fred? In that moment Larry felt an unexpected wave of sympathy for the crook. He too, then, had stumbled by accident or design upon the murderer of Gordon Stuart.

What was that clue? He must find Flash Fred, and find him at once, for this thief might have in his hands a solution to the mystery.

He went home, 'phoned to head-quarters, and discovered that Harvey had made a negative report, took a bath and went to bed. He slept for four hours; and then by his instructions Sunny, who seemed equally able to dispense with the recuperation of sleep, brought him his tea and toast.

"What time is it?" asked Larry, blinking himself awake.

"Nine o'clock, sir," said Sunny. "The postman has come and the papers have been."

"Bring me my letters," said Larry, jumping out of bed.

He looked them through as he sipped his tea.

One had come, evidently delivered by hand, for there was no stamp upon the envelope.

"When did this arrive?" he asked the valet when Sunny returned to the room.

"It was in the box when I got up, sir," said Sunny. "I think it must have come by hand."

"You're a fool, Sunny," snapped Larry. "Of course it came by hand."

"I'm glad you agree with me, sir," said the imperturbable Sunny.

Larry ripped open the envelope and took out a sheet of paper. It began without any polite preliminary:

"You had better interest yourself in another case, Mr. Holt. You will get into serious trouble if you do not heed this warning."

"Oh, yes," said Larry, and rang the bell.

"Sunny," he said, "bring me my coat and the papers that are in the inside pocket."

Larry searched for and found the letter which Flash Fred had received inviting him to call at Todd's Home at six o'clock in the morning and to avoid attracting attention.

He put the letter of warning by its side and compared them. They were in the same handwriting!

The Woman Who Drew the Insurance Money

DIANA WARD, I'm a greatly rattled man," said Larry.

The girl stopped working, her fingers poised above the keys of her typewriter; then she swung round in her chair.

"The case is growing a little clearer to me," she said quietly.

"I wish to heaven it would grow clearer to me," grumbled Larry. "Here is the situation. Let me recapitulate." He ticked off the points on the fingers of one hand as he leant back in his chair. "A rich Canadian, who comes to London apparently to visit the grave of his deserted wife and child, is murdered after seeing a play at the Macready Theatre. The author of that play is John Dearborn, who admittedly writes the worst trash that has ever been seen on the stage. But that doesn't make him a murderer. And, moreover, he is a respectable clergyman engaged in a great humanitarian work amongst the blind. The murdered Stuart leaves, written on the inside of his shirt-front, a will leaving the whole of his property to a daughter, who apparently has no existence, so far as we can discover. Certain clues are found, one a piece of Braille writing, another a black enamel and diamond sleeve-link which is found in the dead man's hand. The Braille writing is stolen from Scotland Yard; the sleeve-links, when they fall into the possession of Flash Fred and are pawned by him for security, are regarded by some person or persons unknown as being of such importance that a burglary is committed at the pawnbroker's shop in which they are pledged, with no other object, I should imagine, than to recover those links. Moreover, the agent of the enemy proceeds first to attempt your abduction, then the murder of Fanny Weldon, who committed the burglary at Scotland Yard, which is understandable, and then the destruction of Flash Fred, which is also within my understanding. As a matter of fact, the only inexplicable point in the whole case," he said with a smile, "is their attempt to strafe you."

She nodded.

"That is a mystery to me too," she confessed.

"We have now discovered," said Larry, ticking off the point on another finger, "that Stuart was heavily insured, at the office of Dr. Judd, of the Greenwich Insurance Company. Dr. Judd makes no secret of the fact that this insurance was effected."

"Have you seen Dr. Judd?" she asked in surprise.

"I have telephoned to him," he said, "and I am seeing him this morning. Perhaps you will come along with me—we can postpone our visit to the Home until this afternoon."

He saw her face brighten up.

"You like to be in this game, don't you?" he bantered her.

"I think it's wonderfully fascinating," she replied, "and I like to be close to things. I had a feeling yesterday that you thought I wasn't keen."

Larry blushed guiltily.

"It was only for a second," he admitted, "and it was very unworthy, and after all, why should you elect to work all the hours that Heaven sends?"

"Because I want to see the murderer of Gordon Stuart brought to justice," she answered steadily, and Larry experienced a little thrill.

Dr. Judd expected one visitor, and was to all appearances surprised agreeably when Larry's companion came into the big managing director's office on Bloomsbury Pavement.

"This is Dr. Judd. My secretary, Miss Ward," introduced Larry. "Miss Ward has a very excellent memory, and it may be necessary for me to have a shorthand note of our talk."

"I should prefer that," said Dr. Judd. Yet he seemed ill at ease at the presence of the girl. If Larry noticed this fact, it did not alter his plans.

"I am glad you have come," said Dr. Judd slowly. "I wanted to talk to you about the man with whom you saw me the first time we met. I am afraid that you received an altogether wrong impression, though as to this I cannot blame you, for the man is a disreputable scoundrel. Have you seen him lately?"

"I have neither seen nor heard of him for weeks," said Larry untruthfully, and the girl found that she had to exercise all her self-control to prevent her looking up in surprise.

"Well," said the doctor, "we can talk about that at some other time. Do you mind my smoking. Miss Ward?" She shook her head with a smile. "I am an inveterate smoker of cigarettes," said the doctor. "I have smoked a hundred a day for twenty-five years, and my robust health gives the lie to all the anti-tobacconists!"

He laughed, and he had a very hearty and pleasant laugh. It was a gurgle of genuine merriment, which was so infectious that Diana found herself smiling in sympathy. The doctor lit a cigarette, then took a folder from his desk and opened it.

"Here are the policies," he said. "You will notice that they are made payable to a nominee who shall be afterwards named. That authorization came to us on the day of Stuart's death. I will show it to you presently. The matter was not brought to my attention until yesterday morning, when my clerk reminded me that we had issued these policies. Simultaneously we received a demand for the money, accompanied by a certificate of death—or rather, a copy of the certificate issued by the coroner."

"Which can be obtained for about five shillings," said Larry, and Dr. Judd inclined his head.

"It was sufficient," he said quietly, "and at any rate, when the legatees called, there was no reason in the world why I should not pay the money, and that payment was made."

"How was it paid? By cash or cheque?"

"By open cheque, at the lady's request."

"At the lady's?" said Larry and Diana together, for she had been surprised into this ejaculation.

Dr. Judd looked at her with a little smile and rubbed his hands gleefully.

"I like a secretary who takes a keen interest in affairs," he chuckled.

"But who was the lady?" asked Larry.

The doctor took two slips of paper from the folder and laid one before the detective.

"Here is the receipt," he said. "You see it is for one hundred thousand pounds."

Larry took up the paper and examined it. It was signed "Clarissa Stuart"!

When Diana Fainted

LARRY could not believe his eyes. He handed the slip to the girl, but she had already seen the signature over his shoulder.

"Clarissa Stuart?" he said slowly. "Do you know her?"

"Never heard of her before," said the doctor cheerfully. "But she was the person nominated to receive the proceeds of the policy."

"What is she like?" asked Larry after a pause.

Dr. Judd was lighting a fresh cigarette from the glowing end of another, and he threw the butt into the fireplace before he replied.

"Young, pretty, fashionably dressed," he said briefly.

"Did she seem—distressed at all?"

"Not at all," said the doctor. "On the contrary, she was rather amusing."

They looked at one another, Diana Ward and Larry Holt, and there was blank astonishment in each pair of eyes.

"Did this lady give any address?"

"No, it was not necessary," said the doctor. "I told you I gave her an open cheque. Well, she seemed a little perturbed at first. She did not want a cheque; so I sent my clerk to the bank to draw the money, and when he brought it back I delivered it to her."

"So it was in cash?" said Larry.

"Literally it was in cash I paid her," said Dr. Judd.

"You have never seen her before?" persisted Larry.

Dr. Judd shook his head.

"She came from nowhere so far as I am concerned," he said. "She was undoubtedly the daughter of Mr. Stuart, or at least, she told me so, and I have no reason to disbelieve her word."

Larry and the girl were out in the street again before he spoke to the girl.

"It is amazing," he said. His cab was waiting and he ushered the girl in. "304 Nottingham Place," he said.

"Where are we going?" asked the girl in surprise.

"We're going to the lodgings that Stuart had," replied Larry. "I left the investigation at that point to Sergeant Harvey, and he is a particularly thorough man, but may have missed something. Surely, if Gordon Stuart learnt on the day of his death that he had another daughter, he must have had some visitor?"

"Do you think the girl saw him?" asked Diana quickly. "Clarissa, I mean."

"It is possible," replied Larry, "but that is to be discovered."

No. 304 Nottingham Place was a big and sedate-looking mansion, of the type which is patronized by American visitors of the better class, and Larry and his companion were shown into a comfortable drawing-room. A few minutes after, a little lady with white hair came in.

"Mrs. Portland, isn't it?" said Larry. "My name is Holt. I am from Scotland Yard."

A look of dismay came to the lady's face.

94

"Oh dear," she said, evidently distressed. "I did hope that the police had finished with me. It gets this house such a bad name, and I've already suffered in consequence. The poor gentleman committed suicide, didn't he? Why he should I don't know," she said, shaking her head. "I have never seen him so cheerful as he was the night just before he went to the theatre. As a rule he was so glum and sad that it depressed me to see him."

"Cheerful before he went to the Theatre?" said Larry quickly. "Unusually so?"

She nodded.

"Had he any visitors in the afternoon?"

"None sir," replied the lady, and Larry's face dropped. "None at all. I told your detective officer who called that he never received visitors. He had been out in the afternoon, and I must confess that he came back a little before we expected him. We had a charwoman in, and she was making his room tidy, and the first I knew about his room was when I passed his door and I heard him having a long conversation with somebody. It was so unusual that I spoke to my head waitress about it."

"Who was the somebody?" asked Larry, and the landlady smiled.

"It was the charwoman," she said. "A woman I used to get in to do odd jobs. I thought it was extraordinary, because he never spoke to anybody."

"How long was the woman with him?" asked Larry.

"Nearly an hour," was the surprising reply.

"An hour?" said Larry. "He was talking with a charwoman for an hour? What did he talk about?"

She shook her head.

"I don't know. I remember it well, because the charwoman left without drawing her wages. In fact, she must have gone straight out after leaving Mr. Stuart's room—and she never came back."

Larry frowned.

"That is important," he said. "Did you tell Sergeant Harvey?"

"No, sir," said the lady in surprise. "I didn't think it was worth while reporting a little domestic incident like that. He asked me if Mr. Stuart had

had any visitors, and I replied truthfully that he had not."

"What was the woman's name?"

"I don't know," said the landlady. "We used to call her Emma. I am surprised she didn't come back, because she left her wedding ring here. She used to take it off before she started scrubbing. It is a peculiar ring for a woman of her position—half platinum and half gold, and—Catch that young lady, sir," she said suddenly.

Larry turned quickly and caught the girl as she fainted.

The Man Who Was Deaf

HE CARRIED her to a sofa and laid her down, and presently she opened her eyes.

"I am an awful idiot," she said trying to rise, but he laid his hand on her shoulder.

"You must lie there a little while. What is the trouble?"

"The room is a little close, I think," she said.

The room was stuffy: Larry had noticed it when he came in, and as the landlady pulled up the window, she apologized.

"I'm always telling the servants to keep this room aired, and they never do," she said. "It's like a furnace. I am very sorry."

Larry had seen many fainting women, but never before had such a phenomenon occasioned him so much alarm.

"I don't remember doing such a stupid thing before," said the girl at last sitting up.

"You had better go home," said Larry solemnly.

She was still very white, but the cup of tea which the landlady brought in revived her.

"I'm not going home," she said firmly. "I am going with you to Todd's. You promised me I should, and as soon as I get into the air I shall be all right. If you were to take me a drive around Regent's Park—it's quite near—I should be as well as ever."

They made the slow round of the outer circle and the colour came back to her face.

"Was it this morning you told me I was overdoing it?" smiled Larry. "My young friend, you are in danger of a breakdown."

She shook her head.

"I shall be very hurt if you insist upon that. I am not so stupid that I would go on if I wasn't fit," she said. "That undignified collapse into your arms will not occur again. Besides," she said mischievously, "if I am liable to having a fit on the mat, don't you think it would be better if you were with me than if I were by myself in my room?"

"There's something in that," said Larry. "But I'm not so sure that visiting Todd's is the best way of spending an afternoon. It's very smelly, and the sights are not quite pleasant."

"They will not worry me," she answered quietly. "Please, please let me go!"

He reached over and took her hand and she did not resist this attention.

"You can go just where you like, Diana," he said, "and—and—as far as you like!"

By now his own flustered feelings had calmed, and he remembered that he had not asked to see the novel wedding ring of Emma, the charwoman. Nor had he made the inquiries which he would have made but for the dramatic interruption of Diana's collapse.

He drove the girl back to Piccadilly, and they lunched together, and then they went on to Scotland Yard. In the restaurant he had telephoned to Harvey, and Harvey had renewed the distress of Mrs. Portland by another visit. He was waiting for Larry at the Yard in Room 47 when they returned.

"I've traced Emma," he said, and his tone was so serious that Larry knew that he was not wrong in giving importance to the interview which the charwoman had with Stuart. "She lives, or lived, in Camden Town," said Harvey. "She lodges with an Army pensioner and his wife."

"Well, have you seen her?"

"No, sir, I haven't seen her. She's no longer there," said Harvey. "She has not been home since the night following the Stuart murder."

Larry made a little grimace.

"That is the real end and the real clue of this crime," he said. "Emma the charwoman is going to supply us with a considerable amount of information. Did she take away her things from her lodgings?" he asked.

"No, sir," replied Harvey. "That is the curious circumstance. The woman neither told her friends that she was leaving, nor did she take any of her clothing or her belongings with her."

"Put her on the list," said Larry, "and warn all stations. No news of Blind Jake?"

"No, sir."

"Nor Fred?"

"No, sir."

"To the already overburdened vigilance of the Metropolitan Constabulary—poor chaps!—" said Larry with a smile, "we will add the name of Miss Clarissa Stuart. Young, pretty, and smartly dressed, probably staying in a good-class hotel. Put a comb through those places where a woman of wealth is likely to be, and report."

Harvey lifted his hat and went out, and Larry walked slowly to his desk and stood for a while looking down at it disapprovingly.

"I don't know why I am given a table in this office," he said. "I never sit at it." Nevertheless he dropped down in his chair and glanced across at the girl. "Well, Miss Ward," he said, "you have a further mystery to add to the others. Emma has disappeared as unexpectedly as Flash Fred or as Stuart, and the man who persuaded Emma to go was the man who nearly persuaded Mrs. Weldon to depart this life."

"Blind Jake?" she asked.

"That is the lad," he replied. "A terrible figure. I can't think of him without a shudder."

"What a confession for a detective to make!" she scoffed. "Of course you can think of him—he's human!"

"And a very sore human, too," smiled Larry. "For Flash Fred was fairly useful with a knife in the days when I was trailing him for carving up Leroux, a rival of his."

"Do you think they have caught him?" she asked.

He shook his head.

"No, Fred has gone to earth. He's gone because he's afraid they'll catch him."

"Then he is not in with them?"

"Fred?" He laughed. "Not Fred. Fred's a lone wolf and plays a lone hand. He preys upon the virtuous and the wicked alike. One of his many boasts is that he has never been a member of a gang, and I dare say that is why he has so far escaped, or partially escaped, the consequence of his rascality. He is in London," he mused, "and I have an idea we shall see him again very soon."

How soon he could not guess.

He worked for an hour, and seemed oblivious both to Diana's presence and the looks she shot across at him—glances which were intended to remind him that he was taking her to Todd's.

He covered sheet after sheet of paper, for it was his practice to write down his cases in narrative form, dovetailing the cause to the effect. They were curious-looking documents, these "statements" of his, abounding in marginal notes and interlinear corrections. Presently he finished writing, dropping the last sheet and slipping the paper into a drawer. Then he got up and stretched himself. He walked to the window and looked out. It was late afternoon and he could glimpse a wonderful picture of the Thames Embankment, a vista of blue bridges spanning a leaden stream, of dim spires looming through the eastern haze, of a long line of green where the trees shaded the broad sidewalk, of chocolate-coloured tram-cars that flashed to and fro—a fragment of London, recognizable even to those who had never seen the great city, or throbbed to its ceaseless pulsations.

Larry Holt scratched his nose unromantically and turned a dubious look to the waiting girl.

"If you still want to go to Todd's, I'll take you," he said. "This is the hour I'd promised myself the pleasure of a visit."

A car took them to the end of Lissom Grove, and they walked down Lissom Lane, which was a cul-de-sac opening from the bigger thoroughfare. Two plain-clothes police officers, who were waiting, joined them, and the party stepped to the side of the street opposite that on which the Home was situated.

"What is the place next door?" asked Larry, nodding at a black-looking house with shuttered windows.

"It used to be a laundry," said the policeman. "There's a yard and a shed at the back."

"Laundry?" said the girl thoughtfully. "Do you remember that it was a laundry van that was outside my flat that night they tried to carry me off?"

"By Jimmy!" said Larry. "So it was!"

"It couldn't have been this laundry, miss," said the policeman. "It has not been doing business for twelve months. They went bankrupt, and somebody bought up the business, but doesn't seem to have made a start yet."

"Those gates lead to the yard, I presume?" said Larry pointing.

"Yes, sir. I haven't seen a motor-van come out of there, and I don't even know that they have one," said the policeman. "But nowadays, when there are so many motor vehicles about, it is impossible to keep track of them."

Larry went up the steps and knocked at the door, and the same little old man opened.

"Four people!" he yelled. "All strangers! What do you want?"

"I want to see Mr. Dearborn," said Larry.

"Oh yes, sir, you were the gentleman that came on Sunday morning at six a.m.," said the little man, and went pattering down the long passage. "Come this way!" he bawled. "All of you. Four of them, sir!"

The Rev. John Dearborn came out of his study to meet the party, and ushered them in.

"Mr. Holt? I think I recognized your voice," he said. His little dictating machine was spinning, and there was a thick pad of typed manuscript on his table. He put his hand lovingly upon it as he passed to his chair. "I have a gentleman who comes in to read for me in the evening," he said, as though guessing Larry's thoughts. "Now what is the object of to-night's visit?" he asked. "Have you found your Blind Jake?"

"I have met him without finding him," replied Larry grimly. "I merely want to see over the house. I have brought a lady with me."

"How interesting!" said the Rev. John Dearborn, rising.

The girl held out her hand instinctively, and the man took it.

"I shall be most happy to show you round. You have some other friends?"

Larry introduced them, and together they went up the stairs, John Dearborn leading the way.

"We will start at the top of the house this time," he said humorously. "Our friend Lew is still in his cubicle."

"Aren't you afraid to keep a man here who is not quite right in his head?"

"He is very weak," said John Dearborn, "and I haven't the heart to send him to the infirmary. I fear that I must do so sooner or later."

Larry had the girl by his side on the landing, and lowering his voice he asked:

"Do you want to see this old man? He is rather——" He did not finish his sentence.

"I want to see him—yes," she said. "You forget that I was nurse in an institute for the blind."

Dearborn led the way to the cubicle. No lights shone, though there were electric globes on every landing. The blind needed no lights, thought Larry.

The old man in the cubicle lay quietly on his back, his hands folded patiently. He was no longer talking, and was, indeed, much calmer than when Larry had seen him last.

"How are you to-day?" asked Larry.

The man made no reply. It was the girl who laid her hand upon his shoulder.

"Are you feeling better?" she asked, and the man started round.

"Who's that? Is that you, Jim?" he asked. "Have you got my supper?"

"Are you feeling better?" said Diana.

"And bring me a mug of tea, will you?" said Lew, and lay over on his back and resumed the same attitude of resignation in which they had found him.

The girl stooped and looked closely at the old man; and, sensing her presence, he put up his hand and touched her face.

"Is that a lady?" he said.

And then Dearborn pressed past them and caught the man's hand in his.

"Are you better to-day. Lew?" he said, and the man winked.

"All right, sir," he replied. "I'm feeling fine, thank you."

Diana Ward walked out of the cubicle, her eyes fixed absently on space, and Larry joined her.

"What is the matter?" he asked.

"That man is dead," she said.

"Dead?" he repeated in amazement. "Of course he's not dead."

She nodded her head.

"Diana, I don't understand you," said Larry. He thought for a moment that her fainting fit had affected her mind and that she was talking lightheadedly.

"Dead," she repeated, and her voice had a passionate thrill which made him gasp. "As effectively dead as if he were lying cold and lifeless on that bed. Oh, it's cruel, cruel!"

John Dearborn and the detectives were still in the cubicle discussing the invalid.

"What do you mean, Diana?" he asked.

"Don't you see? I've seen it happen once before," she said in a low voice that shook. "There were little black marks on the man's ear. Those are powder marks. He has been deafened."

"Deafened?" he whispered, still not grasping the significance of the revelation.

"You told me something of what this man said when you saw him on Sunday," she said, speaking rapidly and almost in a whisper, "and now I see what has happened. This man has had a shot-gun discharged near both ears, and he is dead."

"But, I don't understand."

"Do you realize," she asked, and she spoke slowly now, "what it means to be blind and deaf?"

"Good God!" he gasped.

"That is what has happened to the man they call Lew. Some persons, who for their own purpose desire to spare his life, have made him incapable of testifying against them."

"What do you mean?"

"I mean," she said, "that he was the man who wrote the Braille message found in Gordon Stuart's pocket."

The Disappearance of Diana Ward

WAS IT guess-work? Was it sheer deduction? Was it knowledge? These three questions flashed through Larry's mind, but before he could ask her any further questions, John Dearborn had come from the cubicle and was feeling his way down the stairs.

On the next landing he opened the door of a dormitory which Larry had seen before. It consisted of three rooms which had been knocked into one at some previous period.

Obedient to Larry's instructions, the two detectives did not follow the party in. One strolled down and took his place on the lower landing; the other sat upon the stairs that led to the cubicles above and waited.

"Is it light?" asked Dearborn as he walked into the inner room.

"Quite light," said Larry.

"I am told there is rather a good view from this window," said Dearborn, and pointed unerringly to a view which was neither picturesque nor extensive.

Larry did not reply. It was possibly a polite fiction that the views from the Home were lovely, and he did not desire to hurt, even in the slightest degree, the man who was so proud of a prospect which included six roofs and a hundred chimney pots.

"Is the window closed? I think it is," said John Dearborn. "Will you open it for me?"

Larry pulled up the noisy sash, and a breath of cool, sweet air came into the stuffy dormitory.

"Thank you," said Mr. Dearborn. "Now, perhaps the young lady—"

103

Larry was looking about the room. The girl was not in sight. He walked quickly to the door and the officer on duty stood up from the stairs on which he had been sitting.

"Which way did Miss Ward go?"

"She didn't come out, sir," said the man in surprise. "She went in the room with you."

Larry stared at him.

"Didn't come out?" he repeated in amazement. "Are you sure?"

"Absolutely sure."

He called to the man on the lower landing.

"Did you see Miss Ward?"

"No, sir," said the officer, "she hasn't come out of that door. I can see it plainly from here, and I haven't taken my eyes off it."

Larry went back into the room. It was empty. There were half a dozen plain iron beds, but there was no place of concealment save a cupboard which stood against the wall opposite the fireplace. He was in a panic, and his heart was beating wildly as no danger to himself could have made it beat.

He pulled open the cupboard door. It was empty, except for some old clothing which was hanging on a line of pegs. He flung these out and struck the back of the cupboard. It was solid.

"Have you found the young lady?" asked Dearborn presently.

"No, I have not," said Larry quickly. "Is there any other way out of this room but these doors?"

The clergyman shook his head.

"No," he said in astonishment, "Why do you ask? Oh, perhaps you are thinking we should have a means of egress in case of fire. We have been thinking over that matter——"

Larry was white of face, and he was trembling. He called in one of the police officers.

"You will remain in this room until you are relieved," he said. Then he summoned the other. "Call Scotland Yard in my name and tell them I want twenty plain-clothes men here at once. There's a constable on point duty at the end of Lissom Grove. Bring him here and station him outside the house."

"What has happened?" demanded the Rev. Dearborn anxiously. "These are the only times when my malady distresses me, when I feel that I cannot help."

"Perhaps it would be better if you went to your study," said Larry gently. "I am afraid a crime has been committed under my very eyes."

How could it have happened? He had heard no sound. He thought the girl was behind him. He knew she had gone into the room because he had pushed her in before him; he remembered that distinctly. He remembered her turning to the left to inspect the lower end of the room when he had gone to open the window—that was when it happened!

When he had pulled up the window he had made a noise which had drowned any sound which may have occurred at the further end of the room. But it had all passed so quickly, and she had not left the room.

He began a systematic examination of the walls, looking for secret doorways. The coco-nut matting on the floor was pulled up, but without result. Diana Ward had disappeared as though an earthquake had swallowed her, as though she had dissolved into minutest atoms and had floated out of the window in invisible vapour.

The Laundry Yard

LARRY paced the dormitory, sick with fear, terrified as he had never been before. He had searched the house from roof to cellar, had explored dusty and dark corners of which the occupants of Todd's Home were unacquainted; but searchings and questionings produced nothing—nothing!

Within half an hour a cordon of plain-clothes men had been drawn round the house, and Larry had been relieved from the dormitory and set free to conduct his search elsewhere.

"There is no communication between this house and the next?" he had asked the clergyman.

"None whatever," said John Dearborn without hesitation. "In fact, some years ago the noise from the laundry was so great and disturbing to my men that I compelled the proprietors of the building to put up a new wall, a sort of inner lining, to deaden the sound. It is no longer in the occupation of the company," he said. "They went bankrupt, and the premises were taken over by a firm of provision merchants. I understand that they intended storing their goods in the laundry building."

"That is the small building one can see over the gates at the end of the yard?" said Larry.

"That is so," replied the superintendent.

Larry went up to the door of the empty house and examined it carefully; and a sergeant from Scotland Yard made a close inspection.

"I can tell you this, sir, that nobody has been in or out of this door for a very long time," he said. Over the railings which enclosed a narrow area they could see through the dusty windows into a room which was the quintessence of dinginess. It was quite bare and innocent of furniture. Larry felt his heart sinking with every minute that passed. If he should lose her, if he should lose her!

Only then did he realize what this girl meant to him. She was a friend of less than a week, and yet all other matters and interests—friends, profession, success—none of these meant anything to him, compared with that one slim girl. He would willingly have sacrificed every prospect he had in life to hold her hand once more, or to exchange with her a dozen words. In the power of Blind Jake! He reeled under the thought. It was maddening—grotesquely horrible!

He pulled himself together with a jerk. He would go mad if he allowed his mind to dwell upon that hideous possibility.

He had no time to think upon the Stuart case or its bearing on this disappearance. All his energy and agony of endeavour were concentrated upon one object, one discovery—Diana Ward.

He climbed over the wooden gates and explored the yard of the laundry; and here he found something which set his eyes on the trail again. There were wheel tracks, and they were comparatively new. The tracks of a motor-car, possibly two cars. He looked round the littered yard for a garage, and saw a black-looking door which had the appearance of closing some such building.

Sergeant Harvey, who had followed him over the gate, tried a pick-lock on the door, and after two attempts succeeded in forcing back the bolt of the lock. The doors were fixed on slides, and they went back easily and noiselessly, almost at a touch.

"They have been used recently," said Larry.

There were two cars in the garage—a long-bonneted limousine and a small motor-van. Larry walked in, and there was light enough to see, for the day had not yet failed.

"Look!" cried Larry suddenly, pointing to the hood of the motor-van.

It had been newly painted; but clearly underneath the white paint which covered it was the faint impression of a word, badly and awkwardly painted by an amateur hand—the word "Laundry."

"Do you remember, Harvey, Miss Ward telling us that there was a laundry van outside her flat the night they tried to abduct her? If she can identify this——" He stopped suddenly with a twinge of pain. If she were there to identify anything!

The limousine had recently been cleaned, and he took the precaution of jotting down the numbers of both cars. It might be, of course, that these machines were the legitimate property of the new owners of the building, and had been engaged only in perfectly innocent business. It might have been a coincidence that such a car was waiting in the Charing Cross Road the night Blind Jake tried to abduct the girl.

He closed the doors, and Harvey re-locked them.

'Phone these numbers through to the Yard," said Larry. "Ask the Registration Department to identify them!"

Harvey went off and Larry was left alone in the yard. He went again to the wheel tracks. They had been made that morning, for a shower of rain had fallen in the night, and the newness of the markings was obvious.

He walked along to the laundry building proper—a new erection of brick, with ground-glass windows. Here, too, was a sliding door, and on the stone steps leading up was a foot-mark. He bent suddenly to look at the print.

Larry, in moments of excitement, was wont to act jerkily. And now his movements to an observer would seem sudden and unexpected. As he bent his head—

"Plok!"

It was a sound like a cork being discharged from a gaseous champagne bottle, only a little louder, a little more metallic. There was an answering crash near at hand, a splinter of wood fell upon Larry's neck, and he jumped up with a start. A panel of the door was smashed as by a bullet. If he had not dropped his head at that moment to examine the foot-print—Sunny would have stopped the morning papers! That, strangely enough, was the first thought that struck him.

Larry looked round quickly; he had recognized the sound as soon as he had heard it. There had been no report, but he had been fired at with a rifle or pistol fitted with a Maxim silencer. He had heard that "Plok!" before. His keen eyes ranged the windows of the building behind for a sign of smoke, but whatever there might have been must have been instantly dissipated. Then he noticed for the first time that the dormitory from whence the girl had disappeared commanded a view of the yard. He saw the open window, and with his exact sense of topography located the room. No other shot was fired, and he crossed the yard, keeping his eyes upon the backs of the two houses, ready to drop at the first flash of a rifle.

Harvey, on his way back, had opened a wicket in the bigger gate, and Larry stepped out into the street in a thoughtful frame of mind. He went straight back to the Home. The blind hawkers who used the Home were beginning to arrive. They came in ones and twos, tapping their way with their iron-shod sticks, and as they passed him on their way to the common room, a local officer identified them.

"They're all decent citizens, eh?" said Larry. "None of them is on the crime-index?"

"None, sir," said the man. "They're all quite law-abiding people, and we've never had a complaint against any of them."

Larry went up to the dormitory from whence he believed the shot had been fired. To his surprise, the door was locked and the officer was on duty outside.

"What is the meaning of this?" he asked sternly.

"The superintendent sent a message up, telling me that you wished to see me, sir," said the detective. "I went down and found that he had sent no such message. When I came back, the door was locked."

"From the inside?" asked Larry.

"Apparently, sir. There is no key in the lock."

"Who brought the message?"

"The little fellow who opens the door of this place."

"I know him," nodded Larry. "What explanation did he give?"

"He said that somebody with the superintendent's voice told him to go upstairs with the message."

"Stand on one side," said Larry, and with his foot kicked open the door.

The room was empty, but he sniffed.

"A rifle has been fired in here, probably when you were downstairs," he said. "You understand that you are not to leave this room unless I personally or Sergeant Harvey come to you and bring a man to take your place."

"Very good, sir," said the crestfallen worker.

"But in the circumstances I'm not blaming you," interrupted Larry with a faint smile. "We are dealing with an extraordinary gang, and they will use extraordinary methods—you cannot be expected to meet every move as it comes, let alone anticipate what their next will be."

There was no doubt that the rifle had been fired in this room; he could smell the exploded cordite; the proof came when he found under the bed near the window, the exploded shell of a cartridge. He descended to the superintendent's office and found the Rev. John Dearborn a little perturbed.

"How long do you intend keeping your men here, Mr. Holt?" he asked. "Some of my fellows want to go to their dormitory to sleep."

"I am keeping my men here until I get some proof that Miss Ward is not on the premises," said Larry shortly, "and until I have found the gentleman who shot at me from the very dormitory in which she disappeared.'

"Shot at you?" said the other in surprise. "You don't mean——"

"I mean just what I say," said Larry. "Forgive me if I am brusque. Whilst you were talking to the detective who had been brought downstairs by a ruse, I was shot at from that room and the door was locked."

"It is most amazing," said the Rev. John, shaking his head. "I cannot imagine a situation more trying to myself or more exciting for you."

"Exciting!" repeated Larry, and laughed bitterly. "There will be excitement all right," he said grimly, "but it will come later, when I have unravelled this tangle."

And then his mordant humour asserted itself.

"You should put this situation into one of your plays, Mr. Dearborn," he said, and he thought he saw the colour come to the man's pale face.

"That is quite an idea," replied the superintendent thoughtfully, "and I thank you for it. Have you ever seen any of my plays?"

"No, I have not seen them," said Larry, "but I am going at the first opportunity to pay a visit to the Macready."

The superintendent shook his head.

"I sometimes fear," he said, "that they are not as good as some of my friends think they are, and I am disappointed that you have not seen one. But they go on producing them, and money comes in for the Home."

"Who pays the cost of production?" asked Larry curiously. He welcomed any diversion from the overwhelming misery of his thoughts.

"A gentleman who is interested in my work," replied Mr. Dearborn. "I have never met him, but he has never refused to produce a play of mine. Sometimes I think he does so because he wishes to help this Home."

"He must have some good reason," said Larry.

Conversation flagged after this. Once a telephone buzzed, and the superintendent took up a receiver from his table and listened.

"Yes, I think you had better," he said, and hung up the receiver again. "A mundane question from the kitchen," he smiled. "I have telephones fitted all over the house so far as our means allow us," he added. "It saves so many journeys."

Just then a deputation came from the common room with a grievance. The men of No. 1 Dormitory wish to go into their sleeping-places. Some of them made a practice of sleeping the clock round, and all of them, whether they wanted to retire at once or not, claimed their right to enter their dormitory.

"You hear?" said the superintendent. "It is rather difficult for me."

Larry nodded.

"They can have beds at the nearest hotel," he said, "and I will pay for them. Or they can sleep somewhere else. I don't mind the beds being taken out. But nobody occupies that room until Miss Ward is found."

He strolled out into the passage and walked to the common room. These poor men were entitled to an explanation, and he gave it, stating the case fairly and simply, and there was a chorus of approval even from the most obstreperous.

He had concluded his harangue and was standing in the passage with his back to the wall, his head on his breast, thinking, when he heard a commotion upstairs, and a cry, and leapt up the stairs two at a time. He got to the first landing and was turning, when he saw a sight that brought his heart into his mouth.

Walking slowly down the stairs towards him was Diana Ward. Her blouse hung in rags, so that the under-bodice and the snowy white of her shoulders were visible. She carried in one hand a compact Smith-Wesson revolver, and on her white face was a smile of triumph.

For a second Larry looked at her and then leapt up the remaining stairs to meet her, and caught her in his arms.

"My dear, my dear!" he said brokenly. "Thank God you have come back!"

What Happened to Diana

DIANA WARD had strolled to the farther end of the dormitory and was feeling the texture of the rough sheets. The housewife instinct in her was a strong one, and her nurse's training had given her an additional interest in the means which were adopted to give comfort to these poor blind beggars—for beggars most of them were. She had heard the superintendent ask Larry to open the window, and she was watching idly, when the door of the cupboard behind her opened without a sound and a barefooted man crept out.

The first thing that Diana knew was that something like a piece of wet chamois leather was over her face, and she was being lifted bodily. For a second she was paralysed, and in that second she had passed through the cupboard and the wall behind. Both doors fastened—for the back of the press, as Larry had suspected at first, was a door that moved, pegs and all, outwards. What he could not know was that it was literally a brick door.

She heard its thud as it closed, and, wriggling her face clear of the wet leather, she screamed. Again a hand that was big enough to cover the whole of her face came over her mouth, and she was dragged along in the darkness; another door opened, and she was thrown in. There was a click, and an electric light blazed from above, and she saw her captor and shrank back in terror.

He was tall, bigger than any man she had seen. She guessed he was seven feet in height, and his breadth was in proportion. He was dressed in a shirt and a pair of trousers. His feet and his arms were bare, and she had no need to study that hairy forearm to appreciate its strength. It was as massive as an average man's thigh, and the muscles stood out in swathes. His face was red and large and curiously flat.

His eyes, which did not move when he spoke, were of the palest blue, and a mane of grey hair swept back from his forehead and hung untidily behind. The mouth, heavy and gross, was covered by a short unkempt beard which was neither grey nor yellow, but had something of each in its hue. His enormous ears stuck out from his head almost at right angles, and she thought she had never seen so terrible a creature in her life.

"I'll let ye have a look at me so that ye'll know me again," he giggled. (There was no other word that Diana could think of that so described that shrill laugh of his.) "Where's your gun?" he bantered. "Why don't you fire it at poor old Jake—he told you all about me, I'll bet!"

She knew that he referred to Larry Holt, but made no reply. Her eyes were searching the room for some weapon, but the rough plastered walls were bare and there was not a stick of furniture in the place. The only window was a long narrow slip of toughened glass near the ceiling, flanked on each side by two wall ventilators. She searched her bag, but there was nothing there. She was even without hat-pins, though they would be practically useless against this brute.

"Looking for something to kill me with, are you?" he giggled again. "I hear you! Now you sit down and be patient, young woman," he said. "There's a good time coming, and nobody wants to hurt you."

He did not attempt to approach her, and she had that relief, but his next words told her that the real danger was but postponed.

"Ye're pretty by all accounts," he chuckled. "And them as likes pretty ones might give the world for you. It's a wonder to me that They ain't took ye, my dear, but They haven't any use for women or marriage and the like, so They've given ye to Old Jake."

He giggled again and the girl went cold at the sound. He had a trick of pausing before and emphasizing "They" as though the word stood in capitals in his dark mind.

"I can't see ye, so prettiness don't mean much to me, my little darling. And if your face was like hers"—he jerked his thumb to the ceiling—"it wouldn't make no difference to me."

"You'll never get out of this building," she said, realizing that it was best to show a bold attitude. "Mr. Holt is in the house next door, and by this time the place will be surrounded."

This time his chuckle had a deeper note.

"There are ten ways out of the house," he said contemptuously. "That's why They bought it. There's a hole underneath the cellar where you can walk for miles, and nobody there to stop you but the rats. Rats are afraid of blind men."

There was the hint of a curious, childlike simplicity that ill fitted his monstrous shape.

"Sooner or later he will get you," she said quietly, and then, with a sudden inspiration: "He has already got Lew."

He was on the point of leaving the room, and he spun round, his face working.

"Lew!" he roared. "He's got Lew!"

Then he was silent, and the silence ended in a shout of laughter that seemed to shake the room.

"Lew will tell him a lot!" he said. "How's he going to ask Lew for information when Lew doesn't know where he is, or who he's talking to? He can't read or write. He'd have been dead, too," he nodded sagely, "dead as a door nail, Lew would have been, for the dirty trick he played upon Them. He was the man who put the paper into the pocket of the feller They croaked!"

"We know that," she said boldly, and he seemed to be impressed.

"You found that out, did you?" he said. "But Lew didn't tell ye. He'd have been dead, as dead as a door nail, Lew would, only They didn't want no dead men knocking about. Me and Lew carried him down the steps," he said, nodding his great head. "I can tell you that, because I know the lor. I know the lor properly, I do. You can't tell Old Jake anything."

She was wondering what he meant by this boast of his knowledge of the law.

"A wife can't give evidence against her husband," he said with a little leer. "That's why I tell you all this, little darling."

"A wife!" she gasped, sick at the ghastliness of the suggestion.

"Mrs. Jake Bradford," he chortled. "Bradford is my name, my darling, and you'll be married by his reverence too, proper and in order."

"You fool!" she burst forth in her anger and fear. "Do you think anybody could marry me to a horror like you? Do you think I should stand without protesting and telling all I know, by your side? You're mad."

He bent his head forward and his voice came lower as he spoke, until it was little more than a whisper.

"There's worse than me in this house," he said slowly, "and maybe you won't mind me if you don't see me, young lady. And you may be blind as I am, and deaf too, like Lew." He paused, and she shrank back, holding on to the walls for support. "And dumb, if you're going to talk!" he roared in a sudden fury. "There's nothing I wouldn't do to you if They told me to."

The door opened and closed. A key turned and a bolt was shot, and looking up she saw he was gone, and slid to the floor half conscious, half fainting. Then with an effort she drooped her head low and felt the blood coming back, and presently she was able to stand.

No power of will could stop her hands from shaking, and it was not until she had paced the room for ten minutes that she came back to anything like normal. She knew that it was no idle threat this man had uttered. He would be merciless if his unknown superiors gave the order. He would crush out the youth and the beauty of youth, the sweet senses of life, without compunction at the word of They. He would mutilate and torture, and pity would not come to him. She had to think clearly and think quickly.

She went to the door, but she knew that escape that way was impossible. There was no chair by which she could reach the window, and she could not make her escape without even attracting attention through that slit of wall. There was nothing in the room but the electric light.

She remembered Larry's story of how this man had come toward him with his hands up, and how he had crushed the bulb in his powerful fist. He must be animal strong, she thought. Wasn't there a danger of his being shocked by the electric current?

At that thought she looked up quickly. The light had been fixed without any regard to appearance. The long wire came from the ceiling at one end of the room and was loosely tacked to the ceiling as far as the centre, where it passed over a hook and hung downwards, with a little tin reflector over the pear-shaped lamp. She reached for the lamp and turned it round.

"Two hundred volts," she read, ground upon the crystal glass.

She tried to unhook the wire by throwing up the loose end, but it was some time before she succeeded, and at last the loose part fell and the lamp jerked to the floor and almost touched it. She caught the loose flex in her hand and pulled gently, and the thin wire brackets which held the flex to the ceiling came away without any difficulty. The switch was near the door, and she walked across and turned it off. Putting one foot upon the flex, near to where it entered the aperture of the shade, she pulled with all her might and after several attempts it snapped.

She was in darkness, but her nimble fingers plucked at the loose end of the wire, and with her fingernails she cleared away the rubber casing which enclosed the tiny thread-like strands of copper. Soon she had something that felt like a loose-haired broom in her hands, and she was satisfied. She thought she heard a noise in the passage, and, running to the switch, turned the current on again. She groped in the half-darkness for her bag and found it, took out her gloves and put them on, then felt gingerly for the hanging strands. She took them in her hands and held the "brush" before her, being careful not to touch one exposed strand. Pushing away the shade and the globe with her foot, she waited in the centre of the room. And then the door opened.

"Here I am again, dearie," and her breath came quickly as she heard the door locked from the inside. "You think I'm a funny-looking fellow, don't you?" He did not know that the light was out, for he lived in everlasting darkness.

For a time he made no attempt to come near her. She could just see the shape of him by the evening light which filtered through that narrow window.

"Tony missed him," he said, by way of conveying information. "Missed him!" he said contemptuously. "If I'd had my eyes, I'd have got the devil! I'd get him now with this little gun of mine, blind as I am, if I could hear him move. But we'll have Holty yet, my darling. We'll have him and cut his heart out. He'll wish he was never born."

He lowered his voice, and said something which was not intelligible to the girl. Then he seemed to recall the object of his visit.

"Come to Old Jake, my dear," he giggled, as he walked stealthily toward her, both of his huge arms outstretched. "Come to your old husband, my pretty!"

He was as quick as a cat, and one hand had gripped the shoulder of her blouse before she realized he was upon her—gripped it and tore it from shoulder to hem. She threw herself back, and his other hand came up—and touched the outspread wire. With a yell that was half shriek, half roar, he fell back.

"What did you do?" he asked savagely. "What did you do, you little devil? Did you knife me like that swine?"

He was evidently feeling himself to discover an injury, and then he leapt at her, and this time the wire struck his face, and he fell to the ground like a log.

She heard him stir.

"What is it, what is it?" he whispered. "I can't see it! You oughtn't to treat an old blind man like that, you little—"

His hand shot out and caught her ankle, flinging her to the ground. But again his face touched the electric wire, charged with 200 volts, and he screamed and rolled over. He was mad now, a whimpering lunatic. Again and again he approached her; again and again his hand, his face, his neck, came into contact with the current. And then suddenly he fell again, and the girl thrust the cruel ends of the wire at his throat. She felt like a murderess as he shivered convulsively. But she had to kill him; she knew that nothing short of killing him would save her life.

Presently she took the wire away. He lay very still, and her shaking hands searched his pockets. She found the key, felt the revolver in his pocket and extracted it, and fumbled for the lock. Presently the door was open and she was in the passage which turned to the right, and along here she went. She was in a lighter room with two windows, but she was still in mortal terror; for now she had lost her best weapon of defence.

The door was easy to find. Cleverly concealed it might be in the dormitory of Todd's Home, but here it was well marked. She pulled a handle, and the mass of brickwork swung back and she walked through the door. A man standing in the dormitory spun round, a revolver in his hand.

"Good Lord!" he cried. "Miss Ward, where did you come from?"

Back Again

THAT sense of security, of peace, and of deep happiness was inexpressibly sweet, she thought, as she lay in Larry Holt's arms. Presently she released herself, and in a few hurried words had said enough to send a small battalion of detectives racing to the dormitory and through the brick door, which she had left ajar.

Larry handed the girl to the care of Harvey and followed his men. The room where Diana had been imprisoned was empty. He stopped long enough to switch off the current, then joined the searchers. There was no doubt that this place, for all its unoccupied appearance, had regular tenants. They found rooms that had been built within rooms, a thin wall being erected within a few feet of each window. This meant that the house might be occupied at night, and lights might blaze in every apartment without anybody outside being the wiser.

Blind Jake had said no more than the truth when he had told the girl that there were plenty of ways out of the house. They found one in the cellar that led to an old disused rain-water sewer, and here pursuit was abandoned. None of the party except Larry, who always carried a small flash-lamp, was equipped for a chase through the darkness.

Another exit led directly into the yard where Larry had found the garage. A third communicated with the kitchen of Todd's Home.

Larry, realizing that his quarry had escaped, went back to the girl. He found her sitting in the superintendent's office, the watchful Harvey embarrassingly close to her side—an attitude which was explained when the laughing girl lifted one of her arms, for Harvey, who was taking no risks, had handcuffed their wrists together!

"And very wise too," said Larry with a smile as the detective unfastened the irons. "Now, Mr. Dearborn, I want to have some sort of explanation of the mysterious happenings in this house."

"I don't think anything mysterious has happened here," said Mr. Dearborn quietly. "You cannot hold me responsible for villainy which may have been perpetrated next door. I am told that there are doors communicating between these two houses, but of that I had not the slightest knowledge. If there was a man living next door——"

"There were six men living next door," said Larry. "We found their beds and some of their clothing. From the fact that there were books, some of them open, it is pretty clear that they are not blind."

Mr. Dearborn shrugged his despair.

"What can I do?" he asked. "In this house we are dependent entirely upon the loyalty of our inmates; and though it is possible sometimes to detect the presence of a stranger by his unusual footfalls, his voice or his cough, it is quite possible that these men made the freest use of the Home for the purpose of carrying on their nefarious work, without our having the slightest knowledge of such things."

This argument was so logical that Larry did not contest its truth. These cunning men who formed the gang might use the Home with impunity, if they exercised care in their movements and maintained silence. Frankly, he acknowledged the reasonableness of Mr. Dearborn's argument.

"I quite appreciate the possibility," he said. "It is rather unfortunate for you as well as for me. It might have been a great deal more unfortunate," he added with truth. Though how unfortunately this adventure might have ended he had to learn when the girl told her story on the way to Scotland Yard.

"Dreadful, dreadful!" he shuddered. "My poor, poor child!"

His own relief had been so great that he felt physically ill. But no such reaction was visible in the girl, who grew calmer and brighter as the taxi neared Scotland Yard. She wore his raincoat, and they had stopped in the Edgware Road to allow her to buy a blouse, for she insisted upon going to Scotland Yard first to make her statement.

"I'm rather sorry for Dearborn," he said. "He is a pathetic figure. Men who devote their lives to this kind of work may be excused even their feeble dramatic efforts. Did you notice how eagerly he shook hands with you?"

She looked at him sharply.

"Yes, I noticed that," she said in a strange tone.

"Why, Diana," he said, "what do you mean?"

"Oh, nothing," she said lightly. "I mean that he took my hand, that is all, and shook it very heartily."

"Well, there's nothing in that," said Larry with a smile.

"There is a great deal in that," said the girl, "a great deal more than you can realize."

He leaned back in the cab and laughed softly.

"You're going to mystify me. I can feel it coming on," he said, and she squeezed his arm affectionately.

He sent her up to 47 alone, and she had changed her torn blouse for the new purchase by the time he discreetly knocked at the door.

"By the way," he said, "I forgot to ask you. Where did you dig up that deadly-looking weapon I saw in your hand as you were coming down the stairs?"

"From Blind Jake's pocket," she said. "Ugh! It was horrid touching him, but I wanted to be quite sure that I had some kind of weapon."

"Undoubtedly you have a big end of the story," he said. "We know now that Blind Jake and the man Lew——"

"Have you left him there?" she asked quickly.

He smiled a little wryly.

"I've made too many mistakes in this case to add to them," he said. "No, I have taken this man to another institution where he is being looked after. Lew and Jake were the two men who were employed, either before or after the murder of Gordon Stuart," he went on. "The gang has probably got a hold on Lew, and he was anxious to escape from their clutches or to be avenged upon them for some treachery they have committed, and he wrote the message which we found—on the strip of paper with the Braille characters. That fines the search down to one man, because we can find means of inducing Lew to understand whose hands he is in."

"And the greatest discovery of all you haven't touched," she said quietly.

Larry got up from his chair, laughing, and paced the room, a favourite occupation of his.

"You're an extraordinary girl," he said. "No sooner do I think I have got the case set, than you produce something new, something more important in the shape of clues, and something generally," he added pensively, "that upsets all my previous theories."

"I don't think this will," she said. "I am referring to the woman upstairs."

"What woman upstairs?" he asked, astounded.

"Do you remember I told you that Jake pointed with his thumb to the ceiling, and said if I had a face like hers——" She stopped.

"I'm sorry," he said gently. "I'm a brute and a forgetful brute; but things have happened to-day which have driven the Stuart case out of my mind. And that reminds me," he said, "I want to telephone."

He called a number, and she recognized it as the number of the Trafalgar Hospital.

"I want the matron's office, please," he said, and whilst she was wondering where his mind had led him, he said: "Is that you, matron? It is I, Larry Holt. Yes, how do you do? Are the nurses you send out to cases having a slack time? I mean, are there plenty to go round? There are? Well, will you send a nice motherly lady to my address at Regent's Gate Gardens? You know where I live? No, I'm not ill," he smiled, "but I have somebody with me who isn't too well—yes, a lady."

He hung up the receiver and turned to meet the girl's astonished eyes.

"Have you a lady staying with you?" she asked.

"I haven't, but I shall have," said Larry. "You're not going back to Charing Cross Road to-night except to get the things you require; you're coming up to my flat, and there you're going to stay, chaperoned by a very nice nurse, and you'll greatly oblige me if you'll pretend that you're a little bit under the weather. I must save my face."

"But I can't, it's impossible!" she said, scarlet of face. "I couldn't——"

"Oh, yes, you could," said Larry. "Now you're going to do as I tell you. Otherwise, it means that I must sit outside your flat all night catching my death of cold."

Finally she consented. They dined together, and he took her to see two acts of the Dearborn play. They came out at the end of the second act, bewildered.

"But how could anybody put such awful stuff on the stage?" asked the girl on their way to his flat.

"It is rather amazing, isn't it?"

Then Larry began to chuckle.

"You're easily amused to-day," she said.

"I'm very happy to-night," he corrected. "It just occurred to me that Sunny will have to meet the nurse when she comes."

"Whatever will he say?" she gasped.

"Well," drawled Larry, "if the nurse insists there's a lady ill in the house, Sunny will say, 'Yes, madam,' and will do his best to produce one!"

It was past eleven when they got to the flat. The elevators had stopped running at half-past ten, and they had to walk up the stairs.

"Watch your step," warned Larry. "They light these stairways abominably."

He went first, and she saw him pause on the top step of the second flight.

"Great Scott! Who's that?" he asked.

Against his door a man was lying, doubled up and still. Larry leant over him and rang the bell, and Sunny came to the door.

In the flood of light thrown by the hall lamp, Larry saw the face of the prostrate figure. He was breathing stertorously, and his face and his head streamed with blood.

"Sunny, has the nurse arrived?"

"Yes, sir," said Sunny, looking down at the figure.

"Then she'll be wanted," said Larry quietly.

"Who is it?" asked Diana, peering round behind him.

"Flash Fred," said Larry, "and as near to dead as makes no difference."

"John Dearborn Is Not Blind"

THEY carried the injured man into the sitting-room and laid him on a couch. There was a doctor living in the flat above and luckily he had not gone to bed, and was down in a few minutes.

"He is badly injured," he reported. "There are one or two knife wounds, and the wound in the head looks as though there were a fracture of the skull."

"The man must have been attacked outside my door," said Larry. "He couldn't have walked far in this condition."

"No," said the doctor, shaking his head. "He might have walked two or three yards, but the chances are, as you found him outside the door, that he was there when the attack was made on him. Do you know him?"

"Yes," said Larry, "he is an old acquaintance of mine. Is there any danger of his dying?"

"A very big danger," replied the doctor gravely. "That concussion may be anything. I should send him straight away to hospital, where he can be thoroughly examined and, if necessary, operated upon."

The ambulance had come and gone, and the only evidence of Flash Fred's visit was a few dark stains about the door, before Larry began to think consecutively.

The nurse who had arrived fulfilled all his telephoned requirements. She was stout and jovial and matronly, and the first use Larry made of his freedom from distraction was to tell her in a few words just why she had been sent for.

"Obviously I could not allow Miss Ward to go back to Charing Cross Road after her terrible experience to-day," he said, and Nurse James, who was by no means dissatisfied with having so easy a "case," agreed.

She exercised her authority to the extent of ordering Diana to bed immediately, and the girl meekly obeyed. But she could not sleep. At two o'clock Larry, writing at his table, heard the creak of an opening door and looked up to see her. She was in her dressing-gown, and her hair was braided in a long golden plait.

"I can't sleep," she said restlessly, almost irritably, and he saw that she was overstrung and rose to get an arm-chair for her.

She neither apologized for her attire nor her visitation, and these circumstances struck Larry as curious. But that which was on Diana Ward's mind was of so great an importance that the thought of decorum did not occur to her. She sat there, her hands folded on her lap, and there was no sound save the tick of a clock on the mantelpiece and the squeak of Larry's chair as it turned.

"What is troubling you, Diana?" he asked.

She looked up at him quickly.

"Do you think I'm troubled?" she said.

"If you're not, you're a wonderful girl," said Larry gently. "You've had an awful time to-day, my dear, but somehow I do not think that that is what is on your mind."

She shook her head.

"It isn't," and added, "it is the woman upstairs."

"The woman upstairs? Oh, you mean the woman that Jake spoke about? But, Diana, there was no 'upstairs'. You were on the top floor of that building, which is a story lower than Todd's Home."

But still she was not satisfied.

"Besides," he went on quietly, "if she had been there, the woman may have been—as bad a character as any of the other occupants of that house. The fact that she was unpleasant to look at, as Jake suggested, does not make her innocent."

"Poor soul, poor soul!" said the girl, and then to Larry's horror she began to weep softly. "I can't sleep for thinking of her," she sobbed. "They will keep her, they dare not let her go!"

"Why," he gasped suddenly, "you don't suggest that she is Clarissa Stuart?"

She looked up at that, her face stained with tears.

"Clarissa Stuart?" she repeated slowly. "No, I don't think she is Clarissa Stuart."

"Then who is she?" he asked. "At any rate, who do you think she is?"

"I don't think—I am sure," she said, speaking with painful slowness. "That woman was Emma, the charwoman of the boarding-house," and Larry jumped to his feet.

"The charwoman," he said slowly. "You're right!"

Again the tick of the little clock asserted itself as they sat, each busy with their own thoughts.

"You connect this terrible gang with the Stuart mystery?" he said.

She nodded.

"I also connect them," said Larry, "for very excellent reasons. And yet I cannot see what they gained by Stuart's death, unless they were in league with this girl who calls herself Clarissa Stuart?"

She made a hopeless little gesture and rose.

"I can connect them all," she said. "They are very distinct in their relationships, but then," with a faint smile, "I have an advantage over you."

"You have many advantages over me," said Larry, humouring her. "And now, dear, you must go back and sleep."

But she did not heed him.

"There is only one I did not connect," she went on, "and you have made his case understandable."

"Who is that?"

"Flash Fred," she replied. "He is just a criminal who has touched the fringe of the conspiracy and has been in it without knowing he was in it." She nodded as though she had only at that moment decided her point of view. "But the others? Blind Jake who works for an unknown master; the charwoman, the greatest victim of them all; poor Lew, with his deaf ears and his blistered fingers—you didn't see those. I should have told you, only the doctor interrupted us."

"Blistered fingers?" said Larry in amazement. "No, I didn't see them."

"I felt them," she shuddered, "when he touched my face. His fingers and thumbs have been blistered at the tops."

"But why?"

"So that he shall not read Braille or write Braille," said the girl quietly.

"It's impossible, impossible!" said Larry in horror. "There cannot be such villainy in the world. My child, I have been acquainted with some of the worst crimes that have ever been committed in Europe. I have seen the victims, I have tracked and hanged the criminals. Men are cruel, vicious, unscrupulous and bloody-minded, but they do not commit such cold-blooded deeds as you say have been committed upon that poor blind man."

She smiled again.

"I don't think you realize just how bad these people are," she said. "For if you did, you would never say that it was impossible. For Dearborn——" she began, and he laughed outright.

"Diana, dear, you've reached the stage which we always reach, when you're suspicious of everybody! Not of poor John Dearborn, working for the good of humanity in that slum, and amidst those fearful people?"

She nodded.

"I shook hands with John Dearborn when I went there. I shook hands with him when I came away," she said.

"That doesn't make him a criminal," he smiled.

"And when I offered my hand he took it," she said. "Please remember that I was a nurse in a blind asylum for two years—when I offered my hand he took it."

"Well, why shouldn't he?" asked Larry in surprise.

"He shouldn't have seen it," said the girl, "if he was blind. And John Dearborn is no more blind than you or I!"

Who Runs Dearborn?

SAY THAT again," said Larry slowly. "You offered your hand and he took it?"

She nodded.

"Don't you know that when you shake hands with the blind, you always reach out and take their hand, because they cannot see yours offered; but Dearborn raised his just as soon as I raised mine."

Larry was staring helplessly at her.

"If he is not blind, why is he there?" he asked. "He is a clergyman."

"There is no John Dearborn in the Clergy List," said the girl calmly. "I went carefully through the list; and he is not amongst the Congregational, the Baptist, or the Wesleyan ministers."

Larry looked at her, lost in admiration.

"You're a wonder! But don't forget that he came from Australia."

"The Australian lists are available," said the girl immediately, "and the only John Dearborn is an aged gentleman who lives at Totooma, and is obviously not our John Dearborn."

She had come to the table and had drawn a chair up close. She now leant forward, her hands clasped in front of her.

"Larry," she said—"I'm going to call you Larry out of office hours—has it not struck you as strange that John Dearborn's plays should be produced at a theatre, remembering that he has written a succession of failures?"

"I've always thought that," Larry admitted, and she nodded her head.

"I wish you would look into the directorate of the Macready," she said. "Find out what comprises the syndicate which puts up the money for producing these plays. I don't forget that Mr. Stuart disappeared from that theatre."

"Nor I," said Larry quietly. "But John Dearborn! You amaze me."

She rose.

"I feel sleepy now that I have got that off my mind," she smiled. "Are you"—she hesitated—"watching the laundry?"

"I have two men there who are instructed to stop any car coming out and discover who is the driver and what the car contains."

"Then I can go to bed cheerfully," she said with a little laugh, and passing him, she rested her hand gently on his head. "They will keep—Emma alive for some time yet. The only danger is that they may take her away from the laundry."

"You can rest your mind on that," said Larry quietly, and with this assurance she went to bed and he heard her door close.

The next day was uneventful. The police had made a further search of the laundry, and had discovered a room above that in which the girl had been imprisoned. It was a very tiny attic apartment, but showed signs of having been occupied, though it was empty when the police made their call.

Larry cursed himself that he had not made a more thorough inspection of the premises. He had been so relieved at the discovery of the girl that he had not been as painstaking as he should have been—this he told himself disgustedly.

There were two people whom he desired greatly to meet. The first of these was the man who had lost the little finger of his left hand. That curious individual who had preceded him the day he was investigating the reason for Gordon Stuart's mysterious visits to a country churchyard. The second was the mysterious Emma. In his heart of hearts he knew that Emma would supply the key which would unlock the door to great and conclusive revelations.

"I shall never forgive myself," he told Diana, "if any harm comes to this woman."

She shook her head.

"You need not fear that they will do her harm," she said. "She is much too valuable, and I shall know just when her danger period commences."

"You!" he said in surprise. "Really, Diana, you scare me sometimes."

She laughed, and her laughter was drowned in the rattle of her typewriter.

"Flash Fred has not recovered consciousness yet," he told her, "but there's a big chance that he will. The doctors say that there is no actual fracture, and that there is a possibility that the pressure which now keeps him unconscious will disperse."

"Where is he?" she asked.

"In St. Mary's Hospital," replied Larry. "I have him in a private ward with a police officer on guard. Not that poor Fred could escape," he smiled, "but there are people in this city who will probably be most anxious that he escapes by the only way which leaves them safe . . ."

She did not need to ask which way that was. He put down the pen he had been holding, though he had done very little writing.

"It wouldn't be a bad idea if we went along to St. Mary's and discovered at first hand how the man is," he said. "Will you come?"

128

As she put on her hat before the four-inch square of looking-glass which she had imported into the building, she asked, without turning her head:

"What are you going to do about John Dearborn?"

Larry rubbed his chin.

"I hardly know," he said. "It is not an offence for a man to pretend to be blind if he isn't. Besides," he continued, "he might have had sufficient sight to have seen your hand. There may be a dozen explanations. He could have offered his hand mechanically, almost instinctively."

She nodded.

"It is possible," she said quietly, "but he smiled too when I smiled."

"Who wouldn't?" said Larry gallantly.

In the business-like office of the senior house surgeon at St. Mary's they met the surgeon in charge of the case.

"You've come at a very fortunate moment," he smiled. "Your man has recovered consciousness."

"Can he talk?" asked Larry eagerly.

"I think so. At any rate, I see no particular reason why he shouldn't, if there is urgent necessity for your questioning him. Naturally, he is still very weak, and in ordinary circumstances I should not allow anybody to interview him; but I gather that you have particular police business."

"Very particular," said Larry grimly.

The surgeon led the way to the ward. At the door of the ward the girl hesitated.

"Shall I come?" she said.

"Your presence is necessary," said Larry, "if it is only in a professional capacity. Have you got your note-book?"

She nodded and they went into the little private ward where Fred Grogan lay. His head was swathed in bandages and his face was white and drawn, but his eyes lit up at the sight of Larry.

"I never expected to look forward to seeing you," he said. "But first of all, governor,"—his voice was earnest—"you ought to get hold of that woman in the boiler-house."

"The woman in the boiler-house?" repeated Larry quickly. "What do you mean?"

"Clarissa's nurse," was the staggering reply; "and who 'Clarissa' is, the Lord knows!"

Flash Fred's Story

NOW I'M going to give it to you straight, governor," said Fred, settling himself comfortably in bed. "I won't say that I couldn't tell a lie—that's the one saying of Napoleon's that I've never believed."

"The same period, but another man," said Larry, concealing a smile; "but don't worry about your history, Fred. I want you to get this story off your mind as quickly as you can."

"I've done a lot of reading in my time," said the sick man reminiscently. "Histories and high-class novels—they've got a pretty good library in Portland Prison, but they're not so good as the books you get in Wormwood Scrubs. Anyway, I am going to tell you the truth, Mr. Holt. I might as well start at the beginning, and I know I'm going to put myself in wrong, but you'll have to forget a lot of the things I tell you, because they make me look as if I was a dishonest person."

"I should hate that impression to get abroad," said Larry without a smile, "and I promise you that anything which doesn't relate directly to the murder of Gordon Stuart will be discreetly forgotten."

"Cheerio!" said Fred, visibly brighter. "Well, this story begins about four or five years ago in Montpellier. You don't know Montpellier, perhaps?"

"I know it," said Larry. "You can cut out all the topographical details. I know it from the Coq d'Or to the Palace."

"I happened to be there," said Fred, "looking round and enjoying myself, and I drifted into a little game that was run by a man named Floquart on the quiet. It was baccarat, and I'm very lucky at baccarat, especially when I've made friends with the dealer. But this time the dealer and me weren't on speaking terms, as you might say, and for three days I never felt money that wasn't my own. And each day there was less of my own to feel. Then one night they cleaned me out proper, and I left Floquart's with just enough to get me home to the hotel if I walked.

"I was turning out of the rue Narbonne when I heard a shot, and, looking across the place, I saw a man lying on the ground and another fellow walking away pretty slick. In those days the police arrangements at Montpellier weren't all they could have been, and there wasn't a gendarme in sight. The fellow who was walking must have thought he'd got away with it, when I suddenly came up to him. There was just enough light, for the day was breaking, for me to distinguish his face. A fine-looking fellow he was, with a big yellow beard, and I think he was scared sick when I suddenly stepped out and claimed him as my own. It was not my business to butt into private disturbances, but you understand that I was broke, and I thought that here was a chance of helping a fellow creature in distress to get rid of any incriminating money he might have in his possession. He told me a yarn that the man he'd shot had done him a very bad injury, which I won't refer to in front of the young lady, and then he slipped me about sixteen thousand francs and I let him go, because I was sorry for him."

He glanced slyly up at Larry and grinned.

"Well," he went on, "seeing that no gendarme had appeared, I walked over and had a look at the lad who was shot, though I knew I was taking a risk by being seen in the company of a soon-to-croak. They say he was shot and must have died immediately, but that isn't true: he was alive when I got to him, and when I was bending over him, it was to find out if I could do anything for the poor devil before he passed out. I asked him who had shot him, and he replied"—he paused impressively—"'David Judd.'?"

Larry's eyebrows went up.

"David Judd?" he asked. "Is he any relation to the doctor?"

"His brother," said Fred. "That's how I came to know him. I've always told Judd that I recognized him in the street; as a matter of fact, it was the poor guy on the ground who gave him away. I was trying to find out why he was shot, when he croaked. I knew there was nothing to be gained by being found attached to a murdered man, though fortunately I hadn't a gun in my possession and could have proved an alibi. Then I heard a gendarme's heavy feet coming down one of the side turnings, and I got away as quickly as I could. But the swine recognized me, though, and I had to go before an examining magistrate and prove that I had nothing to do with the murder and that I was going for a doctor when I was spotted. I had the good sense to go for a doctor," he added, "the moment I realized that the copper had seen me."

He paused, finding it rather difficult to explain his subsequent action in language which would be wholly creditable to himself.

"When I got back to London I thought it my duty to call on Mr. David Judd," he said. "He wasn't in his office—he used to have a room at the Greenwich Insurance—but I saw his brother, and I unloaded my trouble."

"Your trouble being to discover how much they'd 'drop' for keeping your mouth shut, I suppose," said Larry.

"You've got it at once, Mr. Holt. What a mind!" said the admiring Fred. "He was terribly upset, was Dr. Judd, and said he would see his brother as soon as he came back from the country. And then happened an event which looked like spoiling all my beautiful prospects. Dr. David died. He caught a cold coming down from Scotland and died in twenty-four hours. I went to the funeral," said Fred, "as a mourner, and I bet that nobody mourned more than I did. Anyway, I must say that Dr. Judd acted like a gentleman. He sent for me after his brother's funeral and said that he wanted to save his brother's memory from disgrace, and offered me a yearly income if I would keep my mouth shut."

"The man who was killed was a clerk, was he not?" asked Larry.

"He was a clerk," said Fred slowly, "a clerk in the employ of the Greenwich Insurance Company, who had blackmailed David Judd."

Larry whistled softly.

"The Greenwich Insurance Company," he said; "and blackmailed David! Why, what crime had David committed?"

Fred shook his head.

"I can't tell you that, Mr. Holt. If I could, I would. But it was something pretty bad, you can bet. Dr. Judd said that this clerk had pinched a lot of money, and I think that's true, because I remember his playing, and playing very high, at Floquart's.

"Well, to cut this story short, I've drawn about four years' income from Dr. Judd. I'm not apologizing or trying to prove to you that I acted like a little gentleman; that doesn't interest you, anyway. The other day I met the doctor at a wedding. He was invited, but I wasn't," explained Fred shamelessly, "but that didn't make any difference: I went. He asked me if I'd go to dinner with him last night at his house in Chelsea. He's got a real fine house, has Dr. Judd, full of wonderful pictures and sparklers. And as he was going to pay me a lump sum to get rid of me, I decided to go.

"There is a man at the doctor's," he said after a pause, "a valet. I don't want to give him away, Mr. Holt, but he's an old lag and was in the next cell to me at Portland."

"His name is Strauss," said Larry. "He takes drugs, and has had three convictions."

"Oh, you know that, do you?" said Fred in surprise. "Well, anyway, I know him. I met him in Piccadilly the other day. He was going to fence a few articles that he'd pinched from his boss, and he dropped me a pair of sleeve-links—"

Larry gasped.

"Oh, that is where they came from; they were Dr. Judd's?"

"I ain't so sure that they were Dr. Judd's," said Fred. "From what I have heard, the doctor has people who stay with him over week-ends, and Strauss may have pinched them from one of these. Anyway"—again he hesitated, finding it difficult to express his plans in such a manner as would save him from the charge of ingratitude—"I had an idea of helping myself to a few souvenirs of Dr. Judd before I went," he explained, "and I'd fixed it up with Strauss so that I could just look over the premises and pick a few things that would remind me of my old friend. So when I was asked to dinner, naturally I jumped at the chance. I don't say that I'd have gone alone to dinner, because the doctor and me aren't quite bosom companions; but he told me that there was a lot of people coming, so I went. I was supposed to go at eight, which is well after dark, but I went at seven, and not to the house but to the opposite side of the street, because I was anxious to see Dr. Judd's guests arrive before I got in. I waited till eight and nobody came. I waited till half-past eight, and then I saw the doctor come out and look up and down the road. I was so hungry that I nearly went over to him, but I didn't see myself dining alone with a fellow that I've been swindling. So I waited and waited, and presently a motor-car drove up and went straight to the gates at the side of the house. I thought he was going to push them in, but the moment the head-lamps touched the gates they opened. 'That's funny,' says I to myself, and I crossed the road and had a look over the top of the gate. It meant a bit of a climb, but I did it without making any noise; and the first fellow that got out of the car was that big stiff who tried to croak me in Jermyn Street."

"Blind Jake?" said Larry.

"I've never been introduced," replied the other sardonically. "I saw him plain for a minute because he passed in front of the head-lamps, and then the lights went out and I saw nothing more. At ten o'clock the gates opened—like magic it was, for there was nobody near them—and a car came out. It passed me, going slow, and I ran behind and jumped on to the luggage-carrier, which was down. I got off as it went into the King's Road, Chelsea, because there is a lot of light there and a copper might have seen me and given me away. But there were plenty of taxis about, and I hired one and told him to keep the car in sight. I wanted to know where Blind Jake—that's his name, is it?—was living, and I didn't have much difficulty in keeping the car in sight. We went up past Victoria, along Grosvenor Place, up Park Lane. I was afraid the car would turn into the park, for private cars are allowed there but taxis aren't, and I should have lost him. But, luckily or unluckily, it didn't. The car went up Edgware Road—Tyburn Tree, where they hanged them in the old days, used to be there," he said, apropos of nothing. "I read that in a book when I was in stir."

"Cut out those memories of Old London," begged Larry.

"I followed up close behind, and then the machine turned into some side-streets," said Fred, "and I took the risk of paying off the cabman and following on foot. I know that district pretty well, and I hadn't been searching for ten minutes before I saw the car pulling up against a gate which was set into a high wall. The driver must have missed the way, because I was there almost as soon as the doctor."

"Dr. Judd? Was he there?" asked Larry.

Flash Fred nodded, and was very sorry for himself that he had done so. It was some time before he could speak again.

"If I don't keep my blinking head still," he said good-humouredly, "I shall lose it. Yes, the doctor was there. I was close up to them; as a matter of fact, I was standing behind the car when they all three got out. Blind Jake was one; a fellow I didn't recognize was another, and the doctor was the third. He had a bag in his hand, and he seemed to be a bit put out.

'I protest against being sent for at this hour of the night,' he said.

"The other man, not Blind Jake, said something in a low voice which I didn't catch.

'Why couldn't you have got another doctor? Remember that you have forced me to come here, and I come under protest. Where is this woman?' he asked, and I don't think the reply was intended for my ears, for the big blind man said, 'In the boiler-house,' and laughed, and the other fellow turned to him with a curse and told him to keep quiet.

"They went through the gates, and presently the car moved on. I think it had to turn, and the street wasn't wide enough. The gate was locked and it had been painted black, but I saw that the word 'Laundry' had been there before the new coat had been put on."

"Did you notice the name of the street?" asked Larry.

"Reville Street," said the other, to Larry's surprise, and then he remembered.

"That is the street behind and running parallel with Lissom Lane," he said. "Go on, Fred."

"Well, I had to slip away; otherwise I should have been seen. I went all round the houses and came back behind it, just as the doctor came out, and this time there were only two of them; the big blind man had gone. I couldn't hear what they were talking about, but presently I heard the doctor say good night and the car drove off. The other man was looking after the tail-lights, and I had nothing to do but to slouch past as though I had been coming along, walking all the time. If there's one bad habit that's worse than another," said Fred reflectively, "it's talking to yourself, whether you talk in your sleep or while you're awake. But there are some men who can't help it. There was a pal of mine in Barcelona—however, I won't talk about him, Mr. Holt. Well, this man that was left standing was one of that kind. A brooder, I should think. And before I got opposite to him, I heard him muttering, as he stood stock-still, his hands behind him, looking after the car; and the words that I heard as I passed were these. I remember them—sort of committed them to memory. And the words were: 'Clarissa's nurse.' He said it twice. I walked on, never dreaming that he'd spotted me, and as I walked I thought: 'Now the best thing you can do, Fred, is to go straight to Mr. Holt and tell him what you've seen and what you've heard.'?"

Larry nodded.

"I was only a few hundred yards from your house, so I made up my mind I'd do it. I hadn't gone very far when I got an uncomfortable feeling that I was being followed. I couldn't see anybody, but I had that creepy sensation that you get when the splits are after you, and I couldn't shake it off. I got into your street and began looking for the block where your flat was. I passed it once and was directed back here; and I think that the people who were following me must have slipped in and got upstairs and were waiting for me when I came up. I remember putting my hand up to the knocker of your flat, and then I don't remember anything more."

The girl had been writing rapidly, and now she closed her book.

"I think that's about all," said Fred weakly. "I'd like a drink."

Ten minutes later two motor-cars laden with plain-clothes officers were on their way westward, and the inhabitants of the little street upon which the laundry backed were interested spectators of another raid.

Edgar Wallace

"What is this wall?" asked Larry of his assistant.

"It is the wall of the laundry building proper," said Harvey. "I inspected it very carefully, but there was nothing there."

"Did you see the boiler-house?"

"Yes, sir, it is a very ordinary underground room with one large boiler and a steam engine."

"Get that door open," said Larry. "You have got some men in Lissom Lane to watch the other gate?"

"Yes, sir," reported the sergeant, and with an expert hand he manipulated the lock and presently the door swung wide.

The room into which the door directly led was in darkness. It proved, when lights were obtained, to be a long brick shed, with a concrete floor, and four rows of trestles down the centre, where, in the days of the laundry, the washerwomen worked. A flight of steps, guarded by a rail, went down to a lower floor, and Larry led the way into the boiler-house.

In the Tubular Room

YOU OUGHT to be ashamed of yourself," said Blind Jake, shaking his huge head.

He sat huddled up at one side of the tubular room, and his remarks were addressed to a wretched-looking woman who sat on the other side, her arms folded on her knees, her head bent in dejection. She was miserably clad; her hanging hair was streaked with grey, and her hands and face were grimy.

The room itself could hardly be described as a room. It was like an enlarged gas main. The floor was littered with fragments of rubble and broken concrete. One end was a steel door, just large enough for a medium-sized person to squeeze through, and the other was a jagged hole torn in the steel wall, and disclosing beyond a black void which, in the light of the candle, was also littered with rubbish.

"You ought to be ashamed of yourself," reproved Blind Jake. "Here are They doing all They can for ye, ye ugly old devil, and ye're whining and snarling! Like a pup who's had his tail bit!"

137

The woman moaned and said something.

"You'd have something to snivel about if I had my way," said Blind Jake. "Don't we feed ye? Didn't we give ye a good bed to lie on, till that dog came nosing about?"

"I want to go away," said the woman. "You're killing me here."

"Not yet," said Blind Jake with a chuckle. "Maybe. They'll want ye killed, and then ye'll be killed, sure."

"I want to go out of this horrible place," cried the woman with a sob. "Why am I here?"

"Do ye want to be down with the rats?" growled Blind Jake. "Didn't ye squeak and squeal when I took ye down in the long passage under the street, because the little fellows squeaked at you? And now ye're safe and sound where a rat couldn't get ye, and to-morrow you're going into a nice house to live, with fine sheets on your bed. You ungrateful old devil!"

She raised her woebegone face and looked at the blind man curiously.

"You talk about 'em as though they were gods," she said. "One of these days they'll betray you——"

"Shut up!" snapped the man. "You don't know 'em! What have they done for me? They've given me a lovely life—all the money I want, everything I can eat and drink. They gave me a young wife," he chuckled, but the chuckle ended with a hideous distortion of face. "I'll have her yet; she nearly killed me, that wench."

"Who was she?" asked the woman.

"Never ye mind. Nobody ye know," said Jake, but did not seem disinclined to talk on the matter. "A young, white, sleek girl she was," he said. "They wanted her because she's police too."

She was silent for so long that he leant forward and touched her with his big hand.

"You're not having a fit, are ye?" he said with a note of anxiety. "Not another one of them fits? We can't always bring a doctor. The next time I'll rouse ye," he said menacingly. "I'll make ye wake." He shook her savagely.

"I'm awake, I'm awake," she said, terrified. "Please don't do that; you will break my arm."

"Well, behave yourself," he grumbled, and then began to crawl slowly towards the farther end of the tubular room. Even the woman, though she was far from tall, could not have stood upright in that cramped space. It was wonderful how a man so big could manœuvre himself through the jagged hole in the steel and crawl into the space beyond. She heard him tossing bricks about and enlarging the cavity at which he had been working all the day. She wondered where she was, for she had been a sick woman when she had been dragged into that terrible chamber, and had no recollection of how she had come in. Only she knew that people were searching for her, and that the awful forces which now held her prisoner were determined that she should not be found. She had been hidden in the depths of the earth, in hideous places alive with terrifying life, and this at least was better.

When he came back she said:

"Mr. Stuart would give you a lot of money if you took me to him."

He chuckled.

"Ye've told me that a hundred times, ye fool!" he said, and mimicked her: 'If you take me to Mr. Stuart he'll give ye a lot of money!' A lot of money he'll give me!"

"I nursed his children," she wailed, "and his poor wife. And when I got married he gave me a beautiful wedding ring."

"Aw, shut up!" snarled the man. "Haven't ye got anything more to talk about? A hundred million times ye've told me about nursing his babies and your blasted wedding ring!"

"When I told him about Clarissa, he said he'd give me a thousand pounds," whispered the woman. "I was that surprised to see him I nearly fell down!"

Blind Jake ignored her. He had heard this story before, and it had lost all its novelty.

"He never knew about the twins, and thought he had no children alive."

"If ye hadn't been a hook or a soak, y' could have told him where she was; but don't worry yer head: They've found her. A fine lady she is, with plenty

139

of money! I heard 'em say that she was a fine lady with plenty of money," he added simply.

His faith in these mysterious employers of his knew no bounds.

"I was fond of my drop," confessed the half-witted woman, "and they sent me to prison for nothing at all. And the home was awful!"

Suddenly Blind Jake lurched forward and dropped his hands upon her shoulders. She opened her mouth to scream, but he put his face close to hers.

"If y' squeal ye're dead, my lady! Be quiet!"

His sensitive ears had caught the sound of footsteps on the floor above, though they were so completely deadened that none but a blind man would have heard them. He crept closer to her side, put one great arm around her shoulder, the other he held just in front of her face.

"If y' squeal, ye're dead," he said again, and then somebody knocked at the little door at the end of the chamber and the voice of Larry Holt demanded:

"Is there anybody here?"

Fred Lends His Keys

IT HAD been Diana Ward who had called Larry's attention to the great rusty boiler at one end of the house, the boiler which had supplied the steam and the power for the laundry. Larry tried the thick iron door which opened into the furnace, but it was fast. He tugged again and it did not move.

"Nobody could be here," he said, shaking his head. "What do you think, Harvey?"

"They would suffocate anyway in there, sir," replied Sergeant Harvey.

The girl was looking distressed.

"Is there nowhere else?" she asked. "I did hope——"

She did not finish her words.

"No, miss, we've searched the whole of the place now," said the sergeant. "Would you like that door forced open, sir?" he asked. "It will take some hours."

Larry shook his head.

"No, I don't think so," he said. "I am inclined to agree with you that if anybody was concealed in the boiler, supposing there were room enough, which is unlikely, they would die of suffocation."

"Do you think," asked the girl as they came away, "that Mr. Grogan was telling the truth? I know he was," she added quickly. "I don't know why I ask such stupid questions."

"Oh, he was telling the truth all right," said Larry. "Fred isn't a model of virtue, but in this case, I believe him. It's just the luck of the game," he said bitterly. "Sometimes I feel that I'm never going to fathom this mystery."

"It will be solved, and solved within a week," she said, and she spoke with such assurance that he could only stare at her.

"Then you're going to solve it," he said, "for I have reached the point, and it is the most dangerous point that a detective can arrive at, when I am suspicious of everybody. Suspicious of Dr. Judd, of the innocent Mr. Dearborn, of Flash Fred, the Chief Commissioner, and you," he added good-humouredly. But she did not smile.

"I wondered how long it would be before you suspected me," she said gravely.

She went off with Harvey and he returned to the hospital, for he had a few more questions to ask the injured crook.

Flash Fred listened attentively, and when Larry had finished:

"God knows I have never trusted a policeman in my life," he said piously, "but I think you're different, Mr. Holt. In one of my pockets you will find the key of my safe deposit. The hospital people have the clothes. It's the deposit in Chancery Lane, and I'm trusting you," he said whimsically. "There are things in that box that I shouldn't like anybody to see, but you will find what you are looking for without disturbing them. There's a bundle of war stock," he said uneasily, "which I bought by the sweat of my brow."

"Somebody sweated, I'll bet," said Larry cheerfully. "You needn't be afraid, Fred, I shan't pry into your secrets, nor shall I use anything I find there to jail you."

Fred was ill at ease.

"I knew I was taking a risk when I told you about this business," he said, "because you were certain to go farther in it, and I was just as certain to help you. If I'd been out and about, it would have been easy, because I could have given you the keys."

"What are the keys?" asked Larry.

"They're duplicates that I had made," said Fred without a blush. "Strauss got them from the doctor's key-ring when he was asleep and took the impressions. Strauss ain't a bad fellow, but he dopes; I never did hold with those evil practices," said the virtuous Fred. "You want a clean eye and a clear brain to get on in life, don't you, Mr. Holt?"

"And eight nimble fingers, plus two nippy thumbs," said Larry.

He secured the keys without difficulty, and half an hour later he walked into Room 47, humming a tune and jingling Flash Fred's nefarious possessions in his pocket.

Diana, after a great deal of persuasion, had been induced to take up her residence under Larry's eye. The motherly nurse had become a permanent institution at Regent's Gate Gardens, a circumstance which was not wholly to the liking of Mr. Patrick Sunny, who found himself forced to sleep on a camp bed in the kitchen.

"I am sorry to inconvenience you, Sunny," said Larry Holt that night, "and it is an inconvenience, I suppose?"

"Yes, sir," said Sunny. "It is an inconvenience."

"Not a painful one, I hope."

"No, sir," said Sunny. "It is not a painful one."

"The lady was in danger," said Larry, and this Sunny knew because the matter had been discussed very freely in his presence, "and it was impossible to leave her in her apartment."

"Yes, sir," agreed Sunny. "What collar will you be wearing to-day, sir?"

"Any old collar," said Larry with a smile. "Anyway, Sunny, the lady is safe sleeping in this flat."

"No, sir," said Sunny, and Larry was shocked, for it was the first time in his life that Sunny had ever disagreed with him.

"No?" he said incredulously. "Didn't you hear what I said? I said the lady is safe here."

"No, sir," said Sunny. "I'm very sorry, sir, and I beg your pardon."

"But no you mean, I suppose? Why isn't she safe?"

"Because you're not safe, sir," said Sunny calmly, "and if you're not safe, the lady's not safe, sir."

Larry laughed.

"All right, have your own way," he said; "and, Sunny—"

"Yes, sir."

"Will you close the kitchen door to-night? I could hear you turning around in your bed and it woke me up."

"Very good, sir, I will close the kitchen door," said Sunny, and in truth he did.

After Larry had gone to bed and the flat was in silence, Sunny carried his little camp-bedstead into the hall, placed it so that its foot was about fifteen inches from the door, balanced a broom, the head against the door, the end of the handle resting on the bed, and then he retired. But he shut the kitchen door.

At two o'clock in the morning a key was placed noiselessly in the lock and the door was pushed open a few inches, and the broom fell ruthlessly on Sunny's head. It might have brained him, but, by a fortunate accident, didn't.

Larry heard three shots fired in rapid succession and leapt out of bed and came into the passage, gun in hand. He saw an empty camp-bedstead, an open door, but Sunny was gone. He ran down the stairs and met that worthy man returning, leading by the collar a diminutive ruffian, upon whose evil face was stamped a twisted grin of pain, for he had a bullet in the fleshy part of his leg.

"Bring him in," said Larry, and closed the door.

Diana was standing in the passage when the man was marched through and hastily withdrew, to reappear again at the informal inquiry which Larry instituted.

It was an inquiry prefaced by a respectful apology on the part of Sunny.

"I beg your pardon, sir, for taking the loan of your pistol," he said, "and as to my bed being in the passage and disturbing you——"

"Say no more about that, Sunny my lad," said Larry with a grateful glance at his valet. "We'll talk about that afterwards. Now, my boy, what have you to say for yourself?" He addressed the unpleasant-looking prisoner.

"He ain't got no right to use firearms," said the man hoarsely.

Larry thought his hoarseness was due to his emotion, but it would seem that it was his natural voice.

"I'm shot, I am! I was coming down the stairs as quiet and as peaceful as possible when this fellow came out and shot me."

"Innocent child!" said Larry, unpleasantly. He felt over the man's pocket and took out a long-bladed knife, the edge of which he tested with his finger and thumb. It was razor-sharp.

Larry looked at the man again. He was about thirty-five, hollow-cheeked and sunken-eyed.

"Let me see your hands," said Larry, and the man with a scowl put them out. "Have you any convictions?"

"No, sir," said the man sullenly.

"Who sent you here?"

"Find out!"

"I am going to find out," said Larry softly, "and you will be a little damaged in the finding. Who sent you here?"

"I'm not going to tell," said the man.

"I think you will," said Larry, and led him into the kitchen and shut the door.

When the police arrived ten minutes later they took charge of a very shaky man.

"He has told all he knows," said Larry. "He was sent here to cover another man who escaped. He swears he does not know who the other man was, but it was evidently not Blind Jake."

"How did you induce him to tell?" asked the girl, a little fearfully.

"I threatened to wash him," said Larry, and he spoke no more than the truth. "It was not the threat of the washing, of course," he explained, "it was the being in that room alone with me and the fact that I could strip off his coat without an effort, and the possibility that the washing was merely a preliminary to some form of horrible torture which I had invented which made him talk—his wound is nothing, by the way. It will probably be healed by the time he sees the divisional surgeon. And now I think we can all go to bed. I want to see you, Sunny, before you retire for the night."

What he said to Sunny set that stolid man strutting for the rest of the week.

A Breakfast Proposal

ATHIN white mist overhung the park and shrouded the deserted stretch of Rotten Row, and the one or two riders who had come out at this early hour for their constitutional merely served to emphasize the desolation of the place.

One of these horsemen was Sir John Hason, Chief Commissioner of Police, who made it a practice to ride before breakfast, and he neither expected nor invited company. He was, therefore, surprised and a little annoyed when a horseman came up from behind him and, checking his mount to a walk, fell in by Sir John's side.

"Hallo, Larry," said John Hason in surprise. "This is an unexpected apparition! I thought you were a ghost."

"I shall be that too, one of these fine mornings," said Larry, "unless I'm jolly careful. I knew you would be riding, so I hired a hack from the local livery stable and came out. Besides," he said, "I want a change of air and I want to talk, outside the stultifying atmosphere of your office."

"Anything new?" asked Sir John.

"There was an attempt at assassination last night, but that's so usual that I hate reporting it as a novelty," said Larry, and told the story of the two o'clock visitation.

"It's the queerest case I've ever heard about," said Sir John Hason thoughtfully. "Not a day passes but somebody new comes in. You still attach importance to the charwoman?"

Larry nodded.

"You know London better than I, John," he said, for between him and his old school-mate there was no formality on such occasions as this. "Who is Judd?"

"Oh, Judd!" laughed the Commissioner. "I don't think you need worry your head about him. He is a man of some standing in the City, though I seem to have heard that his brother was rather a waster. The Judds practically own all the shares in the Greenwich Insurance Company. It is not a very big concern, but it has successfully resisted every attempt on the part of the insurance trusts and the big companies to absorb it. That shows character which I admire. They inherited the shares from their father and built up what looked to be a very shaky concern into a fairly prosperous business."

"I was looking at the board of directors last night," said Larry. "It is in the Stock Exchange year-book. I sat up after everybody had gone to bed and tried to puzzle things out. Do you know that John Dearborn is a director of that company?"

"Dearborn the dramatist?" asked Hason quickly. "No, I did not know. Of course, the directors in a company like that," he smiled, "are merely the nominees of Judd. Judd is a very good fellow, I am told, and spends a lots of money in charity. He practically supports the Home which Dearborn is running. He may have been given an ornamental directorship in order to bring in a little money to his institute."

"I thought of that too," nodded Larry. "Who is Walters?"

"Never heard of him," said John Hason.

"He's another director of the Company, and also an ornamental person, I should imagine. And Cremley? Ernest John Cremley, of Wimbledon."

"He is most certainly an ornamental person," said the Commissioner. "I know him slightly, a man with very little brains and an insatiable appetite for cards. Why do you ask?"

"Because these two men are also directors of the Macready Theatre Syndicate," said Larry quietly. "Judd's name does not appear, but there is another strange name, which is probably a nominee of his."

"Where are we getting to?" asked the Commissioner.

"We're getting here," said Larry, reining in his horse and bringing it round so that he stood side by side and facing his chief, "that Judd controls the theatre where Dearborn's plays are produced. So there is some association between Judd and the superintendent of the Blind Mission in Paddington."

Sir John digested this fact before he spoke.

"I don't see that there is anything particularly blameworthy about that," he said; "after all, Dearborn is only the victim of Blind Jake, and from what you told me in your report last night, Judd is the victim of nobody except our friend Flash Fred. I can well understand why the doctor wanted to save his brother's name," he went on. "Judd adored that younger brother of his, thought he was the finest fellow in the world. I have never seen a case where brothers entertained such affection one for the other. The week David Judd died the doctor shut himself up and would not see anybody. What the—!"

The Commissioner's note of startled surprise was justified, for Larry had suddenly brought round his horse and was riding furiously across the park, taking no small risk from the low railings he leapt.

He had seen a figure, unmistakably tall, muffled to the chin in a pea-jacket, slouching along the path that led to one of the gates of the park.

The man heard the gallop of hoofs and ran as straight and as swift as a deer, gained the gates and ran out into the street. The gate was too small for Larry to ride his horse through, and he flung himself off and, leaving his mount to his own devices, he ran out into the street. He saw no more than a car pull away from the kerb and move rapidly eastward.

He looked around for a cab, but there was none in sight, and with a shrug he came back, found his horse, mounted and trotted slowly back to where Sir John was sitting.

"Where the devil did you go?" asked Sir John.

"I saw a gentleman I am most anxious to meet," said Larry a little breathlessly. "One Blind Jake, who was taking his morning constitutional in the park, with his car waiting to pick him up like a perfect gentleman. If I had had a gun I would have given Tarling another Daffodil Mystery to solve. I should have been glad to have found flowers for Blind Jake!"

Lew

WHEN he got back to the house Diana was dressed and sitting down to breakfast.

"I thought you weren't coming back," she said with a little sigh.

"Why the sigh?" asked Larry.

"Because—I thought you weren't coming back to breakfast," she said.

He told her of the chase in the park.

"That rather upsets my theory that Blind Jake is still at the Home or at the laundry," she said, "because the house is being watched, isn't it?"

"On both sides," said Larry, "but there are a dozen ways this fellow could get out, and the fact that he goes for an early morning constitutional, and the people who are behind him consider that his health is of sufficient importance to put a car at his disposal, rather proves that he is confined during the day."

They were alone, for the nurse chaperon had not finished dressing.

"I don't know how this case is going to end, Diana," said Larry after a little silence, "and this is a most prosaic moment to say what I want to say, but—but—but after this case is ended, I don't want you to remain at the Yard."

She went a little pale.

"You mean I am not satisfactory?" she said. "As a secretary?"

"You're very satisfactory, both as a secretary and an individual," said Larry, trying hard to maintain command of his voice. "I don't like your—I don't like your working."

There was another silence.

"I don't think I shall work after this case," she said quietly. "I thought of leaving, too."

This was an unexpected reply, and it filled him with a sense of panic.

"You're not going away?" he asked, and she laughed.

"You're really a most inconsistent person. You dismiss me in one breath and hope I'm not leaving you in another," she said, and she was treading on dangerous ground and was well aware of the fact. "After all," she went on, solemnly mischievous, "there are so many jobs where competent girls are wanted."

"I know a job where a competent girl is wanted," said Larry, swallowing something, "and her job is to look after a flat and share the modest fortune of a detective-inspector who may be something better one of these fine days."

She was helping herself to a triangular piece of toast when he spoke, and she let the toast drop.

"I don't quite know what you mean," she faltered.

"I mean," said Larry. "I want to marry you—go to the devil!"

She looked up open-mouthed, in time to see the door shut upon the outraged Sunny.

"I'm awfully sorry," stammered Larry. "I didn't mean that last remark for you, dear. I really mean——"

"I know what you mean," she said, and laid her hand on his. "You mean you want me?"

"I want you so much," said Larry, "that I can't find words to make my want plain."

She did not speak. She suffered her hand to stay under his, and her eyes catching the distorted reflection of her face in the polished coffee-pot, she laughed. Larry drew his hand away quickly, for he was a sensitive man.

"I'm rather a fool, I'm afraid," he said quietly. She had not moved.

"Put your hand back." Her voice was no higher than a whisper, but he obeyed. "Now tell me what you were saying. I was laughing at myself in the coffee-pot. I don't look like a person that anybody could propose to at half-past eight in the morning."

"Then—then you know you are being proposed to?" he said huskily.

She nodded, and her shining eyes turned to meet his.

"And—will you?" he asked, finding it difficult to frame the words.

"Will I what—be proposed to?" she answered innocently. "I think I will, Larry dear: I rather like it."

And then she was in his arms, and he was holding her tightly, tightly.

And then Sunny came in, and they did not see him. He stole forth silently and made his way to the landing outside the door and rang the elevator bell. The girl who worked the elevator was a great friend of his and supplied him with much information which was of value.

"Louie," he said, and he was more than usually sober, "can you tell me where I can get lodgings near at hand? I think I shall soon be sleeping out."

"Sleeping out, Pat?" said the wondering Louie. (She called him Pat because it was his name, but more because he had graciously permitted her that liberty.) "Is your master getting a housekeeper?"

"I think so," said Sunny very gravely indeed. "I think so, Louie."

Larry may have walked to the office that morning, or he may have ridden, or floated. He had no distinct recollection of what happened, or how he got there, except that he knew that Diana Ward was by his side and that he was hopelessly, ridiculously, overwhelmingly happy in his love. It had been the most extraordinary courting, and the proposal had been as amazingly unconventional. He had pictured such a scene, but it had been set in a quiet drawing-room under shaded lights, or in some bosky dell, or in the shade of an old tree along some backwater of the ancient river.

"Not at breakfast," he said aloud, "oh dear, no."

"Not at breakfast?" repeated the girl. "Oh, you are thinking—yes, it was funny."

"It was wonderful!" said Larry. "I feel all puffed up."

"Then I'm going to take some of the puffed-up feeling out of you," she said calmly. "I want you to make me a promise."

"I'll promise you anything in the world, Diana," he said extravagantly. "Ask me for the top brick off the chimney-pots, or a slice of the moon——"

"Nothing so difficult as that. I merely want to——And yet perhaps it will be more difficult," she said seriously. "Will you promise me that under no circumstances you will ask to be released from your engagement?"

He turned round to her, and almost stopped in his walk.

"That's an easy one," he said. "Whatever makes you think I should want to break off this wonderful——"

"I know, I know," she interrupted. "It's very wonderful to me, and yet"—she

150

shook her head—"will you promise that whatever happens, whatever be the outcome of the Stuart case, whether you fail or succeed, whatever revelations come, you will not break your engagement?"

"I promise you that," said Larry eagerly. "There's nothing in the world which would induce me to take back a word I've said. I am living in mortal terror lest you discover how you are throwing yourself away upon somebody who is not worthy of you. If you do, I swear I will sue you for breach of promise! My fine feelings are not to be trifled with."

When they reached Room 47 they found two men waiting in the corridor. One was a plain-clothes officer, the other was a wizened little man who sat pensively on a form, his hands on his knees, staring with unseeing eyes at the floor.

Larry stopped at the sight.

"What's this?" he asked.

"Oh, I'm sorry," said the girl penitently, "I should have told you—I sent for him."

"Why, it's Lew!" said Larry in surprise, and Diana nodded.

"You told me that I could call for any witness I wanted," she began, and he stopped her.

"My dear, of course you can," he said.

He looked at the old man curiously, and Lew, oblivious to all things, sat in his dark and silent world, consuming his own thoughts.

"Bring him in," said Larry. "How are you going to make him talk, or convey our wishes to him?" He shook his head pityingly. "I never realized before what a terrible affliction this combination of circumstances might be," he said. "Can you talk to him?"

"I think so," said the girl quietly, "but you must realize that he has no idea where he is. For all he knows, he may still be in that dreadful house of the blind, still under the care of the men who have treated him so cruelly."

Larry nodded.

"When you said he was dead I thought you were mad," he said, "but I understand now."

"I want a shot-gun," said the girl, "and I want a uniformed officer." She turned to Larry. "I am going to see whether I have forgotten all I learnt in the Blind Hospital," she said. She took the old man by the hand and he followed her obediently.

She caught his two wrists gently and raised them to her face.

"A woman," he said; then she took up the little vase of flowers on her desk and held them under his nose.

"Roses, ain't they?" he said. "This is a hospital."

She beckoned the uniformed policeman who stood at the door and again raised the old man's hands, letting them rest lightly on the collar of his tunic, and his buttons, then she raised them to his helmet.

"A copper!" said Lew, and shrank back.

She gave him the flowers again, and again raised his hand and brought the gnarled old hand to her cheek.

"I'm in a hospital and a policeman's looking after me. Am I wanted for anything?"

She took his head between her hands and gently shook it.

"I'm not, eh?" he said, relieved.

Larry was watching the play, fascinated.

"Am I safe from them swine?"

She took his head between her hands and forced him to nod.

"Do you want me to talk?"

She repeated the movement, and pushed a chair up to him, guiding him down to it.

The plain-clothes officer had brought the gun and she took it from him, and lifting Lew's hand passed it lightly over the barrel and the stock. He shivered.

"Yes, that's what they've done to me," he said. "You want them for that, don't you? It was cruel hard on a blind man. What are you pinching my left hand for?"

Again she made him nod, then she pinched the right hand, and without waiting for his question made him shake his head.

152

"I see, I see," he said eagerly. "The right hand is no and the left hand is yes. Is there somebody here—high?"

She signalled yes.

"Do they want me to tell?"

Again she signalled the affirmative, and he began his story.

He and Blind Jake had been companions in misfortune. He had been a slave to the big man, almost since his youth, and had lived a life of terror, dominated by this extraordinary villain.

"He done things that would make you curl up if you knew! Jake did," nodded Lew. "Things that I don't like thinking about, that haunt me at nights."

Then five or six years before Lew's own brother had joined this extraordinary band of criminals.

"A fine big fellow he was, too," said Lew proudly, "and he could see! He used to go round the fairs pretending he couldn't, but he had grand eyesight, could read newspapers and books. A big chap, sir, with long bushy whiskers down to here. A grand fellow was Jim, but a hook."

Then they had come under the influence of this extraordinary power, to which Blind Jake was used to refer in such reverent tones. They had been sent to carry bodies from a house, and Jake had assisted, and so had Jim and Lew. He didn't know that they were murdered, but he thought they were.

"A clever gang they are. Why, six years ago, do you know what they did?" He seemed almost proud of the genius of these terrible men. "We chucked a man in the river with a weight round his legs. You'd think they'd be suspicious, wouldn't you, when they found the body? Not they! What do you think the weight was attached to, guv'nor? A big block of salt, that fitted just round the cove's legs, and as soon as the salt dissolved, up he came."

"Was he alive when you put him in?" asked Larry, and the girl shivered.

The man could not hear, but he answered almost as though he could.

"He may have been dead, I forget," Lew went on. "He didn't holler or anything. God's truth, I didn't know they was going to put him in the water! How was I to know? But in the water he went. And then Jim disappeared. I don't know what happened to him. He just went away and we never saw him again. That was four years ago in May, as far as I can remember."

Lew had got frightened after a while and began to suspect the danger to himself, if he did not know it already, and was fearful of Jake and his threats, more fearful of the mysterious vanishing of his brother. He could not write Braille, but he had got a man in Todd's Home, a "straight 'un," to write the message that he intended putting in the pocket of the next victim. Possibly he had heard from Jake that there was a "job" at hand.

"I think I will go now," said the girl, suddenly white.

Larry took her out into the corridor and brought her a glass of water.

"I'm quite all right," she smiled bravely. "Go back and listen."

Lew was talking when Larry returned, and when he had finished, Larry knew almost all there was to be known about the murder of Gordon Stuart.

That evening there was a conference of all heads of departments, presided over by the Chief Commissioner.

"We may not be able to convict on the evidence of this man," said Sir John gravely; "we will get the warrants if you like, but I think with a little more rope, and the knowledge we have, we could catch them red-handed."

Larry came back to his office—the girl had gone home—in time to hear his telephone bell ringing.

"Is that Mr. Holt?" said a strange voice.

Now it is unusual to receive a call at Scotland Yard from anybody but police or public officials because the numbers of the various departments do not appear in the telephone book.

"I am Inspector Holt," replied Larry.

"Dr. Judd asks you whether you can come to his office at once. He has something important to communicate."

Larry thought a moment.

"Yes, I will come immediately," he said.

He picked up Harvey, and a cab deposited them at Bloomsbury Pavement.

At this hour Larry expected the building to be deserted, but there was a light showing in one of the upstairs windows. The long narrow vestibule was also illuminated.

Larry walked quickly through the vestibule; the porter's little recess was empty. At the far end were the doors of two automatic lifts, one of which was in position.

"Shall I come up with you?" asked the sergeant.

There was no reason why he shouldn't, and yet——

"No, no, stay here," said Larry.

He stepped into the lift and pushed the ivory button marked "Fourth Floor" and the elevator jerked upward. At the fourth floor it stopped and Larry, pushing open the grille, stepped out on to the landing. Immediately opposite him was a glass door, behind which a light shone. The words "Dr. Judd" were written legibly enough, and he turned the handle of the door and stepped into an empty room. He called, but nobody answered him, and, puzzled, he came back to the landing.

Every sense in Larry Holt's system was alert. Dr. Judd was not the kind of individual who would indulge in a silly practical joke, or attempt to hoax him.

Then he had a mild surprise. He had come by the left-hand elevator, which had now disappeared, and in its place was the right-hand lift, which must have been on a higher floor when he had reached the landing. What was more remarkable, the lift door was wide open. Who had come up?

He looked along the corridor, but there was nobody in sight.

"Is everything all right?"

It was the hollow voice of Harvey coming up the elevator shaft.

"I'm coming down," said Larry, and stepped through the open grille into the waiting elevator.

His foot was poised, he was in the very act of bringing it down upon the floor of the lift, when he realized in a flash that what he had thought was solid wood flooring was no more than paint and paper. There was no possibility of drawing back. His balance had shifted, and the full weight of his body was thrown forward.

He had the fraction of a second to think, and then, utilizing every ounce of strength, every atom of impetus he could get from his left foot, which still rested on the solid edge of the landing, he leapt forward and gripped the moulding of one of the panels at the back of the elevator. He had less than half an inch to hold on by, but by the extraordinary strength in his hands he maintained his hold, even as his feet crashed through the paper flooring and the whole weight of his body was flung upon his fingers-tips. He hung thus, suspended in space, a fifty-foot fall upon the stone flags beneath him.

"Quick, come up!" he shouted. "Fourth floor. I'm trapped!"

He heard the rattle of the other lift and the whine of the motor, and at the same time he heard another sound above him, and, glancing up, saw a face looking down from the opening on the fifth floor.

Then something whizzed past him and struck the panelling of the elevator with a crash. For a second he nearly released his hold. He felt the lift shaking unaccountably, and then, to his horror, the ascending lift passed him.

"Here, here!" he shouted.

The face above seemed to be growing dimmer; but again he saw the hand poised, something struck him on the shoulder, he released his hold and fell.

Larry Inspects a House

LARRY jerked open the gates on the ground-floor, and staggered from the lift-shaft to meet the dumbfounded Dr. Judd standing in an attitude of surprise, and incredulity expressed on every line of his countenance.

"Whatever has happened?" he demanded anxiously.

"A miracle!" said Larry, with a touch of grimness. "I seem to have fallen about four feet. You sent for me, Dr. Judd."

Dr. Judd shook his head.

"I'm afraid I don't understand what this is all about," he said. "Will you come up to my office?"

"I don't think that is necessary," said Larry. "You sent a telephone message asking me to come here at once because you had something important to communicate to me. I'm going up," he said viciously. "There's a gentleman on the top floor whose acquaintance I should like to make."

"I assure you, Mr. Holt," said the doctor earnestly, "that I have never sent for you or communicated with you in any way. I sent my porter out on a message and then remembered that I hadn't any cigarettes and foolishly left this great building unattended. You didn't step into the wrong lift, did you?"

A slow smile came to Larry's face.

"I rather fancy I did," said he.

"Good heavens!" gasped the doctor. "Why, you might have been killed!"

"I don't exactly know what happened as it is," said Larry.

"Only one lift is working," explained the doctor. "Something went wrong with the motors and we're working them on balance. That is to say, one elevator comes down while the other goes up. Taking advantage of the fact that to-morrow is Sunday, the workmen were repairing the floor of number two elevator, which has worn rather thin——"

"And spread some pieces of paper and canvas in its place, I presume?" said Larry, who was impolite and well aware of the fact. "Anyway, I'm going up now," he said, and they went together in the sound elevator.

Harvey was half-way down to his chief, and they met him.

"Thank God you're not hurt," he said.

Larry shook his head.

"I could have only been six feet from the ground when I dropped. I didn't realize that this infernal elevator was descending all the time the gentleman was shying things at me."

"Somebody throwing at you, sir? I thought I heard a bit of iron strike the bottom of the shaft."

The elevator only went as far as the fourth floor. The upper floor was reached by a stairway. Larry came up to the darkened landing to find, as he had expected, that his assailant had gone. Which way he had gone there was no need to ask, for in the ceiling at the end of the passage was a square patch of light where a trap-door had been raised, and beneath there was a pair of steps.

"I can't tell you how sorry I am," said Dr. Judd, when they rejoined him.

He looked unusually pale and his voice quavered.

"Some fool must have played a practical joke which might have had very serious consequences. How did you save yourself?"

But Larry was in no mood for narrative, and he left a perturbed Dr. Judd with a curt "Good night."

"And to-morrow, Harvey," said Larry, "I shall be at the office at half-past nine, and I want you to be there to meet me. The clearing-up process begins in earnest to-morrow and this day week, please God, there will be no Stuart mystery."

*

"My dear," said Larry Holt at breakfast the next morning, and his tone was at once paternal and apprehensive, "I said one large prayer last night, and it was one of thankfulness that your prophecy is coming true."

"About capturing the gang?" she asked.

"Something like that," said he, rising.

"Are you going without me?" she asked in surprise as he rose from the table.

"Yes," he hesitated, "I am going to pursue a little clue which may be a very big clue indeed."

She looked at him doubtfully.

"I couldn't come with you, I suppose?" she asked.

He shook his head.

"No, this is a job which I must do entirely on my own," he said. "Anyway it is necessary that I should break the law to make my investigations, and I cannot be responsible for leading you from the straight path."

"I don't think it would worry me very much," she smiled, "but you don't want to tell me, that's it, isn't it?"

"You've guessed it first time," said Larry. "The noble Sunny will look after you and escort you to Scotland Yard, and he will be bulging with weapons of a lethal character."

Sunny blushed, but recovered immediately.

"Yes, sir," said he, "I'm thinking of sending your overcoat to be cleaned for the winter."

"What on earth has that to do with escorting Miss Ward to Scotland Yard?" asked Larry in astonishment.

"Nothing, sir," said Sunny, "except it will be very cold round about November, and they take a long time to clean overcoats."

"In fact," said the girl with a smile, "Sunny is being nicely domestic and is taking a very optimistic view of the outcome of this case. Where will this clue lead you?" she asked. "I'd rather like to know, because——" She stopped. "Well, in case you are ever missing."

"It is leading me to Hampstead," said Larry.

She drew a deep sigh.

"I was dreadfully afraid it was somewhere else," she said.

He wondered why she was afraid, but it was not a subject that he wished to pursue because he had lied outrageously.

Half an hour after he reached the Yard, two slightly soiled men in the shabby uniform of the North Metropolitan Gas Company walked out the Whitehall end of Scotland Yard, one carrying a bag of tools, and boarded a bus. They were set down within a quarter of a mile of their destination and walked the remainder of the journey, stopping to survey the house wherein Larry had decided would be found the solution of Gordon Stuart's death.

It was an unusual-looking house, bare and grim, with few windows, and those heavily barred.

"The man who planned that must have thought he was designing a prison, sir," said Harvey.

"Maybe he was," replied Larry. "Harvey, if what Lew the blind man told us is true, then we have come to the end of the chase."

Harvey was shocked.

"But this is only a look-over, sir?" he said. "You don't really expect to finish the case on this one inspection?"

Larry nodded.

"When I enter that house I am pulling into material shape every dream I have dreamt, every theory I have evolved. I stand or fall by the result."

"Does Miss Ward know——?" began Harvey boldly.

"This is the one thing that Miss Ward doesn't know," smiled Larry. Crossing the road, he mounted the steps and rang the bell.

The door was opened by a manservant, and to him Larry Holt spoke shortly and with authority, and they were ushered into the hall.

"Remember, you are to keep our visit a secret," said Larry.

"You can depend on me, Mr. Holt," said the man, who had turned a sickly green at the detective's appearance.

The hall was wide and lofty, panelled in oak from the tesselated marble floor to the ceiling. The only furniture was a table and a chair, Larry noted. There were no lights visible, and he gathered that illumination was furnished by lamps concealed in the cornices. Other illuminations were furnished by a long, narrow window of frosted glass, through which the shadow of the bars could be seen. There was no stairway leading from the hall, but there was a doorway immediately facing the street door, which Larry guessed concealed the staircase. On the other side of the hall was a second door, and these were the only apparent means of egress from the passage.

He opened the door on the right and found himself in a large and beautifully furnished salon. The walls were hung about with pictures and tapestries, and on the polished floor were a half a dozen Persian rugs, which Larry could see were worth a fortune.

There were six stained-glass windows in this room, and each was a masterpiece. By their side hung heavy velvet curtains which could be so drawn that the window excluded all light. One silver electrolier hung in the middle of the apartment, and there were no other lights, though here again Larry supposed that the main illumination came from concealed lamps.

He walked across to the big fireplace with its silver grate and fixtures, and examined two letters which lay open upon a table by the side of the big arm-chair. They were of no importance, and he continued his search.

From the main apartment another door opened on to a flight of stairs, which led to a suite of bedrooms, a little drawing-room and a large study, which was over the salon and covered practically the same area.

His search upstairs was more or less perfunctory, though his examination of the corridor from whence the bedrooms gave was of a more careful and exacting character. But he came down again to the salon, satisfied in his mind that what had to be discovered was to be looked for on the lower floor.

He found the servant in the room when he came down and dismissed him sharply.

"Go back to the hall," he said, and sulkily the man obeyed.

And now Larry gave every minute to an examination of the panelled walls of the room—particularly that wall which was opposite the door through which he and Harvey had entered. So cunningly had the panelling been arranged that it was a long time before he found the concealed door; and then it was not where he had been looking, but on a level with the stained-glass window. He remembered then having seen from the outside a small semicircular obtrusion from the main wall of the building.

"Here we are, Harvey!" he said exultantly, as he pulled up a carved wreath which seemed to be part of the wall's decorations and disclosed a tiny keyhole. He took the packet of keys from his pocket and tried first one and then the other. At the fourth trial a lock slipped back and the door opened inwards.

He was right! He knew it at that moment. The joy of accomplishment set his heart beating faster—the knowledge that he had at last a tangible something to show, not to the Commissioner, not to his superiors, but to the girl who was more to him than career or life, brought a new colour to his cheeks and a brighter light to his eyes.

He was in a small bell-shaped apartment, with a domed roof, a room so small that the door, when it was opened, touched the opposite wall. It was made of concrete, and a flight of steps leading down to the cellar were also of this material.

The first thing that caught his eye was an electric switch and this he snapped down, illuminating a lower landing. There was another door to the left, and a further flight of steps which disappeared in darkness. No effort had been made to conceal the keyhole of the door, and one of his keys opened it.

He found himself in a low-roofed concrete chamber, about five foot six in height and, as near as he could judge, about ten feet square. He searched for, and found, the electric switch and illuminated the apartment.

"What do you think of this, Harvey?"

"What are they running?" asked Harvey in surprise. "An electric light plant?"

Larry shook his head.

"No," he said, "this isn't a light plant. I know very little about machinery, but I have an idea that this gadget is a pump."

He examined the machinery more carefully.

"Yes, it is a pump," he said, "one of the type which is used in ships to trim the ballast tanks."

A thick cable was suspended on brackets along the wall, and he felt this gingerly.

"Electric," he said. "This is where he gets his power."

On the wall was a switchboard and what seemed an independent lever. He examined this closely and before he went on to yet another machine.

"And this is the ventilating plant," he said, pointing to a barrel-shaped instrument. "You notice the bad-air exhaust?"

"He's a thorough gentleman, this," said Sergeant Harvey.

"Very," agreed Larry, and they walked out of the room, locking the door behind them.

"A door over there leading to the yard," said Larry, pointing to the wall opposite the machine-room.

Harvey saw no door, but followed his leader down a further flight of stairs.

"Ten steps," Larry warned, and then he came against a door. A heavy door of ferro-concrete hung upon hinges of toughened bronze. This Larry confirmed before he went any farther. He expected to find bronze, and would have been surprised if the hinges had been made of any other material. He had two fears: one that the doors would be fitted with bolts and the other that they were impossible to open from the inside. This latter fear, he saw, was groundless, for the keyhole was covered from the outside by a screw cap. He twisted the cover off and opened the door. It swung back heavily, and he measured the edge.

"Four inches thick!" he said grimly. "He takes no chances."

Behind the first door was another of steel, and this too he unlocked. And now he paused and he felt his breath grow laboured.

"Take note of this room to which we are coming," said Larry Holt, "for it was here that Gordon Stuart died!"

The Death Room

HE CARRIED a flash-lamp in his hand, but it was some time before he discovered the switch, which was set high in the wall, near the sloping roof of the stairs on the farthermost side of the door. A click, and the void before them was illuminated. He could see nothing from where he stood save a brass bedstead, destitute of clothing. Down two steps and three paces along a narrow passage, and he was in the room. Floor, roof and walls were of cement-work, and he saw that what he had thought was one was really two rooms, the second being fitted up roughly as a bathroom. There were no windows of any kind, and he had not expected them. The air was heavy and stale, and evidently the two ventilators near the ceiling were not in working order.

But it was not the bathroom nor the bedstead to which his eyes strayed; it was to a great block of granite in the centre of the room. In the stone, which was a cube two feet in each direction, was a large steel bolt, and from this bolt ran a thin rusted chain, also of steel. Each yard of the chain ran through a block of lead, which Larry judged to be ten pounds in weight, and there were three of these. The chain terminated in a brass leg-ring.

"Yes," said Larry, "I think so."

He picked up the ring and examined it, and, trying first one and then the other of his keys upon the little lock, the opening of which was protected by a sliding cover, presently he saw the two catches snap back, and heaved a sigh.

"Thank God for that!" he said. "I was afraid I'd missed the key."

He looked round at Harvey and Harvey's face was a study.

"What is this, Mr. Holt?" he asked, bewildered.

"The operating room of the 'Dark Eyes,'?" replied Larry briefly.

"Do you mean to say that these devils——"

Larry nodded. He was walking around the walls, looking for a place where he could conceal the waterproof bag he carried in his pocket. There was not so much as a crack into which it could be hidden, for the big holes set in the wall near the floor at regular intervals were, he knew, of no value for his purpose. Then his eye fell upon the granite block, and, exerting all his strength, he pulled at it. Slowly it canted away. There had been no necessity to cement to the floor a block of that weight.

"Give me a hand to ease this down, Harvey," he said, and the two men lowered the block on its side.

It had fitted truly, and its base was perhaps only an inch deeper than the floor. Where it had stood the workmen had not taken the trouble to make its foundations secure, and there was a depression in the cement, irregular and shallow, but large enough for Larry's purpose. He took the waterproof bag—it was no more than a sponge bag—from his pocket and began to drop various articles into the bottom. Key followed key and then:

"A handcuff key, if you've got one, Harvey," he said. "I left mine in my room."

Harvey found a handcuff key in his waistcoat pocket and passed it across to his superior.

"And this, I think," said Larry, and took something from his pocket and placed it in the bag.

He smoothed the bag and its contents as flat as possible, and it just fitted into the depression. Then the two men lifted the stone and put it back in its place.

"May I ask," said the bewildered Harvey, "what is the idea?"

Larry laughed, and his laugh sounded hollow in that dreadful room, which had never heard laughter.

"Is the servant in this?" asked Harvey.

"I'm perfectly sure he isn't. This gang wouldn't trust a servant," replied Larry. "No, he probably keeps to his own part of the house, and doesn't even enter the reception-room except when his boss is at home, unless he is sent for. If you notice this house, it has been built for a specific purpose. For example, the room has a vacuum bracket in the wainscot, there is an electric lift from the kitchen, and a private stairway to the bedrooms and study upstairs. My theory is, but I haven't time to confirm it, that the servant lives in practically a house of his own, which has no connection with this part of the building. Did you notice a door opposite what I would call the engine-room? It wasn't easy to spot because it looked like the rest of the wall. In reality, it is of iron, camouflaged as concrete. It is on the ground level and leads to the yard at the side of the house, and incidentally to the garage."

Harvey shouldered his tools.

"This is a horrible place, Mr. Holt," he said with a shudder. "In all my thirty-five years of police experience I have never been so—shocked. It sounds silly to you?"

"Not a bit," said Larry quietly. "I am shocked beyond words."

"You really think that that is the place where these people have been done to death?"

"I'm certain of it," said Larry. "In that room Gordon Stuart went over to the other side."

They went back in the hall now. By the side of the door there was a narrow slit of a window covered by a strip of silk casement cloth, and Harvey went to this and pulled it aside.

"There's a car at the door," he said. "Just come up."

Larry stepped to his side and looked. A man had descended from a taxicab and was paying the driver.

"The Reverend Mr. Dearborn," said Larry. "How interesting!"

Larry hesitated only for a second, then he opened the door, and the Rev. John Dearborn, who had turned from the cab, and whose hand was on the spikes of the gate, bent his head suddenly as though he had remembered something, and beckoned the cabman.

"My friend," he said, "I cannot see you, but are you still there?"

"Yes, sir," replied the cabman.

"I have remembered that I wish to call at the post office. Will you take me there?"

His hand groped out and the cabman took it, and leaning back opened the door again.

Before Larry could get down the steps the cab was on the move. The detective turned back with a little smile.

"David Judd can wait," he said softly.

"David Judd?" said Harvey.

"David Judd!" repeated Larry Holt. "Who said this is not an age of miracles, when the blind can see as John Dearborn sees, and David Judd, dead and buried, is rollicking round London in a taxicab. Harvey, there's a great detective in this city."

"There is, sir," said Sergeant Harvey heartily. "And the name of the same is Holt."

"It isn't, but it will be," said Larry softly.

The Woman in the Garage

WAIT!" said Larry. He was on the point of leaving the House of Death. "We may not get another opportunity of making a leisurely examination of these premises. I am curious about the side door." He led the way to the secret door in the salon, closing it behind him, then down the steps he passed and paused opposite the engine-room.

"Here is the door to the yard, I think," he said, and switched his flash-lamp over the wall.

The keyhole was difficult to find, but he discovered it after a while near the floor in the bottom right-hand corner. As he had expected, it opened on to a covered passageway from the road.

"Clever work," he said in honest admiration.

He was in the yard looking at the wall through which he had come. Nothing like a door was visible. Instead he looked upon something which had the appearance of a window made up of four opaque panes. It stood out from the wall in the most natural fashion, a trim window-box filled with flowers on its ledge.

"Not much like a door!" said Larry, and added, "Clever work!"

He walked back to the gate and examined it closely. Then he returned to Harvey.

"The mystery of the automatic gate is solved," he said. "As I suspected, it is possible to reach the house and enter the yard and garage without the servants knowing anything at all about it. The last time I was here, I noticed what looked to be two peep-holes placed at a distance of four feet apart and rather low. They couldn't have been intended for purposes of observation because they were backed with iron. Did you notice anything about that car we saw in the laundry garage?"

"Yes, sir," said Harvey, "there were two bars sticking out in front under the head-lamps," and Larry nodded.

"I thought at first," he said, "that it was some new kind of motor-car invention, but it is clear now just what they are intended for. A car is driven up to the gate, and those two bars fit in what I called the peep-holes; a lock is pressed back and the door opens, and presumably closes behind them, thus dispensing with the attendance of any servants and avoiding the inconvenience of their coming and going being noted by the people in the house. I think we will look at the garage, and then we will go," he said.

The door of the garage was at the far end of the drive and extended across its whole width. Larry searched amongst his keys, and presently he found what he was looking for.

"I wondered what door this tumbler lock was on," he said.

He slipped the key in the hole and turned it, and as he did so he heard a slight movement within the garage.

"Did you hear that?" he said in a whisper.

Harvey nodded, and drew his truncheon. Then suddenly Larry threw open the gates wide. He saw a car, but apparently the garage was empty of people. The wheels of the car were wet.

"That came in this morning," said Larry.

There was no place where the smallest of men could conceal himself, he thought. And then he heard a scream, shrill and painful, the scream of some one in agony, and he sprang to the door of the big limousine and pulled it open. Then a tornado loosed itself at him—a great, gibbering shape leapt at the two men and by sheer weight flung them down, dropping his huge mass upon them.

Larry was stunned for a second, and then, as he struggled to his feet, he heard the door of the garage slammed and the click of the lock as the key was turned. The two men threw themselves at the door, but it did not give an inch.

"The woman!" cried Harvey suddenly, and pointed to the car.

There was an inert heap lying there, and Larry leapt on to the step and, lifting her out in his arms, carried her to where a ray of light penetrated from the small roof-window.

It was a woman of fifty, grey and bedraggled. Her face had not known soap or water for weeks; her hands were almost black. But now through the grime her white face showed in a deathly grin, and the claw-marks of Blind Jake stood out in purple relief upon her lean throat.

"Get some water, Harvey; there's a faucet there," said Larry, loosening the woman's blouse. "She's alive," he said. And then he realized. "My God!" he said in a low voice. "It is the charwoman!"

Whilst he attended to the poor wretched creature, Harvey had searched the garage and had discovered an axe. In five minutes the lock was smashed and the door was open.

"Take this gun," said Larry, slipping his revolver from his pocket. "It hasn't been much use to me, but if you see that swine, shoot him. Don't argue with him or think you can stop him with your truncheon, Harvey."

But Blind Jake had gone, as he knew. That blind man, with the most precious of his faculties destroyed, had again been a match for him.

The woman was showing some signs of a return to life. Larry had dragged her into the air and was sprinkling water on her neck and face. Her eyes fluttered and opened, and she looked up with a frown.

"Where is Miss Clarissa?" she asked thickly.

"That is what I am going to ask you," said Larry.

The cab came soon after, and they carried the woman through the side door, up the steps, and through the beautiful salon. They paused to set her down in the reception-room, and Larry looked round at the evidence of comfort and luxury, bought with the suffering and misery of God knows how many innocent souls who had died that this villainy should be gilded and scented and live in fragrance.

Then his eyes dropped upon the incongruous figure that lay on a thousand-pound Persian rug, who had done no harm but know and recognize Stuart, and must for that reason be condemned to hide in dark places under the care of a fiend like Blind Jake.

Strauss, the ex-convict butler, waited in the hall, nervously rubbing his hands.

"You're not in this, are you?" asked Larry.

"No, sir," said the man shakily. "I thought when you came that my gentleman had sent you, because I had—found a few things."

"Like a black enamelled link, eh?" said Larry. "How many pairs did he have of those?"

"Two pairs, sir. I had to tell him when he asked me what had become of them, because really I did not steal them—he had half given them to me because three of the brilliants were missing."

"Don't worry, Strauss," said Larry. "He has got them back now, though he had to burgle a pawnbroker's to get them."

A knot of idlers gathered on the pavement to watch the spectacle of two, apparently officials of a gas company, carry an unsavoury woman, who looked seventy, down the steps into the cab.

She had recovered consciousness before the cab had gone far, and was trembling violently, looking from one to the other of the men.

"You're all right now, Emma," said Larry kindly.

"Emma?" she repeated. "Do you know me, sir?"

"Yes, I know you," said Larry.

"Then I'm safe?" she said eagerly. "Oh, thank God for that! You don't know what I've been through. You don't know what I've been through!"

"I can guess," said Larry.

"Where are you taking her?" asked Harvey in a low voice. "I didn't hear what you told the cabman."

"I am taking her to my flat," said Larry, and Sergeant Harvey looked his surprise. "I can't afford to fill the hospitals with the witnesses for the crime," said Larry with a faint smile. "And, besides, this woman is not ill; she's just tired and hungry."

"That's right," said Emma eagerly. "I know I must look terrible, but they never gave me a chance of washing myself. They dragged me from one hole to another. I'm not a common woman, sir, although I've done charwoman's work. I was nursemaid and brought up a little girl, sir—the daughter of my missis. Brought her up like a lady, sir. Little Clarissa Stuart."

"Clarissa Stuart?"

"I called her Clarissa, sir," said Emma. "If I could only see her again!"

"You called her Clarissa," said Larry slowly. "Was not that her name?"

"Yes, sir," said the woman. "Clarissa Diana, but I used to call her Diana."

Larry started back as though he had been shot.

"What is your name?" he asked in a husky voice.

"Emma Ward, sir. Diana Ward I called the young lady, but Diana Stuart is her real name, and her father is in London."

"Diana Stuart!" repeated Larry slowly. "Then Diana Stuart is the heiress to whom Stuart left his money. Diana Stuart!" he repeated in a tone of wonder. "My Diana!"

The Heiress

MRS. EMMA WARD had told him practically all there was to tell about herself before the cab had drawn up at the entrance of the flat.

It was she who had failed to register the birth of Diana and her twin sister, and this failure had, curiously enough, saved her life; for when the gang had discovered, as they did a few hours earlier than Larry, that Gordon Stuart had left an enormous fortune to the daughter whose existence he had discovered through an accidental meeting with the charwoman at Nottingham Place, they lost no time in securing the one witness who could prove the legality and the circumstances of Diana's birth.

Never had Larry so congratulated himself upon any event as he did upon the fact that he had engaged a chaperon for Diana. Once before had that nurse been useful; and now she took charge of the unhappy woman who, to the scandal of the neighbourhood, he brought to his flat; and it was a presentable and tidy lady of middle age who came into his sitting-room an hour after her arrival within reach of hot water and clean towels.

"I am going now to see Miss"—he baulked at the word—"Miss Stuart," he said.

The woman started.

"Do you know where she is?"

"Oh, yes," said Larry. "I know! She has been with me for——" He was on the point of saying "years" and honestly believing the word he framed; and then, with a queer sense of surprise, he realized that weeks, and very few weeks at that, would most accurately describe the length of his friendship with "Miss Diana Ward."

He had thought of telephoning the news to her, but somehow he wanted to tell her himself; and there were other things he had to say—things which were hard to think about. He thought it all over on the way to the Yard. Diana Ward, poor and dependent, was a different girl from Clarissa Stuart, an heiress to millions of dollars. He could ask Diana Ward to marry him and look forward with happiness to a union where each brought to the other only the treasure of love. Diana Stuart was a rich woman. He did not doubt that she would be sweet and generous and desirous that the marriage should go through; but after a time she would realize how enormous were the possibilities which great possessions offer. And then she would regret in a nice way, he told himself; for he defended her even as he accused her. And that was the end of the case, he thought. Kudos would come to him, though he could take no credit for that; and the long-deferred promotion—that also would come and he would sit in the office, an Assistant Commissioner, and exercise his function. But all the success he had secured was Diana's. Hers was the brain that had disentangled the knottiest of the problems and had made the tangle of clues into one straight case.

It was curious that he did not also credit her with having discovered even more. Perhaps it was the natural vanity which is latent in all men, which made him guard so jealously the claim to one achievement—the discovery of her identity.

The end of the case! And the end of all hope for him, as he knew. There was never another woman in the world like Diana Ward. She was the first in his heart and should be the last. He had renounced her in his mind and had drawn a grey veil over the future, by the time he stood outside Room 47 with his hand upon the door-knob, hardly daring to turn it because of the loss which would be his. And his first words expressed aloud the thought that followed that moment of hesitation.

"Diana," he said, "I am the most selfish brute in the world."

She showed all her white teeth in a silent laugh.

"I waited for you for over an hour," she said.

"Good Lord!" he gasped. "I was taking you to lunch."

"Yes," she nodded, "that was what you were talking about?"

He shook his head.

"I wish to Heaven it was," he said. "There I am again, thinking of myself and being sorry for myself, when I ought to be on my knees, thanking Heaven for the good fortune which has come to you."

She jumped up.

"You have found Emma!" she said.

"I have found Emma Ward," he replied slowly, "and I have found—Clarissa Stuart."

He walked towards her, both hands outstretched.

"Oh, my dear, my dear," he said, "I am so glad for you."

She took the hands in hers and lifted one to her cheek.

"Aren't you glad for yourself too?"

He was silent, and she looked at him quickly.

"Larry," she said, "I have known all about this for days and days—ever since the day I fainted at that boarding-house in Nottingham Place. Don't you remember?"

He frowned.

"Of course. But why——"

"Why, you silly," she said, "I knew it was Aunt Emma's ring. I always called her 'aunt,' though I knew she was not my aunt. And then I guessed who Gordon Stuart was. I knew nothing would make her leave her wedding-ring behind. Do you know where she went in such a hurry?"

He shook his head.

"To find me," she said simply. "I guessed that. I knew it instinctively before I had heard of that ring. My father gave it to her. She used to tell me how she was married when she was in my father's service, and how my father presented her with this strange wedding-ring for all she had done for my mother."

"You knew!" he said wonderingly. "But you never told me."

"You went on a chase to-day"—she lifted her finger reproachfully and shook it in his face—"and you never told me! You said you were going to Hampstead and you went to Chelsea."

"You knew that too?" he gasped. "Do I get any credit out of this infernal—this case?" he corrected quickly.

"You get me," she said demurely.

He pressed her hands together.

"Diana, I've got a serious talk coming with you, and it's about——"

"I know what it's all about," she said. "You can save yourself the trouble. You can't marry a rich woman because you're afraid she'll want to keep you. You would much rather marry a poor woman—and keep her, if she would submit to that indignity."

There was fun in the eyes that were raised to his.

"Larry!" She shook his hands with quiet impatience.

"It makes a difference, doesn't it?" he asked.

"Not to me, Larry," she replied. "And anyway, it doesn't matter." She dropped his hands and walked back to her table. "Because you've promised."

"Promised? What have I promised?"

"Hear this man!" she scoffed. "You promised me that, whatever happened, whatever was the outcome of the Stuart case, it would make no difference to our marriage."

"Did you know?" he asked in astonishment. "Was that why you made me promise?"

"Of course I knew. I've been a rich woman for quite a long time, and I'm so used to the feeling that I can hardly restrain myself from taking a cab whenever I see one!"

He walked over to her and laid his arm about her shoulder.

"Diana—" he began, and then asked: "Or is it Clarissa?"

"Diana, always," she said.

He kissed her.

"And always."

The End of Jake

THE MAN who called himself the Rev. John Dearborn sat behind the locked door of his study, and methodically burnt papers in a little fireplace that was at the back of his chair. His blue glasses he had dispensed with, and under his eyes, keen and alert, the heap of manuscripts, old letters, receipts and other data, were sorted, and melted away until there was only a package left small enough to go into his pocket. He slipped a rubber band round these and put them on one side. Then he took up a heavy wad of manuscripts and dropped it into an open bag which was beside his desk; and as he sorted and read and destroyed, he whistled a little tune thoughtfully.

From one of the drawers in the desk he took out a thicker package of manuscript bound in a stiff cover. He turned the leaves of this idly, and sometimes the excellence of the writing induced him to read on and on.

"That's damned good," he said, not once but many times; for John

Dearborn was a great admirer of the genius of John Dearborn.

At last, with an air of reluctance, he closed the manuscript volume and put that more reverently in the bag.

The house was empty, for the hawkers had not begun to stray back; and except for the little man who acted as doorkeeper and kept the Home swept and garnished, and the old cook, who was dozing in her kitchen, the Home was deserted.

Presently he finished his packing and patted first one breast-pocket and then the other, until he found the letter he wanted. He took it out and studied it for a while. It was a brief, hand-written note which Larry Holt had written to him the day after his first visit to Todd's Home. He took up his pen and, with one eye on the copy, he fashioned a word taken from the letter, and compared the two efforts. Then from the open writing-case which lay on the desk he extracted a sheet of headed notepaper and began to write slowly and laboriously, and all the time he wrote he whistled his gay little tune. He finished at last and addressed an envelope, also taken from the writing-case; and when this was blotted, and the letter sealed and put into his pocket, he strapped the case and placed it on the floor by the side of his bag. Then he unlocked a wardrobe let into the wall and took out some clothing, which he laid on the back of a chair; and now he was singing with soft diminuendo, yet with evident enjoyment, one of the "Indian Love Lyrics."

He stripped his sombre clerical garb, tore away his white choker collar, and began to dress. He was a man about town now in smartly tailored tweeds; and he put the clerical costume into the wardrobe and shut the door. Then he sat down at the table, his face in his hands, thinking, thinking.

He had dressed almost mechanically, and he had a strange feeling of dissatisfaction. All the exits would be guarded; even the panel, the roof-path, the way through the boiler-room.

"I'm mad," he said, getting up.

He looked down at the bag and the writing-case, and there was regret in his expression. He peeled his coat and slowly undressed again. This time he did not go to the wardrobe, but to a long black box under the window, and he took out various articles of attire and viewed them with distaste.

"A wretched mountebank," he called himself, and was genuinely contemptuous.

But it had to be this or nothing. Blind Jake could find his way by the underground channel. He had the sharp instincts of the blind, could walk like a cat past the sentinels, and even creep through narrow passages where it seemed impossible that his big frame could go.

John Dearborn dressed and took up a canvas bag from the box, laying it on the table. He turned the contents of his leather grip into this bag, then went to the front room of the Home and looked out into the street. Two policemen, he knew, were guarding the end of the cul-de-sac. Nobody used this front room except himself, for storing odds and ends of furniture, old account-books and the like; but it had the advantage of possessing a door which was only a few feet from the front door.

He put down his sack and came out, closing the door carefully, before he went back to his study and locked himself in. He sat there for ten minutes waiting, and then came a gentle tap-tap on the panel. He crossed the room noiselessly, opened the door just wide enough for the caller to slip through.

It was Blind Jake, and his face was strained and puffed, and on his broad forehead the blue veins stood out.

"I only just got here, governor," he said breathlessly.

The other was eyeing him with a steely look.

"What are you doing here, Jake?" he asked softly. "I told you not to leave the woman under any circumstances until I came."

"Well, you didn't come, master," said the blind man. It was pathetic to hear the pleading, the humility, in his tone. His blind eyes were fixed on the cold man whom he loved so well and had served as men serve fate. A great rough cruel hound of a man, strong enough to crush and maim the master he worshipped, yet ready to cringe and whine at a sharp word. Blind Jake had given all for John Dearborn, had been the readiest minister of his vengeance and the slave of his cupidity. Blood was on his hands, and there were nights when strange faceless shapes came in and out of his room and were visible.

Cold hands touched him on these nights, cold stiff fingers felt for his throat, and he could feel the rough wipings of sodden sleeves and the drip-drip-drip of water.

But none of these things mattered. The sweat poured down his puckered face, his big lips were dropping, and perhaps the blind man felt some thrill in the atmosphere, for he asked with a little whine:

"Is there anything wrong, governor?"

"Where is the woman?" asked Mr. Dearborn, and his words dropped one by one like steel pellets.

Blind Jake shifted uneasily on his seat.

"I left her. I couldn't do——"

"You left her!" Another tremendous pause. "And they found her, eh?" John Dearborn's voice had grown very soft.

"Yes, they found her," said the man. "What could I do? Governor, I'd have done anything for you. Haven't I used my strength for you, master? There's no one as strong in the world as me, old Blind Jake. There's no one who can work as cunning as I can! Haven't I worked for ye; haven't I carried 'em out for ye? Haven't I croaked 'em for ye, with these hands, master?"

He held them out: great cruel hands, knotted and roughened, their backs speckled brown, their palms yellow with callosities.

"You lost Holt," said Dearborn calmly, dispassionately, as a judge might speak. "You lost that woman You lost the girl. And you come and talk to me of what you have done."

"I've done my best," said the man humbly.

"And they'll catch you, too. And you can talk."

"I'll have my tongue torn out before I talk against you," said Blind Jake violently, and smashed his fist down on the table so that it cracked and quivered. "You know that I'd die for you, master?"

"Yes," said Dearborn.

He slipped his hand, the left hand that had no little finger, under his coat, and pulled out a short, ugly automatic pistol of heavy calibre.

"You'll talk," he said. "You're bound to talk, Jake."

The man leant forward, his big face working convulsively.

"If I die——" he began. And then John Dearborn, taking deliberate aim, fired three shots, and that great mountain of muscle swayed and slipped by the table into a heap on the ground. Blind Jake's day had come.

The Get-Away

DEARBORN slipped the revolver in his pocket, unlocked the door and stepped out. The little man who acted as porter was standing, his mouth agape.

"What's wrong?" he said quickly. "Who's shooting?"

"Go out and fetch the police," said John Dearborn calmly. "Somebody has been killed."

"Oh, my heaven!" whispered the little man.

"There are two policemen at the end of the road. Hurry," said John Dearborn sharply, and listened to the flip-flap of the messenger's slippers as he shuffled up the street.

Dearborn waited a while, then entered the front room and closed the door, standing against it listening. He heard the rush of feet, distinguished the policemen, heard them clump through the passage and the chatter of an idle bystander or two behind them; then he opened the door. A policeman was bending over Blind Jake.

"That's him all right," he said. "Jim, clear these people out and stand on duty at the door until the inspector comes. You'd better blow your whistle."

A police whistle shrilled through Lissom Lane, and the little knot of curiosity-mongers who had been turned unceremoniously from the scene of the tragedy grouped about the door.

"What's happened?" asked Mr. Dearborn, and the policeman smiled good-naturedly.

"Now, postman," he said, "you go along and deliver your letters." And John Dearborn flung his bag over his shoulder.

For he had chosen the uniform of a letter-carrier, and it had proved a most effective cloak. He got away within a few minutes of Larry's arrival. The detective was on his way to interview Mr. John Dearborn, and the handcuffs he had in his pocket were expressly intended for that gentleman.

Larry saw the little crowd about the door and knew that something unusual had happened. He came to the study and looked silently upon the massive body of his enemy. Blind Jake had died immediately. He had never known what had struck him, or guessed the vile treachery of the employer he had served so well.

"The man must be in the house somewhere, sir," said the policeman. "This little fellow heard the shots, and the superintendent sent him out to get a policeman. We both came down together, me and my mate."

"Was the front door left unguarded at all?" asked Larry.

"Only for a second, sir," said the policeman. "We both came in together."

"That was the second our friend got away," said Larry. "I don't think it's any use searching the house."

He was accompanied by the officers who had been charged to effect the arrest of Dearborn, and their inspection and examination of the room produced nothing of importance.

Larry drove back to the Yard and interviewed the Chief Commissioner. Then he went to the girl.

"I've heard the news," she said quietly. "Sergeant Harvey has just been in. Do you think Dearborn's killed him?"

"Dearborn is David Judd," said Larry.

"Dr. Judd's brother?" she said in surprise, "But he's dead."

He shook his head.

"That elaborate funeral was well staged, and I am perfectly certain that David even went to the length of providing the body. He is a very thorough gentleman. You remember Lew telling us of his brother who disappeared, a fine-looking fellow with a beard?" She nodded. "That is the man we shall find in David Judd's grave," he said.

"Is Dr Judd——" she began, and there was no need to finish the sentence.

"Dr. Judd is in it up to the neck," said Larry. "The story of Dearborn is explained very easily. Dearborn was a partner of Judd's, and something that happened at the office—either some crime or some murder, perhaps, which David had manœuvred in order to draw insurance—had come to the knowledge of one of the clerks. This man stole a large sum of money and went to Montpellier, and from there began to blackmail David. David went after him and shot him. Probably the murder was unpremeditated, because David is not the sort of man who would shoot in the open square. But at any rate he did shoot, and he was seen by Flash Fred, who reached the body in time to learn from the dying man the name of his murderer. To a man of Fred's calibre, that meant that he had an income for life, and he hastened back to London, saw Dr. Judd, and probably stated the terms on which he would keep his mouth shut. Judd decided that David should conveniently die; and David, you remember, was a fine-looking man with a beard. Of their hirelings or acquaintances they chose Lew's brother as being the nearest in physical appearance to David, and he was unceremoniously destroyed and buried as David. Incidentally, a very large sum of money was drawn from the underwriters on the heavy insurance policy which had been issued to David.

"They must have had this scheme in mind for some time, for a month before David's death Dr. Judd had completed the purchase of Todd's Home. It was not so much a charitable institution as a business proposition, for Todd's Home had deteriorated into a kind of superior doss-house, frequented by the lowest of the low amongst the blind mendicants of London. It was there that the famous Dark Eyes had their head-quarters, and it was from them that David must have learnt of Todd's.

"The Home was bought, and the day after David's 'death' the Rev. John Dearborn appeared as the new superintendent. It is perfectly true that he cleared out all the bad characters and had certain structural alterations made; but he only did this because he wanted to clear the taint from Todd's Home, to give it a good character, and to employ the house as his head-quarters without fear of police visitations. When the laundry company went broke, it was Judd who bought the premises, and the alterations were carried out by David himself with the assistance of his gang. David, I might remark, is an architect and built the house in which his brother lives. We know they employed foreign workmen, and that that house was built for one specific purpose," he said gravely.

"With the laundry premises in their possession the Dark Eyes came back to Lissom Lane, and came and went amongst the blind, who could not see them and who were ignorant of their presence."

"What about Dr. Judd?" she asked.

"I am arresting him," said Larry. "And I am arresting him in the very place from whence your father disappeared—in that famous Box A at the Macready Theatre."

"Will he be there?" she asked in surprise.

He nodded.

"He is there almost every evening," he said quietly.

"But why not take him now?" she asked, puzzled.

"Because Box A and its mystery has yet to be cleared up," said Larry; "and I have an idea that I shall clear it."

At eight o'clock that night he walked into the vestibule of the Macready Theatre.

"Dr. Judd, sir?" said the attendant. "Yes, he's in Box A. Is he expecting you?"

Larry nodded. Harvey was for accompanying him, but the other shook his head.

"I'll go alone," said Larry.

He went swiftly down the passage and, stopping only for a second outside Box A, he turned the knob of the door and stepped in.

Dr. Judd's eyes were fixed on the stage, and the detective had stopped to speak to him when something dropped on his head, something fleecy and warm. It felt like a bag lined with wool. It had been saturated with a chemical which took his breath away and momentarily paralysed him. Then he felt a string pulled tightly round his neck, and whipped out his pistol. Before he could use it, it was gripped. Something sharp hit the hand that held it, and he let go with a cry of pain, muffled in the bag. Every breath he took choked him. He struck out, but his arms were seized from behind, and he was flung forward on the floor. Dimly he heard the voice of Dearborn.

"The atomizer, Peter!"

A nozzle was pressed under his chin into the bag, and something pungent was sprayed under his nostrils. He tried to fight his way out of their grip, but a knee was in the middle of his back, and then he lost consciousness.

"You're really a genius, David," said Dr. Judd almost ecstatically. "So perfectly timed, so beautifully done! Wonderful, dear fellow, wonderful!"

"Open the door and look out, Peter," said David, and the doctor obeyed.

The passage was empty. Immediately opposite the door of Box A a curtain was draped on the wall, and through this he disappeared, and there came a rush of cold air as he opened the fire-exit door which led to the side street, where a car was waiting.

A minute later David Judd had picked up the detective as easily as though he were a child, had lifted him into the interior of the limousine and had taken the place at the wheel.

He came to the house in Chelsea, and brought the car with a sweep straight to the closed gates of the covered driveway. In that solid gate were the two big circles, and before David Judd's car were two steel bars that projected beyond the line of the lamps and just beneath. Slowly and skillfully he brought the car up the inclined slope from the roadway, so that the ends of the two bars rested in the "peep-holes." Then he drove the machine forward. There was a click and the gates swung open. The car rolled in, and as the wheels passed over a narrow transverse platform that gave slightly under its weight, the doors closed again.

David Judd stopped opposite the door that looked like a window, opened it and, lifting Larry in his arms, passed inside. The lights were burning on the stairs leading to the cell, the doors of which were wide open.

He threw the detective on the bed, picked up the bronze anklet and snapped it about one of Larry's ankles; and then, and only then, did he pull off the heavy leather bag which covered Larry Holt's head. It stank of formaldehyde, and he threw it into the bathroom.

Larry's face was purple; he had all the symptoms of one who had been strangled, but as the night air reached him he gasped. David leant over and felt his pulse, opened his eyelids and smiled.

He went out softly, locking the two doors, and paused at the first landing, to enter what Sergeant Harvey had called the "machinery room." He turned over a switch and the electric ventilating apparatus hummed drowsily.

David went again into the yard, stopping only to lock the doors behind him. He had no time to lose; the engines of his car were still running, and he jumped into his seat and began to go slowly backward. As the wheels reached the narrow weighbridge, the gates opened again. They would remain open twenty seconds and would then close of themselves; and the car had hardly backed on to the road before they came together noiselessly.

Swiftly the car sped back. This time it turned northward and jolted to a standstill opposite Larry Holt's flat.

A Letter from Larry

DIANA had gone home—it was queer how in a few days she had come to regard Larry's flat as her home—before dinner. Her work was done, and there remained only the stern, grim processes of arrest to be accomplished. At any moment she expected the telephone bell to ring and to hear Larry's voice telling her that the brothers were under lock and key.

She had a book on her lap, but she was not reading. Her nurse and chaperon was sewing in her room. Sunny was standing outside the door of the flat, which was ajar, discussing certain matters with Louie, the lift girl, in a low voice. Probably Sunny had secrets of his own, but it was certain that the discovery of a person who agreed with him in most of the things he said, and most of the statements he made, had fascinated this agreeable man.

Diana sat, her head bent, her hand softly caressing her throat, and her mind was on the future rather than upon the tragic past. She rose once and went into Sunny's little room, where the woman she had called "aunt" was sleeping peacefully; and she smiled as she walked back along the passage at the thought of this female invasion of Larry's bachelor quarters.

She had taken up the book when Sunny knocked and came in.

"There's a note for you, miss," he said, and handed a letter to the girl. It was in Larry's writing, and she tore open the envelope and read:

"Dear Diana,—The most extraordinary mistake has occurred. Dr. Judd has given an amazing version of the death of your father. Will you get into the car which I have sent and come down to his house at once—38 Endman Gardens, Chelsea.—Larry."

She glanced at the embossed note-heading. Larry had written from Endman Gardens.

"Is there any answer, miss?"

"Yes," said the girl. "Tell the chauffeur I will come down at once."

"Are you going out, miss?" said Sunny dubiously.

"Yes, I am going to Mr. Holt," she said with a smile.

"Would you like me to come with you, miss?" said Sunny. "The master doesn't wish you to go about alone."

"I think I'm all right this evening, Sunny," said the girl kindly. "Thank you very much for your offer."

She dressed quickly and went downstairs. The limousine was waiting at the door, and the chauffeur touched his cap.

"Miss Ward?" he asked. "I'm from the doctor's." He spoke in a gruff voice as if he had a cold.

"I am Miss Ward," she replied, and sprang into the limousine.

The car stopped before a dark and silent house.

"Is this the place?" she asked.

"Yes, miss," said the man. "If you go up those steps and ring the bell, the servant will take you to the gentlemen."

It was Dr. Judd himself, jovial and smiling, who opened the door to her and ushered her into a magnificent room.

"You don't mind waiting here a little while, Miss Stuart?" he said.

The name sounded oddly to her, and he laughed.

"I suppose you're not used to being called that name, eh?" he said with excellent humour. "Now I'm going upstairs to see our mutual friend, and I will bring him down to you. Perhaps you could amuse yourself for ten minutes. Our little conference is not quite ended."

She nodded, and settled herself in the chair. The ten minutes passed, and twenty minutes, and the twenty minutes became forty minutes, and nobody came to her. The silver-toned clock on the mantelpiece chimed sweetly.

"Ten o'clock!" she said in surprise. "I wonder what is keeping him?"

Yet she had no fear, and did not doubt for one moment that Larry was in the house.

The room was luxurious, beautiful, more beautiful than any Diana had ever seen. She sat by the side of a great open fireplace where a small fire was burning, for the night was chilly, and she looked round approvingly upon the pictures, the tapestries, the rich hangings, and the soft panelling which was the background for all. There was not an article of furniture in that room, she thought, that had not been chosen with care and judgment. The rugs upon the floor were antique Persian; the carved table might have been looted from an Eastern emperor's palace.

She lay luxuriously in the depths of a great chair, an illustrated newspaper on her knees, and brought her gaze back to the fire and her thoughts to Larry. She wondered what important matters he was discussing and what was the explanation which the doctor had offered. After a while she looked up at the clock again. Half-past ten! She put down her paper and walked restlessly about the gorgeous apartment, and then she heard the click of a door and Dr. Judd came in from the hall.

"I hope you haven't been lonely," he said. "He will be in very shortly."

She took it for granted that the "he" to whom the doctor referred was Larry Holt.

"I was getting worried," she smiled. "What a beautiful room this is!"

"Yes," he said carelessly, "it is beautiful, but one day we will have a more wonderful saloon to show you."

"Here he is," said the doctor; but it was not Larry who came in. She sprang to her feet with an exclamation of alarm. The man who had entered was John Dearborn. He made no pretence now. His glasses were gone, and his fine eyes were surveying her with amusement.

185

"Where is Mr. Holt?" she asked.

Dearborn laughed softly.

"You would like some supper," he said, and slipped back one of the panels by the side of the fireplace, revealing a silver tray on which a meal for one had been laid.

"We do not eat at night." He carried the tray to the table and spread a lace cloth.

The girl's colour had gone. She was in mortal peril, but her voice did not quiver.

"Where is Mr. Holt?" she asked again.

"Mr. Holt is quite happy." It was the doctor who spoke. "We will let you see him later."

The strange words and the stranger tone frightened her, and she got up from her chair and picked up her wrap.

"I don't think I will stay any longer, if Mr. Holt is not here, Dr. Judd," she said, addressing that jovial man. "Can you take me home?"

The doctor did not reply. He had pulled open a drawer of a lacquer bureau and had taken out a thick pad of papers and handed them to Dearborn with a broad smile.

"You're going to have a delightful time, Miss Stuart," he said. "Really, David, it is most good of you. I thought you would be too tired to-night."

The girl looked from one to the other, not daring to credit her own senses. Dr. Judd, who had hitherto been polite to a point of obsequiousness, was ignoring her.

"I don't think you heard me, Dr. Judd," she said steadily. "I want you to take me back to my—to Mr. Holt's flat."

"She is thinking of her clothes," murmured the doctor, addressing his brother. "You will see that they are sent for, won't you, David?"

"Sent for?" gasped the girl. "What do you mean?"

David Judd—already she had ceased to think of him as "Dearborn"—had settled himself in the chair which she had lately occupied, and was turning the leaves of his manuscript book.

"I think you had better eat first. You must be very hungry."

"I will eat nothing in this house until I know what you mean by saying that my clothes will be brought here," she said hotly. "I am going back alone."

"Dear young lady,"—it was the doctor who laid his big hand on her arm—"please do not distract David. He is going to read one of his beautiful plays to you. Do you know that David is the greatest dramatist in the world—the supreme force in modern drama, rivalling, and indeed excelling, the so-called genius of Shakespeare."

David looked at his brother and their eyes met.

He was so earnest, so self-convinced, that she had no words for a moment. Then:

"I am not in a mood to hear plays read, however beautiful they are," she said. She had to keep a tight hold on herself, for instinct warned her that her plight was desperate.

"I don't think she will go back to-night," said the doctor, almost regretfully. "Perhaps to-morrow, when you are married to her?"

He spoke timidly, pleadingly, and there was a question in his statement.

"I shall not marry her," said the man called Dearborn sharply. "I thought we had arranged that, brother? Jake is dead, but there are others. Does it matter who marries her?"

Diana was dumb with indignation and horror. They were discussing her marriage with one of them, each trying to induce the other to wed her with a calmness and an assurance which left her speechless. At last she found her voice.

"I do not intend marrying either of you," she said. "I am engaged to—Larry Holt."

Both men were looking at her, and in the doctor's rubicund face there was an expression of distress.

"It is a pity," he said. "The whole thing could be arranged if Mr. Holt were with us. Unfortunately, though he is with us in the body, we are spiritually as far as the poles apart."

"With us in the body?" she repeated, and was seized with a violent fit of trembling. She had realized that the letter which lured her to this terrible house was a forgery, and her hope of rescue was centred on the certainty that Larry would discover her absence and come after her.

And then the two men exchanged glances, and Dearborn rose and put down his book with an air of resignation. He beckoned her and passed to the other end of the apartment, and there found a door which Larry had overlooked; for the edge of the panels which covered it so overlapped that no crevice was visible.

"I designed this house myself," he explained simply, "and built it myself with only twenty workmen from Tuscany."

Later she was to find much of that was true. The chamber in which she found herself, led by the fascination of a growing horror, was unfurnished and unadorned. She heard a strange humming sound and a curious vibration beneath her feet. Then David stopped, fumbled with something on the floor, and opened a little trap-door less than a foot square. It revealed a pane of glass, and when her eyes had become accustomed to the unexpected perspective, she saw beneath her a small room, evidently lighted from the ceiling.

She had no time to take in the details of the room; her eyes were focused upon the figure that sat on the edge of the bed. With his handkerchief he was binding a wound in his hand, and at first she did not recognize him. Then he looked up, for, though he could not see the occupants of the room above, he had heard the sound of the trap opening.

She stared and screamed, for it was Larry Holt who sat there, and he was chained by the ankle.

Diana Pulls a Lever

DEARBORN put his arm about her waist and dragged her from the room into the saloon. When he released her, her knees gave way under her and she dropped to the floor.

"Everything must be seemly," said Dr. Judd gravely. "We cannot countenance a vulgar scene. Do I speak your mind, brother?"

"Exactly, my dear," answered David Judd.

Diana stared up at him from the floor, resting her shaking body upon her arms.

"What are you going to do with him?" she asked wildly.

Again the brothers looked at one another.

"You tell her, Doctor," said David gently.

Dr. Judd shook his head.

"I think you should tell her, my dear David," he answered. "You are so very delicate in these matters, bless you—and remember," he added, "that she is your wife."

David had seated himself and was leaning over the arm of the chair, his immobile face fixed upon Diana's.

"When I have finished with him," he said, "I shall drown him."

She started up, her hand to her mouth.

"My God!" she breathed.

The dreadful truth came upon the girl with a rush. These men were madmen! Madmen who preserved all the outward appearance of sanity, who day by day and for years had conducted a business with sane men and never once betrayed the kink in their unwholesome minds. She shrank back from them, farther and farther back until she was against the panelling of the opposite wall. They were her father's murderers! She thought she was going to faint, but dug her nails into her palms in a tremendous effort to keep her senses. Mad, and the world rubbed shoulders with them and never suspected!

"Shall I read?" asked David quietly.

"Yes, yes, read," she said eagerly.

They were to kill Larry when he had finished reading!

That was the thought which obsessed her as she turned her drawn face to the man. The vanity of this monomaniac was flattered, and he betrayed his agitation in his stumbling speech as he read the first two pages of his manuscript.

Then his voice grew calmer, and the girl understood in a wondering way that he was imparting into these dead and lifeless words a beauty which only his mind could see, but which, in some extraordinary way, he was conveying also to her.

Dr. Judd had slipped from his chair to the big bearskin rug before the fire and sat with his legs crossed, his hands clasped before him, his large, eager face turned to his brother. And here was another curious circumstance which the girl noted numbly. Those lines which seemed brilliant to David were brilliant also to the other, and when he paused self-consciously, as if for applause, it was always the doctor who anticipated his desire.

"Wonderful, wonderful! Is he not a genius, Miss Stuart?" asked Stephen.

She glanced quickly at the other, expecting to find him embarrassed, but he sat bolt upright, a complacent smile upon his heavy face, a benevolence in his eyes. And they were planning murder! They had murdered many men in this terrible house, she thought, and wondered. Had they sat here whilst their victims fought their last fight in that horrible dungeon, the one reading and the other listening to these trite sentences, these age-worn situations which both believed were the work of a supreme genius?

"This is not my best work," said David, as though reading her thoughts. "You like it, of course?"

"Yes," said the girl in a low voice. "Go on, please."

She hoped to keep them occupied throughout the whole of the night. She knew that the police would be searching for Larry, and perhaps one of them knew this house in Chelsea. But those hopes were to be shattered, and her heart gave a wild leap as she saw David close the manuscript book and put it tenderly on the table beside him.

"Brother," he said, "I think——?"

The doctor nodded.

"And it would be a gracious thing, and a picturesque beginning for all the happiness which lies ahead of us, if this fair hand——" He took the unresisting hand of Diana in his, and again he did not complete his sentence.

He took his keys from his pocket, the keys that Flash Fred had so carefully duplicated, and Larry had duplicated again, and walked to the door through which the girl had entered the room. He smiled to himself as he inserted the key and the door swung open.

"Will you come this way, dear girl?" he asked. She hesitated, then, summoning her courage, followed him down a flight of steps.

Again there was a door at the end. A little room filled with machinery she saw, when he put on the light. He walked to a switch.

"You shall have the honour of releasing our friend—we bear him no malice—Mr. Holt."

"Release him?" she asked huskily. "Do you mean that?"

She hesitated, her hand upon the black lever in the wall.

"Why do you not open the door and let him out?" she asked suspiciously.

"That will open the door and release him. Believe me, my dear, I would not in this hour deceive you."

It was the doctor who spoke in his softest tone, and she hesitated no longer. Her brain was in a whirl. She could not analyse either their motives or their sincerity, nor could she appreciate the fact that to these men deception was a habit of thought. She swung the lever back and it came more easily than she had expected. Then she looked at the door.

"Let us go and meet him," said the doctor, and put his arm round her shoulders.

She shivered, but did not attempt to escape, and so he led her up the stairs and back into the salon, closing and locking the door behind him.

Then, before she could guess or anticipate his intentions, the arm about her shoulders had become a grip as firm as a vice, and she found herself pressed closely to the big man.

"My wife, I think, brother," he said.

"Undoubtedly your wife," said the doctor; "for the world is yours to pick and take from, my dear."

"My wife," repeated Dearborn without emotion, and brought his lips to hers.

She was frozen with terror, incapable of movement. Why did not Larry come? Then, as suddenly as he had seized her, the doctor released his hold and took her cold hand in his.

"Come back to the fire, wife," he said. "I will finish the third act of this great work of mine, and by that time Mr. Holt will be dead."

In the Trap

LARRY sat on the iron bedstead of the cell, his aching head between his hands. He had anticipated many ends to that night's adventure, but never did he imagine that he would be trapped like a rat, and that the mystery of Box A would be solved in so startling a fashion. So that was the explanation of Gordon Stuart's death. He had accepted the invitation of Dr. Judd to go with him in his box, and there had met the sinister figure of Dearborn. He had either been drugged or clubbed to insensibility and had been carried in John Dearborn's strong arms through the emergency door in the passage and whisked away to the House of Death.

If he had not anticipated such an end to the evening, he thought, he had at least made some preparations. Instinctively he had known that of all places on the face of the earth where his quarry would be run down and "Finis" might be written to the Stuart case, no other spot was so likely as in this terrible mansion which the Judds had built for themselves, and the object of his visit that morning had been twofold. He desired to know and to see with his own eyes the evidence of the men's wickedness; but he had also a wish to understand the ultimate danger to himself and to the girl.

He smiled as he thought of Diana, sitting snugly at home, and wondered what she would feel if she knew his position.

His captor had taken from him every weapon he carried, but that did not worry Larry overmuch. He got up from the bed and walked about the room, but the weight of chain at his ankle made it necessary that he should gather a yard of it slack in his hand. He gave one glance at the black holes in the wall near the floor, for it was from these that danger would come. Well and truly had these men planned their execution-room. No cry for help, no sound he might make, would penetrate through these concrete walls. The light in the ceiling was protected by a thick and heavy globe of glass. It reminded him of a bulkhead light.

He wanted to test the length of the chain, for he had ample time, he thought. Dearborn would be in the house by now. He heard the click of the trap-door above and looked up, but saw nothing. He waited for another half-hour, then pushed over the big block of stone to which the chain was fastened. Before his eyes could fall upon the bag he had left there in his earlier visit, the light went out.

Curiously enough, he had not provided for that contingency, and he drew a sharp breath. The bag was there: his fingers touched and pulled it out, and he groped inside for the keys. Had there been light, there would have been no difficulty in selecting that which unlocked the anklet; but now he tested three, and none of them fitted the bronze clamp about his ankle.

He heard a sound, a low, gurgling sound, such as water makes when it is poured from a bottle; and then about his feet came an eddy of cold air. He tried another key, and that too failed him. Worse still, it remained fixed in the lock, and he could not pull it out.

He heard the rush of the water coming through the small holes in the wall, and the dull throb of a pump. He tugged at the key, great beads of sweat running down his cheeks, and then, with a sigh of relief, it came out. The water was over his boots now and rising rapidly.

There was only one more key to try; the rest were too big for the purpose. He drew that out, but the ward caught in the string of the bag in which he had put them, and the key fell into the water. He groped down; it had gone! Again and again he flung his hand through the swirling water, and his fingers groped along the rough concrete floor. Presently with a cry he felt it and, lifting his ankle with an effort, he inserted the key. It turned. The anklet opened, and he was free.

There were still the two doors, and he knew that, with the pressure of water, it would require his utmost efforts to open them.

The water was up to his waist now, and he waded along the passage and up the two steps, holding the waterproof bag between his teeth. The key turned easily enough, but there was no handle to pull, and every second increased the pressure of the water. He set his teeth and, gripping the key in both hands, he pulled steadily, steadily . . .

The Passing of David

DIANA had heard the dread words without understanding them at first. "By that time Mr. Holt will be dead!"

She opened her mouth to scream, but no sound came. She had killed Larry! Her hand had pulled the lever which drowned him! That was the word Judd had used. Drowned him—but how? As the thought took more definite shape she swayed toward the doctor and gripped his shoulder for support. She would not faint, she told herself; she would not faint! There must be a way of saving Larry. She looked around for some weapon, but there was none; and then she grew calmer. They were madmen and must be humoured. But the time was short.

Again she assumed an attitude of attention, but her mind and eyes were busy, and as David Judd leaned forward she saw something that brought a thrill of hope to her heart. His jacket was open and showed just a glimpse of white shirt where his arm passed through the waistcoat, and against that strip of white was a sharp black line. She looked again and saw it was an automatic pistol, worn in a holster under the armpit. She remembered reading of desperadoes who carried their guns that way, so that they might be ready to hand; and possibly David had read too.

He was in the midst of an impassioned love scene when her hand darted forward and closed over the butt. With a jerk she pulled it free and stepped back, overturning the little table on which her supper tray had been laid.

"If you move I'll kill you," she said breathlessly. "Open that door, and release him!"

The two men were on their feet, staring at her.

"You—you interrupted my reading," cried David, in the tremulous voice of a hurt child. He did not seem to be conscious of any danger.

"Open the door," she breathed, "and release Larry Holt, or I'll kill you!"

David frowned and put his hand on the mantelpiece. She saw his fingers touch a button, and as the lights went out she fired.

The explosion deafened her. A second later his strong arms were around her and he had flung her into the chair and stood glaring down at her.

"You interrupted my reading," he almost sobbed, and Dr. Judd, a frowning figure, looked anxiously from her to his brother. "And now," said David petulantly, "I will not marry you."

His big hand gripped the edge of her bodice and dragged her to her feet. His eyes were wet with tears, the tears of pride, of humiliation. Then, with the sudden caprice of a madman, he released her.

"He is dead now, I should think, brother," he said, turning to the doctor, and Dr. Judd drew a sigh of relief and nodded.

"Yes, he is dead now," he said. "The water rises at the rate of one foot in two minutes, I think."

"One foot in a minute and fifty seconds," said David.

"Spare him for God's sake!" cried the girl hoarsely. "I will give you anything—anything in the world you want! If it is money, you shall have it!"

"I think she ought to see him," said David, ignoring her frenzied appeal.

"There is no light," said the doctor and shook his head.

"Of course not. How stupid of me! We always put the light out," said David, whose fit of anger seemed to have passed. "Then the water comes up through the little holes at the bottom of the cell very, very quickly. It is pumped from the roof of the house. We have a large tank there, you know," he went on, "and the person we drown cannot rise because of the weight of his feet. Once a man got on the bed—do you remember?"

"I remember," said the doctor in a conversational tone. "We had to put nine feet of water into the cell before he died."

She listened numbly. It was a nightmare, she told herself, and presently she would wake.

"And that takes a long time to pump out. It was very thoughtless of him. So much had to be done," David continued, and his brother was looking at him for the first time anxiously.

"We had to dry the bed," David went on, "and did you notice the chain was rusty, brother? That isn't right. It is an eyesore to me."

He turned and looked at Diana thoughtfully.

"My wife," he said in a low voice, and there was a sudden fire in his eyes which terrified her. "My wife," he said again, and caught her to him with a horrible animal cry that set her shrinking.

"I want you, Judd!"

He spun round. Some one had come into the room and was standing now with a pistol aimed straight at the man's heart.

It was Larry Holt.

The End of the Chase

DON'T MOVE," said Larry. "Resistance is useless. Listen to that."

There was the faint sound of a crash in the hall.

"Those are police officers, and they are inside the house," said Larry laconically.

Slowly David pushed the girl away from him and faced the intruder, looking at him from under his heavy brows. Larry did not see the man's hand move, so quick was the motion. A wind fanned his cheek, a panel splintered, and the two shots sounded like one to the half-fainting girl.

David Judd stood for a moment erect, then staggered a little.

"My beautiful plays!" he said, and choked.

Then, without another word, he crashed to the floor, dead.

"David, David!" Dr. Judd threw himself upon the body. "David, don't act! I will get you beautiful actors for your work. I don't like to see you doing it, David! It frightens me. Tell him not to!"

The big man, his florid face gone white, looked up appealingly at Larry Holt, who stood with his smoking pistol in his hand, his eyes fixed upon the two.

"Mr. Holt, you have influence with him," whined the doctor, his face streaming with tears. "Tell him, please, not to do this! It frightens me when he acts. Sometimes he acts for hours in this room—little pieces from his own wonderful plays. You must ask him to read you some, Mr. Holt. David—!" He shook the body, but David was beyond the voice of his brother.

Edgar Wallace

Then the doctor stood up. He came across to Larry, laying his large hand on the other's like a frightened child. Larry was so overwhelmed by the tragedy of it all that he could not speak. This grown man, whose brilliant brain had conceived and dared so much, was for a moment like a little child.

Suddenly the doctor's head came up.

"I am sorry," he said huskily. "Poor boy!"

He looked at Larry Holt long and steadily.

"Mr. Holt," he said, "I have been behaving childishly, but I am perfectly sane. I accept full responsibility for all my acts—and all the acts of my brother. I know quite well what I have done."

Harvey had burst into the room and stopped dead at the scene, until Larry beckoned him forward.

"Take him," he said.

"I wish we had finished you," said Dr. Judd as they led him away.

The girl was in Larry's arms now, her face hidden against his shoulder.

"This is the end of the bad road," he whispered, and she nodded. As they came into the vestibule, one of the police officers who filled the hall saluted him.

"We've taken the servant, sir. He was locked up in another part of the house."

"He knows nothing about it," said Larry. "You can safely release him. And, anyway, I haven't taken the trouble to get a warrant for him."

A tall man came out of the broken doorway which Larry discovered led to the servants' quarters, and took the girl's hand in his.

"You've had a terrible experience, Miss Stuart," he said, and she recognized the Police Commissioner, and tried to smile. "I have my car here. You had better come along, Larry. Harvey can charge Dr. Judd."

They drove back to Scotland Yard, and Larry said very little on the journey. He sat by the girl's side, her hand in his, and answered the questions the Commissioner put to him briefly and without elaboration. It was when they were back in the Commissioner's office that Larry spoke.

"John," he said, "I hope you are not going to report this matter to the

197

Government as an achievement on my part."

Sir John looked at him with an inquiring frown.

"Of course I shall," he said. "Who else takes credit?"

Larry put his hand on the girl's shoulder.

"Here is the best detective we have had in Scotland Yard for many years," he said simply.

Diana laughed.

"You silly man," she scoffed, "of course I am not. Who was the best detective you could have had to deal with this case?"

"You," he said.

She shook her head.

"The best detective was Dr. Judd, if you could have secured his services. And he was best because he knew most of this matter, knew all the secrets which we were trying to discover. I was in very much the same position; I was inside the game. Once I knew, as I did, that Clarissa Stuart was myself, I was able to mystify you. For when it was clear that poor Emma—I nearly called her aunt—poor Emma Ward was the charwoman who had seen my—my father, and had left in such a state of great agitation, there was no doubt whatever in my mind that it was my father. And when that was clear, the rest was rather easy. I knew then that I was the objective of the gang. No, Larry, you are and you have been wonderful."

Larry shook his head, with a smile.

"Anyway," said the Commissioner dryly, "does it matter who gets the credit?"

"Why?" asked Larry in surprise.

"I mean, so long as it goes into the family," said Sir John, and the colour came to the girl's face.

"There's a great deal in that, Sir John," she said, "and now I am going to take him home."

That night, after she had gone to bed, and Larry sat before his little fire, his bright brier between his teeth and his mind at peace, Sunny came in to him, bearing an armful of laundry.

"Two of your collars are missing, sir."

"And the man who wears the collars was nearly missing, Sunny," chuckled Larry. "Do you know, one of the first things I thought about in that infernal place was whether you'd get the news in time to stop the papers."

"I could have always sent them back, sir," said Sunny gravely.

"You're a cheerful soul," said Larry. "Well were you named Sunny! And Sunny," he said, "I want to tell you that I'm going to be married."

"Yes, sir," said Sunny, and his brows knit in thought.

"Well?" said Larry.

"Well, sir," said Sunny slowly, "I think you'll want some new socks. They dress very smartly at Monte Carlo."

"By Jove!" said Larry, and then his face fell. "We can't go to Monte Carlo in the summer, you silly ass. It would be too hot. No, I'm going to Scotland for—for—after I'm married."

Sunny was interested.

"Then you'll be wanting a kilt, sir," he said.

Three Cigarettes

TWO MONTHS later, Dr. Judd sat on the edge of a very small bed and smoked three cigarettes, one after the other. It was a rainy morning, and the square of glass which gave light to the cell seemed to collect all the greyness and drabness of the day and transmute the faded light of heaven into a lead.

The doctor smoked luxuriously, for he had not tasted a cigarette for the greater part of two months. Presently the door of the cell opened, and Larry came in. Judd jumped up to his feet and greeted the visitor with a smile.

"It's awfully good of you to come, Holt," he said. "I intended saying nothing, but in the circumstances it seems to me only fair to a man of your position, who has put in such a large amount of earnest and excellent work, that you should know the truth."

He was altogether sincere: Larry knew that.

"My brother David and I—and this you will understand—were on the most affectionate terms from our early childhood. David was my care and my responsibility, and he was also my joy. We had both been left by our mother at a very early age, and our father was an eccentric gentleman who had very little use for children. So we grew up and went to the same public school and to the University together, and I think I am right in saying that we were wholly sufficient for one another. I had an admiration and a love for David beyond anything that is human," said the doctor, lowering his voice and looking down.

Larry nodded. He had recognized this quality in the two men.

"I hope you will not think that I owe you a grudge because you killed David," he said. "Far from it. I recognize the inevitability, and in my heart I know that nothing could have saved David. He died as he would have wished; and in some respects I am very glad for all that has happened. At the trial I made every effort to prove to the judge and the jury that I was perfectly sane, and your evidence helped to secure the conviction which I knew was inevitable. I thank you for it. As I say——" he went back to the story of his early life, and told stories of the childhood of he and his brother.

"When my father died," he went on, "he left us the Greenwich Insurance Company, a small impoverished concern which was then on the verge of bankruptcy. I can safely and honestly say that I have never respected the sanctity of human life. To me a human being is like any other animal—a kind of dumb Lew," he explained easily, and Larry could hardly restrain a shudder at the light-hearted way he referred to this human wreck.

"I tell you that before I go any further, lest you expect anything in the shape of an apologetic attitude on my part. If you do, you will be disappointed. The business to which my brother and I succeeded was bankrupt, and I think we got our first idea for the subsequent operations when we had to pay out a risk which had been taken by my eccentric father, and a risk which he should never have undertaken.

"The idea of the scheme was partly mine and partly David's. We began our experiments three months later, when we drowned a man, whose name I need not tell you, since it would serve no useful purpose and no person is under suspicion for his death. We had insured him in our own office—a very simple process—without his being any the wiser. I myself had signed the medical report, and David, who was a clever draughtsman, in addition to being a brilliant engineer—the career for which he was trained—signed all the necessary forms in his name. We chose the man carefully. He was one who had no friends and was regarded as being something of a recluse. The policy was made payable in favour of a fictitious name which my brother had taken in Scotland, where he had furnished a small house and where he lived for the purposes of collection.

"We made a large sum of money by this death, for we had reinsured the life and there was little to do but to collect from the underwriters. My brother was always something of a poet, and when he was at Oxford he wrote two or three plays, which the managers of the London theatres rejected. I need hardly tell you," he said with the utmost gravity, "that they were wonderful plays, though not, of course, as good as those I produced later at the Macready Theatre."

"The Macready was your property, was it not?" said Larry, and the doctor inclined his head.

"I bought it some time ago for the purpose of producing dear David's dramas," he said. "It was the one thing for which I lived: to establish David's name. He had very early on taken the name of Dearborn, and it is curious that you had not compared the name that appeared on the playbills six years ago with the Rev. John Dearborn."

"They were compared," said Larry, "and our conclusions were drawn, but not until a late stage in the investigations."

"Our next experiment was on a man named—well, I need not give this name, either," he said. "We had to wait a reasonable time before we bled the underwriters. And here occurred an unfortunate thing. One of our clerks discovered that the person to whom the money was paid was my brother. He found it out by the veriest accident, and began to blackmail David, and finally, fearing the consequence of this line of action, he stole a considerable sum of money from the office and went to France. David followed him and shot him in Montpellier. You know that part of the story very well, Mr.

Holt," he said with a good-humoured smile. "Flash Fred saw the act committed, and lived on me for years, but only because he never accepted an invitation to dinner in my house," he added with a little smile.

"And now I come to the Stuart case. David, who did a great deal of investigation of his own, had, as you know, disappeared as the result of Flash Fred's recognition. We gave him a very handsome funeral, and——" He hesitated.

"And the body was the brother of Lew," said Larry quietly.

"Quite right," agreed the doctor. "He was an awkward man, and he—had to go! The whole thing had been simplified by now," he explained. "My brother had built our beautiful house, and the death chamber with its water, its pump and its ventilator, had been created by his genius. It was my idea that we should buy up Todd's Home, and curiously enough, I had completed the sale before it became necessary for dear David to disappear. Mr. Grogan has not told you, in all probability, that we sought by every means in our power to induce him to come to the Macready Theatre to see a representation of one of my brother's dramas. He saved himself, not by any superhuman cleverness, but because he had the low cunning of the rat which walks around the cage of a trap, knowing that the trap is there, yet unable to realize just how it works.

"I will return to Stuart," he said. "We had laid our plans when Stuart came into the box, and our plans did not include any injury to him whilst he was in the theatre, because we thought it would be a simple matter to persuade him to pass through the fire door into the car which was waiting in the private road which is the property and stands upon the grounds of the theatre.

"Stuart came. My brother, of course, was not there, though he was near enough at hand if I wanted him. Boxes A, B and C were never let to the public, by the way. To our surprise he came in the most exalted mood, and told us that he had discovered a daughter. And then, for the first time, we knew that he was not an obscure stranger, but a very rich man. We took him back to the house and he went willingly, and there we had a discussion, dear

David and I, as to what should be done. We came to the conclusion that there was nothing definite to be secured from this man if we let him live, and it was very necessary, indeed vitally necessary, that money should come in at once. I had spent a great deal of money, some hundred thousand pounds," he said airily as he lit his second cigarette, "on art treasures, and another hundred thousand upon the theatre, and we were being pressed very hard. We decided that Stuart should go."

He puffed at his cigarette and blew a ring to the ceiling.

"He showed fight," he said briefly. "By the way, I have reason to believe that one of the cuff-links which were torn off my shirt in that struggle was retrieved by you, Mr. Holt. Where did you find it?"

"In the dead man's hand," said Larry, and Dr. Judd nodded.

"I was afraid I had not been very thorough," he said, "but I am relieved, because I thought that David was to blame—David was careless in some matters.

"He had told us, had Stuart, all about his charwoman, had given us her address; and there and then we decided to find this Clarissa and marry her to some one." He shrugged his shoulders. "It did not matter whom, so long as we could first of all prove her birth and then control her money. The next day my brother went to confirm the man's story, but he found difficulty. The woman in charge of the nursing home—it was a converted farm, if you remember, where Mrs. Stuart died—had disappeared. And even the offer of a reward did not produce any results. We had no difficulty in finding and capturing the charwoman. Blind Jake, who was a faithful servant of ours—and nobody regrets his death more than myself, but I also realize that it was necessary, or had the appearance of necessity—Blind Jake, I say, hurried her away, and from the information she was able to supply us with, I could trace Clarissa Stuart as Diana Ward. I might add, for your information," he said, addressing Holt, "that the inquiries did not take more than half a day."

"There is one question I should like to ask you, doctor," said Larry quietly. "The lift accident was arranged by whom?"

"By David," said the doctor with a little smile as though he were amused at something. "David was on the floor above, and it was David who dropped things on your head. They didn't reach your head, of course, which was unfortunate. Then he had an easy exit along the roof to the next building, and I never admired you so much as when you refrained from going up those steps left so invitingly under the open trap-door. You would have come down very quickly," he added significantly. "And that, gentlemen, really concludes my story." And he took up the third cigarette, for the second had been smoked very vigorously.

"Why did you spare Lew?" asked Larry. "He was one of your helpers and knew your secrets."

"I was prepared to spare almost anybody unless my life was endangered," said Dr. Judd. "Certainly I did not want to find all my good plans tumbling to the ground through the death of some wretched beggar who was quite harmless. I only killed when it was necessary or profitable," he said. "Blind Jake had his own vendettas, and his attempt upon Fanny Weldon was a purely private affair in which we were not interested."

A man came in through the door of the cell, a short, stocky man who was bareheaded, and Dr. Judd took one long whiff of his cigarette, dropped it on the floor of the cell and put his foot upon it.

"The executioner, I presume?" he said pleasantly, and turned round, putting his hands behind him.

The stocky man strapped him tight, and the white-robed clergyman, whose ministrations he had refused and who was waiting outside the cell door, came in and walked slowly by the doctor's side.

And so he went out of sight of Larry, who waited behind. He saw the broad shoulders for the last time as they passed through the narrow door leading from the prison hall to the exercise yard, and he waited, feeling inexpressibly and unaccountably sad.

A minute passed, and then there was a crash that came like thunder to his ears and made him start. It was the crash of the falling death-trap. Dr. Judd had met his brother.

The Vampire of Wembley

and Other Tales of Murder, Mystery, and Mayhem

Contents

The Vampire of Wembley

THE gentle Tressa was remarkable in one respect: she never found bad people interesting.

When Lady Mary Midston told her about the burglar, Tressa was politely interested but not enthusiastic.

"Daddy was in Paris, otherwise I should have called him when I heard the noise in the hall. He's simply furious with me for not calling Thomas. When I got downstairs there was a light in the drawing-room and a little man was tying up the silver in a tablecloth. I must say, Tressa, that he was awfully decent, and when he told me about his sick wife and his poor little children I hadn't the heart to call any of the staff."

"And you let him go?" said Tressa, coldly for her. "My child, you have a certain duty to society—I suppose you realise that? I know you acted as your own kind little heart dictated, but a burglar is a burglar, no matter what the state of his wife's health—"

"That's what daddy said," remarked Mary complacently.

She was a slim, pretty girl, with flawless colouring and anybody but Mike Long would have spent sleepless nights in the fear of losing her. Mike, for the moment being in the grip of the Wembley Vampire, spent his evenings composing letters breaking off the engagement and his mornings in tearing them up.

"My dear Tressa, you are most original! Of course I let him go! And he was an honest man, apart from his burglaries, for he gave me his address, and when I went—"

"You went to his house?" gasped Tressa.

Mary nodded.

"Of course I went I wanted to know whether his story was true. And, darling, it was! He's got two of the sweetest children, and a wretched, washed-out kind of wife without an 'h' to her name. And I've asked my cousin Arkwright, who's in the City, to find him a job, so that he will never have to go out burgling any more."

Tressa sighed; and then, after a pause:

"Perhaps you're right," she said, "and I am wrong. But I must confess that I do not like the most picturesque of burglars, and he doesn't seem to have been particularly attractive. Bad people do not appeal to me."

Mary said nothing, but thought a great deal, and Tressa, who was something of a thought-reader, smiled and went on:

"Meeting bad people in one's own circle is unavoidable; and besides, there's just a chance that one may be able to switch them on to the right track."

Mary sniffed.

"If you can switch Lila Morestel on to the right track, I shall be both surprised and pleased," she said.

The taunt was not without justification, for Lila had been a constant visitor at the Piccadilly flat in the past few weeks.

"That is one of the things I cannot understand about you, Tressa. Everybody knows about Mrs. Morestel. Why, they took her name off the books of the Jacara Club and they are pretty broad-minded."

"Lila is in trouble and wanted my help," said Tressa shortly.

*

LILA MORESTEL was frequently in trouble: and as frequently, in her helpless, agonised way, appealed for the assistance of her friends. Sometimes the assistance was such that it could not be rendered without damage to the reputation of the helper.

Her history was a curious one. She had been a shop assistant in an Oxford Street establishment, and her beauty attracted the attention of Vivian Morestel. Nobody knew how Vivy earned his living. It was supposed that he sold cars on commission, and that he acted as agent for a firm of bookmakers in various members' enclosures. He had other sources of income, which only the unfortunate young men who accepted invitations to play cards in his flat knew anything about, and they were naturally reticent.

For some inexplicable reason his hectic courtship of Lila culminated within a few weeks of his meeting her in a visit to the Marylebone Registry Office, where they were joined together in the business-like bonds of matrimony.

Lila's social progress was amazing. There were vague stories in circulation of tremendous adventures with wealthy members of the British aristocracy, and the officials of the Royal Courts of Justice could tell of divorce suits begun by Vivy and 'settled out of court' for a consideration. Generally the sum was about £20,000, and Mr. and Mrs. Vivy Morestel grew opulent, bought Flynn Hall at Wembley, and lived there alternately.

Vivy had discovered a method of earning a livelihood more effective than the most cleverly manipulated pack of cards could give him. There were minor scandals within scandals. Big, bluff Scherzo, the maître d'hôtel at the Fourways Club, complained bitterly that he had introduced Lila to a rich Brazilian and that, no sooner had Lila got her landing hooks into his banking account, than she persuaded him to patronise another establishment—a dead loss to Scherzo of £100 a week, for the Brazilian was a liberal spender.

By mutual consent the two young people lived apart, and only met either in consultation, to decide for how much they could bleed Lila's latest friend, or else to cut up the profits over a pleasant dinner. This sounds incredible, but it is true, and the partnership might have continued for a very long time, with profit to both but Vivy made the mistake of falling in love with somebody, and decided on a real divorce.

That is the story of Lila, known to every clubman in London. It is the story behind the dazzling picture of her published in the daily and weekly press. Into the web of Flynn Hall many bloated flies had flown and struggled helplessly, and had been duly blooded. And now the king fly was buzzing nearer and nearer to the viscid threads.

"I can only tell you, Tressa, that if she gets Mike I'll—I'll murder her!"

Tressa laughed softly.

"Mike's much too sensible," she said, conscious of her own hypocrisy, for she had told other women that other men were 'much too sensible,' and had had to watch the ruin of hopes and ambitions that littered the trail where the triumphant Lila had passed.

She decided in this particular case that it would be wise to see Mike himself; but days passed before she met him, and then the opportunity—it was at the opening match at Hurlingham—was not a particularly good one.

Mike listened, obviously ill at ease, whilst Tressa expatiated on the virtues and sweetness of his fiancée.

"Yes, of course, that's all right," he said awkwardly at last. "Mary is a dear—much too good for me, and all that sort of thing. I wouldn't hurt her for the world. But I'm not so sure that our marriage would be the best thing for her in the long run. Honestly, Tressa, I'd give a million pounds if she'd get fed up with me and break it off."

"Why?" asked Tressa.

Mike fumbled with his tie, ran his hand through his fair hair, pulled at his aristocratic nose, and stammered something about incompatability.

"The point is, Tressa," he said at last. "Mary's much too sweet a girl to marry a rough-and-tumble fellow like me. She's unsophisticated, and it would simply hurt me most damnably to upset her. She's a child. I feel that I ought to marry a girl who has—well, suffered—give her a sort of safe harbour after the storm."

"In fact, Lila Morestel," said Tressa brutally, and Mike went very red.

"Well, yes; I'm awfully fond of Lila, and she's had a perfect hell of a time with that awful husband of hers. You've no idea, Tressa, what that girl has suffered."

"I have a pretty shrewd idea, I think," said Tressa drily, and Mike grew a little peevish.

"Of course, if you are one of the people who believe all these awful stories that are told about her, there's no use in continuing the argument," he said. "'Malice loves a shining mark', Tressa, and naturally these beastly women who invent all kinds of stories about the poor girl...."

Tressa realised that this was not the moment to give her views on Lila Morestel and her sufferings. More especially she was embarrassed by the knowledge that she had been the unwilling recipient of that lady's confidence.

When she got home she wrote a little note asking Lila to come and see her, and the next morning came a telephone call from Flynn Hall.

"Is it very important, darling? I'm simply rushed off my feet. I have to see my solicitors today or tomorrow—or perhaps it's next Monday: I'm not quite certain. But anyway, I'm fearfully rushed! You know just how terrible I'm feeling about the whole business."

"Can you come tomorrow?" insisted Tressa, and there came from the other end of the wire a reluctant agreement.

"You know I'm selling Flynn Hall?" she added, just as Tressa thought the conversation was ended and was about to replace the receiver.

*

IT was perfectly true that Lila contemplated the sale of Flynn Hall. She discussed the matter with Vivy, who came to lunch that day, and he completely agreed with her plans. They sat together in the beautiful, panelled library that looked out on a stretch of lawn and a well tended garden. Lila was at her desk, and had before her a neat array of title deeds and accounts; for she was a business woman of extraordinary ability, methodical to a painful degree—it pained Vivy at any rate—even going so far as to keep the records of many strange but thrilling incidents in a steel filing cabinet. Because, as Lila told her husband:

"You never know when these things may be useful."

A cigarette drooped from Vivy's thin lips, his pale blue eyes surveyed the pleasant vista in a melancholy stare, his hands were thrust deep into his pockets, and his shoulders humped—a favourite attitude of his when he found himself in hopeless conflict with his businesslike partner.

"Well, have it your own way, Lila," he said, "only tell me when you've made the decision. I've never known you to be so undecided before. It seems a perfectly easy thing to do: you can bring a petition: I'll not defend it; and that will be the end of it."

She looked at him thoughtfully.

"I'm not sure that is the best way," she meditated. "Mike and I went to the El Moro last night and had a long talk. He's worth three millions, Vivy, but the money is so tied up that I can't see myself handling a great deal of it."

"Here, what do you mean?" asked Vivian, galvanised to activity in his alarm. "You're not going to cry off? I've promised that dear girl—"

"Never mind what you've promised that dear girl," snapped Lila. "And how you can bring yourself to fall in love with her is beyond me. I'm not going to cry off—I want to marry Mike."

"Isn't he engaged or something?" asked Vivy, with a flicker of interest. "I thought he was tied up with Lady Mary Midston— rather a pretty girl, too."

"He's tied up with nobody," said Lila decisively. "He likes her, and I suppose he is sort of engaged to her. I know he's rather worried about breaking it off, but that's nothing. The point is this"—she folded her hands on the desk and looked him straight in the eyes—"will it be the best for me to divorce you or for you to divorce me? If I bring the action, there's nothing in it for either of us, and there's always a chance that he might back out. On the other hand, if you bring the action, Mike's got such a strange sense of honour that he's certain to marry me and, what is more, there would be a settlement."

Now settlements had been the foundation of Lila's fortune and, incidentally, of Vivy's and they were now on ground familiar to both.

"Only this time, of course," Lila went on, "there would be no cut. Whatever I got would be mine, and I think, with a bit of luck, we could induce Mike to pay a hundred thousand pounds out of court. The only thing is that is mustn't be settled on me, otherwise it might affect my marriage settlement."

Vivian was now thoroughly alert, and for an hour they discussed ways and measures. At the end of that time Lila made a neat little memorandum of the arrangement, cursed her husband for his rapacity—he had ultimately accepted an eight per cent commission—and there, so far as the vampires were concerned, the matter was satisfactorily ended.

To Tressa, the next afternoon, she gave her own version of the agreement.

"My dear, the most terrible thing has happened! Vivy is filing a suit for divorce."

Tressa was staggered.

"He is divorcing you?" she said incredulously. "I thought—"

"I know, I know," said Lila, wringing her hands. She was a tall, svelte woman, with a willowy figure, an over-large chin and eyes of melting blue.

"Isn't it too dreadful, Tressa! And after all I have done for him, the sacrifices I have made, after all my subterfuges to keep his name clean!"

"Of course, Mike will defend the action, and you will counterpetition?" said Tressa.

Lila shook her head sadly.

"I could do that, of course," she said mournfully, "but my dear, think of the publicity—I would make any sacrifice for Mike's sake. In fact, I've just seen him and told him so. You can't realise what this means to me, Tressa."

"But," said the incredulous Tressa, "You're not allowing Vivian to bring this action and offering no defence, are you?"

"What can I do?" wailed Lila. "I have to consider Mike. It's the awful publicity of a defended action that I'm thinking about." Tressa frowned.

"Is your husband asking for damages?" she demanded suspiciously.

"I don't know what he's doing. My head is in a perfect whirl, and I'm positively sick with worry and anxiety," said Lila. "Mike has been awfully good about the whole thing. Of course, it's come as a great blow to the poor darling, especially as he is, in a manner of speaking, innocent; and he's threatened to kill Vivy. But he realises that he's been seen about with me so much, and under the circumstances he feels, as I do, that the thing to avoid is publicity—"

"How much is Vivy asking?"

Lila threw out tragic and despairing hands.

"I haven't the slightest idea, darling," she whimpered. "Please don't ask me! The thing is so sordid and horrible that it doesn't bear speaking of."

Mike Long, a very dazed and serious young man, sat down that night and sent a letter which took him two hours to compose; and Mary Midston read it in bed and did not shed a tear. She read it twice, read it again, and then, reaching out of bed, lifted the telephone and called Tressa.

"Have you heard the news?" she asked.

Tressa, who had come in to breakfast early in the expectation of this call, replied cautiously:

"What news is this, Mary?"

"I've had a letter from Mike," said Mary, and her voice was singularly even for one whose engagement had been so unceremoniously broken off. "I won't read it to you, but it's all about my youth and innocence, and the horrible unworthiness of Mike. In fact, Tressa, he's ditched me!"

Tressa winced: she had never taken to the argot of the streets.

"And he's going to marry the Vampire. In fact, Mr. Vampire is bringing an action for divorce, and Mike is the Foolish Third."

There was a long pause.

"What are you going to do?" asked Tressa.

"I'm going to do all that I'm not expected to do," said the cool voice at the other end of the line. "I should be sobbing into my pillow, or writing a tear-stained letter. But, Tressa, I'm not going to allow that poor child—"

"Which poor child?" asked the startled Tressa.

"Mike," was the calm reply. "Do you know anybody who better fills the description? I'm not going to allow him to be ruined by that unspeakable reptile. I'm supposed to be unsophisticated but, Tressa, though I neither dope nor drink, nor indulge in the peculiar pleasures of our mutual friends, I know just enough of the wicked world and its ways to stop this divorce."

"How?" asked Tressa.

"Ha ha!" said the voice, so sardonic that for the second time within twenty-four hours Tressa was staggered.

"I know something about Lila," Mary went on, "and I'm going to learn a little more. Do you remember how she once settled a dispute we had at dinner, as to who won the money when we all went to Ascot with the Gladdings, by producing a four-year-old race-card with all the accounts neatly pencilled on the back?"

"But what on earth has that to do with the divorce?" asked Tressa in amazement.

"We shall see," said Mary, and rang off.

Mike Long was on the point of going out that night when the visitor was announced, and he almost collapsed at the sight of the girl in shimmering blue and white who confronted him in the drawing-room.

"Mary!" he stammered. "My dear, I'm sorry you came. I don't think it's wise of you to distress yourself."

"I'm not distressing myself at all," said Mary. "I thought I would come along and make your mind easy. I'm consoling myself with Social Snaps".

"With what?" gasped Mike.

Had his brutal conduct turned this unfortunate girl's brain?

"You may not have heard of Social Snaps, she said apologetically. "It isn't a very high-class paper—in fact, daddy says that it is a very low- class paper. It has been advertised for sale in the Press for months—you must have read the announcements. I bought it—daddy lent me the money."

"But why in the name of fate do you want to go in for that sort of thing?"

He was so astonished that he forgot the painfulness of the interview.

"You're not a journalist—you can't write—"

"Can't I?" she said darkly. "Oh, can't I!"

He looked at her uncomfortably.

"I'm glad—I mean, I'm glad that you have taken things so well. The whole business is rather awful, isn't it? Vivy is a so-and-so, but I've got to go through with it. You don't know how terrible I'm feeling...."

He babbled further inanities, and she heard him through. Then she made a statement, and he went red and then white.

"You mustn't say that sort of thing about Lila: she's as innocent as a child, and all these stories about her are lies. It is infamous to suggest that she has lived on blackmail—wicked!"

"You must subscribe to my paper, Mike," she said at parting. "Can you drop me at the comer of Russett Street, Lambeth? I saw your car at the door."

"Where!" he squeaked. "Russett Street—why that's one of the lowest neighbourhoods in London!"

"We journalists have to go to strange places," said Mary.

*

IT was on the fourth day of the second week after this interview that Lila stalked tragically into Tressa's room and dropped onto a chair.

"If I could only find the man I'd give him five thousand pounds," she

214

groaned. "The fool didn't trouble to take my jewel case."

"But why should a burglar trouble to rob your library?" asked Tressa, who had read the account of the burglary in the morning newspaper.

"Because—I don't know!" snapped the Vampire. "Oh my God, why did he? Every paper taken from my safe, every letter stolen from my file! He must have spent hours. And there were two of them. The fool of a policeman said that he saw a little man and a woman coming down the drive and got into a car that was waiting on the road."

"Who was the woman?"

Lila could only wave despairing hands.

Tressa was genuinely puzzled for a day or two, and then one morning there came to her breakfast table a small weekly journal. She tore off the wrapper to examine Mary's initial effort as a journalist, and the first thing that caught her eye was a black letter announcement.

In our next issue we shall tell the story of:
The Vampire of Wembley
and publish extracts from correspondence between
this sinister woman, her wretched victims, and her horrible husband.
We shall also give the confessions of a converted burglar who,
owing to the influence exercised by a young and charming society
woman, was induced to return to the paths of virtue.
Order Your Copies Now

And then Tressa understood.

Lila read the marked paragraph sent to her by registered post and also understood.

She got on the telephone to Vivy.

"That Midston girl has got the letters, Vivy. I don't know what you'll do, but I'm going to California till things look brighter. I think that is the only way to stop publication. Oh, yes, Mike has a copy of the worst letters. I called him up a few minutes ago, and his valet told me that he was not at home to me."

Halley's Comet, the Cowboy and Lord Dorrington

LORD DORRINGTON was a middle-aged man. He showed no evidence of mental decrepitude, and the alienist who was invited on one occasion to dine with his lordship—the invitation came from anxious relatives, who feared that, unless the poor dear fellow was placed under proper control, he would dissipate the fortunes of the Dorrington family—this alienist wrote so cheery a report upon Dorrington's health that the question of the payment of his fifty-guinea fee was seriously debated. It was felt by a select committee, composed of the beneficiaries under Dorrington's will, that the alienist had not done his duty. They called him (the alienist), disrespectfully, the 'mad doctor', and decided that his report upon Dorrington's sanity was a remarkable proof of the generally-accepted theory that all alienists become mad themselves—in time.

The reason for their fears for Lord Dorrington's reason is understandable. He was an enthusiastic seeker after light. He was a spiritualist, a student of thaumaturgy, theurgy, electro-biology, and something of a Shamanist in an amateur kind of way. He believed that unlikely things happened.

It must be understood that he was, in many ways, a practical man. He once had a butler who neglected the silver horribly. The butler's somewhat ingenious excuse that he also was given to occult studies, and was, moreover, a cadet in the practice of demonology, was received coldly. Further, explained the butler, the silver was cleaned every day, but by night there came a little devil who smeared his dirty paws all over the polished surface of the plate. 'A little devil named 'Erbert, me lord,' said the butler pathetically, 'who cursed me when I was born.'

'You have been reading German fairy tales,' said his lordship, with chilly hauteur, 'and your impudent excuses decide me: I shall not give you a character.'

It was obviously absurd and unthinkable that even a little devil should condescend to consort with a mere butler, and Lord Dorrington very properly resented the assumption of his servant.

Dorrington was a rich man and a shrewd man. The Dorrington belt was the eighth wonder of the world, as any guide-book to the castle will tell you. It was the belt presented by an English king to a lady who was the founder of the family. It was six inches broad, and made of diamonds—not large diamonds, but very saleable diamonds. The Dorrington strong-room was the strongest strong-room in England, for many people desired those gems, the market value being somewhere in the neighbourhood of £80,000.

Lord Dorrington, as I say, was very practical in such matters, and where many a less fanciful man might have contented himself with phylacteries, his lordship, though a student of phylacteries, pinned his faith to doors of chilled steel and Chubb locks.

It would occupy a great deal too much space to give at any length the number of attempts which were made upon those strong-rooms at Dorrington Castle.

There was the still-room maid, who came with forged credentials from an eminent domestic agency, whose box contained diamond drills and a portable axe. There was the groom of the chambers, so suave and polite, with a hundred-pound 'kit' of well-tempered, safe-breaking tools. There was the Swiss valet, who was so very satisfactory until he was discovered one sad night walking cautiously in his stockinged feet in the direction of the strong-room. His explanation that, as a connoisseur of paintings, he desired an uninterrupted study of his lordship's 'Ribera Espanolito' in the east gallery was not accepted by a sceptical bench of magistrates, who gently pointed out that the skeleton keys found in his possession were not consistent with his statement.

These and many others I could name.

Whatever views his relatives might have concerning his mental balance, I am happy to say that in select criminal circles the acumen and intelligence of Lord Dorrington was held in the greatest respect.

'Not that he's so wonderfully clever,' said Billy the Boy (sometimes called Willie the Nut), 'for, in spite of his electric bells and alarms, three men working together could open the safe—only the devil of it is that it's as much as we can do to get one man inside.'

His companions in crime—they were dining at Figgioli's, in Conduit Street, and were beautifully arrayed—nodded their heads in approval.

'They tell me,' said Augustus (nobody knew his other name), 'that a New York crowd are thinkin' about—'

'Let 'em think,' said Billy contemptuously. 'If we can't do the job, they can't.'

There was some justification for such arrogance, for Billy the Boy was a master of his craft, and one remarks, with a glow of national pride, that for scientific burglary England's old supremacy stands unassailed.

I record this conversation that you may have a true appreciation of Lord Dorrington's contadictory qualities, and because he occupied a position of some fame a month or so later, and every scrap of information concerning him is of interest. He was, too, something of a biologist, but that has nothing whatever to do with this story.

You may remember that the year 1910 was chiefly remarkable for the visitation of Halley's comet, and for the fact that the world passed through the tail of our celestial visitor. Now, in spite of lucid articles appearing over the signatures of eminent astronomers, and set forth prominently in the popular organs of public opinion, proving beyond doubt that you might take the tail of Halley's comet and fold the whole of it into a grip sack, there were hundreds of thousands of people who shook in their shoes at the mere thought of the phenomenon they were to witness. As one pseudo-scientific writer querulously pointed out, nobody had ever packed the tail into a portmanteau, so that it was ridiculous to say that such a thing could be done without creasing the tail and ruining it beyond repair. But the most important contribution to the literature on the subject was a letter signed 'Dorrington', which appeared in The Times. It began: 'There is something more than a material aspect to the approaching comet...' and went on to deal with the extraordinary happenings which had coincided with its appearance in former years.

For my own part, (concluded Lord Dorrington soberly) I anticipate remarkable results from the visitation. For the first time in the world's history we have the scientific equipment to register and convey simultaneously the observations of psychists the world over....

There were gross and sordid writers in Fleet Street who guffawed loudly on reading this; worse, they wrote sarcastic paragraphs and little poems, and generally shocked the psychic world by their levity.

But their confusion came quickly.

The comet came, growing brighter and brighter nightly, and, as the superb spectacle increased in splendour, the world began to take the comet more and more seriously.

The earth entered the comet's tail on May 18th, and quite a number of people sat up all night destroying so much of their correspondence as, being recovered from the week of the world, might tend to make them look ridiculous.

But nothing happened on the night of the 18th, and the sun rose on the 19th in very much the same way as usual.

The busy world awoke, and went about its work. Factory horns hooted the toiling millions to labour, trim maids knocked at innumerable doors with tea and buttered toast, and the charwoman reigned supreme in the City of London.

At 7.15, PC Albert Parker, of the City Police, came leisurely out of Shoe Lane into Wine Office Court. He turned the corner of the court, and came to a narrow stretch which leads into Fleet Street. On the left is the white-bricked wall of the Daily Telegraph paper store, on the right is the dingy facade of the Press Club. Lying between the Press Club and the far end of the court was the body of a man. 'Lying' is hardly the word, for he sprawled face downward, with arms and legs outstretched in spread-eagle fashion.

PC Parker hastened his steps, and came up to the prostrate figure.

It was clad in the most extraordinary garments. The trousers were of undressed sheepskin, with the woolly side outermost; a dark blue shirt was on his back, and round his neck was a gaudy neckcloth of great size. Under his baggy trousers he wore top-boots, and two large silver spurs stuck up, sparkling in the sunlight. Add to this a broad-brimmed hat, which lay at some distance from the figure, and a huge revolver at his side.

The constable knelt down and felt the man's face; it was quite warm. He turned the figure over on its back. The man was breathing regularly, his heart was strong and normal; he appeared to be in a deep sleep.

PC Parker frowned, and smelt his breath. No, he was not drunk, and the policeman shook the man by the shoulder.

'Come along,' he said sternly; 'you can't sleep here.'

The man drew a long breath, sighed, and opened his eyes, blinking at the light. He stared at the policeman, and the policeman stared at him. The stranger was about thirty years of age; he was unshaven, and his face was covered with a faint coating of white dust.

'Gee!' he said, and sat up, scratching his head. Then he yawned, stretched himself, and rose a little shakily. 'Whar's that all fired hoss of mine?' he demanded sleepily.

'Look here,' said the policeman, 'what's this—a circus performance?'

The stranger stared coolly at the officer of the law.

'Say,' he repeated, 'whar's that old greaser of mine?'

Then he seemed of a sudden to realise that something had happened.

He looked up and down the deserted court curiously. He allowed his eyes to wander along the buildings, then they came back to the policeman with a scared look.

Then he passed his hand over his forehead wearily.

'I was goin' out to brand a steer,' he said, in a dreamy voice, 'an' that old light, she came prancin' over the prairie—she was a sure enough comet's tail, an' she hit me good. Where am I?' he asked suddenly.

'You're in the City of London,' said the police constable; 'and I'm going to take you along to the station.'

The strange sleeper staggered back.

'City of hell!' he roared. 'I'm in Colefax, Texas. Whar's my horse?'

Four policemen, hastily summoned by a shrill whistle, hustled the cowboy—for such he evidently was—to the Bridewell, and two hours later, charged with being 'a suspected person' the man in the sheepskin chapperos came up at Guildhall before the alderman.

That he told the same story, only more coherently, of the 'sure enough comet which came prancing over the plains about Colefax, Tex.,' is evidenced by the fact that at noon there was not a newspaper bill in London which was not screaming the news of the extraordinary occurrence. I give you the headlines of one of the more sedate of the evening newspapers:

AMAZING DISCOVERY IN THE CITY
COWBOY CAUGHT UP BY THE COMET'S TAIL
DEPOSITED IN LONDON
ASTRONOMER-GENERAL SAYS IT IS IMPOSSIBLE.

It was the one great splash of news of the day—nay, it was the most amazing happening of the century. Astronomers became apoplectic in their attempt that the whole thing was impossible. Yet—but let me quote The Evening Advertiser:

...Another extraordinary fact is that when the man was taken to Bridewell his face and hair were covered with thin, white powder. The City surgeon, who was called to examine the man, took the trouble to brush some of this powder off, and submit it to analysis. It proved to be a fine alkaline matter, such as a man might accumulate in a ride across the alkali plains which abound in that part of the world from which the man said he came. Moreover, on being searched, he was found to be in possession of ten five-dollar bills, a Mexican five-dollar piece, some loose American money, and, most remarkable of all, a receipted hotel bill. The bill was for 'one night bed' at Golden South Hotel, in a town in Texas, and was dated May 17th, 1910. There was also a note of some laundry work done on the same date, and some thin hide laces, wrapped up in an American newspaper, which, although the title was undecipherable or torn off, has the date fairly legible, and that date is May 18th.

This, and other evidence of the extraordinary character of the visitor, may be found in The Psychical Magazine, if it is not destroyed—but I rather fancy that that particular number of the publication in question has been burnt.

It is no exaggeration to say that England talked of nothing else but 'the man the comet brought', and that there was not a psychical society in the world but hastily assembled to gather data upon the remarkable visitation.

Excitement was at its height, when a new and even more sensational discovery was made.

The particulars may be given in the words of The Sussex Times:

A sensational affair has happened at Eastergate, which has caused great local excitement. It appears that a number of horses from Mr Alfred Knight's training establishment were proceeding along the road in the direction of the downs, when the leading horse, Master Hopmoon, shied at the figure of a man lying by the side of the road. It is by no means a strange thing to observe tramps sleeping out at this time of the year, but the remarkable fact about the present case was that the figure was that of a Chinaman. The boy cantered back to where Mr Knight and his head lad were riding, behind the exercising horses, and informed his master. Mr Knight immediately rode forward and, dismounting, examined the man. Apparently the Chinaman was sleeping. He was dressed in the costume of his country, and Mr Knight informed our representative that the man was evidently one of the labouring class of China.

As might be expected, the newcomer did not speak a word of English. He seemed dazed and terrified, and was with difficulty persuaded to accompany Mr Knight to the Eastergate Drill Hall, where temporary accommodation was found for him until the police were communicated with. Much greater difficulty was found in persuading him to get into the train at Barnham Junction, to accompany the police to Arundel. The man was in a condition of abject fright, jabbering and gesticulating as though he had never seen a railway train in his life. Fortunately, there lives in Arundel the Rev J. Wiggs, who has, until recently, been a missionary in China, and the rev. gentleman had no difficulty in conversing with the Celestial.

So much for The Sussex Times. It was after that memorable conversation with the Rev J. Wiggs that the story of the Chinaman acquired a larger value. No man in England read that interview with greater interest than Lord Dorrington. He read it in the The Morning News, and straightway took a train for London, and thence to Arundel.

'It is quite true, my lord,' said the Rev J. Wiggs, a little bewildered by the extraordinary experience of the previous day. 'I saw him as soon as he arrived. He is a Chinaman from the province of Yste-Yang; so far as I can make out he is a boatman. His story is so remarkable that my head whirls with it.'

'What is it?' demanded Lord Dorrington, not unprepared for the answer.

'Virtually he tells the same story as was told by the cowboy who was, as your lordship may know, discovered two days ago in the City of London.'

Lord Dorrington nodded.

'He says,' continued the returned missionary, 'that in the cool of the morning he was walking through a rice-field, in the direction of the village of Lung-tsi-lang, where he had made an appointment to meet a moneylender, who wished to marry his daughter. He had noticed, with fear, the apparition of the comet, and as he walked he faced that portion of the sky where the tail of the comet showed dimly. If anything, as he says, the comet was less brilliant than it had been. But on the horizon he observed a curious light. According to his account, it was a 'great wall of silver dust', which rose higher and higher, and became more and more brilliant, until, terrified by the apparition and by the almost blinding dazzle of the vision, he stopped, covering his face with his hands. He heard a whistling roar and lost consciousness, and the next thing that he knew was that he was lying on a soft, grass bank, and a foreign devil was talking to him in a strange tongue.'

Later, Dorrington saw the Chinaman, very sullen, and showing as much evidence of his fear as his natural imperturbability of countenance allowed.

Lord Dorrington returned to London to find a small crowd of reporters awaiting him at Victoria, to face innumerable cameras, and to answer a hundred questions.

'No,' he said, shaking his head, when questioned by the special representative of The Morning News, 'I am not in a position to give my theories as to the remarkable happenings of the past two days. I have my own ideas concerning them, but they are not sufficiently definite to give to the world. I intend bringing both men to Dorrington Castle, and, through an interpreter as far as the Chinaman is concerned, collect as much data as possible before these victims of astral phenomena are returned to their homes.'

'Do you think that these comet translations have occurred elsewhere?' demanded the reporter.

'I do,' replied his lordship. 'In a day or so, in a few hours perhaps, we shall have further manifestations of the comet's power.'

The newspapers had, by this time, reversed their attitude of amused scepticism, and awarded Lord Dorrington's statement the dignity of leaded type.

His prophecy, and the story of its fulfilment, appeared side by side, for, whilst his lordship had stood in the centre of the interrogating pressmen, the third, and, so far as can be ascertained, the last of the strange visitations, came.

The third was even more dramatic in its circumstances than were the others.

Dorrington had arrived at Victoria at 10 o'clock on the night of the 20th, which fell on a Saturday, and whilst he was giving his views on the phenomena with which all England was ringing, a curious scene was being enacted in one of the theatres.

The curtain had just gone up for the second act of Our Miss Gibbs, at the Gaiety, and the stage was filled with beautiful women, picturesquely grouped, when there entered from one of the wings a figure which brought the play to an immediate standstill, which left the very conductor petrified with upraised baton.

The figure was that of a man, of medium height and enormously stout. He was in evening dress, stained and dusty. His shirt front, in which glittered a huge diamond, was crumpled and grimy, and as he came waddling down the stage, rubbing his eyes and yawning, the immaculate chorus fell back on either side.

He looked around with a puzzled frown, and then addressed a question to the actor nearest to him.

'Señor,' said he, in the dialect of the Estremadura, 'will you, in the names of the blessed saints, inform me where I am?'

The actor, who did not understand a word of Spanish, shook his head, and glanced appealingly to the wings, and the curtain was rung down amidst some excitement.

This, indeed, was the third visitant!

José Sebastian Lopez, to give him the name by which he described himself, was a Brazilian, on a holiday visit to Spain. His story, inscribed in Lord Dorrington's neat handwriting, is not the least interesting of the memoranda on the men who were hit by the comet:

I am (says this document) a native of Brazil, although I cannot tell you what part of Brazil, for the time being, for I seem to have lost my memory. I arrived in Madrid on the night of the 16th, and stayed at the Hotel de Paris, on the Puerta del Sol. On the 17th, I believe, though I am not certain in my mind, I saw a man with whom I had some business relations. Who he was, or what was the nature of his business, I forget, but probably, when my head is less clouded, I shall recall the matter. The next day I spent in walking about Madrid. I have a dim idea that I went to the Prado, and that I spent some time admiring the old Spanish masters. In the evening I know that I dressed for dinner, and, the evening being a warm one, I went out without my overcoat, to the Casino. I left the Casino late. It must have been in the early hours of the morning but there were a number of people about and most of the cafés were open. I went up to my room and sat by the open window, smoking a cigar. It was then that over the houses, to the west side of the Puerta del Sol, I noticed a strange white light in the sky, resembling a pillar of white fire, which expanded in breadth visibly as I watched it. It grew broader and broader, and I pinched myself, thinking I must be dreaming. I sat with open mouth, paralysed, and the light grew fiercer and fiercer, till I felt it envelop me. I had no sensation of warmth, only a strange feeling of lightness, as though I could step through the window into the street below without hurt—and that was all I remember. When I awoke I found myself in a strange building. There was above me a skylight, which was open, and through which I must have fallen. I knew that I was in a theatre, for the curtain was raised, and the seats were all shrouded in holland, but I had no feeling of curiosity. All I wanted to do was sleep, sleep, sleep. I climbed over the orchestra on to the stage and wandered around, looking for a place in which to lie, for I was like a man drunk with sleep.

*

Lord Dorrington steadfastly refused to receive any reporters, although some of the best men journeyed down to High Dorrington to secure his views.

'The only thing I can say is this,' said his lordship to a select deputation, whose persistence had secured for themselves a short interview. 'I have, as you know, the three men here at Dorrington Castle. We are, through the instrumentality of interpreters, collecting and comparing everything they say bearing upon their transmigration. I can tell you this much, that their stories tally in every respect, but the full account of my investigations will be published at a very early date. The cowboy seems to have the most vivid recollection of all that happened, and I am certain that we have at last a manifestation of an occult mystery which will convince the most sceptical.'

Saying this, his lordship ushered the Pressmen from the room, and returned to his strange investigations.

We have not, unfortunately, the minutes of that inquisition, although it has been stated on most reliable authority that they covered reams of foolscap. We may guess that an irritated cowboy, a wondering but impassive Chinaman, and a most voluble gentleman from Mexico sat and suffered as Lord Dorrington, with the cold persistence of the enthusiast, extracted from them the particulars of their varying sensations.

It was the night of the reporters' visit that the fourth and the most inexplicable of the comet's vagaries was recorded. The three men, after a lengthy examination, had retired to their separate bedrooms, and Lord

Dorrington sat alone in his study, revising the notes he had made.

Engrossed in his labours, he did not regard time, and time, utterly independent of Lord Dorrington's patronage, moved ruthlessly forward.

Looking up, in a passionate attempt to find a synonym for 'extraordinary' and 'remarkable', his lordship was astounded to observe that the hands of the clock pointed to half-past two.

He put away his papers, locked them in his desk, lit his bedroom candle, and extinguished the light in the study. Then he made his way along the silent hall toward the big stairway that led to his sleeping suite.

Then, of a sudden, when he was half-way along the broad passage, there came a blinding white flash of flame. It leapt to him, and, as he staggered back, something struck him on the head, and he went to the floor like a log.

Some say that he was stunned, but others aver that it was blue funk that kept his lordship lying on the floor of the hall until an early-rising servant discovered him, and assisted him back to the study.

His first act—and here he showed the soul of the true scientist—was to send for the three men to compare their sensations with his.

There came no answer to the knockings of Lord Dorrington's hired servants. An examination of the rooms led to the discovery that the men were gone. Their beds had not been slept in; there was no sign of their presence.

Lord Dorrington stood before the door of the cowboy's room, a water compress about his head, wrapped in deep thought. The tremendous character of the new phenomenon impressed even him.

He returned to his study, and sent thirty-six telegrams to thirty-six different newspapers, but the wire was in every case the same.

> THREE ASTRAL VISITORS AGAIN TRANSMIGRATED.
> I MYSELF HAVE EXPERIENCED POWER OF COMET.
> SEND REPORTER.—DORRINGTON.

Long before the reporters could possibly respond to the invitation, a tall, clean-shaven man, with bushy eyebrows, came flying up to the great door of the Dorrington demesne, and demanded imperiously to see his lordship.

He spoke with a strong American accent, and, when ushered into Dorrington's presence, nodded curtly.

'You have come,' began my lord, 'to ask about the men—'

'One was a Chink,' interrupted the other rudely, 'one a Spanish fellow, one a tough from our side, I think?'

'That is so,' said Lord Dorrington gravely, 'but a phenomenon which—'

'Phenomenon nothing,' said the brusque stranger. 'They are the Denver three—the cleverest devils that ever held up a bank. Where are they?'

'Gone,' said his lordship, staring at the man.

'Gone!' roared the other. 'Oh, steaming Hades! Gone! See here,' he went on rapidly, 'I'm Torken, of Pinkerton's. I've got a warrant for the lot; they're bank robbers. We've been after them for a year. They're the people who impersonated the Chinese delegation last fall, and got away with the British ambassador's jewels—'

'Jewels?' repeated his lordship faintly.

'Jewels,' said the vigorous American.

Lord Dorrington, supported on the arm of the detective, led the way to the strongest strong-room in England.

Outwardly it appeared as though nothing unusual had occurred, but when his lordship had inserted his key he found the operation was unnecessary, for the door was unlocked and the Dorrington belt was gone.

The Forest of Happy Thoughts

BAILMAN made things snug for the night in his own characteristic fashion: walked round the tent; saw to the guide ropes; put his lantern over the strands of barbed-wire pegged firmly into the ground; carefully inspected his mosquito-net for signs of a stray musca; then turned his attention to the boys. They were squatting round their fire—a voluble, light-hearted assembly.

"Hast night your noise disturbed me," he said, as he passed them. "To-night, when the lo-koli sounds, you will sleep, and, if I be awakened, I will come with my whip, and you will feel great shame."

He spoke in the sonorous tongue of the Bo-mongo people, and, despite the awfulness of his threat, a titter of amusement ran round the circle. Bailman himself grinned into the darkness as he made his way down to the river, not that he would hesitate to use his chicotte upon a disobedient servant. He had too full an acquaintance with the Congo folk to be overmuch exercised at the necessity for employing the stick; but he grinned because twelve months in the wilds had made him half a savage, and he appreciated the humours of pain.

By the river side the little steamer was moored. There was a tiny bay here, and the swift currents of the river were broken to a gentle flow; none the less, he inspected the shore-ends of the wire hawsers before he crossed the narrow plank that led to the deck of the Zaire. The wood was stacked on the deck, ready for tomorrow's run. The new water-gauge had been put in by N'kema, the engineer, as he had ordered; the engines had been cleaned, and Bailman nodded approvingly. He stepped lightly over two or three sleeping forms curled up on the deck, and gained the shore. "Now I think I'll turn in," he muttered, and looked at his watch. It was nine o'clock. He stood for a moment on the crest of the steep bank, and stared back across the river. The night was black; but he saw the outlines of the forest on the other side. He saw the jewelled sky, and the pale reflection of stars in the water. Then he went to his tent, and leisurely got into his pyjamas. He jerked two tabloids from a tiny bottle, swallowed them, drank a glass of water, and thrust his head through the tent opening. "Ho, Sokani!" he called, speaking in the vernacular, "let the lo-koli sound!"

He went to bed.

He heard the rustle of men moving, the gurgles of laughter as his threat was repeated, and then the penetrating rattle of sticks on the native drum—a hollow tree trunk. Fiercely it beat—furiously, breathlessly, with now and then a deeper note as the drummer, using all his art, sent the message of sleep to the camp.

In one wild crescendo the lo-koli ceased, and Bailman turned with a sigh of content and closed his eyes... he sat up suddenly. He must have dozed; but he was wide awake now.

He listened, then slipped out of bed, pulling on his mosquito boots. Into the darkness of the night he stepped, and found N'kema, the engineer, waiting.

"You heard, master?" said the native.

"I heard," said Bailman with a puzzled face, "yet we are nowhere near a village."

He listened.

From the night came a hundred whispering noises, but above all these, unmistakable, the faint clatter of an answering drum. The white man frowned in his perplexity. "No village is nearer than the Bongindanga," he muttered, "not even a fishing village; the woods are deserted—"

The native held up a warning finger, and bent his head, listening. He was reading the message that the drum sent. Bailman waited; he knew the wonderful fact of this native telegraph, how it sent news through the trackless wilds. He could not understand it, no European could, but he had respect for its mystery.

"A white man is here," read the native; "he has the sickness."

"A white man!"

In the darkness Bailman's eyebrows rose incredulously.

"He is a foolish one," N'kema read; "he sits in the Forest of Happy Thoughts and will not move."

Bailman clicked his lips impatiently. "No white man would sit in the Forest of Happy Thoughts," he said, half to himself, "unless he were mad."

But the distant drum monotonously repeated the outrageous news. Here, indeed, in the heart of that loveliest glade in all Africa, encamped in the very centre of the Green Path of Death, was a white man, a sick white man... in the Forest of Happy Thoughts... a sick white man....

So the drum went on and on, till Bailman, rousing his own lo-koli man, sent an answer crashing along the river, and began to dress hurriedly.

In the forest lay a very sick man. He had chosen the site for the camp himself. It was in a clearing, near a little creek that wound between high elephant-grass to the river. Mainward chose it, just before the sickness came, because it was pretty. This was altogether an inadequate reason, but Mainward was a sentimentalist, and his life was a long record of choosing pretty camping places, irrespective of danger. "He was," said a newspaper, commenting on the crowning disaster which sent him a fugitive from justice to the wild lands of Africa, "overburdened with imagination." Mainward was cursed with ill-timed confidence; this was one of the reasons he chose to linger in that deadly strip of the Ituri which is clumsily named by the natives "The Lands-where-all-bad-thoughts-become-good-thoughts," and poetically adapted by explorers, and daring traders, as "The Forest of Happy Dreams." Over-confidence had generally been Mainward's undoing—over-confidence in the ability of his horses to win races; over-confidence in his own ability to secure money to hide his defalcations—he was a director of the Welshire County Bank once—over confidence in securing the love of a woman who, when the crash came, looked at him blankly and said she was sorry, but she had had no idea that he felt towards her like that....

Now Mainward lifted his aching head from the pillow and cursed aloud at the din. He was endowed with the smattering of pigeon-English which a man may acquire from a three months' sojourn, divided between Sierra Leone and Grand Bassam.

"Why for they make 'em cursed noise, eh?" he fretted. "You plenty fool-man, Abiboo."

"Si, senor," agreed the Kano boy calmly.

"Stop it, d'ye hear; stop it!" raved the man on the tumbled bed; "this noise is driving me mad—tell them to stop the drum."

The lo-koli stopped of its own accord, for the listeners in the sick man's camp had heard the faint answer from Bailman's.

"Come here, Abiboo—I want some milk: open a fresh tin; and tell the cook I want some soup, too."

The servant left him muttering and tossing from side to side on the creaking camp bedstead. Mainward had many things to think about. It was strange how they all clamoured for immediate attention; strange how they elbowed and fought one another in their noisy claims to his notice. Of course there was the bankruptcy and the discovery at the bank—it was very decent of that inspector fellow to give him the tip to clear out—and Ethel, and the horses, and—and...

The Valley of Happy Dreams! That would make a good story if Mainward could write, only, unfortunately, he could not write. He could sign things, sign his name "Three months after date pay to the order of—" he could sign other people's names... he groaned and winced at the thought.

But here was a forest where bad thoughts became good, and, God knows, his mind was ill-furnished. He wanted peace and sleep and happiness—he greatly desired happiness. Now suppose "Fairy Lane" had won the Wokingham Stakes? It did not, of course (he winced again at the bad memory), but suppose it had? Suppose he could have found a friend who would have lent him £16,000, or even if Ethel....

"Master," said Abiboo's voice "dem puck-a-puck, him lib for come."

"Eh, what's that?"

Mainward turned almost savagely on the man.

"Puck-a-puck—you hear 'um?"

But the sick man could not hear the smack of the Zaire's stern wheel, as the little boat breasted the downward rush of the river; he was surprised to see that it was dawn, and grudgingly admitted to himself that he had slept. He closed his eyes again and had a strange dream. The principal figure was a tall, tanned, clean-shaven man in a white helmet, who wore a dingy yellow overcoat over his pyjamas.

"How are you feeling?" said the stranger.

"Rotten bad," growled Mainward, "especially about Ethel; don't you think it was pretty low down of her to lead me on to believe that she was awfully fond of me, and then at the last minute to chuck me?"

"Shocking," said the strange white man gravely; "but put her out of your mind just now: she isn't worth troubling about What do you say to this?"

He held up a small greenish pellet between his forefinger and thumb, and Mainward laughed weakly.

"Oh, rot!" he chuckled faintly, "you're one of those Forest of the Happy Dreams johnnies; what's that? a love philter?" He was hysterically amused at the witticism.

Bailman nodded.

"Love or life, it's all one," he said, but apparently unamused, "swallow it."

Mainward giggled and obeyed.

"And now," said the stranger—this was six hours later—"the best thing you can do is to let my boys put you on my steamer and take you down river."

Mainward shook his head. He had awakened irritable and lamentably weak. "My dear chap, it's awfully kind of you to have come—by the way, I suppose you are a doctor?"

Bailman shook his head.

"On the contrary, I am a journalist," he said flippantly, "I'm Bailman, the special correspondent, of The Megaphone. I've been doing atrocities for a year—you know the stuff that is associated with the Congo—but you were saying?"

"I want to stay here—it's devilish pretty."

"Devilish is the very adjective I should have used—my dear man, this is the plague spot of the Congo; it's the home of every death-dealing fly and bug in Congo Land."

He waved his hand to the glorious vista of fresh green glades, of gorgeous creepers that hung their garlands from tree to tree.

"Look at the grass," he said; "it's homeland grass—that's the seductive part of it; I nearly camped here myself—come my friend, let me take you to my camp."

Mainward shook his head obstinately.

"I'm obliged, but I'll stay here for a day or so. I want to try the supernatural effects of this pleasant place," he said with a little smile. "I've got so many thoughts that need treatment."

"Look here," said Bailman roughly, "you know jolly well how this forest got its name; it is called Happy Dreams because it's impregnated with fever, and with every disease from beri-beri to sleeping sickness. You don't wake from the dreams that you dream here. Man, I know this country, and you're a new comer; you've trekked here because you wanted to get away from life and start all over again."

"I beg your pardon." Mainward's face flushed and he spoke a little stiffly.

"Oh, I know all about you—didn't I tell you I was a journalist? I was in England when things were going rocky with you, and I've read the rest in the papers I get from time to time. But all that is nothing to do with me. I'm here to help you to start fair. If you had wanted to commit suicide, why come to Africa to do it? Be sensible and shift your camp; I'll send my steamer back for your men—will you come?"

"No," said Mainward sulkily. "I don't want to, I'm not keen; besides, I'm not fit to travel."

Here was an argument which Bailman could not answer. He was none too sure upon that point himself, and he hesitated before he spoke again.

"Very well," he said at length, "suppose you stay another day to give you a chance to pull yourself together. I'll come along to-morrow with a tip top invalid chair for you—is it a bet?"

Mainward held out his shaking hand, and the ghost of a smile puckered the corners of his eyes. "It's a bet," he said.

He watched the journalist walk through the camp, speaking to one man after another in a strange tongue. A singular, masterful man this, thought Mainward. Would he have mastered Ethel? He watched the stranger with curious eyes, and noted how his own lazy devils of carriers jumped at his word....

"Good-night," said Bailman's voice, and Mainward looked up. "You must take another of these pellets, and tomorrow you'll be as fit as a donkey-engine. I've got to get back to my camp tonight, or I shall find half my stores stolen in the morning; but if you'd rather I stopped?"

"No, no," replied the other hastily. He wanted to be alone. He had lots of matters to settle with himself. There was the question of Ethel, for instance.

"You won't forget to take the tabloid?"

"No. I say, I'm awfully obliged to you for coming. You've been a good white citizen."

Bailman smiled. "Don't talk nonsense," he said, good-humouredly. "This is all brotherly love. White to white, and kin to kin, don't you know? We're all alone here, and there isn't a man of our colour within five hundred miles. Goodnight, and please take the tabloid—"

Mainward lay listening to the noise of the departure. He thought he heard a little bell tingle. That must be for the engines. Then he heard the puck-a-puck of the wheel—so that was how the steamer got its name.

Abiboo came with some milk. "You take um medicine, master?" he inquired.

"I take um," murmured Mainward; but the green tabloid was underneath his pillow.

Then there began to steal over him a curious sensation of content. He did not analyse it down to its first cause. He had had sufficient introspective exercise for one day. It came to him as a pleasing shock to realise that he was happy.

He opened his eyes and looked round. His bed was laid in the open, and he drew aside the curtains of his net to get a better view.

A little man was walking briskly toward him along the velvet stretch of grass that sloped down from the glade, and Mainward whistled.

"Atty," he gasped. "By all that's wonderful."

Atty, indeed, it was: the same wizened Atty as of yore; but no longer pulling the long face to which Mainward had been accustomed. The little man was in his white riding-breeches, his diminutive top-boots were splashed with mud, and on the crimson of his silk jacket there was evidence of a hard race. He touched his cap jerkily with his whip, and shifted the burden of the racing saddle he carried to his other arm,

"Why, Atty," said Main ward, with a smile, "what on earth are you doing here?"

"It's a short way to the jockeys' room, sir," said the little man. "I've just weighed in. I thought the Fairy would do it, sir, and she did."

Mainward nodded wisely. "I knew she would too," he said. "Did she give you a smooth ride?"

The jockey grinned again. "She never does that," he said, "but she ran gamely enough. Coming up out of the Dip, she hung a little, but I showed her the whip, and she came on as straight as a die. I thought once The Stalk would beat us—I got shut in, but I pulled her round, and we were never in difficulties. I could have won by ten lengths," said Atty.

"You could have won by ten lengths," repeated Mainward in wonder. "Well, you've done me a good turn, Atty. This win will get me out of one of the biggest holes that ever a reckless man tumbled into—I shall not forget you, Atty."

"I'm sure you won't, sir," said the little jockey gratefully; "if you'll excuse me now, sir?"

Mainward nodded and watched him as he moved quickly through the trees.

There were several figures in the glade now, and Mainward looked down ruefully at his soiled duck suit. "What an ass I was to come like this," he muttered in his annoyance. "I might have known that I should have met all these people."

There was one he did not wish to see; and as soon as he sighted Venn, with his shy eyes and his big nose, Mainward endeavoured to slip back out of observation. But Venn saw him, and came tumbling through the trees, with his big flabby hand extended and his dull eyes aglow,

"Hullo, hullo!" he grinned, "been looking for you."

Mainward muttered some inconsequent reply. "Rum place to find you, eh?" Venn removed his shining silk hat and mopped his brow with an awesome silk handkerchief.

"But look here, old feller—about that money."

"Don't worry, my dear man," Mainward interposed easily. "I can pay you now."

"That ain't what I mean," said the other impetuously; "a few hundred more or less docs not count. But you wanted a big sum—

"And you told me you'd see me—"

"I know, I know," Venn put in hastily; but that was before Kaffirs started jumpin'. Old feller, you can have it!"

He said this with grotesque emphasis, standing with his legs wide apart, his hat perched on the back of his head, his plump hands dramatically outstretched, and Mainward laughed outright.

"Sixteen thousand?" he asked.

"Or twenty," said the other impressively. "I want to show you—"

Somebody called him, and with a hurried apology he went blundering up the green slope, stopping and turning back to indulge in a little dumb show illustrative of his confidence in Mainward and his willingness to oblige.

Mainward was laughing, a low, gurgling laugh of pure enjoyment. Venn of all people! Venn, with his cursed questions and talk of securities. Well! well! Then his merriment ceased, and he winced again, and his heart beat faster and faster, and a curious weakness came over him.

How splendidly cool she looked.

She walked in the clearing, a white, slim figure: he heard the swish of her skirt as she came through the long grass... white, with a green belt all encrusted with dull gold embroidery. He took in every detail hungrily—the dangling gold ornaments that hung from her belt, the lace collar at her throat, the....

She did not hurry to him: that was not her way.

But her eyes dawned a gradual tenderness—those dear eyes that dropped before his shyly.

"Ethel!" he whispered, and dared to take her hand.

"Aren't you wonderfully surprised?" she said.

"Ethel! here!"

"I—I had to come."

She would not look at him, but he saw the pink in her cheek and heard the faltering voice with a wild hope. "I behaved so badly dear—so very badly."

She hung her head.

"Dear! dear!" he muttered, and groped toward her like a blind man.

She was in his arms, crushed against his breast, the perfume of her presence in his brain.

"I had to come to you—" Her hot cheek was against his. "I love you so."

"Me—love me? Do you mean it?" He was tremulous with happiness, and his voice broke—"dearest."

Her face was upturned to his, her lips so near; he felt her heart beating as furiously as his own. He kissed her—her lips, her eyes, her dear hair....

"O God, I'm happy," he sobbed, "so—so happy...."

Bail man sprang ashore just as the sun was rising, and came thoughtfully through the undergrowth to the camp. Abiboo, squatting by the curtained bed, did not rise. Bailman walked to the bed, pulled aside the mosquito netting and bent over the man who lay there.

Then he drew the curtains again, lit his pipe slowly, and looked down at Abiboo.

"When did he die?" he asked.

"In the dark of the morning, master," said the native.

Bailman nodded slowly. "Why did you not send for me?"

For a moment the squatting figure made no reply, then he rose and stretched himself.

"Master," he said, speaking in Swaheli—that is a language which allows of nice distinctions—"this white man was happy; he walked in the Forest of Happy Thoughts: why should I call him back to a land where there was neither sunshine nor happiness, but only night and the pain of sickness?"

"You're a philosopher," said Bailman irritably.

"I am a follower of the Prophet," said Abiboo, the Kano boy; "and all things are according to God's wisdom."

A Raid on a Gambling Hell

I HAVE had to deal with all classes of society, high and low, rich and poor, and number amongst clients several millionaires, crooks, peers and peeresses, and servant girls. It is my boast that nothing surprises me, yet I must confess feeling a mild tinge of excitement at receiving, on the letter-head of the Ministry of the Interior, a request that I would call at eleven o'clock upon

Mr. George Tresham, the Minister in question.

The Right Honourable George Tresham was a name to conjure with on the day I received that summons. A comparatively young man who had won his way to the foremost Cabinet rank by sheer ability and courage, he had as solid a following as any Minister in the House.

'I have sent for you, Dixon,' he said, 'on a very delicate private matter. A matter,' he went on, 'which affects my personal honour—indeed, affects my whole future career.'

Motioning me to a chair, he began the narrative which is set down below. Of course, I am not giving the real names of persons and places.

George Tresham, in addition to being a popular statesman, was something of a man about town. He had a host of friends, mostly younger than himself, and his interest in the theatre had extended to the writing of a four-act drama, which had been produced with moderate success in the West End. It was during his brief incursion into the realms of dramatic authorship that he made the acquaintance of Bart Philipson—the Honourable Bartholomew Philipson—who, at the time this narrative was told me, had succeeded to his father's very small and very heavily encumbered estate as Lord Colesun.

Bart Philipson, as he was then, had an interest in the theatre wherein Mr. Tresham's play was produced.

The two became fast friends, for George Tresham was a large-hearted, lovable soul, who was attracted rather than repelled by the other's cynicism and worldliness. Tresham was, of course, enormously wealthy.

The two friends were talking at their club one night, and the conversation drifted round to gambling hells. Bart gave a very vivid word-picture of one he had visited in London, and Tresham expressed his surprise that such places existed, and also asked his friend to take him to see one some night.

About a month later, on a Thursday evening, when Tresham had finished his solitary dinner, the telephone bell rang, and his butler told him that Lord Colesun was on the telephone.

'I say,' said Bart's voice, 'are you still keen on seeing one of those places we were speaking about the other night?'

'Rather!' said Tresham, who was bored, and welcomed any diversion.

'Well, there's a new place opened in Montacute Square,' said Bart's voice. 'I don't know very much about it, except that I've got the password and the right of entrée for a friend. I am told it is unique in many respects.'

'All right. I'll come along.'

Tresham ordered his car, picked up Bart, and dismissed the car at the corner of Montacute Square. The two walked on. It was a foggy night, but Bart knew the way.

'Here we are,' he said, and, ascending a short flight of broad steps, he knocked in a peculiar manner on the door.

It was opened by a servant in quiet livery, and after a glance at Bart the two were passed into a hall which was dimly lighted and escorted up a stairway to a landing above. A pair of folding doors confronted them. On this the servant knocked. The door opened a few inches, and a keen eye scrutinised the pair.

'All right; come in, gentlemen,' said the owner of the eye, and they were admitted into a large saloon, blazing with light and richly furnished.

But it was not the appointments which made Tresham stare. It was not even the green table in the centre of the room, around which a dozen men were playing. It was the other questionable occupants. Men and women, the latter in wildly extravagant costumes, were sitting at little tables, taking no notice of the players. They all had the appearance of being under the influence of drink, and very far under at that.

'How perfectly beastly!' Tresham said. 'A perfect saturnalia! Let us get out of this, Bart.'

'I quite agree,' said the phlegmatic Lord Colesun. He was turning to the door, when it burst open, and a wild-eyed servant dashed in.

'The police! The police!' he gasped, and had hardly got the words out of his mouth when two or three policemen burst into the room after an inspector, and were followed by a dozen men in plain clothes. Immediately began a stampede, a kicking over of tables, a screaming of women, a shouting of men. Somebody cried, 'Put out the lights.' One man attempted to unshutter the window, and was pulled back by a constable, and in the end the inspector made his voice heard.

'Ladies and gentlemen,' he said, 'you will all consider yourselves under arrest. I shall take you to Bow Street Police Station.'

'My God! What shall I do?' said Tresham. 'It is ruin, Bart.'

'Keep quiet,' said Bart in a low voice. 'I'll see what I can do.'

He went across to the inspector, and at first the officer would have nothing to say to him. Then Bart said something in a low voice, and the two men stepped aside into a corner of the room, and for a few moments conversed together. Presently Bart strode back to Tresham.

'A policeman will take us out of the door,' he said. 'I've squared him.'

A constable approached and the two men were pushed unceremoniously on to the hall landing and escorted down the stairs.

'All right,' said Bart to the constable and slipped something into his hand.

'Hold hard, sir,' said the policeman, 'I seem to know that gentleman's face.'

'Never mind what you know,' said Bart.

'It's all right, sir. I hope there's no offence,' said the policeman, 'but if that isn't Mr. Tresham, I'm a Dutchman.'

Tresham looked at the man, but could not see his face. He noted, however, that one of his front teeth was broken. In a few moments they were out in the street, Bart cursing himself for having led his friend into such a mess. Tresham stopped him.

'Don't be a fool, Bart,' he said, 'it was my own stupid curiosity which is entirely responsible. What did you say to the inspector fellow?'

'I said a thousand pounds,' said Bart briefly, 'It was the only argument I could think of.'

'Of course I'll pay that,' said Tresham. 'In fact, it's cheap at the price. What about that infernal policeman? Do you think he'll talk?'

'I'll have to go back and see him,' said Bart. 'Otherwise, I don't think there's anybody there who recognised you, not even the inspector.'

George Tresham got home at 11.30, spent a restless night, and when, passing along Whitehall the next afternoon, he saw on the newspaper placards the announcement of a gambling raid, his heart beat faster. Fortunately it was scrappy, merely mentioning the fact that a raid had been made on a house in Montacute Square, that a certain number of people had been arrested, the proprietor had been fined and imprisoned, and that two servants who assisted in the conduct of the house had also been sent to prison. There was no mention of the unpleasant things he had seen; and that afternoon, when Bart came by appointment, the reason was explained.

'I saw the inspector again this morning,' he said, 'and I asked him to keep that part of it quiet, in case it ever came out that I was there. But I'm afraid we're going to have trouble with the policeman,' he went on, shaking his head. 'He's a man named Bowker, a shrewd and unscrupulous fellow, who has been in trouble before, and apparently has already announced his intention of resigning from the force to live upon a private income.'

'What does he mean by that?'

'He means you are the private income, I am afraid.' said Bart grimly.

'Blackmail?' demanded Tresham.

'That's what it amounts to,' said Bart.

'This is dreadful,' said Tresham with a despairing gesture. 'Have you seen this policeman?'

'That's what it amounts to,' said Bart.

'I've just come from him,' said Bart. 'I've found his address—he lives in Bayswater—and made a call. As I feared, he intends making us pay.'

'Did he mention a figure?'

'He did,' said Bart. 'He asked for fifty thousand pounds!'

'Fifty thousand pounds!' Even Tresham was startled.

'Seventy really,' said Bart. 'Fifty from you and twenty from me. Heaven knows where I'm going to get my twenty from.'

Tresham thought for a while.

'When does he want his answer?' he demanded.

'Tomorrow evening at the latest,' said Lord Colesun. 'I have an appointment to meet him on Hammersmith Broadway.'

It was after his friend's departure that Mr. Tresham sat down and wrote the letter that brought me to his study.

I listened in silence and sympathy to the narrative.

'Have you told Lord Colesun that you have sent for me?' I asked.

He shook his head.

'No,' he replied; 'but, of course, I shall tell him.'

'I would rather you didn't,' said I. 'I prefer working under one pair of eyes and with only one set of theories to combat.'

'Namely, mine?' he smiled faintly.

'Namely, yours, sir,' I said. 'You can afford to pay fifty thousand pounds, although I don't suppose anybody can afford to part with such an enormous sum. But Lord Colesun—is it humanly possible that he can pay?'

The Minister shook his head.

'Did he give you the address of the policeman?' I asked.

'No; it is somewhere in Bayswater, but he is meeting him tonight at Hammersmith. You will have to work with Lord Colesun, because he knows the man, and will be able to introduce you if necessary,' he said.

'What do you want me to do?' I asked.

The Minister hesitated.

'Well, I hardly know, except that I should like you to see the fellow and beat his price down. Maybe you could scare him?'*

I shook my head.

'That kind of man isn't easily scared,' said I. 'He is evidently a thoroughly bad lot, and, being a policeman or an ex-policeman, as he will be in a day or two, he knows the law just as well as I, and he would be a difficult man to bluff. Now, if you'll be advised by me, Mr. Tresham, you will not say a word to Lord Colesun as to having seen or employed me.'

'But what can you do?' he asked. 'You do not even know the policeman's address.'

'I'll make a few inquiries which will help me to clear up the mystery of the drunken people.'

'Mystery?' he said. 'There was no mystery about it; they were there.'

'Exactly,' said I with a smile: 'but that is the mystery. Don't you realise, Mr.

Tresham, that in gaming houses drunkenness is as rare as at a revival meeting?'

I thereupon left him and pursued my investigation.

Scotland Yard very kindly gave me a few particulars, and the Home Office the necessary permission to see the proprietor of the raided gambling-house. He was in Wandsworth Gaol, and to Wandsworth I drove, handed in my order, and was taken to where a stout, elderly man sat on the edge of his seat.

'I want to talk to you about this raid of yours,' said I. 'How did they come to catch you?'

'How? Why, I was given away,' he said vehemently, 'and what's more, I know the man that gave me away.'

'Who was it?' I asked.

'You find out,' he snapped. 'I name no names; I keep my opinions to myself. I was running one of the quietest, best-conducted little joints in London, and it's a shame they couldn't leave me alone.'

'I like your idea of well-conducted little joints,' said I, and in a few brief words I gave him my own opinion of the class of establishment he kept.

'That's a lie,' he said. 'If there were a lot of lushers lying about don't you think the police would have brought it out?

'Anyway, I'm glad they raided me when they did, if they were going to raid at all,' he went on. 'If they'd come a couple of hours later we should have been in full swing. As it was, they caught a few. The police messed it, as they mess everything. Fancy raiding a gaming house at half-past nine at night!' he said contemptuously. 'You're a split, aren't you?'

'I am a sort of detective,' I admitted.

'Well, don't think I've got anything against the police, because I haven't,' he said. 'Inspector Ericson was decent to me, and I don't suppose he'd have raided me, if that swine hadn't given me away. I'll "Bart" him when I come out.'

'What name was that?' I said quickly.

'Never mind,' he replied evasively, and try as I did, he could not be induced to say any more.

Now, Inspector Ericson is one of the straightest men in London. No Robespierre was more incorruptible. He was certainly not the kind of man who would accept a thousand pounds to allow a detected gambler to go scot free.

Ericson was not at the station when I called, and I took the liberty of driving over to his house, and found him preparing to go on night duty.

'I wanted to see you, inspector, about the raid you made the other night.'

'Oh, did you?' he said, with his hard little smile.

'When you made the raid why did you choose half-past nine?'

'Well, the raid was made in accordance with instructions we received from headquarters. The gentleman who gave the house away told us that at half-past nine it was crowded, and, what's more, he had arranged with the doorkeeper to let us in at that hour.'

'Another question, Ericson. When you made the raid, did anybody offer you a thousand pounds to let them out?'

'I think not. Otherwise it would have been as good as paying me to put them in!' he said.

'I happen to know,' said I, 'that the gentleman who gave you the information which led to the raid was Lord Colesun.'

'You do, do you?' said he. 'Ah, well, you know a lot!'

'Well, I won't ask you whether it was he or somebody else,' said I. 'But tell me this—was your informant present when the raid was made?'

'I can answer you very emphatically that he was not,' replied Ericson.

'Just one more question, Inspector. Do you know whether there are any other gambling houses in Montacute Square?'

'I can tell you that there are not,' said the inspector, 'it is funny you should ask that. It was the same question asked by one of my detective-sergeants who was watching the place we raided. He reported that a lot of people had gone in to No. 27. The house we raided was No.43, farther along. He went over to make an inquiry, but found there was a fancy-dress ball on or something. In fact, he mistook a dressed-up policeman, as he thought, who was going into the house as a real one.'

'Thank you, that's all I want to know,' said I, and went back to the office to get the report of my assistants, who had spent that afternoon making inquiries in knowledgeable circles in the city.

Their reports were very satisfactory from my point of view, and I was in the midst of reading them when Mr. Tresham rang through and asked me to come and see him.

'I hope I haven't annoyed you, Mr. Dixon, but I have had to tell Lord Colesun. I thought it was hardly fair to him. Will you come over?'

'Is he with you?' I asked.

'He is with me now.'

I gathered up the reports and read the last two on my way to Whitehall. Lord Colesun I had not met before.

He shook hands with me warmly on my introduction.

'Glad to meet you, Mr. Dixon. I have heard about you, and I am extremely glad that my friend Mr. Tresham has called you in. I was a little ratty when I heard in the first place, but since then I agree that it was wise to take professional advice. Mr. Tresham and I have been talking the matter over, and we have decided that the best thing to do is to pay this infernal policeman and let the matter rest.'

'I think it is the best thing to do,' broke in Mr. Tresham. 'I did have a wild idea that it would be better if you met the policeman, but on consideration I have decided that Bart—Lord Colesun—should carry the thing through himself.'

'I never expected to meet this policeman,' said I. 'At least, not in his role as a policeman. You said, Mr. Tresham, that although you did not see the policeman's face you noticed that he had one of his front teeth broken.'

Mr. Tresham nodded. I turned to Lord Colesun.

'May I ask you,' I said, 'if you know any person who has a front tooth broken?'

'I probably know several. I don't notice the teeth of policemen, however.'

'I am not talking about policemen,' I insisted. 'Do you know any other person with a broken front tooth?'

I had seen the young man's face change, and now he picked up his hat from a settee and walked towards the door.

'I'd like you to excuse me for a little while; I'm not feeling very well,' he said in a low voice.

'Wait!' said I, 'I have to finish my story.'

'Then you'll finish it alone,' snarled the man at the door, and went out, slamming it behind him.

The Minister looked at me in bewilderment.

'What does it all mean.'

'It means this,' said I. 'Your friend Lord Colesun has for months been on the verge of bankruptcy. Moreover, he has been taking funds from a company with which he is connected, which must be made good by tomorrow morning.'

'Good God! You don't suggest—' he began.

'I suggest that the gambling hell and the supposed police raid were got up for your special benefit. The gamblers and the police were members of a provincial touring company, who were brought to London to play their part by Lord Colesun, who told them that he was having a joke on one of his friends. The house was hired furnished—'

'But why the drunkenness?' asked Mr. Tresham.

'That was intended to make you all the more disgusted and all the more anxious to keep your name out of the case. To make the deception seem more real, your friend arranged for a gaming club, which undoubtedly existed in Montacute Square, to be raided the same night—as a matter of fact, an hour and a half before the sham raid was made. The policeman with the broken tooth was Lord Colesun's valet.'

'Then you suggest,' said Mr. Tresham in a low voice, 'that Bart was blackmailing me, and that the fifty thousand pounds was for himself?'

'I not only suggest that, but I advance it as a fact,' said I. 'The valet is a man who has been hand-in-glove with his Lordship in every dirty piece of business in which he has been engaged. Your friend arranged for a raid on a genuine gaming club in order that you should be able to read something in the next day's paper. The sham police who "raided" were in one of the rooms downstairs waiting until you were safely inside the saloon.'

The Minister sat at his desk, his head on his hands. At last he rose.

'Well, Mr. Dixon,' he said with a smile, 'you have saved me fifty thousand pounds, but you have cost me a very dear illusion.'

'You will not prosecute, of course?' said I.

He shook his head.

'If there is any of his father's spirit in the man, there will be no necessity for a prosecution,' he said quietly.

Tresham was right as it happened, for the first announcement I read when I opened my paper the following morning was that Lord Colesun had shot himself.

The Devil Light

I

Some men have an aversion to cats, others shrink back in horror from a third floor window and fight desperately to overcome the temptation to throw themselves into the street below. For others the mirror holds a devil who leers a man on to self-destruction. But for Hans Richter that cruel and puzzling light which he interpreted into E Flat held all that there was of threat and fear.

If you say that the obsession of little Hans savoured of madness, tell me something of yourself. Squeak a knife-edge along a plate, or knife-edge against knife-edge and watch the people shudder and grimace. They also are mad of the same madness. Some men and women grow frantic at the rustle of silk; others may not pass their palms over certain surfaces (such as plush or velvet) without a shivering fit. Exactly why, nobody knows.

There are undreamt of horrors in commonplace objects for some of us—Hans Richter had the advantage of hating and fearing that which was not commonplace.

He played second violin at the Hippoleum. He had little spare time with a daily matinée and a twelve o'clock rehearsal every Monday, but he utilized that spare time with great profit, being a most earnest student of colour values, and, moreover, a worshipper of heroes.

You had no doubt as to what manner of heroes qualified for his adoration. Nature had built him short and clumsy, with a pink, round face and blue eyes. She had built him cheap as a builder runs up a cottage out of the material left over from a more pretentious job.

'Well buttressed, but poorly thatched,' he described himself, and indeed the great Dame had been mean in the matter of head-covering, for his hair, sandy and fine, was in a quantity less than was necessary. His moustaches were mere wisps, but in the shape to which he trained them you read his mind, his faith and his pride.

He was a gentle soul, with strange and unusual views on lights, and a certain pride in his intimate knowledge of London. It was his boast that there was not a street in the metropolitan area which he had not visited, not a historic monument upon which he could not enlarge at length; and once on a more than ordinarily poisonous night of fog he had led Sam Burns by the hand from Holborn Town-Hall to Paddington Station, and never bungled a single crossing, never so much as mistook the entrance of a blind alley, though the fog was so thick that Sam could neither see his guide nor the pavement under his feet.

Oh, no, he was no spy—he hated the Prussian, as so many Bavarians did before the war (he was from Nurnberg). He was German all through, but neither favoured bureaucracy nor militarism.

They lived together, this curious pair, in a tiny house off Church Street, Paddington—in a neighbourhood of strange smells and of Sunday morning markets. Sam Burns was 'Mr Burns' in law, and entitled (did they but know it) to the respectful salute of policemen, for he was a naval gunner on the reserve of officers, and held the King's warrant.

They had one quality in common—that they were simple men — and because of this No 43 Bebchurch Street was a haven of peace.

For Sam directed such casual help as he could secure in his best quarter-deck manner, had a gift for spying out untidy corners and hurried scrubbings, a vigilance which earned for him the hatred and slander of the charladies of Paddington, and resulted in a constant melancholy procession of new servants.

They sat together by an open window on a Sunday evening in June 1914, taking the air. Sam's lean red face was one great scowl, for he was reading a thrilling murder case—facial contortion was part of the process of his reading.

'Murder's a curious thing,' he said at last, setting the paper down on his knee. 'I've killed men in my time—natives and that sort of thing—but always in what I might term the heat of battle. I wonder how it feels?'

Hans turned his mild face to the other and stared through his gold-rimmed glasses.

'Herr Gott!' he said. 'That you should talk about such subjects, Sam—who could think of murder on such a night? It is a night for thought—exalted thought!'

He stopped suddenly, pursing his lips and looking thoughtfully out of the open window, and upward to the patch of western sky which showed above the mean housetops.

'G minor,' he said abstractedly, and Sam grinned.

'You're mad on lights, Hans!" he chuckled. 'G minor!—what the dickens is G minor?'

Without turning his head or relinquishing his gaze the musician whistled a soft sweet note sustained, and full of sorrow.

Sam frowned.

'I'm beginning to see,' he admitted, 'yes—that's the kind of light it is. You're a crank on lights, Hans—'

The other swung round in his chair and reached for his violin and bow that lay on the table near him. He drew the bow across the muted strings and a gloomy stream of thick sound filled the little room.

'Purple,' he said, and played another long note—a joyous blatant note of arrogant triumph.

'Scarlet,' he smiled, and put the instrument back.

'Lights are horrible or beautiful—terrifying or adorable – listen.'

He seized the instrument again and sent the bow rasping across the strings.

'For God's sake don't make that infernal noise!' growled Sam shifting uneasily, for the note shrill and menacing carried terror in its volume.

Hans had the instrument on his knees. His lids were narrowed, his plump jaw outthrust.

'That is white light—the devil's light—cruel and searching. It stares and shrieks at me. There is a beckoning devil in that light. You see it on the stage—I have seen it a hundred times. It strips young girls of their modesty, it reveals the lie, it mocks the passé. You can see them staring at it—blinded and yet staring, their white teeth glittering, their red lips smiling like children smile when they are in pain—it is the light of war, and cruelty and suffering—phew!'

He flung the violin away and mopped his damp forehead with a big green handkerchief.

Sam rose from his window chair slowly.

'Hans, you're a fool,' he said, 'and I'm going to put a B major match to the A flat lamp.'

Hans laughed and rose too with the remark:

'And I'm going to a ten o'clock rehearsal—the show opens to-morrow—Gott! It is a quarter to ten already!'

*

It was not a happy rehearsal for the little German. There was a new American producer at the Hippoleum, a burly man in a grey sweater, who was quick to wrath, and had a wealth of unpleasant language.

In the third scene the lights went wrong. Four specially erected electric projectors had been fixed in the gallery, and on a certain chord, at the end of a song number, they had to concentrate upon the principal, who was singing. And they just didn't. One wandered off to the second entrance. One wavered undecidedly too far up stage, and the other two did not appear at all.

'Say, what's the matter with you?' exploded the producer. 'Are you crazy up there? Is this a joke?'

He said other sarcastic things, and said them through a megaphone, which somehow made them worse.

A hollow and apologetic voice answered from the deserted gallery.

'Put all your lines down—now put 'em on the proscenium arch—now put 'em all together up stage—now put 'em on the bald-headed fiddler in the orchestra—'

There was a gentle titter of laughter from the weary chorus—but it was short-lived.

The bald-headed fiddler was standing up facing the light, his face distorted with rage, his wild eyes glaring like a trapped animal, as his clawing hands flung out at the light.

A torrent of words, German and English, poured from his twisted mouth.

'Take it off! Take it off! Take it off!' he screamed.

There was an instant and a painful pause. The lights dimmed and an outraged producer strode down the central aisle of the theatre and confronted the second violin.

'For the lord's sake!' he said, mildly enough, 'have you gone mad, mister?'

The little man, one trembling hand curved about the orchestra rail, shook his head. He was very white, and the American, a judge of men, and kindly enough out of business hours, dropped his big hand on the other's shoulder.

'You go right along home and have a sleep, son,' he said gently; 'don't you worry—go right along home.'

'It's the light, sir,' faltered Hans, and blinked fearfully up at the gallery. I do not like the light—'

'Sure!' soothed the other; 'now you go right away and have a rest — there's nothin' comin' to you, son—on the square. I get just crazy like that myself.'

Hans did not lose his job—he played second fiddle on the opening night of that brilliant success, There You Are, Bunny! and would have gone on playing through the inevitable run but for certain great happenings in Europe. A prince of an Imperial house was killed, and when the message came to six chancelleries six separate and distinct ministers demanded of their war offices, 'How soon can you mobilize?'

Hans did not know this, but later he was to have misgivings.

'I must go home,' he said doggedly. 'I am too old to be of any use – but who knows?'

He looked wistfully at the red-faced Mr Burns, who sprawled across the table gloating over a newspaper chart which showed the relative proportions of the world's fleets.

Sam looked up.

'They'll want me,' he said with quiet satisfaction. 'My old captain will hoist his flag—he's vice admiral now—and he promised me that if ever there was a kick-up he'd take me. Who made the Penelope the best gunnery ship in the home fleet? Me, Hans!'

He thumped his thick chest and his eyes were puckered with proud laughter.

'I'm not too old for sea-going, but if I am there are lots of jobs for a man who ain't too old to spot a damned—'

He stopped in confusion. The eyes of Hans were set and the dominant expression in those eyes was envy.

'Gott!' he said with a sigh, 'I am no good—I hate war – it is terrible to think about—it is like the white light, a devil! But I must go back. Perhaps I may take the place of one—if He wants me!'

He left the next day—an exhilarating day for Mr Burns, for he had received a notification that 'my lords of the Admiralty' had accepted his offer of service.

Hans, with his brown ulster and his aged violin, came, packed his cheap gripsack and two brown paper parcels, paid his share of the expenses which were current, and went off in a taxicab.

'Good-by, Sam.'

'Good-by, Hans—good luck!'

The little man's grief was undisguised.

'I shall think of you—as a soft golden light, Sam,' he choked.

'That's right,' replied his less imaginative friend, 'yellow for me, Hans.'

Poor old Hans! So thought Mr Gunner Burns with a sigh...anyway, they weren't likely to meet. The little musician would scarcely be found amongst the ships' companies which the marksmanship of Gunner Burns foredoomed to destruction.

So passed Hans, and as for Sam, after a spell at Whale Island teaching the young and impetuous naval marksman how to shoot, he came back to Somewhere in England to more important duties.

II

There was a noise like the roll of a trap drum—an even 'br-r-r-r' of sound.

Gunner Burns standing in the darkness, dropped his head sideways and listened.

It was faint at first, but grew louder with every second that passed, and the noise came from the air.

Sam peered over the parapet in a swift, keen scrutiny of the sector south of the position. Somewhere beyond the inky belt of darkness which blotted out the nearest features of the landscape was London—London the vast and wealthy, a gigantic, flat hive buzzing and droning, unconscious of the danger.

As the watcher looked he pressed the electric button which was fixed to the wall near his hand, and almost instantly a second figure joined him.

The trap drum noise was now loud and angry, and the men craned their necks and searched the skies through their night glasses.

'There she is, sir!' said Sam in a low voice, 'the biggest they've got ... '

The officer at his side had his glasses on the lean shape that blotted no more than two or three stars at a time.

'What's her range?' he asked with the regret in his voice of one who anticipates an answer which will dash his hopes.

'Three or four thousand yards—shall I light her up?'

The other's hands had closed on the telephone receiver in the little recess beneath the parapet.

' 'Lo—that you, Shepherds Bush? Zep coming over, I'm going to light her up—no, only one as far as I can see. She'll start circling in a minute, looking for the small-arms factory as usual...Right!'

He turned to the man at his side with a grunted order. Something hissed and spluttered. Little bubbles of light outlined a big barrel shape somewhere in the rear of where he stood, and there leaped into the air a solid white beam of dazzling light which moved restlessly from side to side till it settled on something which looked for all the world like a silver cigar.

'She's just beyond range—but give her one for herself, Burns,' said the young officer. 'She's turning!'

The deafening crash of a gun woke the still night—a drift of smoke passed between the observer and his objective. As it cleared a tiny point of vivid light flicked and faded beneath the big silver cigar.

'Five hundred yards short,' was the bitter comment.

'She'll take some hitting! Keep the light on her—Shepherds Bush will pick her up in a minute...'

WHOOM!

The shock and pulsation of the explosion came to them. The trees rustled as though they had been stirred by a gust of wind, and the concrete parapet under the officer's hands trembled and shook again.

The old gunner at his side drew a sharp breath.

'Addlestone—that is!' he said. 'Fancy Addlestone! Good God, it doesn't seem real, does it? Why, when I was a kid I went to school at Addlestone...'

Another report followed, fainter than the first, and then over toward Addlestone came a red glow in the sky, a glow which gathered in brightness until it was almost golden.

'Them thermite bombs are pretty useful,' said the gunner with reluctant admiration. 'Hot! You can't get near a fire that's been started by one of them. I've seen men and women roasted to death by 'em, and they never knew what killed 'em. There's Shepherds Bush, sir!'

From the south two white beams had shot into the air and focused instantly on the fast moving cigar. She turned to the westward, and the lights followed. She moved in one majestic sweep to the east—but the lights did not leave her. They were the two great eyes of the dark world staring their wrath at the night bird.

'She wants that cloud dam' badly,' said the young naval officer. 'Put your light over the cloud—yes, it's big enough.'

He took up the telephone.

' 'Lo, Shepherds Bush...She's going for the cloud on the left. She's about level—no, I can't keep her lit up for much longer—she's getting beyond my range.'

The sky shape was now blurred and indistinct, for it had reached the misty edges of the cloud—in ten seconds it had disappeared. But now flashed into the air not two but a dozen searching eyes. They grew from the dark void beyond the hillcrest to the south, slender white spokes of light that criss-crossed incessantly. The cloud glowed yellow where the beam came to a dead end, and once it sparkled at a dozen points, For all the world, as Gunner Burns said, as if some one were striking a match along its under surface and had done no more than raise a shower of sparks.

'Shrapnel,' said the old authority approvingly; 'that'll rattle her a bit. Nothing like a nearby shell burst to make you take your eyes from the compass—there she is!'

Out she came from the same cloud-wall into which she had dived – into the gleam and glare of the searchlights. Left and right, beneath and at the side of her the light splashes came and went. They were as soft and as sudden as the glow the fireflies make.

The great machine turned again, her nose rose slowly into the air and her tail went down. The watchers could see the cloud of oily smoke at the stern as her speed increased.

'She's got to climb for it, and climb quick,' said the gunner.

A quick fan of light leapt up from the ground over by Golders Green. WHOOM!

'A keepsake,' said the lieutenant grimly.

The telephone bell tinkled and an urgent voice demanded his immediate attention.

'She's going back to you, Carter—keep your light on her. She's twelve thousand seven hundred feet up and rising—shoot her off or she'll give you hell!'

'Ay, ay, sir!' the officer swung round. 'Light her up!'

Again the searchlight stabbed the dark, and again the cigar floated in a halo of soft radiance.

Then from the north came a new sound. It was not the 'br-r-r-r' they had heard before, but a purring note—a far-off motorcycle could reproduce the gentle din.

High above, the merest midgets in the vast space of starlit sky, three specks of earth-dust moved slowly across the field of the watchers' vision, and as they moved, in the limitless dome of the heavens a red ball of light lived and died. The young officer sought the telephone.

'Three aeroplanes up—they have signalled "shut down searchlights,"' he called breathlessly.

Two seconds passed, and then, as though one hand controlled the light shafts that swept the skies, they vanished.

They waited in the dark. The never-ceasing roar of the Zeppelin engines neither increased nor grew fainter. She was cruising laterally for some reason—the Golders Green telephone explained.

'We've hit her, sir—first or second compartment. Think one of her fore tractor screws is out of action...Yes, she got near us, but now she's drifting your way.'

'Her fourth visit,' said Sam.

'And every time she's gone straight to the place she wanted to reach,' added the officer with an impatient and wondering little 'ch'k' of his tongue. 'That fellow must know London like a book—he must know it blind to pick out his target with all the lights shaded and faked.'

Sam nodded and thought of a certain Hans Richter.

Poor old Hans! Fancy making Hans the focus of ten three-thousand candle-power searchlights! Sam grinned in the darkness.

Three...four...five minutes passed, then from the sky shot a thin beam of light that seemed from the viewpoint of the gun position to be aimed horizontally from the airship.

'Got her blinders on,' commented Sam. 'Aeroplanes are up to her level—there they are! Right ahead of her! They can do nothing with the light in their faces. She'll climb if she ain't climbing already.'

Another minute passed. Then a speck of red fire appeared in the black heavens, another red followed and then a green.

'Aeroplanes coming down—she's blinded 'em,' he said rapidly. 'Stand by to light her up—keep 'em off the aeroplanes...Now!'

From every point of the horizon the beams sprang until the sky was a thick jungle of converging light stalks. They beat fiercely, remorselessly, upon the big cigar as she zigzagged her way to safety and the north-west.

A thousand feet above the guns the landing lights of an aeroplane burnt blue, and the great bird swooped to earth. They ran out to him as the guns of Golders Green began a frantic bombardment of the disappearing Zeppelin.

It was Burns who helped the pilot to alight, and the boy who jumped to the ground was shaking from head to foot.

'Did you see it...did you see it?' he croaked. 'It was awful!'

They got him to the shelter of the position and to the little room behind. The airman was pinched and blue of face, but it was not his cold ride which had set him a tremble. He drank the cup of hot coffee they gave him, and as he did so his teeth were chattering against the edge of the mug.

'Awful!' he said at last; 'did you see it?'

'The Zep?'

He shook his head impatiently.

'No—after we gave the signal for the light, and they all came up—we were under the angle, and I looked up and suddenly a man—' he shivered and closed his eyes, 'a man leaped and straight out of the fore cabin...leaped and turned over and over...'

*

In the morning they made a search and found, in the big Mill Pond by Addlestone one who had in his lifetime been Hans Richter — the man who knew London and hated lights. Especially lights that could be translated into E flat.

Edgar Wallace

The Man from the Stars

IN THE SUMMER of 1915, I received a request from Berlin which somewhat surprised me. I was instructed to send to Holland as many good maps of London as I could buy, and I was told also to prepare one special map, marking the areas which the street-lamps had been darkened. This was followed (or it may have come I the same dispatch, I forget) by a request that I should instruct my men to discover how it was that the British Government knew we contemplated an air-raid on London.

I myself wondered what information the British Government had secured and how they had secured it. For months the streets had been lit as gaily as pre-war days. The theatre signs glowed and flashed, the West End streets were bathed in radiance and then, almost by a touch of the magician's wand London "went dark." Street lamps were shaded, the light signs outside the theatres were extinguished and it was almost impossible to pick your way through the streets.

I suppose my excellent friend, the High-Born Baron von Hertz-Missenger would have said, "English Secret Service." He reminds me of a character Charles Dickens the great English poet, who invariably thought that his head was the head of King Charles II!

The explanation I offered was, that some of our too impetuous airmen must have betrayed the fact by shouting with haughty insolence to the English airmen they met in the air. As this has never been denied, it is probably true.

At any rate I set myself to work upon a map. It was a long business, and very unsatisfactory, because the whole of London was dark, and no place was more light the another. This I reported, forwarding the maps by special courier.

And then I received a request from our Headquarters that I should arrange light-signals which should be seen by Zeppelins. The idea was to post three lights so that they formed a triangle, one near Albany Park, one near Maidstone Road, and a third in the east, near Shepherd's Junction. The triangle thus made would contain all the valuable city area which it was our

Zeppelins' intention to utterly destroy.

Of the first raid in September, it is not necessary for me to tell. Of how the cowardly Englishmen trembled beneath the midnight hail of bombs, you have read. I myself did not witness the raid, because, on receiving information on the afternoon Zeppelins were due, I had left London for Cornwall. Since it was impossible for the brave fellows who piloted our good Zeppelins to distinguish between a patriot and a hateful enemy, I thought that in the interest of the Fatherland, it was necessary that I should be as far away as possible when the dread visitation came.

I returned to London the next morning and arrived at eleven o'clock. Oh what consternation there was. Oh what vile language these unkultured Londoners used, what epithets, what adjectives, the A's, and B's, and C's, and D's, they called us—but of that anon!

I was in some anxiety before my journey's end was reached as to whether I should have to walk a part of the journey, and I was greatly relieved on questioning the conductor to learn that Paddington Station had escaped the holocaust. When I arrived at Paddington everything was going on as usual. To my amazement buses were running and cabs were plying for hire.

"Where was the raid ? " I asked.

"In the East End and the City," was the reply. So, I thought, my triangle had proved efficacious, and calling a cab, I said: "Will you please drive me to the ruined area?"

The poor, ignorant fellow thought at first that it was the name of a public-house, and I bad to enlighten him.

"Where the bombs struck," I said.

"Oh, yes," he said, brightening up, "I will ask a policeman where they fell."

"Do you mean to tell me," I inquired, "that you don't know? Perhaps you haven't been to the City?"

"Yes sir," he replied in the true boorish cabman spirit. "I've been to the city three times but I ain't seen no place where the bombs fell."

This of course was "eye-wash." For my part I had removed all my archives from my office, and as that was on the edge of the City, I drove there first and as pleased to find that my office had not been touched. I drove up Ludgate Hill and apparently everything was as usual, and it was not until he had driven farther on and. had penetrated a side street that I saw the wreckage of a house. It was pleasing and yet disappointing. A number of windows had been smashed, one house was in ruins and there was a big hole in a court-yard, but the damage was as such as might have been caused by an explosion of gas.

It took me a long time before I found the second place where a bomb had fallen, and there again the results were not as I expected. I spent the whole of that day wandering about looking for devastation. I went east and south, and north, and although I saw some damaged houses, the results of our gallant Zeppelins' visit left much to be desired.

Returning to my office I was called on the phone and a code message was sent through to me. As I expected, it was from Berlin asking for full particulars of the damage done, and very faithfully I described what I had seen, coded it and passed it on to the proper quarters.

To my wrath and humiliation, the next evening brought a peremptory demand from Berlin. It had been sent by radio, picked up off the coast by a little steamer plying the flag of –, and was brought to me from an East Coast port by one of he couriers we employed for that purpose. The message was, as I say, peremptory, and there were tears in my eyes, tears of sorrow and injury as I read it.

"Cannot understand your message. Our pilots report Westminster Abbey as bombed. Whole streets of the City are in flames, Houses of Parliament partly destroyed, also London Bridge and Tower of London. Several ships in docks hit and sunk. Please personally investigate and report."

Of course there was a chance that these cunning English had, by means of scene painters and workmen labouring through the night, removed all sign of the destruction, but I walked over London Bridge without any difficulty, and as far as I could see the Tower of London was uninjured.

I reported the same, and three days later, had this message back:

"Be on south side of Three Mile Wood, north-north-east Saffron Walden, at eleven o'clock on the night of October 7th."

I could not understand this message, and my new assistant, who had arrived from America, Herr Wilhelm Peters, was as much puzzled as I. However, on the 7th of October, I journeyed to Saffron Walden, which is a little town in Essex, and by studying a map I discovered that Three Mile Wood was inaccurately named because it was about seven miles from the town. I decided to walk, and arrived in the neighbourhood of the wood at about ten o'clock at night. Having ascertained by consulting my compass which was the south side, I made my way across fields and muddy ditches to a big meadow which was exactly placed to the south of the sparsely-wooded little forest.

It was a clear night with a thin ground haze and was rather cold. I had brought one of those walking-sticks, the top of which forms a seat, and this found very comfortable; for the inner man I had a flask of brandy and some liver sandwiches, and I settled myself down to my vigil, wondering what on earth ad induced Headquarters to send me upon this wild adventure.

Then suddenly my heart began beating at a tremendous rate as I divined the reason ! It was intended this night for our airships to reach London, and they desired that I should be a witness. What folly! What folly! What incomparable insanity to risk the life of a high Officer of Intelligence, to place him in such horrible jeopardy. I felt myself grow pale, but then with an effort I braced up. I was a German!

We Germans fear God and nothing else, and, besides, I thought there might not be an air-raid after all.

But what satisfaction I got out of that thought was quickly dissipated. Suddenly an ominous sound came to me. A double "boom! " far away an the east, was followed by three staccato explosions. Another bomb fell, suddenly the whole of the eastern sky was illuminated by the tracing fingers of searchlights.

"Boom!" The sound was growing nearer and my mouth was dry. I was choking. I loosened my collar and mopped the sweat from my forehead and stood up, my knees trembling.

I have thought the matter over since and I have come to the conclusion that my agitation might be explained in this way, that I was trembling with pride in the fearless exploits of our gallant airmen, those intrepid messengers of death who sailed the midnight skies fearless of foe; that I perspired because the liver sandwich was perhaps a little too highly flavoured. Anyway, the cursed things were corning closer and who knows what mistakes a blundering fool of a pilot might make. The searchlights were suddenly extinguished, the guns were silent and for ten minutes I heard no sound save a faint but ever-growing-nearer hum of an engine in the sky. Then there was a shrieking whistle, a crash that seemed to shake the very earth, a blinding fan of flame and, then silence.

In my rage I shook my fist at the sky.

"Stupid jackasses, miserable, bat-eyed swine-hound! " I cried. "Have you not the highest instructions in your pockets to avoid bombing an Intelligence Officer?"

The cursed thing passed overhead. It was roaring like a railway train passing through a tunnel. I saw the bulk of it outlined against the stars and then I saw something else, a little black dot that moved and swayed against the sky. I thought it might be some infernal machine and I nearly fainted.

Understand that my chief thought was of Germany. I had no fear for myself, I was merely a cog in the wheel of the great machine and stood ready at any hour and all days to sacrifice myself for our dear Deutschland. Fortunately, there was a fallen tree in my neighbourhood, and under this I crept, looking out from time to time to see what had happened to the strange thing in the air.

Then I heard a thud, a rustle, and an oath, and I jumped up, bruising the back of my head against the tree-trunk, and ran towards the sound, for that oath was in good German.

"Wer da?" called a sharp voice. "It is I, Heine," I replied.

"Oh, good," said the voice in German. "You are on the spot, I see. Help free me from this doubly rotten parachute."

I made my way to him and helped unbuckle some of the straps that fastened him, and presently he was free.

"Have you got a pocket lamp?" he asked. "No, perhaps you had better not use it. Where can I put the parachute?"

I suggested the tree under which I had been—I won't say hiding, let me rather say taking cover.

"Have you a car?" he asked.

"No," I replied.

"You are an ass," said he; "why haven't you a car?"

I knew by the imperiousness of his tone that he was a true German gentleman probably highly born and connected by many social ties with an old family of Prussia.

"I am the Baron von Treutzer," he said, as though answering my thoughts "and I have been sent here to survey the damage that was done in the last raid."

"Your Excellency will discover that I have spoken nothing but the truth," I said humbly. The sound of the Zeppelin's engines, which had diminished, was now increasing in volume.

"Is the airship returning?" I asked.

"Yes, yes," he said testily. He took from his pocket a small electric lamp and flashed it three times in the air and immediately after three tiny sparks of light showed in the sky.

"They won't be dropping any more bombs, Herr Baron?" I asked carelessly.

"Good heavens! What does it matter if they do? " he boomed—he was a booming kind of man, born to command, typical of our virile aristocracy which has placed Germany in the forefront of world-nations.

"I only asked," I said. "I am a mere observer."

"We only dropped a few bombs," he said, "just to explain our presence. The real business of our visit is here." I heard him slap his chest in the darkness.

"I did not know where the raid was intended," I said, "or I would have arranged for a leader."

"A leader?" he asked. "What the devil do you mean?"

"Evidently Herr Baron is not a member of the Zeppelin crew," I said humbly, "or he would know that the Zeppelins are 'led' to their destination by motor-cars with strong head-lamps."

"Of course I am not a member of the Zeppelin crew," he said in deep disgust, "I am a Royal Lieutenant of the 31st Regiment of the Prussian Guard."

"Does your Excellency intend staying here very long?" I asked, as we trudged along the country road.

"For a week," he replied, "after that I return —"

"By—?"

"That is my business," he replied, "if a Zeppelin can bring me here, a Zeppelin can take me away."

Though I had never heard of parachutes that go up, I know all things are possible owing to the inventive genius of our nation, so I questioned him no further. Outside Saffron Walden we stopped while I went to the hotel to collect the handbag which I had left there.

Needless to say the people in the hotel were in that condition of cowardly funk which our Zeppelin always inspires. The children were crying because they had not seen the airship, and again I heard in the common bar of the hotel those terrible words which my modesty would only allow me to designate by using certain letters of the alphabet.

I rejoined the Baron and we made our way to the railway station, which was in darkness. Fortunately the train which came in was also darkened and remained that way until we reached London and I was able to bring the Baron to my flat without observation. He was a tall, handsome gentleman, dressed in civilian clothes of a noble cut and rich texture, and over a glass of whisky he graciously unbent and told me that he had come to England by this curious method to discover the extent of the damage, not only of the first raid, but of a raid which was projected and by which it was hoped to lay London entirely in ruins.

"On what day will that occur? " I asked.

"You will be notified in due time. It may be to-morrow, and it may be the next day," he replied.

"I only asked," I said carelessly, "because it is necessary for me to see one of my agents in North Devon one day this week, and I should not like to miss the raid."

"You will stay here until I go. That is an order. Why are you looking so pale?"

"It is the pressure of work, your Excellency," I replied. "I am afraid I have rather taxed my strength. My doctor suggested that I ought to go away at once to Cornwall or perhaps Scotland."

"We hope to bomb Scotland," said the Baron thoughtfully. "It would not be a bad idea if you were there."

"When I said Scotland," I said hastily, "I should have said that my doctor suggested I should go to Scotland in the spring. This of course is the very worst weather. Are you likely to bomb Wales?"

"We cannot reach there. It is beyond our reach," said the Baron.

"I only ask," I said, "because he also suggested that I should go there."

"When the raids are over you can go to the devil. I only want your assistance when they are on."

"Did you say raids or raid?" I asked.

"There may be two," he replied callously.

The next morning he expressed his intention of going through the City and the East End to photograph the worst of the damage. I did not offer to accompany him, and indeed, had he suggested that I should do so, I should have firmly declined. Fortunately, he knew London very well, for he had been an attaché the German Embassy a few years before the war broke out, so ha had no need my assistance or guidance.

He left the flat at eleven o'clock and I arranged to meet him at a restaurant in Piccadilly for lunch. I need hardly say that he was armed with a passport not only very completely filled in, but endorsed with an exact imitation of rubber stamps which were used in those days by examining officers at Folkestone when passengers landed.

I was waiting for him at one o'clock, but he did not arrive. Half-past one came, a quarter to two, two o'clock, and I began to feel seriously alarmed, and was thinking what an excellent text his arrest would provide for a letter to Potsdam on the futility of sending amateurs, when he came through the swing doors.

He uttered no word till we were sitting at the table, and the waiter had served the soup.

"These English people are very clever," he said at last.

"In a way they are clever," I said, "but by the side of the German—"

"Don't talk nonsense. Our German people are merely slavish imitators of everybody else in the world. If Germany was not a nation of slaves we should never have an army."

This put an end to the easy flow of conversation, but presently I ventured ask: "Why does your Excellency think the English are clever?"

"I am referring to the way they have cleared up the mess we made and have run up new buildings." He looked up at me curiously as he spoke.

"Don't you agree?"

"Naturally," I said heartily, "I have reason to believe that hundreds thousands of workmen have been working day and night to restore tube damage.'

He laughed.

"In addition to being a fool, you are a liar," he said, and I could only smile the good humour and buoyant frankness of this high-born officer who was in a probability in the entourage of the All-highest himself and, at any rate, as I have since learnt, had frequently dined with that exalted Prince whom we call the Hope of Germany.

"No," Baron von Treutzer went on, "the Zeppelin did little or no damage. It caused nothing of the smash that we expected it would. We will see what tonight's raid brings out."

"To-night?" I said, half-rising from my seat.

"Did I say to-night?" he said in an off-band way. "Well, whenever it happens."

But I knew that in a moment of incaution he had spoken the truth.

"By the way, I shall want you with me to-night," he said.

"To-night?" I repeated. "I am very sorry but this is the one night I can not be with your Excellency. I have an important messenger coming from Ireland with particulars of a rising, and the Foreign Office has particularly asked me—"

"I shall want you to-night," repeated the Herr Baron, "and you will meet me at ten o'clock, let us say, in St. Paul's Churchyard."

"Himmel! Herr Baron!" I exploded, "that would be in the very centre the raid!"

"Did I ever say that it would not?" he asked coolly, "Of course it will be in the centre of the raid. You understand, at ten o'clock. The War Office require a detailed account by eye-witnesses of the damage which is done,"

"But my messenger arrives at Fishguard to-night," I said with a tremor in my voice, "Forgive me if I am agitated, Herr Baron, but I realize the terrible importance, the absolute necessity, of meeting that boat."

"At ten o'clock you will be in St. Paul's Churchyard," said the Baron.

How I loathed and hated this tyrant. We Germans are naturally lovers of freedom. We despise the sycophant and the toady. Tyranny to us is a pestilential disease to be stamped out with an iron heel. Woe to those who endeavour to enslave the Germans, for they are biting on granite!

I told the Baron that I would meet him at the appointed time.

"Don't come before ten," he said. "We will remain until the raid is over."

I lifted my hat and bowed as I parted from him in Piccadilly, and I prayed most fervently, that the earth would open and swallow this pig, whose abominable manners and low attitude to men not so well born as himself (though of that I am not sure, for there were many stories about my mother's friendship for the Graf von Maldesee, which I sometimes reflect upon with a certain amount of satisfaction) aroused in me the deepest scorn.

I could eat no dinner that night, I could do no work that afternoon. I sat in my office until a quarter to ten, suffering, I think, from a touch of malaria and ague which I contracted in America. I arrived in St. Paul's Churchyard, dark and gloomy and silent, on the stroke of ten. I had arranged to meet the

Baron at the corner of one of the lanes which slope down to Upper Thames Street, and here I took my station.

At a quarter past ten he had not arrived. At twenty minutes past ten a hundred searchlights flashed into the sky and the first gun-shot woke the sleeping city. The Zeppelin was coming straight to the City, but was west of where I stood. I heard the thud of its bombs and the devil's chorus of the guns. I saw the skies speckled with shrapnel bursts, but much of what happened in that brief space of time between its appearance and its disappearance is blotted from my memory.

I could only stand crouched in a friendly doorway, my hands before my eyes, thinking of my dear friends, and particularly of a certain girl in Chicago with whom I had exchanged photographs, of my dear home, my little brothers, in fact all my life passed before me. I dare not go out to look for the Herr Baron.

How I envied him, that hardened man of war to whom this terrible concatenation of sound was as the gentle zephyrs; who could stand uncowed and watch with his stern military eye the destruction that was going on about him, uncaring, unafraid, contemptuous of danger, seeking only the information he required for his superiors!

In that moment I almost loved the man, even though I hated to meet him lest he mistook my ague for a more ignoble emotion, but presently I plucked up courage and went out to look for him. He was not at the corner of the lane nor was he on the pavement at all.

I made a circuit of the Cathedral without meeting him and then I realized that the Zeppelins had not been near St. Paul's but had passed westward. Naturally he would have been informed at the last moment and would have been on a spot where they would pass.

I did not attempt to join the throngs that gathered about the places where the bombs had fallen, but made my way homeward. At one o'clock he had not returned; two, three, and four passed. I still listened and then the horror of the possibility seized me. This gallant man had perhaps paid for his temerity with his life and I bought an early morning paper as soon as one was procurable and searched in vain for some indication of his fate.

Such a man could not be stricken down without attracting attention, but there was no reference whatever to such a one as he. In a fever of anxiety I paced my room. I called up my various agents but they could give me no information and I had almost abandoned hope when, at half-past eleven, the Baron came, debonair and calm, into my office.

"You had a good view," were the first words he said.

"Oh, Herr Baron," I said. I grasped his hand and shook it (a most presumptuous thing to do); "I am so glad to see you back! If you missed me I was on the spot."

"I didn't miss you," he said.

"Where were you?"

"I was at Fishguard, meeting your man, but apparently without success, for he did not come."

"You were at Fishguard?" I gasped.

"Naturally," he said, "you don't suppose I am such a silly fool that I am going to stand under a bomb to see it burst, do you?"

Such a man was this mean-souled dog, von Treutzer!

Thank heaven! He disappeared in a week. He may have been picked up by a descending Zeppelin. He may have been taken off by a near-approaching submarine. I have had no news, but if I hear he got back to Germany alive, I, Heine, will be sorry.

The Looker and the Leaper

FOLEY, the smoke-room oracle, has so often bored not only the members of the club, but a much wider circle of victims, by his views on heredity and the functions of the hormones—for he has a fluent pen and an entree to the columns of a certain newspaper that shall be—nameless—that one is averse to recalling his frayed theories.

He is the type of scientist who takes a correspondence course in such things as mnemonics, motor engineering, criminology, wireless telegraphy, and character-building. He paid nothing for the hormones, having found them in an English newspaper report of Professor Parrott's (is it the name?) lecture. Hormones are the little X's in your circulatory system which inflict upon an unsuspecting and innocent baby such calamities as his uncle's nose, his father's temper, and Cousin Minnie's unwholesome craving for Chopin and bobbed hair. The big fellows in the medical world hesitate to assign the exact function of the hormones or even to admit their existence.

Foley, on the contrary, is prepared to supply thumb-nail sketches and specifications. When you go to the writing-table in the "Silence" room, and find it littered with expensive stationery, more or less covered with scrawly-wags, it is safe betting that Foley has been introducing his new friend to some wretched member whom he has inveigled into an indiscreet interest.

But Hormones apart, there is one theory of evolution to which Foley has clung most tenaciously. And it is that the ultra- clever father has a fool for a son.

Whether it works the other way round he does not say. I should think not, for Foley senior is in his eightieth year, believes in spiritualism, and speculates on margins.

Foley advanced his theory in relation to Dick Magnus.

John Seymour Magnus, his father, is popularly supposed to be in heaven, because of the many good qualities and characteristics recorded on the memorial tablet in St. Mary's Church. Thus: He was a Good Father, a Loving Husband and a Faithful Friend, and performed Many Charitable Deeds in This City.

There is nothing on the memorial tablet about his Successful Promotions or Real Estate Acquisitions. He was bracketed first as the keenest business man of his day. A shrewd, cunning general of commerce, who worked out his plans to the minutest detail, he ran his schemes to a time-table and was seldom late. All other men (except one) would comprehend the beginning and fruition of their schemes within the space of months. John Seymour Magnus saw the culmination of his secret politics three years ahead.

There was one other, a rival, who had the same crafty qualities. Carl Martingale was his contemporary, and it is an important circumstance that he supplied, in his son, a complete refutation of all Foley's theories. Carl and John died within twelve days of one another, and both their great businesses went to only sons.

Dick took over the old man's chair, and was so oppressed by his uncongenial surroundings that he sold it for a ridiculous figure to Steven Martingale. The two were friends, so the sale was effected over a luncheon for which Dick paid.

Steven had arranged the lunch weeks ahead, had decided upon the course of conversation which would lead up to the question of sale, and had prepared his reply when Dick was manceuvered into offering the property. For Steven was his parent, and worse. Old Carl was a selfmade boor, with no refined qualities. Steven had the appearance and speech of a gentleman and shared certain views on life with the anthropoid ape.

Ugly stories floated around, and once old Jennifer came into the club in a condition bordering on hysteria and drank himself maudlin. He had hoped to bag Steven for the family, and had allowed his pretty daughter Fay a very free hand.

Too free, it seems. Nothing happened which in any way discommoded Steven. The old fellow owed him an immense amount of money, and Steven knew to a penny the exact strength of these financial legirons.

He was a strikingly handsome fellow, the type the shop-girls rave about—dark, tall, broad of shoulder and lean of flank, an athlete and something of a wit. A greater contrast to Dick could not be imagined, for Dick was thinnish and small, fair haired, rather short-sighted (Steven's flashing eye and long lashes were features that fascinated) and languid.

But he did not develop his left-handedness until after he was married.

Both Dick and Steven courted Thelma Corbett, and never a day passed but that their cars were parked in the vicinity of the Corbett ménage. Corbett being on the danger-zone of bankruptcy was indifferent as to which of the two men succeeded in their quest, and Thelma was in a like case.

She was one of those pretty slender creatures whom. meeting, leave you with a vague unrest of mind. Where had you met her before? Then you realized (as I realized) that she was the ideal toward which all the line artists who ever drew pretty women were everlastingly striving. She was cold and sweet, independent and helpless, clever and vapid; you were never quite certain which was the real girl and which was the varnish and the finishing-school.

To everybody's surprise, she married Dick. Steven had willed it, of course. He half admitted as much one night between acts when we were smoking in the lobby of the Auditorium. Dick had at that time been married for the best part of a year and was childishly happy.

"I can't understand how Dick came to cut you out, Steven," I said. He was feeling pretty good toward me just about then, for I had pulled him through a sharp attack of grippe.

He laughed, that teasing little laugh of his.

"I thought it best," he said, a statement which could be taken two ways. That he was not exposing his modesty or displaying the least unselfishness, ho went on to explain:

"She was too young, too placid. Some women are like that. The men who marry them never wake them up. Some go through life with their hearts asleep and die in the belief that they have been happy. They have lived without 'struggle,' and only 'struggle' can light the fire which produces the perfect woman. I figured it that way."

I was silent.

"I figured it that way"—a favorite expression of his—explained in a phrase the inexplicable.

"That is why you find the most unlikely women running away with the most impossible men," he went on; "the heavens are filled with the woes of perfect husbands and the courts shudder with their lamentations. They are bewildered, stunned, outraged. They have showered their wealth and affection upon a delicate lady, and in return she has fled with a snubnosed chauffeur whose vocabulary is limited to twelve hundred words and whose worldly possessions are nil."

I said nothing, and soon after the bell rang and we went back to our seats.

273

He drove me home that night and came up to my den for a drink, and I reopened the subject of Dick and his wife.

"Dick is one of Nature's waste products," he said. "He has neither initiative nor objective in life. How could old Magnus breed such a son? He was the cleverest, shrewdest, old devil in the City. Dick is just pap and putty—a good fellow and a useful fellow for holding my lady's wool or carrying my lady's Chow, but—"

He shook his head. "No 'struggle' there, Steve?" I asked. "Foley's theory works out in this case."

"Foley is a fool," smiled Steven. "What about me? Aren't I my father's son?"

I admitted that.

"No, Dick lives from breakfast to supper, and could no more work out a scheme as his father did than I could knit a necktie."

"And there is no 'struggle' in the establishment?" I repeated, and he nodded gravely. "There is no 'struggle,'" he said, and although he never said the words I felt him saying "as yet."

Steven became a frequent visitor at the Magnus' house—Dick told me this himself. "He's an amusing person," he said—I met him in the Park, and he stopped his car to talk"—and I can't help feeling that life is a little dull for Thelma."

It was much duller for people who were brought much into contact with Thelma, but I did not say so. She was the kind of hostess who wanted entertaining.

Everybody loved Dick in those days, and he was welcomed wherever he went. Later, when he passed through that remarkably awkward stage, a stage which we usually associate with extreme adolescence, he was not so popular, and I was a little bit worried about him. It grieved me to see a man with all the money in the world making a playtime of life, because people who live for play can find their only recreation in work, and he never expressed the slightest desire to engage himself in the pursuit which had built up his father's colossal fortune. He rode well, he shot well, he played a good game of golf, and it was a case of "Let's get Dick" for a fourth at bridge.

"The fact is," said Dick, when I tackled him one day, "heavy thinking bores me. Maybe if I had to, I would. Sometimes I feel that I have a flash of my father's genius, but I usually work out that moment of inspiration in a game of solitaire.

"One afternoon he took me home to tea, arriving a little earlier than usual. He was evidently surprised to find Steve's car drawn up near the house. He should have been more surprised when he walked through the French windows opening from the lawn to the drawing-room, and found Steve and Thelma side by side on a settee examining Medici prints. It may have been necessary for the proper study of Art that Steve's hand should be upon the girl's shoulder. Evidently she did not think so, for she tried to disengage herself, but Steve, much more experienced in the ways of the world, kept his hand in position and looked up with a smile. As for me, I felt de trop.

"Hello, people!" said Dick, glaring benignly into the flushed face of the girl, "do my eyes behold a scandal in process of evolution? Or have I interrupted an exposition on the art of Michael Angelo?"

Steve rose with a laugh.

"I brought Thelma some pictures," he said, "they're a new lot just published; they are rather fine, don't you think?"

Dick looked at the pictures and, having no artistic soul, said that they struck him as a little old-fashioned, and I saw the girl's lips curl in disdain of her husband, and felt a trifle sad.

Another time (I have learnt since) Dick found them lunching together at Madarino's, a curious circumstance in view of the fact that she had said she was going to spend the day with her mother.

Then one afternoon Dick went home and sounded his motor-horn loudly as he swept up the drive, and discovered his wife at one end of the drawing-room and Steve at the other, and they were discussing Theosophy loudly.

After tea Dick linked his arm in Steve's and took him into the grounds.

"Steve, old boy," he said affectionately, "I don't think I should come and see Thelma unless somebody else is here, old man."

"Why in Heaven's name shouldn't I?" asked Steve. "What rubbish you talk, Dick! Why, I've known Thelma as long as I've known you."

Dick scratched his chin.

"Yes, that seems a sound kind of argument," he said. "Still, I wouldn't if I were you. You know, servants and people of that kind talk."

But Steve smacked him on the back and told him not to be a goomp, and Thelma was so nice that evening that, when during a week-end Dick surprised his wife and Steve one morning walking with linked hands along an unfrequented path through the woods, he did no more than give them a cheery greeting, and passed on with a grin.

It was about this time that Dick started on his maladroit career. He became careless in his dress, could not move without knocking things over, went altogether wrong in his bridge, so that you could always tell which was Dick's score by a glance at the block. There was usually a monument of hundreds, two hundreds, and five hundreds erected above the line on the debit side, and when men cut him as a partner they groaned openly and frankly.

Harry Wallstein, who is a lunatic collector, gave him a rare Ming vase to examine, and Dick dropped it, smashing the delicate china into a hundred pieces. Of course he insisted upon paying the loss, but he could not soothe Harry's anguished soul. He had a trick too, when he was taking tea with some of his women friends, of turning quickly in a drawing-room and sweeping all the cups on to the floor. In the street he escaped death by miracles. Once he stood in the center of a crowded thoroughfare at the rush hour to admire the amethystine skies. A motor lorry and two taxicabs piled themselves up on the sidewalk in consequence, for it had been raining and the roads were slippery.

Dick footed the bill for the damage and went on his awkward way. It is extraordinary how quickly a man acquires a reputation for eccentricity. People forgot the unoffending Dick that used to be, and knew only the dangerous fool who was. When he called on Mrs. Tolmarsh, whose collection of Venetian glass has no equal in the country, the butler was instructed never to leave his side, to guide him in and out of the drawing-room, and under no circumstances to allow him to handle the specimens which Mrs. Tolmarsh invariably handed round for the admiration of her guests. Nevertheless he managed to crash a sixteenth-century vase and a decanter which had been made specially for Fillipo, Tyrant of Milan, and was adorned with his viperish crest.

And in the meantime Steven gave up his practice of calling three times a week on Mrs. Magnus and called every day.

Dick did not seem to mind, although he took to returning home earlier than had been his practice. I might have warned Dick. I preferred, however, to say a few words to Steven, and I got him alone in a corner of the library and I did not mince my words.

"I shall not moralize, Steven," I said, "for that is not my way. You have your own code and your own peculiar ideas concerning women, and so far you've got away with it. I do not doubt that you will get away with this matter because Dick seems to be drifting down the stream towards imbecility—but there are, thank Heaven, a few decent people in this town, and if you betray Dick you are going to have a pretty thin time. I won't commit the banality of asking you to look before you leap, because I know you're a pretty good looker!"

"Leaper!" he corrected. "No person who looks very carefully leaps at all. The world is divided into those two classes—lookers and leapers. Anyway, I am not very greatly concerned by what people think of me. If I were, I should have entered a monastery a long time ago. You've been straight with me, Doctor, and I'm going to be straight with you. My affairs are my affairs and concern nobody else. I shall do just as I think, and take a line which brings me the greatest satisfaction."

"Whosoever is hurt?" I asked.

"Whosoever is hurt," he said, and meant it. "I know just what is coming to me. I have figured it out."

There was no more to be said. To approach Dick was a much more delicate matter, for he was impervious to hints.

A week after I had talked to Steven I met Hariboy, who is a banker of standing and the president of my golf club. I met him professionally, for I had been called into his house to perform a minor operation on one of his children, and I was cleaning up in his dressing-room when he strolled in, and after some talk about the child he said:

"Steven Martingale is going away."

"Going away?" I repeated. "How do you know?"

"I know he has taken steamship accommodations for Bermuda. My secretary and his secretary are apparently friends, and she told my girl that Steven is doing a lot of rush work, and that he is leaving for a long holiday on the 18th."

"Do you know by what line?" I asked, and he told me.

Luckily the manager of the shipping office was a patient of mine, and I made it my business to call on him that afternoon.

"Yes, the ship leaves on the 18th," he said, "but I haven't Mr. Martingale on my passenger list."

We went through it together, and I traced my finger down the cabin numbers and their occupants.

"Who is this in No. 7 suite?" I asked. He put on his glasses and looked.

"Mr. and Mrs. Smith. I don't know who they are. It's not an uncommon name," he added humorously.

So that was that!

I do not think I should have moved any further in the matter if I had had the slightest degree of faith in Steven's honesty. But Steven was not a marrying man. He had once told me that under no circumstances would he think of binding his life with that of any woman, and had expounded his philosophy with that cold- blooded logic of his, which left me in no doubt at all that whatever fine promises he might make to Thelma Magnus, only one end of that advenlure was inevitable.

I sought Dick all over the town, and ran him to earth in the first place I should have looked—the card-room of Proctor's Club. I entered the room in time to hear the peroration of a violent address on idiocy delivered by Dick's late partner. His opponents were too busy adding up the score to take any interest in the proceeding.

Dick sat back in his chair, his hands in his pockets, a little smile on his thin face.

"Fortunes of war, old top," he murmured from time to time.

"Fortunes of war be—" roared Staine; who was his victim. "You go four spades on the queen, knave to five, and not another trick in your hand...!"

"Fortunes of war, old top," said Dick again, paid his opponents and rose, upsetting the table and scattering the cards in all directions.

"Awfully sorry," he murmured; "really awfully sorry!"

That "awfully sorry" of his came mechanically now.

"Now, Dick," said I, when I'd got him into my car, "you're coming straight home with me, and I'm going to talk to you like an uncle."

"Oh, Lord!" he groaned. "Not about Thelma?" I was astounded, and I suppose looked my astonishment. "Everybody talks to me about Thelma," said Dick calmly. "She's a dear, good girl, and as honest as they make 'em. I'm not a very amusing chap, you know, Doctor," he said mournfully, "and Steven is the kind of fellow who can keep a room in roars of laughter."

"But, my dear, good man," I said impatiently, "don't you realize that a man of Steven's character does not call daily on your wife to tell her funny stories?"

"I don't know," said Dick vaguely. "Thelma seems to like him, and I've really no grudge against old Steve. He's a leaper too," he said, with a quick, sidelong glance at me, "and that makes him ever so much more interesting to the women." lie chuckled at my astonishment. "He was telling us the other night about that amusing conversation he had with you."

"He did not tell you the whole of the conversation, I'll swear," said I dryly, but Dick showed no curiosity.

"Old Steven is a good fellow," he repeated. "I like him, and I tell everybody who comes to me with stories about him and Thelma that he is my very best friend."

I groaned in the spirit.

"Then," said I in despair, "it is useless telling you that Steven has booked two berths by the steamer which leaves on the 18th for Bermuda."

He nodded. "I know; he is taking his aunt," he said. "I got the same yarn from Chalmers, and I asked Steven, and he told me, yes, he was going away—"

"In the name of Smith?" I asked pointedly.

"In the name of Smith," repeated Dick gravely. "After all, he's a big power in the financial'world, Doctor, and it is not good business for him to advertise his comings and goings."

After that there was no more to be said.

"We're having a little party on the 17th at the house. I wish you would come along," said Dick before I left him. "I've particularly asked Steve to come. It will be a send-off for him, though of course nobody must know that he is going abroad."

The dear, simple fool said this so solemnly that I could have kicked him. What could I do? I had a talk with Chalmers, who is as fond of Dick as I am, and he could offer no advice.

"It's hopeless," he said, "and the queer thing is that Dick has arranged to go out of town on the night of the 17th. So we can't even drag him to the ship to confront this swine!"

"Do you think he'll marry her?" I asked after a long pause in the conversation.

"Marry her!" scoffed Chalmers. "Did he marry Fay Jennifer? Did he marry that unhappy girl Steele? Marry her!"

It was a big party which Dick gave. His house lay about twenty miles out of town and is situated in the most gorgeous country. It was a hot autumn day, with a cloudless sky and a warm gentle breeze, the kind of day that tempts even the most confirmed of city birds into the open country.

I do not think it was wholly the salubrious weather that was responsible for the big attendance. Half the people, and all the women who were present, knew that on the following day Steven Martingale was leaving for Bermuda, and that Thelma would accompany him.

I saw the girl as soon as I arrived, and noted the bright eyes, the flushed cheek, and the atmosphere of hectic excitement in which she moved. She was a little tremulous, somewhat incoherent, just a thought shrill.

All Dick's parties were amusing and just a little unconventional. For example, in addition to the band and the troupe of al fresco performers and Grecian dancers, he usually had some sort of competition for handsome prizes, and the young people, particularly, looked forward to these functions with the greatest enjoyment. On this occasion there was a revolver-shooting competition for ladies and gentlemen, the prize for the women being a diamond bangle, and for the men a gold cigarette case.

Most men imagine themselves to be proficient in the arts which they do not practice, and nine out of ten who have never handled a gun boast of their marksmanship.

Dick sought me out and took me into the house and upstairs to his own snuggery.

"Doctor," said he, as he dropped into an easychair and reached for his cigarettes, "spare a minute to enlighten me. What was the Crauford smash? I only heard a hint of it last night, and I'm told that dad was positively wonderful."

It was queer he had never heard of Ralph Crauford and his fall. Old Man Magnus and he were bitter enemies, and whereas Crauford must nag and splutter from day to day, Magnus was prepared to wait. As usual he laid his plans ahead, and one morning failed to turn up at his office. The rumor spread that he was ill, and there was suport for the story, because you could never pass his house without seeing a doctor's waiting car. It was a puzzling case, and I myself was fooled. So was every specialist we brought in. For weeks at a time Magnus would be well, and then he would have a collapse and be absent from his office for days.

And all the time the Crauford crowd were waiting to jump in and smash two of the stocks he carried. We had advised a trip abroad, but it was not till the end of a year of these relapses and recoveries that he consented. He went to Palermo in Sicily, and after a month it was announced that he had died. Then the fun started. Crauford jumped into the market with a hammer in each hand, figuratively speaking. Tyne River Silver fell from 72 to 31, and all the time the executors of the estate were chasing one another to discover their authority to act. This went on for three days and then the blow fell. Old Man Magnus appeared on 'Change, looking a trifle stouter, a little browner, and infinitely cheerful.

Crauford had "sold over." It cost him his bank balance, his town house, and his country estate plus his wife's jewelry to get square with Magnus.

Dick listened to the story, his eyes beaming, interrupting me now and again with a chuckle of sheer joy.

"Wonderful old dad!" he said at the end; "wonderful old boy! And he was foxing all the time. Kidding 'em along! The art of it, the consummate art of it! Specialists and sea voyages and bulletins every hour!"

He stood up abruptly and threw away his cigarette.

"Let's go and see the women shoot," he said.

There was the usual fooling amongst the girls when their end of the competition started. In spite of their "Which-end-shall-I- hold-it?" and their mock terror, they shot remarkably well.

I had caught a glimpse of Steven, a silent, watchful, slightly amused man, who most conspicuously avoided Thelma, but came down to the booth and stood behind her when she fired her six shots for the prize. Incidentally not one bullet touched the target, and the wobbling of her pistol was pitiful.

Steven's shooting was beautiful to watch. Every bullet went home in the center of the target and the prize was assuredly his.

"Now watch me, Steve," said Dick, and at the sight of Dick with a gun in his hand even his best friends drew back.

He fired one shot, a bull's-eye, the second shot was a little bit to the left, but nevertheless a bull's-eye, the third shot passed through the hole which the first had made, the fourth and fifth were on the rim of the black center—and then he turned with a smile to Steven.

"My old pistol is much better than the best of the new ones," he said.

He had refused to shoot with the weapons provided, and had brought a long ungainly thing of ancient make; but as he was not a competitor in the strict sense of the word, there had been no protest.

The sixth shot went through the bull and there was a general clapping.

"How's that?" said Dick, twiddling his revolver.

"Fine," said Steven. "The Looker shoots almost as well as the Leaper," laughed Dick, and pressed the trigger carelessly. There was a shot and a scream. Steve balanced himself for a moment, looking at Dick in a kind of awed amazement, and then crumpled up and fell.

As for Dick he stood, the smoking revolver still in his hand, frowning down at the prostrate figure.

"I'm sorry," he muttered, but Steven Martingale had passed beyond the consideration of apologies. He was dead before I could reach him.

*

That old-fashioned revolver of Dick's had seven chambers, and people agreed both before and after the inquest that it was the kind of fool thing that Dick would have.

"He ought to have seen there were seven shots when he loaded the infernal weapon," said Chalmers. "Of course, if it was anybody but Dick I should have thought that the whole thing was manoeuvred, and that all this awkwardness of his had been carefully acted for twelve months in order to supply an excuse at the inquest and get the 'Accidental Death' verdict. It is the sort of thing that his father would have done. A keen, far-seeing old devil was John Magnus."

I said nothing, for I had seen the look in Dick's eyes when he said "leaper."

At any rate, the shock wakened Dick, for his awkwardness fell away from him like an old cloak, and Thelma Magnus must have found some qualities in him which she had not suspected, for she struck me as a tolerably happy woman when I met her the other day. But I shall not readily forget that hard glint in Dick's eyes when he spoke the last words which Steven Martingale was destined to hear. I had seen it once before in the eyes of John Seymour Magnus the day he smashed Crauford.

Maybe some of the old man's hormones were working. I should like to ask Foley about it.

The Speed Test

MISS JANE IDA MEAGH was prepared to brain the first misguided person who addressed her by either of her given names, and had accepted with gratitude at a very early age the appellation suggested by the combination of her initials—Jim. And from "Jim" to "Jimmy" is but a short step.

In the census return Jimmy described herself as a "stenographer." So might Edison have marked himself "electrician" or Napoleon "soldier." For there was no stenographer like Jimmy. She was at the very head of her profession, and was booked ahead like a film-star or a Harley Street specialist.

If there was one person in the world whom Jimmy hated and loathed with all her soul, that person was Henry Obbings. Henry was a limp youth who gave you the impression that he had shaved in a bad light. He was famous in the social circle in which he moved for his ready wit and a gift of repartee. He invariably recounted with a wealth of detail his encounters with Jimmy, and repeated with great effect the things he had said to Jimmy on these occasions.

It is true that the majority of his pert replies were those he remembered long after he had left Jimmy, and it is also a fact that he never quite gave a faithful account of what Jimmy had said to him. There were some things which Henry could never bring himself to repeat.

Henry Obbings was the pet speedster of the Rat-a-plan Typewriter Co. Ltd., and from time to time there were issued by him or on his behalf challenges to the whole of civilised mankind, man or woman, to meet him in a speed contest, the only conditions being that Mr. Obbings should operate on a Number 6 Silent Rat-a-plan, "the writer that writes."

For the purpose of this challenge Jimmy regarded herself as inhuman; she steadfastly and resolutely declined to beat Mr. Obbings privately or publicly, and sneered openly at Mr. Obbings's portrait in the newspapers. These appeared from time to time, for the Rat-a-plan had an excellent Press agent, and they revealed Mr. Obbings working at his machine, a sycophantic attendant standing by with an oil-can. It was a legend that he worked so fast that after half-an-hour's use the bearings of the machine became so hot that it was necessary to open the door and windows of the room in which he worked, to let the temperature cool down.

There were also pictures of Mr. Obbings in his moments of leisure and recreation, sitting at a table, with his head upon his clenched fists, looking at a book with a studious, even sad expression.

One morning there came to Jimmy a further challenge by Mr. Henry Obbings. There was an annual exhibition at which business appliances of all kinds were shown, and it was a feature of this event that a diploma and a gold medal were competed for by stenographers. So far it had resulted in a walk-over for Henry.

Jimmy had turned down every such artful move and invitation, and she now dropped the letter into her waste-paper basket with an exaggerated gesture of disgust. Nor did the information that the Rat-a-plan Typewriter Co. offered an additional money prize of substantial value to anyone who could exceed the speed of Mr. Obbings produce a trace of irresolution to her decision.

She got up from her breakfast-table briskly and looked at her engagement-book. Jimmy was booked ahead, as has been remarked before, like a fashionable physician. Her amazing quickness, her accuracy, her unquestionable integrity justified the big fees she received, and incidentally confirmed her wisdom when she set out to be a specialist stenographer.

Her first call that day was on Dr. John Phillips, who was also a specialist in his way; and Dr. John, who looked a little tired under the eyes, as well he might be, for he had been up all night with a dying patient, received her at his morning meal.

"Thanks, no, doctor," said Jimmy. "I've just breakfasted."

"This is my supper," growled the doctor. "Jimmy, I've the details of fourteen cases to dictate to you, and I hope you feel fitter for the job than I. By the way," he said curiously, "where did you get your extraordinary knowledge from? You've never yet spelt a medical term wrongly."

"I got them out of a book, the same as you," said Jimmy.

The doctor looked at her admiringly.

For the next hour and a quarter she was absorbed in the gruesome and sorrowful business of recording the histories of cases, every other one of which ended: "The patient died at 11.45," or whatever the hour might have been.

"Don't any of your patients get well?" asked Jimmy as she snapped the band round her note-book.

"Just a few," said Phillips. "Don't forget, I'm only called in at the very end in lots of cases. I think some of them expect me to bring my trumpet, under the impression that I am the Archangel Gabriel."

"A rotten life!" said Jimmy thoughtfully. "I'd sooner have my job."

The doctor looked at his watch.

"I must hurry. I've got to go to Greenwich," he said.

Nevertheless, and in spite of his hurry, he sat down again at his desk and lit a cigarette, offering one to Jimmy, who shared a common match.

"Jimmy, do you think that a young man with brilliant prospects, but no money, should marry a very nice girl and start family life on—that!" He snapped his fingers to indicate a microscopic income.

"It all depends upon the prospects," said Jimmy cautiously. "If there's only a prospect of raising a largo family, I should say no."

"And I said no, too," said the specialist with a sigh.

He was a youngish man, remembering the position he occupied in the medical world, and that he could still sigh over the follies of his fellow-men was a wholesome tribute to his youth.

"He's a pal of mine. We were at University together," he said.

Jimmy guessed that the unknown He was the patient at Greenwich. Dr. John was looking at the ceiling thoughtfully.

"I was talking to him about you yesterday."

"About me?" said Jimmy in surprise.

"Yes, about you. I don't think he has a great deal of money—in fact I know he hasn't," said Phillips frankly, "and it's hard luck that at a time when he's really ill—he's had a bad nervous breakdown—he should have had a good offer from one of the technical journals for a series of articles."

He paused and blew a ring of smoke to the rafters.

"Jimmy, I know your fees, and they are beautifully exorbitant. God bless you for keeping the specialist beyond the reach of common people. But if he asks you to go down—for I think he could dictate these articles; he certainly could not write them—I wish you'd charge him a sum which is not ridiculously low, but which is not your ordinary rate. One minute," he said as she was going to speak. "I want you to put the rest of your fee on my bill."

"I'll do nothing of the kind, doctor," said Jimmy quietly. "I'd do this job for nothing, but I suppose he wouldn't like that. Anyhow, I'll do it at an ordinary typist's fee, and as to putting the rest of the charge on your account, that's ridiculous, unless you send me a bill for doctoring my throat last spring and for giving me several helpful pieces of advice about my heart, lungs, and other important parts of me."

He laughed as he rose.

"I must go, Jimmy. I'll let you know about Fennell."

*

THAT morning Miss Jane Ida Meagh was the victim of a trick. She had been engaged by a firm of manufacturer's agents to copy a long document dealing with the cork harvest of Spain. She had to do the work at the agent's office, and it was urged upon her that it was vital, was indeed a matter of life and death that she should get to the last word of that report in the briefest possible space of time.

It was a brand new typewriter, of a brand new make, at which she sat. The keyboard was, of course, universal, and most of the gadgets were of a type with which she was unfamiliar, though their manipulation was very easily learnt.

She had fixed the tension to her liking, and then—the machine grew eloquent under her lightning fingers.

"There's your report," she said, and observed that the agent had a stop watch in his hand.

"Five thousand words in forty-two minutes 15.2 seconds," he said breathlessly but exactly.

"I dare say," said Jimmy. "Shall I send you a bill or are you one of those never-owe-nobody people?"

The agent for this occasion was of the latter variety. Jimmy collected her cheque and left, and there the incident appeared to have closed.

But the next day she passed a shop window in which was a typewriter. And beneath the typewriter was a large sign:

THE PLATEN TYPEWRITER
on which
MISS JANE IDA MEAGH
(the world's champion stenographer)
wrote 5,347 words in 42 min. 15.2 secs.
A Record For The World.
Come Inside and Look at This
New Marvel of Engineering Science:
"THE MACHINE WITH A MIND."

"God bless my soul!" said Jimmy, and despite this pious invocation went red with wrath.

She swept into the shop and demanded to see the manager.

"Take my name out of your window," she said peremptorily when that gentleman made his appearance.

"But, my dear young lady—"

"Take it out or I'll sue you for libel," she said. "Anyway, it's a lie. I took an hour and a quarter to do the work, on the worst brand of machine that I've ever handled. And what's more, I shall make an affidavit to that effect."

"It's a good machine," he protested; "there are only three in existence; they're show samples, and—"

"Three too many!" snapped Jimmy.

"Mr. Brown said—

If Brown is the nom-de-guerre of the Armenian who engaged me to copy the cork serial," said Jimmy, "I don't want to hear what he said. Now, do you take out that placard, or do I tell the Press all my troubles?"

"I'll take it out," growled the manager. "I must say, though, that you're not very considerate. You'll remember that I gave you a lot of work last summer—"

"You can give it to somebody else next summer," retorted Jimmy promptly. "Perhaps she'll do it on 'The Platen.' It's a fairly good machine for two-finger typists. Try 'em with 'Now is the time for all good men to come to the aid of the party'!"

She fired this invitation as she left him, and there was a sting in it which only a real typist will understand.

The placard was removed, and there the matter would have ended, for Jimmy was discretion itself, and she was in no mood to advertise the trick that had been played upon her. What annoyed her most was that the machine was really good and a distinct improvement on any she had ever used.

Unfortunately, the manager was not so discreet, and the news came to a wandering reporter. The reporter, who was a clever young reporter, wrote a most amusing story that covered the Platen Typewriter, without mentioning its title, with shame and ignominy, so that in every office where girls groped for keys and dreamt dreams of making Miss Jane Ida Meagh look like a pickled walnut, the Platen Typewriter became synonymous with foolishness.

The publicity had the effect of spurring Mr. Henry Obbings to a further challenge, to whom Jimmy was stung to a reply:

Dear Sir,

You ask me whether I will make on exhibition of myself, and urge as a reason the fact that you intend making an exhibition of yourself. The only inducement I can see for me so far forgetting myself is the paragraph in which you tell me that I should work at one end of the building and you at the other. The knowledge that we were as far apart as possible would be an inducement were it not for the fact that the certainty that I was under the same roof as yourself would make me sick.

Yours sincerely,

J. I. Meagh.

It was a very rude letter, such a letter as Mr. Obbings explained to his friends, no lady would write. Possibly he was justified.

"The truth is," said Mr. Obbings… "no, Percy, I won't show you the letter, it's too disgraceful for words—the fact is she knows jolly well I could lick the stuffing out of her in spite of her vaunted speed."

Yes, Mr. Obbings used the words "vaunted speed."

"Perhaps she'll enter at the last minute?" suggested the friend.

"I'm afraid not." Mr. Obbings shook his head with the sad smile of a tiger deprived of a meal.

*

A FEW days later Jimmy was rung up on the 'phone. It was Dr. Phillips.

"Can you go down there to-day, Jimmy?" he asked. "Fennell thinks he could dictate the article, and he has got together most of the data."

"I'm free this afternoon," said Jimmy.

"I'll wire that you're coming then. Be there at half-past two," said the doctor, and gave her the address.

That morning Jimmy had a great idea. Here was an invalid. She did not know much about invalids except that they lay in bed and refused delicate food. Sometimes they nibbled at a grape or swallowed a mouthful of chocolates, but now and again by a miracle they could be tempted to negotiate some particularly appetising dish, whereafter they put on weight and recovered with the greatest rapidity.

That morning Jimmy stood in her private kitchen, her sleeves rolled up, a cookery-book propped against a milk-bottle, and the light of battle in her eye.

No man or woman knew her ghastly secret. Even Mr. Obbings in his wildest moments never dreamt that her vice was the mangling and cremation of flour and fruit. Her lips moved as she followed the directions in the book.

"Flour, two spoonfuls…. Fresh butter… put in a dry, warm place… bake in a slow oven…."

She drew a long sigh and switched on her electric oven. She ate a hurried lunch, dashing backward and forward to the kitchen to examine the little thermostat which regulated the heat of the oven, and to compare the watch which lay open on the dresser with a note of the minute and the second that her work had gone to a warmer climate, written in pencil on the edge of the cookery-book.

She opened the oven, and with a cloth drew out the steel plate on which four beautiful confections lay, and the fragrance of them was as incense to her nostrils.

She looked at her work, then opened the cookery-book and examined the coloured plates, on which was a life-like representation of the little cakes she was baking. They were exact! If anything her creations were an improvement upon the book. She bore them to her room, and on her face was a look of holy exaltation. Each one she wrapped in white tissue and packed them into a small box and put the box into her attaché case.

She arrived at Greenwich in the afternoon. The Fennell's house was a small one and poorly furnished, she saw at a glance.

A girl met her at the door, a smiling bright-eyed girl who had laughed at poverty so long that it had become a habit.

"You're Miss Meagh, aren't you?" she said. "It is very good of you to come so far."

Jimmy, who was somewhat at sea on occasions like this, smiled and was glad to get an awkward situation over. She found her client lying on a sofa in a somewhat bare parlour. He was a man of thirty, and he looked terribly ill, Jimmy thought. A low table near by was piled high with books, newspaper cuttings, and blue-covered reports.

"My husband has been ill," explained Mrs. Fennell. "But he's much better now, aren't you, Frank?"

"Oh, much! I'm just loafing now," said the man with a grin. "I think I can dictate the best part of the article this afternoon, Miss Meagh."

"Fire away," said Jimmy, and produced her book.

Fennell's estimate of his strength had erred on the optimistic side. After three-quarters of an hour of dictation he was exhausted.

"I'm sorry," he said ruefully. "I thought I was stronger."

"Don't worry," said Jimmy. "You've dictated quite a lot. Anyway, I can come down to-morrow afternoon."

"It's a long way out of town," he said doubtfully.

"Rubbish!" said Jimmy, and that settled the matter.

They pressed her to stay to tea, and she needed very little pressing. She had not had the opportunity she had sought, and as tea was to be served in the drawing-room she thought that this was a chance not to be missed. In the interval of waiting she was introduced to the Fennell baby, and as usual, when babies swam into her ken, she became incoherent and foolish.

"I always get maudlin over babies," she said apologetically. "Of course, it is every girl's pose that she loves them, but I'm honest. I admit it."

The maid brought in the tea, a plate of bread and butter, some jam sandwiches, and a large sponge-cake. Jimmy waited breathlessly.

"No, thanks, dear, I won't eat anything," said Mr. Fennell with a little shiver as he ran his eyes over the meal. "No, thank you," he said again as though he had asked himself and refused.

"Really, you ought to eat something, Frank," said his pretty wife, looking concerned.

Jimmy coughed. "A friend of mine makes rather good pastries," she said carelessly. "She's rather a good cook, and curiously enough she sent me..."

She opened her attaché case and took out the box with fingers which shook a little.

Would they have retained their beautiful shape and appearance? Before now Jimmy had known the most remarkable changes to occur between oven and eating. She removed the wrappings from one with a reverent touch. It was as it had been! Fennell's eyes fastened upon it.

"That does look good!" He reached out his hand. "Have you one to spare?" He took the pastry between his finger and thumb and bit into it.

Jimmy held her breath and half closed her eyes.

"Splendid!" he said. "This is the most wonderful thing I've had for years."

"Would you like one, Mrs. Fennell?" asked Jimmy in a hollow voice. Her heart was thumping. She could have wept at that moment.

"Really, it's so extraordinary to see Frank eat that I can hardly take my eyes from him," laughed Mrs. Fennell.

She nibbled at the cake.

"It's really delicious. Your friend must be very clever."

"Oh, very!" said Jimmy huskily. "Perhaps she will send me some more to-morrow."

"Aren't you eating any yourself?" asked Fennell.

"No," said Jimmy eagerly, and fumbled for the other two. "Would you like them?"

Mr. Fennell not only liked them, but he ate them. He, an invalid, who had refused the choicest productions of the O.K. Cake Company (or the label about the sponge-cake lied), was eating with every evidence of relish the creature of her brain and hand.

"You can come to-morrow, can you?" asked Mrs. Fennell.

"I can come," said Jimmy, speaking under stress of great emotion, "if—if you want me."

It was a lame conclusion. The conversation drifted away from cakes, and Mrs. Fennell took the girl into her confidence.

"We've had a lot of bad luck, haven't we, Frank?"

"Just a little," ho said.

"Do you know that a week ago I thought we were going to be quite wealthy," the girl went on. "Frank is an inventor, and he has invented one of the best typewriters that has ever been put on the market, and just fancy, because some stupid girl refused to work it, the manufacturers turned it down!"

"I think she was right," said Fennell. "Apparently they got her to do a speed test by means of a trick, and they rather over-reached themselves."

"They were going to give Frank a big sum of money on account of royalties, but now we hear that a lot of orders, which had been booked, have been cancelled."

Jane Ida Meagh did not swoon. She sat up straight and stared at the girl-wife.

"What was the name of that machine?" she asked faintly.

"I called it 'The Platen,' because the . . ." He explained why it was called "The Platen," but Jimmy did not hear.

She had ruined them—these lovely people of taste and refinement! This poor man stretched upon a bed of sickness! Jimmy's eyes filled with tears, and she gulped at the extravagant picture of misery she drew. She had done it! And from sheer caprice and femininity. Jimmy had always hated femininity, and now it seemed the most loathsome of weaknesses.

"You'll come to-morrow, and don't forget those cakes," said Mrs. Fennell.

*

JIMMY went on the next day, and the cakes she took were even more delicious than the last, for she had mercifully refrained from improving upon the recipe—which was occasionally Jimmy's super-weakness.

That evening on her return to town she went into the shop where the "Platen" had been exhibited, and the manager, standing with his hands behind him in the middle of the floor space, greeted her with a grave but reserved nod.

"Good afternoon, Miss Meagh," he said.

"Good afternoon, Mr. Salter," for that was the manager's name.

"How is the trade in 'Platens'?" asked Jimmy briskly.

"Well, you smashed that for us," said Mr. Salter bitterly. "But, still, I don't mind so much, because I am thinking of taking over the Rat-a-plan agency for their improved portable machine."

"Don't do it," said Jimmy. "What are you charging for the 'Platen'?"

He named the price, and she produced her cheque-book.

"You're not going to buy a machine?" he cried in amazement.

"There are two other ways I can get one," said Jimmy. "One is by stealing it, and the other by accepting it as a gift—both of which methods are objectionable to me."

"But you're—"

"Get that flat-footed boy of yours to carry this to my cab, will you? I'm not so strong as I was twenty years ago." Which was true, for Jimmy's age was twenty-four.

The flat-footed boy, who was now a scowling flat-footed boy, carried the instrument to the waiting taxi, and Jimmy placed it on her table that night with determination in the set of her jaw, and the light of battle in her eye.

*

MR. HENRY OBBINGS sat in a gaily-decorated stand, surrounded by a large crowd of admiring stenographers, and demonstrated, what time a smooth and silky-voiced lecturer dilated upon the staggering qualities of the Rat-a-plan.

"Un-for-tun-ate-ly," he said, "we have not the op-por-tun-ity of test-ing the rela-tive speed of the Rat-a-plan with any of its com-pet-i-tors." He spoke as though each syllable was separated from its fellow. "Our challenge extended to the whole of the civilised world has not been accepted by any of our rivals, for reasons which I think need no explanation. Tonight, we had hoped there would be a competition for the Inter-Trades Diploma and Medal, together with the money prize offered by my company, but you are deprived of that interesting demonstration. As you will see, we are the only entrants in the competition."

He pointed to a large bulletin board where the name of "Mr. Henry Obbings, The Rat-a-plan Typewriter," was visible.

It was at that moment that the secretary of the exhibition pinned beneath the notice:

"J. I. Meagh, The Platen Typewriter."

THE contest will remain in the minds of all interested in the delicate art of stenography. The two competitors sat, not at either end of the building, but at the same bench, each with the matter to be copied neatly stacked on their left and a pile of virgin white paper as neatly stacked on their right, and at the word "Go!" both struck simultaneously at the keys.

The test was for half-an-hour's continuous work, and in that thirty minutes Jimmy wrote 4,630 words without a mistake, beating the baffled Henry Obbings by exactly twelve hundred words.

Incidentally, she established the name of the Platen Typewriter, so that to-day there is scarcely an office in the City where the peculiar tick-tick of its keys cannot be heard.

The Junior Reporter

IF the junior reporter approached the platform with awe and reverence, it was because he was the junior reporter.

You must understand that Sir Thomas was in the chair, and Mr. Hilldry (Lord of the Manor) was prominently displayed in the front row of the platform.

Miss Cicily was there, too—they say down at Taunborough that she has half-a-million in her own right—and the canon and goodness knows what other celebrities.

The junior reporter, who was born and bred in Taunborough, looked round the crowded audience, and his heart swelled with pride that Taunborough had risen to the occasion; that Taunborough had been worthy of itself; and it may be that in this his melting mood a youthful tear glistened in his eye. He rather hoped that Sir Thomas would recognise him, but somehow Sir Thomas had no eyes for the line of young men that sat at the reporters' table sharpening their pencils.

Naturally enough, with Mr. Hilldry contesting the seat, rendered vacant by the retirement of his brother, local feeling ran high. Indeed, the junior reporter, telegraphing to his newspaper at Bristol, had said so in exactly those words. Naturally, too, the junior reporter reflected that shade of political opinion so ably represented by Mr. Hilldry.

Because it was an important by-election, there were reporters from London and from Plymouth, and between a Londoner and weary Devonian the junior reporter found himself.

They were both very pleasant young men, especially he who came from

London. He had a shock of hair and wore pince-nez, and before Sir Thomas rose to open the meeting he leant across to his colleague from Devonshire and asked:

"What's it worth?"

"This?" said the Devonshire man, sharpening his pencil. "Oh, about a short half for us."

"Two sticks for us," grumbled the gentleman from town, "unless," he added, hopefully, "there's a riot."

"There'll be no riot," said the other contemptuously, "Taunborough's the slowest place on earth!"

The junior reporter listened resentfully; for his part, so far from a "short half," this meeting would be recorded in five closely-set columns.

"Who's Sir Thomas?" asked the London man.

The junior reporter would have been delighted to volunteer the necessary information, but the Devon man anticipated him.

"Oh, Sir Thomas," he said offhandedly, just as though he'd been discussing some ordinary man, "is a local person, a little tin god in his way—he'll bore your head off."

The junior gasped.

"If he speaks for an hour," the Devon man went on gloomily, "there won't be two lines you can report; but perhaps," he reflected, "he won't speak."

"What is the candidate like?"

"Shocking," said the Devon man frankly.

The junior reporter found his voice.

"Perhaps, gentlemen," he said with elaborate sarcasm, "the candidate's views do not coincide with yours."

The London man regarded him curiously.

"Speaking for myself, they don't," he confessed. "That is partly because I have no views; so far as the political colour of my paper is concerned, we are red-hot supporters of the candidate."

"Politics," said the Devonshire oracle, "means one set of rotters trying to chuck another set of rotters out—"

"Ladies and gentlemen…" (Roars of cheering).

Sir Thomas was on his feet, and the junior reporter poised his pencil over virgin pad.

"Ladies and gentlemen. I am sure—I am quite sure that you do not expect me, that you are not expecting a speech, a long speech from me tonight, this evening. We all know, most of us know, in fact we all know, we are all well acquainted with our friend and neighbour Mr. Hilldry Simes-Patrick. (Cheers.) I've known him, that is, I remember him when he was a little boy, quite a small boy in frocks. (Laughter.) I remember his father…."

"He's started," groaned the gentleman from Devonshire.

A sibilant whisper ran along the reporters' table.

"Somebody wants you," said the Devon man, and the Londoner leant forward and looked down the table.

"You taking this?" asked the whisperer hoarsely.

"No," said the London man.

"Good," said the whisperer, "I was afraid you were—how long will he talk…."

Sir Thomas had stopped speaking and was glaring at the audience.

A thin old man with big gig-lamp spectacles on his nose, and clutching a bundle of notes, was standing up, to the indignation of his scandalised neighbours.

"… I would like to ask Sir Thomas," he piped.

"I cannot answer you—wait until I have finished my speech," said Sir Thomas, very red in the face.

"… Will you explain the attitood of Mr. Chamberlain in the year 1875, when he said…."

"Sit down! Sit down, sir!"

"… Speakin' at the town 'all Birmingham on March 10th he referred to the dooty of the proletariat…."

No man cried "Sit down!" more fiercely than did the junior reporter; no partisan applauded Sir Thomas more vigorously, and certainly no journalist took so complete and copious a note of the great man's speech as did that representative of the press.

"A quarter of an hour," said the Devon man gratefully, when the chairman resumed his seat amidst loud and continued cheering. (I quote again from the script of the junior reporter.)

A burst of wild cheering: "For he's a jolly good feller" in several keys, and a smiling figure at the chairman's table.

"This," said the London man, apprehensively, "is, I presume, His Nibs!"

"That's him," said young Devonshire, ungrammatically.

Those excerpts I have been able to take from the junior reporter's book enable me to fit in the speech—as I heard it.

"... the pendulum has swung back, and the pendulum has swung true."

"A little bit mixed up in his metaphor," said the Devonshire reporter.

The junior, who thought the figure of speech beautifully apt, scowled.

"... We are going forward to a winning cause, the goal is in sight and we will not turn back—(cheers)—the prosperity of the country is in the hands of the people, let there be no...."

"What did he say after 'people,'?" asked the London man.

"I don't know," said the Devon man in despair. "Whatever he said doesn't matter much."

The junior reporter could have told them, but he spitefully covered the passage "let there be no wavering in the ranks of progress" with the palm of his hand.

The gentleman from London ran his fingers through his hair wearily.

"There were three jobs I might have taken," he said deliberately. "I might have done a memorial service, or the opening of the Oyster Fishery Exhibition, or the Brixton murder; and to think," he soliloquised bitterly, "to think that I chose this!"

"... whatever might be the opinion of a few self-seeking politicians with axes to grind—(cheers)—the vast majority of the electorate is in favour of...."

"I rather like funerals," mused the Devon man, "you get such a splendid opportunity of ringing the changes on 'sombre magnificence' and 'gloomy grandeur'—why didn't you take the memorial service?"

The London man yawned and shook his head wearily.

"... we cannot put back the clock—(cheers)—we cannot—er—identify ourselves with an anachronism...."

The junior reporter, with a rapt frown, scribbled down the burning words, faithfully, religiously, literally.

"....if you send me to the House of Commons—"

Above the speaker's monotonous voice rose a shrill cry. A cry that sent an indignant flush to the junior reporter's cheek, that brought a bright light to the eye of the London man, that jerked a dozen bored metropolitan journalists to their feet seeking the face of the interrupting member of the audience.

Again the thin voice.

"Votes for wimmin!"

"Madam," muttered the London man under his breath, as the uproar began, "from the bottom of my heart I thank you!"

"So" (I quote the junior reporter again) "the meeting concluded in great disorder, owing to the unseemly conduct of two ladies." And after "ladies" the junior reporter put marks like this: (?), but his all-wise editor cut them out.

If—?

THE war had soured Hector Smith. It had drawn a line between comparative youth and comparative middle-age. It had burst inconveniently, as wars have a habit of bursting, upon more than one half-matured scheme of his, and had scattered them to bits and left him the poorer. To be exact, it had left Mary the poorer, because it was Mary's money that went, of which fact it had become a habit of hers to remind him.

But more souring, bits of boys, the merest urchins, to be patronized or ignored in the old days, had obtruded themselves upon his and the public's attentions. The balance of life was over-set. The inconsiderable factors (in which category he included these boys who now strutted consciously be-ribboned through his world) had grown to such importance that they overshadowed the real big things of life, such as his handicap at golf, his bridge hands, the remarkable poverty of intelligence on the part of his partners, and the like.

There was a time when Arthur, for example, would have been carried to the seventh heaven by a timely half-sovereign, and would have run his long legs off in his haste to reach the confectioner's before the cream buns were sold. Now Arthur was a straight-limbed youth with "wings," and a record of good service in France.

And Arthur and Mary—

Pshaw! It was absurd! Why, he remembered this dirty little kid when he was so high! Yet, it was a fact that Mary spent most of her time with Arthur, raved about his dancing, his beautiful manners, his perfect sympathy. Pshaw!

Hector Smith cursed the war that forced him to listen to gruesome stories in which he was not interested.

He opened the drawing-room door and stalked in, then stopped with a little grimace. The inevitable Arthur was there, and the inevitable Arthur with an embarrassed giggle made his escape with a mumbled reference to the weather. As for Mary, she looked too good to be true.

"Hasn't that bird got a perch of his own?" snarled Hector.

"How can you speak of a man who has been wounded—?" began his indignant partner.

Mr. Smith laughed contemptuously.

"Wounded! The first time he tried to fly he crashed, and the second time he tried to fly he crashed, and the third time he tried to fly he crashed!"

She tossed her head.

"I'd like to see you do it!"

Mr. Smith shrugged.

"Oh, I know it's a mistake to talk disrespectfully of your hero," he sneered.

He was not feeling at his brightest.

"What do you mean?" she demanded with ominous calm.

"I mean, I'm fed up, that's what I mean," he snapped, and she flamed round on him.

"And so am I!" she cried. "You're vulgar and stupid and tyrannical. The life I've lived with you is abominable. When I married you I had money—"

He bowed.

"That's right," he said, encouragingly, "throw that in my face! Didn't I invest it for you?" It was an unfortunate question.

"Yes, you did," she said, bitterly. "You put it into a luminous sign business. Luminous signs! And a month after war was declared! And the only thing you could get out of showing a luminous sign was six months' imprisonment!"

"How did I know there was going to be a war?" asked the exasperated man.

"You might have guessed it," she replied, illogically.

"Could I guess that London was to be plunged in darkness? I did my best. I should have made a million out of that fuse factory I started this year—"

"Yes, if it hadn't been for the armistice," she scoffed.

"How did I know there was going to be peace?" he roared.

She flounced past him on her way to the door.

"Oh, you never know anything!"

"There's one thing I know," he shouted after her.

"What's that?"

"One of these fine days I'll run away to America!" Her scornful laugh came back through the slammed door. He threw himself upon the settee. The money was gone and the wife remained. That was his luck. If it had been the other way about—! If only it had been the other way about! If he could only live the years over again! If he could only be five years younger and knew what he knew!

He sat staring at the newspaper in his hand. There was a critique of a new play, a fairy play.

Bah! Fairies were nonsense!

He laid the newspaper down on his knees.

But suppose there were such things as fairies, and suppose they moved about this prosaic, industrialized world as in the old days they moved through the woodland glebes; suppose by a wave of a magic wand a man could be transplanted back, back, back; and suppose that it were possible that the clock should be put back, and one had consciousness of all the things that were going to happen, the horses that were going to win races, the stocks which were going to rise, all the great events which must occur!

He heaved a deep sigh and looked up. He half-rose from the couch, for there before him, a bright and radiant figure in the dusky room, stood a brilliant presence. He knew it was a fairy because it was dressed as fairies should be dressed, and bemuse she was bathed in a flood of silvery light which seemed to come from nowhere in particular. The little hands grasped a wand which twinkled and glittered with light.

Recovering from his initial astonishment he looked at her aappraisingly. He felt it would be undignified and ill-bred to regard her as a phenomenon.

"Hector Smith," said a sweet, low voice,

"I am your fairy godmother!"

"Oh, yes." said Hector Smith, politely.

"You have expressed a wish to be five years younger. Be happy, for to-morrow you will awake in 1914."

"Eh?" said Hector, sitting up. "I say, do you really mean that?"

She inclined her head.

"Wait a moment," said Hector, eagerly. "I must be the only one who knows it. D'ye understand? Because if everybody else knows it I shall be in the cart again."

She raised her wand and waved it slowly above his head.

"I must be the only one who knows that there's going to be a war and all that sort of thing," said Hector, drowsily. A sense of languor was rapidly overcoming him. "I don't want...."

His head fell on his chest.

He did not know how long he had slept when he awoke with a jerk. He had a confused dream in which figured fairies and brilliant wands, and low, sweet voices mingled, and then he remembered that he had to see Tomkins who was liquidating his ill-fated fuse factory. He went to the study and 'phoned Tomkins, but, amazingly enough, Tomkins was not on the 'phone. He asked

Exchange to connect him with Smith's Patent Fuse Factory, but Exchange was ignorant that such a place had ever existed.

"The telephone service," said Hector Smith, as be hung up the receiver, "is becoming more and more abominable."

He decided to write to the newspapers on the subject. He paused outside the drawing-room door, for he heard his wife moving about inside, and it was necessary to brace himself up for the ordeal. He was a little scared of Mary in her tantrums, and more scared that his apprehension should be known to her. But the girl who came across the room to meet him had no frown, no reproaches. She was one beaming smile, and she ran towards him and laid her hands upon his shoulders.

"Dearie!" she kissed him, ecstatically: then noting the gloom in his face, "darling, whatever is the matter?"

"Matter?" he answered, suspiciously. "What's that you did? What's the matter with you?"

She looked at him in wonder.

"Nothing is the matter with me. I just kissed you, that's all."

He heaved a sigh. How did she know he had received his directors' cheque that day?

"How much do you want?" he asked, with resignation.

"Naughty boy, why do you say that?" she pouted. "Don't you love your diddlelums any more?"

He stared at her.

"Look here. What's up?" he asked, desperately. "I'll buy it! What's wrong with you?"

"Wrong?"

She was frankly astonished.

"Everything has gone wrong to-day," he growled. "I went to call up that fellow about the fuses—"

She frowned.

"Fuses? What are fuses?"

His suspicions returned. "Don't pull my leg," he said, coldly. "I'm not in a mood for it. Try it on the other fellow."

"What other-fellow?" He jerked his head to the door.

"He was heme just now. I heard his voice."

A smile of understanding dawned on her face.

"Who, little Arthur?"

"Yes, little Arthur," he snarled, "the little hero!"

"Don't be silly, Hector," she laughed.

"Arthur a hero!"

His rising wrath moderated. Evidently what he had said to her had done some good. Still suspicious, and with a horrid sense of unreality, he slipped his arm about her waist and led her to the couch. It was all unreal and unexpected, he thought, as her golden head rested on his shoulder.

"It's a. long time since we did this," he said. "It reminds me of the raid nights."

She straightened herself up.

"The what nights?"

"The raid nights."

She laughed. Hector in the full ardour of that period which was neither youth nor middle-age, had been a tempestuous lover.

"Dear, you use such queer expressions!"

"Do you remember the siren?" he asked, after a pause, and her head nodded vigorously.

"Yes, the cat—but I got you away from her."

"And how we used to go down into the cellar?" he mused. It seemed a thousand years ago. She straightened up. It was she who was suspicion.

"We never did," she protested. "Really, Hector! I hope you're not thinking of somebody else?"

Before he could answer Jane came in, and Jane, curiously enough, looked much younger.

"Will there be three to dinner, madam?" asked the maid.

Mary nodded.

"Who is the third?" demanded Mr. Smith.

"Oh, no one," said his wife, airily. "I asked Arthur to stay."

He sprang to his feet.

"Arthur! Confound the fellow, hasn't he gone? I won't have him. Do you understand. Marv. I-won't-have-him!"

Again the look of blank astonishment on her face.

"But why not?"

"He's such a nice little gentleman, sir," pleaded Jane. "He sat on my knee and told me such funny stories."

Hector glared from the maid to his wife.

"There you are!" he said, triumphantly. "That's the sort of fellow he is! Sits on her knee and tells her funny stories!"

To his amazement she laughed.

"It's not worth while getting angry—he can dine in the kitchen."

"In the kitchen!"

"Of course, he doesn't care," Mary went on, calmly, "so long as he goes to the White City."

"With whom?"

"Well, I'll take him," said Mary, indifferently. "I rather like the Roly-Poly and the Wiggle-Wag."

With a mighty effort Mr. Smith controlled himself.

"You can't go to the White City. It's been requisitioned by the Government four years ago," he said. "The White City is closed, I tell you. It's where the C3 men get their A1 gratuity—everybody knows that."

There was a strained silence, during which Jane tip-toed from the room.

Hector saw something in his wife's eyes that looked like fear, and failed to diagnose its cause.

"I'm sorry I lost my temper," he said, penitently; "the fact is I'm jealous."

The fear was replaced by a gleam of interest.

"Jealous? Of whom?"

He made a little gesture to cover his discomfort.

"Of you—and Arthur."

"But you're mad," she gasped; "at his age—"

"At his age." said Mr. Smith, icily, "I had been thrown out of the Empire twice."

He did not explain the degree of worldliness which this experience implied, but he left her to gather that it represented a particularly lurid form of precocity.

"I don't understand you to-night," she said, shaking her head.

"I don't understand myself," said Mr. Smith, rising. "I think I'll run down to the club, I promised to meet an ace."

"An ace? I thought you'd given up cards."

"You don't understand me—this fellow brought down thirty."

"Thirty what?"

"Boche."

"It isn't 'bosh'!" she exploded. "How did he bring them down?"

Hector groaned.

"He got on their tails and crashed them," he explained, patiently.

She was shocked.

"Poor things! I suppose they broke quite easily?" she asked.

He looked at her.

"I don't know what you are talking about," he said, irritably. "I am speaking about a fellow who has been 'mentioned' six times."

She shook her head.

"This is the first time you have mentioned him to me," she said; "what has he done?"

"Done? Why, in the early days before he started flipping, he took a pill-box all by himself!"

Her mouth opened.

"A whole box?" she gasped.

"You see," he explained, "he was in a tank, and when they went over the top—"

"Over the top of the tank?" she asked, hazily.

"No, the tank went over the top and a minnie dropped in front of him."

She was interested again.

"Poor girl," she said, sympathetically, "and did he help her up?"

"No; you see, a dying pig burst just behind him."

"But what did he do with Minnie?" she demanded.

She could not grapple with pigs that flew, but Minnie was someone tangible.

"Oh, she got him in the leg," he stated, carelessly.

She was grave now.

"I see, she wasn't a lady?"

"Of course she wasn't a lady," he wailed.

"I have told you it wasn't a lady! It was a minenwerfer."

She did not want to hear about Miss Werfer or even of a low person to whom he made glib reference—a Miss Emma Gee. This friend of her husband's seemed to have low tastes. He crashed people, he got on their tails.

"And Big Bertha—" Hector was saying when she stopped him.

"I don't think I want to meet your friend," she said, and made for the door.

He didn't understand her. Usually she was as full of the jargon of the war as the most ardent subaltern. Now she professed ignorance and demanded an elucidation of the most commonplace phrase.

He was pondering on this fact when the maid came into the room. She stood nervously waiting, and Hector guessed her errand.

"Well?" he growled.

"I-I thought I would ask you, sir," she faltered; "I was going to ask the mistress if-if she would give me a little rise."

"A rise again!" he groaned. This was the third or was it the fourth time...?

"But, sir?"

"Now listen to me," he said, severely, "I know that living is expensive, and coals are dear, and I am willing to give you another rise. But this must be the very last time. You can have five pounds a month, but not a penny more."

She did not swoon. She was too well-bred a servant.

"Five pounds a month! Oh, thank you, master, thank you! Oh, you are most good—" she grew incoherent.

Hector raised his eyebrows. He thought she was unusually grateful. His wife returned at that moment to hear his news.

"By the way, dear, I've just raised Jane's wages."

Usually she objected to his interfering in her domestic affairs, but now she was most amiable.

"I promised her I would—she seems a nice girl."

"Yes," said Hector. "I'm giving her five pounds a month."

His wife grasped a chair for support.

"Are you mad?" She beckoned Jane, for her earlier suspicions were now certainties.

"Fetch a doctor," she said, under her breath. "The master isn't well. I only pay her eighteen pounds a year."

She tried to say this in a light conversational tone, but her voice shook.

"You only—?" Something was very wrong, and he called the maid to him. "Ask Dr. Sawyer to step round. Mrs. Smith isn't quite herself," he said.

"Get Dr. Thomas." demanded Mary, sharply.

Thomas! Thomas was in Mesopotamia! It was clear now. The worry of the past years had turned her brain. It was a flattering explanation for the preference she had lately shown to Arthur. They watched one another apprehensively after the girl had gone, then:—

"Feel better, ducky?" he asked, huskily.

"Has that nasty wuzzy feeling gone, lovey?" her voice was a nervous squeak.

Dr. Thomas had the flat opposite, and Dr. Thomas was coming out of his flat when the frightened maid had literally flung herself upon him.

"They're both mad," she babbled, and the startled doctor followed her to where two people, each standing at the extreme end of a long drawing-room, were watching one another in silence. Hector saw him and uttered an exclamation of astonishment.

"By Jove. I thought you were in Bagdad?"

The doctor laid his soothing hand on the other's shoulder.

"Of course—Bagdad! Ah, that's the place—we'll soon put you right, old man."

Ignoring the implication that he wasn't right, Mr. Smith whispered something in the other's ear.

"Of course she is," replied Thomas, indulgently, and caught Mary's eye and Mary's significant signal.

It was at that moment that Arthur came in—Arthur in his Eton suit, with his cherubic face stained with jam. Hector looked at him and his jaw dropped.

"What the devil have you dressed like this for?" he demanded.

"Because I'm going to school, Mr. Smith."

"To school? How old are you?"

"Fourteen—nearly."

"Fourteen!" repeated Hector, hollowly.

"Is it possible—?"

On Mary's desk was a calendar and to this he walked.

"Nineteen fourteen! Mary, I understand all. I will explain. You're not mad—it was the fairy—who put back the clock!—my wish was granted!"

The doctor looked at Mary and Mary looked at the doctor. "I'm going to prophesy," Hector went on, excitedly. "We are going to war! The Kaiser will abdicate! The British Army will be seven millions strong! We shall win the war, thanks to Beatty, Haig, and Foch!"

He saw the round face of Arthur and—smack! Arthur sprawled on the door, blubbering.

"Why did you do that?" asked the terrified Mary.

"He's going to cause me a lot of trouble," said Hector, prophetically.

The Death Room

'DO you believe in spiritualism, Mr Gillette?'

Detective-Inspector John Gillette now frowned a little terrifyingly at the girl who sat on the opposite side of his desk. When an official of Scotland Yard receives a newspaper reporter he does not expect to be cross-examined on his hobbies. And spiritualism was a hobby of this dour man.

'You see,' Ella Martin broke in eagerly, 'I have taken up a case for the paper. The editor did not like the idea at all, and said that my job was to write nice, chatty little pars about what Lady So-and-So wore at the Devonshire House ball, and all that sort of thing, but I rather insisted.'

John Gillette concealed a smile—and he very seldom felt the inclination to smile. She was very young and very pretty, and very unlike any newspaper reporter he had ever seen.

'How did you know I was interested in spooks?' he asked.

'From the evidence you gave in the Marriot case years and years ago. It was amongst the cuttings in the library.'

Detective-Inspector John Gillette was not an easy man to interview. Against that, however, was the fact that very few, other than those officials at police headquarters whose business brought them in touch with him, regarded him as worth interviewing. His name rarely appeared in print, for he was an 'office man' and a consultant rather than a practitioner in the art of crime detection.

He was a man of thirty, and a bachelor in a double sense of the word, for he held a degree from the London University.

'Spiritualism?' he repeated slowly, 'Well, yes and no. Certain phenomena are inexplicable. Animal instinct, for example. I have seen sheep terrified before the door of a new slaughter-house, and one that has never been used before. I have known dogs to be frantic with fear hours before an earthquake. In fact, I have seen my old terrier shivering with fright three hours before a raid warning was received. Explain that! It is as easy to explain as spirit manifestations. There is a something. The mediums feel it, and, dissatisfied with its faint message, they must interpret the whisper as a shout! They see things dimly, and in their impatience or enthusiasm they insist that you shall see plainly. With this result—that they fake. They rip along ahead of the thing they should pursue, and are mad with you when you prove that all that is following them is their own silly shadows! But why are you so interested? It doesn't seem a very healthy subject for a young lady to discuss with a police officer! What is the stunt behind your question?'

She smiled.

'Have you ever heard of Mr Jean Bonnet?' she asked.

The inspector's forehead puckered.

'Bonnet! Do you mean the stockbroker?'

She nodded.

'That is the gentleman. He is a millionaire, and has a big, rambling place, Tatton Corners, near Reading.'

Gillette pushed himself back from the table and frowned again.

'A Russian died there the other day. I remember! So that is your stunt? What were the circumstances of the death? All the details were not in the newspapers, and I wasn't very much interested.'

'So I gather,' said the girl, with a little smile. 'Otherwise you would not ask why I want to know something about spiritualism. The Russian's name was Dimitri Nicoli, a financier, who was associated with Mr Bonnet. Nicoli, who lived in Paris, seems to have been a furtive, secretive man. He had no relations and very few friends, certainly nobody who enjoyed his confidence. He had a leaning towards the shadier side of finance, and undoubtedly during the War he dabbled in one or two questionable enterprises which yielded him a huge profit. About four weeks ago Nicoli came to London, and to a man who knew him and who remembered him in town, he confided the fact that he was engaged in a transaction with Mr. Bonnet which would yield him "milliards." The character of the transaction he never discussed, and the next day he left for Tatton Corners, where he arrived and was entertained by Mr Bonnet. He spent a week there, talking over some business. Mr Bonnet says it was the flotation of a culture pearl company on an extensive scale; at any rate, Nicoli left at the end of the week for Paris.

'He returned in the early part of last week, and, at his own request, was put in what the servants at Tatton Corners call "the haunted room".'

'The haunted room?' repeated Gillette. 'Of course! I remember now. There was a headline about it in your newspaper.'

She nodded.

'Apparently one of the rooms—and, curiously enough, it is one of the newest rooms in the most modern wing of the house—is believed to be haunted. Mr Bonnet, who studies spiritualism, and who, like so many people

312

who take up the study, is a hard-headed business man'—she shot a swift glance at Gillette, and for the second time he smiled—'told our reporter that he has seen dark shapes come and go down the corridor, and even through the closed door of the room. He has never mentioned the fact before for fear of frightening the servants.

'The morning after Nicoli's return he was found dead in his bed, and had the appearance of a man who had been strangled, though there were no marks at all upon his body. Suspicion immediately fell upon a mysterious Frenchman, or, at any rate, a man of foreign appearance, who had arrived in the neighbourhood at the same time as Nicoli, and who stayed at the little inn in the village and spent his nights wandering about the country, and was seen by Mr Bonnet's gardener in the grounds of Tatton Corners itself.'

John Gillette tapped the table impatiently.

'You will think we are asleep at Scotland Yard, but I had forgotten all about it! I remember now. But the local police were perfectly satisfied that nothing was wrong. Could this foreigner have reached Nicoli through the window?'

She shook her head.

'I have seen the plans of the house. That wing is newly built, and it is almost impossible for anybody to have got into the room without leaving some trace.'

'And the mysterious Frenchman?'

'Has disappeared entirely. He gave the name of Binot. And now comes the remarkable part of the story. Mr Bonnet sent for one of our reporters yesterday and told him that he had had a communication with the dead man, who had appeared to him that night by the side of his bed with the news that Binot was the murderer!'

'H'm!' growled the detective, settling back in his chair. 'That sounds to me like a disordered digestive apparatus, aggravated by an attack of nerves. I shouldn't take that too seriously if I were you, Miss Martin. Your editor, now—was he interested?'

'Not very,' said the girl; 'but it occurred to me that there might be a bigger story behind it all.'

Detective-Inspector John Gillette was silent for a while, absorbed in his own thoughts.

'I should like to see this haunted room,' he said at length, and her eyes lit up.

'I hoped you would,' she said. 'You see, Mr Gillette, I am not frantically impressed by the spirit theory; whilst I can't help feeling that there is something just a little uncanny, I am certain that there is also something scientific behind it too. And science rattles me.'

The detective looked at the eager face and his heart went out to the girl. There was something very naive and appealing in her youth, something that stirred a chord in his nature that had never been touched before.

'Briefly, what is the stunt?' he asked, and she hesitated.

'I was going to do it myself, and then I got a little frightened and realized that detective work isn't as easy as it seems. I thought I would go to Tatton Corners, pretending that I was a fellow countryman of Mr Nicoli—a niece who was interested in his fate. They say Mr Bonnet is awfully kind and unsuspicious.' She hesitated again.

'And when you have taken advantage of his innocence and secured an entry to his house, what then?' asked Gillette, with a twinkle in his eyes.

She pulled a little face.

'I don't know,' she said vaguely. 'Probably get permission to sleep in the haunted room.'

It was Inspector Gillette who hesitated now. He really was not interested in a newspaper mystery which was probably no mystery at all, but he was very much interested in Ella Martin.

'I hate helping the Press,' he said, 'but I'll go with you, though I've an uncomfortable feeling that I'm being a fool. Of course, nobody will invite you to stay, and probably I shouldn't let you if they did. It's a mad adventure, and I look like being turned out of the Force for helping you!'

II

A BITTERLY cold wind was blowing, and there was a smell of snow in the air when they arrived at Tatton Corners. In their assumed character of Russians they were wearing fur coats and hats.

Mr Bonnet, a slight, sad-looking man, was playing patience in his drawing-room when the station fly clattered up the drive. The thin, almost aesthetic-looking face of the financier, the high forehead and the straight grey eyebrows, held the detective's attention. It was the face of a dreamer, of the spiritualist rather than one who had been the shrewdest financier in the country.

Mr Bonnet listened in sympathetic silence whilst the girl (with a glibness which amazed the detective) explained the object of the visit.

'A relation?' asked Mr Bonnet gravely, and she nodded. 'I would, of course, do anything for a relative of my poor friend Nicoli,' said Mr Bonnet with a little sigh, 'though it saddens me even to discuss the tragedy. Perhaps Mr—' He looked at the inspector inquiringly.

'Gillette,' said that gentleman, and Mr Bonnet bowed.

'I had a fear at first that you were reporters, although I am hardened to that now,' said the financier, as he led the way out of the room into the chill of the garden. 'I seem to have lived in the company of policemen and newspaper reporters all my life. Here is the room.'

Tatton Corners was a sixteenth-century farmhouse, to which its owner had made certain ruthless additions, none of which was calculated to improve it from the point of view of the artist. The new wing was of red brick, and some half-hearted attempt had been made to keep the annexe in harmony with the remainder of the structure.

Gillette looked up. A broad window, the top sash of which had been dropped down a foot, a window box, and—

'What is that red square underneath the window?' he asked.

'That is a ventilator,' replied Mr Bonnet. 'I had the new wing built on the soundest hygienic principles, and I fixed these patent ventilators in every room. There is another, you will notice.' He pointed to a window.

He led them round the grounds, which must have been beautiful in summer, and all the time Gillette's eyes did not seem to leave the house.

'You are utilitarian at the cost of good architecture,' he laughed. He pointed to a large red tank which the girl had mistaken for a turret structure.

'I hoped nobody would ever notice that,' said the melancholy Mr Bonnet. 'The water supply here isn't sufficient, and we are inclined to dry up during the summer. So I store my rainwater, and at that height we can get sufficient pressure to reach the farthest part of the grounds.'

They passed into the house, and Mr Bonnet led the way to the haunted room. It lay at the end of a passage, from which opened two other doors, leading, as the host showed them, to spare bedrooms. The door was unlocked, and Bonnet flung it open wide.

The detective saw a very ordinary bedroom, comfortably furnished. Beside the bed in the corner there was a dressing-table, a writing-desk, two or three chairs and a small but handsome Persian rug upon the polished floor.

'There, you see, is the other side of the ventilator.' Mr Bonnet pointed to the grille in the wall. 'It is a curious thing that this room should be haunted, because it has rather haunted me.' He smiled pathetically. 'I intended this to be my own sitting-room, but somehow I could never work in it. I experimented with every kind of lighting.' He pointed to the electrolier fastened to the ceiling (a little too rich, the girl thought, for so commonplace a room). 'First I tried lighting it from the walls, and then from the roof; then I tried hand lamps, but somehow I could never settle down to work here, and so I turned it into a spare bedroom. The view sometimes tempts me to come up, or used to tempt me'—he shivered—'until this hideous tragedy got rid of any desire I had to spend my afternoons here.'

Absent-mindedly John Gillette fingered the silver electric switches near the door. Suddenly the light blazed in the roof. He turned another switch, but there was no further illumination.

'The wall lamp is out of order. I am going to have it wired,' said Mr Bonnet. 'I feel I don't wish to do anything to this room now that my poor friend—' He turned away his head.

Ella Martin found herself ushered into the passage and into the hall, and felt for a moment desperate. She had come determined to stay the night, but the absence of women servants, no less than the failure of her host to issue an invitation, made the plan look just a little mad—as mad as Gillette thought it was.

Mr Bonnet accompanied them to the waiting fly.

'I was hoping,' he said, 'that you good people would have stayed the night. But I am very lonely here; half my servants have left, and the new ones are already terror-stricken.'

The detective, with one foot on the step, turned and looked at Ella thoughtfully.

'It would be no great hardship, staying a night in this lovely house. And the hotel doesn't seem to be a very inviting one. Perhaps we can lay the ghost.'

Ella hesitated. For a moment her courage forsook her. The adventure had lost a little of its attractiveness. A glimpse of Gillette's face decided her.

'I'll send the driver back to the hotel to bring a suit-case,' said Gillette. 'I'm glad you asked me. I would rather like to stay here. By the way, are you making a rockery garden, Mr Bonnet?'

'Yes,' said the other in surprise. 'Why?'

'I saw a heap of broken marble at the back of the house,' said the detective. 'But why rockery gardens should not have gravel under foot, and must have unpleasantly sharpened, pointed marble pebbles, heaven only knows!'

They talked of gardens and gardening, and the evening passed so quickly that the girl was surprised to discover it was eleven o'clock.

'I am afraid you will have to be accommodated in the haunted wing,' said Mr Bonnet, smiling for the first time. 'I hope your nerves are good.'

'Excellent,' said the detective. 'I undertake to lay any ghost I find.'

The other became instantly grave.

'I don't think I should speak slightingly of these things, if I were you, Mr Gillette,' he said. 'I am only a child in the science, but I have seen amazing things happen.' He seemed to stop himself with an effort, as though he were afraid of placing too great a strain upon their credulity.

'And the young lady?' He looked at the girl dubiously.

'The young lady...' Ella found her breath coming more quickly; she had to force the words.

'The young lady would like to sleep in the haunted room itself,' she said a little unsteadily, and Mr Bonnet stared at her.

'In the haunted room?' he gasped. 'Impossible, my dear young friend! Why, you would be frightened.'

He looked appealingly at Gillette, and then beckoned him aside.

'I do not know, sir, in what relationship you stand with this young woman,' he said in a low voice, 'but I beg that you persuade her to change her mind.'

An hour before the detective would have been in a dilemma. Now, however, his mind was very clear on all matters except Miss Ella Martin.

'I think I should allow the young lady to sleep where she wishes,' he said calmly, and Mr Bonnet was obviously nonplussed.

'Very good,' he said with a shrug. 'But I must prepare the room—no servant will go into it after dark.'

For a moment the girl's resolution wavered, but her host was gone before she could change her mind.

'I'm scared to death,' she said in a low voice.

'Don't be,' said Gillette, and tapped three times on the table.

'You hear that?—remember it, and when you hear that sound on your bedroom door open and let me in. You'll stay up all night, of course?'

'But—' she began, bewildered.

'You wanted an adventure,' he said grimly, 'and you wanted ghosts. You have bewitched a respectable police officer into acting the fool to that end, and I rather fancy that—'

He had heard Mr Bonnet's footsteps in the room above the library where they were talking, and then:

'Whoo-oo-oo!'

It was a moan that rose to a wail, and then to a shrill shriek ... and silence.

And at that moment Mr Bonnet came slowly down the stairs towards them.

It was Gillette who asked the question.

Mr Bonnet shook his head.

'I don't know,' he said simply. 'I hear it often—it is the sound which frightens the servants. Your room is ready, Miss Nicoli,' he said, using the name she had given. And with reluctant feet she walked upstairs.

The bed had been made and she sat down, looking fearfully about the room. It was nearly twelve o'clock before a tap brought her heart to her mouth, and she opened the door to admit the detective. He seemed to be amused at something as he turned and locked the door. He carried a bag in his hand, and this he opened and took out a small black cardboard box. From this he extracted two tin candlesticks, into which he fitted two short candle lengths.

'Are you preparing for the lights to go out?' she said in a whisper.

'Not exactly. I am preparing for their coming on,' said the other. 'Will you oblige me by sitting bolt upright, Miss Martin. Sit on a pillow and keep very, very quiet, because this ghost hates noise.'

He walked to the window and tried to open the lower sash, but it had been fastened, and he remembered Mr Bonnet apprising him of the fact. The top sash, however, he pulled down.

'Not that it will be much use,' he said.

He took off the silken shade from the wall bracket.

'Why, there is no electric bulb in it,' said the girl in surprise. 'That is why it doesn't light.'

'I didn't think there would be,' said the other, replacing the silk shade.

Pulling down the blind he lit the two candles and placed them on the floor; then he switched out the light.

'Watch the candles,' he whispered.

III

THE girl sat, watching and watching, until there seemed a dozen dancing candles, until her very head ached from weariness. No sound broke the stillness of the night; the faint roar and rattle of distant trains came to them at intervals, but there was no other sound. Once Gillette turned his head and looked at the wall bracket, but that was the only movement he made, and then, for no reason whatever, one of the candles went out.

The girl stared at the remaining light. Whilst she looked that too went out. 'Don't move!' hissed Gillette.

Suddenly there was the flash of an electric torch.

'Hold that,' he whispered. He took a box of matches out of his pocket, lit one, steadied it until the flame had taken hold and then slowly lowered the light toward the candle. An inch from the top of the wick the light went out.

'Take off your shoes,' whispered the detective, and switched on the lights. 'No, no, don't stoop, put your feet up on the bed. That's right.'

Tiptoeing to the door he turned the key softly and pushed. The door did not give by so much as a millimetre. She saw the frown gather on his face as he turned the handle.

'The ghost has bolted us in,' he said nonchalantly. 'I was a fool not to look for bolts.'

He lit the candles again and slowly lowered one to the floor. It went out just below the bed level.

'I always carry candles in my kit,' he said conversationally. 'I wish I carried an axe.'

He went to the window and examined the panes.

'Toughened glass strengthened by wire,' he said. 'We must have time.'

She saw him glance up at the wall bracket, and then, kneeling on the bed, he screwed up a piece of paper and leisurely plugged the open end of the fixture.

Over the open window sash he vaulted, lowering himself to the ledge without.

'Come here and bring your scarf,' he ordered, and, wondering, she obeyed. 'Hold up one hand.'

In an instant he had knotted an end of the scarf about her wrist, and drew up the slack until the strain on her arm was almost painful. Then he fastened the other end to the hinge of the outside shutter.

'What are you doing?' she gasped.

'Women faint,' said Mr Gillette coolly, 'and I particularly wish you not to faint until I return.'

A second later he disappeared.

Her wrist pained her; the agony was almost as much as she could bear, and she seemed in danger of fulfilling his prophecy when she heard the rasp of wood against the window ledge and he appeared.

'A ladder,' he said, and helped her over the open sash.

She saw nothing, but he guided her to the ladder's head.

How she got down she could never remember. She was trembling in every limb when at last she reached the ground. Still she could see nothing. The night was pitch black. Large, wet snowflakes brushed against her cheek, and an icy wind swept through the tree-tops, filling the night with a dismal sound, and chilled her to the bone despite her heavy fur coat.

'I'm afraid I shall have to carry the ladder, but in a little while your eyes will get used to the darkness,' he said, 'and you will see ahead.'

He shouldered the ladder, and she followed blindly. No light showed in the house, but presently they came to a corner which was, she remembered, the corner where first she had seen the red tank.

'Will you stay here or come with me?' he asked in a low voice.

'Where are you going?' she whispered fearfully.

'Looking for ghosts,' was the grim reply, and then she laughed a little hysterically.

'I think I had better see them too,' she said.

He was planting the ladder against a wall unbroken by windows. Presently she heard the grate of his feet on the rungs. Biting her trembling lip she gripped the sides of the ladder and began to climb. Half-way up an attack of vertigo almost brought her down, and the man above her must have been possessed of supernatural senses, for, even as she swayed, he caught her.

'A little farther,' he whispered, and with his aid she scrambled to the top.

She could see now clearly; she was on a flat leaded roof.

'Take off your shoes,' he whispered, and she obeyed.

They crept forward to the very middle of the oblong patch, and there she discerned something which looked like a small platform raised a few inches above the roof level.

'This may not be the place at all,' he whispered in her ear, 'but I've been drawing a mental plan of the house, and I imagine my guess is right.'

Stooping, he gripped the edge of the platform and drew it up an inch. No light showed, and, peering down, he saw that the trap covered a glass fanlight. Cautiously he lifted the trap still farther and laid it back, the girl at his side. Then from the room below came a sudden brilliant flash of light, and they looked down speechless, for in that flash was revealed the hideous paraphernalia of destruction.

The room was long and narrow, lined with white-glazed brick. In the centre was a large retort, near which was a heap of those marble chips that they had seen in the garden that afternoon. Attached to a pipe leading from the retort was a small electric pump which worked ceaselessly.

The girl could only stare in amazement. The significance of the retort and the working pump did not come to her. Her eyes were fixed upon a bearded man who lay, strapped to a narrow table, gagged and helpless.

'Binot!' she gasped.

The detective gripped her arm so fiercely that she winced. His eyes were on Bonnet, who stood in his shirt-sleeves, his hands thrust in his pockets, a smile of sardonic amusement upon his face, as he caught the glaring eyes of the prisoner on the table.

He was saying something, but the sound did not penetrate through the glass, or rise above the moan of the wind.

Gillette stooped and felt desperately for the edge of the fanlight. To his surprise it was not locked, but came up in his hands, and the queer, sickening odour of the room struck him in the face and made him choke.

'My friend,' Bonnet was saying in French, 'I suffer from a plague of detectives. First there was you, whom our admirable friend Nicoli brought to Tatton Corners because he feared, very rightly, that I would steal the eight million francs he brought with him. And you, I admit, were difficult! Then we have the admirable Detective-Inspector Gillette, accompanied by a girl who has a cock-and-bull story of being a relative of Nicoli.'

He laughed softly, and took up the long knife that lay upon a table near the bench and felt the edge with his finger. Then he laughed again.

'Our Gillette is dead by now,' he said calmly. 'I watched him join his young lady, and it is better to be dead than compromised. The beauty of it is that nobody will ever discover—'

He walked across to where the glaring Frenchman lay, and tried his knife again ...

Gillette flung open the fanlight and leapt upon the madman.

IV

'BEFORE I came upon this perilous adventure I looked up Mr Bonnet in an old work of reference, and I found that his hobby was chemistry,' said Inspector Gillette, as they were travelling back to town, 'and when I discovered that the electric wall lamp was fixed on the end of a hollow pipe I began to wonder where the pipe led to. Obviously in building the wing, and for this especial room, Bonnet connected the wall bracket with a hollow pipe which led to his laboratory. Bonnet must have planned the murder some time ago; he had been in correspondence with Nicoli, an old confederate of his, for more than a year. That is to say, before the builders put trowel to brick on the new annexe.

'By some means which we may discover, but very likely shall never know, he persuaded Nicoli to bring an enormous sum of money to London, and the bait must have been a fairly golden one. Nicoli mistrusted his former friend, or else had no desire to travel with so much money without an escort, and he engaged Binot to follow him and watch him. When Binot found his master was dead, and there was no mention of the money, instead of getting back and reporting to Paris to the French authorities he decided to wait and investigate independently. I am not imputing any motive to Binot,' said Gillette, shaking his head, 'but human nature being what it is, I should imagine Binot wanted to get the money that his master had. He came, was captured, and he has been a prisoner for a month.

'To-night Bonnet decided to kill three birds with one stone. I am not sure,' said Gillette thoughtfully, 'whether it was just carbonic acid gas, or whether it was carbon monoxide. They are both very heavy gasses. They are both odourless, tasteless, and they could both be poured into a room while a man was sleeping or sitting.'

'But the moaning ghost?' asked the girl.

Gillette chuckled.

'The moaning ghost put me on to it. Obviously it was an electric fan placed behind the ventilator and operated from Bonnet's room. He turned a switch and the fan began to revolve. He touched a switch and it stopped. The fan, of course, was to clear the room of the gas, so that any person coming in afterwards would not detect the slightest trace of it. The other ventilators were fakes. The death room was designed for Nicoli and his millions—how many millions we may never know.

'Last night I had a talk with Bonnet, and dropped a hint that I knew his game, without exactly intimating that I understood the method he adopted. I did mention the fact that a fairly deadly gas can be made from marble chips treated with hydrochloric acid, and I guess that hit home, for he is sane enough to be annoyed by the ease with which he was bowled over. There would have been a sad accident last night, my young friend, if you had gone to sleep in that room without the warning candle—nothing burns in either carbonic acid or carbon monoxide—and without the knowledge that our dear friend was spending the night profitably in generating the real spirit of the death room.

'I hope I shall see you again,' said Gillette at parting, and held her hand. 'I can't promise you ghosts, and I won't advise you to look round the Black Museum. Do you ever write stories?'

'Sometimes,' she smiled.

'Tell me, is it a convention of literature that a girl marries the man who rescues her from—er—death and all that sort of thing?'

She went very red, but did not take her eyes from his.

'It is a convention—in detective stories,' she said.

Which seemed to Gillette, in the circumstances, a completely satisfactory answer.

Edgar Wallace

The Sodium Lines

MR HERBERT FALLOWILL made his final entry on a square card almost covered with his neat and microscopic writing, took up the dead end of his cigar from the edge of the ash-tray and lit it. He was a square-built man, clean-shaven, except for a fiery moustache, and his reddish hair ran back from a forehead that was high and bald.

'You leave for Queenstown to-night?' he said, and the thin-lipped woman who bore his name nodded.

'The passports?'

'Yours is in the name of "Clancy",' he said. 'Mine is fixed. I shall leave as arranged by the Aquitania. You'll meet me at the apartment on 44th Street—I shall be there at eleven-fifteen. This is the time-table—'

He fixed a pair of pince-nez on his thick nose and consulted the card.

'At nine o'clock Dorford will give me the cheque; at nine- thirty it will be cashed, and I shall move to Southampton—quick! I have relay cars waiting at Guildford and Winchester. The Aquitania leaves dock at twelve-thirty—I shall make it, with time to spare. The old man will not expect to see me again on the Saturday or Sunday because I've told him I'm going away. Monday is a holiday and the banks are closed. The earliest he can discover anything is by Tuesday morning.'

She took out the cigarette she was smoking and blew a cloud to the ceiling.

'That old man is certainly dippy!' she said, shaking her head.

Mr Fallowill smiled indulgently.

'There never was a pure scientist that wasn't,' he said. 'Only so very few of 'em have the stuff.'

Professor Dorford had no illusions about himself. Business of all kinds worried him, and he accounted himself fortunate that, after a succession of incompetents, heaven had sent him a most capable middle-aged secretary, who combined an exceptional knowledge of finance with a capacity for knowing just what the Professor would say in answer to people who pester a rich man with requests for subscriptions or charitable assistance.

He would have gone farther and favoured his secretary with a power of attorney which would enable him to draw small cheques for the tradespeople, but here Gwenn Dorford, a nineteen-year-old graduate, put her small foot down very firmly.

'My dear lamb!' she said, and when the Professor was addressed as a dear lamb in that tone of voice, he invariably shivered.

'Fallowill is a most excellent man,' he protested feebly.

'I don't like Mr Fallowill, and I loathe his wife,' said Gwenn, 'but I realize that I may be prejudiced—and, after all, a woman can be a good wife and still be a cat to everybody else. Mr Spooner, the bank manager, says—'

'Spooner is an interfering jackanapes,' said the Professor testily. 'I am seriously thinking of taking my account away from the Gresham Bank. To—er—impugn Fallowill's—er—honour is monstrous! He had letters from eminent people in Australia and the United States.'

Nobody knew better than Gwenn Dorford that her father had not verified these excellent references, but she did not press the matter to an argument.

She did, however, tell Johnny Brest for the fortieth time, and for the fortieth time Johnny sympathised with her. But then, Johnny would. He was tactful, as became an officer in the Public Prosecutor's department and a lawyer at that; he was sympathetic, because—Gwenn was very pretty and he carried her portrait in his cigarette case.

'He may be all right,' he said. 'I went over to New Scotland yard and tried to find out whether anything was known about him—he is quite a stranger to police headquarters.'

'I don't wish him to become acquainted through us,' she said firmly. 'He may be the nicest man in the world, but the way daddy trusts him makes my hair stand up! And now, Johnny, you can take me a long drive in your pot boiler.'

Johnny Brest was the owner of a steam car, because that was the only kind of car he could afford to buy. Not that such machines are cheap. They were certainly rare in England—so rare that, when one was offered for sale by auction, Johnny, who had drifted into the rooms out of curiosity, heard the car offered at so ridiculously low a figure that, in a moment of recklessness, he bid, and found himself the proprietor of a machine that nobody understood. It was only then that he discovered the secret of its propulsion.

Mr Fallowill watched the noiseless white car slip down the drive and disappear from view, as he had watched it scores of times. He felt easier in his mind when the antagonistic daughter of his employer was away from the house, and more especially was he relieved that afternoon.

Returning to his desk, he cleared off his correspondence and went in search of Professor Dorford. The Professor looked up as his secretary entered. He was a grey, bent man with a vague manner and a trick of ignoring the immediate. Fallowill said of him, with truth, that he lived from three days to ten years behind his time, and certainly it was the fact that most days were gone before John Dorford was aware that they had arrived.

'Ah, Fallowill! Come in, come in, please. Will you get on to Sir Roland Field—Cambridge 99 or 999—or perhaps it is some other number—'

'Cambridge 9714,' said the secretary.

'Of course! I was sure you would remember. Will you be so good as to ask him if I am—er—mad in supposing that the sodium lines disappeared from the spectrum this morning? It is an extraordinary fact, my dear Fallowill, that when I was making a very superficial examination of the sun's spectrum, those lines appeared and disappeared, and finally vanished altogether for the space of twelve minutes!'

Fallowill inclined his head and adopted the requisite expression of amazement. The peculiarities of the sun's spectrum meant nothing to him. Inwardly he cursed his employer's dislike of the telephone, for he knew his own limitations, and a scientific discussion on a long-distance wire was beyond him.

'Certainly, sir. Did you think any more about the matter I mentioned to you?'

The Professor scratched his head in perplexity.

'The matter—now what was that, Fallowill?'

'The question of transferring your balance to the Wales and Western bank.'

Professor Dorford sighed—he always sighed when money was a subject of discussion.

'Yes, yes, of course, Fallowill. I quite agree, and I shall certainly act on your advice. I will make the transfer—when?'

'Saturday is the end of the month!' suggested Fallowill.

Even Gwenn paid a grudging acknowledgement to Mr Fallowill's financial genius, and justly so. For, in various names and in divers countries, he had so manipulated the finances of confiding investors that it had been necessary from time to time to make startling changes in his appearance. And now he had rendered the Professor an immense service. Foreseeing the industrial slump, he had induced his employer to turn all but his government stock into money.

'Saturday? Yes,' said the Professor. 'When is Saturday?'

'To-morrow,' replied the other. 'Brighton Rails are down to three. We got out of those in time! I was calculating to-day that, if you hadn't started selling when I suggested, you would have been eight thousand to the bad. You can't make a mistake by holding the cash instead. Short term loans pay very little interest, but you have the money to jump into the market when it strikes bottom.'

'Exactly,' murmured Mr Dorford agreeably. 'I'm greatly obliged to you, Fallowill. And now will you get Sir Roland?'

Waiting for the call to come through, the sturdy secretary marshalled his knowledge of the spectrum. He knew that when the rays of the sun passed through a prism it threw bands of variegated light on a screen. He knew that there was a more complicated apparatus which showed in the rainbow hue bright and dark lines which indicated the presence in the sun of certain elements. To keep pace with his employer's requirements, he had struggled through various text-books on the subject, and knew, therefore, that sodium was one of the more important of the solar elements.

It was some time before he got his call through to Sir Roland, and that aged gentleman, who shared his fellow scientist's dislike of the telephone, was in his most irritable mood.

'What's that? Sodium—who wants sodium? Is it Dorford himself? What do you want, my good fellow?'

'The Professor wishes to know if you have observed the absence of sodium lines in the spectrum,' said the patient Fallowill.

'No, I haven't,' snapped the other. 'Nor has he! You've made a mistake. Get back and tell him to write!'

Crash! went the telephone receiver, and Fallowill went back to his employer to report the result of the conversation. Professor Dorford rubbed his chin nervously.

'Perhaps I was wrong,' he said. 'It may have been some trick of eyesight, but certainly the sodium lines disappeared at eleven-sixteen this morning.'

'Remarkable, sir,' said Fallowill politely.

He lived in West Kensington, and travelled home by tube. His mind was so occupied with the possibilities which to-morrow held that, although he read his evening newspaper, he did not comprehend a single word until his eye was held by a headline: 'Extraordinary Traffic Block.' And then the figures '11.15' arrested him.

*

At 11.15 this morning a most extraordinary traffic block occurred in the heart of the City. By an amazing coincidence, three motor-buses stopped of their own accord in the narrowest part of Cheapside, and could not be moved for a quarter of an hour. As it was the rush hour, the street was soon filled with stationary cars. This in itself might not have been remarkable, but the same phenomenon was witnessed in the Strand, on Ludgate Hill and in other parts of the City.

*

He was waiting on the platform for the car to slow into South Kensington Station when the conductor, whom he knew by sight, looked at the paper he was carrying.

'Queer thing, that traffic stoppage,' he said. 'It happened down here.'

'On the tubes?' asked Fallowill in surprise, and the man nodded.

'Yes, we slowed down and all the lights went out. Somebody told me that it was a magnetic storm. I know the telegraph lines weren't working.'

'Queer,' agreed Fallowill, and went home to help his wife pack.

*

GWENN DORFORD did not as a rule see her father before the lunch hour. He was an early riser, and usually closeted himself in his study until midday, and it was a rule of the establishment that he should not be interrupted. She was passing his room an hour before lunch and, seeing the door open, looked in. The Professor was standing at the window, his hands in his pockets, staring moodily into the sunlit street.

'Good morning, daddy. Aren't you working?'

He looked round with a start.

'No, no, my dear,' he said a little nervously. 'I'm—er—not working. I'm going out. Who is that?' He stared past her. 'Oh, it is you, Johnny—Come in, come in. Are you staying to lunch?'

'I'm taking Gwenn to Hampton Court,' said Johnny Brest.

'So you are! Of course, I remember.'

Dorford looked at his watch, and for some remarkable reason the girl felt a little twinge of alarm.

'Where is Mr Fallowill?' she asked.

'Gone to the bank,' said the Professor a little huskily. 'And, Gwenn, the sodium lines are gone again. Remarkable! Sodium has disappeared from the sun!'

'Why has Mr Fallowill gone to the bank?' she asked, not interested for the moment in sodium and its eccentricities.

The Professor looked appealingly to the young man.

'I think I have been rather a fool, Gwenn. It is extraordinary that I should think so, but I do. Though I'm sure Fallowill is as honest as the day, but—'

'What have you done?' she asked quickly.

'I've given him—er—a cheque for eighty-four thousand pounds—he is transferring my account,' said the Professor, and the hand that went up to his mouth was shaking. 'You see, I have a whole lot of fluid capital, and Fallowill thought that it would be better in another bank.'

She gasped.

'You've given him the cheque? But will Mr Spooner pay?'

'I wrote a letter also. Spooner telephoned up to ask if it was all right, and I said yes.'

'To what bank was it to be paid, Mr Dorford?'

'The Wales and Western.'

'We can easily find out,' said Johnny, and took up the telephone. He jerked the hook for a long rime, and then: 'Your phone is out of order.'

'I know.' The Professor nodded. 'I tried to get the bank five minutes ago.'

He was still looking out of the window, his mind apparently concentrated on the fruitless efforts of a chauffeur to start a car on the opposite side of the road.

'That is strange,' he said.

'But, father, why don't you drive round to the bank and ask?'

'I thought of doing that,' he said. 'In fact, I've sent Mary to get a taxi, and here she is.'

A hot and flustered housemaid appeared in the doorway.

'None of the taxis are going, sir,' she gasped.

'Going? What do you mean?'

'The street's full of cabs and cars and they're all standing still! They can't move them, sir. And if you please, sir, none of the telephones are working... a man told me the electric lights have gone too...'

*

WITH a large wad of American bills in his inside pocket, Mr Fallowill moved out of town, exercising that caution which experience had taught him was profitable. An annoyed traffic policeman might make all the difference between the success and failure of his scheme. Once beyond Barnes and out of Kingston, he stepped on the accelerator and the big car roared along the Portsmouth road at sixty miles an hour. Beyond Cobham there was a hill to negotiate, and, reaching the crest, he turned the car at full speed down the steep slope.

And then he heard something and frowned. The engine had stopped, and the car was running downhill under its own weight and impetus. If he had any doubt, it was settled when he came to the foot of the slope. A slight rise a hundred yards along slowed the car, and he had to put on the brakes to prevent the machine from running backwards. Fortunately, there was a wayside inn within a hundred yards, and, after making an ineffectual effort to restart the machine, he walked to the hostel.

To his relief, he saw a telephone wire connecting the house with the main lines.

'I want to telephone to Guildford—' he began.

The landlord shook his head.

'The 'phone is out of order,' he said. 'At least, it was a minute or two ago when I tried to get a call through to Esher.'

Fallowill's heart sank.

'Where is the nearest?' he asked.

'There isn't one within six miles,' said the landlord. 'What is the matter?'

'My car has broken down, and it is absolutely necessary that I should be in Southampton in two hours,' said Fallowill.

He was desperate, but he must risk giving a clue to the police that would lead them eventually to Southampton. Then, to his relief:

'I have an old flivver here that'll run you into Guildford. You will be able to hire a car from there,' said the landlord, and Fallowill could have fallen on his neck. At Guildford the relief car was waiting, thanks to his foresight.

He followed his host out into the yard, where a dilapidated machine stood underneath a shed, and together they pushed the car into the stable yard, whilst a hastily summoned youth struggled into his coat.

'Take this gentleman to Guildford. Where did you leave your machine, sir?'

'At the bottom of the hill.'

'I'll have it brought up,' said the landlord. 'You can call for it on your way back.'

The youth dropped into the driver's seat and Fallowill followed.

'I can't get her to start!' said the surprised chauffeur a few minutes later.

Neither self-starter nor handle had the slightest effect, and after a quarter of an hour Fallowill, white-faced and shaken, stepped to the ground.

*

MANY strange things happened that day. The streets and roads of England were littered with useless motor-cars. Every electric train, above and below ground, had come to a standstill, and from the black tunnels of darkened tube stations poured processions of frightened passengers.

Johnny Brest drove his steam car along Whitehall. The sight was amazing. Motor-cars, motor-buses, great lorries, tiny motor-cycles, stood derelict, and the pavements were crowded with their passengers.

Nowhere was there a telephone or telegraph working, he learnt from the technical expert, who, with the police chiefs, had been summoned to a conference at the Home Office.

And then Johnny saw on his chief's table a big magnet, and wondered who had brought it there.

'Look at this!' said the chief, and, picking up the magnet, held it against a little desk-knife.

'What is the matter?' asked Johnny in perplexity. 'It doesn't seem to be attracting the steel.'

'It has lost its properties, for some extraordinary reason,' said the chief. 'That is why the streets are filled with standing cars. Every piece of metal in the world has become demagnetized!'

For a long time the young man could not grasp the significance of this simple statement.

'We have had electric storms before,' said the technical expert. 'Storms which, for some reason or other, have disorganised telegraphic communication. But this is something worse. Electricity, as created and applied by man for his service, has ceased to exist. Communication throughout the country has practically stopped.'

'But the railways are working.'

The other smiled.

'They are certainly working,' he said drily. 'Trains are being flagged from station to station, and since the telegraph service is out of order, trains will be restricted to two or three a day on the main lines until we can organise some method of signalling by semaphore. There isn't an aeroplane in the sky—the London-Paris service went out of action at ten- forty- five, and we can only hope that the London-Paris machines got down without mishap—there is no means of knowing.'

Later, they were to learn that ships were feeling their way into port, their compasses having ceased to function. Even the gyroscope compass, which depended upon a little electric motor, was valueless under the new and strange conditions.

On the Sunday the Cabinet, which had dispersed for the week- end, reached town, the Premier coming down from Yorkshire by a special train, which took twenty-six hours to do the journey. The Home Secretary, more fortunately placed, came up from Devizes on a steam trolley.

No newspapers appeared on the Sunday—everybody depended upon electric current for its motive power, and the great power works were out of action. Only the streets which were lit by gas had any illumination. On the Monday morning a steam-driven press issued the momentous tidings.

*

The scientists have discovered that an extraordinary revolution is taking place in the sun. The sodium lines have disappeared from the spectrum, and it is an astonishing fact that, for some reason which cannot be understood by the cleverest brains in the world, sodium has been absorbed by some other element, the sun's spectrum revealing amazing chemical changes in the sun's composition. A limited mail service will be carried on by steam tractors, and the Minister of Transport is mobilising all the horses in the country to augment the main railroads, and every effort is being made to secure the food supply. The country must, however, reconcile itself to the possibility that what we know and call electricity, as applied to the service of mankind, may never return to use during the lifetime of the present generation. Fortunately, very few of our collieries are equipped for electric hauling, and all, with the exception of a dozen, are working at full speed to cope with the increased demands of the gas plants.

On the Monday, when the Stock Exchange was opened, scenes of the wildest excitement were witnessed. The oil market suffered the most extraordinary collapse in its history, despite the warnings which were displayed, that all heavy locomotion was practically unaffected by the sun's eccentricity. Rail shares jumped on the rumour that a new method of light signalling had been successfully adopted on the Western region. But the most sensational advance of all was in the gas market. Here stocks soared to undreamt-of prices.

It was humanly impossible to learn what was happening in other parts of the globe. Cable and radio communication were suspended.

*

PROFESSOR DORFORD was a beggar. Before him stretched such a vista as would have reduced an ordinary man to despair, but in the new world problem his own personal misfortune was so insignificant that it was lost to sight.

On the fourth night of the solar disaster, Johnny Brest called to give the latest news.

'Fallowill is still in the country,' he said. 'A car was stranded on the Portsmouth Road, near the Red Lion, on the day the juice went west, and the landlord identified the man—luckily, I stopped at the inn to get water for my magnificent machine—I was offered a thousand pounds for it to-day, by the way.'

'You think he will be found?' asked the girl quickly.

'Certain—he is hiding in the neighbourhood of Guildford. I suppose it will make a big difference to the Professor if the money cannot be recovered?'

She nodded.

'At present he is so absorbed in that wretched sodium that he doesn't realise that he is ruined,' she said. 'Listen!'

From the study came the sound of a booming voice.

'Sir Roland Field,' she said. He came—don't laugh, Johnny—by steam-roller! There are no trains from Cambridge.'

'There is no doubt,' Professor Dorford was saying at that moment with some satisfaction, 'that the only places unaffected by this solar disturbance are the wild villages of Africa.'

'But why sodium?' boomed Sir Roland.

He was an irascible old man, who regarded this phenomenon of nature as a direct affront to himself.

'Why sodium, my good friend? If the iron had gone from the sun, or the magnesium, or any other infernal element, I could understand, but why sodium? What the devil has sodium got to do with electrical energy?'

'I don't know,' admitted Dorford.

'Of course you don't know!' roared the old gentleman. 'It's an absurdity! There isn't a scientist in the world who will not tell you that it is an absurdity! Now, if it were iron or nickel...'

'Is it not possible,' interrupted Professor Dorford, 'that the disappearance of sodium brought about through, let us say, such a chemical conversion as we see every day in our laboratories, may have—'

'No, sir, it isn't possible!' bellowed Sir Roland.

Johnny listened and grinned. He was a busy man. His steam car was one of the most popular means of locomotion in the country. Attached by his chief to the Intelligence Department of the War Office—for the troops were under arms everywhere, guarding the food markets, and augmenting the police, on whom the darkened towns of England threw an additional burden—he had little leisure.

The next day he was on his way to Winchester with despatches to the officer commanding the troops. It was a glorious afternoon, and, peering up at the unclouded brilliance of the sun, he found it hard to believe that that bright friend of the world had played so low a trick upon humanity.

Eight miles from Winchester he saw the gleam of a little river on his right and a huddle of squat factory buildings, and wondered who had laid down an industrial plant in the heart of the smiling countryside. And then he saw a figure walking in the shade of a hedge. It might have been a tramp, so dusty and begrimed was Mr Fallowill, for the fear of detection had kept him to the woods and the hedges.

As he had realised the immense advantages which the failure of the telegraph and mechanical propulsion gave to him, he had grown bolder. No message could warn the police of the towns through which he passed, no swift cars could overtake him. His wife, he guessed, was on the seas and safe; he himself was sufficiently ingenious to devise methods of escape. He touched the pad of crisp papers in his breast pocket and smiled.

And then he heard the soft purr of the steam car and whipped round. As Johnny jumped to the ground, the man turned and, leaping a hedge, ran across the fields toward the little river.

Instantly John Brest was in pursuit. He was younger, more athletic, but the man out-distanced him rapidly. Fallowill reached the river's edge and looked round for some method of crossing. He could not swim, and there was no boat. Hesitating, he looked around. A few hundred yards along the river was some sort of factory building, and, crossing the stream a little way down, was a thick cable supported on either bank by iron trestles.

Darting along the tow-path he gained the first support, climbed, and, catching the cable, went hand over hand across the river.

By the time the pursuer reached the trestle, Fallowill was across. Johnny watched him; saw him reach out his hand to grip the second trestle.

There was no scream, no sound, only a flicker of white light, and Fallowill dropped to the ground a bundle of smoking clothes.

When John Brest, swimming the stream, came up to him, he was dead, and the packet of notes in his pocket was singed brown. For he had crossed by a power cable at the very moment that scientists the world over saw the sodium lines come back to the spectrum of the sun.

The Face in the Night

Contents

Edgar Wallace

The Edgar Wallace Super Pack

The Man from the South

The fog, which was later to descend upon London, blotting out every landmark, was as yet a grey, misty threat. The light had gone from the sky, and the street-lamps made a blurred showing when the man from the South came unsteadily into Portman Square. In spite of the raw cold he wore no overcoat; his shirt was open at his throat. He walked along, peering up at the doors, and presently he stopped before No. 551 and made a survey of the darkened windows. The corner of his scarred mouth lifted in a sardonic smile.

Strong drink magnifies all dominant emotions. The genial man grows more fond of his fellows, the quarrelsome more bitter. But in the man who harbours a sober grievance, booze brings the red haze that enshrouds murder. And Laker had both the grievance and the medium of magnification.

He would teach this old devil that he couldn't rob men without a come-back. The dirty skinflint who lived on the risk which his betters were taking. Here was Laker, almost penniless, with a long and painful voyage behind him, and the memory of the close call that had come in Cape Town, when his room had been searched by the police. A dog's life—that was what he was living. Why should old Malpas, who had not so long to exist, anyway, live in luxury whilst his best agent roughed it? Laker always felt like this when he was drunk.

He was hardly the type that might be expected to walk boldly up to the front door of 551 Portman Square. His long, unshaven face, the old knife wound that ran diagonally from cheek to point of chin, the low forehead, covered with a ragged fringe of hair, taken in conjunction with his outfit, suggested abject poverty.

He stood for a moment, looking down at his awkward-looking boots, and then, mounting the steps, he tapped slowly at the door. Instantly a voice asked: "Who is that?"

"Laker—that's who!" he said loudly.

A little pause, and the door opened noiselessly and he passed through. There was nobody to receive him, nor did he expect to see a servant. Crossing the bare hall, he walked up the stairs, through an open door and a small lobby into a darkened room. The only light was from a green-shaded lamp on the writing-table, at which an old man sat. Laker stood just inside the room and heard the door close behind him. "Sit down," said the man at the far end of the room. The visitor had no need for guidance: he knew exactly where the chair and table were, three paces from where he stood, and without a word he seated himself. Again that grin of his twisted his face, but his repulsive-looking host could not see this. "When did you come?"

"I came in the Buluwayo. We docked this morning," said Laker. "I want some money, and I want it quick, Malpas!"

"Put down what you have brought, on the table," said the old man harshly. "Return in a quarter of an hour and the money will be waiting for you."

"I want it now," said the other with drunken obstinacy. Malpas turned his hideous face towards the visitor. "There's only one method in this shop," he said gratingly, "and that's mine! Leave it or take it away. You're drunk, Laker, and when you're drunk you're a fool."

"Maybe I am. But I'm not such a fool that I'm going to take the risks I've been taking any more! And you're taking some too, Malpas. You don't know who's living next door to you."

He remembered this item of information, discovered by accident that very morning.

The man he called Malpas drew his padded dressing-gown a little closer around his shoulders, and chuckled.

"I don't know, eh? Don't know that Lacy Marshalt is living next door? Why do you think I'm living here, you fool, if it is not to be next to him?"

The drunkard stared open-mouthed. "Next to him... what for? He's one of the men you're robbing—he's a crook, but you're robbing him! What do you want to get next to him for?"

"That's my business," said the other curtly. "Leave the stuff and go."

"Leave nothing," said Laker, and rose awkwardly to his feet. "And I'm not leaving this place either, till I know all about you, Malpas. I've been thinking things out. You're not what you look. You don't sit at one end of this dark room and keep the likes of me at the other end for nothing. I'm going to have a good look at you, son. And don't move. You can't see the gun in my hand, but you've got my word it's there!"

He took two steps forward, and then something checked him and threw him back. It was a wire, invisible in the darkness, stretched breast-high from wall to wall. Before he could recover his balance, the light went out.

And then there came upon the man a fit of insane fury. With a roar he leaped forward, snapping the wire. A second obstruction, this time a foot from the ground, caught his legs and brought him sprawling.

"Show a light, you old thief!" he screamed as he staggered lo his feet, stool in hand. "You've been robbing me for years—living on me, you old devil! I'm going to squeal, Malpas! You pay or I'll squeal!"

"That's the third time you've threatened me."

The voice was behind him, and he spun round and, in a frenzy of fury, fired. The draped walls muffled the explosion, but in the instant's flash of flame he saw a figue creeping towards the door, and, stark mad with anger, fired again. The reek of burnt cordite hung in that airless room like a veil. "Put on the light; put on the light!" he screamed. And then the door opened and he saw the figure slip through. In a second he was out on the landing, but the old man had disappeared. Where had he gone? There was another door, and he flung himself against it.

"Come out!" he roared. "Come out and face me, you Judas!"

He heard a click behind him. The door of the room whence he had come had closed. A flight of stairs led to another story, and he put one foot on the lower stair and stopped. He was conscious that he was still holding the little leather bag that lie had taken from his pocket when he came into the room, and, realizing that he was going away empty-handed, with his linsiness incomplete, he hammered at the door behind which he guessed his employer was sheltering.

"Aw, come out, Malpas! There'll be no trouble. I'm a bit drunk, I guess."

There was no answer.

"I'm sorry, Malpas." He saw something at his feet, and, stooping, picked it up. It was a waxen chin, perfectly modelled and coloured, and it had

343

evidently been held in position by two elastic bands, one of which was broken. The sight of this tickled him and he burst into a yell of laughter.

"Say, Malpas! I've got a part of your face!" he said. "Come out, or I'll take this funny chin of yours to the police. Maybe they'll want to recover the rest of you."

No answer came, and, still chuckling, he went down the stairs and sought to open the front door. There was no handle, and the keyhole was tiny, and, squinting through, he could see nothing.

"Malpas!"

His big voice came echoing down from the empty rooms above, and with a curse he flew up the stairs again. He was half-way to the first landing when something dropped. Looking up, he saw the hateful face above, saw the black weight falling, and strove to avoid it. Another second and he was sliding down the stairs, an inert mass.

The Queen of Finland's Necklace

There was a dance at the American Embassy. The sidewalk was spanned by a striped awning, a strip of red carpet ran down the steps to the kerb, and for an hour glittering limousines had been bringing the distinguished and privileged guests to join the throng already gathered in the none too spacious saloons that form the forty-ninth state of the Union.

When the stream of cars had dried to the merest trickle, a compact, jovial-faced man stepped down from a big machine and walked leisurely past the fringe of sightseers. He nodded genially to the London policeman who kept the passage clear, and passed into the hall.

"Colonel James Bothwell," he said to the footman, and made his slow progress to the saloon.

"Excuse me." A good-looking man in evening dress took his arm affectionately and diverted him towards a small ante-room fitted as a buffet, and at this early hour deserted.

Colonel Bothwell raised his eyebrows in good-natured surprise at this familiarity His attitude seemed to say: You are a perfect stranger to me,

344

probably one of these queerly friendly Americans, so I must tolerate your company. "No," said the stranger gently.

"No?" Colonel Bothwell's eyebrows could not go any higher, so he reversed his facial processes and frowned.

"No—I think not." The grey eyes smiling down into the Colonel's were twinkling with amusement.

"My dear American friend," said the Colonel, trying to disengage his arm. "I really do not understand... you have made a mistake."

The other man shook his head slowly. "I never make mistakes—and I am English, as you very well know, and you are English too, in spite of your caricature of the New England accent. My poor old Slick, it is too bad!"

Slick Smith sighed, but gave no other evidence of his disappointment.

"If an American citizen can't make a friendly call on his own Ambassador without lashin' the bull-pen to fury, why, sump'n's wrong, that's all. See here. Captain, I got an invitation. And if my Ambassador wants to see me I guess that's no business of yours."

Captain Dick Shannon chuckled softly. "He doesn't want to see you. Slick. He'd just hate to see a clever English crook around here with a million dollars' worth of diamonds within reach. He might be glad to see Colonel Kothwell of the 94th Cavalry on a visit to London and anxious to shake him by the hand, but he has no use at all for Slick Smith, Jewel Thief, Confidence Man and Super-Opportunist. Have a drink with me before you go?"

Slick sighed again. "Grape juice," he said laconically, and indicated the bottle which was otherwise labelled. "And you're wrong if you think I'm here on business. That's a fact. Captain. Curiosity is my vice, and I was curious to see Queen Riena's diamond necklace. Maybe it's the last time I'll see it. Go easy with that water, George—whisky can't swim."

He stared gloomily at the glass in his hand before he swallowed its contents at a gulp.

"But in a way I'm glad you spotted me. I got the invitation through a friend. Knowing what I know, my coming here was the act of one who imagines he is being followed by black dogs and poisoned by his spiritual adviser. But I'm curious. And I'm cursed with the detective instinct. You've heard of them nuts, Jekyll and Hyde? That's me. Every man's got his dreams, Shannon. Even a busy.*"

[* A "busy" or "busy fellow" is, in the argot of the underworld]

"Even a busy," agreed Dick Shannon.

"Some men dream about the way they'd spend a million," Slick went on pensively. "Some men dream of how they'd save a girl from starvation and worse, and be a brother to her until she got to love him... you know! Between jobs I dream of how I would unravel deadly mysteries. Like Stormer —the busy thief-taker that gave me away to you. They've got something on me."

It was perfectly true that Shannon had had his first intimation of Slick's character from that famous agency.

"Do we meet now as brother detectives?" he asked, "or are we just plain busy and... ? "

"Say 'thief—don't worry about my feelings," begged Slick. "Yes, I'm a busy tonight."

"And the Queen's diamonds?"

Slick drew a long breath.

"They're marked," he said. "I'm curious to know how they'll take 'em. There's a clever gang working the job—you won't expect me to give names, will you? If you do you've got a shock coming."

"Are they in the Embassy?" asked Dick quickly.

"I don't know. That's what I came to see. I'm not one of these professionals who take no interest in the game. I'm like a doctor—I like to see other people's operations; you can learn things that you'd never guess if you had nothing to study but your own work."

Shannon thought for a moment. "Wait here—and keep your hands off the silver," he said, and, leaving the indignant Slick, he hurried into the crowded room, pushing his way through the throng until he came to a clear space where the Ambassador stood talking to a tall, tired-looking woman, whose protection was the main reason for his being at the Embassy ball. From her neck hung a scintillating chain that flashed and glimmered with her every languid movement. Turning to survey the guests, he presently singled out a monocled young man engaged in an animated conversation with one of the secretaries of the Embassy, and, catching his eye, he brought him to his side...

"Steel, Slick Smith is here, and he tells me that there will I if an attempt made to 'pull away' the Queen's necklace. You are not to allow her out of your sight. Get an Embassy man to verify the list of guests, and bring any to me that can't be accounted for."

He went back to Slick and found him taking his third free drink.

"Listen, Slick. Why did you come here, if you knew the robbery was planned for tonight? If you are not in it, you'd be suspected right away."

"That certainly occurred to me," said the man. "Hence my feeling of disquiet. That's a new word I learnt last week."

From where they stood, the main doorway of the saloon was visible. People were still arriving, and, as he looked, a big-framed man of middle age came in, and with him a girl of such remarkable beauty that even the hardened Slick stared. They were gone out of sight before Dick Shannon could observe them closely.

"That's a good-looker. Martin Elton isn't here, either. That girl goes about a whole lot with Lacy."

"Lacy?"

"The Honourable Lacy Marshalt. He's a millionaire—one of the tough sort that started life in a rough house and is always ready for another. You know the lady, Captain?"

Dick nodded. Most people knew Dora Elton. She was one of the smart people you saw at first nights, or met in the ultra-fashionable supper clubs. Lacy Marshalt he did not know save by repute.

"She's a good-looker," said Slick again, wagging his head admiringly. "Lord! What a good-looker! If she were a wife of mine she wouldn't run around with Lacy. No, sir. But they do that sort of thing in London."

"And in New York and Chicago, and in Paris, Madrid and Bagdad," said Shannon. "Now, Percy!"

"You want me to go? Well, you've spoilt my evening, Captain, I came here for information and guidance. I'd never liave climbed into a white shirt if I'd guessed you were here."

Dick escorted him to the door and waited until the man's hired car had driven away. Then he returned to the ballroom to watch and wait. A guest strolling negligently into an unfrequented passage of the Embassy saw a man sitting reading, pipe in mouth.

"Sorry," said the intruder. "I seem to have lost my way."

"I think you have," said the reader coolly, and the guest, a perfectly honest and innocent rambler, retired hastily, wondering why the watcher should have planted his chair beneath the switchboard from which all the lights in the house were controlled. Shannon was taking no risks.

At one o'clock, to his great relief. Her Majesty of Finland made her departure for the hotel in Buckingham Gate, where she was staying incognito. Dick Shannon stood, bareheaded, in the fog till the rear lights had gone out of sight. On the seat by the driver was an armed detective —he had no fear that majesty would not reach its bedroom safely.

"That lets you out. Shannon, eh?"

The smiling Ambassador received his report with as much relief as the detective had felt.

"I heard an attempt was to be made, through my own detectives," he said; "but then, one always hears such stories in connection with every function of this character."

Dick Shannon drove his long touring car back to Scotland Yard, and he drove at a snail's pace, for the fog was very thick, and the way intersected with confusing cross-roads. Twice he found himself on the sidewalk; in Victoria Street he all but collided with a bus that was weatherbound and stationary.

He crawled past Westminster Abbey, and, guided by the booming notes of Big Ben, navigated himself to the Embankment and through the archway of Scotland Yard.

"Get somebody to garage my car," he instructed the policeman on duty. "I shall walk home—it's safer."

"The inspector was asking for you, sir—he's gone down the Embankment."

"A pleasant night for a walk," smiled Dick, wiping his smarting eyes.

"T. P. are searching for the body of a man who was thrown into the river tonight," was the startling rejoinder.

"Thrown—you mean jumped?"

"No, sir, thrown. A Thames police patrol was rowing under the Embankment wall when the fog was a little thinner than it is now, and they saw the man lifted up to the parapet and pushed over. The sergeant in charge blew his whistle, but none of our men was near, and the chap, whoever it was who did the throwing, got away—they're dragging for the body now. Just this side of the Needle. The inspector asked me to tell you this if you came in."

Dick Shannon did not hesitate. The lure of his comfortable quarters and the cheery fire was a lure no longer. He groped his way across the broad Embankment, and, with the long parapet to guide him, went quickly along the riverside. The fog was black now, and the mournful hoot of the river tugs had ceased as their baffled captains gave up the struggle.

Near the obelisk that records the past glories of Egypt, he found a little knot of men standing, and, recognizing him at close quarters, the uniformed inspector advanced a pace to meet him.

"It is a murder case—T. P. have just recovered the body."

"Drowned?"

"No, sir: the man was clubbed to death before he was thrown into the water. If you'll come down to the steps you'll see him."

"What time did this happen?"

"At nine o'clock tonight—or rather, last night. It is nearly two now."

Shannon descended the shallow steps which lead to the water on either side of the obelisk. The bow of a row-boat came out of the fog and swung round so that the Thing which lay huddled in the stern was visible in the light of the pocket lamps.

"I've made a rough search," said the sergeant of the patrol. "There's nothing in his pockets, but he ought to be easy to identify —there's an old knife wound across his chin."

"Humph!" said Dick Shannon, looking. "We'll make another search later."

He went back to headquarters with the inspector, and the entrance hall, which he had left silent and deserted, was now bustling with life. For in his absence news had come through which set Scotland Yard humming, and brought from their beds every reserve detective within the Metropolitan Area.

The Queen of Finland's car had been held up in the darkest part of The Mall, the detective had been shot down, and Her Majesty's diamond chain had passed into the fog. Nor was it to be found again until a certain girl, at that moment dreaming uneasily about chickens, came to the glare and sorrow of the great city to visit the sister who hated her.

Audrey

"Peter and Paul fetched four shillin's each," reported old Mrs. Graffitt, peering near-sightedly at the coins as she laid them on the table. "Harriet, Martha, Jenny, Elizabeth Queenie and Holga—?"

"Olga," corrected the girl sitting at the table, pencil in hand. "Let us be respectful, even to hens."

"They fetched half a crown each from Mr. Gribs the butcher. It's unchristian to call hens by name, anyhow."

Audrey Bedford made a rapid calculation.

"With the furniture that makes thirty-seven pounds ten shillings," she said, "which will about pay the hen-feed man and your wages, and leave me enough to get to London."

"If I had my rights," said Mrs. Graffitt, sniffing tearfully, "I'd get more than my wages. I've looked after you ever since before your poor dear mother died, obliging you as no other mortal woman would. And now I'm cast aside without a home, and I've got to live with my eldest son."

"You're lucky to have an eldest son," said Audrey, unmoved.

"If you gave me a pound for luck... ? "

"Whose luck? Not mine, you dear old humbug," laughed the girl. "Mrs. Graffitt, don't be silly! You've been living on this property like a —a fighting cat! Poultry farming doesn't pay and never will pay when your chief of staff has a private sale for the eggs. I was working it out the other day, and I reckoned that you've had forty pounds' worth of eggs a year."

"Nobody have ever said I was a thief," quavered the old woman, her hands trembling. "I've looked after you since you were a bit of a girl, and it's very hard to be told that you're a thief." She wept gulpily into her handkerchief.

"Don't cry," said Audrey; "the cottage is damp enough."

"Where will you be going, miss?" Mrs. Graffitt tactfully passed over the question of her honesty.

"I don't know; London, perhaps."

"Got any relations there, miss?"

Perhaps, at this the last moment, the late owner of Beak Farm would be a little communicative. The Bedfords always were closer than oysters.

"Never you mind. Get me a cup of tea and then come for your wages."

"London's a horruble place." Mrs. Graffitt shook her head. "Murders and suicides and robberies and what-nots. Why. they robbed a real queen the other night!"

"Goodness!" said Audrey mechanically. She was wondering what had happened to six other chickens that Mrs. Graffitt had not reported upon.

"Robbed her of hundreds of thousan's' worth of diamonds," she said impressively. "You ought to read the papers more—you miss life."

"And talking of robbery," said Audrey gently, "what happened to Myrtle and Primrose and Gwen and Bertha—?"

"Oh, them?" For a second even Mrs. Graffitt was confused. "Didn't I give you the money? It must have slipped through a hole in my pocket. I've lost it."

"Don't bother," said Audrey. "I'll send for the village policeman —he's a wonderful searcher."

Mrs. Graffitt found the money almost immediately.

The old woman shuffled into the low-roofed kitchen and Audrey looked around the familiar room. The chair on which her mother had sat, her hard face turned to the blackened fireplace, Audrey had burnt. One charred leg still showed in the fire.

No, there was nothing here of tender memory. It was a room of drudgery and repression. She had never known her father, and Mrs. Bedford had never spoken of him. He had been a bad lot, and through his wickedness had forced a woman of gentle birth to submit to the hard life that had been hers.

"Is he dead, Mother?" the child had asked.

"I hope so," was the uncompromising reply.

Dora had never asked such inconvenient questions, but then she was older, nearer in sympathy to the woman, shared her merciless nature and her prejudices.

Mrs. Graffitt had brought her tea and counted her money before she wailed her farewell.

"I'll have to kiss you before I go," she sobbed.

"I'll give you an extra shilling not to," said Audrey hastily, and Mrs. Graffitt took the shilling.

It was all over. Audrey passed through the December wreckage of the garden, opened a gate, and, taking a short cut to the churchyard, found the grave and stood silently before it, her hands clasped.

"Good-bye," she said evenly and, dry-eyed, went back to the house.

The end and the beginning. She was not sorry; she was not very glad. Her box of books had already gone to the station and was booked through to the parcels office at Victoria.

As to the future—she was fairly well educated, had read much, thought much, and was acquainted with the rudiments of shorthand —self-taught in the long winter evenings, when Mrs. Graffitt thought, and said, that she would be better employed with a knitting- needle.

"There's tons of time," growled the village omnibus driver as he threw her bag into the dark and smelly interior. "If it wasn't for these jiggering motor-cars I'd cut it finer. But you've got to drive careful in these days."

A prophetic saying.

The girl was stepping into the bus after her bag when the stranger appeared. He looked like a lawyer's middle-aged clerk, having just that lack of sartorial finish.

"Excuse me. Miss Bedford. My name is Willitt. Can I have a few words with you this evening when you return?"

"I am not returning," she said. "Do I owe you anything?"

Audrey always asked that question of polite strangers. Usually they said "yes", for Mrs. Graffitt had the habit which was locally known as "chalking up".

"No, miss. Not coming back? Could I have your address? I wanted to see you on a—well, an important matter."

He was obviously agitated.

"I can't give you my address, I'm afraid. Give me yours and I will write to you."

He carefully blacked out the description of the business printed on the card, and substituted his own address.

"Now then!" called the aggrieved driver. "If you wait any longer you'll miss that train."

She jumped into the bus and banged the door tight.

It was at the corner of Ledbury Lane that the accident happened. Coming out on to the main road, Dick Shannon took the corner a little too sharply, and the back wheels of his long car performed a graceful skid. The bump that followed was less graceful. The back of the car struck the Fontwell village omnibus just as it was drawing abreast of the car, neatly sliced off the back wheel and robbed that ancient vehicle of such dignity as weather and wear had left to it.

There was a solitary passenger, and she had reached the muddy road before Dick, hat in hand, had reached her, alarm and penitence on his good-looking face.

"I'm most awfully sorry. You're not hurt, I hope?"

He thought she was seventeen, although she was two years older. She was cheaply dressed; her long coat was unmistakably renovated. Even the necklet of fur about her throat was shabby and worn. These facts he did not notice. He looked down into a face that seemed flawless. The curve of eyebrows or set of eyes perhaps, the perfect mouth maybe, or else it was the texture and colouring of the skin... He dreaded that she should speak, and that, in the crude enunciation of the peasant, he should lose the illusion of the princess.

"Thank you—I was a little scared. I shan't catch my train." She looked ruefully at the stricken wheel.

The voice dispelled his fears. The ragged princess was a lady.

"Are you going to Barnham Junction? I am passing there," he said. "And anyway, if I hadn't been going that way, I must go to send relief for this poor lad."

The driver of the bus, to whom he was referring in such compassionate terms, had climbed down from his perch, his grey beard glittering with rain, his rheumy eye gleaming malevolently.

"Why don't you look where you're going?" He wheeaed the phrases proper to such an occasion. "Want all the road, dang ye?"

Dick unstrapped his coat and felt for his pocket-book.

"Jehu," he said, "here is my card, a Treasury bill and my profound apologies."

"My name's Herbert Jiles," said the driver suspiciously; he took the card and the money.

"Jehu is a fanciful name," said Dick, "and refers to the son of Nimshi, who 'driveth furiously'."

"I was nearly walking," said the indignant Mr. Jiles. "It was you as was driving furiously."

"Help will come from Barnham," said Dick. "Now, young lady, can you trust yourself alone with me in this car of Juggernaut?"

"I think so," she smiled, and, rescuing her bag from the bus, jumped in at his side.

"London is also my destination," said Dick, "but I won't suggest that you come all the way with me, though it would save you a train fare."

She did not answer. He had a feeling that she was being prim, but presently she cleared away that impression.

"I think I will go by train: my sister may come to meet me at the station."

There was no very great confidence in her tone.

"Do you live hereabouts?"

"At Fontwell," she said. "I had a cottage there. It used to be mother's, until she died. Have you ever tried to live on eggs?"

Dick was startled.

"Not entirely," he said. "They are extremely nutritive, I understand, but—?"

"I don't mean eat them; I mean, have you ever tried to get a living by poultry-farming?"

He shook his head.

"Well, don't," she said emphatically. "Hens are not what they used to be. Mrs. Graffatt—she kept house for me and absorbed my profits —says that a great change has come over hens since the war. She isn't sure whether it's Bolshevism or Spanish influenza."

He laughed. "So you've given it up?"

She nodded several times.

"I can't say that I've sold the old home; it was sold by bits in the shape of mortgages. That sounds pathetic, doesn't it? Well, it isn't! The old home is ugly and full of odd comers that bumped your head, and smells of a hundred generations of owners who never took baths, except when the roof leaked. And the drainage system goes back to the days of the Early Britons, and none of the windows fit. My sympathies are entirely with the grasping mortgagee—poor soul!"

"You're lucky to have a nice sister to meet you at the station," he said. He was thinking of her as seventeen or perhaps a little younger, and his manner was a trifle paternal.

"I suppose I am," she said without enthusiasm. "This is the beginning of Barnham, isn't it?"

"This is the beginning of Barnham," he agreed, and a few minutes later, brought the machine before the station entrance.

He got down after her, carrying her pitiably light baggage to the platform, and insisted upon waiting until the train came in.

"Your sister lives in London, of course?"

"Yes: in Curzon Street."

It was queer that she should have told him that. Nobody in the county was even aware that she had a sister.

Dick did not show his surprise.

"Is she..." It was a delicate question. "Is she—er—working there?"

"Oh, no. She is Mrs. Martin Elton."

She wondered at herself as she said the words.

"The devil she is!" he was startled into saying.

The train was signalled at that moment, and he hurried off to get her some magazines for the journey.

"It is Awfully kind of you, Mr.——? My name is Audrey Bedford."

"I shall remember that," he smiled. "I've a wonderful memory for names. Mine is Jackson."

He stood watching the train until the dull red of the tail-lamps swung round a curve out of sight. Then he went slowly back to his car and drove to the police station to notify his accident.

Mrs. Martin Elton, and that was her sister! If he had given her his real name, and she had gone to Curzon Street and told pretty Dora Elton that she had passed the time of day with Captain Richard Shannon, the harmonies of the bijou house in Curzon Street might very well have been disturbed.

And with good reason. Dora Elton was the one crook in London that Dick Shannon was aching to trap.

The Hon. Lacy

Lacy Marshalt was once a Senator of the Legislative Council of South Africa, therefore he was by courtesy called "Honourable"—a fact which was, to Mr. Tonger, his gentleman, a source of considerable amusement.

He came out of his bathroom one drear morning, simply attired in trousers and silk singlet, under which the great body muscles showed plainly. Thus, he had less the appearance of a legislator than what his name had stood for in South Africa—the soldier of fortune who had won at least this guerdon of success, a palatial home in Portman Square.

He stood for a long time staring moodily down into the square. Rain had followed the fog as a matter of course; it always rained in England —doleful, continuously, like a melancholic woman. He thought longingly of his sun-washed home at Muizenburg, the broad, league-long beach and the blue seas of False Bay, the spread of his vineyard running up to the slopes of Constantia...

He turned his head back to the bedroom with a jerk. Somebody was tapping softly on the door.

"Come in!"

The door opened and his old valet sidled in with his sly smile.

"Got the mail," he said unceremoniously, and put a handful of letters on the little writing-table.

"Say 'sir'," growled Lacy. "You're getting out of the habit again."

Tonger twisted one side of his face in a grin. "I'll have to get into it again," he said easily.

"You'd better: I can get a hundred valets in London for a quarter of what I pay you—younger men and twenty times as efficient," threatened his master.

"I dare say, but they wouldn't do what I do for you," he said; "and you couldn't trust 'em. You can't buy loyalty. I read that in a book the other day." 'Lacy Marshalt had chosen one letter from the others, a letter enclosed in a pique-blue envelope and addressed in an illiterate hand. He tore it open and read:

"O.I. Breaking Sown"

There was no signature.

The big man grunted something and tossed the letter to the valet.

"Send him twenty pounds," he said.

Tonger read the scrap of paper without the slightest hesitation.

"Breaking down?" he mused. "H'm! Can he swim?"

Lacy looked round sharply.

"What do you mean?" he demanded. "Of course he can swim—or could. Swim like a seal. Why?"

"Nothing."

Lacy Marshalt looked at him long and hard.

"I think you're getting soft sometimes. Take a look at that envelope. It has the Matjesfontein postmark. So had the last. Why does he write from there, a hundred miles and more from Cape Town?"

"A blind maybe," suggested Tonger. He put the scrap of paper in his waistcoat pocket. "Why don't you winter in the Cape, baas?" he asked.

"Because I choose to winter in England."

Marshalt was putting on his shirt as he spoke, and something in his tone riveted the man's attention.

"I'll tell you something, Lacy: hate's fear!"

The other stared at him.

"Hate's fear? What do you mean?"

"I mean that you can't hate a man without fearing him. It's the fear that turns dislike into hate. Cut out the fear and it's... well, anything —contempt, anything you like. But it can't be hate."

Marshalt had resumed his dressing.

"Read that in a book, too?" he asked, before the glass,

"That's out of my own nut," said Tonger, taking up a waistcoat and giving it a perfunctory snick with a whisk brush. "Here, Lacy, who's the fellow that lives next door? I've meant to ask you that. Malpas or some such name. I was talking to a copper last night, and he said that it's believed that he's crazy. He lives alone, has no servants and does all his own housework. There's about six sets of flats in the building, but he won't let any of them. Owns the whole shoot. Who is he?"

Lacy Marshalt growled over his shoulder:

"You seem to know all about it: why ask me?"

Tonger was rubbing his nose absent-mindedly. "Suppose it's him?" he asked, and his master spun round.

"Suppose you get out of here, you gossiping old fool!" Tonger, in no wise disconcerted by the magnate's ferocity, laid the waistcoat on the back of a chair.

"That private detective you sent for the other day is waiting," he said, and Lacy cursed him.

"Why didn't you tell me?" he snarled. "You're getting useless, Tonger. One of these days I'll fire you out—and take that grin off your face! Ask him to come up."

The shabby-looking man who was ushered in smiled deferentially at his employer.

"You can go, Tonger," growled Marshalt.

Tonger went leisurely.

"Well?"

"I traced her," said the agent, and, unfolding his pocket-book, took out a snapshot photograph, handing it to the millionaire.

"It is she," he nodded; "but it wasn't difficult to find her once you knew the village. Who is she?"

"Audrey Bedford."

"Bedford? You're sure?" asked the other quickly; "Does her mother live there?"

"Her mother's dead—five years ago," said the agent.

"Is there another daughter?"

The agent shook his head.

"So far as I can discover, she's the only child. I got a picture of her mother. It was taken at a church fair in 1913, one of a group."

This was the flat parcel he was carrying, and the paper about which he now unfolded. Lacy Marshalt carried the picture to the light...

"That is she!" He pointed to a figure.

"God, how wonderful! When I saw the girl I had a feeling... an instinct."

He cut short the sentence.

"You know her, then, sir?"

"No!" The answer was brusque almost to rudeness. "What is she doing? Living alone?"

"She was practically. She had an old woman in the house who assisted her with a poultry farm. She left for London yesterday. From what they tell me in the village, she is broke and had to sell up."

The millionaire stood in his favourite attitude by the window, staring at nothing, his strong, harsh face expressionless. How wonderful! "Hate is fear," whispered the echo of Tonger's voice—he shook off the reminder with a roll of his broad shoulders.

"A pretty girl, eh?"

"Lovely, I thought," said the detective. "I'm not much of a judge, but she seemed to me to be out of the ordinary."

Lacy grunted his agreement. "Yes... out of the ordinary."

"I got into a bit of trouble at Fontwell—I don't think anything will come of it, but you ought to know in case it comes back to you." The man showed some signs of discomfort. "We private detectives find we work much better if we give people the idea that we're the regular goods. I had to pretend I was looking for a chicken thief—down at the Crown Inn they thought I was a Yard man."

"There's not much harm in that, Mr. Willitt," said the other with his frosty smile.

"Not as a rule," said Willitt, "only, by a bit of bad luck, Captain Shannon happened to stop at the inn to change a tyre."

"Who's Shannon?"

"If you don't know him, don't look for him," said Willitt. "He's the biggest thing they've got at the Yard. The new Executive Commissioner. Up till now the Commissioners have been office men without even the power of arrest. They brought Shannon from the Indian Intelligence because there have been a few scandals lately—bribery cases. He gave me particular hell for describing myself as a regular. And his tongue... Gee! That fellow can sting at a mile!"

"He didn't discover what you were inquiring about—the girl?"

The agent shook his head.

"No. That's about the only thing he didn't discover. You'd think he had all his mind occupied with the Queen of Finland's necklaces, wouldn't you?"

Apparently Lacy did not hear him speak. His mind was concentrated upon the girl and the possibilities that followed.

"You allowed her to go without getting her address? That was pretty feeble. Go down and get it. Then follow her up and scrape an acquaintance. You can be a business man on the look out for investment—lend her money—all that she requires—but do it in a way that doesn't frighten her."

He took from his pocket-case half a dozen notes, crushed them into a ball and tossed them into the outstretched hand. "Bring her here to dinner one night." he said softly. "You can be called away on the 'phone."

Willitt looked hard at him and shook his head in a halfhearted fashion.

"I don't know... that's not my line..."

"I want to talk to her—tell her something she doesn't know. There's five hundred for you."

The private detective blinked quickly. "Five hundred? I'll see..."

Left alone, Lacy went back to the window and his contemplation of the reeking square.

"Hate is fear!"

It was his boast that he had never feared. Ruthless, remorseless, he had walked over a pavement of human hearts to his goal, and he was not afraid. There were women in three continents who cursed his name and memory. Bitter-hearted men who brooded vengeance by night and day. He did not fear. His hatred of Dan Torrington was... just hate.

So he comforted himself, but deep down in the secret places of his soul the words of the old valet burnt and could not be dimmed—"Hate is Fear."

Slick-Philosopher

"It is nothing," said Shannon, surveying the battered mudguard.

"Had a collision?" asked Steel, his assistant, interested.

"Yes—a very pleasant one. In fact, the best ever!" They went into the narrow passage that was the approach to Dick Shannon's apartment.

"No, I haven't been waiting long," said Steel, as Dick unlocked the door of his sitting-room. "I knew you would come back here. Did you see the Bognor man?"

"Yes—he split... after a little persuasion. Steel, do you know anything about the girl Elton's relations?"

"I didn't even know that she had any," said the other.. "Perhaps Slick knows. I've told him to be here at six."

"I wonder if she got to town all right?"

"Who?" asked the other in surprise, and the Commissioner was for the moment embarrassed.

"I was thinking of... somebody," he said awkwardly, and hanged the subject. "Has the body been identified?" he asked...

Steel shook his head.

"The man was from abroad, probably South Africa," he said. "He was wearing veltshoen, a native-made boot, very popular amongst the Boers, and the tobacco in his pouch is undoubtedly Magaliesberg, There's no other tobacco like it. He may have been in England some weeks, but, on the other hand, it is likely that he has just landed. The Buluwayo and Balmoral Castle arrived last week, and in all probability he came on one of those ships. In fact, they are the only two that have come from South Africa in the past fortnight. Did the Bognor man know anything about the Queen's jewels?"

"Nothing. He said that Elton had quarrelled with him some time ago, and they did no business together. Mainly the talk was, as is usual in these cases, parable and metaphor. You can never get a thief to call a spade a spade."

He stood looking down at the table deep in thought, and then:

"I suppose her sister did meet her?"

Steel blinked.

"Whose sister, sir?" he asked, and this time Dick Shannon laughed.

"It is certain she did," he said, continuing his train of thought. "At any rate, she'd stop her coming to Curzon Street, and would shepherd her off to some hotel."

A light dawned upon Steel.

"I see, you're talking about Elton?"

"I'm talking about Elton..." agreed Captain Shannon, "and another. But the other won't interest you. You're having the house watched?"

"Elton's? Yes. We've had to go very carefully, because Elton's a shrewd fellow."

Dick bit his lip.

"Nothing will happen before a quarter to nine tonight, unless I'm greatly mistaken. At that hour the Queen of Finland's necklace will leave Curzon Street, and I personally will follow it to its destination, because I'm most anxious to meet the fifth member of the gang, who, I guess, is a foreigner."

"And then?" asked Steel when he paused.

"Then I shall take Dora Elton with the goods. And that's just what I've been waiting for for a long time."

"Why not Bunny?" asked Steel, and Dick smiled.

"Bunny's got plenty of courage: I'll give him credit for that; but not that kind of courage. It requires valour of an unimaginative kind to walk through London with stolen property in your pocket and the knowledge that half the police in town are looking for you. That isn't Bunny! No, his wife will do the trick."

He looked at his watch impatiently, then took up a timetable from his writing-desk.

"Are you going away?" asked Steel in surprise.

"No," impatiently, "I am seeing what time her train arrives."

He turned the leaves and presently ran his finger down a column, then looked at his watch again as though he had forgotten what he had already seen.

"She arrived half an hour ago. I wonder..." Steel was wondering too. He had never seen Dick Shannon in that mood before. But any explanation was denied by the arrival of Mr. Slick Smith. He came without diffidence, a very self-possessed, neatly dressed man, whose unlined face, twinkling eye and expensive cigar advertised his peace with the world. He nodded to Steel, and received a sympathetic grin in reply. Not until he had taken his departure did Dick come to the point.

"I sent for you, Slick, to ask your advice. The robbery came off all right."

"So I see by the morning newspapers," said Slick, "though I do not place too great a credence in the morning press. Personally, I prefer the afternoon variety; they haven't time to think up trimmings, and you get your news without dilution."

"Elton was in it, you know."

Slick raised his eyebrows.

"You surprise me," he said politely. "Dear me! Mr. Elton? He is the last person in the world one would suspect of larcenous proceedings."

"Let's cut out the persiflage and get right down to cases," said Dick, pushing the decanter towards his visitor. "What do you know about Mrs. Elton?"

"A most charming lady! A most de—lightful lady! Though it would be an exaggeration to describe her soul as of the white virginal variety. I don't mind confessing that, when I think about souls at all, I prefer them delicately tinted, rose du barri, eau de nil—anything but lemon."

"What was she before she married?"

Slick shrugged his shoulders.

"Gossip and scandal are loathsome to me." he said reluctantly. "All I know about her is that she was a good woman but a bad actress. I think she must have married Elton to reform him. So many of our best women do that sort of thing."

"And has she?" asked Shannon sarcastically.

Again Mr. Smith shrugged.

"I heard the other day that he was strong for prohibition. Is that reform? It must be, I suppose."

He poured out a liberal portion of whisky and sent the seltzer sizzling into the glass.

"You can't say anything in favour of booze, however clever you may be. You may say: 'Oh, but I'm a moderate drinker: why should my allowance be curtailed because that horrible grocery man gets drunk and beats his wife?' To which I reply: There are fifty thousand babies in England under the age of six months. Babies who would welcome with infantile joy a nice, bright razor to play with. And you might give them each the razor. Captain, and not more than one in fifty thousand would cut his or her young throat. Must we then deny the other forty-nine thousand and odd the joy and happiness of playing with a hair-mower because one fool baby cut his young head off? Yes, sir, we must. Common sense tells us that what happened to one might just as well happen to the fifty thousand. Do I speak words of wisdom? I do. Thank you—your very good health."

He smacked his lips in critical appreciation. "Liqueur, and at least twenty years old. Would that all whisky was like that—there would be fewer suicides."

Dick was watching him closely, well aware that he was delicately shifting the conversation into another channel. "Has she a sister?"

Mr. Smith finished the remainder of his glass. "If she has," he said, "God help her!"

The Sisters

Audrey spent a quarter of an hour waiting on Victoria station, alternately making short excursions in search of Dora and studying the new bills, which were given up to the Robbery of the Queen of Finland and the new clues that had accumulated during the day. Twenty minutes passed, and Dora had not appeared. Mrs. Graffitt had an exasperating habit of forgetting to post letters, and she remembered she had entrusted the announcement of her plans to the old woman.

Her stock of spare cash was too small to rise to a taxi, and she sought information from a policeman whose knowledge of bus routes was evidently encyclopaedic. After waiting for some minutes in the drizzle she found one that was bound for Park Lane, from which thoroughfare Curzon Street runs. London was a place of mystery to her; but by diligent searching she at last found the little house and rang the visitors' bell. A short delay, and the door was opened by a smart maidservant, who looked askance at the shabby visitor.

"Mrs. Martin Elton is engaged. Have you come from Seville's?"

"No, I've come from Sussex," said the girl with a faint smile. "Will you tell Mrs. Elton that it is her sister?"

The maid looked a little dubious, but ushered her into a small, chilly sitting-room and went out, closing the door. Evidently she was not expected, thought Audrey, and the uneasiness with which she had approached the visit was intensified. Their correspondence had been negligible. Dora was never greatly interested either in her mother or what she magniloquently described to her friends as "the farm"; and when the younger girl had in her desperation written for assistance, there had come, after a long interval, a five-pound note and a plain intimation that Mrs. Martin Elton had neither the means nor the inclination for philanthropy.

Dora had gone on to the stage at an early age, and had made, a few weeks before her mother's death, what had all the appearance of a good marriage. In the eyes of that hard, unbending woman, Dora could do no wrong, and even her systematic neglect never altered the older woman's affection, but seemed rather to increase its volume. Day and night, year in and year out, Dora had been the model held before her sister. Dora was successful; that, in Mrs. Bedford's eyes, excused all shortcomings. She had been successful even as an actress; her name had appeared large on the bills of touring companies; her photograph had appeared even in the London papers. By what means she had secured her fame and founded her independence, Mrs. Bedford did not know and cared less.

The door opened suddenly and a girl came in. She was taller and fairer than her sister, and in some ways as beautiful, though her mouth was straighter and the eyes lacked Audrey's ready humour.

"My dear girl, where on earth have you come from?" she asked in consternation.

She offered a limp, jewelled hand, and, stooping, pecked the girl's cold cheek.

"Didn't you get my letter, Dora?"

Dora Elton shook her head. "No, I had no letter. You've grown, child. You were a gawky kid when I saw you last."

"One does grow," admitted Audrey gravely. "I've sold the cottage."

The elder girl's eyes opened: "But why on earth have you done that?"

"It sold itself," said Audrey. "In other words, I pawned it bit by bit until there was nothing of it left; so I disposed of the chickens —probably the only eggless chickens in the country, and worth a whole lot of money as biological curiosities."

"And you've come here?" There was no mistaking the unwelcome in Dora's tone. "That is very awkward! I can't possibly put you up here, and I don't think it was particularly kind of you, Audrey, to sell the farm. Dear mother died there, and that in itself should have made the place sacred to you."

"All things associated with mother are sacred to me," said Audrey quietly, "but I hardly think it is necessary to starve myself to death to prove my love for mother. I don't want very much from you, Dora—just a place to sleep for a week, until I ran find something to do."

Dora was pacing the little room, her hands behind her, her brows knit in a frown. She wore an afternoon frock, the value of which would have kept Audrey in comfort for a month; her diamond ear-rings, the double rope of pearls about her neck, were worth a small fortune.

"I've some people here to tea," she said, "and I'm having a dinner-party tonight. I don't know what on earth to do with you, Audrey. You can't come to dinner in that kit."

She looked contemptuously at the girl's uncomely wardrobe.

"You had better go to an hotel. There are plenty of cheap places in Bloomsbury. Then make yourself smart and come and see me on Monday."

"It will cost money to make me smart on Monday or Tuesday or any other day in the week," said Audrey calmly, "and two nights at a third-rate hotel will exhaust my supplies."

Dora clicked her lips.

"It's really too bad of you, dropping down from the clouds like this," she said irritably. "I haven't the slightest idea what I can do. Just wait—I'll see Martin."

She flung out of the room, leaving behind her a faint I fragrance of quelques fleurs, and Audrey Bedford's lips curled into a faint smile. She was not sorry for herself. Dora had behaved as she had expected her to behave. She waited for a long time; it was nearly half an hour before the door-handle turned again and her sister came in. Some magical transformation had occurred, for Dora was almost genial, though her good-humour sounded a little unreal.

367

"Martin says you must stay," she said. "Come up with me."

She led the way up the narrow stairs, past an entry behind which there was the sound of laughter and talk, and on the second floor stopped and opened a door, switching on the light. Audrey guessed that it was the second-best bedroom in the house, and reserved for the principal partakers of the Elton hospitality.

"You have no friends in London, have you, old girl?" asked Dora carelessly. She stood watching in the doorway while the girl put down her bag.

"None," said Audrey. "This is a pretty bedroom, Dora."

"Yes, isn't it? Anybody know you've come up?"

"Mrs. Graffitt knows I've come to town, but she doesn't know where."

She had expected her sister to leave her as soon as she had been shown into the room, but Dora lingered in the doorway, having apparently something to say.

"I'm afraid I've been rather a brute to you, Audrey," she said, laying her hand on the girl's arm. "But you're going to lie a good, sweet angel and forgive me, aren't you? I know you will, because you promised mother you would do anything for me, darling, didn't you?"

For a second Audrey was touched.

"You know that I would," she said.

"Some day I'll tell you all my secrets," Dora went on. "I ran tell you because you're the one person in the world I can trust. Mother used to say that you were so obstinate that the devil couldn't get you to speak if you didn't want to."

Audrey's eyes twinkled in the ghost of a smile.

"Dear mother was never flattering," she said dryly.

She had loved her mother, but had lived too near to her petty tyrannies and her gross favouritism for love to wear the beautifying veil of tenderness. Dora patted her arm and rose briskly.

"The people are going now. I want you to come down and meet Mr. Stanford and Martin. You've never seen Martin?"

"I've seen his photograph," said Audrey.

"He's a good-looker," said Dora carelessly. "You'll probably fall in love with him—'Bunny' will certainly fall in love with you. He has a weakness for new faces." She turned at the door. "I'm going to trust you, Audrey," she said, and there was an undercurrent of menace in her voice. "Curzon Street has its little skeletons as well as the farm."

"You may say what you like about the farm," said Audrey, her lips twitching, "but the word 'skeleton' can never be applied to those chickens! They ate me to ruin!"

Dora came back to the drawing-room, and the two occupants searched her face.

"Where is she?" asked the taller of the men.

"I've put her in the spare bedroom," said Dora.

Mr. Elton stroked his smooth, black moustache.

"I'm not sure in my mind whether she ought to be here just now. Give her the money and send her to an hotel."

Dora laughed.

"You've been arguing all afternoon as to how we shall get the stuff to Pierre. Neither of you men want to take the risk of being found with the Queen of Finland's necklace—?"

"Not so loud, you fool!" said Martin Elton between his teeth. "Open the window and advertise it, will you?"

"Listen!" commanded Big Bill Stanford. "Go on, Dora. I guess what you say is right enough. It may be a lifer to the man caught with that stuff—but Pierre has got to have it tonight. Who'll take the necklace?"

"Who? Why, my dear little sister!" said Dora coolly. "That girl was born to be useful!"

The Plot

Big Bill was no sentimentalist, but in the thing that passed for a soul there was a certain elementary code, the rudiments of what had once been a sense of honour and decent judgment.

"Your sister! Suffering snakes, you couldn't allow a kid like that to take such a risk?"

Dora's smile was her answer. Her husband was biting his nails nervously.

"There may be no risk," he said, "and if there is, isn't it ours, too?"

Standford stirred uneasily. "That's so. But we're in this for the profit—and the risk. Suppose they caught her and she squealed?"

"That is the only real risk," said Dora, "and it isn't a big one."

The big man looked thoughtfully at the carpet.

"That stuff has to get out of this house and out of the country —quick!" he said. "It is too big to hold and break up here, and I never pass a newspaper boy but I don't hear the squeal that the papers are putting up. Lock the door, girl."

She obeyed. On the mantelpiece was a beautiful gilt and enamelled clock, surmounted by a statuette of a fawn.

Gripping the statuette firmly, he lifted out the greater portion of the clock's interior, without in any way affecting the functions of the timepiece, which ticked on. Pressing the spring, one side of the bronze box opened and showed a tightly fitting package of silver paper. This he laid on the baize cloth and unrolled. Instantly there came from the table such a flicker of leaping fires, blue and green and purest white, that Dora's mouth opened in wonder and awe.

"There's seventy thousand pounds there," said Stanford, and thrust out his lower lip thoughtfully. "And there's also ten years for somebody —seven years for the theft and three years for outraged majesty. You cannot rob a visiting queen without putting something on to the sentence."

The dapper man shivered. "Don't talk about sentences, my dear fellow," he said petulantly. "If Pierre does his part—"

"Pierre will do his part. He'll be waiting at Charing Cross station at nine-fifteen. The question is, who's going to take the stuff?"

There was a silence.

"Audrey will take it," said Dora at last. "I was a fool not to think of it when I saw her. Nobody knows her, and nobody will suspect her. Pierre is easy to recognize. And then, Bunny, out of this business for good." She nodded emphatically. "There's a little old story about a pitcher and a well; and there's 'Daisy Emming's Life in Prison', published in the Sunday Globe—taking them in conjunction I read a Warning to Girls."

"Perhaps Mr. Lacy Marshalt will give Martin a directorship," sneered the big man. "When you people get next to what looks like good, easy, honest money, it's surprising how quickly you reform."

"I scarcely know the man," said Dora sharply. "I told you about him. Bunny. He's the man I met at the Denshores' dance. He's a South African and rich, but you couldn't pry loose a red nickel without dynamite."

Martin Elton looked at her suspiciously.

"I didn't know you knew him—" he began.

"Get back to this stuff," snapped Stanford. "There's one thing I want to know—suppose she's caught?"

Another long and painful silence.

"Why not keep it here till the squeal dies down?" asked Elton. "There's no ghost of a suspicion that they connect us with the job."

Stanford looked him straight in the eye.

"Twelve months ago," he said slowly, "when Leyland Hall was cleaned up, you got most of the stuff out of the country through a receiver at Bognor. He gave you a little trouble, didn't he?"

"Yes," said the other shortly; "that is why I hadn't thought of him in connection with this job."

"And you're wise," said Bill, nodding. "Dick Shannon has been spending the greater part of the day with your friend at Bognor!"

Martin Elton's pale face went a shade paler.

"He wouldn't squeal," he said unsteadily.

"I don't know. If a man would squeal to anybody, he'd squeal to Shannon. The English detective service has gone to blue blazes since they introduced gentlemen. I like police whom you can reason with." He jiggled the loose coins in his pocket suggestively. "That's why I say that you can't keep the stuff at this house. Bennett may not have squeaked. On the other hand, he may have emitted squeak-like noises. What do you say, Dora?"

She nodded. "The stuff ought to go: I've recognized that all along," she said. "Make a parcel of it, Martin."

They watched the man as, wrapping the necklace again in cotton-wool, he packed it in an old cigarette-box and tied it about with brown paper, and then Stanford asked: "If it comes to squealing, what about your sister?"

Dora considered before she replied.

"I am sure of her," she said.

"Let us see her," said Stanford when the parcel had been firmly tied and hidden under a sofa cushion, and the top of the clock replaced.

Audrey was sitting in a deep, low chair before the gas-fire, pondering her strange welcome, when she heard Dora's footsteps on the stairs.

"You can come down now."

She looked at her sister and made a little face, and, for all her subtlety, could not hide the disparagement in the glance.

"You're a human scarecrow, Audrey! I shall have to buy you some clothes straight away."

Audrey followed her down to the floor below and into the big drawing-room that ran the width of the house. A tall, broad-shouldered man stood with his back to the fire, and on him Audrey's eyes first rested. He was a man of fifty, whose hair was cropped so close that at first she thought he was bald. His deep, forbidding eyes fixed and held her as she entered.

"This is Mr. Stanford," introduced Dora. "And this is my little sister."

He held out a huge hand and took hers in a grip that made her wince.

The second man in the room was slight and dapper, and his unusual pallor was emphasized by the small, black moustache and the jet-black eyebrows. Good-looking, she thought, almost pretty. So this was the great Martin about whom she had heard so many rhapsodies.

"Glad to meet you, Audrey," he said, his admiring eyes never leaving her face. "She's a peach, Dora."

"She's prettier than she was," said Dora indifferently, "but her clothes are terrible."

It was not like Audrey to feel uncomfortable. She was so superior to the trials of poverty that ordinarily she would have laughed good- naturedly at the crude comment. But now, for some reason, she felt embarrassed. It was the unwavering stare of the big man by the fire-place, the cold appraisement of his gaze.

Stanford looked at his watch.

"I'll be going," he said. "I'm glad to have met you, miss. Perhaps I'll be seeing you again."

She hoped sincerely that he would not.

The Arrest

Dora signalled to Martin Elton to retire with their guest, and it was when they were left alone that Dora had her story to tell.

It was the story of an injured wife, who had been obliged to fly from the country because of her husband's brutality, leaving behind her the miniature of her child.

"I don't mind confessing to you that we have secured the miniature, Audrey," said Dora in an outburst of frankness. "I don't think we were strictly legal in our actions—in fact, Martin bribed the servant in Sir John's house to bring it to us. He guesses we have it, and has had us watched day and night, and any attempt we make, either through the post —we are sure he has notified the postal officials—or by messenger, is likely to lead to failure. A friend of this poor dear Lady Nilligan is coming to London tonight, and we have arranged to meet him at the station and hand him the miniature. Now the question is, Audrey, will you be a darling and take it to him? Nobody knows you; his sleuth-hounds will not molest you; and you can render this poor woman a great service. Personally, I think there's a little too much sentimentality about it, for I don't see why one miniature should be more valuable than another. But evidently this demented lady thinks it is."

"But what an extraordinary story!" said Audrey, frowning. "Couldn't you send one of your servants? Or couldn't he come here?"

"I tell you the house is watched," said Dora, never the most patient of individuals. "If you don't want to do it—?"

"Of course I'll do it," laughed Audrey.

"There is only one point I want to make," her sister interposed, "and it is this: if by any chance this comes out, I want you to promise me that our name shall not come into it. I want you to swear by our dead mother—"

"That is unnecessary," said Audrey, a little coldly. "I will promise —that is enough."

Dora took her in her arms and kissed her. "You are really a darling," she said; "and you've grown so awfully pretty. I must find a nice man for you."

It was on the tip of Audrey's tongue to suggest that her sister might very well try some other ground of search than that which produced the pallid Martin Elton, for whom she felt an instinctive dislike.

"Of course I'll take it, my dear," she said. "It seems such a little thing to do. And if I meet the grumpy husband, why, I'll just talk to him firmly!"

Apparently Dora's feasts were of a movable kind, for, although Audrey had her dinner in her room, the party of which her sister had spoken did not materialize. At half past eight Dora came up for her, carrying in her hand a small, oblong package, tied and heavily sealed.

"Now remember, you do not know me, you have never been to 508 Curzon Street in your life..." She repeated the admonition, and described in detail the mysterious Pierre. "When you see him, you will go up to him and say, 'This is-for madam'—that, and nothing more."

She repeated the instructions, and made the girl recite them after her. Audrey was at first amused, then a little bored. "It seems an awful lot of bother to make about so small a thing, but you have succeeded in arousing that conspirator feeling!"

With the package secure in an inside pocket of her coat, she went out into Curzon Street and walked quickly in the direction of Park Lane. She had hardly disappeared before Martin Elton came out. Keeping her in sight, he watched her board a bus, and, hailing a taxicab, followed.

To Audrey the adventure was mildly exciting. She knew neither of the parties of this family quarrel, and found it difficult even to speculate upon their identity. They were probably two very plain, uninteresting people.

Edgar Wallace

Family quarrellers usually were. But she was glad of the opportunity of earning her board and keep, and it relieved her of a sense of obligation, for which she was grateful.

The bus put her down opposite Charing Cross station, and, crossing the congested road, she hurried through the courtyard into the station building. There were hundreds of people in the big approach; the night mail was beginning to fill, and passengers and their friends stood in groups before the harriers. She looked for a considerable time before she saw Mr. Pierre, a short, stocky man with a square, flaxen beard, who seemed to be wholly absorbed in the animated spectacle. Moving to the other side of him to make absolutely sure, she saw the little mole on his cheek by which she was to identify him. Without further ado, she took the package from her pocket and went up to him.

"This is for madam," she said...

He started, looked at her searchingly, slipped the package in his pocket, so quickly that she could hardly follow his movements.

"Bien!" he said. "Will you thank monsieur? And—?"

He spun round quickly, but the man who had caught his wrist possessed a grip which was not lightly to be shaken. At the same moment somebody slipped an arm in Audrey's.

"I want you, my young friend," said a pleasant voice. "I am Captain Shannon of Scotland Yard."

He stopped, staring down at the frightened face turned up to his. "My ragged princess!" he gasped.

"Please let me go." She attempted to free herself. She was horribly frightened and for a second felt physically sick. "I've got to go to—" She checked herself in time.

"To see Mrs. Elton, of course," said Shannon, scrutinizing her.

"No, I haven't to see Mrs. Elton. I really don't know Mrs. Elton," she said breathlessly.

He shook his head. "I'm afraid we'll have to talk about that. I don't want to hold your arm. Will you come with me?"

"Are you arresting me?" she gasped.

He nodded gravely.

"I'm detaining you—until a little matter is cleared up. I'm perfectly sure you're an innocent agent in this, just as I am equally sure that your sister isn't."

Dora? Was he talking about Dora, she asked herself with a sinking heart. His tone, the hard judgment in the voice, told the girl something she did not want to know. Something that shocked her beyond expression. Then, forcing every word, she said: "I'll talk the matter over with pleasure, and I won't make any attempt to get away. But I have not come from Mrs. Elton's, and she is not my sister. The story I told you this afternoon was untrue."

"But why?" he asked, as they walked together through the stone corridor to the courtyard.

"Because"—she hesitated—"I knew you were a detective."

He signalled a cab, gave directions and helped her inside.

"You're lying to shield your sister and Bunny Elton," he said. "I hate using the word 'lie' to you, but that's what you're doing, my child."

Her mind was in a turmoil, from which one clear fact emerged. It was not a miniature that she was carrying from Dora to the mythical wife; it was something more important. Something horribly serious.

"What was in the parcel?" she asked huskily.

"The Queen of Finland's diamond necklace, unless I'm greatly mistaken. Her carriage was held up in The Mall four nights ago, and the jewels were stolen from her neck."

Audrey sat up with a grimace of pain. It was as though he had struck her. Dora! She had read something of the affair in the newspaper which he had bought for her at Barnham Junction. Mrs. Graffitt had spoken of the crime. For a spell she sat paralysed with horror.

"Of course you didn't know what it was," he said, and he was speaking to himself. "It's a hateful thing to ask you to do, but you must tell me the truth, even if it brings your sister to the place, that has been waiting for her these many years."

The cab seemed to go round and round; the stream of lights and traffic through the window became a confused blur.

"Do what you can for Dora..." Her mother's insistent lesson, almost forgotten, was ringing in her ears. She was trembling violently; her brain had gone numb and would give her no guidance. All that she knew was that she was under arrest... she, Audrey Bedford of Beak Farm! She licked her dry lips.

"I have no sister," she said, her breath labouring. "I stole the necklace!"

She heard his soft laughter, and could have murdered him.

"You poor, dear baby!" he said. "It was a job carried out by three expert hold-up men. Now let me tell you"—he patted her hand gently —"I'm not going to allow you to do this mad, quixotic thing. Didn't you know that Dora Elton and her husband are two of the most dangerous crooks in London?"

She was weeping, her face to her hands.

"No, no," she sobbed, "I don't know anything... She is not my sister."

Dick Shannon sighed and shrugged his shoulders. There was nothing to do but to charge her.

Pierre had arrived at the station before them, and she watched, with fascinated horror, the process of his searching, saw the package opened on the sergeant's desk, and the flash and glitter of its contents. Presently Shannon took her gently by the arm and led her into the steel pen.

"The name is Audrey Bedford," he said. "The address is Fontwell, West Sussex, The charge"—he hesitated—"is being in possession of stolen property, knowing the same to be stolen. Now tell the truth," he whispered under his breath.

She shook her head.

Disowned

Audrey woke from a restless, troubled sleep and, struggling to her unsteady feet, rubbed her shoulders painfully. She had been lying on a bare plank, covered with the thinnest of blankets, and she ached from head to foot.

The sound of a key turning in the cell lock had awakened her; it was the matron, who had come to conduct her to the bathroom. She had returned to her cell a little refreshed, to find coffee and bread and butter waiting for her, and she had finished these when the door opened again, and she looked up to meet the grave eyes of Dick Shannon. He nodded to her.

"I want you," he said. Her heart sank. "Am I going before—before a judge?" she faltered.

"Not yet," he said. "I'm afraid that eventually you will go before a judge, unless—?"

She waved aside the suggestion with an impatient hand. She had settled that matter definitely in the silence of the night.

The man's heart ached for her. He knew well enough that she was innocent, and he had sent a man into Sussex that morning to prove the matter, as he hoped, beyond question.

"Here's somebody you know, I think," he said, and, opening a door, drew her into a room.

There were two occupants: Dora Elton and her husband. Audrey looked; she had to dig her finger-nails into her palms to control herself, and she succeeded wonderfully.

"Do you know this girl?" asked Shannon.

Dora shook her head.

"No, I've never seen her before," she said innocently. "Do you know her, Martin?"

The haggard-faced Martin was equally emphatic.

"Never saw her before in my life," he said.

"I think she is your sister."

Dora smiled. "How absurd!" she said. "I've only one sister, and she is in Australia."

"Do you know that both your mother and your sister lived at Fontwell?"

"My mother never lived at Fontwell in her life," said Dora calmly, and, in spite of her self-possession, Audrey started. "There were some people who lived at Fontwell who were"—she shrugged—"pensioners of mine. I helped the woman once or twice. If this is her daughter, she is a perfect stranger to me."

All the time she spoke her eyes were fixed on Audrey, and the girl thought she read in them a mute appeal. In a flash she realized that what Dora had said might very well be true. She had married in her stage name, and it was quite possible that none of the neighbours identified her with Mrs. Bedford's daughter, for she had not visited the place, and Audrey's mother was one of the reticent kind that made no confidences.

"What Mrs. Elton says is quite true," she said quietly. "I do not know her, nor does she know me."

Dick Shannon opened the door, and the girl went out again to the waiting matron. When she had gone, he faced the Eltons.

"I don't know how long she'll keep this up," he said. "But if she sticks to the story from first to last, Elton, she'll go to jail." He spoke deliberately. "And I'm going to tell you something. If that child is sent to prison, if you allow her to sacrifice herself, I will never rest night or day until I have brought you both to the penal settlement."

"You seem to forget to whom you're speaking," said Dora, a bright light in her eyes.

"I know I'm speaking to two utterly unscrupulous, utterly depraved, utterly soulless people," said Dick. "Get out!"

*

Lacy Marshalt sat in his breakfast-room. A newspaper was propped up before him; his face was puckered in a frown. He looked again at the picture taken by an enterprising press photographer. It was the portrait of a girl alighting from a taxicab. In the background a blur of curious spectators. A policeman was on one side of her, a broad-shouldered wardress on the other. It was one of those pictures fairly familiar to the newspaper reader. A fleeting snap of a criminal on her way to trial.

There was no need to compare the newspaper with the photograph in his pocket. The name of the prisoner would have told him, even if there bad been no photograph.

Tonger came in, slipping through between door and post.

"You didn't ring, did you. Lacy?" he asked.

"I rang ten minutes ago. And I'm telling you for the last time to forget that

'Lacy' of yours. There is a limit to my patience, my friend."

The little man rubbed his hands gleefully. "Heard from my girl today," he said. "She's doing well in America. Clever kid that, Lacy."

"Is she?" Lacy Marshalt returned to a survey of his newspaper.

"She's got money—always writes from the best hotels. Never thought things would turn out that way."

Lacy folded his paper and dropped it on the floor.

"Mrs. Martin Elton will be here in five minutes. She will come through the mews to the back door. Be waiting for her and bring her through the conservatory to the library. When I ring for you, show her out the same way."

Tonger grinned.

"What a lad for the girls!" he said admiringly.

Lacy jerked his head towards the door.

Less than five minutes later Dora Elton pushed open the heavy wicket gate and, crossing the courtyard, mounted the iron stairs to the "conservatory"—a glass annexe thrown out at the back of the house above the kitchen and scullery of the establishment. She was dressed in black and heavily veiled. Tonger detected signs of nervousness as be opened the conservatory door to her.

"Have you come to breakfast?" he asked amiably.

She was too used to his familiarities to resent his manner.

"Where is Mr. Marshalt?"

"In the library—readin' Christie's Old Organ," suggested Tonger humorously.

Lacy was reading nothing more informative than the fire when she was shown in. "I had an awful trouble getting here," she said. "Wouldn't it have done this afternoon? I had to tell all sorts of lies to Martin. Aren't you going to kiss me?"

He stooped and brushed her cheek. "What a kiss!" she scoffed. "Well?"

"This jewel robbery," he said slowly. "There is a girl implicated. I understand that the police are under the impression that she is your sister."

She was silent.

"I know, of course, that you are on the crook," he went on. "Stanford is an old acquaintance of mine in South Africa, and he's one of your gang. But this girl, is she in it?"

"You know how much she is in it," she said sulkily. She had not come, at some risk, to Portman Square to discuss Audrey. And at the thought of risk...

"There was a man watching this house at the back when I came along the mews," she said. "I saw him by the back door. When he saw me he walked away."

"Watching this house?" he said incredulously. "What sort of a man?"

"He looked a gentleman. I only just saw his face—very thin and refined-looking. He had a limp..."

Lacy took a step towards her, and gripped her by the shoulders. His face was grey, his lip quivered. For a moment he could not speak, then:

"You're lying! You're trying to put one over on me!"

She struggled from his grip, terrified.

"Lacy! What is wrong with you?"

He silenced her with a gesture.

"I'm nervy, and you startled me," he muttered. "Go on with what you were saying. That girl is your sister? I want to know."

"My half-sister," she said in a low voice.

He stopped in his pacing.

"You mean... you have different fathers?"

She nodded.

He did not speak again for so long that she began to feel frightened.

"She'll go to jail, of course, and she's shielding you." He laughed, but there was no mirth in his laughter. "That is best—I can wait," he said.

A month later, on a bright March morning, a pale girl stood in the spacious dock of the Old Bailey, and by her side a square-shouldered Belgian, the first to be sentenced.

Coming out of court towards the end of the case, sick at heart and weary of the solemn machinery of vengeance which was grinding to dust so frail a victim. Shannon saw a familiar figure ensconced in one of the deep- seated benches where, usually, witnesses sat waiting.

"Well, Slick, have you been in court?"

"I have," said the other carefully, "but the illusion of the successful detective wore through, and that big pen was certainly hungry-looking. I tore myself away. Other people haven't any sensitive feelings. I saw Stanford amongst the ghouls."

Shannon sat down by his side.

"What do you think?"

"Of the case? Little Miss Quixote—pronounced Key-o-tey, they tell me—is going down." He pointed significantly at the tiled floor.

"I'm afraid she is," Shannon said after a pause, and sighed. "But that is as far as they'll get her," mused the crook. "She'll come up just as she went down—sweet. That kind doesn't sour easily. Say, Shannon, ever heard of a man called Malpas?"

Dick, who was thinking of something else, started. "Yes, he's an eccentric old man who lives in Portman Square—why?"

Slick Smith smiled blandly. "He's in it somewhere," he said. "I am speaking in my capacity as a detective. That case has finished mighty suddenly."

A policeman was beckoning Shannon, and he hurried into court in time to hear the sentence.

"What is your age?" asked the judge, pausing, pen in hand, and looking over his glasses.

"Nineteen, my lord." It was Shannon. "And I may say that the police are perfectly satisfied, in spite of the evidence, that this girl is an innocent victim of other people who are not in custody."

The judge shook his head.

"The evidence does not support that view. It is very dreadful to see a young girl in this position, and I should be failing in my duty to society if I did not deal severely with so dangerous an agent. Audrey Bedford, you will go to prison with hard labour for twelve months."

Edgar Wallace

The Truth

On a gloomy morning in December the wicket gate of Holloway Prison opened, and a slim girl, in an old brown velour coat, came out, and, looking neither to the left nor right, passed through the waiting friends of prisoners to be released, walked quickly up the Holloway Road towards Camden Town. Crossing the road, she boarded a street car, and at that moment Dick Shannon's long machine swept past, and she did not see it. He arrived three minutes too late to intercept her.

She had a few shillings left as the result of her year's work and, getting down at the tram terminus, she went along the Euston Road till she came to a small restaurant.

The face was a little finer-drawn, the eyes graver, but it was the old Audrey who ordered extravagant portions of devilled kidneys and egg. For nine months the prison routine had ground at her soul; for seventy-two hours a week she had associated with the debased dregs of the underworld, and had neither grown down to their level nor experienced any sense of immeasurable superiority. There were bitter nights when the black treachery to which she had been subjected overwhelmed her, and she closed her eyes to shut out the hideous realities. Nights of torture, when the understanding of her own ruin had driven her to the verge of madness.

Yet it did not seem unnatural that Dora had acted so. It was almost a Dora-like thing to have done, consonant with all that she knew and all that she had heard of the girl. A horrible thought to Audrey (and this alone saddened her) was that the qualities in her sister were those which had been peculiarly noticeable in her mother. With a half-checked sigh she rose, and, taking her bill, paid at the cashier's little box.

Where should she go now? To Dora, she decided. She must be absolutely sure that she had not wholly misjudged her. She could not go in the daytime; it would not be fair to the girl. She spent the rest of the morning looking for lodgings, finding them at last in a top back room in Gray's Inn Road. Here she rested through the afternoon, straightening the rags of her future. When dark came she made her way to Curzon Street.

The servant who opened the door to her was the same girl that had been there on her first visit.

"What do you want?" she asked tartly.

"I want to see Mrs. Elton," said Audrey.

"Well, you can't," said the girl and tried to shut the door.

But Audrey's nine months of manual work had had results. Without an effort she pushed the door open and stepped in.

"Go up and tellyour mistress I am here," she said.

The girl flew up the stairs, and Audrey, without hesitation, followed her. As she walked behind the servant into the drawing-room she heard her sister say: "How dare she come here!"

She was in evening dress, looking particularly lovely, her fair hair shining like burnished gold. She stared at the girl as if she were a ghost, and her eyes narrowed.

"How dare you force your way into this house?" she demanded.

"Send away your servant," said Audrey quietly, and, when the girl had gone and she had made sure that she was not listening on the landing, she walked across to Dora, her hands behind her. "I want you to say 'thank you'," she said simply. "I did a mad, foolish thing, because I felt that I wanted to repay mother for anything that I owed her, and which I had not already paid."

"I don't know what you're talking about," said Dora, flushing.

"You've got a nerve to come here, anyway!" It was the sleek Martin. "You tried to drag us into your—your crime. You hold your—Mrs. Elton up to the scorn of the world, and then you calmly walk into our house without so much as a please or by your leave. Damned nerve!"

"If you want money, write," said Dora, and flung open the door. "If you come here again I'll send for a policeman."

"Send for one now," said the girl coolly. "I'm so well acquainted with policemen and wardresses that you can't frighten me, my dear sister."

Dora closed the door quickly. "If you want to know, we're not sisters. You're not even English!" she said in a low, malignant voice. "Your father was mother's second husband, an American! He's on the Breakwater at Cape

Town, serving a sentence of life!"

Audrey caught the back of a chair for support.

"That's not true," she said.

"It is true—it is true!" stormed Dora in a harsh whisper. "Mother told me, and Mr. Stanford knows all about it. Your father bought diamonds and shot the man who betrayed him. It is a felony to buy diamonds in South Africa. He disgraced my mother—she changed her name and came home the day after his arrest. Why, you're not even entitled to the name of Bedford. She hated him so much that she changed everything!"

Audrey nodded.

"And, of course, mother left him," she said, speaking to herself. "She didn't stay near to give him the comfort and sympathy that a wife might give to the vilest of men. She just left him—flat! How like her!"

There was no malice, no bitterness in her voice. Audrey had the trick of seeing things truly. She raised her eyes slowly until they met Dora's.

"I ought not to have gone to prison," she-said; "you are not worth it. Nor mother, I think."

"You dare to speak of my mother!" cried Dora in a fury.

"Yes, she was my mother too. She's beyond my criticism or your defence. Thank you. What is my name?"

"Find out!" snapped the woman.

"I'll ask Mr. Shannon," said the girl.

It was the only malice she showed in the interview. But it was worth the effort to see the change that came to the two faces.

Mr. Malpas

Dick Shannon had a flat in the Haymarket, an apartment which served as home and office, for, in the room overlooking one of London's busiest thoroughfares, he got through a considerably larger volume of work than he disposed of in his uninspiring bureau on the Thames Embankment.

Steel, his assistant, christened the flat "Newest Scotland Yard", and certainly had justification, for here, more often than not, were held the conferences which brought the Big Five—an ever-changing quantity—about the council board.

Something in the nature of a sub-committee was sitting on the day that Audrey Bedford was released from prison. Sergeant Steel, who specialized in society cases—it was the Yard's boast that he was the best-dressed man in London—and Inspector Lane, late of Bow Street, now of Marylebone, was the third.

"You didn't see her?" asked the inspector.

Dick Shannon shook his head.

"By the time I got to the Governor and discovered she had been released, it was useless looking for her. I've given instructions to the stations that the moment she reports—she hasn't completed the whole of her sentence—they are to report to me."

He suppressed a sigh.

"There was a miscarriage of justice, if ever there was one!" he said. "And yet, for the life of me, I can't see what other verdict the jury could return."

"But if she was innocent," said Steel, puzzled, "what was easier than for her to speak? It is not innocent to hide the guilty."

"Let us lift this discussion out of the base realm of metaphysics," said Dick testily. "What about Mr. Malpas?"

"He's a mystery," said Lane unnecessarily, "and the house is more so. So far as I can find, he has been in occupation of 551 Portman Square since January 1917, and has been there most of the time. Nobody has seen him. We had a complaint last year from Mr. Lacy Marshalt, who lives next door, that he was disturbed by knocking at nights, but we could only advise him to take a summons. He pays his bills regularly, and when he came into the house (which is his own property, by the way) he spent a considerable sum in renovations. A big Italian firm of Turin fitted the house with electric lighting, burglar alarms and various other gadgets, though I can't trace any furniture going in."

"Are there any servants?"

"None: that's the strangest thing. No food goes into the house, which means that he must eat outside or starve. I've had men to watch the back and front of the house, but he has slipped them every time, though they've seen a few interesting things."

Dick Shannon smoothed his chin. "It isn't an offence to be a recluse," he said, "but it is an offence to engage in a conspiracy. Bring in the girl, Steel."

Steel went out, to return with an over-powdered young lady, who nodded coolly to the company, and took the chair which Steel, with an air, pushed up to her.

"Miss Neilson, you are a professional dancer–disengaged?"

"I'm that," she said laconically.

"I want you to tell us about your visit to 551 Portman Square."

She was not particularly anxious or willing to talk.

"If I had known I was speaking to a detective when I got so talkative the other night, I wouldn't have said so much." she admitted frankly. "You haven't any right to question me."

"You practically accused a gentleman who holds a responsible position of attempting to engage you in a conspiracy," said Dick. "That is a very serious accusation to make."

"I didn't say it was a conspiracy," she denied quickly. "All I said was that the old gentleman, who was a perfect stranger to me, asked me if I would start something at Mr. Marshalt's house–that's next door. He wanted me to go to there one evening and make a fuss–to start screaming that Mr. Marshalt was a scoundrel, break a window, and get arrested."

"He didn't tell you why?"

She shook her head.

"No. It wasn't my job, anyhow. And I was only too glad to get out –the man gave me the creeps." She shivered. "You've heard of ugly men? Well, you don't know what ugliness is. And scared! You have to sit at a table one end of the room whilst he sits at the other. And the room is all dark except for little light on the desk where he sits. The house is full of ghosts–that's how it seemed to me. Doors open by themselves and voices talk to you from nowhere. When I got out on to the street again I could have gone down on my knees and said a prayer of thanksgiving."

"If you were a stranger to him, how did he come to know you?" asked Dick, puzzled and suspicious.

Her explanation was logical. "He got my name out of a theatrical newspaper—I'm in the 'want engagement' columns," she said.

Lane questioned her closely, but her story held, and presently they let her go. "Queer," said Dick Shannon thoughtfully. "I should like to see Mr. Malpas. You have had other complaints?"

Lane hesitated.

"I wouldn't call them complaints. The inspector of income tax made a little trouble about not being able to see the man. He returned his income at what Inland Revenue thought was too low a figure, and he was summoned to appear before the inspector. And, of course, he did not appear, sending, instead, permission to inspect his banking account. I happened to know of this and took the opportunity of sharing the inspection. It is the simplest account I have ever seen: a thousand five hundred a year paid in —by cash; a thousand five hundred a year paid out. No tradesmen's cheques. Nothing but taxes, ground rent, and substantial sums for his current expenses."

"You say he has had visitors?" asked Dick.

"Yes, I was going to tell you about these. At intervals, never longer than two weeks, he has a visitor, sometimes two in the course of the day. Generally it is on a Saturday. The caller never comes until it is dark, and doesn't remain longer than half an hour. So far as we have been able to learn, the same man never comes twice. It was only by accident that we discovered this: one of our officers saw a man go in and come out. The next Saturday, at precisely the same hour, he saw a visitor arrive and, after an interval, take his departure. This was seen again a few weeks later, the caller being a negro. Our man 'tailed him up', but could get nothing out of him."

"Malpas must be placed under closer observation," said Dick, and the inspector made a note. "Pull in one of his visitors on some pretext or other—see what he has in his possession. You may find that the old man is nothing more alarming than a dispenser of charity—on the other hand, you may not!"

That almost exhausted the subject of the mysterious Mr. Malpas, and they passed to the matter of a providential fire that had saved an insolvent cabinet-maker from bankruptcy.

Mr. Malpas might not have come up for discussion at all but for the story that the dancer had told to a sympathetic and official listener. That this sinister figure should be associated with the events which, under his eyes, were moving to a climax, that the ragged princess whose image had not left his mind for nine months would shortly come into the old man's ken and find her fate and future linked with his, Dick Shannon could not dream. Mr. Malpas was "an inquiry", an arresting circumstance to be questioned and probed. Soon he was to loom upon the scene, blotting out all other objects in Captain Shannon's view.

Audrey Bedford had made an interesting discovery. There was an essential thing in life about which she had never heard. It was a mysterious something called "a character"; some-times it was more genteelly styled "references".

Without one or the other (and they were really one and the same thing) it was impossible to secure employment. There were leering men who said, "Never mind, little woman, we'll get along without that"; other men who did not leer and were apparently shocked when she told them she had just come from prison, but who bore up well enough to engage her and ask her to come to dinner with them; and there were others (and she liked these best) who said curtly, "We have no opening for you."

Her little stock of money was dwindling. There dawned a Christmas Day when she woke with a healthy appetite to breakfast on water and one very stale slice of bread that she had saved from the night before. And this was to be her luncheon, and would have been her supper too, only there occurred that night, in a little street off Gray's Inn Road, a light between two viragos, one of whom thrust a small and greasy package into the girl's hand that she might deal more effectively with her rival. The police came instantly, there was a wild scrimmage, the battlers were haled off to Theobalds Road Police Station, and Audrey carried the parcel home and supped royally on fried fish and potatoes. It was heavenly.

On Tuesday morning her landlady came up the stairs and Audrey heard the heavy foot of the woman with a sense of blind panic.

"Good morning, miss. There's a letter for you."

Audrey stared. Nobody knew her address—she had never reached the address stage in any of her essays at finding employment.

"I hope it's good news," said the landlady ominously. "I don't charge much for my apartments, but I like it regular, We've all got to live, and I've had a party after this very room this very morning. Not that I'm going to turn you out. I'd sooner make up a bed for you on the sofa," she added.

Audrey was not listening. She was turning the letter over in her hand. Tearing it open, she found an address and a few lines of pencilled writing. She read the message in bewilderment.

Come at 5 o'clock this evening. I have work for you.

The note was signed "Malpas".

She knit her forehead. Who was "Malpas", and how had he discovered her whereabouts?

The Interview

AUDREY BEDFORD held the soddened slip of paper nearer to her eyes to assure herself of the address. The writing, in pencil, was worn now to a faint and almost indecipherable smear. In the failing light of a grey December afternoon it would have been difficult enough to read, but to all other disadvantages was added the drive of wind and sleet. Her old coat was already saturated. It had been wet before she had walked a mile; the brim of her black velvet hat drooped soggily.

She put the paper back in her pocket and looked a little fearfully at the grim door of No. 551 Portman Square. This forbidding house, with its dingy stone front and blank, expressionless windows, might hide interiors of comfort and luxury, but there was little promise in the outward appearance.

What would be the end of this essay, she wondered, with a calmness which seemed strange, even to herself. Would it go with the others and end in dismissal, or, what was worse, an engagement on terms unspoken but none the less clearly understood?

Portman Square was empty of pedestrians. Down one side of the open space the great red buses rumbled and closed taxis and cars sped past at intervals. Drawing a long sigh, she walked up the two steps and looked for the bell. There was none. The door was innocent of knocker—she tapped gently with her knuckles.

"Who is there?"

The voice seemed to come from the side stone doorposts. "Miss Bedford," she said. "I have an appointment with Mr. Malpas."

There was a pause, and then, as the door opened slowly: "Come upstairs—the room on the first landing," said the voice.

It came from a small grating let in the wall. The hall was empty. One yellow globe supplied the illumination. Whilst she was looking around the door closed again, by no obvious agency. For a second she was seized with a sudden unaccountanle fear. She sought the handle of the door: there was none. The black, heavy portal was closed upon her irrevocably.

Audrey's hands were trembling; cold and fear combined to break her courage—cold and fear and hunger, for she had taken nothing that day but a piece of bread and the remains of a coffee left over from the previous night.

She looked around the hall. Of furniture there was none except an old chair against the wall. The marble floor was thick with dust, the discoloured walls innocent of pictures or hangings.

With an effort she controlled her shaking limbs and walked up the stone stairs. On the first landing was a polished rosewood door—the only interior door she had seen—and, after a pause to summon the reserves of her courage, she knocked.

"Is that Miss Bedford?" This time the voice came from over her head. Looking up, she saw a second grating in the recessed doorway. It was placed so that any visitor knocking would stand immediately underneath.

"Yes," she answered, holding her anxiety in check. Instantly the rosewood swung open, and she passed into a broad, well-lit hall. Facing her was a second door, ajar.

"Come in, please." This time the voice spoke from the room; it was less distinct.

She hesitated, her heart thumping painfully. The room seemed to be in darkness save for one faint reflection. Pushing open the door, she walked in. It was a large room, about thirty feet in width, and almost twice that length. The walls, so completely draped by velvet curtains that it was impossible to tell where the windows were hidden, ran up into gloom; the visitor must guess where the black ceiling began and the walls ended. Under her feet was a rich, deep carpet, into which her halting feet sank as she took three steps, stopped and looked open-eyed.

In the far corner of the room a man sat at a desk, on which a green- shaded lamp afforded the only illumination the gloomy chamber possessed.

A strangely revolting figure. His head was narrow and bald; his yellow face, innocent of hair, was puckered in a thousand wrinkles and seams; the nose was big and pendulous. His long, pointed chin moved all the time as though he were talking to himself.

"Sit in that chair," he said hollowly.

The chair she saw when her eyes grew accustomed to the darkness: it stood behind a small table, and slowly and painfully she sat down.

"I have sent for you to make your fortune," he said, in his mumbling voice. "Many people have sat in that chair and have gone away rich."

In the green light that fell athwart his face from the lampshade he looked like some hideous imagining of a Chinese artist. She shuddered, and gazed steadily past him.

"On the table—look!" he said.

He must have pressed some button on the table, for instantly she found herself sitting, the focus of a powerful yellow light that fell from a bell-shaped shade above and threw a circle of bright radiance on the floor around her. And then she saw on the table a thin package of money.

"Take it!" he said.

After a second's hesitation she stretched out her hand and took the notes, shivering from head to foot. The light above was slowly dimming. Presently it faded altogether, and she sat in the darkness, her hands unconsciously gripping the wealth that had come to her. And a key—she did not realize that until, later, he referred to the fact.

"Audrey Bedford. That is your name?"

She made no reply.

"Three weeks ago you were released from prison where you served a sentence of a year, or nine months of a year, for being accessory to a robbery?"

"Yes," said the girl quietly. "I should have told you that in any event. I have invariably told that when I have applied for work."

"Innocent, of course?" he asked.

There was no smile on his expressionless face, and she could not judge whether his tone was ironical or not. She guessed was.

"Yes: I was innocent," she said evenly.

"Faked charge... a frame-up, eh? Elton had it all fixed for you. You knew nothing of the robbery? Just an innocent agent?"

He waited.

"I knew nothing of the robbery," she said quietly.

"Did you say that at the trial?"

She did not answer. He sat so still that she could have believed that he was a waxen figure, worked by some drug-crazy artist.

"You are badly dressed... that offends me. You have money; buy the best. Come this day week at this hour. You-will find a key on the table: this will unlock all doors, if the control is released."

Audrey found her voice.

"I must know what my duties are," she said, and her voice sounded dead and lifeless in that draped room. "It is very good of you to trust me with so much money, but you will see how impossible it is to accept unless I know what is expected of me."

Famished as she was, with the prospect of a supperless night, and before her eyes the drab ugliness of her little room and the reproachful face of her landlady, it required more than an ordinary effort to say this. Hunger demoralizes the finest nature, and she was faint for want of food.

He spoke slowly.

"Your task is to break a man's heart," he said.

She almost laughed.

"That sounds... rather alarming. You are not serious?"

He offered no reply. She felt a cold draught behind her, and turning, experienced a little thrill of fear to see the door opening. "Goodnight."

The figure at the end of the room waved a hand towards the door. The interview was over.

She had put one foot on the stairs when the door closed again, and she went down to the hall, her mind in a state of chaos. The front door was not open: evidently he expected her to use the key. With trembling fingers she tried to press it into the microscopic slit which, after a search, she discovered. In her haste the key slipped and fell. It was so small that she could not find it at first. The force of her pressure had sent it into a corner of the hall. She found it after a search, and found something else too—a pebble, the size of a nut. Attached was a blob of red sealing-wax and the clear impression of a tiny seal. It was so unusual an object that she forgot for the moment her very urgent desire to get out of the house. The bizarre has a fascination for the young, and there was something very unusual about that common piece of stone so carefully sealed...

Audrey looked up the stairs, hoping to see the old man and ask him if this queer find of hers had any interest for him. Then she remembered that she would see him again in a week, and she dropped the pebble into her little handbag.

So doing, she became aware that one of her hands was' gripping a package of notes. Six hundred pounds! There were three of a hundred, four of fifty, and twenty of five.

Audrey drew a long breath. She thrust the money out of sight and turned the key in the lock—in another second she was facing the realities of a blizzard. The taxicab that was crawling leisurely towards her had no significance at first. Then it came upon her that she was an enormously rich woman, and, her heart beating a little faster, she put up her hand to signal the cab, walking rapidly to meet, it as it drew in to the kerb. "Take me to —?"

Where? First food; then, in the sanity which food might bring, a few minutes of quiet contemplation.

"She's had one over the eight," grinned the driver.

Audrey's first impression was that the man was speaking of her, and she wondered what he meant. But he was looking beyond her, and, following the direction of his eyes, she saw a sight that first sickened and then moved her to pity. Clinging to the rails that bordered the area was a woman. She held tight with one hand, swaying unsteadily, whilst with the other she was manipulating the knocker of the front door of the house next to that place of mystery which she had left.

Her pathetic finery, the draggling imitation paradise plume of her hat, the wet and matted surface of her fur coat, ludicrously fashionable in cut, made an unforgettable picture. Drunkenness was loathsome to the girl; she realized its horror to the full when she saw it in a woman. Somehow the fighting viragos of Gray's Inn Road were infinitely less repulsive than the spectacle of this poor creature with her red, swollen face and her maudlin mutterings.

Audrey had withdrawn her foot from the step of the cab, intending to go to her, when the door was flung open violently, and she saw a thin, elderly man appear.

"Here—what's the row? Coming here making this fuss at a gentleman's house. Go away or I'll send for a copper!"

Tonger's voice came down to the girl through the shrill whistle of the wind.

"Going in—" gasped the wreck, and lurched towards the open doorway.

Audrey, watching, saw him try to hold her, but she collapsed on to him. "Here, hold up!"

There was a little struggle, and suddenly Tonger jerked the woman into the hall and the door slammed.

"That's Mr. Marshalt's house," said the cabman. "He's the African millionaire. Where did you say you'd like to go, miss?"

She was inspired to name a little dressmaker's shop in Shaftesbury Avenue, a shop before whose windows she always lingered when her search for work brought her westward. Later, she would consider the propriety of spending this terrible old man's money. For the moment her creature needs dominated. Opposite the dressmaker's was a shoe shop; two blocks away was a snug hotel.

"I'll come out of this dream some time," said Audrey, looking through the blurred windows at the shops that flashed past, "but I'm coming out with dry clothes and a bed that isn't nobbly!"

Bunny Talks Straight

It is sometimes difficult to rule a line across a human life, and say with exactness, "Here began a career." Martin Elton had become a criminal by a natural sequence of processes, all related one to the other, and all having their foundation in a desire, common to humanity high and low, to live without working.

The product of a great school, he had found himself, at an early period of his life, with no other assets than a charming manner, the ability to converse pleasantly, and a host of exploitable friends. He went where his accomplishments paid the biggest dividends; and being unhampered by a conscience or handicapped with a too stringent sense of honour, he came naturally to the society of men and women who lived by their sharpness of intellect. He had run gambling houses (at one of which he had first met Dora and found in her a partner equally free from stupid scruples); he had manoeuvred intimate robberies that had something of blackmail in them; he had dabbled in race-track frauds of an unobtrusive character, and had made his many enterprises profitable.

Between the second and third acts of a play to which Dora had taken him, he strolled out into the lobby. There were people who knew and nodded to him, only one who made any effort to get into conversation, for Martin was not of the gregarious kind. He preferred the company, of his own thought at any time, most of all tonight.

"'Lo, Elton!"

He smiled mechanically and would have moved on, but the man who had intercepted him was wilfully blind to his desire for solitude.

"Stanford's gone to Italy, they tell me—that fellow is certainly the bird that's in two places at once. Anything doing?"

"Nothing," replied Martin pointedly. "London has been very dull since Melilla Snowden's rooms at the Albemarle were burgled and her pearls lifted."

Slick Smith laughed softly.

"Not guilty," he said, "and anyway, they were props. The burglary was more genuine, but the scream her press agent raised is just publicity. My opinion of Melilla, both as an actress and a woman, has gone right down to the mezzanine floor. A vamp that can only vamp up Luk-lik-Reels ought to be teaching Sunday school. If you got any kind of work I can do, let me know. But it must be honest."

"Come round one day and fix my kitchen stove," snarled Martin, who was not in the best of humours.

"Stoves are my speciality," said Slick, unperturbed. "Have a good cigar?" He offered his case.

"No!"

"Maybe you're right," agreed the other. "They were a Christmas present. I can't get anybody to try 'em out. It will be tough on me if I have to do the pioneer work. Seen Shannon?"

Martin sighed heavily.

"My dear fellow, I haven't seen Shannon and I don't want to see Shannon. More to the point, I'm not in the mood for conversation."

"That's a pity," said Slick regretfully. "I'm feeling chatty, and I'm tired of talking to myself. I pall on one."

"You're in danger of palling on me," Martin smiled in spite of himself.

"I felt that too. I'm responsive to atmosphere. There's a whole lot in this aura theory. Lacy Marshalt's not like that."

There was no especial emphasis to his words. He was lighting an experimental cigar as he spoke, painfully and apprehensively.

"I don't know very much about Marshalt," said Martin shortly.

"Don't suppose you do. I know him slightly. He's a thief too. And the things he steals leave a kind of gap. You're a pretty good fellow, Elton."

The seeming inconsequence of the last remark was not lost upon his hearer.

"I don't think I'd go any farther if I were you," said Martin Elton quietly. "You're trying to be kind, aren't you?"

"Not trying. I do these things naturally." Slick Smith's smile was broad and disarming. "There goes the bell—I wonder if she married the duke and sent her village swain back to the family woodpile? I guess she didn't—they never do in plays."

That raw night, as he was driving home, he thought of Slick. He had not enjoyed the play, neither had Dora, and a sense of restraint had fallen upon both. The drive was unrelieved by any spoken words. He followed her up to the drawing-room, well prepared for the outburst which was due and, unless he was mistaken, was coming.

"What is the matter with you, Bunny? You've hardly spoken a word this evening. I'm tired of your sulks! You make me so nervous I hardly know what I'm doing!"

He bit off the end of a cigar and lit it, his attention on the match.

"I'm not sulking, I'm just thoughtful, that's all," he said, throwing the stick into the fire before he sat down in a corner of the roomy settee. "Have you heard any more of your sister?"

"No, I haven't," she snapped, "and I hope to God I never hear from her again! The whining little jail-bird!"

He took his cigar from his mouth and examined it carefully.

"I don't remember that she whined; and if she's a jail-bird, we made her so," he said.

She stared at him in amazement.

"That's a new tone for you to take, Bunny. You practically threw her out of the house last time she was here."

He nodded.

"Yes, I haven't forgotten that," he said quietly. "London is a rotten place for a pretty girl to be alone in, without money, or friends. I wish I knew where she was."

A slow smile dawned on her lovely face.

"You seem to have had a visit from R. E. Morse, Esquire," she said ironically. "But then, you always fell for a pretty face."

He made a gesture of distaste. There were moments when the groundings of Wechester College started up from their sleep and made themselves evident.

"Her prettiness weighs less with me than her helplessness at this moment. She didn't write?"

"Of course she didn't write," said his wife scornfully. "Is that what has been making you so glum? Poor Bunny!" she mocked. "He has a soft heart for beauty in distress!"

He looked at her for a second, a cold scrutiny which aroused her to fury.

"What's wrong?" she demanded, her voice trembling with anger. "Tell me what's in your mind—there's something!"

"Yes, there's something," agreed Bunny Elton; "in fact, there are several somethings, and Audrey is one of them. The girl may be starving. God knows what may have happened to her."

"Let us leave her to His keeping," she said with mock piety, and his eyes narrowed.

"I've been thinking lately," he said, "that, if you behave this way to your own sister, what sort of treatment should I get if things went wrong, and you had to make a quick decision between me and safety?"

"Safety would win," she said coolly. "I'll not deceive you, Bunny. 'Sauve qui peut' is my family motto."

She kicked off her shoes and was pulling on the red morocco boudoir boots that stood before the fire.

"And is that all? Is it only the thought of the poor little girl driven from home that is worrying you?" she sneered.

"That's one thing," he said. He threw his cigar into the fire and rose. "Dora"—his voice was like ice—"Mr. Lacy Marshalt is an undesirable acquaintance."

She looked up, her eyes wide open.

"Isn't he honest?" she asked innocently.

"There are a whole lot of honest people that no respectable lady thief can dine with in a private room at Shavarri's," he said deliberately. "Lacy Marshalt is one."

Her eyes dropped to the fire again; her colour came and went...

"You've been watching me, have you? Marshalt may be a very useful man to know in certain eventualities."

"He is no use to me in any eventuality," said Martin Elton; "and he is never so useless as when he is dining furtively with my wife."

A long silence followed.

"I only dined with him once at Shavarri's," she spoke at last. "I intended telling you, but I forgot. Hundreds of people dine privately at Shavarri's," she said defiantly.

He nodded. "And I'm particularly anxious that you should not be like any of those hundreds," he said. "You've dined with him twice, as a matter, of fact—twice I know about; probably more often. Dora, that hasn't to happen again."

She did not answer.

"Do you hear?"

She shrugged her shoulders.

"I get precious little out of life," she said with a little sob. "The only people I meet are Stanford and you and the little crooks you pull into your various games. I like to meet somebody who isn't that way —at times. It's like a breath of fresh air that makes me forget the rotten atmosphere in which I live."

She did not see his cynical smile, but, knowing him, she could guess how he would receive her excuse.

"Intensely pathetic," he said. "The picture you have drawn of the pure child, striving to regain the memory of her lost innocence, touches me deeply. But if you want to get back to nature, I suggest some other means than tete-a-tete dinners at Shavarri's. They are sophisticated, Dora. You won't go again."

She looked up quickly.

"If I want to go—" she began defiantly.

"You will not go again," he said, his voice little above a whisper. "If you do, I will look up Mr. Lacy Marshalt and put three bullets through the pocket in which he carries his excellent cigars. What I shall do to you, I don't know," he said in a matter-of-fact tone. "It depends entirely upon my mood and your—your propinquity. I rather fancy it will be a triple tragedy."

Her face was a ghastly white. She tried to speak, but could not put her words in order. Then, suddenly, she was at his feet, her arms clasping his knees. "Oh, Bunny, Bunny!" she sobbed. "Don't talk like that; don't look like that! I will do what you wish... there was no harm... I swear there was nothing in it. Bunny... I just went out of devilment."

He touched her golden hair.

"You mean a lot to me, Dora," he said gently. "I haven't given you the very best training, and I guess I've thrown overboard every one of the good old moral maxims that guide most people. But there's one to which I am holding like death—it's 'honour amongst thieves', Dora... honour amongst thieves!"

She had been in bed two hours, and he still sat before the remains of the fire, the stub of an unlighted cigar between his white teeth, his eyes fixed moodily upon the dull embers. Two bitter hours they had been, when he had stood face to face with the naked truth of things, and had brought his philosophy to join experience in judging the woman he loved. This good-looking young man, with his flawless skin and his dandified attire, was very human.

He rose, unlocked a drawer of the writing-table, took out a small Browning, and sat for a quarter of an hour before the fire, the pistol resting on the palm of his hand, his grave eyes fixed upon the weapon. He heard a rustling sound outside, and slipped the gun into his pocket as Dora in her neglige came into the room.

"It's past two o'clock, Bunny," she said anxiously. "Aren't you coming to bed?"

He rose stiffly and stretched himself.

"You're not worrying any more, are you, Bunny?" she asked apprehensively. Her eyes were still red with weeping; the hand she laid on his arm shook. He took it in his and patted it.

"No, I'm not worrying any more," he said. "We'll start afresh."

"But, Bunny," she wailed, "there's no need to start afresh. I swear to you—"

"We'll start afresh," said Bunny, and kissed her.

A Chance Meeting

Dick Bannon tapped furiously on the glass of the cab that was carrying him down Regent Street, and, dropping the window, leaned out.

"Turn round and go up the other side. I want to speak to that lady," he said.

The Ragged Princess! It was she—he would have known her anywhere—but a different ragged princess.

"Which lady, sir?"

The taximan screwed his body to shout the query through the open window as he brought the cab to the edge of the opposite sidewalk. But Dick had the door of the cab open and had leaped to the pavement before the car came to a standstill.

"Miss Bedford, I presume?" he laughed. "This is a very pleasant surprise."

It was, in more senses than one. All traces of her poverty had vanished; the girl was well dressed, well shod, and, in the now setting, was so lovely to look upon that she had passed through a lane of turning heads.

The surprise was mutual, and, by the light that came to her ryes, the pleasure was no less.

"I have been searching London for you," he said, falling in by her side and oblivious of the taximan's alarm at the threatened bilk. "By rank bad luck I lost you on the morning you came from Holloway. I arrived a few minutes after you had left. And queerly enough, I made the mistake of thinking that it was necessary that you would have to report to the police."

"Like other dangerous criminals," she smiled. "No—I am spared that. I saw you once or twice in Holloway. You were there on business."

The business that had taken him to the woman's prison had been to catch a glimpse of her and to learn of her well-being. There were small privileges that could be obtained for her, an allocation of less unpleasant tasks. She had often wondered why she was so abruptly taken from the drudgery of the laundry and given the more congenial work of librarian, and had not connected the fugitive visits of Dick Shannon with the change of conditions.

They turned into the less congested area of Hanover Square. She had had no intention of going to Hanover Square, and was, in fact, on her way to an Oxford Street store, but she surrendered her will to his in this small matter without exactly realizing why.

"I am going to talk to you like a Dutch uncle," he said, slowing his pace. "You're not a mason; neither am I. But masons have confidences and keep one another's secrets and talk 'on the square' with the greatest frankness."

There was laughter in the eyes that she turned to his.

"And from knowledge that I have acquired, in a place that shall be nameless," she said, "policemen are artful! And under the guise of loving-kindness—?"

She saw the flush come to his face and the droop of his brows.

"I'm awfully sorry; I didn't really mean to be rude. Go on, be candid—I'll be recklessly truthful, but you mustn't ask me anything about Dora, and you really must not raise the question of that unfortunate Queen's jewellery."

"Dora Elton is your sister, isn't she?"

She was silent for a moment. "She isn't exactly my sister, but I was under the impression that she was," she said.

He stroked his chin thoughtfully.

"Anyway, it stands to her credit that she's looking after you now."

The girl's soft laughter answered him.

"Do you mean to say that she isn't?" He stopped and frowned down at her.

"Dora and I are no longer on speaking terms," she said, "and very naturally.

It isn't good for Dora that she should be on speaking terms with a woman of my low antecedents. Seriously, Captain Shannon, I do not wish to speak about Dora."

"What are you doing?" he asked bluntly.

"I was walking up to Daffridge's, only I was arrested and taken—"

"Tell me seriously, what work are you doing?"

She hesitated. "I don't know, except copying letters for a very unpleasant-looking old gentleman, and being paid at extravagant rates for my services."

In spite of the flippancy of her tone he detected the doubt in her voice, and knew that behind her pose of light-heartedness she was worried.

"Hanover Square isn't the quietest place in the world." he said. "I'll drive you to the Park and we'll have a real heart-to-heart talk."

He looked round for a taxicab. There was one crawling behind him, and the driver's face was strangely familiar. "Oh, lord! I'd forgotten you," he gasped.

"I hadn't forgotten you!" said the taximan grimly. "Where do you want to go to?"

In the desert of Hyde Park they found two dry chairs and a desirable solitude.

"I want first to hear about this unpleasant-looking old gentleman," said Dick, and she gave him a brief and vivid narrative of her experience with Mr. Malpas.

"I suppose you'll think it was despicable of me to use the money at all; but when a girl is very hungry and very cold, she has neither the time nor the inclination to sit down and work out problems of abstract morality. I certainly had no intention of breaking anybody's heart, but I didn't examine my duties too closely until I was comfortably installed in the Palace Hotel, with two day dresses, three pairs of shoes and a lot of other things that would be complete mysteries to you if I mentioned them! It was not until the next morning that my conscience became awfully busy. I had written the night before to Mr. Malpas, telling him my new address, and I was half-way through a second letter in the morning, explaining that, whilst I was ready and willing to render any service, however menial, I had discovered that heart-breaking was not amongst my accomplishments, when a note came from him. It didn't look like a note: it was a bulky envelope, containing about ten pencilled letters, which he asked me to copy and return to him."

"What kind of letters?" asked Dick curiously.

"They were mostly notes declining invitations to dinners and other social functions, which had evidently come from intimate friends, because he merely signed the letters with his initial. He said they could be written on the hotel note-paper, and that they must not be typewritten." Dick Shannon was very thoughtful.

"I don't like it very much," he said at last.

"Do you know him?"

"I know of him. In fact, the other day I was having a long talk about him with some—friends. What is your salary?"

She shook her head.

"That we haven't mentioned. He gave me this lump sum, told me to report next week, and since then I've done nothing but copy the documents which come to me every morning by the first post. Today the letters were longer. I had to make a copy of correspondence between the Governor of Bermuda and the British Colonial Office. This time the document was printed—it had evidently been torn from an official Blue Book. What am I to do, Mr. Shannon?"

"I'm hanged if I know," he said, puzzled. "One thing you must not do, and that is to go alone to that queer house next Saturday, or whatever is the day of your appointment. You must let me know the exact hour, and I will be waiting in Portman Square, and when the door opens for you it will be easy for me to slip in." And then, noticing her alarm, he smiled. "I'll remain in the hall within shouting distance, so you need have no qualms that I'm using you for my vile police purposes. We haven't anything against Mr. Malpas, except that he is mysterious. And, in spite of all that has been written to the contrary, the police hate mysteries. By the way, were any of the letters you wrote addressed to Mr. Lacy Marshalt?"

She shook her head.

"That is the African millionaire, isn't it? He lives next door. The taxi-driver told me."

She narrated the queer little comedy she had witnessed on the doorstep of Mr. Marshalt's house.

"H'm!" said Dick. "That sounds like one of the old man's petty schemes of annoyance. I think the best thing I can do is to see friend Marshalt and ask him what Malpas has got on him—that there is an enmity between the two is very clear."

A cold wind was blowing, and, warmly clad as she was, he saw her shivering, and jumped up.

"I'm a selfish dog!" he said penitently. "Come and drink a flagon of steaming hot coffee, and I will continue my famous 'Advice to Young Girls Alone in London'."

"Perhaps at the same time you'll begin it," she said demurely. "So far, we have only had your equally famous lecture on 'How to Get Information from Reformed Criminals'!"

The Man Whom Lacy Did Not Know

Tonger opened the door to Dick Shannon. Tonger had the knack of forestalling the footman and welcoming visitors who had the slightest pretensions to importance, and Dick recognized him by the girl's description. Audrey had said he was bird-like, and certainly there was a strong resemblance in this little old man, with his head perked on one side, his bright eyes, his quick, jerky movements, to an inquisitive sparrow. His keen eyes looked the detective through and through.

"Mr. Lacy Marshalt is in—yes," he said, standing square in the doorway. "But you can't see him without an appointment. Nobody can see Mr. Lacy Marshalt without an appointment, not while I'm around."

The utter lack of respect amused Dick Shannon. Evidently this was more than an ordinary servant.

"Perhaps you'll take my card to him?"

"Perhaps I will," said the other coolly. "But it's just as likely that I won't! All kinds of queer people want to see Mr. Lacy Marshalt, because he's kind and generous and big. That's the sort we train in South Africa, even if we don't breed 'em there. Open-handed, free- hearted—?"

He paused to take the card that Dick offered, and read.

"Oh!" he said, a little blankly. "You're a detective, are you? Well, step inside, Captain. Have you come to pinch anybody?"

"Is it possible that anybody requires pinching in this beautifully ordered house, where even the footmen are so polite and deferential that it is painful to trouble them?"

Tonger chuckled.

"I'm not a footman," he said. "You've made a slight error."

"The son of the house?" suggested Dick good-humouredly. "Or perhaps you are Mr. Lacy Marshalt?"

"God forbid!" grinned the man. "I shouldn't like to have his money and responsibility. Step this way. Captain."

He ushered the visitor into the drawing-room, and, to Dick's surprise, followed and closed the door.

"There is nothing wrong, is there?" he asked, a note of anxiety in his voice.

"Nothing that I'm aware of," said Dick. "This is a purely friendly call, and you needn't go down to the pantry and count the spoons."

"I'm not the butler either," corrected Tonger. "I'll tell the governor."

He slipped out of the room and in a few minutes returned, preceding Mr. Lacy Marshalt He would have remained, but Marshalt pointedly opened the door for him.

"I hope that fellow hasn't been fresh, Captain Shannon?" he said when they were alone. "Tonger has grown up with me, and has never been wholly civilized in consequence."

"I thought he was rather amusing," said Dick.

Mr. Lacy Marshalt grunted.

"He doesn't amuse me at times," he said dourly. "One can pay too big a price for loyalty—there are times when Tonger puts a very heavy strain upon my patience."

He had the detective's card in his hand and now looked at it again.

"You are from Scotland Yard, I see. What can I do for you?"

"First I want to ask you if you know Mr. Malpas, your next-door neighbour?"

Marshalt shook his head. "No," he said. "Is this call in reference to a complaint I made some months ago—?"

"No, I think that was settled by the local police. I've come to see you because I have information that this man Malpas is running some sort of a feud against you. You say you do not know him?"

"I have never seen him, so I can't tell you if I know him or not. Certainly I know nobody whose name is Malpas. Won't you sit down, and will you have a drink?"

Dick refused the drink but pulled up a chair, and the other followed suit.

"What makes you think that Malpas has a grudge against me?" asked Lacy. "It's very likely that he has, because I made a complaint against him, as you evidently know. He was such a noisy beggar that he disturbed my sleep."

"What kind of noise did he make?"

"Hammering, mostly. It sounded as though he were tapping on the wall, though possibly I was mistaken there, and it was more likely that he was closing packing-cases."

"You have never seen him?"

"Never."

"Have you had any description of him," asked Dick, "that would enable you even remotely to identify him as somebody, you knew in South Africa?"

"No, I know nobody," said Lacy Marshalt, shaking his head. "One has enemies, of course: it is impossible to achieve any measure of success without attaching these disagreeable appendages to life."

Dick considered for a moment. He was dubious about the advisability of taking the millionaire entirely into his confidence, but he decided that, at the risk of subsequently giving himself a great deal of trouble, he would tell

Marshalt all he knew.

"Malpas is employing somebody, or is intending to employ somebody, to annoy you, and to cause you inconvenience of a petty character. For example, I am under the impression that the drunken woman who came here a few days ago was sent by him."

"Woman?" Marshalt's brows lowered. "I never heard of any drunken woman coming here."

He got up quickly, rang the bell, and Tonger came in almost immediately.

"Captain Shannon says that a few days ago a drunken woman called at this house and made some sort of disturbance. You never told me."

"Do I tell you everything?" asked Tonger wearily. "A woman certainly did call, and she was certainly oiled."

"Oiled?"

"I mean soused, or, to use a vulgar expression, drunk. What a lady! She fell into the hall, and she fell out again quick. She said she was Mrs. Lidderley from Fourteen Streams..."

Dick Shannon was looking at the man's employer as he spoke, and saw Lacy Marshalt's face go grey.

Shannon Pays a Call

"Mrs. Lidderley!" said Marshalt slowly. "What sort of a woman was she?"

"She was a little thing." Tonger's eyes were fixed absently on the detective. "But my word, wasn't she wiry!"

There was relief in Marshalt's sigh.

"A little woman? She was an impostor. Probably she knew the Lidderleys. The last time I heard from South Africa, Mrs. Lidderley was very ill." He looked hard at his servant. "You knew the Lidderleys, Tonger?"

"I didn't know Mrs. Lidderley. The old chap married after we left the Cape," said Tonger, "if it's Julius Lidderley you mean. Anyway, I pushed her out."

"Did you get her address—where she was staying?"

"Who am I that I should take the address of a soused lady?" asked Tonger, his eyebrows rising. "No, Lacy—?"

"Mr. Marshalt, damn you!" flamed the other. "How many times am I to tell you, Tonger?"

"It slipped out," said the other, unabashed.

"Follow its example," growled Lacy Marshalt, and slammed the door behind his disrespectful servitor.

"That fellow exasperates me beyond measure," he said. "I've had him so many years, and it is certainly true that we were 'Lacy' and 'Jim' to one another in the old days, and that makes it more difficult. I feel a horrible snob when I insist upon his showing me a little courtesy, but you will see for yourself how extremely embarrassing the volatile Mr. Tonger can be!"

Dick laughed. He had been an amused spectator of the scene. Tonger was a type that he had met before in other households—the pet dog that nobody had the heart to destroy, despite its awkward qualities.

"As to Malpas," Marshalt went on, "I don't know anything about him. He may be, and probably is, somebody on whose corns I have stepped at a period of my life, but if I have to pass that category in review, why, I shall be suspicious of a hundred! Have you any description of him?"

"None that you would recognize," said Dick. "The only thing I know is that he's an elderly man, very ugly, and that lie commissioned a cabaret singer to molest you, an action which to me seemed hardly worth the trouble, unless you have a peculiar objection to cabaret singers."

Lacy Marshalt paced up and down the big drawing-room, his hands behind him, his chin on his breast.

"The whole thing is inexplicable to me," he said, taking the news with greater calmness than Dick had expected, "and I can only imagine that at some remote period I have done Malpas an injury beyond forgiveness. Why don't you call and see him. Captain Shannon?" he asked, and added quickly: "It is nerve on my part to make suggestions to you! But I'm curious to have this gentleman identified."

But Dick Shannon had already made up his mind that he would see the mysterious Mr. Malpas, and the suggestion was unnecessary.

Tonger was waiting in the hall when he came out, and opened the front door for him.

"Is anybody to be pinched?" he asked pleasantly. "We've got a cook we could do without. Come one day and try her pies!"

Dick went out into Portman Square chuckling. He strolled along to the door of the next house and looked up at the blank windows. This was not his first visit to the residence of the eccentric Mr. Malpas, but never before had he sought an interview. He looked for the bell, failed to find it, and tapped on the door. There was no answer. He knocked more loudly, and jumped when a voice spoke apparently at his ear.

"Who is that?"

He looked round in bewilderment. There was nobody within twenty yards of him, and yet the voice... And then he saw the small grating let into the stone-pillar of the doorway, and found a solution to the mystery. Behind that grating was a loud-speaking telephone.

"I am Captain Richard Shannon from Scotland Yard, and I want to speak to Mr. Malpas," he said, addressing the invisible instrument.

"Well, you can't!" snarled the voice, and there was a faint click.

Dick tapped again, but, though he waited for five minutes, no voice spoke to him from the pillar, and the door resisted his pressure. There must be a way to get into touch with this man, and his first act was to search the telephone directory. The name of Malpas, however, did not occur as a resident of Portman Square, and he went back to his flat a little baffled. The day, however, had not been unprofitably spent. He had met the Ragged Princess—ragged no longer—and knew where she was to be found. Dick Shannon was resolved that she should be found, and found as often as he could in common decency call.

Tonger Assists

Few servants enjoyed the freedom and comfort which were Jim Tonger's. The top floor of the house in Portman Square was his own. There he had a bedroom, a sitting-room, a bathroom, specially fitted by his indulgent employer, and here it was his wont to spend long periods of the evening, engaged in endless mathematical calculations with the aid of a small roulette wheel; for Tonger had occupied the greater portion of his life's leisure in perfecting a system which would one day strike terror and consternation into the hearts of those responsible for the management of the Casino at Monte Carlo.

He was otherwise engaged that night when the bell over the doorway shrilled, and he went out of the room hurriedly, locking the door behind him, and came into the presence of Lacy Marshalt, who was awaiting him in his study, with greater haste than that gentleman imagined.

"Where the devil have you been?" growled Lacy.

"You rang for me in my room—so I must have been in my room. I was playing solitaire," said Tonger. "I'm glad you called me, because I've tried the darned thing thirty times and it hasn't come out. That means bad luck for me. Have you ever noticed. Lacy, that if you can't work out a game of solitaire, nothing goes right with you? I remember the day before I found that diamond patch on Hope River, I got a 'demon' patience out six times in succession—?"

"I want you to let in Mrs. Elton at seven-forty-five," interrupted Marshalt. "She'll drive her own car. Be waiting for her in the mews, and take the machine to the Albert Hall: there's a concert there tonight. Park it with the others, and after the show is over, bring the car straight back to the mews."

Tonger whistled. "A bit dangerous, isn't it, after the letter that Elton wrote you?"

Marshalt's eyes narrowed. "What do you know about the letter that Elton wrote me?" he demanded.

"Oh, you left it about; I couldn't help seeing it," said the servant coolly.

"So far from leaving it about, I put it in the drawer of my desk. I suppose you took it out and read it?"

"It doesn't matter how I saw it—I saw it," said Tonger, "and I tell you that it's dangerous! You don't want to figure in any court case."

"With you as a witness," sneered the other. Tonger shrugged his thin shoulders.

"You know I'd never go on to the stand and talk against you, Lacy," he said. "That's not my line. But if a fellow like Eilton wrote and told me that if I saw his wife again he'd shoot me, why, I guess I'd be interested."

"Mrs. Elton and I have certain business to discuss," said Marshalt shortly. "The thing is, I want you to be outside the yard gate at a quarter to eight. As soon as Mrs. Elton gets out of her machine, you get in and drive off." The man nodded.

"So that, if she's being followed and watched, there's the car at the Albert Hall to prove she was there all the time!" he said admiringly. "What a brain! Lacy, what did that busy fellow want?"

"I can't keep track of your slang. What does 'busy fellow' mean?"

"I'm talking about the detective. I take naturally to the argot of the country where I'm living. I wish we were in New York," he said regretfully; "it's a richer language."

Mr. Marshalt's lips curled. "He came to inquire about that crazy man next door," he 'said. "Apparently he is an enemy of mine."

"Who isn't, Lacy?" asked the other with a sigh. "What have you been doing to him?"

"I don't know. I haven't the slightest idea who he is, and I'm not worried, I assure you," said Marshalt carelessly. "Why did you think he called?"

"Over Mrs. Elton," said the other coolly. "She's a crook; so is Elton; everybody knows that. You can't touch pitch—not that kind of pitch—without getting your hands black, so black that no Oojah Magic Cleanser can clean them."

A pause.

"I suppose Elton is a'crook, but Mrs. Elton is quite innocent—"

"So innocent," broke in Tonger, "that angels turn down side streets so as not to feel small when they meet her."

Marshalt checked the angry retort that rose to his lips.

"That is all," he said curtly, and then, as Tonger was going, with unexpected meekness: "I am dining at home tomorrow, and if I have any luck I shall have rather an interesting guest."

"Who is she?" asked Tonger, himself interested.

"I didn't tell you it was a 'she'."

"There ain't any other kind of interesting guest," said Tonger coolly. "Have you found that girl?" he asked suddenly. "The girl you set the private detective to find?"

Marshalt started.

"How did you know?"

"I'm a wonderful guesser. Is she to be the belle of the ball tomorrow?"

"I'm hoping she'll come to dinner. And, by the way, you needn't be so much in evidence on that occasion, my friend. I want the parlourmaid to be very visible and to wait at table."

"Thus inspiring confidence in the heart of the young and foolish," said Tonger. "All right, governor. What time is this woman coming tonight?"

"Mrs. Elton is coming at a quarter to eight: I told you before. And I'd like you to refer to her in those terms, my friend. 'This woman' doesn't sound good to me."

"You're too sensitive. Lacy, that's what's wrong with you," was the valet's parting shot.

*

He was waiting in the dark mews when the little car came bounding over the cobble-stones and jerked to a stop before the door. He helped the slim, muffled passenger to alight, and, contrary to his usual practice, did not speak to her, taking her place in the machine and sending it through the mews in Baker Street.

As he came out into the main road his sharp eyes detected a watcher standing at the corner of Portman Square, and he grinned to himself. It may have been a casual party to an assignation, but there was something in the patient pose of the figure which suggested private detective. Possibly Mr. Elton was not satisfied that his threat would produce the desired effect.

At eleven o'clock he drew out of the phalanx of parked cars and made his rapid way homeward. Almost as soon as he stopped before the back gate of

551 the door was opened and the girl came out.

"Did you see anybody?" she asked in a low voice. "Anybody you knew?"

"No, ma'am," said Tonger, and then: "I don't think I should do this again if I were you."

She made no reply, slipping into the car and taking her place at the wheel, but Tonger stood with the open door in his hand.

"There are some things that are not worth while, ma'am, and this is one of them."

"Shut the door," she said curtly, and he obeyed, and watched the car until its red tail-lamps turned the comer. Then he went back to his master.

Lacy Marshalt was in his study standing before the fire, deep in thought.

"Want me any more?"

Marshalt shook his head.

"Think you're being clever. Lacy?"

The other looked up quickly. "What do you mean?"

"Do you think it's clever to fly in the face of providence over a girl you don't care a whole lot about, unless I misunderstand you?"

Instead of the angry reply which Tonger expected. Lacy laughed.

"There is such a thing as wanting the forbidden because it is forbidden," he said. "These things are not very palatable without the salt of risk."

"Ever tasted salt—neat?" asked Tonger. "It's rotten! I'm not going to roust you. Lacy, because every man's got his own idea of what's worth while. But Elton's the kind that shoots. You can laugh! I know the talkative ones, and I know just how Elton feels, because I've felt that way myself —?"

"Get out!" snapped the other, and Tonger went without haste.

Lacy Marshalt's study and bedroom were on the first floor, and were shut off from the rest of the house by a door which cut off a portion of the passage and gave him that complete privacy which his peculiar temperament required. There were moments when he was really unapproachable, and Tonger was quick to recognize the symptoms of that particular mood, and sufficiently wise to leave his sometime friend in peace whilst the fit was on.

He went back to his room to continue where he had left off that game of patience which would not come out.

Dora Elton got home to find that her husband, who had been out to dinner, had arrived before her.

"Well, was your talk satisfactory?" she asked brightly as she came into the drawing-room.

He looked up from the sofa on which he lay at full length, and shook his head almost imperceptibly.

"No, we shall have to close the establishment. Klein wants too big a share, and he's holding the 'black' up as an inducement. I don't take much notice of that." He pulled at his cigar thoughtfully. "Klein knows that there isn't much money to be had out of the police for shopping a gambling house. There are too many of them. Still, I'd hate to close Pont Street, because it brings steady money and big money, and it's got the kind of clientele that makes a straight game profitable." He looked at his watch. "I was expecting Bob Stanford. Do you want to see him? He's returning from Italy."

She was taking a cigarette from a silver box on the mantelpiece. "I don't care," she said indifferently. "Do you want a private interview?"

"No," he said after thought. "I saw Audrey tonight."

"Where?" She looked at him in astonishment.

"She was dining at the Carlton Grill."

The match was half-way to the cigarette, and stopped.

"With—?"

"Shannon—and very cheery. You needn't be afraid. Audrey's not the kind of girl who would give you away."

"I wasn't thinking about that."

"Maybe you were worrying about the impropriety of her dining without a chaperon; and if there was a chaperon there I did not see her," suggested Bunny.

The girl shot a quick, suspicious glance at him. "I like you least when you're funny," she said. "Was she—well dressed?"

He nodded. "A most prosperous-looking lady." And added inconsequently: "I never realized she was so beautiful. Shannon hardly took his eyes from her."

"Apparently you were smitten too," she said with a little smile. "I enjoyed the concert immensely. Bunny. Kessler was wonderful. I don't as a rule like fiddlers—?"

"Kessler didn't appear," he said evenly as he blew out a cloud of smoke. He was not looking at her. "He caught a cold and was unable to perform—the fact was announced in the late editions of the evening newspaper: I wonder you didn't see it."

Only for a second was she thrown off her balance. "I don't know one fiddler from another," she said carelessly. "Anyway, the man they sent in his place plays gorgeously."

"Probably Manz," he nodded.

She was relieved to hear the door-bell ring. What a fool she had been not to make herself completely acquainted with the artistes who had appeared that night! Tonger could have attended and made her acquainted with the programme.

Big Bill Stanford came in, a very weary man, for he had spent thirty- six hours in the train, having come direct from Rome. He reported without preliminary.

"The Contessa leaves on Thursday. She breaks her journey in Paris and will be here on Tuesday night. I've got photographs of the tiara and the pearl rope. I think they can both be duplicated in less than a week, and if we can do that the rest will be easy. Stigman has got friendly with the maid—his Italian is grand: you'd think he was a pukka Wop! She'll give him a chance of 'ringing' the stuff—?"

"I thought we weren't going to touch this kind of job again?" said Dora petulantly.

"I'm not," drawled her husband. "We take an outside interest; and, Bob, if you bring so much as a pearl into this house I'll brain you!"

"Am I mad?" asked the big man contemptuously. "Did the last job pay so well? No, thank you! Not one link of one platinum chain comes this way. It is going to be easy, Elton."

"I don't want anything to do with it," Dora broke in. "Bunny, why can't we cut this cheap thieving altogether? It is making a nervous wreck of me. I hate it!"

He looked at her.

"Why not?" he asked lazily. "What is ten thousand to you and me? We could live without this kind of work!"

"I could, at any rate," she muttered.

"How? With your needle? Or possibly by giving piano lessons to the musical bourgeoisie? Or perhaps by your art! I forget how much per week you were earning when I drifted across you."

She looked away from him, her lips tightly pressed together.

"Was it three pounds or four pounds a week?" he went on. "I remember that it was some fabulous sum. You were not particular how you climbed into the big type and the principal's salary."

"You might discuss this when we are alone," she said, with a resentful glance at Bill Stanford.

"Bill knows all about it. I've known William longer than I have known Dora, and, speaking generally, he has played the game a little straighter."

She leapt up from her chair, her face white with passion, a "How dare you say that!" she stormed. "I have stood by you through thick and thin! You pretend to let bygones rest, and then you throw your beastly suspicions up in my face. Is that your idea of playing the game?"

He made no reply, his dark eyes looking at her speculatively.

"I am sorry," he said, but without any great heartiness. "You see how absurd it is to talk about cheap thieving? There isn't any other kind. I am a thief by nature—with talents beyond the ordinary. It sounds as though I am being foolishly boastful, but it is true to say that I am the cleverest burglar in London. There isn't a house I couldn't get into or escape from. I can climb bare walls like a cat—but it isn't necessary that I should. I prefer genteel robbery—which is just robbery, anyway. I stole you into prosperity, and even the price of the wedding ring goes back to a larceny. Lots of men would have got honest just about where that ring had to be bought. Think that out."

She was about to say something but changed her mind, and stalked out of the room without a word.

She was in bed when he came into the room, and pretended to be asleep. She saw him gather his pyjamas, dressing-gown and slippers, and go out, closing the door softly behind him, and the sound of the second bedroom door opening and closing came to her. Dora sat up in bed suddenly, a panic in her breast. Martin Elton had never done that before.

Lacy Entertains

There came to Audrey Bedford a letter in a strange handwriting. She tore open the envelope expecting no more than one of those artistic advertisement cards which come inevitably to an hotel guest. Instead she found a letter.

Dear Miss Bedford,

You will be surprised to hear from one who is a stranger to you, but finding your name by chance in the register of the Palace, and thinking that I might be of some service to you, particularly in view of the monstrous miscarriage of justice in which you were a victim, I am writing to ask you if you will come and see me tomorrow evening at 7.30 at the above address. I think I can find you congenial employment—if you are not in need of that, to offer you at least the good offices of a disinterested friend.

Sincerely,

Lacy Marshalt.

P.S.—Will you send me a wire if you can come?

She puzzled over the letter all the morning. Lacy Marshalt's name was known to her. He belonged to that branch of politico-social world whose names recur in the press. She sent a telegram before lunch, announcing her acceptance of the invitation, after looking up his name in Who's Who and discovering that there was a Mrs. Marshalt. Mrs. Marshalt appeared in all works of reference, but here her tangibility ended. For twenty-five years she had been a most convenient invention. Early in his career, Lacy had discovered that, whilst the wealthy bachelor might be run after, certain complications followed his attempt to apportion his attentions equally. The wealth of welcome which was his in one quarter was levelled down by the chilling politeness which greeted him elsewhere. "Mrs. Marshalt" came into existence to his profit. No longer amongst the eligibles, he retained his place as an amusing companion and gained something in respectability. He never spoke of his wife: when other people made direct or oblique reference to her, he smiled sadly. Without knowing more, the world decided that, if there was an estrangement, Mrs. Marshalt was to blame.

Just before half past seven a cab deposited Audrey before the door of Lacy Marshalt's house, and she was admitted by a neatly uniformed maid. She was wearing a simple black dinner frock that she had bought in Shaftesbury Avenue, and, innocent of jewels as she was, there was something so regal in her carriage that Lacy Marshalt stared at her in amazement and admiration. She was infinitely more beautiful than he had thought.

She, for her part, saw a hard-faced, distinguished-looking man, but, what was more to the point, she saw no other guest, and the "Mrs. Marshalt" she expected was equally invisible.

"You are Miss Bedford? I am very glad to meet you."

He took her little hand in his, and did not make the mistake of holding it a second longer than was necessary.

"I hope you don't very much object to a tete-d-tete dinner. I hate crowds. Twenty years ago, when I was younger, I disliked solitude as intensely."

The subtle emphasis of his age had the effect of quietening the unease in the girl's mind.

"It was very kind of you to ask me, Mr. Marshalt," she said with her quick smile. "It isn't everybody who would want to meet a person with my record!"

He shrugged his broad shoulders to indicate his indifference to the opinions of the world.

"You were, of course, perfectly innocent," he said. "Anybody but a congenital idiot knew that. And, what is more, you were screening somebody." He raised his hand. "No, I'm not going to ask you whom, but it was very plucky of you, and I admire you. And I think I can help you. Miss

Bedford. A friend of mine needs a secretary—?"

"I don't want you to think that I have no work," she smiled. "I am, in fact, employed by a neighbour of yours, though I am not particularly happy about the work."

"A neighbour of mine?" he asked quickly. "Who is that?" And, when she told him: "Malpas? I hadn't the slightest idea that he was human enough to employ anybody. What is he like?—forgive my curiosity, but I'm rather interested in the gentleman."

"He is—not very pretty," she said.

A sense of loyalty made the discussion of her employer a little difficult, and, apparently recognizing her embarrassment, he did not press his inquiry.

"If you aren't happy, I think I can get you a position where you'll be most comfortable," he said. "In fact, I can almost promise you the post."

Just then, dinner was announced, and they passed out of the drawing-room, along the corridor, through a second door that was opened and which cut off a section of the house, into a small and elegantly furnished dining-room.

As they passed into the room, Lacy stopped to speak to the servant in a low tone, and Audrey heard the murmur of his voice, wondered… and feared.

For a moment she was alone in the room. She looked up and caught a glimpse of her troubled face in the mirror over the mantelshelf.

And then it occurred to her that she was looking at the wall which divided the room from the home of her mysterious employer. Even as this thought came to her…

"Tap, tap, tap!"

Somebody in the house of Malpas was rapping on the wall.

"Tap, tap, tap!"

It sounded like a warning, yet how could the old man know?

The first part of the meal passed off without any unusual incident. Her host was politeness itself, and when he learnt that she did not drink wine, filled her glass with water. He himself showed no denial in the matter; he drank liberally, without the wine seeming to have the slightest effect upon him, though, when the third bottle of champagne was uncorked by the waiting maid, Audrey began to feel a little uneasy. The sweets came and the coffee, and Lacy pushed a golden box towards her.

"Thank you, I don't smoke," she smiled.

"You have all the virtues, Miss Bedford," he said gallantly. "Mr. Malpas does not like you smoking, probably?"

"I have never consulted him," she replied.

"What does he pay you a week?"

She was on the point of answering the question when its cool impertinence came home to her.

"The wage is not settled yet," she said, and looked at the clock on the mantelpiece. "You won't mind if I go early, Mr. Marshalt?" she said. "I have some work to do."

The hand that held the big cigar waved impatiently.

"That can wait," he said. "I have a lot to say to you, young lady. I suppose you realize that your job with Malpas will not last for ever? He's an eccentric old devil, and the police are after him."

This was news to the girl, though she did not feel the surprise she showed.

"I have reason to believe," Marshalt went on slowly, "that the old man only gave you this job in order to get acquainted with you, and to have an opportunity of studying you, with the idea of a closer acquaintance."

"Mr. Marshalt!" she cried indignantly, and came to her feet.

"We were talking as friends," pleaded Marshalt. "I am trying to tell you all I know—?"

"You have invented that! You don't even know Mr. Malpas; you practically told me so just now."

He smiled. "I have access to information," he said cryptically, "which puts me beyond the possibility of error. Please sit down, Miss Bedford."

"I must go," she said.

"Wait a little longer. I wanted to talk this matter over with you, and nine o'clock isn't so very late, you know," he laughed.

She sat down again reluctantly.

"I've known you for longer than you can guess. I knew you before this trouble came to you. You probably don't remember seeing me at Fontwell? And it is true that not a day has passed that you have been absent from my thoughts. Audrey, I am very fond of you."

She rose, this, time in less haste, and he followed her example.

"I can make life very smooth for you, my dear," he said.

"I prefer a harder road," she answered with quiet dignity, and moved towards the door.

"One moment," he begged.

"You are wasting your time, Mr. Marshalt," she said coldly. "I very dimly understand your proposal, and I can only hope that I am mistaken. I very foolishly came here because I thought you were a gentleman who really was anxious to help one who had suffered—unjustly, as you suggested."

And then his tone altered.

"You came here because I sent for you," he said, "and nobody in their senses will suggest that I am dining tete-d-tete with you against your will."

She eyed him gravely.

"You seem to forget that you wrote me a letter, and that that letter—" she stopped.

"Is in your handbag," he smiled. "No, my dear young lady, you've got to be sensible. And don't, please, try to go, because this portion of the house is shut off from the rest of the premises, and only one privileged person has the key. If you're a sensible girl, you will be that privileged person."

She ran into the passage. The door leading to the entrance hall was closed. She pulled at the handle, but it did not budge. In another second his arm was round her, and, lifting her as though she were a child, he carried her, struggling, back to the little dining-room.

With all her strength she beat at the face pressed down to hers, and, with a superhuman effort, flung herself free. Her eyes fell upon a sharp-pointed carving-knife that lay upon the buffet, and, snatching it up, she stood at bay.

"I will kill you if you touch me!" she said breathlessly. "Open that door!"

At heart Lacy Marshalt was a coward, and before the threat of the knife he drew back.

"For God's sake don't be a fool," he cried. "I—I only want to help you."

"Open the door!"

He fumbled in his pocket at his key chain, and pulled out a bunch. She heard the click of the lock turning and went out, passing him quickly as he stood with the door in his hand. Beyond was the dimly lit passage.

"Will you forgive me?" he whispered.

She made no reply, but swept past him, dropping the knife on the carpet.

"To the right," he whispered, as if giving her directions. Obeying him, she turned into a narrow passage, though her instinct and her memory told her that the way to safety lay straight ahead. Before she realized her danger, he was behind her. Only a second she hesitated, and then fled down the narrow corridor. At the end was a flight of stairs, and up these she flew, the man in pursuit. In absolute darkness she was climbing what was evidently a servants' stairway. How many flights she traversed in her terror she did not know. Suddenly she stopped: the footsteps were no longer following her. Above her head was a skylight, out of reach. There was nothing to do but to retrace her steps, and stealthily she walked down the carpeted stairs. She had reached the landing below when she heard a thin wail of sound, the sound of a woman sobbing.

The acoustic properties of the stairway were such that she could not locate the sound. It might come from underneath, from above; it might be penetrating the partition wall which separated her from the next house —the house of Mr. Malpas!

She listened intently. The sobbing died to a low wail, and then was silent. Only for a moment was her attention distracted from her own imminent peril. There was no sound or sign of Lacy Marshalt, and she descended a second flight, peering nervously into the darkness, to which her eyes had now grown so used that she was able to see distinctly. She came to the floor where the little dining-room was situated, and to the narrow hall, beyond the entrance to which lay freedom. Still no sign of Lacy.

And then, as she stepped cautiously into the corridor, a hand came round her waist, another covered her mouth; she was carried bodily back to the dining-room, and the door clicked behind her.

"Now, my little jail-bird!" Lacy Marshalt's voice was tremulous with triumph. "You and I will have an intelligent talk!"

He thrust her down into a deep arm-chair, and she sat, dishevelled, breathless, her unflinching eyes never leaving his face.

"If my servants had not strict orders to confine themselves to the servants' hall, there would have been the beginnings of a scandal. Are you going to see my point of view? If I'd known what a little wildcat I was going to entertain, I should have had a chaperon," he said humorously.

He poured out a glass of wine and pushed it to her.

"Drink this," he ordered.

On the point of collapse, she felt her strength slipping from her, and, risking everything, she drank the wine greedily.

"It's not drugged; you needn't look at it twice," he said. "Audrey, are you going to be a good girl? I want you, my dear. You're the one woman in the world that I have ever wanted, and I never realized that fact until tonight. I can give you everything that heart can desire—money beyond your dreams—?"

"You're wasting your time now, Mr. Marshalt," she said. The wine had steadied her, had given her a new strength. "I won't tell you how greatly you have insulted me: such words would be empty and meaningless to you. I'm going back to the hotel, and I shall call up Captain Shannon, and tell him what has happened."

He laughed.

"In other words, you're going to fetch a policeman! Well, that is a very old-fashioned kind of threat which doesn't frighten me. Shannon's a man of the world; he knows that I wouldn't invite a lady from Holloway to dine with me, unless... well, use your intelligence, my child. And he knows that you wouldn't accept unless you expected to be made love to. You think I'm a brute, but the caveman method saves a lot of time and a lot of stupid preliminaries. Generally speaking, women prefer it to all others."

"Your kind of woman may, but I am not your kind," she said.

"By God, you are!" he said in a low voice. "You are not only my kind, but you are all women to me—the very quintessence of womanhood!"

He stooped and lifted her up, his strong arms about her, one hand behind her head, and she gazed in horrified fascination into the deeps of his black soul. Only for a second, then his lips were pressed to hers. She was helpless; consciousness was slipping from her; life, and all that made life, was going out to the drum-beats of her broken heart, when she was faintly conscious of a movement at the lock; somebody was fitting a key. He heard it too, and, releasing her so suddenly that she dropped to her knees on the floor, spun round as the door opened slowly. A woman in black was standing there, her brooding eyes looking from the man to the dishevelled girl on the floor.

It was Dora Elton, and Audrey, looking up, saw the hate in her sister's eyes and shivered.

The Story of Joshua

"I seem to have come at an awkward moment," said Dora Elton in a metallic voice.

She met the blazing fury in Marshalt's eyes without flinching.

"You are rather partial to our family, Lacy," she said.

Audrey had struggled to her feet and, gathering her wrap, walked unsteadily past her sister into the hall and to the cold clean air of the night.

Not a word was spoken till the thud of the front door told them that she was gone, and then: "I'm not going to ask you for an explanation, because it is fairly obvious," said Dora.

He poured out a glass of wine with a hand that shook, and gulped it down before he spoke.

"I asked her to come to dinner, and she got a little fresh—that's all. There was nothing to it," he said.

She smiled.

"I can't imagine the gentle Audrey 'getting a little fresh', but women are queer creatures under your magnetic influence, Lacy." Then she went off at a tangent. "Bunny knew I was here the other night—the night I was supposed to be at the concert."

"I don't care a damn what he knew," growled the man. "If you get so rattled about what Bunny thinks and what Bunny knows, you'd better give up coming here."

Again she smiled.

"And you would like the key, of course? Bunny would find it handy. It opens the back gate and the conservatory door and this dear little sanctum sanctorum. Bunny has rather a passion for pass-keys."

"I don't want you to think there was anything between your sister—"

"She is not my sister, but that doesn't matter. And as for there being anything between you... Lacy, you beast!"

The air of amused indifference had dropped from her. Rage shook her from head to foot, bereft her of speech for a while, though presently it came in full and spiteful flood.

"I've risked everything for you. I've lied and deceived; oh, you vile thing! I've always hated her. God, how I hate lier now! And you want her to take my place? I'll kill you first! I'll shoot you like a dog. Lacy—"

"You shoot me every day," he interrupted with an angry laugh. "Either you or your husband. I'm a human target for the Eltons. Now be sane, Dora."

He took her by the shoulders and drew the bead of the sobbing girl to his breast.

"If you think I'm in love with that kid, you're mad. I'm going to make a confession, and you've got to believe me this time."

She murmured something that he could not hear, but he could guess, and he smiled over her shoulder.

"Well, this is the truth—for once! There's one man in the world I hate worse than any other, and that man is Audrey Bedford's father. That makes you jump!"

"Her name is not Bedford," she said with a gulp. She was drying her eyes with a little handkerchief.

"You're right that much. Her name is Torrington, though yours was not. Dan Torrington and I are old enemies. I've got a big score to wipe off, and it's not cleared yet."

"Her father is a convict." There was still a sob in her voice.

Lacy nodded.

"He's on the Breakwater at Cape Town, serving a life sentence," he said. "If my gun had thrown straight, he'd have been a dead man. He was lucky; I got his leg and lamed the swine. If the detectives hadn't claimed him at that moment, I'd have been dead, I guess."

"Then you had him arrested?" she said, looking up in surprise.

He nodded. "Yes, I was running the secret service for the Streams Diamond Mining Corporation, and I discovered that Dan Torrington was engaged in illicit diamond buying. I trapped him, and that's about the whole of the story, except that he got his extra time for shooting at me."

She pushed herself clear of him and, womanlike, walked to the mirror above the mantelpiece.

"Look at my eyes!" she said in dismay. "Oh, what a fool I was to come! I don't know whether to believe you or not, Lacy. How could you revenge yourself upon Torrington by making love to this girl?"

He laughed. "Well, maybe it isn't as obvious as it looks," he said. "I was a fool, anyway, to try to carry her off her feet. I should have gone slowly and steadily, and then she would have married me."

"Married you?" she gasped.

He nodded.

"That was the general idea."

"But—but you said you would never marry—?"

He pointed to a chair by the table, and she sat down.

"Here's a story that sounds as if it had been taken from a book," he said. "When Torrington was buying diamonds from the natives, he was the owner of a farm called Graspan. There are thousands of Graspans in South Africa, but this particular Graspan stood on a river, one of those after which Fourteen Streams is named. He had hardly been sent down to penal servitude before a big pipe was discovered on the farm, and by 'pipe' I mean a diamond pipe. I never knew this till a short time ago, because the property has been worked in the name of his lawyers, Hallam and Coold. In fact it is called the Hallam and Coold Mine today. Dan Torrington is a millionaire; he is also a dying millionaire. Ever since I've been in England I've had one of the warders on the Breakwater send me a monthly report about the man, and the last news I had was that he was slowly sinking."

"Then if you marry Audrey—?"

He laughed again.

"Exactly! If I marry Audrey, I shall be an extremely wealthy man."

She looked at him puzzled.

"But you're rich now!"

The smile left his face.

"Yes, I'm rich now," he said brusquely, "but I could be richer."

A tap at the door arrested him. "Who is that?" he called sharply.

The maid's voice answered: "A gentleman to see you, sir. He says his business is urgent."

"I can see nobody. Who is it?"

"Captain Shannon, sir."

Dora's mouth opened in an "Oh!" of horror.

"He mustn't see me! Where can I go?"

"Through the conservatory and out the back way, the way you came," snapped Lacy.

He had hardly pushed her into the darkened library and returned to his room before Dick Shannon walked through the doorway. He was in evening dress, and there was a look on his face that was not pleasant to see.

"I want to speak to you, Marshalt."

"Mr. Marshalt," snarled the other, sensing the antagonism.

"Mr. or Marshalt, it's just the same to me. You invited a lady to dine with you tonight."

A light dawned upon the African.

"Suppose the lady invited herself to dine with me?" he said coolly.

"You invited a lady to dine with you tonight, and you offered her the deadliest insult a man can offer to any woman."

"My dear fellow," drawled Marshalt, "you're a man of the world. Do you imagine this girl came here with her eyes shut to—to possibilities?"

For a second Dick Shannon stared at him, and then he struck the man across the face with the back of his hand, and Marshalt fell back with a roar of fury.

"That is a lie which must not be repeated," said Dick Shannon in a low voice.

"You call yourself a policeman—is that part of your duty?" screamed Lacy.

"I know the duties of the police very well," said Dick sternly. "They are carved over the face of the Old Bailey, remember them, Marshalt! 'Protect the children of the poor and punish the wrongdoer'."

Dick Shannon came out from Marshalt's house a little cooler than he had been when he entered. Glancing up—an almost mechanical act —at the next house, he saw a slit of light in one of the windows, and despite his absorption in Audrey's wrongs and his own murderous feelings towards Lacy Marshalt, he was so struck by the unaccustomed sight that he crossed the road to get a better view. He had been examining the house when Audrey came out and literally ran into him, and there had been no sign of life then. Somebody was peering down through the slit; he saw a vague movement, and then the light went out.

Crossing the road again, he tapped on the door, but there was no answer. Waiting, his mind still occupied with the tearful Audrey, he thought he heard a faint sound in the hall. Was the mystery man coming down after all? He took a step down to the pavement and drew a little flash-lamp from his pocket. But if the uncouth Mr. Malpas had intended coming into the open, he changed his mind.

For ten minutes Dick Shannon waited, and then gave up the vigil. He wanted to see Audrey that night and get from her a statement in greater detail than the incoherent story she had told him.

Walking to the Baker Street side of the square, he glanced left and right for a taxi. There was none in sight, and he looked back along the way he had come. Was it his imagination, or did he see a dark figure emerge from the mystery house and, crossing the road with a curious limping gait, hurry towards the far end of the square? The figure was real enough. The question was, were his eyes tricking him to the belief that it had emerged from the home of Mr. Malpas?

He walked swiftly in pursuit, his rubber-soled shoes making no sound. The quarry was making a circuit that would bring him to the Oxford Street end of the square, and had reached the corner of Orchard Street when Shannon came up with him.

"Excuse me."

The limping stranger turned a keen, thin face to the detective. Behind the gold-rimmed spectacles two searching eyes scrutinized the newcomer, and almost imperceptibly his hand had dropped into the depths of his overcoat pocket.

"You're a friend of Mr. Malpas, aren't you?" asked Dick. "I saw you coming out of his house!"

Shannon experienced queer flashes of telepathy at odd times—he was conscious of one such manifestation now. As the man looked at him, he read his thoughts as clearly as if he had spoken. The stranger was saying:

"You were a long way off when you first saw me, otherwise you would have overtaken me before. Therefore, you are not certain as to which house I came from."

In actual words he said: "No, I don't know Mr. Malpas. The fact is, I am a stranger to London and was trying to find my way to Oxford Circus."

"I didn't see you in the Square until a few minutes ago."

The spectacled man smiled.

"Probably because I came in from this end and, finding that I was wrong, retraced my steps. There is a certain amount of amusement to the idle stranger in being lost in a great city."

Dick's eyes never left his face.

"Are you living in town?"

"Yes—at the Ritz-Carlton. I am the president of a South African mine. By the way, you will think I am rather foolish lo give this information to a chance acquaintance, but you are a detective—Captain Richard Shannon, unless I am mistaken."

Dick was staggered. "I don't remember meeting you, Mr—? He paused expectantly.

"My name cannot possibly interest you—my passport is in the name of Brown. The Colonial Office will supply you with particulars. No, we have not met before. But I happen to know you."

Dick had to laugh in spite of his chagrin. "Let me put you in the way of finding Oxford Circus—a taxicab is the quickest method of reaching the place. I will share one with you; I am going to Regent Street."

The old man inclined his head courteously, and at that moment a disengaged taxi came into view and was captured.

"The apparent prosperity of London astounds me," said Mr. Brown with a sigh. "When I see these platoons of houses, each inhabited by somebody who must enjoy an income of ten thousand pounds a year, I wonder where the money came from originally."

"It never struck me that way," said Shannon.

With the help of the street lights he had taken a good look at the man. There was little about him that could be regarded as sinister. His hair, which was plentiful, was white, his shoulders were slightly bowed, and although his thin hands were knotted and gnarled like a manual labourer's, he had the appearance of a gentleman.

At the corner of the Circus the cab stopped, and the old man alighted painfully.

"I'm afraid I'm rather a cripple," he said good-humouredly. "Thank you, Captain Shannon, for your assistance."

Dick Shannon watched him as he limped into the crowd about the entrance of the Tube station.

"I wonder?" he said aloud.

A Message from Malpas

Audrey was waiting for him in the lounge of the Palace, and all trace of her distress had vanished.

"I hope I haven't kept you from bed," he said apologetically.

All the way down Regent Street he was hoping most devoutly that he had.

She was reluctant to return to her unpleasant experience of the evening, but he was firm on the point.

"No, I am not going to make any further trouble."

She silently noted the word "further", but wisely did not press him for an explanation.

"Marshalt has a pretty bad private reputation, and had I known that you contemplated meeting him, I should have stopped you."

"I thought he was married," she said ruefully, and he shook his head.

"No. That is his famous 'safety first' stunt. It prevents his lady friends from resting their hopes too high. He is an unmitigated scoundrel in spite of his wealth, and I'd give a lot to deal with him—adequately! Audrey, you've got to leave Portman Square severely alone."

"Audrey? I don't mind really, though I feel I ought to be a little more grown-up. In Holloway they called me '83', or, if they were being more than usually kind, just plain 'Bedford'—I think I prefer Audrey from people who aren't likely to hold my hand and get sentimental."

He tried hard to be annoyed and failed.

"You're quaint. I'll call you Audrey, and if I ever grow sentimental, just say 'business', and I'll behave. And you will leave Portman Square."—

She looked up quickly.

"You mean Mr. Malpas?"

He nodded.

"I don't know how many of his hundreds you have spent—"

"Sixty pounds," she said.

"I'll give you that, and you can send him back his money."

He felt her resistance to this proposal before she spoke.

"I can't do that, Captain Shannon," she said quickly. "I must make my own arrangements. When I see him on Saturday I will ask him to specify the wage he is paying, and tell him frankly how much I have spent, and that I want to return the balance to him. When that interview is over—?"

"And it had better not last long, princess," said Dick grimly, "or I'll be stepping into his grisly drawing-room—?"

"Why do you call me princess?" she asked with a little frown, and he went red.

"I don't know... Yes, I do! I'll change my habits and tell the truth! I think of you as the—as the Ragged Princess. There is an old German legend, or maybe it is Chinese, about a princess who was so beautiful that she was by law compelled to dress in rags to prevent everybody from falling in love with her to the disturbance of domestic peace and happiness, and the first time I saw you I was reminded of the story, and christened you so."

"And that ends your interview," she said severely.

She was by no means annoyed, though he did not know this. In the privacy of her room she laughed long and softly at the story and the compliment it held.

She was preparing for bed when she saw the note which had been left on her dressing-table. The scrawled writing she knew at once and tore open the envelope.

"I congratulate you on your escape." (it ran). "You should have used the knife."

She gasped. How did Malpas know what had happened behind the locked doors of Lacy's sanctuary?

Audrey had left Dick Shannon in no doubt as to her real mind before he took his departure, for she was a bad actress. Walking home, he arrived at the door of his flat a little after eleven o'clock, when the theatres were turning out and the streets were lively with rushing cars, and just as he was going in he was aware that standing on the edge of the sidewalk was a man whom he had met before that evening. He walked back to the motionless loiterer.

"Are you still lost, Mr. Brown?" he asked pleasantly.

"No, I'm not," was the cool reply. "It occurred to me after I left you that I would like to have a little talk with you."

A moment's hesitation, then: "Come in," said Dick, and ushered his visitor into his bureau. "Now, Mr. Brown," he said, pushing forward a chair, into which his visitor sank with a sigh of relief.

"Standing about or walking is a little painful to me," he said. "Thank you, Captain Shannon. What do you know about Malpas?"

The directness of the question took the detective aback.

"Probably less than you," he said at last.

"I know nothing," was the uncompromising reply, "except that he is a gentleman who keeps himself very much to himself, doesn't interfere with his neighbours, and doesn't invite interference from them."

Was there a challenge in the tone? Dick found it difficult to answer the question.

"The only thing we know about him is that he has strange visitors."

"Who hasn't?" was the reply. "But is anything known to his detriment?"

"Nothing whatever," said Dick frankly, "except that we are constitutionally suspicious of elderly people who live alone. There is always a chance that some day we shall have to force an entrance and discover his tragic remains. Why do you think I know anything about him at all?"

"Because you were watching the house before the young lady came out of Marshalt's and distracted your attention," was the cool reply.

Dick looked hard at him.

"You told me you had just walked into the square and out again," he said.

"One has to prevaricate," was the calm reply. "Even in your business it is not possible to preserve an even candour. The truth is, I was watching the watcher, and wondering what you had against Malpas."

"You weren't watching from inside the house by any chance?" asked Dick dryly, and the man chuckled.

"It would certainly be the best post of observation," he replied evasively. "I've been wondering, by the way, what happened to that unfortunate girl. Marshalt had a reputation for gallantry in the old days. One supposes that he has not wholly reformed. Have you ever seen anything like this?"

He went off at a tangent, and putting his fingers into his waistcoat pocket produced a small brown pebble, to which was affixed a red seal. Dick took it in his hand and examined it curiously.

"What is that?" he asked.

"That is a diamond in the rough, and the red seal is the mark of our corporation. We mark all our stones of any size in that way, using a special kind of wax that hasn't to be heated."

Dick looked at the diamond and passed it back.

"No, I've not seen anything like it. Why do you ask?"

"I was wondering." The old man was watching him closely. "You're sure nobody has brought that kind of stone to you—the police come into possession of curious properties."

"No, I have not seen one before. Have you lost a stone?"

The old man licked his lips and nodded.

"Yes, we've lost a stone," he said absent-mindedly. "Have you ever heard of a man called Laker? I see that you haven't. An interesting person. I'd like to have introduced him to you. A clever man, but he drank rather heavily, which meant, of course, that he wasn't clever at all. There is nothing clever about booze, except the people who sell it. Laker, sober, was a genius; drunk, he was the biggest kind of fool. You never saw him?"

The eyes rather than the voice asked the question.

"No, I don't know Laker," confessed Dick Shannon, "which means that officially he is unknown."

"Oh!" The old man seemed disappointed, and rose as abruptly as he had sat down. "You will begin to think that I'm something of a mystery myself," he said, and then, in his brisk way: "Did anything happen to that young lady?"

"Nothing, except that she had a very unpleasant experience."

Mr. Brown showed his teeth in a mirthless smile.

"How could one meet the Honourable Lacy and not have an unpleasant experience?" he asked dryly.

"You know him, then?"

Brown nodded.

"Very well?"

"Nobody knows anybody very well," the other said. "Good night, Captain Shannon. Forgive me for intruding upon you. You have my address if you want to find me. Will you please telephone first, because I spend a considerable time in the country?"

Dick went to the window and watched the limping man pass out of sight. Who was he? What feud was there between Marshalt and him? He almost wished he was on speaking terms with the South African, that he might satisfy his curiosity.

Martin Elton Predicts an Inquest

Lacy Marshalt came to breakfast in the blackest mood. The mark of Dick's knuckles still showed redly on his face; his eyes were hollow from want of sleep. Tonger recognized the symptoms, and was careful not to draw upon himself the wrath of his employer. Yet, sooner or later, that rage was to burst forth. Something of a philosopher, the valet waited until Marshalt had finished a fairly substantial breakfast, and then:

"Mr. Elton called to see you—I told him you weren't up. He's coming back."

Marshalt glowered at him. "You can tell him I'm out of town," he rasped.

"He happens to know you're in town. It's not for me to give you suggestions, Marshalt, but that's a bad habit you've got into, standing before the window before you're dressed. He saw you."

Lacy Marshalt felt an inward twinge at the mention of Martin's name; but if there was to be any unpleasantness, it were better that it was disposed of whilst he was in his present mood.

"Bring him in when he comes," he said. "And if he asks you any questions about Mrs. Elton—?"

"Am I a child?" said the other contemptuously. "Besides, Elton isn't that sort. He was trained as a gentleman, but broke down in training. That kind does not question servants."

If Elton was coming in a truculent mood, he could deal with the matter once for all. Dora was beginning to bore him. Lacy's ideal woman was self-reliant, and free from sentimentality. He had thought Dora was of this

437

type, but she was leaning more and more upon him, bringing problems for his examination which she might dispose of herself, and, worse than all, showing a cloying affection which both alarmed and annoyed him.

He had not long to wait for the advent of Dora's husband. He was half-way through the first leading article of The Times when Tonger came in and said, in sepulchral tones:

"Mr. Elton, sir."

He looked up, trying to read the sphinx-like face of the debonair young man who came into the room, silk hat in one hand, ebony walking- stick in the other.

"Good morning, Elton."

"Good morning, Marshalt."

He put down his hat and stripped off his gloves slowly.

"Sorry to interrupt your breakfast." Bunny pulled a chair from the table and sat down. His face was pale, but that was not unusual; his dark eyes were normally bright. "I wrote you a letter some time ago, about Dora," he said, playing with a fork that lay on the table. "It was a little direct; I hope you didn't mind?"

"I don't remember receiving any letter of yours that offended me, Elton," said Marshalt with a smile.

"I hardly think you would forget this particular epistle," said Martin. "It had to do with Dora's little dinner-parties; and, if I remember aright, I asked you not to entertain her again."

"But, my dear fellow..." expostulated the other.

"I know it looks stupid and tyrannical and all that sort of thing, but I'm rather fond of Dora. One gets that way with one's wife. And I want to save her from the hideous experience of explaining her relationship with you before a coroner's jury." He met Lacy's eyes and held them.

"Naturally," he went on with a little smile, "I wouldn't risk a trial for killing you, unless you passed out in such circumstances as threw no suspicion upon me. I wish to avoid, if possible, the vulgarity of felo de se, for I have still so much respect for my family that I would spare them the publicity which the more sensational newspapers would give to the case."

"I don't understand you. I'm afraid—" began Lacy.

"That I can't believe," Martin Elton interrupted him. "I'm sorry you make it necessary for me to say this. Dora has visited you twice since that warning came to you. There must be no third visit."

"Your wife came to me last night with her sister," said the inventive Lacy. "She was not here a minute."

The other's eyes opened.

"With her sister? You mean Audrey? Was she here?"

"Yes, she was here. Didn't Dora tell you?"

Lacy Marshalt determined to brazen the matter out. He could telephone to Dora after her husband left and acquaint her with the story he had told.

"Yes, Audrey was dining with me alone, and Dora got to hear of it, came to fetch her away, thinking that my company would contaminate her." He smiled largely.

Martin thought for a long time. "That doesn't sound like Dora," he said. "As a matter of fact, she told me she hadn't been here at all, but that little piece of deception I can understand. You know Audrey?"

The African shrugged. "I can't say that I know her; I've met her," he said.

"But Audrey was not here on the night of the concert at the Albert Hall, was she?"

Lacy made no reply.

"I don't think you will be able readily to invent a chaperon for that occasion. I think that is all I, want to say."

He walked across to where he had put his hat and his stick and picked them up.

"You're a shrewd fellow, Marshalt—a little on the crook side, unless I'm greatly mistaken, and I'm sure it's not necessary for me to indulge in the heroics proper to this occasion, to impress upon you the advantages of being a live millionaire over—well, other things. The jury will probably pass a resolution of condolence with your relatives, and in that you will have the advantage over me. But it is ever so much more satisfactory to read about somebody else's demise than to be the chief figure in your own. Good morning, Marshalt."

He paused at the door.

"You need not telephone to Dora—I took the precaution of putting the instrument out of order before I left the house," he said, and nodded a grave farewell.

A Proposal

It was a bright wintry morning. A blue sky overhead and yellow sunlight flooding Audrey's room—cheerful—such a day as says "Come out of doors" and lures the worker to idleness.

Audrey surveyed her task with no great relish. A small pile of pencilled notes, written on every variety of paper, had to be copied and returned by that evening. The work itself was practically nothing: it was the monotony, the seeming uselessness of the task, which distressed her. And she had an uncomfortable feeling, amounting to certainty, that her employer was merely finding little jobs to occupy her time, and that the real service which he had in mind would be revealed in a more unpalatable light.

She opened her window, looked down into the busy street, in a desire to find some attraction that would give her an excuse for putting off a little longer her work. But interest failed, and, with a sigh, she went back to her desk, dipped the pen in the ink and began. She finished by lunch-time, enclosed copies and rough notes in a large envelope and, addressing them to "A. Malpas, Esq., 551 Portman Square", dropped them in the hotel letter-box.

Who was Mr. Malpas, and what was his business? she wondered. Youth hates the abnormal, and Audrey was true to her age. She was looking forward with some dread to the interview, which might very well end embarrassingly for her; but all her thoughts and her speculations were coloured by one uncomfortable undercurrent which she would not allow herself to put into shape. Not the least of the shocks of the previous evening had been the discovery she had made of Dora's friendship with Marshalt. She was more than shocked; she was horrified. She had a new view of her sister, the ugliest view yet. Had it been she whose sobs she heard? That was unlikely.

Audrey had wondered since whether that sound of weeping was not a trick of imagination, conjured by her own terror. Whenever she allowed her mind to halt at the contemplation of Dora, she felt nauseated, and hurried on to a thought less painful.

Then it came to her, as it had come to her in prison, that Dora was almost a stranger to her. She had always regarded their relation as an irrevocable something which gave them, automatically, identical interests. They were two hands of the same body. Yet, if Dora had always belonged elsewhere, the estrangement so violently emphasized had not produced so great a shock as this new discovery.

On her way to the restaurant the hall-porter gave her a letter which had just arrived by messenger. One glance at the pencilled address told her that it was from Malpas. He had never before sent a message in the daytime, and she had a little spasm of apprehension that he wished to see her. The note was brief and puzzling.

"I forbid your seeing Marshalt again. The offer he is making to you today must be rejected."

She gazed at the peremptory lines in astonishment, resenting alike the tone and the calm assumption of authority. What offer was Marshalt making? It mattered very little; without this order, she would reject the most alluring proposition that the ingenuity of the South African could devise.

The nature of the offer she was to learn. Half-way through luncheon, the page brought her the second letter, and she recognized Lacy Marshalt's flowing hand. The letter began with an abject apology for his boorishness of the previous night. He would never forgive himself (he said), but prayed that she would be more merciful. He had known her for longer than she imagined, and...

... I chose the most awkward, the most stupid way of meeting you. Audrey, I love you, sincerely and truly, and if you will consent to be my wife you will make me the happiest man in the world.

An offer of marriage! It was the last thing she expected from Lacy Marshalt, and she lost no time in replying, leaving, her lunch unfinished to pen the answer.

Dear Sir—I thank you for what is evidently intended as a compliment. I have no regret in refusing to consider your offer. Sincerely, Audrey Bedford.

"Send that by express messenger," she said, and went back to her luncheon with a feeling that the day, so far, had been well spent.

The offer had had an effect. It had brought from the background of her thoughts a matter which she had partly suppressed. She had a sudden impulse and acted upon it.

A cab dropped her before the little house in Curzon Street, and this time her reception was more gracious than that which had been accorded on her previous visit. And for a good reason. The servant did not recognize her.

"Mrs. Elton, miss? I will see if she is in. What name?"

"Say Miss Audrey."

Evidently the servant did not recognize the name either, for she showed her into the chill room where she had been received before.

Audrey waited until the girl had gone upstairs, and followed her. She had no illusions about Dora's attitude.

"Tell her I am not at home," said Dora's voice. "If she doesn't go, send for a policeman—"

"I'll not keep you long," said Audrey, coming into the room in that moment.

For a breathing-space Dora stood motionless, her eyes blazing. With an effort she controlled herself and sent away the servant with a gesture.

"Every second you are in my house is a second too long," she said at last. "What do you want?"

Audrey walked slowly to the fire-place and stood with her back to it, her hands behind her.

"Does Martin know about Lacy Marshalt?" she asked.

Dora's eyes narrowed until they were dark slits.

"Oh... it's about Marshalt..."

"I want you to give him up, Dora."

"To you?"

The woman's voice was husky; Audrey saw the trembling lips and knew the symptoms. Not for the first time was she watching the gathering of a storm which would presently break in wild, tempestuous fury.

"No. I think he is despicable. I don't know any man that I like less. Dora, you can't love him?"

No answer; then: "Can't I?... Is that all?"

"That isn't all. I'm not going to preach at you, Dora, but Martin is your husband—isn't he?"

The girl nodded.

"Yes, Martin is my husband. Is that all?"

The agony in her voice touched Audrey for a second, and she took a step towards her sister—but Dora drew back with an expression of such loathing and hatred that the girl was stricken motionless.

"Don't come near me. Is that all? You want me to give up a man I love and who loves me. Give him up to you? That is why you have come here today?"

Audrey drew a breath, "It is useless," she said. "I want you to be happy, Dolly—?"

"Call me Dora, you sneak! You jail-bird—you... ! You've finished, haven't you? You came here for my good. I hate you! I have always hated you! Mother hated you, too—she as good as told me once! Give up Marshalt! What do you mean? I'm going to marry him when I've got rid of—when the time comes. Get out of here!"

She flew to the door and crashed it open. White as death the rage in her eyes smouldered like live coals. "I'm going to fix you, Audrey Torrington —?"

"Torrington!" gasped the girl.

Dora pointed to the open doorway and with a gesture of despair Audrey walked through. She went down the stairs to the hall, her sister at her heels, and all the time the elder girl was muttering like one demented. Audrey heard snatches of her talk and shivered. The mask was off —all restraint was thrown to the winds.

"You spy! You smug, hypocritical thief! He's going to marry you, is he? Never, never, never!"

Audrey heard the scrape of steel and swung round. On the walls of the hallway hung two trophies of Scottish armour. A steel buckler, a dirk and two crossed pikes.

"Dora—for God's sake!"

In the woman's hand flashed a long steel dirk. She stood at the foot of the stairs, crouched like a wild beast about to spring. The woman was mad with jealousy and hate. Audrey was conscious that behind her was the scared parlourmaid, twittering in her fear. She grasped the handle of the little waiting-room, but before she could turn it Dora was on her. She struck savagely; instinct made the girl stoop, and the dirk point buried itself in the wood of the doorpost. Wrenching it free she stabbed again, and Audrey in her panic stumbled and fell.

"I've got you now!" screamed the maddened woman, and the dirk went up.

And then a hand gripped her wrist, and she wrenched herself round to meet a pair of the most amused eyes that ever shone in a dimpled, dishonest face.

"If I'm interrupting a cinema picture, lady, I'm sorry," said Slick Smith; "but I'm nervous of steel—I am, really!"

Slick Hints

The door had closed upon Audrey before Dora Elton recovered some of her normality. She was trembling from head to foot, her head was swimming. Slick Smith took her arm, led her into the little sitting-room and pushed her down into a chair, and she did not resist him.

"Get your lady a glass of water," he said to the agitated parlourmaid. "These rehearsals of amateur theatricals are certainly fierce."

Dora looked up wonderingly.

"I've been a fool," she said shakily.

"Who hasn't?" asked the sympathetic Mr. Smith. "Every woman makes a fool of herself over some man. It's too bad when he's not worth it, lady —too bad!"

The maid came back with the water, and Dora drank greedily. Presently she pushed away the glass that he held.

"She was to blame," she gasped. "She... she... oh, she is hateful!"

"I won't argue with you," said Mr. Smith diplomatically; "it would only make you worse. She always seemed to me to be a very nice girl. She went to prison to save you, didn't she?"

Dora looked at the man again and began to realize dimly that he was a stranger. In her elementary passion she had seemed to know him.

"Who are you?" she asked.

"Your husband knows me. I'm Smith—Slick Smith of Boston. Shannon thinks I'm bluffing when I say that I operated in America, but he's wrong. I'm English born and Boston bred; the most elegant combination known to humanity—class and culture. Lady, he's not worth it."

He changed the direction of his speech so quickly that she did not grasp his meaning at first.

"Who... who isn't worth it?"

"Marshalt—he's dead wrong; you don't want me to tell you that? He'd use his first-born for shoeleather if he wanted boots. I like Martin—he's a good fellow. And I'd just hate to see somebody club him just as he was turning his gun on himself. Those kind of accidents happen. And maybe you'd go to the trial and he'd smile at you when the Awful Man put on the black cap before he sent Elton to the death cell. And you'd be sitting there frozen... thinking what a skunk Marshalt was, and how you'd brought both men to the grave. There's only three clear Sundays after a man's sentenced. Three Sundays, and then he toes the T mark on the trap. You'd go and see Martin the day before, and he'd try ever so hard to cheer you up. And then you'd have a night of hell, waiting... And when the clock struck eight—"

"For God's sake, stop!" She jumped up and pushed both her hands across his mouth. "You're driving me mad! Martin sent you—?"

"Martin hasn't seen me today and hasn't spoken to me. You don't know what a cur Marshalt is, Dora. I'll say you don't! There's no part of his heart that'd pan a trace of gold."

She lifted her hand to arrest the curiously soothing stream of sound.

"I know... please go now. Did you come to see me about that? How strange! Everybody knows I care for him."

Slick gently closed the door behind him, tiptoed down the passage and came into the street in time to see Martin alighting from a cab. At the sight of the crook his brows met.

"What the devil do you want?" he asked aggressively.

"I haven't time to tell you—but an income, a grand piano and a manicure set come nigh top of the list. Elton, you jump too quick. You jump on me because I make a call; you jump on feather-headed young people because they want variety." His bright eyes were fixed on Martin, and he saw the young man change colour. "You jump at easy money from Italy because that big stiff Stanford told you there had never been anything like it..."

Martin was white enough now and without words.

"Mind you don't jump into bad trouble. That just-as-good money was offered to me. Giovanni Strepessi of Genoa makes it, and certainly there's a lot in circulation. As a sideline burglary is less risky, and a little baccarat game a blooming sinecure!"

"I don't know what you're talking about," said Martin at last. "Stanford went to Italy to buy jewellery..."

"Maybe there was somebody in the room you didn't want to know when he told you that," said Slick. "Don't go, chauffeur—you can take me home. And, Elton..." He lowered his voice. "Even the graft of the old man Malpas is better than Stanford's new hobby."

"What is his graft?"

"Malpas?"

Slick pondered the matter a moment.

"I don't know exactly... but never see him in his house done," he said. "I saw him once—but he didn't see me. That's why I'm alive, Elton."

Edgar Wallace

The Swimmer

Mr. Lacy Marshalt had been a very preoccupied man these past few days, and the shrewd Tonger, susceptible to his employer's humours, had not failed to observe the fact. Ordinarily, very little troubled the South African millionaire, and certainly the threat of Martin Elton, who would not hesitate, as he well knew, to give his hatred expression, did not disturb his sleep or trouble his waking mind.

He was not greatly troubled now, only he was very thoughtful. Tonger surprised him half a dozen times a day deep in a reverie. Late on the Saturday night the valet brought a bundle of letters to Lacy Marshalt's study, and put them down on the writing-table by his side. The South African turned them over rapidly and frowned.

"There's none from our friend of Matjesfontein," he said. "I haven't heard from that fellow for a month. What do you think is the matter?"

"Maybe he's dead," said Tonger. "People do die, even in South Africa."

Marshalt bit his lip.

"Something might have happened to Torrington," he said. "Perhaps it is he who has died?" and Tonger smiled.

"What the devil are you laughing at?"

"You always were an optimist, Lacy. That's half your charm!" He thought a while. "Perhaps he can't swim after all," he said.

Lacy looked up sharply.

"That is the second time you've referred to his swimming. Of course he can swim. I don't suppose even his lame leg would affect him. He was one of the finest swimmers I knew. What do you mean?"

"I was only wondering," said Tonger. He delighted in his mystery, and was loath to reveal it. "A High Commissioner's children should be able to swim, too," he said.

Marshalt turned his suspicious eyes to the man and scrutinized him closely.

"And if they can't swim," Tonger went on, "they shouldn't be allowed to go sailing boats round the Breakwater, especially in the summer, with a south-easter blowing—you know what a rip-snorting wind the old south-easter

447

is."

Lacy swung round in his chair and faced his servant.

"I've had enough of this," he said. "Just tell me what you're driving at. High Commissioner's children? You mean Lord Gilbury's?"

The man nodded.

"About eighteen months ago, Gilbury's kids took a sailing boat and went out into Table Bay. Off the Breakwater the boat capsized, and they'd have been drowned if one of the convicts who were working on the quay hadn't seen them and, jumping into the water, swum out and rescued them."

Lacy's mouth was wide open.

"Was it Torrington?" he asked quickly.

"I have an idea it was. No man was mentioned, but the Cape newspapers said that the convict who rescued the children was a lame man, and there was some newspaper talk about getting up a petition for his pardon."

Lacy Marshalt began to understand.

"Eighteen months ago?" he said slowly. "You swine! You never told me."

"What could I tell you?" demanded the other, aggrieved; "No names were mentioned, and how could I know? Besides, the warder would have given you the tip if he'd been released, wouldn't he? What are you paying him for?"

The big man made no reply.

"Unless," said Tonger thoughtfully, "unless—?"

"Unless what?"

"Unless the warder was pensioned off and was living in Matjesfontein, and didn't want to lose a steady income. In that case, he wouldn't know what had happened on the Breakwater, and would go on sending you reports."

Marshalt leapt to his feet and struck the writing-table with his fist.

"That is it!" he said between his teeth. "Torrington has been released! I see now what has happened—they wouldn't make a fuss about it, and naturally his lawyers would not advertise his release."

He paced up and down the room, his hands clasped behind him. Suddenly he stopped and confronted the valet.

"This is the last time you play a trick on me, you dog! You knew!"

"I knew nothing," said the aggrieved Tonger. "I only put two and two together and suspected. If he was released he would have come here, wouldn't he? You don't suppose Dan Torrington would leave you alone if he was at liberty?"

That idea had already occurred to the millionaire.

"Besides," Tonger went on, "it's not my business to worry you with all sorts of rumours and alarms, is it? You've been a good friend of mine, Lacy. I dare say I give you a lot of trouble at times, but I owe a whole lot to you. You stood by me in the worse time of my life, and I've not forgotten it. You talk about betraying you! Why, if I wanted to betray you, there are a hundred and one facts stored up there"—he tapped his forehead—"that would put you on the blink. But I'm not that kind. I know the best side of you, and I know the worst. And didn't Torrington play the dirtiest trick on me that any man could play? Wasn't he running away with my little Elsie, the very day you get him pinched? I haven't forgotten. Look here."

He dived his thin hand into his inside pocket and took out a worn note-case. From this he took a letter which had so often been handled that it was almost falling to pieces.

"For years I've read this letter whenever Torrington has come into my mind. It's the first she sent me from New York. Listen:

"Dear Daddy—I want you to believe that I'm quite happy. I know that Torrington has been arrested, and in some ways I am glad that I carried out his instructions and came on here ahead of him. Daddy, will you ever forgive me, and will you please believe that I am happy? I have found new friends in this great city, and the money Torrington gave me has enabled me to start a little business which is prospering. Some day, when all this is an unhappy memory, I will come back to you, and we will forget all that is past."

He folded the letter, put it carefully back in the case, and replaced it in his pocket.

"No, I've got no reason to love Torrington," he said steadily. "I'd plenty for wanting to do him a bad turn." The big man was staring blankly at the floor.

"Hate's fear," he said slowly. "You're afraid of him too."

Tonger chuckled.

"No, I don't hate him, and I'm not afraid of him. Maybe it was for the best. Isn't my little girl doing well in America, with a millinery store of her own, and offering to send me money if I want it?"

Lacy walked slowly back to his desk and sat down, his hands thrust into his trousers pockets, his moody eyes still staring into vacancy.

"Mrs. Elton said she saw a limping man—" he began.

"Mrs. Elton gets that way," interrupted the other. "These nervous women are always seeing things. Lacy, do you think I ought to hate Torrington? Do you think I ought to feel so mad at him that I'd kill him? You're a bigger man than me, and take a different view. If you had a daughter that some fellow had made love to, and got her to run away with him, would you want to kill him?"

"I don't know," said the other testily. "She seems to have done well for herself."

"But she mightn't. She might have lived a perfect hell of a life —what then? For the matter of that," he went on, with Ins whimsical smile, "she mightn't have run away at all! What's that?"

He turned as Lacy sprang to his feet and glared at the wall of the room. Muffled and distinct came three slow taps. "It's that old devil in the next house," said Tonger. And then a strangled exclamation from his employer made him turn his head. The face of Lacy Marshalt was livid. From his open mouth came strange noises that were hardly human. But it was his eyes that held the valet spellbound; for they held terror beyond his fathoming.

The Call to Paris

"What—what is it?" stammered Lacy, his hands trembling, his face ashen.

Tonger was staring owlishly at the wall as though he expected the solid masonry to open and reveal the knocker.

"I don't know—somebody tapping. I've heard it before, a few days ago."

The noise had now ceased, but still Lacy stood transfixed, his head thrust forward, listening...

"You've heard it before, have you? Somebody knocking?"

"Once or twice," said Tonger. "I heard it the other night. What do you think the old man is doing—hanging up pictures?"

Lacy licked his lips and, with a shake of his broad shoulders, seemed to rid himself of the terror which the noise had inspired. He went reluctantly back to his writing-table.

"That will do," he said curtly, and Tonger accepted his dismissal.

He was at the door when Lacy lifted his head and checked him with a word. "I shall want you to go an errand for me this afternoon," he said, "to Paris."

"Paris?" The valet's eyebrows rose. "What's the good of sending me to Paris? I don't speak French, and I hate the sea. Haven't you got anybody else? Send a district messenger; they take on jobs of that kind."

"I want somebody I can trust," interrupted his employer. "I'll ring up Croydon and have an aeroplane ready to take you, You will be back before night."

Tonger stood fingering his chin dubiously. The request evidently worried him, for his tone had changed.

"Aeroplanes are not in my line, though I'm willing to try anything once. What time shall I be back—if I ever get back?"

"You'll leave at twelve; you'll be in Paris by two, deliver the letter, and you'll be on your way back by three. That will bring you to London at five."

Still Tonger was undecided. Walking to the window, he looked up at the skies a little fearfully.

"Not much of a day for aeroplane travelling, is it, Lacy?" he grumbled. "It's cloudy and there's a lot of wind... All right, I'll go. Have you got the letter ready?"

"It will be written in an hour," said the other.

After Tonger had gone, he walked to the door and locked it, returned to his table, took up the telephone and put through a call to Paris. When this had been registered, he gave another number.

"Stormer's Detective Agency? I want to speak to Mr. Willitt at once. Mr.

Lacy Marshalt speaking. Is he in the office?"

Apparently Mr. Willitt was on hand, for presently his voice greeted the millionaire.

"Come round and see me immediately," said Marshalt and, hanging up the receiver, began to write.

It was a time of crisis for him, as he well knew. Within reach of him was a man whom he had wronged desperately, one who would not hesitate to act; a man cunning and remorseless, waiting his moment. Instinct told Lacy Marshalt that that moment was near at hand.

He finished his letter, addressed an envelope, and heavily sealed the flap. Then he unlocked the door, just in time, for Tonger came to usher in the private detective whom Lacy had previously employed.

"I haven't taken the trouble to inquire before, but I suppose you are the head of this agency?"

Willitt shook his head. "Practically," he answered. "Mr. Stormer spends most of his time at the New York Branch. In America we hold a much more important position. Stormer's run Government inquiries and protect public men. Here—?"

"That's the commission I'm giving you," said Lacy grimly. "Have you ever heard of Malpas?".

"The old man who lives next door? Yes, I've heard of him. We had a commission to discover his identity—our clients wanted a photograph of him."

"Who were they?" asked Lacy quickly.

Mr. Willitt smiled. "I'm afraid I can't tell you," he said. "It is part of our job to keep our clients' secrets."

Lacy took his inevitable roll of notes from his pocket, gripped two and, laying them on the desk, pushed them across to the detective, who smiled awkwardly as he took them.

"Well, I suppose there's no reason why we should make such a secret about this case. It was on behalf of a man named Laker who disappeared some time ago."

"Laker? I don't know the name. Were you able to get a line on the old man?"

Willitt shook his head. "No, sir, he's closer than an oyster."

Lacy thought for a long time before he spoke again.

"I want you to have relays of men watching Malpas. I want the front and back of his house under observation day and night; and I want a third man on my roof."

"That will mean six men in all," said Willitt, making a note. "And what do you wish us to do?"

"I want you to follow him, identify him, and let me know who he is. If possible, get a photograph."

Willitt noted his employer's requirements.

"It will be much easier with your co-operation," he said. "The job we had was not big enough to employ so many men. In fact, we only had one detective engaged on the work. When do we start?"

"Right now," said Lacy emphatically. "I'll arrange for the man whom you put on the roof to be admitted—my man Tonger will see after his comfort."

The dismissal of the detective was hurried by the Paris 'phone call coming through, and for ten minutes Lacy Marshalt was issuing instructions in voluble French.

The Woman in the Park

There were times when Audrey looked back with a certain amount of regretful longing to the days of her chicken farm and the peccant Mrs. Graffitt. Chicken-raising had a drawback; for somehow the caprices of the domestic hen, yielding, as they did, a starvation return, were more attractive than those of the unattractive old man who lived and operated in the sinister atmosphere of 551 Portman Square.

She had not seen Dick Shannon for two days, and harboured a wholly unjustifiable grievance against him, though he had given her his telephone number, and a call, as she well knew, would bring him immediately. Once or twice she had taken up the instrument, hesitated with the receiver in her hand, and put it down again.

On one matter she had reached a decision. Her second interview with Mr. Malpas was due that night, and she would make an end of their association. Morning after morning his budget had arrived, had been copied and returned to him—she had even carried the letter back to Portman Square in the hope of seeing him before the hour of the interview; but though she had knocked, no reply had come, and she had perforce pushed the letter through the narrow letter-slit and heard it thud into the steel letter-box.

On the afternoon that Tonger made his reluctant journey to Paris she went for her favourite walk. Green Park on a cold January afternoon was something of a desert. The ponds were frozen, save near the edges, where the park-keepers had broken the ice for the benefit of the winged creatures who live in the little islands and the shelter of the bush-grown banks. The branches of the trees were bare, and only the dull green of laurels and holly bushes remained to justify the park's title.

She walked briskly past the kiosk, following the path that skirts the lake, and came eventually to the footbridge which spans the water. A chill north wind was blowing: the blue sky was flecked with hurrying clouds; snow was coming: she experienced the indescribable smell of it.

She was half-way across the bridge when a heavy gust of wind half turned her, and she decided that this was no day for pedestrian exercise, and, pushing down the skirts that the wind had raised, and with one hand gripping her hat, she turned and walked back the way she had come. Ahead of her she saw a man strolling, a thick-set saunterer who twirled a walking-stick, and the scent of whose cigar reached her long before she came up with and passed him. A wider sweep of the twirling stick almost struck her, and, glancing round in alarm, the cigar almost dropped from his teeth in his contrition... "I'm sorry, madam," he said.

She smiled and, uttering some brief commonplace, hurried on. And then, on one of the garden seats that are set at intervals facing the lake, she saw a woman sitting, and her attitude, even at that distance, was remarkable. She lay back in the seat, her face upturned to the sky, her hands outspread, gripping the seat. Something like fear stirred in the girl's heart.

The pose was so unnatural, so queerly disturbing, that she checked her pace, fearful of passing the figure, and, so slowing, The stick- swinging saunterer came up to her. He also had seen.

"That is queer," he said, and she was glad of his company. "What is the matter with that woman?"

"I was wondering," she said.

He quickened his step, and she followed at his heels, for some reason fearful of being alone.

The woman on the seat was between thirty and forty; her ryes were half closed, her face and hands blue with the cold. By her side was a little silver flask, from which the stopper had been removed, so that over the bars of the bench was trickling a tiny pool of liquid that had flowed from the bottle. Audrey looked and shivered.

There was something strangely familiar in that dreadful face, and she racked her brains to identify her. She had seen her somewhere—a glimpse in a crowded street, perhaps? No, it was something more intimate than that.

The stout man had thrown away his cigar, and was sliding his hand tenderly under the head.

"I think you had better go and find a policeman," he said gently, and at that moment a patrolling officer came into view and saved her the search.

"Is she ill?" asked the policeman, bending down.

"Very ill, I guess," said the man quietly. "Miss Bedford, I think you had better go."

She started to hear her name pronounced by the stranger, and looked more closely at him. She had never seen him before within her recollection, but his eyes, as he glanced meaningly along the path, were eloquent; he wanted her to go.

"You'll see another constable on point duty opposite the Horse Guards Parade, miss," said the policeman. "Do you mind sending him along to me and asking him to ring the ambulance?"

Glad to escape, she hurried off, and was gone before the policeman remembered certain stringent police instructions.

"I forgot to ask her her name. You know her, don't you? Miss—?"

"Yes, she's Miss Bradfield. I know her by sight: we used to work in the same office," said Slick Smith glibly.

He picked up the little silver flask, closed the stopper carefully and handed it to the policeman. "You may want what's in this," he said; and then, warningly, "I shouldn't let anybody take a sip unless you've got a grudge against them."

"Why?" asked the policeman, aghast. "Do you think it's poison?"

Smith did not reply, "Can you smell anything?" He sniffed at the woman's lips. "Like almonds..."

The policeman frowned, and then: "You don't think she is dead, do you?"

"As dead as anybody will ever be," said. Smith quietly.

"Suicide?" asked the constable.

"I don't know. You'd better take my name—Richard James Smith, known to the police as Slick Smith. They know me at the Yard. I'm on the register."

The man in uniform regarded him with suspicion.

"What are you doing round here?" he asked. He was a dull man and his questions were mechanical.

"Helping you," said Smith laconically.

The second policeman arrived, and soon after the wild clang of the ambulance bell brought a curious crowd. The doctor who came made a brief examination.

"Oh, yes. She's dead. Poison—hydrocyanic or cyanide."

He was a young man, just through the schools, and consequently dogmatic, but here his first diagnosis was to be borne out by subsequent inquiry.

The news came to Dick Shannon by accident, and beyond the interest which the name of Slick Smith aroused, he saw nothing in the matter which called for his personal interference till the officer in charge of the case came to make inquiries about Smith.

"Yes, I know him; he's an American crook. We have nothing on him here, and he has no English record. Who was the woman?"

"Unknown, so far as we can trace."

"Nothing in her clothes or handbag to identify her?"

"Nothing. It looks like a suicide. This is the second we've had in Green Park since Christmas."

That night at dinner, Audrey, glancing through the evening paper, saw a three-line paragraph:

"The body of an unknown woman was found in Green Park this afternoon. It is believed that she committed suicide by poisoning."

She was dead! Audrey went cold at this confirmation of her private fears. How dreadful! It must have been very quick, for the woman had not been there when she had passed along the footpath a minute or two before. Who was she? Audrey was certain she had seen her somewhere...

And then with a gasp she remembered. It was the woman that she had seen a week before, the drunken virago who was hammering at Lacy Marshalt's door!

She left her dinner unfinished and went to the telephone. Here, at any rate, was an excuse for talking to Dick Shannon. The pleasure in his voice when he answered her gave her, for some reason, a warm little feeling of happiness.

"Where have you been? I was expecting you to call me up... Is anything wrong?"

The last words were in a more anxious tone.

"Nothing. I saw in the paper tonight that a woman had been found dead in the Park. I saw her. Captain Shannon—I mean I was there when she was found, and I think I know her."

There was a pause.

"I'll come along now," said Dick.

He was with her in a few minutes, and she told him what she had seen. "Yes, I knew Slick Smith was there. There was a report that a lady, a Miss Bradfield, was present: that was you, of course? But you say you knew her?"

She nodded. "You remember my telling you of the woman who knocked at Mr. Marshalt's door?"

"The Annoyer!" He whistled. "An agent of Malpas."

"But why—?"

"He has been employing people to worry Marshalt, for some mysterious reason which I cannot fathom; I rather think that this unfortunate creature was one of them. I made inquiries about her when I was at Portman Square the other day. Apparently Tonger threw her out, and that was the last that was seen of her."

He looked at the girl thoughtfully.

"I don't want you in this case," he said, "either as witness or in any other capacity. You had better remain the unknown witness until the inquest is over. Smith will supply all the evidence we require—I'll see Tonger tonight. By the way," he said suddenly, "when do you visit your ancient boss?"

It was on the tip of her tongue to say that she was going upstairs to dress for the interview at that moment.

"Tomorrow," she said instead.

He looked at her keenly.

"You're not telling the truth, young lady," he said. "You are going tonight."

She laughed. "I am really," she confessed. "Only I thought you would make a fuss."

"Indeed I shall make a fuss. What time is your interview?"

"Eight o'clock."

He looked at his watch.

"I will kill two birds with one stone," he said. "I'm going to Marshalt's house now, and I will meet you at the north side of Portman Square at three minutes to eight."

"Really, there's no reason why you should. Captain Shannon—" she began, but he stopped her.

"I think there's a good reason," he said; "and what I think goes —for this night only."

She hesitated.

"You promise me you will not go to the house until you have seen me?" he insisted.

She had so intended, but his earnestness was a little impressive.

"I'll promise," she said, not wholly without relief that she would have him on hand during the interview which would follow.

The Betrayal

Martin Elton looked up from the newspaper he was reading, and for the twentieth time his grave eyes fell upon his wife, who had drawn a low chair up to the fire and sat, elbow on knee, her face in her hands, gazing moodily into its red depths. This time she turned with a start and met his scrutiny.

"I thought you were going out?" she said.

"I am."

He folded the paper and put it down. The hands of the clock above the mantelpiece showed twenty minutes after seven.

"What's the matter with you, Dora? You ate nothing at dinner."

"I'm not feeling very well," she said with a shrug, resuming her contemplation of the fire. "What time will you be back?"

"I don't know—about midnight, I suppose."

"You are going to see Stanford?"

"I've seen Stanford once today: I don't want to see him again."

A long interval of silence.

"Did he bring that money here?" she asked, without looking round at him.

"No," said Martin Elton.

She knew him too well to be convinced.

"He brought something in a bag: was it the money that man Smith spoke about?"

This time Martin spoke the truth.

"Yes, he brought three million francs. It's good stuff and there's no danger in it. Klein can get rid of it. And it's all profit."

Her shoulders moved almost imperceptibly.

"It is your funeral, Martin; if you like to take the risk it has nothing to do with me. I'm sick of everything."

"There is no risk," said Martin, and took up the paper again. "The Italian

459

is a genius, and with me it is only a sideline." He was almost apologetic. "I don't intend making a hobby of putting phoney money into circulation."

"Where is it? I want to know."

Her voice was unusually peremptory. She had been suffering from an attack of nerves all that day, and he had done his best to humour her.

"It's in the mattress under my bed," he said. "But don't let it worry you, Dora. I'll have it taken away tomorrow."

He went out of the room and came back presently, wearing his overcoat and gloves.

"Will you go out?" he asked.

"I don't know—I may," she said without looking round. She heard the street door slam, and returned to her unhappy thoughts. She was afraid of Martin; afraid, not for herself, but for the man she loved. Martin had become an intolerable burden. He was watching her all the time, suspecting her... slighting her. In these past few days she had come to hate him with a malignity which frightened her. It was he who had dragged her down, who had brought her into contact with the underworld, and moulded her in his image. So she thought, forgetting, conveniently, all that he had done for her, and the life from which he had saved her, and his many kindnesses, his invariable generosity.

If Martin were out of the way! She sighed at the thought; her unconscious mind, moving like a magnet beneath the screen of conscious thought, dragged in its path The Idea, and after a while she found herself thinking deliberately, cold-bloodedly, of a plan that, until then, she had not dared tell, even to herself.

He would kill Lacy Marshalt; she nodded as she considered this certainty. And he was holding the threat over her. She hated him worse for that. And how was she to escape? How might she shake off the burden which Martin had imposed? There was only one way. All day long, all night long, she had been engaged in reconciling herself to the deed of shame.

Martin had been gone a quarter of an hour when she ran up to her room, put on her coat and hat, and came quickly downstairs.

The sergeant in charge at Vine Street Police Station was chatting with Chief Detective Gavon when a pale girl came quickly through the doorway into the bare charge-room. Gavon knew her and nodded pleasantly.

"Good evening, Mrs. Elton. Do you want to see me?"

She nodded. Her mouth was dry; her tongue seemed to be in a conspiracy against her.

"Yes," she gasped at last. "There is a man in Italy"—her voice was shrill and jerky—"who forges notes on the Bank of France. There's a lot—in circulation."

Gavon nodded.

"Yes, that's true. Why, do you know anybody who has this stuff?"

She swallowed something.

"There's a whole lot in my house," she said. "My husband brought it there. It is in the mattress in his room. There's a little drawer near the head of the bed... it runs into the mattress. You'll find it there."

Gavon nearly collapsed.

"Your husband?" he said incredulously. "Is it his property?"

She nodded.

"What will he get?" She gripped his arm fiercely. "They'll give him seven years for that, won't they, Gavon?"

Inured as he was to the treachery of jealous women, Gavon was shocked. He had seen betrayals before, but never had he dreamt that Dora Elton's name would appear in the secret squeal book at Vine Street.

"You're sure? Wait here."

"No, no, I must go," she said breathlessly. "I must go somewhere... somewhere! My servant will let you into the house. I give you permission."

In another second she was flying down the street.

Fast as she went, someone followed faster, and as she turned up a side street that somebody was at her elbow. She heard the footsteps and turned with a scream.

"Martin!" she cried.

He was looking at her, his eyes blazing, and she shrank back, her hands raised as though to ward off a blow.

"You've been in Vine Street—why?" he asked in a whisper.

"I—I had to go," she stammered, white as death.

"You went to squeal. About the money?"

She looked at him, fascinated.

"You were watching?"

He nodded.

"I was on the other side of the street. I saw you go in—and guessed. I've been waiting for you to do this, though I never dreamt you would. You can save the police a whole lot of trouble by going back and telling them that there's no money there. You've been itching to catch me for a week!"

"Martin!" she whimpered.

"You think that with me out of the way," he went on remorselessly, "things will be easy for you as far as Marshalt is concerned, but you're wrong, my girl. I'm settling with Lacy this night! Go back and tell that to your police friends."

"Where are you going?"

She clung to him, but he thrust her aside and strode along the street, leaving a half-demented woman to stagger to the nearest telephone booth, there to ring in vain Lacy Marshalt's number.

The House of Death

Five minutes after his interview with the girl. Shannon's car brought him to the imposing portals of Marshalt's house. Tonger opened the door to him. Usually the valet affected some kind of livery—a tail coat and striped waistcoat—but now he was wearing a tweed suit with a heavy overcoat, and looked as though he had just returned from a journey.

"Marshalt's out," he said brusquely.

"You look pretty sick: what's the matter with you?" asked Dick.

He walked into the hall uninvited, and closed the door behind him; Tonger seemed amused.

"You've said it! Ever been in an aeroplane?"

Dick laughed.

"So that's where you've been, eh? Well, I sympathize with you, if you're a bad sailor—it's a novel but unpleasant experience. I want to see you more than Marshalt. Do you remember a woman who came here a week back—the woman you fired out?"

Tonger nodded.

"Come into the drawing-room, Captain," he said suddenly, and opened the door, switching on the lights. "I've only this minute got back. You almost followed me in. Now what about the lady?"

"This afternoon," said Dick, "a woman was found in the Park, dead. I have reason to believe that it was the same person who made the row."

Tonger was staring at him open-mouthed. "I shouldn't think so," he said. "In the Park, you say? It may have been, of course. But I know nothing about her, where she is or anything."

"You said it was Mrs. somebody from Fourteen Streams."

"That's the name she gave; I didn't know her. Would you like me to see her?"

Dick considered. The man was obviously suffering from the effect of his journey, and it would be unfair to subject him to another ordeal that night.

"Tomorrow will do," he said.

He did not wish to prolong the interview, anxious to keep his appointment with the girl, and Tonger accompanied him to the door.

"Ships are bad," he said, "and little boats are worse, but, my Gawd! aeroplanes are sure hell, Captain! Next time Lacy sends me to Paris, I'll go by boat—all the way if I can! How did she die, that woman?" he asked unexpectedly.

"We think it was a case of suicide by poisoning. A silver flask was found by her side."

He was standing on the doorstep, and as he spoke the door was gently closed on him. Evidently Mr. Tonger had merely shown a polite interest in the discovery, and was more concerned with his own inward distress.

"Your manners, my friend, require improvement," said Dick as he went down the steps, half annoyed, half amused.

As he came to the pavement a woman passed him. He had seen her move through the little halo of light that one of the street lamps threw a dozen yards away, and now, as she came abreast of him, something in her walk arrested him. She was dressed in black; a wide-brimmed hat hid her face. Yet he knew her, and, acting on the impulse of the moment, called her by name.

"Mrs. Elton."

She stopped as if she had been shot, and half turned towards him.

"Who is it?" she asked in a quavering voipe. "Oh—you!" Then, eagerly, "Have you seen Marshalt?"

"No, I haven't."

"I've been trying to get at him, but he must have changed the lock on the back door. Oh, God! Captain Shannon, what will happen?"

"What is likely to happen?" he asked, amazed at the agitation in her voice.

"Martin isn't there, is he? What a fool—oh, what a fool I've been!"

"No, there is nobody there, not even Marshalt."

She stood brooding, her hand at her mouth, her white face drawn and haggard. Then, without warning, she went off at a tangent.

"I hate her, I hate her!" she almost spat the words, and her voice was vibrant with passion. "You would never dream she was that kind, would you? The wretched little hypocrite! I know he is meeting her! I don't care what Martin does, I don't care what he knows; but if Lacy is playing me false—he changed the lock—that proves..." Her voice died to a sob.

"What on earth are you talking about?" he asked astounded.

The woman was in a pitiable condition of hysteria; he could see her shivering in the intensity of her hopeless fury. "I'm talking about Lacy and Audrey," she wailed.

And then, without another word, she turned and fled along the way she had come, leaving Dick to stare after her in wonder.

By the time he had reached the end of the square, Audrey was waiting for him.

"To whom were you talking?" she asked as he walked by her side in the direction of 551.

"Nobody—at least, nobody you know," he said.

She would have left him near the house.

"Don't come any farther, please," she begged.

"I'm coming inside that house with you," he insisted, "or else you do not go inside—I certainly have no intention of allowing you to go alone."

She looked at him thoughtfully. "Perhaps that is best, though I feel that I shouldn't allow you. He may be a dreadful old man, but I owe him something."

"By the way, have you the money with you?"

"All that is left," she said with a little smile. "I've been very mean. I paid my board for a week in advance at the hotel. I suppose you realize that I've got to get another job on Monday, and probably Mr. Malpas will send for the police if I do not account for the money I've spent."

"Let him send for me," said Dick.

By this time they were opposite the door of 551, and, after a moment's hesitation, Audrey tapped. There was no reply and she tapped again. Then the hard voice spoke from the door pillar.

"Who is that?"

"It is Miss Bedford."

"Are you alone?"

She hesitated, Dick nodding furiously.

"Yes," she said.

The words were hardly spoken before the door opened slowly, and she slipped in, followed by the detective. A dim light burnt in the hall.

"Wait here," whispered the girl as the door closed behind them.

Dick mutely agreed, though he had no intention of waiting so far out of reach. She had scarcely got to the first landing of the stairway when he was following her, his rubber-soled boots making no sound. She saw him as her hand was raised to knock on the landing door, and frowned him back. Twice she knocked, and her hand was raised for the third time when, from the room within, came the sound of two shots in rapid succession.

Instantly Shannon was by her side, and had pushed her back. Throwing his weight against the door, it opened suddenly. He was in the well- lighted lobby, and ahead of him was the open door of the dark room. And dark it was, for no glimmer of light showed inside.

"Is anybody here?" he called sharply, and heard a stealthy movement.

"What is it?" asked the frightened voice of the girl.

"I don't know."

There was in that room some terrifying influence. He felt the hairs at the back of his neck rise, and a crawling sensation run along his scalp.

"Who is there?" he called again.

And then, most unexpectedly, two lights went on; a table-lamp and a heavily shaded light above a small table and a chair within reach of his hand. For a second he saw nothing unusual, and then, lying on the carpet in the very centre of the room, the figure of a man, face downwards.

He ran forward. A wire caught his chest, another trip wire nearly brought him down; but his flash lamp revealed the presence of a third, and he broke it with a kick. In another second he was kneeling by the man's side, and had turned him over on his back. It was Lacy Marshalt, and above his heart the white shirt-front was smudged black with the gases of a pistol fired at close quarters. The out-flung hands were clenched in agony, the eyes, half closed, were fixed glassily on the sombre ceiling, and now a thin ooze of blood reddened the smoke stain on his breast.

"Dead!" gasped Dick.

"What is it, what is it?" asked the terrified voice of the girl.

"Stay where you are," commanded Dick. "Don't move from the room."

He dared not trust her out of his sight in this house of mystery and death. Picking his way to the shadow of the desk, he found, as he expected, within reach of the old man's hand, the little switches which controlled the doors. He turned them back one after the other, and then rejoined the girl.

"I think the doors are open now," he said, and, taking her by the arm, hurried her down the stairs.

"What has happened?" she asked again. "Who was that—that man?"

"I'll tell you later." The front door was wide open, and he ran out into the street. The dim lights of a taxicab were visible in the square, and his shrill whistle brought the machine to the sidewalk.

"Go back to your hotel," he said, "and stay there until I come to you."

"You mustn't go into that house again," she said fearfully. She gripped him by the arm. "Please, please don't! Something will happen to you—I know it will."

He gently loosened her hands. "There is nothing to worry about," he said. "I'll bring a whole lot of policemen on the scene in a minute, and—" Crash! He looked round in time to see the front door close.

"There is somebody still in the house!" she whispered. "For God's sake don't go in! Captain Shannon—Dick! Don't go in!"

He leapt up the steps and flung his weight against the door, but it did not so much as tremble.

"It almost looks as if they've settled the matter for me," he said. "Now go, please."

He hardly waited for the cab to move before he was hammering at the door. He expected no answer. Then his blood went suddenly cold as in his very ear there sounded a peal of insane laughter.

"Got him, got him, got him!" screamed the voice, and then silence.

"Open the door!" cried Dick hoarsely. "Open the door: I want to speak to you."

There was no reply.

A policeman, attracted by the sound of his thunderous knocking, came from the darkness of Baker Street, and he was joined by another man, whom Dick instantly recognized as Willit, the private detective.

"Anything wrong, Captain Shannon?" asked the latter.

"What are you doing here?" asked Dick.

"I'm watching the house. I have a commission from Mr. Marshalt."

This was staggering news.

"Marshalt told you to watch here?" asked Dick quickly, and, when Willitt had replied: "Have you anybody watching the back of the house?"

"Yes, Captain Shannon, and I've got another man on the roof of Mr. Marshalt's house."

Dick made his decision.

"Go along to your friend at the back and join him. Have you any kind of weapon?"

The man seemed embarrassed.

"That means you've got a gun without a licence! I won't press the question. Get round to the back, and don't forget that you're dealing with a murderer, an armed murderer who will not think twice about shooting you, as he shot Marshalt."

"Marshalt?" gasped the man. "Is he shot?"

"He's dead," Dick nodded.

He sent the constable away to gather reinforcements and the inevitable police ambulance, and made a quick survey of the front of the house. Separated from the pavement by a wide, spike-railed area were two windows which, as he knew, were shuttered. To reach them would be possible with the aid of a plank, but once he was in the room, the chances were that the door of the hall (he remembered the door) was as difficult to force as the street entrance. He had considered and rejected before that possible method of ingress. Leaving the policeman, who had returned, he went round to the back of the house and joined the two men who were watching.

In the narrow mews behind Portman Square there was little to be seen except a high wall pierced by a door, which apparently had been used, for there was none of the dust and rubbish which so easily accumulates and hardens against the bottom of a door that is not opened.

Willitt's man helped him climb to the top of the wall: by the aid of his flash-lamp he saw a small courtyard and a second door, which he guessed was quite as unmovable as any of the others. He got back to Portman Square as a police taxi, crowded with detectives and uniformed police, came into the square, and the first man to leap out was Sergeant Steel. One of the men carried a big fire-axe, but the first blow on the door told Dick that this method must be abandoned.

"The door is faced with steel: we shall have to blow it out," he said.

"Blowing it out", however, presented unusual difficulties. The keyhole was minute, and it looked as though the introduction of explosives into the lock would be a complicated and even dangerous business.

And then, when he was consulting the inspector in charge, the miracle happened. There was a click and the door slowly opened.

"Wedge it back," ordered Dick, and raced upstairs into the death-room.

The lights were still on; he stood in the doorway, paralysed with amazement. The body of Lacy Marshalt had disappeared!

Mr. Malpas's God

"Search every room," ordered Dick. "The man is still in the house. He's been here." He pointed to the desk. The papers which lay about in confusion bore traces of blood.

Dick began his search of the walls for another exit, and: "For the Lord's sake!" he breathed.

At the end of the room near the desk was an alcove which the velvet curtains screened from view. Drawing these aside, Shannon and his companion gazed in amazement at the thing they saw.

It was a great idol of bronze that squatted on a broad pedestal. Behind the figure, and encrested on the wall, was a huge golden sun, the leaping flames of which were set with thousands of tiny rubies that, in the light, gleamed like living fires.

Flanking the obscene idol were two cat-like animals cast, as was the figure, in bronze. Their eyes sparkled greenly in the light of the hand-lamps.

"Emeralds, and genuine emeralds," said Dick. "We seem to have stepped into Ali Baba's cave. The god beats me. He is something between Plutus and the Medusas—look at the snakes in his hair!"

It was a hideous figure. The head was monstrous, the gaping jaws, with their jagged ivory teeth, seemed to move as they looked.

"The old gentleman seems to have added devil-worship to his other accomplishments," said Dick, pointing to two small braziers, black with smoke, that stood on either side of the figure.

"That's blood!"

It was Steel who made the discovery. On the black pedestal the rays of his lamp showed a damp impression, and, drawing his finger across it, he displayed a red smear.

"Push the thing and see if it moves."

Three men put their shoulders to the plinth, but it was unmovable. Dick looked at his subordinate.

"Where have they put Marshalt's body?" he asked. "It is somewhere in this house. You take the upper rooms. Steel; I will search the ground floor and cellars."

Steel was sniffing.

"Do you notice any peculiar smell in the room. Chief? It is as though there has been a smoking fire here—the smell that soft coal makes."

Dick had been puzzled by the same phenomenon.

"I detected it when I came in," he began, when one of the uniformed men interrupted him.

"There's something burning on the carpet," he said, and the lamp showed a blue spiral of smoke.

Dick slipped on a glove and lifted it up. It was a hot coal, now dull and lifeless, though the carpet was smouldering.

"How did that get here?" he demanded.

Steel had no solution to offer.

The curtains concealed other points of interest. Behind one, in a corner of the room, he found a little door. Apparently this was not governed by the switch controls, and here the fire axe was brought into play with great effect, and a little stone stairway was revealed. It led downwards to the ground floor, through a door into the front room that lay behind the shuttered windows. At some time or other the drawing-room had been a very noble establishment; it was still furnished, though every article was so covered with dust and so moth-eaten as to give the apartment an air of utter wretchedness. Here was in odd comers a medley of incongruous articles. Bundles of skins, stacks of Zulu assegais, and a queer collection of African idols in every degree of ugliness. The skins were moth-eaten, the spearheads red with rust.

Last, and not least remarkable, of his finds was a deep Egyptian coffin, brilliantly painted, with a lid carved in the semblance of a man. He lifted the hinged lid—it was empty.

"Lacy Marshalt's body is in the house," he said, as he returned to the room above; "and his murderer is here. Have you looked for communication between the two houses?"

"There is none," said Steel. "The walls are solid: I've tried them on every floor."

Returning to the room where the body had been found, he discovered the police inspector seated at Malpas's desk.

"What do you make of this, sir?"

He handed the paper to Dick. It was a half-sheet of note-paper, and, reading it, Dick Shannon's blood went cold. The paper bore the address of Audrey's hotel, and the handwriting was undoubtedly hers. He read:

"Will you come and see me tonight at eight o'clock? Mr. M will admit you if you tap at the door."

It was signed "A".

Audrey! Only for a second was he thrown off his balance, and then the explanation came to him immediately. This was one of the notes that the old man had asked her to copy. It was the lure that had brought the millionaire to his death.

He took Steel aside and showed him the letter.

"I can explain this," he said; "it is one of the letters which Miss Bedford copied on the old man's instructions." And then, "I'll go along and break the news to Tonger."

He had forgotten all about Tonger and the effect which the news would bring to the house next door.

A small crowd had gathered before the front door when he came out, for the news of the tragedy had spread with that rapidity peculiar to such events. A light showed through the glass panelling in the hall of Marshalt's house, and he rang the bell. Tonger would be shocked. He had grown up with the dead man, fought with him and felt with him. Scoundrel as he was, the valet would know some good of his old employer.

No answer came to his knock. Looking over the area railings, he saw a light in the kitchen downstairs and rang again. And then he heard Steel calling him, and went back to meet his subordinate.

His foot was on the pavement, he had half turned to his subordinate, when, from the interior of Marshalt's house, came a shot, followed by two others in rapid succession.

He was at the door in a second. From somewhere in the basement came the sound of screams, and the kitchen entrance was flung open.

"Murder!" screamed a woman's voice.

In an instant he was running down the steps. A fainting woman fell against him, but he thrust her aside, darted through the kitchen and ran up the stairs which, he guessed, led to the hall. Here he came into a group of three hysterical maid-servants and a woman who was evidently the cook, and who proved to be the calmest and most intelligible, though she could give little information except that she had heard shots and the voice of Mr. Tonger.

"From there, sir!" A girl pointed with shaking fingers upwards. "Mr. Marshalt's study!"

Shannon went up the stairs two at a time, and, turning at right angles, saw that the door of the study was wide open. Across the threshold lay the body of Tonger, and he was dead.

Tonger! Passing his hands under the man, he lifted him without an effort and laid him on the sofa. He, too, had been shot at close quarters —there was no need to call a doctor. Death had been instantaneous.

Going to the door, he called one of the maids.

"Bring a policeman in here at once."

This time the unknown murderer should not spirit away the evidence of his deed.

He waited until the body had been removed before he made a rough search of the study. Two exploded shells told him that the murder had been committed with an automatic. But how had the murderer escaped? A thought occurred to him, and he went in search of a maid. "When I came up from the kitchen the front door was open—who opened it?"

Neither the girl nor any of her fellows knew. The door had been open when they erupted from the basement. A superficial examination of the house told him nothing, but one clear fact emerged: Malpas had a confederate, and if either escaped it was the second man. That Malpas was in his house after the murder of Marshalt he was certain.

Dick went back to 551 to continue his search there. Every room had been investigated except one on the top floor, which defied the efforts of the police to enter.

"The door must be opened," said Dick decisively. "You must get crowbars. I'll not leave this house till every room has been combed out."

He was alone in the black-draped room where Marshalt had been shot, and was speculating upon the extraordinary character of the disappearance, when he was conscious that somebody was moving behind him, and he spun round. A man was standing in the doorway. The first view of him Dick Shannon had was the gleam of his spectacles. It was "Brown", the limping lover of London whom he had seen that night in Portman Square, and who had been so interested in diamonds. A suspicion shot through Shannon's mind.

"How did you get here?" he asked curtly.

"Through the door," was the bland reply. "It was wide open and, being a member of the crowd bolder than the others, I came in."

"Isn't there a policeman on duty at the door?"

"If there is, I didn't see him," said the other easily. "I'm afraid I'm de trop, Captain Shannon."

"I'm afraid you are," said Dick, "but you won't go till I discover how you got in."

The elderly man showed his white teeth in a smile.

"Don't say that I'm suspect," he said mockingly. "That would be too bad! To be suspected of killing my old friend Lacy Marshalt!"

Dick did not like his sly smile, saw nothing of humour in the tragedy of the evening, and, as he accompanied the man downstairs, his mind was busy.

The constable on the door had not seen him enter; swore, at any rate, that nobody had passed him whilst he was on duty.

"What does this mean?" Dick looked at the visitor.

"It means the constable is wrong," said the other coolly. "He will perhaps remember going out on to the sidewalk to move the crowd farther back." The man admitted he had done this.

"You might have seen that happen from the inside of the hall or from the stairs," said Shannon, unconvinced.

"I saw it from the outside, but I well understand that if a man is foolish enough to come into a place where a murder has been committed, he only has himself to blame if he is suspected."

"Where are you staying?"

"I am still at the Ritz-Carlton. I will remain here if you wish, but I assure you that the most heinous crime to my discredit is, in this instance, an ungovernable curiosity."

Dick had already verified the man's statement that he was a guest at that fashionable hotel, and the intruder was sent about his business.

"I don't like it at all," said Shannon to his assistant, as they went back to Malpas's room. "He may have come in, as he said; on the other hand, it is quite likely that he was in the house when the murder was committed. How long will they be opening that door? Let me see it."

He followed Steel up to the top landing, where two constables were standing before a stout door which had neither key nor handle.

"How is it made fast?" asked Dick, examining the door curiously.

"From the inside, sir," said one of the policemen. "There's somebody in there now."

"Are you sure?" asked Dick quickly.

"Yes, sir," said the second policeman; "I heard him too. A sort of thudding noise, and a sound like a table being dragged across the floor."

He raised a finger warningly to his lips, and bent his head. Dick listened; at first he could hear nothing, and then there came to him the faintest of creaks, like a rusty hinge turning.

"We've tried it with the axe," said Steel, pointing to deep gashes in the wood, "but there was no room to swing. Here come the men with the crowbars."

"Hear that?" asked the policeman suddenly. He would have been deaf had he not: it was the sound of a falling chair, and was followed at an interval by a deep thud as though something was falling. "Get that door open, quick!" said Shannon.

Taking one of the crowbars in'his hand, he forced the thin edge between door and lintel and tugged. The door gave slightly. The second crowbar found a purchase, and as the two were pulled together the door opened with a sharp crack.

The garret into which they burst was empty, and unfurnished except for a chair, which lay overturned on the floor, and a table. Jumping on to the table, Dick pushed at the skylight above his head, but it was fastened. At that moment he flashed a ray from his hand-lamp upwards. Staring down at him, he saw, through the blur of the grimy window, the outline of a face. Only for a second, and then it vanished.

A long, pointed chin, a high, bulging forehead, a hideously big nose...

The Cigarette-Case

"The crowbar; quick!" he shouted, and attacked the heavy framework.

In a few minutes it was open, and he had drawn himself up on to the flat, lead-covered roof. He stepped cautiously round a chimney-stack, and then: "Hands up!" called a voice, and, in the light of his flash-lamp, he saw an overcoated man, and remembered that Willitt had told him that a guard had been set on the roof.

"Are you Willitt's man?" he shouted.

"Yes, sir."

"I'm Captain Shannon from headquarters. Have you seen anybody pass here?"

"No, sir."

"Are you sure?" asked Dick incredulously.

"Absolutely sure, sir. I heard a noise of somebody walking before I heard the skylight break—I suppose it was the skylight—but that came from the other end of the roof."

Dick hurried back beyond the opening, taking the opposite direction, until he was brought to a standstill by the wall of the next house, which was a story higher than 551. He threw a ray up to the coping: it was impossible that anybody could have climbed that bare face.

And then he saw, hanging over the low parapet which enclosed the rear of the roof, a knotted rope, its ends secured round a chimney-stack. He peered down into the darkness.

"If the fellow went that way, he certainly moved," he said, and went back to interview the sentinel.

The man said he had heard nothing, except a sound which might have been the skylight being opened, and there had been no violent noise of breakage until Dick's crowbar had got busy.

"You're an American?" said Shannon suddenly.

"Yes, sir, I'm an American," said the man. "I've been doing this kind of work on the other side."

There must be some other hiding-place on the roof, but though Dick spent a quarter of an hour prying and peering, even hammering at the solid brick chimney-stack, he found no place of concealment, and lowered himself down to the little room, leaving Steel to complete the investigation.

Steel's search was leisurely but thorough. With the aid of his hand-lamp he began a systematic examination of the lead. His first discovery was a small brass cylinder, obviously an automatic shell and one recently discharged. The second, and the more important, find did not appear until he had almost given up the search. It lay in a little rain gutter running on to the parapet, and it was the glitter of its golden edge that betrayed its presence. He fished it out of the stagnant water and brought it down to the top landing.

It was a small gold case and contained three sodden cigarettes. In one corner was an initial. Wiping the case dry, he brought it down to his chief. Dick Shannon read the initials.

"I think we have the man," he said soberly.

Martin Elton Comes Home

Dora Elton heard her husband's key in the lock and braced herself for the shock of meeting. She was shivering, though she still wore her fur coat and the temperature of the room was above moderate. Tensely strung as she was, all sound was amplified, and she heard him put his walking-stick into the hall cupboard, the rustle of his feet on the carpet, and waited. Once she had read of a man (or was it a girl?) who had done the will of a hypnotist, obeying him blindly. And then, one day, the victim felt a joyous sense of freedom and relief and knew that his master was dead.

And Lacy Marshalt was dead. Even if she had not stood on the margin of the crowd and heard the news passed back over the heads, she would have known by that sudden thunderous withdrawal of her obsession. She felt as a murderer feels on the morning of his execution.

The meanness, the stupidity of the crime—the terrific and disproportionate punishment which must be inflicted upon his dearest; the utter futility of past hates—

The handle of the door turned and Martin Elton came in. At the sight of him her hand went to her mouth to stifle a scream. His face and hands were grimy, his dress suit patched and stained with dust; a strip of cloth hung from one trouser, showing his bruised knee beneath. His face was drawn and old-looking, the bloodless lips twitched convulsively.

For a second he stood by the door, looking at her. Neither malice nor reproach was in his glance.

"Hallo!" he said, closed the door, and came forward. "So the police came after all?"

"The police?"

"You sent them here to find some money. I saw Gavon: he seemed inclined to make a search. You haven't forgotten, have you?"

She had. So much had happened since then! "I stopped them. Gavon thought I was hysterical."

He spread his uncleanly hands to the fire. "I think you were." Looking down at the dilapidation of his garments, he smiled. "I'll take a bath, change my things, and get rid of these clothes—it was rather a stiff climb."

Suddenly she moved to him, and dropped her hand into the pocket of his jacket. He made no protest, and when the hand came out holding the squat Browning, the sight of it seemed to interest rather than distress him.

With shaking hands, and eyes that saw mistily through tears, she examined the pistol. The chamber was empty, the magazine that should have filled the butt was missing. Smelling at the barrel, her face puckered into a grimace of pain. The pistol had been fired, and recently. The stink of cordite still clung.

"Yes, change, please," she said, and then: "Were you seen?"

He pursed his lips thoughtfully. "I don't know—I may have been. What are you going to do?"

"You had better change; if there is anything you want, will you call me?"

When he had gone out of the room, she examined the pistol again. There was nothing to distinguish the weapon from a thousand others, except the number that was stamped upon the barrel, and that would not help the police. Bunny had bought it in Belgium, where purchases are not so carefully registered. She slipped the gun into her pocket, and went up to his room and knocked at the door. "I am going out for a quarter of an hour," she said.

"All right," came the muffled reply.

She knew a terrace turning out of the Edgware Road. The terrace faced a high wall behind which ran the Regent Canal, and half-way along the thoroughfare was a flight of iron stairs to a bridge that spanned the water. A taxi dropped her at the foot of the stairs and was dismissed. From the centre of the bridge she dropped the pistol and heard a "smack!" as it struck the thin ice.

She came to the corresponding terrace on the other side of the canal and in five minutes had found another taxi.

Martin was in his dressing-gown, sipping a steaming cup of coffee before the drawing-room fire, when she came in. He guessed where she had been.

"I'm afraid I made you look rather a fool—about that money," he said, looking at her across the edge of the cup. "I thought better of it. When Stanford came I made him take the stuff away. Gavon came whilst we were out—Lucy told me. You didn't know that?"

"She told me something," said Dora indifferently. "I heard, yet didn't hear. What have you done with your clothes?"

"In the furnace," he said briefly. He had recently installed a system of heating in the house: the furnace was a large one.

"I am going to bed," she said, and came to him to be kissed.

Martin heard the door of her room close and looked thoughtfully at his torn hands.

"Women are queer," he said.

He did not go to bed. His suit was spread in his room ready for the hasty dressing that would follow the expected summons. Throughout the night he sat before the fire, thinking, wondering—but regretting nothing. The grey light of morning found him there, his chin on his breast, sleeping before the cold ashes.

At seven o'clock a sleepy servant woke him.

"There's a gentleman downstairs to see you, sir—Captain Shannon."

Martin rose and shivered.

"Ask him up," he said, and Dick Shannon came almost immediately into the room.

"'Morning, Elton. Is this yours?"

He held in his hand a thin gold cigarette-case. Martin looked.

"Yes, that is mine," he said.

Dick Shannon put the case in his pocket.

"Will you explain how that came to be found last night near the place where Lacy Marshalt was murdered?" he asked.

"Indeed?" said Elton with great politeness. "At what time was the murder committed?"

"At eight o'clock."

Martin nodded. "At eight o'clock"—he spoke deliberately —"I was at Vine Street Police Station, explaining to Inspector Gavon that my wife had moments of mental aberration. Moreover, until you told me at this moment, I did not know that Lacy Marshalt was dead."

Dick stared at him.

"You were at Vine Street Police Station? That fact can easily be verified."

"I should have thought it would have been verified before you came," said Martin gravely.

Both men looked at the door as it opened, to admit Dora. The hollow eyes and pallor told of a restless night. She glanced from Shannon to her husband.

"What has happened?" she asked in a low voice.

"Shannon tells me that Lacy Marshalt is dead," said Martin calmly. "This is news to me. Did you know?"

She nodded.

"Yes, I knew. Why has Captain Shannon come?"

Martin smiled. "I rather fancy he suspects me."

"You!" She glowered at the Commissioner. "My husband did not leave the house last night—?"

Martin's low chuckle was one of pure amusement.

"My dear, you are making Captain Shannon suspicious. Of course I left the house. I've just told him that I went to Vine Street, and was at that public institution at the moment the murder was committed. In some mysterious way my cigarette-case spirited itself to the roof of the Malpas establishment."

"I didn't say it was there," interrupted Dick sharply, and for a moment Martin Elton was nonplussed.

"It must have been telepathy—I am psychometric. It was on a roof, at any rate—"

"I didn't even say that," said Dick Shannon quietly.

"Then I must have dreamt it."

Elton was unperturbed by the series of faux pas, which would have landed any other man into a welter of embarrassment and confusion.

"I want you to be frank with me, as far as is consistent with your safety, Elton," said Dick. "I can't imagine that you would put up so stupid a bluff as

Edgar Wallace

this story of your being at Vine Street at eight o'clock unless there were some substantial grounds for your claim. How came this cigarette-case on the roof of 551 Portman Square?"

"I—I put it there." It was Dora. "I borrowed it. Captain Shannon, a few days ago—you know I was a friend of Lacy Marshalt, and that I—I sometimes visited him."

Dick shook his head. "It was not on Lacy Marshalt's house that it was found. It was on the roof of the Malpas house." His enquiring eyes sought Elton's.

"I left it there," said Bunny Elton calmly, "earlier in the evening. I intended breaking into Marshalt's place and settling a small account with him. But Marshalt's house is unscalable—it was fairly simple to get to the roof next door. The difficulty began when I tried to find a way into Lacy's castle. It was much more difficult last night because I discovered there was a man—a detective, I imagine—stationed on the roof."

"How did you get down again?" asked Dick.

"That was the astounding thing. Somebody had most providentially provided a rope, which was tied round the chimney-stack and knotted at every foot—in fact, it was as easy to negotiate as a ladder."

Shannon considered for a few seconds, and then: "Get dressed," he said. "We will go along to Vine Street and verify your story."

He had no doubt in his mind that the whole statement was untrue: but the first shock of the day came when they reached police headquarters. Not only was Martin's story proved to be true, but in the record book, where all visits were timed with scrupulous accuracy, was the entry: "M. Elton called with reference to counterfeit charge," and against this: "Eight o'clock." It was staggering.

"Now," said Martin, enjoying the chief's discomfiture, "perhaps you will ask the night inspector how I was dressed."

"You didn't seem to be dressed at all to me," said that officer. "In fact, I thought you'd come from a fancy dress ball. He was in rags when he arrived. Had you been in a rough-house, Elton?"

481

Martin smiled quietly.

"On a rough house would be more accurate," he said, and then, to Dick: "Are you satisfied?"

The alibi was unimpeachable. Dick looked in his perplexity at the station clock. "Is that time right?"

"It is now," said the inspector.

"What do you mean?" asked Dick quickly.

"The clock stopped last night; I think it must have been the cold, for it didn't want winding when we started it again. In fact, it stopped round about the time you were here, Elton. It was after you left that the constable drew my attention to it."

"Too bad," murmured Bunny. He accompanied Dick Shannon back to the house, and no word was spoken until they turned into Curzon Street.

"That fool clock will probably save your neck, my friend," said Shannon. "I've a warrant to search your house, which I'm now going to execute."

"If you find anything that is of the slightest value to you," retorted Martin, "I shall be the first to offer my congratulations!"

The Letter

Of all the newspapers the Globe-Herald gave the most accurate account of what had happened on the previous night:

"Within the space of ten minutes last night. Senator the Hon. Lacy Marshalt of South Africa was shot to death, his body being carried away, and his confidential valet was killed, obviously by the same hand. The first of these tragedies occurred in the Portman Square house of A. Malpas, recluse and reputed millionaire. Malpas, a man of eccentric habits, has disappeared, and the police are searching for him.

The story of the crime, gathered by Globe-Herald reporters, reads more like a chapter from Edgar Allan Poe than the record of an event which occurred in the fashionable quarter of London last night. At five minutes to eight, Detective Commissioner Shannon accompanied Miss Audrey Bedford, Malpas's secretary, to 551 Portman Square. At this hour Miss Bedford had an appointment with the missing man, and Mr. Shannon, having made several futile efforts to interview Malpas, decided that this was an opportunity of gaining admission to a house so carefully guarded. It is now known that the doors and windows of the establishment were operated on an electrical control, and that by means of loud-speaking telephones Malpas was able to interview all callers without their seeing him. At eight o'clock precisely the door opened, and Miss Bedford and the Commissioner entered the house. At that time it is certain that Malpas was on the premises, for his voice was heard and recognized. Miss Bedford was in the act of knocking on the door of the old man's private apartment, when two shots were heard from within. Gaining admission, Mr. Shannon discovered, lying on the floor of Malpas's study, the dead body of Lacy Marshalt.

Here followed a fairly faithful record of all that was discovered subsequently.

"The police are face to face with an almost unfathomable mystery, or rather a series of mysteries, which may be briefly summarized.

"(1) How came Marshalt in the carefully guarded house of the recluse, who, as it is now known, hated him, and of whom Marshalt was so afraid that he had employed private detectives to protect himself against the old man's machinations? It is clear that some very strong inducement must have been offered to the dead man to come into this house of mystery.

"(2) In what manner, after his killing, was the body of Lacy Marshalt removed from No. 551?

"(3) Who killed Tonger, the valet, and with what object? The police theory is that the murderer is a man who has been equally injured by both the victims of this terrible outrage.

"(4) Where is Malpas, and has he too fallen into the hands of the shadowy criminals?"

Dick read the account, and paid a silent tribute to the accuracy of the reporter's record. There were certain points, however, that had been missed, and for this he was grateful.

At ten o'clock he interviewed Marshalt's cook, a stout middle-aged woman, the least distressed by the tremendous happenings of the previous night.

"What time did Mr. Marshalt go out?" was his first question, and she was able to give him exact information.

"At half past seven, sir. I heard the front door slam, and Milly, who is the first parlourmaid, went upstairs to the kitchen, thinking that it was Mr. Tonger who had come back. Then, deciding it must be the master, she went into the study, and found he had gone."

"Had there been any kind of trouble at all in the house?"

"You mean between Mr. Tonger and Mr. Marshalt?" She shook her head. "No, sir. Though they were always bickering at one another, Mr. Tonger wasn't like an ordinary servant; he knew Mr. Marshalt so well that sometimes the maids have heard him call him by his Christian name. They were very good friends."

"Did Tonger have his meals in the kitchen?"

"No, sir, they were all taken up to his room. He had a suite on the top floor, away from the servants' quarters. We slept at the back of the house; he had the front."

Dick consulted the questionnaire he had hastily pencilled. "Was Tonger an abstemious man? I mean, did he drink at all?"

She hesitated. "Lately he used to drink a lot," she said. "In the early days I used to send up water or lemon-squash with his lunch and dinner, but for the past few weeks he's had a lot of drink up in his room, though I've never seen him the worse for it."

The woman told him little more than he knew or suspected. He must see Audrey and discover whether she could fill any of the gaps.

She was taking a belated breakfast in the sparsely tenanted dining-room of the hotel when Dick came on the scene.

"I waited up till two o'clock last night, and then, as you didn't arrive, I went to bed."

"Sensible girl," he said. "I promised to come and see you, but I hardly had a second. You know all about it?" he said, glancing at the paper that was folded by the side of her plate.

"Yes," she said quietly. "They seem to have made a lot of discoveries, including the fact that I was with you."

"I told them that," said Dick. "There was nothing to be gained by making a mystery of your presence. Do you remember this?"

He laid a sheet of paper before her—it was the letter that had been found in Malpas's room.

"That is my writing," she said instantly. "I think this was one of the letters I copied for Mr. Malpas."

"You don't remember which one? Can you recall the text?"

She shook her head.

"They were all meaningless to me, and I copied them mechanically." She knit her brows in, thought. "No—it was not an unusual note. Most of them were a trifle mysterious. Why, where did you get this?"

He did not wish to shock her, so passed on without answering the question.

"Has Malpas any other house? Have any of the letters any reference to a possible hiding-place?"

"None," she said, and suddenly: "What have I to do with the money he gave me?"

"You had better keep it until his heir turns up," he said grimly.

"But he's not dead, is he?" she asked in alarm.

"He will be dead seven weeks from the day I lay my hand on the old devil," replied Dick.

He asked her again what the old man was like in appearance, and wrote down the description as she gave it. It was the man whose face he had seen through the skylight!

"He is in London somewhere, probably in the house at Portman Square. The house is full of possible hiding-places."

There were at least two he did not know: had he found the second of these, the mystery of Portman Square would have been a mystery no longer.

In the Outer Circle

To say that Audrey was shocked is to describe, in mild and inadequate terms, the emotion which her experience had called into existence. Lying down on the bed after Dick had gone—she was still very tired and sleepy—she recalled, with a rueful smile the ancient Mrs. Graffitt's warnings against London. What would that old lady think of her? she wondered. For she did not doubt that the story of her criminal career had lost nothing by repetition. Possibly the farm had already become notorious as the sometime home of a shrewd and ingenious, indeed romantic, law-breaker. Perhaps they would put a tablet on the wall, she mused, half asleep, "Here lived for many years the notorious Audrey Bedford..."

She woke from her doze with a start. Her door was ajar: she was certain she had closed it—equally certain that it had been pushed open by somebody outside. Jumping up from the bed, she walked out into the corridor. There was nobody in sight; she must have been mistaken.

Then she saw on the floor at her feet a letter, and at the first view of the address her breath almost stopped. It was from Malpas!

She tore open the envelope with trembling fingers. Inside was the untidy spread of scrawled lines, three words to the line:

Lacy and his satellite are dead. You will go the same way if you betray my confidence. Meet me without fail tonight at mm o'clock at the entrance of St. Dunstan's, Outer Circle. If you tell Shannon, it will be the worse for him and you.

She read the letter again, and the hand that held the paper trembled. St. Dunstan's was a landmark in London, a home for blind soldiers, on the loneliest part of the Outer Circle. Should she tell Dick? Her first impulse was to disregard the warning; her second thought was of his safety.

Putting the letter in her handbag, she went out to find the floor clerk. That superior young lady had not seen any man, old or young, in the corridor, except, apparently, people who were well authenticated.

Audrey was so used to mysteries now, that this new terror which had been sprung upon her was part of the normal. Who was this mystery man, this grey shadow, that flitted unseen, coming and going at his will? As far as the hotel was concerned, his work was easy. There were two entrances, each leading to a different street (there were stairways and elevators in both wings of the building) and it was, as she knew, a fairly simple matter to slip up and down without observation.

She read the letter again, and liked it less. One thing she must not do, and that was ignore the summons. She must either go to the appointment, or else she must tell Dick and risk what followed. There were many reasons why Dick Shannon should not be taken into her confidence at the moment—he was seeking Malpas, and, though she could lead him direct to the man, she could as easily lead him to his death!

Throughout the day her troubled mind grappled with the problem, to which was added a new discomfort. From the moment she left the hotel in the afternoon, until her return, she had the feeling that she was under observation. Somebody was trailing her, watching her every movement. She found herself looking round fearfully, and stepping back with suspicion to stare into the faces of perfectly innocent and unoffending people.

It was characteristic of her that the memory of the tragic sight she had witnessed did not keep her from her favourite walk, though she had to screw up her courage to go along the footpath where she had seen the unknown suicide in her death hour.

The seat was not in view from the far end of the walk; it was placed at the elbow of the path, and came into sight gradually... She stopped dead, her heart thumping fiercely, when she caught her first glimpse. She saw the blue skirt of a woman, and two small feet, motionless.

"You're a fool, Audrey Bedford," she said. The sound of her own voice drove her forward to discover, sitting in the place of doom, a nursemaid cuddling a rosy-cheeked baby!

The nurse looked up to view with interest a very pretty girl, who laughed aloud as she walked past. Annoyed, the nurse sought the mirror in her handbag to see what the girl was laughing at.

On the way back to the hotel Audrey stopped to buy a weekly devoted to the interests of the poultry-keeper—all whimsical thought of hers, but a wise one, for in the well-remembered jargon of its pages, in the extravagant promise of its advertisements, she found her balance.

She hoped Dick would call that afternoon, but he was far too busy, and in a way she was glad, because she could not have seen him without telling him about her intended errand. Nor did he appear at dinner, and she retired to her room to map out her plans.

Firstly, she would leave all her money behind with the reception clerk in the hotel strong-room; and secondly, she would choose the strongest-looking taximan she could find, and she would not leave the taxi. That seemed a very sensible and satisfactory plan. If she could only have borrowed a weapon of some kind, her last remaining fears would have been removed; but amongst the mild and innocuous members of the public whom she saw in the lounge, there seemed none who would be likely to carry lethal weapons on their persons.

"And I should probably shoot myself!" she thought.

The desirable taxicab-driver took a whole lot of finding. Some sort of creeping paralysis appeared to have overtaken the profession, and, standing under the portico of the hotel, she watched fifty decrepit old gentlemen crawl past, before a providential giant came her way and was beckoned eagerly.

"I'm going to meet a man in the Outer Circle," she said hurriedly. "I—I don't want to be left alone with him. Do you understand?"

He didn't understand. Most of the young ladies he had, driven to the Outer Circle to meet men had desires quite the other way round.

She gave him directions, and sank back in the seat with a sigh of relief that an unpleasant adventure was on its way to completion.

It was a snowy, boisterous night, and the roads of the Circle were black and white, the swaying trees alone refusing to hold the wet flakes that were falling. The Outer Circle excelled itself in gloom—in five minutes' driving she saw no human soul on its sidewalks. For an interminable time the cab continued on its way before it drew up to the kerb.

"Here's St. Dunstan's, miss," said the driver, getting down and standing by the door. "There's nobody here."

"I expect they will come," she said.

She had hardly spoken before a long car came noiselessly into view and slowed a dozen yards behind the cab. She saw a bent figure step painfully to the sidewalk, and waited, her breath coming a little faster.

"Audrey!"

There was no mistaking that voice. She went reluctantly a few paces and looked back at the taximan.

"Will you come here, please?" she asked with an assumption of firmness.

He walked slowly towards her, until she saw, above the white muffler around his neck, the big nose and the long chin she had so graphically described to Dick that morning.

"Come here," he said impatiently. "Send your cabman away."

"He's staying," she said loudly. "I can't remain long with you. You know that the police are looking for you?"

"Send the cabman away," he snapped again, and then: "You've got somebody in that cab! Curse you! I told you—?"

She saw the glitter of steel in his hand and shrank back.

"There's nobody there—I swear there's nobody there! Only the taxi-driver," she said.

"Come here," he commanded. "Get into my car."

She turned and slipped on the icy sidewalk, and in another second he had gripped her by both arms and was standing behind her.

"Here, what's this?" shouted the cabman, and came threateningly towards him.

"Stand where you are."

Before the muzzle of the pistol the big driver halted.

"Take your cab and go. Here!"

A handful of coins fell almost at his feet, and the driver stooped to recover them. As he did so, the pistol rose once and came down with a crash upon the unprotected head, and the man fell like a log.

All this happened before Audrey realized her extreme danger—happened without her being able to see the face of the murderer, as she knew him to be; for he stood behind her all the time, and struck at the cabman over her shoulder. As the cabman fell, she found herself lifted from her feet.

"If you scream I'll cut your throat!" hissed a voice in her ear. "You're going the way Marshalt went and Tonger—the way Dick Shannon will go, unless you do as I tell you!"

"What do you want of me?" she gasped, struggling hopelessly to free herself from his hold.

"Service!" he hissed. "All that I've paid you for!"

Mr Brown Offers Advice

The hand of Malpas was over her mouth as he lifted and dragged her towards the car, and she was fast losing consciousness when suddenly the grip relaxed, and she fell, half swooning, to the ground. Before she realized what was happening, the lights of Malpas's car flashed past her. She saw three men running, heard a rattle of shots, and then she was lifted to her feet. There was something oddly familiar in the clasp of the arm about her, and she looked up into the face of Dick Shannon.

"You're a wicked girl," said Dick severely. "Lord! But you have given me a fright!"

"Did you—did you see him?"

"Malpas? No, I saw his rear lights, and there's a chance that they may have caught him at one of the gates, but I confess it is a very remote chance. My man missed you; it was only by luck that he picked you up again just as you were driving through Clarence Gate. He got on to me at Marylebone Lane by 'phone, or else..."

She shuddered.

"Did he tell you anything material?" he asked. She shook her head.

"No, he made a number of unpleasant promises, which I hope he won't fulfil. Dick, I'm going back to my chickens!"

Shannon laughed softly. "Even the fiercest of your hens would be inadequate to protect you now, my dear," he said. "Malpas, for some reason

Edgar Wallace

or other, thinks it is necessary to remove you. Why he didn't shoot you without any preliminary, I can't for the life of me understand."

And there and then he relieved her mind.

"Yes, you've been followed all day, but not by the sinister Mr. Malpas. Two painstaking officers of the C.I.D. have been watching your goings-out and comings-in. The nursemaid in the park scared you, they tell me?"

Audrey was human enough to blush.

"I didn't notice anybody following me," she confessed.

"Because you weren't expecting to see those particular people. You were looking for a nasty old man with a long nose."

He saw her safely to her hotel, and went on to the Haymarket. And then for the second time he saw the man Brown. He was standing in exactly the same spot as he had been the night Dick had taken him into his flat.

"My friend, you haunt me," said Shannon. "How long have you been waiting?"

"Four minutes, possibly five," said the other coolly, with a good-natured smile.

"May I suggest that, if you wish to see me, you knock at my door? I employ people who will admit you. I suppose you do want to see me?"

"Not particularly," said the other surprisingly. And then, "Did you catch him?"

Dick spun round. "Catch whom?"

"Malpas. I heard you were chasing him tonight."

"You hear a great deal more than an innocent man should," said Dick.

Mr. Brown chuckled.

"Nothing annoys the police worse than to be supplied with information which they fondly imagine is their own private secret! When you remember that your gun-play has driven the peaceful inhabitants of Regent's Park into a condition of frenzied alarm, you can hardly say that your unsuccessful attempt to capture the devil-man hasn't been well advertised."

"The devil-man, eh? You know Malpas?"

"Remarkably well," said the other immediately. "Few people know him

491

better."

"And probably you knew the late Mr. Lacy Marshalt?"

"More intimately than I knew Malpas," said Brown. "Better acquainted, in fact, than I was with the late Mr. Laker."

"Come into my flat," said Dick.

He was not sure that the man was following, he walked so softly, despite his injured leg, until, glancing behind him, he saw him at his heels.

"Laker is a name you have mentioned before: who is he?"

"He was a drunkard, a thief and a trainer of thieves. He was not so well acquainted with Malpas that he didn't make a mistake. You only make one with Malpas, and his was to call on his boss when he had looked upon red wine—it was the night of Laker's death!"

"His death? Then he's dead?"

Mr. Brown nodded.

"His body was taken out of the river some time ago. I thought you would associate the cases."

Dick jumped up from the chair in which he had sat. "You mean the man who was clubbed and thrown over the Embankment?"

Brown nodded.

"That was the intemperate Laker," he said, "and he was I imagine, destroyed by Malpas or one of his agents. At the moment I haven't any exact news as to whether such an agent was employed, and I think you'd be on the safe side if you marked Laker down as Malpas's own personal handiwork."

Dick looked at him in silence.

"You're asking yourself whether it is possible that there could be such a—what is the expression?—'fiend in human shape' is popular—who would murder his way out of all his difficulties? Why not? Commit one murder, and find no cause for remorse, and all the others are not only simple but a natural consequence. I have met many murderers."

"You have met them?" said Dick incredulously.

The man nodded.

"Yes; I was a convict for many years. That rather startles you, but it is nevertheless true. My name is Torrington. I had a life sentence but was pardoned for saving the lives of two children—the children of the High Commissioner of the Cape. That is why I am allowed a passport in a false name. I am, in fact"—his quick smile came and went—"one of the privileged classes! I am interested in Malpas; I was much more interested in the late Mr. Marshalt, but that is a point I need not labour. Criminals interest me, just as a train that has jumped the rails interests one. While it keeps to the rails and carries on its humdrum business, it is hardly worth while noticing unless you are a railway engineer; but when it has jumped the rails and becomes a hopeless wreck, or plunges along some track of its own making to destruction, then it becomes a fascinating object."

"You did not like Mr. Marshalt." said Dick, eyeing him keenly.

Brown smiled. "I did not"—a long pause—"like him. That is true. De mortuis nil nisi bonum is a stupid tag. Why shouldn't you speak ill of the dead? For if they die, their acts still circle out on the pool of fate. You want to be careful, Captain Shannon." His hard, bright eyes transfixed the detective.

"Careful about—?"

"About Malpas. One killing more or less isn't going to bother him, and he has an especial reason for getting at you. Remember, he is a genius, with a deplorable sense of the theatrical." His eyes did not leave Dick's face. "If I were you, I should leave him alone."

Shannon laughed in spite of his irritation.

"That's fine advice to give to an executive police officer," he said.

"It is good advice," said the other, but did not pursue the topic. "Where do you think they have taken the body of Marshalt?"

Dick shook his head.

"It is in the house somewhere. But I don't know why I should give you my theories."

"I don't think it is in the house at all," said Brown. "I have an idea—however, I have said too much already. And now you're coming round to my hotel for a nightcap, Captain."

493

Shannon declined laughingly.

"Well, at any rate, you'll come along and escort me?" said the other with his tremulous smile. "I am a feeble man and in need of police protection."

Dick sent him down to the street whilst he telephoned to discover that no further trace of Malpas had been seen. When he joined his companion he found him in his accustomed place on the edge of the kerb, looking up and down the Haymarket with bright, quick, bird-like jerks of his head.

"Are you expecting anybody?"

"I am," said the other, but did not trouble to explain whom.

There was one curious fact that Dick noted on the way to the hotel, and that was that Mr. Torrington's limp was not so pronounced sometimes as it was at others. It was almost as though he had lapses of memory, and forgot to drag his foot. Shannon remarked upon it just before they reached their destination.

"I think a great deal of it is habit," said Torrington without embarrassment. "I've been so used to dragging my leg that it has almost become second nature."

He looked past Dick with the same strange intentness that he had shown before.

"You still expect to see somebody?"

Torrington nodded. "I am looking for the shadow," he said; "he hasn't let up once today, so far as I can discover."

Shannon chuckled. "You don't like being shadowed—it was smart of you to detect him."

Torrington stared at him. "You mean the policeman who has been following me? That is he on the corner; I know all about him. No, I was talking of the man who has been trailing you."

"Me?" asked the Commissioner, and Torrington's eyebrows rose.

"Didn't you know?" he asked innocently. "Bless my soul—I thought you knew everything!"

Edgar Wallace

The Feet on the Stairs

Slick Smith lived in lodgings in Bloomsbury. He had the first floor of a house which had been the latest thing in dwellings somewhere around the time when George II was swearing in broken English at his ministers. Now, in spite of improvements introduced by the landlord. No. 204 Doughty Street was a little out of date.

In some respects the archaic arrangements suited Smith remarkably well. There was, for example, a cistern outside his bedroom window, and the constant drip and hiss and gurgle of water would have driven a more sensitive man to madness. Smith, being neither sensitive nor a martyr to nerves, found the noise soothing and the cistern itself a handy getting- off place. Through the window to the cistern support was a step, to the top of a wall was another. An agile man could get from Slick's bedroom to a side street in less time than it would take him to descend the stairs and pass through the front door like a law-abiding citizen. And he could return the same way almost as easily. Therefore he endured the cistern and the low roofs and the twisting stairway, where you bumped your head against a three-hundred-year-old beam if you were a stranger. And though the smoke of the kitchen fire occasionally came up to him via the open window of his sleeping apartment, he told the apologetic landlord that on the whole he preferred smoke to the more delicate perfumes.

Nobody in the house knew his business. He was generally regarded as one who had more money than duties. He spent most of his nights away from his rooms and slept the greater part of the day behind a locked door. He had few visitors, and those usually came at the hour the landlord dined, and were admitted by himself. They did not knock or ring—a soft whistle in the street brought him to the door.

When he went out, as he did every evening, he was usually in evening dress, and, almost as though it were part of a ritual, he followed the same route. A bar in Cork Street, a small and not too savoury night club in Soho, a more fashionable club in Coventry Street and so on, to a point where he vanished and left no trace. Night after night expert watchers from Scotland

Yard had missed him, and always at the same spot—on the corner of Piccadilly Circus and Shaftesbury Avenue, the best-lighted patch of London.

He had reached the Soho stage of his wanderings on the night that Audrey had made her adventurous journey to meet Malpas, and, seated at a little table at the far end of the room, he listened to the efforts of three instrumentalists who were doing a bad best to keep time with the dancers who thronged a floor as defective in quality as the orchestra.

A little man with a thin, vicious face edged his way to the watcher's side, drew a chair slyly forward and sat down, beckoning the waiter.

"Same as him," he grunted, indicating the bock before Mr. Smith, who did not even look round. Until...

"Slick, there's a dame at the Astoria with a carload of stuff. French and divorced. You could straighten the maid for half a monkey."

"Cease your gibberish, child," said Slick wearily. "What is half a monkey? And which half?"

"Two hundred and fifty... the maid's a Pole..."

"What more appropriate for a monkey than a Pole?" asked Smith. "Or even half a monkey and half a Pole? Tempt me not. You mean Madame Levellier? I guessed so. Her stock's worth twenty thousand—net! And dollars at that. She carries most of it appliqued to her person. And every cheap grab-it in London knows all about it. You're as interesting as last year's Book of Omens and Prophecies."

The informer was not abashed. He was a "spotter", a gatherer of valuable information, and had never stolen in his life. Keeping to the company of valets and servants, he located rich pockets for other men to mine.

"There's a fellow from the North staying at the British Imperial. He's an ironmaster, and has stacks of money. Today he bought a diamond tarara—"

"Tiara—yes, for his wife," said Slick, still watching the dancers. "His name is Mollins; he paid twelve hundred for the jewel —it is worth nine. He carries a gun, and his bulldog sleeps on the end of his bed—he has a great mistrust of Londoners."

The spotter sighed patiently. "That's all I know," he said, "but I'll have a good job for you in a day or two. There's a fellow coming from South Africa with a fortune. He's been here before..."

"Let me know about him," said Slick, in a changed tone. "I've heard about that guy, and I want to get better acquainted."

He laid his hand palm downwards on the table and moved it carelessly in the spotter's direction. That gentleman took what was underneath and was grateful.

Soon after this, Smith left. But at every stage of the journey the same thing happened. Sometimes the spotter was a woman; once it was a hard- faced young girl—and they all told him about the French woman at the Astoria and the ironmaster at the British Imperial, and he listened courteously and helped them out when their information was deficient.

"Listen, Mr. Smith." This was at his last place of call, and the informant was an over-dressed young man who wore a diamond ring. "I've got it for you. There's a dame at the Astoria—?"

"This story must be true," interrupted Slick. "She's got a million dollars of diamonds and a Polish maid, and she's divorced."

"That's right—I thought I had this on my own."

"It will be in the papers tomorrow," said Slick. It was curious how little was the interest taken by professional circles in the Portman Square murder. Never once did he hear it mentioned, and, when he introduced the topic, they wandered straight away.

"It's like getting a cinema star to talk about someone else," he said to an acquaintance.

"They naturally dislike crime," said that worthy, and had the laugh to himself.

When he finally made his disappearance he was without news. That came later. At two o'clock in the morning a tramp shunted into the mews at the back of Portman Square, and half an hour later Dick Shannon was called from his bed by telephone.

"Steel, sir... I'm speaking from 551... I wish you would come down —the queerest things are happening here."

"Queer... how?"

"I'd rather you came than explain over the telephone." Dick knew that his second would not call him from bed at that hour without good cause, and he dressed quickly. When he got to the house. Steel and a policeman were waiting in the open doorway.

"The fact is," confessed the sergeant, "either I have an attack of nerves or else there is something confoundedly wrong."

"What has happened?"

They were in the hall and the door was shut. Steel lowered his voice.

"It started at midnight—the sound of somebody walking up these stairs. I and the constable were in Malpas's room—I was teaching him picquet. We both came out on the landing, expecting to find either you or the inspector from Marylebone Lane. There was nobody. We couldn't both have been mistaken—"

"Did you hear it, too?" asked Shannon, addressing the stolid policeman.

"Yes, sir; it fair gave me the creeps... a sort of stealthy—"

He turned his head and stared up the bare staircase. Dick heard it, and for a second a shiver ran down his spine.

It was the sound of slippered feet on stone steps.

"Sweesh, sweesh..."

Then there floated up to them a muffled laugh.

Shannon crept up to the foot of the stairs. Above, on the landing and out of sight, a solitary light was burning, and, as he looked, there passed across the wall the shadow of a monstrous head. He reached the first landing in a second—no sign of head or owner.

A Vision of Marshalt

"Curious," he mused aloud. "This is the sort of thing calculated to scare Aunt Gertrude."

Steel heard the "Aunt Gertrude". It was the agreed-on code—outside the house and within hail was a policeman specially posted. The man ran across in answer to the flash-lamp signal.

"'Phone the superintendent that the chief requires all divisional reserves—and a cordon! He will understand if you say 'Gertrude'."

He came back to find Dick inspecting the big room which Malpas used as an office. The curtains had been removed from the panelled walls —from everywhere except the alcove that concealed the strange bronze god and those that covered the windows. Against the wall facing the window was a long oaken sideboard, the only article of furniture in the room except the two chairs, the little table at which the guests of Malpas had sat, and the writing-desk.

"Somebody has been here," said Steel. He pointed to a litter of cards on the floor. "I left those stacked on the desk; I was just going to deal a hand when we heard the footsteps on the stairs. I should think they've gone now."

Suddenly Dick gripped his arm, and the three men waited, straining their ears. Again it came, those shuffling, slippered feet on the stone stairs, and this time Dick Shannon signalled them to remain motionless.

Louder and louder, until the feet halted, as it seemed, in the lobby outside. The door was ajar, but, as they looked, it began to open slowly. Shannon's hand dropped to his hip. In another instant the muzzle of his revolver covered the doorway; but nothing else happened, and when he sped softly across the room and dashed out into the lobby, it was empty.

The policeman took off his helmet and wiped his warm forehead.

"Flesh and blood I can stand," he said huskily. "There isn't a man alive that I won't tackle. But this is getting me rattled, sir!"

"Take this lamp and search the rooms up above," said Dick.

The uniformed man took the torch reluctantly.

"And don't hesitate to use your stick."

The policeman pulled his truncheon from his pocket and looked at it with a certain amount of misgiving.

"All right, sir," he said, taking a long breath. "I don't like it, but I'll do it."

"An excellent motto for all police services," said Dick cheerfully. "I don't think there's anything upstairs except empty rooms, but give a shout if you see anything, and I'll be up in two twinks."

He heard the heavy-footed policeman walking up the stairs, and if he had been unaware that the man had no heart in the job, his pace would have told him. Suddenly the footsteps ceased, and Dick walked to the foot of the stairs.

"Are you all right?" he called.

There was no answer, only a queer shuffle of feet and a sound such as a roosting chicken would make, a short, throaty growl. And then something round and dark came over the banisters, fell on the stairs and bounded to Dick's feet. It was the policeman's helmet.

Followed by Steel, he ran up the stairs, and, in the light of his lantern, he saw something swaying on the upper landing—something that swung and struggled and kicked impotently. It was the policeman, and he dangled to and fro from the end of a rope noosed about his neck and fastened to the landing above. The man was on the point of collapse when Steel, springing forward, cut the rope above his head. They got him back to Malpas's room and laid him on the floor, whilst Steel forced brandy between his clenched teeth. It was ten minutes before he had recovered sufficiently to tell what had happened, And of that he knew very little.

"I was turning to go up the next flight when a rope dropped over my head from above. Before I could shout, it was pulled tight, and I could see somebody hauling from the landing. I had the presence of mind to throw my helmet over the banisters, or I'd have been a dead man. Men I can tackle, Mr. Shannon, but ghosts..."

"What is your weight, my friend?"

"A hundred and seventy, pounds, sir."

Dick nodded. "Find me the ghost that can lift a hundred and seventy pounds at the end of a rope, and I'll become a spiritualist," he said- "There's the inspector. Steel; go down and let him in."

Steel went to the desk, put his hand on the switch that controlled the door, and withdrew it with a yell.

"What's wrong?"

"There's a short circuit somewhere," said the sergeant; "Lend me your glove, sir."

But Dick saved him the trouble. Reaching out, he turned over the switch, to find that leather was no protection—he felt the paralysing shock of 250 volts, but the switch was turned.

"There you are," he said. "You needn't go down; they will come in." They waited, but the knocks were repeated. The men looked at one another.

"The control doesn't seem to be working," said Dick, and at that minute the lights went out.

"Keep to the wall, and don't show your light," said Shannon in an undertone.

But Steel had already pressed the button of his electric torch. No sooner did the light flash than a pencil of flame leapt from the other room, something whistled past his head, and there was a smack as the bullet struck the wall.

Dick fell flat, dragging his subordinates with him. Down below, the hammering on the door echoed thunderously through the bare hall.

Shannon shuffled forward, his lamp in one hand, his gun in the other, and Steel followed his example. The darkness of the room was impenetrable. Shannon stopped to listen.

"He's there, in the corner near the window," he whispered.

"I think he's against the wall," whispered Steel. "My God!"

A queer green oblong of light had appeared in the panelled wall behind the level with the sideboard, and in the strange radiance they saw a figure lying. The light grew in intensity, revealing every horrible detail.

It was a man in evening dress, his shirt-front black with powdered smoke. The face was pallid and waxen; his two hands were clasped on his breast. Motionless, awful... Shannon felt a momentary thrill of fear.

"It's a dead man!" croaked Steel. "My God! It's Marshalt! Look —look. Shannon—it's the body of Marshalt!"

The Buffet Lift

The figure lay motionless, fearful to look upon, and then the green oblong of light dimmed and went out, and to their ears came a hollow rumble of sound like distant thunder.

Dick stumbled to his feet and ran across the room, but his groping hands felt nothing but the carved panelling. The strange apparition had vanished!

As he felt, he heard the sound of feet in the hall below.

"Anybody here?" shouted a voice.

"Come up. Use your lamps: the lights are gone."

As though his words were a signal the lights flared up again.

"Who opened the street door?" asked Dick quickly.

"I don't know, sir. It just opened."

"There's another set of controls somewhere. Steel, that axe: it's upstairs. No, one of you men get it: find it in the little room on the top landing. Use your lamps, and club anybody you see."

The axe was procured without any untoward incident, and Shannon attacked the panelling. In a few minutes he had laid bare the cavity where he had seen the body of Lacy Marshalt was lying.

"A buffet lift," he said. "They have them in some of the houses —the width of the sideboard and on the sideboard level."

He reached in and felt the twin steel cables that operated the elevator. The kitchen was in the basement, and the stout door had to be forced—since Steel had visited the place earlier in the evening, somebody had shot the bolts. When an entrance was made he found, as he expected, the buffet lift at rest. But there was no sign of Marshalt.

"That's how they got the body away in the first case, leaving the lift suspended between this room and the kitchen. I searched this place before. If you notice, Steel, the opening even here is so carefully masked by the panelling."

The detective led the way through the scullery into the little courtyard to the rear of the house. The door behind was open; so too was the gate into the mews.

"Marshalt's body is in the house: there's no doubt about that," said Dick. "They couldn't have got it away. Where's your cordon. Inspector?" he asked sharply, looking up and down the deserted mews.

The second half of the cordon were late in arriving, apparently, for they were not on the scene until ten minutes after Dick had returned to Malpas's sanctum.

"This room must never be left without a guard," he said "If there is one thing clearer than another, it is that the old man isn't playing ghosts from sheer mischief. There is a good, solid reason behind his antics, and the reason is that there is something in this room he wants to get at."

He inspected the narrow stairway that led below to the old drawing- room, but found nothing except clear evidence that this system of serving- stairs was general throughout the house.

"You notice there are no servants' stairs at all?" He pointed out the fact to Steel. "Probably this house was built long after that on the left and the right of it, and the architects had to design a method of working in a second staircase without encroaching upon the room space."

"But there are no stairs from the drawing-room to the kitchen," said Steel, and tapped the wall where the stairway ended on the drawing-room level. To his surprise it sounded hollow.

"That's a door with a concrete face," suggested Dick. He put his shoulder against it, and it turned easily. "That is the way our friend came and went. Come up here." He ascended a dozen stairs and stopped. "We are now moving parallel with the main stairway. Listen."

He tapped at the wall.

"You could almost put your finger through it," he said. "That accounts for the slippered feet on the stairs—an old theatrical trick. If you give me two pieces of sandpaper I'll show you how it's produced."

They went back to the big room again.

"And here's a second door." Again Dick tapped at what was apparently a solid wall. "This takes him to the next floor, and he was up there waiting to noose our policeman."

"Where is he now?"

"A sane question," said Dick dryly, "but I'm not prepared to answer you. I should say that he was some miles away. If that cordon had been in its place, there would have been one ghost less in the world." He examined his lamp. "I'm going to have another shot at the roof, though it is unlikely that our bird will be nesting there. By the way, Willitt's detectives have been withdrawn?"

"As far as I know, sir. Willit is still under the orders of Marshalt's lawyers, who have put a caretaker in the house."

A search of the roof revealed no more than that the detective was still on duty. They saw the red glow of his cigar end before he himself was visible.

"Rather unnecessary, isn't it, your being here?" said Shannon.

"From my point of view, yes," was the reply. "But I carry out instructions from my Chief as you carry out yours."

"You've seen nobody?"

"No, sir. I'd have been mighty glad to have had even a ghost to talk to. This is surely the coldest and most lonesome job on earth."

"You've heard nothing happening below?"

"I heard somebody come out of the back just now: I thought it was you. There has been a big car waiting there for the last hour. I looked over, but I didn't see who it was. He was dragging something heavy. I heard him grunt as he got through the gate and loaded it into the car. I thought it was one of your sleuths."

To Dick Shannon it seemed impossible that one man should have carried the body without assistance; and there was something unnatural about the thing. When he came back to Steel, he found that-the sergeant had made a discovery which was eventually to solve the mystery to some extent.

"I found this in the courtyard," he said. "Our friend must have dropped it in his flight."

It was a flat leather case, and, opening it, Dick saw an array of tiny phials, a hypodermic syringe and two needles. The syringe had evidently been put away in a hurry, for it was half, filled with a colourless liquid, and the velvet bed on which it lay was wet, where it had leaked.

"It looks as if it had been used recently," said Steel.

"The needle certainly gives that impression," agreed Shannon, examining the thread-like steel. "Send the contents of the syringe straight away for analysis. I am beginning to see daylight!"

Stormer's

Stormer's Detective Agency occupied the first floor of a new City building. That it was a detective agency at, all was not apparent, either from the discreet inscription on its doors or from the indication in the hall, which said simply "Stormer's", and left the curious to guess in what branch of commerce Stormer's was engaged.

That morning, Mr. John Stormer paid one of his fugitive visits to his English headquarters. He came, as usual, through his own private door, and the first intimation Willitt had that his Chief was in the building was when the buzzer on his desk purred angrily. He passed down the corridor, unlocked the door of the sanctum, and went in. Mr. Stormer, his Derby hat on the back of his head, an unlighted cigar between his strong white teeth, sprawled in his office chair with an open copy of The Times in his hand.

"Give me an English newspaper for news every time," he said with a sigh. "Do you know, Willitt, that it will be fair but colder, that there's a depression to the south-west of Ireland and another depression to the north-east of Ireland, that will probably cause rain in the West of England? Do you know that visibility is good, and that the sea crossing is rough? The newspapers over here give more space to the weather than we give to a Presidential election."

He put the newspaper down on the floor, fixed pince-nez on his broad nose, and looked at his subordinate.

"What's doing?" he asked.

"There are five new cases in this morning, sir," said Willitt. "Four of them husband-and-wife stuff, and one a lady who is being blackmailed by a moneylender." Stormer lit the stub of his cigar.

"Don't tell me about it; let me guess," he said. "She borrowed the money to save a friend from embarrassment, and her husband doesn't like the friend."

Willitt grinned.

"Very nearly right, sir."

"I should say it was very nearly right," said Mr. Stormer with a grimace. "Women never borrow money for themselves: they always borrow it for somebody else. There's never been a bill signed by a woman that didn't have a halo over it. Now what's the latest from Portman Square?"

Willitt gave a long and accurate description of recent developments.

"Last night, eh? Do you know what the trouble was?"

"I don't know, sir. Wilkes reported that Shannon came on the roof, and that the house was surrounded by police."

"Humph!" said Stormer, and there and then dismissed the mystery of Portman Square, and devoted his mind and thoughts to the routine of his business.

He very seldom made his appearance in his London office, but when he did he worked like ten men; and it was not until the City clocks were striking nine that night that he signed his last letter.

"About that business of Malpas," he said; "the old instructions hold until they're cancelled by Marshalt's lawyer. The house is to be watched, a man remaining on the roof, and one of our two best men always to be on the heels of—Slick Smith! You understand?"

"Yes, sir."

"It's too bad Slick should have to be trailed this way, but I'm taking no risks. Cable me if anything develops."

Willitt made a note of the order.

"By the way, how do we come"—Stormer frowned up at the other —"how did we come to be acting for Marshalt at all?"

"He wanted a girl traced and came to us."

Stormer smacked the table with his hand. "Of course—the girl! Did you ever discover what was behind his interest in Miss Bedford?"

Willitt shook his head.

"No, sir: he was that kind of a man. You remember I told you he wanted me to bring her to dinner with him? I don't think there was any other interest."

"Don't you?" Stormer emphasized the first word. "That is surely strange—wanting that girl located. Her name is Bedford, I suppose?"

Willitt smiled.

"You've asked me that before. Yes, sir. She was very well known in the village of Fontwell—lived there all her life practically."

"And Elton—was her maiden name Bedford?"

"Yes, sir: she was married in that name."

"H'm!"

Mr. Stormer had a trick of sweeping the palm of his hand across his mouth when he was perplexed.

"I hoped... however. The girl's in town. now, eh? Staying at the Regency, your report said... hum!"

He beat a tattoo on the desk with his pencil.

"Ever thought of pulling her into this business? We want a woman sleuth badly, and she's the kind who'd pay for dressing. Malpas's secretary too! She's out of a job, isn't she?"

"I've got an idea that Shannon is sweet on her," said Willitt.

"Oh?" Mr. Stormer was not impressed. "Any man is sweet on a good-looking girl. There's nothing to it."

He looked at the telephone thoughtfully, and pulled it towards him.

"I'd like to talk to this man Shannon." he said. "Where will I get him?"

Willitt opened a little pocket-book and searched its pages.

"Here are two numbers: the first is his flat, the second is his office, I think you're more likely to get him at the flat."

Stormer called the flat without success. He then tried the Treasury number which connected him with Scotland Yard.

"Captain Shannon has gone home; he has been gone ten minutes."

"We'll try the flat again," said the detective chief, and this time he had better success, for Dick had just come in.

"It's Stormer speaking. That Captain Shannon?"

"Stormer? Oh, yes, the detective agency."

"Yuh. Say, Captain Shannon, I've been able to help you from time to time—you'll remember I put you on to Slick Smith when he came East?"

Dick, who had forgotten that fact, laughed. "He's been an exemplary criminal since he's been on this side," he said.

"That is how Slick always looks," replied Stormer dryly, "but he's making a living somehow. But that isn't what I wanted to talk to you about, Captain. I understand that my people have got a commission from the late Mr. Marshalt to watch his house. Seems fairly foolish, now he's dead, but the instructions hold, I guess; and I'd be ever so much obliged to you if you'd give my men a little consideration. One of them tells me you questioned his right on the roof of this house in Portman Square, and certainly it looks a little unnecessary. What I want to say is that I've given orders that they are to give the police any help they can, and to put no obstacles in their way."

"That is very kind of you, and I quite see your difficulty."

Stormer smiled to himself. "I guess you don't," he said. "Have you met the caretaker that Marshalt's lawyers have appointed to look after his house?"

"I've seen him."

"Take a good look at him," said Stormer, and rang off before Dick could frame an inquiry.

Mr. Stormer was chuckling to himself as at a good joke, all the way back to the restaurant where he dined that night. For he liked his mysteries; liked better the illusion of omnipotence that he was able to create.

He chose to dine that night at the hotel where Audrey Bedford was living, and after dinner strolled from the dining-room to the vestibule, where he interviewed the reception clerk.

"I find I shan't be able to get home tonight," he said. "Could you let me have a room?"

"Certainly, sir," said the clerk, wondering where was the home of this obvious and patent American. He searched the register. "461?"

"That is a little too high for me. I'd like a room somewhere on the second floor."

Again the clerk consulted his register. "There are two rooms empty, Nos. 255 and 270."

Edgar Wallace

"I guess I'll take 270. Seventy's my lucky number," said Mr. Stormer. The number of Audrey's room was 269.

The Face in the Night

The girl had spent that day looking for work, and greater success was promised her efforts than in the days when she was the Ragged Princess, and had nothing but a prison record and a threadbare costume to recommend her. She had not told Dick Shannon of her plans; she was anxious, as far as possible, to dispense with his assistance. The desire for independence is innate in every woman, and her willingness to accept help from a man is in inverse ratio to her regard for him. Audrey Bedford liked him enough to shrink from his help.

There was a certain amount of humour in her ultimate choice of occupation. Once, in the days of Beak Farm, she had written to a weekly journal, which laboured under the cumbersome title the Amateur Poultry-Keeper and Allotment-Holder. There had developed between Audrey and the editor a long and intimate correspondence about the diet of sick hens, and it had occurred to her that even the Amateur Poultry-Keeper and Allotment-Holder did not appear week after week without some professional assistance. She wrote a letter to the editor, was remembered, and summoned to his untidy office, and there and then offered a position on his staff.

"We want somebody to deal with the poultry correspondence," he said.

The theory that professions influence appearances had some support in the fact that he looked rather like an elderly hen himself.

"I think you will be able to tackle that. We want two columns a week for the paper: the rest you can answer privately. If you find yourself up against some proposition that you can't solve, refer to your reply on the subject in our issue of March 1903. It will give you time."

The salary was not large, certainly insufficient to maintain her in the splendid state which had been hers; but she utilized the remainder of the day to find lodgings, and discovered a very cheery room near to her work. On her way she announced the fact to the assistant manager of the hotel.

"I'm sorry you're leaving us, Miss Bedford," said that gentleman with professional regret. "You'll be giving up your room as from tomorrow at twelve o'clock. We hope to see you again."

She, for her part, hoped he wouldn't. The hotel had unpleasant associations for her, and she was looking forward eagerly to the quietude of her own little room.

Dick had called early to see her, expecting to find her still suffering from the shock of her unpleasant experience of the night before. He was agreeably surprised to learn that she had gone out. Later, one of his men reported that the girl had secured an appointment, and he hurried round to congratulate her.

"You've saved me telephoning for you."

"Why?" he asked quickly. "Has anything happened? You haven't had another communication from—?"

"No." She shook her head. "I don't think I shall; and if I do I shall certainly send for you. I've splendid news."

"You're going back to the poultry business—the editorial side." He laughed at her surprise.

"Of course, your shadow—that is what you call him, isn't it? It's awfully romantic, but a little embarrassing at times, to have a man chasing one. I'd forgotten his existence."

"Why did you want to see me?" She opened her handbag, took out a little pebble, and laid it on his outstretched hand.

"That," she said. "I meant to have told you before."

He stared at the thing open-mouthed, turned it over, and examined the tiny red seal.

"Where on earth did you get this?"

"Is it important?" she asked. "I meant to have told you before, I found it in the hallway at 551, the first time I went to see Mr. Malpas. I dropped the key when I was trying to unlock the door, and, searching for it, I found this little stone."

Dick's mind flashed back to his interview with Brown, or Torrington, who had shown him a similar "stone".

"What is it?" she asked again.

"It is a diamond in the rough. Its value is something like eight hundred pounds."

She gasped. "Are you sure?"

He nodded. Carrying the diamond to the window, he made a closer inspection of the seal.

"You're certain it's a diamond?"

"It is a diamond all right, and the seal is that of the mining company. May I keep this?"

She was relieved. "I wish you would."

"Does anybody else know you have it?"

She shook her head.

"Nobody, unless Mr. Malpas knew, and that isn't likely, is it?"

Dick considered the possibilities. "Nobody else has seen it?"

She thought for a long time.

"I don't think so," she said slowly, "unless—yes, I remember. I went the other day to the reception clerk for the key of my room, and it wasn't there, and I turned everything out of my bag on to the counter, and found it—the key, I mean—in the torn lining."

"That's when he saw it—and when I say 'he', I mean either he or his agent. I should think this partly explains why he tried to get you last night."

Audrey sighed.

"Every day and in every way I am more and more sorry I left my peaceful farm!" she said. "You don't know what a warm feeling I had when my dear poultry editor asked me if I knew how to cure moulting hens!"

She went up to her room that night in a happier frame of mind than she had had in years. She felt that, with her new work, she was leaving behind her the unwholesome atmosphere in which she had moved and lived since her coming to London.

She locked the door of her room, and in her relief was asleep almost as soon as she turned her head on the pillow. And so she slept through the early part of the night, and did not wake till something cold and clammy touched her face.

"Audrey Bedford, I want you," said a hollow voice.

She sat up with a shriek. The room was in complete darkness, except... Not a yard away from her was a face, suspended, it seemed, in mid-air—a face strangely and dimly illuminated...

She stared at the closed eyes, the pain-creased face of Lacy Marshalt!

The Guest Who Disappeared

"The young lady is in a state of collapse. I've sent for a doctor and a nurse."

"Do you know what happened to her?" asked Dick. He was standing by the side of his bed in his pyjamas, telephone in hand.

"No, sir. The porter, who was on the floor below, heard a shriek. He ran upstairs and found Miss Bedford's door open; he saw she had fainted, and sent for me. I was down in the hall below."

"No sign of Malpas?"

"None whatever, sir. There must have been somebody trying to get at her, because the gentleman in the room next to Miss Bedford's was found at the end of the passage, knocked out. He had evidently been clubbed, probably with a rubber stick, for the skin wasn't broken. He has gone off to hospital to have his head dressed."

Dick was at the hotel in five minutes, and the girl was sufficiently recovered to receive him. She sat before the gas fire in her dressing- gown, very white, but, as usual, perfectly self-possessed.

"There's nothing to tell, except that I saw Mr. Marshalt."

"You saw him too, did you?" Dick bit his lip thoughtfully.

"Have you seen him?" she asked in amazement. He nodded.

"Yes, we had a vision of him last night. Do you remember no more?"

"I'm afraid I fainted," she said ruefully. "It was a dreadfully feminine thing to do, but one gets that way. The porter told me that the man in the next room was badly hurt. Oh, Dick, what does it mean?"

"It means that Marshalt is alive and in the hands of this old devil," said

Dick. "Last night we found a hypodermic in the house; we had the stuff analysed and discovered it to be a drug that would have the result of reducing a man to complete unconsciousness—a mixture of hyoscin, morphia and another drug that hasn't been identified. Tonight I had a letter from Malpas." He took out a sheet of typewritten paper. "This is a copy; the original has gone to the Yard for finger-print tests."

She took the letter in her hand, and there was no need for her to ask who had written those straggling lines:

Unless you're a fool, you discovered something last night. Lacy Marshalt is not dead. Knowing him, I ought to have realized that he would take no risks. The bullet-proof singlet he wore under his shirt turned the bullet, as you would have discovered if you had made an examination, instead of being concerned with getting the girl out of the house. I am glad he is alive—death was too good for him, and he will die in my time. If you wish him to live, withdraw your watchers and spies from my house.

"Everything I have found in the house confirms the view," said Dick. "Marshalt is being kept under the influence of this drug, and is either taken on his own feet or carried wherever, Malpas goes."

"It did not seem like a real face to me," interrupted the girl.

This was a new idea to Dick Shannon.

"You mean, it might have been a mask? That might be an explanation. Yet, if it were so, why should this man write as he does? No, I think his letter is true. The reference to the hypodermic suggests that he was forced into telling the truth by Steel's discovery. It is a quaint case altogether. I'm going now to see after our unknown friend—I presume your scream aroused him and he came upon both Malpas and his burden—if burden it was—and was clubbed for his pains."

The injured visitor had left the hotel, for a hospital, as he said. His name on the register was "Henry Johnson, of South Africa". The clerk who had received him was not on duty, so Dick had to be content with that information; and, leaving instructions that he was to be notified when the unknown guest returned, he went home. He drove on to Portman Square, there to learn that nothing exceptional had happened. The inspector and three men were in the house; he saw Willitt's watcher in the street outside.

Leaving, he remembered Stormer's reference to the caretaker, and, early the next morning, Dick Shannon was a caller at Marshalt's house. He had had very little time to consider the effect of Marshalt's disappearance upon his household, but he knew, as a matter of fact, that the man had given very exact instructions as to what should happen in the event of his death. Within a few hours of the news being published, a representative from Lacy's lawyer had visited the house, taken complete control, and removed Marshalt's papers. It was on the following day Dick heard that a caretaker had been appointed in accordance with Lacy Marshalt's wishes, but he had had no occasion to call, the police work being in the hands of the local inspector, and, so far as he was concerned, the caretaker had remained invisible.

A servant, whom he remembered, opened the door and showed him into the drawing-room where he had last seen poor old Tonger.

"I suppose things have changed very considerably with you?" he said to the maid.

"Oh, yes, sir. The whole house has been upset; cook has gone, and there are only Milly and I left. Wasn't it dreadful about poor Mr. Tonger, and poor Mr. Marshalt too?"

It was evident to Dick that the death of Tonger had distressed the house considerably more than the fate that had overtaken its owner.

"You have a caretaker now?"

The girl hesitated.

"Not exactly a caretaker, sir," she said. "The gentleman was a friend of Mr. Marshalt's."

"Indeed?" said Dick, to whom this was news. "I had no idea that Mr. Marshalt—" He checked himself, not wishing to speak disparagingly of the woman's employer. "I did not know that. Who is it?"

"A Mr. Stanford, sir."

Dick's jaw dropped. "Not Bill Stanford?"

"Yes, sir; Mr. William Stanford. I'll tell him you're here, sir; he's upstairs in master's study."

"Let me save you the trouble," said Dick with a smile. "Mr. Stanford and I are old acquaintances."

Bill was sitting in front of a big fire, his feet on the silver fender, an enormous cigar in the corner of his mouth, and on his knees a sporting newspaper. As he looked round, he rose with an embarrassed smile.

"Good morning. Captain. I was expecting to see you before."

"So you're the caretaker?"

Bill smiled. "I'm the man in charge," he said. "Nobody was more- surprised than I when his lawyers came for me, because he wasn't exactly a friend of mine. We were not in the same set, so to speak."

"You knew him in South Africa, of course?" nodded Dick.

"That's it; that's how I came to know him at all. Why I should have been sent for... but there it was in black and white, with my full name- and address written down—William Stanford, of 114 Backenhall Mansions, with the amount I was to be paid and everything."

"A will, one presumes?"

"No, sir, it wasn't a will. It looked as though Marshalt expected to be called away suddenly one of these days. It said nothing about his death; it only said 'if he should disappear from any cause whatsoever, the said William Stanford, etc., etc.'"

Bill Stanford! The friend, and by some considered to be the confederate, of the Eltons! Dick pulled up a chair and sat down.

"What does Martin think of this?"

Stanford shrugged his shoulders.

"I should worry about what Martin thinks," he said, with a curl of his lip. "Martin's a bit sore at me because—" He hesitated. "Well, he thought I knew a lot more than I did know. He got an idea that I was friendly with Lacy and knew all his secrets. I'll give Lacy this credit, that when it came to love affairs, he never told."

Dick didn't ask for any further information on that subject.

"It's dull, especially at night. I'm allowed to go out in the afternoon for a couple of hours, but there's a creepiness about this house that certainly gets on my nerves."

It almost seemed as if he were sincere; his voice dropped to a whisper, and involuntarily he looked round.

"I don't know what your boys get up to next door, but there are some quaint noises on the other side of the wall," he said; "And last night, Moses! I thought the house was coming down. Something happened, too. When I looked out of my bedroom window—that's Lacy's old room—I saw the street full of flatties—I beg your pardon, policemen."

"Call them 'flatties' if it pleases you," said Dick. "Yes, there was something doing. You didn't by any chance have an overflow meeting of ghosts in this house?"

Stanford shivered.

"Don't talk about ghosts, Captain," he begged. "Why, last night I thought I saw—well, that's foolish anyway."

"You thought you saw Marshalt."

"No—the other man, Malpas. How did you know?" asked the other, surprised.

"Malpas is the busiest ghost in London. Where did you see him?"

"Coming out of the store-room—at least, standing in the doorway. Only for a second."

"What did you do?"

Bill smiled sheepishly.

"I got upstairs as fast as I could and locked myself in," he said. "Back chat with ghosts ain't in my repertoire."

Shannon got up.

"I'll take a peep at that store-room if you don't mind."

"You're welcome," said Stanford, pulling out a drawer and taking a large bunch of keys. "It's a fool room that old Tonger used to use for keeping the governor's cartridges and guns, and junk of that kind."

It lay, Dick found, at the end of the hall-passage, and was filled with an indescribable medley of guns, saddles, old boxes, cleaning materials, dilapidated brooms, and all the equipment that untidy cleaners thrust away out of sight. It had one small window, heavily barred, and there was a fire-place, covered up now. At the far end of the room was a rough bench, on which was a gas-ring, a small, rusty vice, and a few tools. There was nothing remarkable about the apartment except its untidiness, and...

"What are in these boxes?"

"I don't know; I haven't looked," said Stanford.

Shannon pulled back the sliding lid of one of the wooden receptacles, and disclosed a number of small, green-labelled cartons.

"Revolver ammunition," said Dick, "and one package has been removed recently."

The under packet was free from dust, he saw.

"What makes you think it was Malpas?"

"I don't know: it was just the description I've had of him," said Stanford vaguely. "I've never seen him in my life."

He evidently expected Dick to take his departure and with difficulty concealed his annoyance when the Commissioner led the way up the broad stairs to the study. Dick stopped to examine the door which shut off Marshalt's private apartment.

"This still functions?" he asked.

"As far as I know," said the other sulkily. "It's no good asking me questions about this house. Captain Shannon: I'm a lodger."

"So you are," said Shannon sympathetically, and turned, as if to go. The man's relief showed in spite of himself.

"I really believe you are anxious to get rid of me," bantered the detective.

Stanford murmured something about not caring one way or the other.

"And how are our friends the Eltons?"

"I don't know anything about the Eltons," said Stanford, resigned. "They have never been great friends of mine."

And now the unwelcome visitor really took his departure. Stanford went downstairs with him and closed the door with a grimace of satisfaction. He returned to the study, locking the partition door behind him, opened a second door which communicated with the little dining-room, and a man stepped out.

"You've got good ears, Martin," he said. Martin walked to the window, and through the heavy gauze curtain that covered the lower pane followed Dick Shannon with his eyes until he was out of sight.

"Early or late, I fall against that bird," he said without heat. "Yes—I've good hearing. I knew it was he the moment I heard voices in the hall. How long are you staying here? There's a job coming along—"

Stanford spread out his arms in a gesture of regret.

"Can't take it, Martin—sorry. Somehow I feel that I ought to play square with poor Lacy. The money's nothing, but I'll stay here just as long as they want me. I regard it as a duty."

Martin laughed softly.

"What did Lacy leave in the way of money?" he asked.

"So far as I know, nothing," said the other in a grieved tone. "It's not pickings I'm after. I was a friend of Lacy's—?"

"You never told me."

"I told you I knew him," protested the other. "Dora knows we were old friends."

"Do you know Malpas?"

The man's eyes narrowed. "Yes—I know Malpas." He dropped his voice until it was almost inaudible. "And if it comes to pickings, I know just where to pick!"

There was doubt and suspicion in the face turned towards him.

"Where is he?" he asked, and Stanford laughed loudly. "Think it out, Elton," he said. "Think of all the people who hated Lacy with good reason, think of all the clever men and women who could act an old man at a minute's notice—think it out, boy, and then take three guesses!"

A Job for Audrey

Mr. Stormer arrived at his office at an unusually early hour. He was on the premises long before any of his clerks or his manager put in an appearance;

and Willitt was amazed to hear the buzzer sounding as he came into his own bureau. He found his Chief lying on a sofa, looking something of a wreck.

"Are you ill, sir?" he asked in alarm.

"Not ill, but dying," growled Stormer. "Get me some strong coffee and a keg of phenacetin. Oh, my head!"

He touched his scalp gingerly and winced.

"My brain capacity has increased to the extent of one cubic foot," he said. "There's a lump here as big as an egg, and no chicken's egg, either. And talking of chickens, go after that girl Bedford. No, sir, this is an ostrich's or a dinosaur's."

"Did you get into trouble last night?"

"Did I get into trouble last night?" repeated his Chief wearily. "Would I be lying here like a sick cow if I hadn't been in trouble? Do gaiety and lightheartedness grow eggs on a man's head? Yes, sir, I was in trouble. Get me some vinegar. And listen! You're in a secret. Nobody is to know that this affliction has come upon me, and if anybody makes inquiries, I am in the United States—where I ought to be."

Willitt hastened out and brought all his Chief required. "Now 'phone up a barber; go round to the nearest collar shop and get something to make me look respectable."

"Is it cut?"

"No, sir, it isn't cut. I have concussion of the brain, but I am not cut."

He winced as he sat up and took the coffee from the tray where Willitt had placed it.

"You're aching to ask me what happened," he groaned as he sipped the coffee. "Well, I'll tell you. I had a fight with a ghost—at least, he, or somebody who was with him, did all the fighting."

"Who was it?"

"I don't know; I saw nobody. I heard a scream and went out to see what was happening, and saw one, two, three, or maybe it was six, people running down the corridor, and I went after them. The same number of people lammed me on the head, and I came to earth in time to prevent the hotel detective stealing my watch. Maybe he was only opening my collar, but I mistrust hotel detectives. Now, you're not to forget that girl. She's got a job at the Hen's Herald, a paper run in the interests of introspective fowls, and I guess she's not going to like it. You know her, don't you?"

"Yes, sir; I've met her."

"Well, see her again and offer her a good job. Any salary that seems to her on the generous side which may suggest itself to you, but you've got to fix her—you understand?"

"Yes, sir."

"Here comes the barber, and after he's gone I'm going to sleep, and it will be death to any man who disturbs me. When does Miss Bedford start work?"

"This morning."

"Get to her as soon as you can. She'll probably come out to lunch, and that'll be your opportunity. You can tell her I've got a job that she can do in a cosy chair with her feet on the fender. I want her to watch Torrington, who calls himself Brown. And, believe me, that guy wants watching! Make it appealing—get into your mind that you're giving something away. And, say, Willitt, don't come back here with a tale of failure; I'm that ill I'd be very offensive to you."

It was a novel experience for Audrey to find herself "going to work"; to be one of the crowd that fringed the subway platform, to struggle for her strap or to fight for a place on a bus already overcrowded. The novelty of it did not quite compensate for its discomfort, but she had a very satisfactory feeling when she eventually reached the out-of-the-way office of the little paper, and found herself established in a corner of the editorial sanctum.

Mr. Hepps gave her a cold and perfunctory greeting, and flung over a heap of letters that had evidently accumulated on his desk for weeks. He was a gaunt, somewhat unclean-looking man, and, she was to discover, a confirmed grumbler. Apparently he was one of those men who believed that praise given to subordinates would arouse in their bosoms a passionate desire for increase of wages. Indeed, the Mr. Hepps she had interviewed the day before and the Mr. Hepps who now barked his instructions, and wrangled about the length of her paragraphs, were two entirely different persons.

She found also that she was expected to work into every answer a small boost for an advertiser.

"Chippers Feed nothing!" he snapped. "What do you want to talk about Chippers Feed for? They don't advertise with us. Cut that out, and tell 'em to use Lowker's."

"Lowker's is poison and death to young chickens," said Audrey firmly. "I would sooner feed them on sawdust."

"What you'd rather do and what I tell you to do are two different things," he roared. "I tell you Lowker's—Lowker goes in!"

Audrey looked at the back of his head. There was a jar of paste within reach. For a second she contemplated a violent assault.

The climax came that afternoon when, having mastered the contents of previous numbers, and having discovered that the announcements of the Java Wire Corporation had appeared in the advertisement columns, she recommended its employment in all sincerity. The paragraph came under his notice, and he stormed at the mouth.

"Java netting is out!" he shouted. "I'd sooner close the paper than boost that business."

"But they advertise."

"They don't advertise any more—that's what! Just say wire net. And your paragraphs are too long. And I don't like your handwriting, miss; can't you use a typewriter? You've got to smarten up if you want to hold this job. Where are you going?" he asked in surprise, as she rose and took down her coat from a peg on the wall.

"Home, Mr. Hepps," she said. "You have shaken my faith in chickens. I never thought they could be put to such base uses."

He stared at her. "I close down here at six."

"I close down at four," said Audrey calmly. "I've had no lunch except a glass of milk and a bun, and the atmosphere of this office is stifling. I'd prefer to work in a hen-house."

"If I'd known you were coming," he said sardonically, "I'd have had—"

"You'd have had the place enlarged—I know. Excuse me if I don't laugh. The fact of the matter is, Mr. Hepps, I am through with this job."

"You can go!" boomed Mr. Hepps, glaring at her over his lop-sided pince-nez. "I'm only sorry I didn't get your character before you came."

"If you did you would have found I'd been in prison," she said.

At his look of horror she gurgled with laughter.

"In prison?" he gasped. "What for?"

"Chicken-stealing," she said promptly, and here ended her first day's employment.

She reached the street, feeling famished, and went straight across the road to the popular tea-shop at which she had looked longingly through the window of her office many times during the course of the day. A man waited whilst she bought a newspaper and followed her in, sitting down at the same marble-topped table. Glancing at him out of the corner of her eye, she thought she had met him before, but was immediately absorbed in the newspaper account of "The Strange Affair at the Regency Hotel", and there learnt that the police had been unable to trace a guest who had been wounded in what had been accurately described as "a midnight affray". Her own name, she was glad to see, was not mentioned. She was referred to as "a young lady of wealth", a description which tickled her. "Excuse me. Miss Bedford." She looked up with a start. It was the man who had followed her into the tea-shop.

"I think we have met before. My name is Willitt; I came down to Fontwell to make a few inquiries."

"Oh, I remember," she smiled. "It wasn't a long interview, was it? I was leaving for London."

"That's right, miss. I represent Stormer's Detective Agency. Maybe you've heard of it?"

She nodded. Stormer's was one of the best known and best respected of these private agencies, which are not very greatly encouraged by the police, and receive little patronage except at the hands of suspicious husbands and wives.

"Mr. Stormer sent me along to have a talk with you."

"With me?" she said in surprise.

"Yes, Miss Bedford. You've heard of our agency? It stands pretty high in the matter of credit and respectability."

"I've heard of it, of course; everybody has heard of it," she said. "What does Mr. Stormer want of me?"

"Well, Miss Bedford"—Willitt had to proceed cautiously, not knowing how she would accept the suggestion—"the truth is, we're short-handed. A lady who did a great deal of work for us got married and left the business, and we've never been able to replace her. Mr. Stormer wondered whether you would like to come into the office?"

"I?" she said incredulously. "You mean, become a woman detective?"

"We shouldn't give you any unpleasant work to do. Miss Bedford," said Willitt earnestly. "We'd put you on to society cases."

"But does Mr. Stormer know my record?"

"You mean about the jewel robbery? Yes, miss, he knows all about that."

The corners of her mouth twitched.

"And is he proceeding on theset-a-thief-to-catch-a-thief principle?"

Even the solemn Willitt laughed. "No, you'll not be asked to catch thieves. We want you for one special job—to watch a man named Torrington."

Audrey's face fell.

"Watch Torrington? And who is Torrington?" she asked.

"He is a very wealthy man, a South African. You are interested in South Africa?"

He saw her flinch.

"Yes, I am rather interested in South Africa," she said, "if all the stories I have heard... are true."

She never had quite believed Dora's bitter gibe, that her father was an American serving a life sentence on the Breakwater, and yet a doubt had been sown in her mind that had not been entirely dispelled. "I don't know how to watch people. Does it mean following them wherever they go? Because I'm afraid I'm unsuitable for that kind of work. Besides"—she smiled—"we have one detective in the family."

And then she went very red.

"That's a joke, Mr. Willitt," she added hurriedly. "I'm in rather a humorous mood today, having spent the day in the bright atmosphere of a chicken murderer."

She gave a brief but vivid account of her day's work, and in Willitt she found a sympathetic listener. When she came again to his offer, he was in a hurry to assure her.

"You won't be asked to follow Tomngton around," he said. "Your job is much easier than that. You will be expected to get acquainted with him."

"What is he—a burglar?"

"No," confessed Willitt, "he's not exactly a burglar."

"Not exactly!" she said, aghast. "Is he a criminal?"

"That was an unfortunate expression of mine," Willitt hastened to assure her. "No, miss, he's perfectly honest; only we want to keep tag of the people who come after him, and we feel that we might get you employed in the same capacity as Mr. Malpas."

"I can't do it. I'd love the work—it sounds thrilling; and there would be a certain amount of fun in it for other reasons."

He didn't ask the reasons, but he could guess the satisfaction Audrey Bedford would feel in revealing herself to a certain high police official.

"Will you consider it?" he begged. "At any rate, we want you in the office."

"Can I see Mr. Stormer?"

"He's gone back to America," said Willitt glibly, "and his last instructions were to secure you at any price."

Audrey laughed.

"I'll try it," she said, and Mr. Willitt breathed a sigh of relief, for if there was one thing in the world he didn't wish to do, it was to make excuses to Stormer.

Returning to headquarters, he found John Stormer in a more amiable frame of mind, and reported his success. "So she kicked at the Torrington job? I guessed she would, but I knew we'd land her!"

Willitt, to whom his employer's prescience was a standing wonder, ventured to put a question. "You seemed sure of getting her—how did you know that she wouldn't be satisfied with the job? Hepps treated her badly, bullied and found fault with her until she couldn't stick it any longer. The man is a brute!"

"Brute, is he? Well, he's changed considerably since I knew him last. I got his son out of pretty bad trouble once—the usual vamp case, with letters and poetry and everything. And then he was mild enough —he doesn't take three baths a day, but he's mild. I guess he must have been crossed in love—maybe his chickens have turned him down. They're mean creatures. That will do, friend."

When Willitt had gone, he used the telephone.

"That you, Mr. Hepps? Stormer speaking. Thank you very much indeed for your help."

"I hated doing it," said the regretful voice of Hepps. "She seems a very nice girl and remarkably capable. I've lost a very good assistant, and, I am afraid, got a very bad name for myself. Personally, I set my face against boosting advertisers in the news columns, and after my treatment of Miss Bedford I feel I can never look a nice girl in the face."

"Maybe they'll be glad," said Stormer.

Mr. Hepps evidently missed this point, for he went on:

"She said she had been in prison—for chicken-stealing. That can't be true, can it?"

"Yuh—that's so," said Stormer. "She's one large hen-roost brigand. Yes, sir. Miss anything in your office, let me know."

He hung up with a large and delightful smile.

The Spotter

Mr. Torrington's suite at the Ritz-Carlton—he was Mr. Brown on the register—was one of the most expensive in an hotel which did not err on the side of cheapness. He saw very few visitors, and, for the matter of that, he was not often visible to the hotel authorities, and, except the manager and the floor-waiter who served his meals in his private dining-room, very few of the staff knew him. It was generally understood that he did not wish to see callers; and when a shabby little man came to the reception bureau and asked that his name should be sent up, the clerk in charge favoured him with an uncomplimentary scrutiny.

"You had better write," he said. "Mr. Brown doesn't see anybody except by appointment."

"He'll see me," said the little man eagerly. "You ask him if he won't. And I've got an appointment with him too."

The clerk was obviously sceptical.

"I'll find out," he said curtly. "What is your name?"

The man told him, and the clerk disappeared into the small room behind the counter, where the wishes of a guest could be discovered without the caller overhearing very often an unflattering description of himself. He came back in a few seconds.

"Mr. Brown has no appointment with you. Where are you from?"

The little man thought rapidly. "I'm from—" He named a famous diamond corporation in Kimberley.

Again the clerk disappeared, and, returning, beckoned a page.

"Take this gentleman up to Mr. Brown's suite," he said, "and wait in the corridor to bring him down again."

Mr. Brown was writing letters when the man was shown in, and he transfixed the visitor through his gleaming glasses.

"You're from De Beers?" he said.

"Well, not exactly De Beers, Mr. Brown," said the little man with an ingratiating smile, "but the truth is, I used to know you in South Africa."

Brown pointed to a chair.

"When was this?" he asked.

"Before you got into trouble, Mr. Brown."

"You must have been young, then, my friend," said Brown with a half-smile.

"I'm older than I look. The fact is, Mr. Brown, I'm on my beam ends, and

I thought you'd like to help an old friend who's fallen on bad times, if I might use that expression—?"

"I'll help you all right, if your story is true; but I confess I don't believe you. I've an excellent memory for faces, and I certainly never forget my friends. Where did we meet?"

The visitor made a shot at random.

"Kimberley," he said. He knew that Kimberley was the centre of the diamond-mining industry.

"I was in Kimberley," said the other; "but then, everybody in the diamond business has been to Kimberley at some time or other. You will, of course, remember my name in those days?"

But the visitor was equal to the occasion. "I remember it," he said firmly, "but nothing would induce me to say it. If a gentleman wants to be called Mr. Brown—well, Mr. Brown's good enough for me. The truth is"—here an inspiration came to him—"I was doing a sentence at the same time as you."

"Fellow jail-birds, eh?" said the other good-humouredly, and put his hand in his pocket. "I don't remember you, but I've taken a great deal of trouble to forget a lot of people I met on the Breakwater."

There was a letter on the table which the old man had just finished writing. The visitor saw the flourishing signature, but the note-paper was too far away from him to read. If he could find some excuse for going to the other side of the table he would be absolutely sure that his information was correct, and, moreover, be in possession of a fact that not even the Clever Ones knew.

The old man pulled out his case and put a Treasury note upon the table. "I hope you have better luck," he said. The little man took the note, rolled it into a ball, and, before the astonished eyes of his benefactor, tossed it into the fire-place that lay directly behind him. Mr. Brown turned in amazement, and in that second the signature was read.

"I don't want your money," said the little man. "Do you think I'm only here for what I can get out of you? You can keep your money—Torrington!"

Daniel Torrington looked at him sharply. "You know my name, then, eh? Pick up that money, man, and don't be a fool. What do you want if you don't want money?"

"A shake of the 'and," whined the other, but nevertheless picked up the crumpled note, which he had been careful to toss no further than was consistent with its safety.

Torrington showed him to the door and closed it upon him. Then he came back to his chair, trying to recall the man's face. Nobody had known him in prison as Torrington; he had had a number for many years, but nothing else, until one of the guards had addressed him as "Brown" in a facetious moment, and that name had stuck. How did this man—?

Then his eyes fell upon the letter, and he understood. What did he want? What had been the object of the visit? He had never heard of spotters and their audacity, of the risks run by these reporters of the underworld. There were others who found them most useful.

Dora Tells the Truth

Martin walked home, after his visit to Marshalt's house, outwardly unperturbed. Dora had not come down and he refused breakfast for himself. There were half a dozen letters for his discussion, but he no more than glanced at them, until he turned to their contents for relief. He was making a halfhearted attempt to write a letter, when Dora came into the room. She was in her neglige—she seldom dressed before lunch unless she had very urgent business indeed. One quick glance at her told him that she had not slept very well—there were shadows under her fine eyes and tiny crow's-feet that had never shown before.

He gave her a simple "good morning" and tried to make a job of his letters. He put his pen down at last. "Dora... what sort of work were you doing before I met you?"

She looked up from the paper she was scanning idly. "What do you mean? Acting."

"What sort of acting—how did you start? I've never asked you before, my dear."

She returned to the contemplation of the morning news, expecting him to press the question. When he did not: "I started with Marsh and Bignall on the road: chorus girl. Marsh went broke, and left us flat in a No. 3 town, with not enough money to pay our fare back to London. I went with a trick-shooting act for three months, and then got into Jebball's fit-up show. I was everything from leading woman to props! I learnt more about electric wiring than most mechanics know—" She stopped suddenly. "I did everything," she said shortly, and then: "Why do you speak of this?"

"I was wondering," he answered. "It is queer, but I never thought of you except as..."

"The clinging ivy? When you met me I was on the way to provincial fame. It wouldn't have got me far. A provincial star doesn't make a lot of money, and I guess I'd never have reached a pretty little house in Curzon Street—honestly. But I was doing well by comparison. Why do you ask?"

"Where did you meet Marshalt?"

She had gone back to her newspaper, he saw her hand tremble and did not press the question. But after a while:

"Here in London. I wish I had died before I did." He was on more painful ground here, no less for himself than for her.

"Dora, are you fond of him?" She shook her head.

"'I hate him—hate him!" she said, with such vehemence that he was taken aback. "You think that means... something? You've got it fixed in your mind that I haven't been a... a good wife to you. I know you feel that. I'll tell you the worst that happened. I loved him. I had ideas of breaking with our life and getting you to let me divorce you. But I was good. I was so good that I wearied him. But I'm old-fashioned in a way. And besides, goodness pays. Easy women are like easy money—they don't last long, and when they're expended a man goes after something new. A woman can only keep a man by his wantings. Bunny, when he died, I knew. I don't mean his death in the flesh—but I felt the tremendous change in him. Just as I felt when Audrey died... yes, she died—the old relationship, bad as it was, had a meaning."

He lay back in his chair, looking at her from under his black eyelashes.

"You don't think he is dead?" The quick, impatient lift of her hands was an answer, even if she had not spoken.

"I don't know. He doesn't feel that way to me. And I care nothing."

She was sincere; he was sure of this.

"Did he ever speak to you of Malpas?"

"The old man? Yes, he often spoke of him. The only time I have seen him really nervous was when he talked about 'the man next door'. Malpas hated him. He used to pretend to the police and people that he knew nothing about him, but he did. He said Malpas and he were partners in the old days and that he ran away with Malpas's wife—I forget all he told me. Did you see Stanford?"

He nodded.

"Did he say anything? Of course, I knew they were acquainted."

"Acquainted?" He laughed. "Bosom friends, I should think. Stanford was never a communicative sort of person, but I should have thought he would have told me that he was a friend of Marshalt's."

He got up, walked across to the back of the settee where she was sitting, and laid his hands on her shoulders.

"Thank you… for all you've said. I think you and I will get straight. How are you feeling towards Audrey?"

She was silent.

"You still feel sore? But why? That is a little unreasonable isn't it? If this man was the only trouble?"

"I don't know." She shrugged her shoulders. "My dislike of Audrey is ingrained, I'm afraid. I was brought up to dislike her."

"I'm sorry," said Martin, patted her gently on the shoulder, again, and went out.

He had an appointment in the City. Funds were running low; one of his gambling houses, the most lucrative, had been raided, and it had cost him the greater part of a thousand pounds to hush up his connection therewith. But the fact that he had been blackmailed by his nominee neither surprised nor shocked him. It was one of those inevitable contingencies for which he was always prepared. There was something like a recognized scale in such cases.

He owed something to Dora in one respect, he remembered, as his car threaded the busy City streets: she had made it impossible to handle the clever handiwork of a certain Italian engraver who specialized in mills notes, so perfectly printed that even the Bank of France was deceived. Stanford had passed them on to another purchaser and that gentleman had been caught with the goods and was now awaiting trial.

Martin lived on "touches", and "touches" had been scarce. It seemed that all the suckers in the world had suddenly been put under lock and key, and it looked, too, as though he were to be reduced to the expedient –the last resort of every crook—of running a bucket-shop and selling those oil shares which look so good on paper. It was not a profession that appealed to him; and though he met his man and settled the preliminaries of the new business, he had no heart in it.

He lunched alone at a restaurant in Soho, and there appeared the inevitable "spotter". At another time he would have shaken off the sly- faced man who sidled up to his table with an apologetic smile and took a seat uninvited. But now Martin's finances were in such a state that he could not afford to miss any chance; and although he expected little from the informer, he wanted to hear what that little was.

The spotter's approach to Martin Elton was slightly different from the direct method he employed with such notorieties as Slick Smith.

"Glad to see you, Mr. Elton. Haven't seen you for a long time… thank you, I'll have a brandy. Things are pretty bad round here, Mr. Elton."

"Round here" meant round almost any place where men were not troubled with too stringent a regard for mine and thine…

"I thought trade was looking up?" said Martin conventionally.

"Ah, your trade might be." The spotter shook his head sorrowfully. "I'm thinking about the poor hooks and crooks, Mr. Elton. Not that I've got any good word for them—they're low people. Even with them, trade wouldn't be so bad if they knew all I knew."

"And what do you know?" asked Elton, keeping up the pretence.

The spotter sunk his voice. "I've got something for you—and I'm the only spotter in town that's got next to it! Found it out myself too. The Clever Ones are always talking about it, but it took me to clean up the way in!"

He smiled complacently.

"That fellow who is supposed to be coming from South Africa has been here over a year! He's been in 'bird'—got a lifer—but he's as rich as—" He mentioned a number of eminent financiers. "And richer!"

"In 'bird'? What did he do?"

"Shot a fellow or sump'n. But he was released more than a year ago, and I tell you he's worth a million—and more! The Clever Ones got the office that he was coming out, but they didn't know that he was here in England—in London. It shows you that the Clever Ones don't know everything."

"Clever Ones" was a vague description—Martin knew it to signify the gangs that did not depend upon the little man for their information.

"From South Africa, you say?" he asked, suddenly interested. "He's been in prison—on the Breakwater? Was it for I.D.B.?"

"It's something to do with buying diamonds. There's a law in South Africa that sends a man to the Awful Place for years and years if he buys diamonds. I can't understand the Clever Ones not finding him. He's a lame man—"

"Lame?" Martin half rose to his feet. "What is his name?"

"Well, he goes by the name of Brown, but his real name's Torrington —Daniel Torrington. And, Mr. Elton, that fellow's easy—"

Martin slipped some money to the man, paid his bill and went home. Dora was going out, and was on the doorstep when h arrived. "I want you for one minute, Dora," he said.

He took her up to the drawing-room and closed the door; "You remember last time Audrey was here? You taunted her with having a name which didn't belong to her; you told her her father was a convict on the Breakwater for diamond-stealing. Was that true?"

"Yes," she said in surprise. "Why?"

"I asked you that night about him, and you told me he was shot before his arrest, and was lame. What was the name of Audrey's father?"

She was frowning at him suspiciously.

"Why do you want to know?"

"My dear"—a little impatiently—"it is not caprice that makes me ask. Will you tell me?"

"His name was Daniel Torrington," she said.

Martin whistled.

"Torrington? I wonder! It must be the same man. He's here in London."

"Audrey's father?" she gasped. "But he's in prison: he's there for life! Marshalt told me that. That is why he wanted to marry Audrey."

"He knew that she was Torrington's daughter? You never told me that."

"There are so many things I didn't tell you," she said petulantly, "that it is hardly worth while going over them now." And then, in sudden contrition: "I'm sorry I snap so, Martin: I so easily lose patience in these days. Yes, Torrington was serving a life sentence."

"He was released more than a year ago," said Martin, "and has been in London most of that time."

He saw the expression that came to her face, and asked quickly: "Did Marshalt know that?"

She shook her head.

"No; if he had known, he wouldn't have been so happy. Oh!" Her hand went up to her mouth. "Malpas!" she whispered.

He gazed at her in amazement, as there occurred to him the same thought that brought the word to her lips.

"Marshalt must have known, or guessed," she said in an awe-stricken whisper. "He was in the next house all the time. Bunny, Malpas is Torrington!"

The New Heiress

"Torrington! That can't be," said Martin. "What object would he have, a man of Torrington's wealth? A story like that is all right in novels and poetry, but I'm satisfied with the cold statistics of the prison service, which show that crimes of vengeance represent about one in five thousand of the cases that are tried in England. A man doesn't hate so much that he'll spend twenty years of his life planning how to get the better of an enemy. Especially Torrington, who is looking for his daughter."

Her eyes met his.

"Is that why he's here—are you sure?" she asked quickly, and he shrugged his thin shoulders.

"I know nothing; I am merely going on the probabilities of the case. What is more likely than that Torrington has been spending his money to locate your mother and his child?"

She shook her head. "You're wrong," she said quietly. "Torrington thinks Audrey is dead. Mother told him that, and so did Marshalt. He knew mother in the old days. She only received one letter from Torrington in prison—it was all about the child. It was on the advice of Marshalt that mother wrote and said that Audrey had died of scarlet fever. Marshalt wrote at the same time with the news. He never told me what he put into the letter, but he was out to hurt Torrington. Why, there's a tablet up to her memory in a church in Rosebank, in the Cape Peninsula! Torrington arranged with the prison chaplain for the slab to be put up. I am sure because Marshalt told me a whole lot after he discovered that Audrey was my sister. If Torrington isn't Malpas, then Lacy had another enemy."

Martin Elton was pacing the room, his hands in his pockets, a far- away look in his eyes.

"What do you think Torrington is worth?"

"Over two million pounds," she said.

"What do you think he'd pay to know—the truth?"

She snapped round on him in a fury.

"Give Audrey—that!" she said between her teeth. "Give her a father and millions to play with, whilst I'm down here in the gutter, with a crook for a husband, and the riff-raff of the underworld for friends! Are you mad? You're not to do it, Martin!"

She came up to him and brought her face and her hard eyes so close to his that he stepped back a pace. "Not for all the money in the world would I do it. If Torrington is her father, let him find her. He will have some job!"

"What is her name?"

"Dorothy Audrey Torrington. He doesn't know she is called Audrey. She hadn't been christened when Torrington was taken to prison. He chose Dorothy and wrote of her as Dorothy, but she was never called by that name."

He was looking at her.

"What do you think?"

"She need never have it," he said slowly. "Write to her!"

She stared at him in helpless anger.

"Write to her, or see her—better write to her first, Tell her to come to tea," he said. "Tell her the shock of Marshalt's death has made all the difference, and you want to express your sorrow for all the unkind things you've said and all the—lies you have told."

"I'll never do it, Martin, not for you—?"

"Say that twice in your letter—all the lies you have told about her parentage. And when she comes, tell her that what you've said about her was true of yourself."

"I'll see you—?"

"Wait—why wasn't she called by the name he chose?" She made an impatient gesture.

"How could she be? It was mine—he didn't know my second name was Dorothy, and mother didn't realize it until after Audrey was registered. We couldn't have two Doras in the family."

"And where can I get Audrey's birth certificate?" She knit her forehead.

"I wonder if I have it," she said. "If I have, I've never seen it; but mother left a lot of papers that I've never looked at from the day they came into my hands. Get them down, Bunny; they're on the top shelf of my wardrobe."

He came back with an old tin box; it was locked and there was no key, but Bunny opened it without trouble. It was packed full of photographs, old share certificates that in some way or other had come into Mrs. Bedford's possession, and which Dora, who knew the woman's story by heart, was well aware were worthless. In a blue envelope at the bottom of the box she found two papers.

"That is my birth certificate," she said, "and this is Audrey's."

He spread it open on the table.

"Dorothy Audrey Torrington," he read, and his eyes were gleaming. "What is your name, Dora?"

"Nina Dorothy Bedford—it was mother's name before she was married to Torrington."

"I could turn that 'Audrey' into something else—Audrey will not do. Your name would stand. You'll write to her, Dora," he said deliberately, "and you'll tell her, with or without the accompaniment of tears, that she is your elder sister."

"But that is impossible—" she began.

"You'll tell her this. Age isn't provable. And if she remembers too distinctly—" His face was set and hard. "I've got a soft place in my heart for a girl in trouble, and I'll tell you that, if I could have helped Audrey, if I could help her now, I would. But there's a million in this, and I'm going out for it."

"You mean—" Her voice was scarcely above a whisper.

"I mean, you're Dorothy Torrington."

"But suppose she does remember? And she will, Bunny. Why, I had my hair up long before she!"

He nodded. "Then she's got to go somewhere and forget," he said. "Nobody knows that Audrey is Torrington's daughter—?"

There was a tap at the door and the maid came in.

"Will you see Mr. Smith, sir?" she said. "Mr. S. Smith of Chicago?"

Mr. S. Smith Brings News

There was a silence, and then Martin said:

"Show him up here. You know this fellow, don't you?" he asked.

"I met him once; you know when. I don't think I'll wait."

"You'd better," said her husband. "He is one of those shrewd crooks that would put two and two together and make it ten. I wonder what he wants?"

To say that Mr. Smith was in a genial mood is merely to state that he was normal. He had the appearance of having come from a fashionable wedding. His well-fitting morning-coat, his polished boots and white spats, no less than the silk hat he put so tenderly on a chair, were alike splendid.

"Sorry to interrupt you. You going out, ma'am?"

He looked at the door. Dora was dressed for the street, for she had been on her way out when Martin had arrived.

"I'd have got here before, but I had to shake a trailer."

Martin's face darkened.

"Might I suggest that, in those circumstances, you might have kept your trail from passing through my front doorway?"

"I shook it." Mr. Smith smiled blandly. "There isn't an amateur detective in the world who can trail me, once I give my mind to the business of beating him. Not even Stormer's sleekest sleuth can get his nose down on me."

With a flourish he pulled a grey silk handkerchief from his breast pocket, patted his lips gently, and replaced the handkerchief.

"I was going out, if you'll excuse me—?"

"That is unfortunate," said Mr. Smith gravely. "I had a few words to say to you, and I'm thinking it will interest you, too, to know that a member of the ancient house of Bedford has joined the unholy congregation of Busy Bees."

"What are you getting at?" asked Martin.

"I'm getting at a revelation which I should like to make as dramatic as possible. Audrey, your respected sister-in-law, has joined the police."

Martin frowned. He was not quite sure about this man, except in one respect: that he could dispense alike with his co-operation and his company.

"What stuff are you giving me?" he asked gruffly. "Audrey joined the police?"

"When I say 'the police' I exaggerate, although Stormer's are as near to the official blues as you can get in this country."

"You mean she's joined Stormer's staff?" asked Martin. J Mr. Smith nodded.

"I discovered it by accident," he said. "Saw her going into Stormer's office with Willitt—that's the child's portion of cheese who is Stormer's vice-regent on earth. Now I know Stormer's; they seem to have had me trailed since I was so high. I don't remember the time when Stormer's didn't intrude in my life or obtrude upon my profession; and naturally I'm deeply interested in those birds. I know Stormer's methods. He's introduced into England a system that has never been here before, and isn't recognized, anyhow—the badge system. Every Stormer man has one, a little silver star with his name stamped on the back. I suppose they do it here because it is done in America. Though badges in this country mean no more than fraternity pins. I watched the girl go in and come out again with Willit, and round they went to Lobell's, the jewellers on Cheapside, and I happen to know that Lobell's supply this Star of Hope. There wasn't any need for me to go in; you could see them inside the shop from the ring section of the window, and sure enough there was her ladyship cooing with joy. They parted at the door. Willitt went to the nearest telephone box, and what do you think he did?"

"Telephoned," said Martin laconically, and Mr. Smith beamed his admiration.

"You've a brain, Elton. Yes, sir, he telephoned—to the Ritz- Carlton. 'Phoned to the Ritz-Carlton for a suite for the lady."

Again he drew his handkerchief, this time to dust his immaculate boots.

"Mr. Brown, or Torrington, is staying at the Ritz-Carlton," he said, apropos of nothing.

And so staggered were Martin and his wife by the news that they did not simulate an ignorance of Mr. Torrington.

"Thought I'd tell you. Maybe it'll be useful to know that young Miss Bedford can be very dangerous, especially to the folk that Wily Wilfred has sent chasing Torrington's millions."

Martin knew that he was referring to the spotter in these terms, and was visibly uncomfortable.

"He's a good fellow," Smith went on, "but given to syndicating his news, and that's where his value drops to nothing. I've got out of him this afternoon that he put you on to Torrington... I thought perhaps you'd like to know."

"Thank you," Martin found his voice to say. "I take very little notice of the stories these men tell."

"And you're wise," agreed Smith.

His bright eyes were fixed on Dora. "Nice girl, your young sister," he said.

Martin almost dropped. The man might have been standing outside the door, listening to the conversation that took place before his arrival. Dora was less liable to be thrown off her balance.

"You mean Audrey?" she asked, and laughed. "People invariably amuse me when they refer to Audrey as my younger sister. I am exactly a year younger than she."

Dora was a perfect opportunist.

"What makes you think we're interested in Audrey Bedford's movements, Smith?"

The crook suspended his boot-dusting operations for a second, and looked up.

"Family affection," he said, "plus the precarious nature of our mutual profession. She's going to give trouble, mark my words. The bogey- man nearly caught her the other night, and if it hadn't been for a certain person he would."

"You mean Malpas? Was she the lady at the Regency?"

Mr. Smith nodded.

"That was nothing. His big try was on the Outer Circle in the park. She's popular. That's the third man who's tried to catch her, and the third man that's failed. I've an idea I shall be going to the funeral of the fourth. She's hoodoo for all honest crooks."

And that seemed to complete his business, for he found no excuse for staying.

"I'll get along now," he said, "having done what I conceive to be my duty. That young sister of yours is certainly mustard, Mrs. E."

He did not emphasize "young", but Martin Elton knew that he had used the word deliberately, and when he had gone he turned to his wife.

"Smith wants a 'cut'. If we pull off this job, it'll cost us twenty thousand to keep him quiet—perhaps more. It all depends what happens to Audrey."

In a Haymarket Flat

The ceaseless thunder of traffic, the never-ending rumble of heavy buses, and the pandemonium of cab-horns and newsboys notwithstanding, Dick Shannon's Haymarket flat was a quiet spot. The ear can grow accustomed to sounds which at first deafen and bewilder, and, as growing accustomed, can filter them out of hearing.

The first intimation Dick Shannon had that the Portman Square case was getting on his nerves was the discovery that the sound-filter no longer functioned. Noises came up from the street to disturb and irritate him; the banging of a taxi-cab door made him jump.

He was engaged in a cold-blooded review of all the circumstances attending the disappearance of Lacy Marshalt and the death of his servant, and he had scribbled on a pad before him four links of the chain that refused to fit.

First of these was the battered man who had been recovered in the fog from the river. Second, the woman found dead in the park. Third, Tonger's death, and the fourth the passing of Marshalt himself.

Stanford was a new factor, unconsidered until then; a shadowy figure in the background, known well enough to the police, but associated with gangs that he had thought Marshalt could not have known but for his friendship with Dora Elton.

He opened a loose-leaf binder, packed tight with typewritten manuscript, and turned the leaves slowly. There was the very detailed story of the man who was evidently Laker; shorter and less satisfactory particulars of the unknown woman of the park; and the longest dossier of all was that which dealt with Tonger. He read to refresh his memory, though almost every word of the report he knew by heart.

"Tonger wore a grey tweed suit, black slippers, blue-striped shirt, white collar... pockets contained 7 in English money, 200 francs, the stub of a return ticket by Instone Line to Paris (Note—Tonger went to France on the morning of his death to deliver a letter to unknown addressee, returning same day, verified by Customs, Paris, and Customs, Croydon); old gold watch. No. 984371, gold chain, two keys, pocket-case containing prescription for bromide of potassium mixture (Note—Prescription issued by Dr. Walters of Park Street, Tonger having described himself as in a highly nervous state and unable to sleep); three 5 notes and a triangular bodkin...”

Dick looked up at the ceiling. Triangular bodkin? That home-made bodkin had puzzled him before; but though he kept it in the house, hoping that a constant view of it would suggest to him its use, no inspiration had come.

He opened a little safe in the corner of the room, took out a flat box and examined the bodkin now, with the aid of a magnifying glass. Expert engineers had already examined and measured it, and had supplied a great deal of meaningless data. He picked the tiny rod up and looked at it curiously. The instrument was four inches in length, blunt at the point, and terminating in a handle like a corkscrew. Near this the steel widened until at a place where it fitted into the wood it was nearly an inch across; and here the evidence of amateur work was clear even to the non- technical observer. Dick remembered the vice and files in the store-room, and guessed that this queer tool was fashioned there. But for what purpose?

The almost flat handle was detachable. Nevertheless, the bodkin must have been of an inconvenient shape to be carried in a pocket-book, as the bulging leather of the case told him.

There was nothing in Laker's dossier, nor in that of the unknown woman, which offered any possible hope of identification. Nor had Marshalt's papers, before they were removed by the lawyer, given him any hint that was of value. Dick had examined the missing millionaire's banking account, but apparently he had banked with various establishments; for in the only one traceable there was nothing to suggest great possessions. Marshalt's few directorships yielded him very little income, for they were either struggling concerns or were actually on the verge of bankruptcy.

A search of Malpas's house and an inspection of his passbook had been even less informative. He put away the casebook, filled and lit a pipe, and, leaning back in his chair, went over and over the case until his brain reeled.

Suddenly he sat up with a start and looked towards the curtained window. He had heard a rattling of stones against the glass. It was early in the evening, and it seemed an unnecessary method of attracting attention, when a perfectly good electric bell was available.

Drawing aside the curtains, he pushed open the casement and looked out, and saw nothing but passing pedestrians hurrying through the rain, about their business. A little way down the street excavators had been laying new gas mains, and there were several heaps of gravel within reach of the nimble passer-by. He went back to his work. It might have been a few stones thrown up by the wheels of passing traffic, but he was hardly seated before the signal came again, and this time he went downstairs. There was nobody at the door, and he stepped into the street. He saw only a sprinkle of people hurrying through the downpour. Left or right there was no loiterer. He waited a moment, closed the door, and went back to his room, and rang the bell for the man who was valet and chauffeur and, at a pinch, cook.

"Somebody is amusing himself by throwing pebbles up at my window, William. Go out by the back way, and come round by the opposite side of the road and keep watch," he said. "If it is a small boy, you needn't trouble to chase him —?"

"Swish!"

Again the rattle against his window. He sprang across the room, threw open the casement and looked out. There were two men walking under an umbrella, a girl hurrying down the hill in a shining wet mackintosh, a third man walking slowly with a girl, also under an umbrella, and they exhausted all the possibilities. He beckoned the servant.

"Sit here," he said, "so that your shadow falls on the blinds."

He pushed a chair half-way between the window and the table, and crept downstairs, opened the door half an inch and listened. Presently he heard the rattle of stones and sprang out. It was the girl in the mackintosh, and he gripped her by the arm.

"Now, young lady, what is the joke?" he demanded sternly, and found himself looking into the laughing face of Audrey Bedford. "What on earth—? he gasped.

"I was being mysterious! I hope I didn't frighten you. But I wanted to see you, and as detectives never ring bells—"

"What the dickens are you talking about? Come inside. You certainly scared me. What were you throwing up—chicken-feed?"

"I've done worse than that; I've thrown up the job," she said. "Happily, I can come in unchaperoned because you are One of Us."

He dismissed his servant, who would have preferred to stay.

"Now, young lady, having fulfilled your heart's desire, and having very completely mystified me, perhaps you will tell me what you mean by 'One of Us'."

She dived into her mackintosh pocket, took out a little silver star, and laid it dramatically on the table. He picked it up, read the inscription on the face, and turned it over.

"Stormer's?" he said, as though he did not believe the evidence of his eyes. "But surely… ? I thought you were safely installed in your journalist coop?"

"I am finished with chickens," she said, as she took off her streaming coat. "They are fatal to me. You are evidently not used to receiving lady visitors, and that is to your credit."

She rang the bell, and when the man appeared:

"Very hot tea and very hot toast, and you can boil me an egg—no, on second thoughts, I'd rather have something less reminiscent. When a lady calls on you," she explained, after the astonished valet-chauffeur-cook had gone, "the first thing you do is to ask her if she wants to drink tea, and the second thing is to ask her if she's hungry. You then push up your cosiest chair to the fire, and express your anxious hope that she hasn't got her feet wet—to which I reply I haven't. You may be a good detective, but you're a poor host."

"Now tell me your day's adventure," he begged.

Complying with her instructions he pushed forward a chair, and she stretched her damp shoes to the blaze. She described her experience with Mr. Hepps in a few pungent sentences, but her incursion into the realms of crime-detection was not so easily retailed.

"I don't know what I've to do, except to live in a nice hotel and keep a fatherly eye upon an old gentleman of sixty, who doesn't even know me, and in all probability would bitterly resent my guardianship. But it is respectable, and Mr. Stormer is certainly more attractive than Mr. Malpas—and more human."

"How did he come to hear of you?"

"He hears of everything—he's a real detective," she said. "Honestly, I don't know, Captain Shannon. By the way, I feel I ought to touch my hat to you, you're so far above me in point of rank and influence. I'd seen Willitt before. He came to me at Fontwell the day we met—or rather, the day your car met my bus—and I had an idea afterwards"—she hesitated—"that he was sent down by Mr. Marshalt. I've no reason for believing this, it is sheer instinct, and I'm depending a whole lot upon my instinct to make me a good detective."

He was laughing now. "You're a queer child," he said.

"I hate the superiority in that word 'child'," she smiled. "As a detective I know I'm not going to be any good, but it is rather fun."

"And it may be rather unpleasant," said Dick, as all the possibilities began to appear. "This inoffensive old gentleman—by the way, what is his name?"

"He's a millionaire."

"Even that seems no adequate reason for his being watched," he said.

The man came in with tea just then, and put the tray down on the table preparatory to laying a cloth. Dick dispensed with that formality.

"It is a profession," he said thoughtfully, "but not a nice one for a girl, though if you're well directed, you may never see the unpleasant side. At any rate, I'm glad you're with Stormer's, I don't know exactly what to advise you," he said. "I certainly have a plan for your future, and I wish you could find something amusing and free from all possible risks, until I've settled this Portman Square mystery, and have Malpas under lock and key. And then ..."

"And then?" she repeated as he paused. "I hope then you will let me settle your affairs," he said quietly, and there was something in his eyes that made her get up quickly.

"I must go home," she said. "The tea was lovely, and thank you!"

"You haven't finished the toast."

"I'm due to eat a large and substantial dinner in an hour."

He rang for her mackintosh, which had been taken to the kitchenette.

"What will you say when I take your future in hand?"

She shook her head.

"I don't know. I don't think I've reached the place where I want my future to be in anybody's hands but mine. You mustn't think I'm being ungrateful. I very much appreciate—all you've done, and could do—"

She laughed nervously. It may have been the red lampshade that was responsible for the colour in her cheeks. They were certainly of the same hue. Just then the man came back with her coat, and Dick helped her. He heard the faint ring of the bell.

"Somebody at any rate knows the way to get in without breaking my windows," he said.

"Did you mind?" She laughed softly to herself. "I was a pig to do it, when you are so worried. It was so easy; nobody saw me lift my hand and throw the stones."

Williams was back again, and behind him came Steel.

He nodded to the girl, then to Dick.

"What are these?" he asked, and pulled from his pocket a handful of yellow pebbles of varying sizes. Some were as big as hickory nuts, one was even larger. Handful after handful he poured on the table.

"What are those, sir?" he asked again triumphantly.

"Those," said Dick carefully, "are diamonds. About a quarter of a million pounds' worth."

"And three times as many more in Malpas's room," said Steel. "The idol is full of them! Now I know why the ghost walks!"

The Idol

"I lit upon the cache by accident," said Steel. "Finding things were a little dull, I was making a loafer's examination of the big idol in the alcove. If you remember, Captain Shannon, this god, or mumbo-jumbo or whatever he is, is supported on each side by a bronze animal that looks something between a cat and a panther. I've often wondered whether they were there as ornaments, or whether they had any especial use. This afternoon I gave one an extra strong tug to see if it was firmly fixed, and, to my surprise, it began to turn by itself with a noise that suggested that I'd started some sort of clockwork machinery on the grand scale. Nothing happened, however, except that the cat turned half-right —she had previously been facing squarely into the room. I tried the other cat in the same way, and exactly the same thing happened.

"Whether I touched a spring, or whether that jerk set the machinery moving, I don't know. At any rate, the cat on the left of the figure turned half-left; and the moment it stopped, an extraordinary thing happened. The upper part of the statue has a starved look about the ribs; all the bones show—it looks as though they had been moulded on over the figure. The moment the cat stopped, the chest of the idol opened in the centre like double doors. I got up on to the pedestal and put my lamp inside, and I swear to you the body is half filled with stones as big as, and bigger than, any of these! I took a handful and put them in my pocket, and came straight away to see you. I didn't dare to telephone, for fear somebody cut in and heard more than I wanted them to know."

Dick was examining the diamonds. Each bore a little red seal that showed the place of its origin.

"Malpas must have had a good haul," said Steel, "but what I can't understand is why he didn't get rid of this stuff."

"I think I could explain that," said Dick. "There's been a pretty bad slump in the past few years in the diamond trade; the market is so loaded with stones that prices are down to their minimum. That kind of slump often occurs in diamonds. His supply was greater than his opportunities for disposal. There is another thing to be remembered; diamonds are an investment, and the most portable form of wealth. A man who contemplated a hurried retirement from the country could have no better form of swag—he could carry a couple of millions in a handbag! Have you closed the door of the idol?"

Steel nodded.

"Fortunately, there was nobody in the room but myself at the time. The inspector was on the landing outside, talking to the two men. I pushed the cats back in their positions and the doors closed."

Shannon picked up the diamonds and, pouring them into a prosaic sugar-bowl, locked the vessel away in his safe.

"The other stones must be removed tonight," he said. "We'll collect them, put them in a bag, and take every stone to the Yard."

Audrey had been a silent and amazed audience, and Shannon had almost forgotten that she was present, "You will come along, won't you, Audrey? You'd like to see what a million pounds' worth of diamonds looks like?"

She stood undecided. "I don't know that I want to see that room again," she said, "but curiosity is one of my weaknesses."

Giving strict instructions to his servant to remain in the sitting- room and not to move until he returned, Dick piloted his party downstairs, and, calling a taxi from the rank in the middle of the road, followed the girl and his assistant. The drive up Regent Street was unrelieved by any kind of conversation. Each was busy with his or her thoughts. For some extraordinary reason, the bodkin with the corkscrew handle occurred and recurred to Dick Shannon's mind, without his being able to explain what association there was in that instrument with the discovery of the evening.

He had brought with him a stout leather grip to carry the stones.

"I doubt whether that will hold them all," said Steel—an idea which secretly amused Shannon.

Steel had left two policemen on duty in the room; the third was in the hall, and the inspector came down from the Upper floor to meet them.

"I think we'd best get all the men in the room, in case there happens one of those curious accidents which invariably occur when we run counter to the wishes of friend Malpas."

He went up to the alcove and drew the curtain aside. It was the first time Audrey had seen the dread figure of the idol, and she shuddered at the fearful sight. It seemed to her that the emerald-green eyes of the cats were fixed balefully upon her—an illusion which most people had who had seen them.

Steel tugged at one of the animals; there was a whirr of machinery, and the cat moved slowly to the right and stopped. He did the same with the other, and a similar movement occurred. As it came to a standstill, the two breasts of the figure opened.

"Here we are," said Steel with satisfaction, and, planting a chair against the pedestal, Dick mounted.

He thrust his hand into the opening and brought out a heap of yellow stones.

"They are up to sample, I think," laughed Steel, trembling with excitement.

"They certainly are," breathed Dick. "They most certainly are!"

He got down, dusted his hands, and, opening the bag, planted it on Malpas's desk.

A sound made him look round. Both cats were turning to their original positions. Presently they stopped, and the doors closed with a click.

Steel was gaping at the statue.

"There's a mechanism there I don't understand," he said. "Wait —I'll fix it again."

He had taken a step, when the lights went out and the room was plunged into darkness.

"Stand by that door," said Shannon quickly. "Let nobody in, or out. One of you men feel your way along to the buffet, and keep your truncheon against the panelling. If it moves, hit out! Where are the lamps?"

He heard Steel curse softly as he groped in the darkness, and then:

"The lamps are on the landing table, sir," came the inspector's voice.

"Get them. You man at the door, let the inspector pass, and make sure that it is he who comes back."

Audrey felt her heart going at double speed, and instinctively her hand sought Shannon's arm.

"What is going to happen?" she whispered fearfully.

"I don't know," he answered in the same tone. "Keep close behind me, and take my left arm."

"The door's shut." It was the inspector again. Dick had forgotten that the secret controls affected the doors as well as the illumination.

"A match, somebody. What is happening here?"

It was Steel's voice, speaking from the floor, as he crawled towards the idol.

"Did you hear anything, sir?"

"I thought I heard a wailing sound. Can you feel the idol?"

"I am—Oh, my God!"

The girl's blood froze at the cry of agony which followed.

"What is it?" asked Dick.

"I touched something almost red-hot. The base of the idol, I think."

They heard his stifled cry of pain.

"There's something burning," whispered the girl. "Can't you smell —the scent of hot iron?"

Dick had already detected the curious, sickly aroma. He put the girl gently from him.

"I'm going to discover what has happened," he said.

And then a policeman at the far end of the room struck a match, and at that moment the lights came on again.

Apparently nothing had been moved. The idol still turned its malignant face to the room; the green eyes of the cats glared unchangingly. "What has happened to you, Steel?"

The man was nursing his hand. Right across the palm was a red and black weal, an inch wide. "It's a burn," he groaned.

Dick ran forward and felt the base of the pedestal—it was cold, ice-like.

"It wasn't that, sir," said Steel. "It was something else that came up out of the floor, a sort of hot barrier—?"

"Barrier or no barrier," said Dick, "I'm going after those stones."

He jerked the cats round, the little door opened. Leaping on to the pedestal, he put his hand inside.

The body was empty!

A Bag

"This, I think," said Dick, "is where we get off. To be robbed under our eyes is just a little more than public opinion will stand."

He examined the floor carefully, even going to the length of pulling up the carpet, but there was no sign of a trap-door. Where the searing hot bar came from was a mystery.

He looked round at the girl and smiled wryly.

"If you're not going to make a much better detective than I have been," he said, "you'll be a pretty poor one—we have seen the worst."

But the amazing happenings of that evening were not yet completed.

"There's nothing to be gained by whining," said Dick. "Did the panelling move, Constable?"

"No, sir; I had my stick here." He pressed his murderous-looking club against the panelling, which must have moved if the visitor had used that method of entrance.

As it proved, this way into the room was no longer practicable.

"I had the elevator cables cut," said Steel. "The buffet lift doesn't move any more. Whew!"

Audrey was making an extemporized bandage with two handkerchiefs to keep the air from the raw wound.

"Jehoshophat! I never knew a little thing could be so painful!" he groaned.

"Let every man carry his own lamp in future, Inspector," said Dick. "Better recover them now."

It seemed almost as if those words were a signal, and the unknown had decided that the arrival of the hand-lamps must be prevented at any cost, for the lights went out for the second time, and the door to the lobby closed with a thud before the nearest policeman could reach it.

"Matches, somebody, quick!" said Dick, feeling frantically in his pockets. He heard the rattle of a box.

"Strike one, confound you!" he roared.

"I'm trying to," said the meek voice of Audrey.

A scratch, a splutter of flame, and the lamps blazed on simultaneously with the lighting of the match.

"This is uncanny," said Dick, "and—?"

Audrey-saw his jaw drop and his eyes open wide. He was staring at the idol. And well he might; for on the floor before the figure was a leather bag. It was big and new.

"Where did that come from?"

Dick jumped at it, and, lifting it with some difficulty, placed it on the table by the side of the grip he had brought to transport the diamonds...

"Be careful, sir," warned Steel. "You don't know what is in there!"

Shannon went over the outside of the bag with a quick, professional touch. "If it's a bomb, it's a new kind of bomb," he said, and-jerked the bag open.

He nearly swooned. The deep interior was almost filled with the yellow stones he had seen in the idol's breast!

He drew a deep breath, and beckoned Steel forward.

"I think that's about all that was there?"

Steel, dumbfounded, could only nod, and Dick, taking the bag in his hand, bowed profoundly to the gaping figure of bronze.

"You're a queer chap and a terrifying chap, but you're also a very obliging chap, and—thank you for the grip! We'll take the bag straight to my flat," he said in an undertone. "When we've collected the other stones I'll lock them away at headquarters. I shan't feel safe until they're behind shell-proof doors!"

"But how did it come?" asked the bewildered Steel, so completely knocked out by the recovery of the stones that he forgot the pain he was suffering.

"They take the stuff away... and send it back in a bag! It's incredible!"

But Shannon had no inclination to discuss the matter.

"Let us get out of this place quick, before they discover their mistake," he said. "Inspector, tell your men to collect their belongings. I'm withdrawing your guard from the house."

The inspector was apparently relieved. "That is the best news I've had for a long time, sir. I'd sooner do six months' duty than one night in this place."

They filed out into the street. Dick was reaching out his hand to pull the door shut, when it closed violently of its own volition, and through the fanlight he saw the lights go up.

"Now they've discovered their mistake, and there is going to be serious trouble." He looked longingly at the door. "I'd give something to be on the other side," he said.

"You're scared!" whispered a voice in his ear. "I'd give something to run, but I haven't the courage."

They crossed the road to the shadow of the railings. Presently a line of light showed at the window. Somebody had pulled the curtain aside and was looking out. As they did so, a devil stirred in Shannon's heart —a wild, insane desire to make a quick end to the mystery that was breaking him. "I'll take a chance," he said.

His gun went up and three staccato shots rang out as one. There was a crash of glass; the streak of light disappeared.

"This is where I get into very serious trouble," said Shannon with a mirthless smile. "But, gosh! I hope I killed him!"

"Who?" asked the frightened girl.

But Dick did not reply.

You may not outrage the laws of the Metropolis, even though you be the highest Commissioner in the land. There was a shrill of police whistles, the sound of hurrying feet; three helmeted figures appeared from nowhere in particular, and behind them the crowd that comes from the air on all such occasions as these. Doors and windows were opening in Portman Square. Such a monstrous happening had not occurred within the history of this sedate place.

Commissioner or no Commissioner, Dick had to give his name, the registered number of his automatic, and his address, and submitted without protest because it was the rules of the game. The shots, at any rate, brought the taxi they wanted, and, getting in first, he planted the bag squarely on his knees. As the weight pressed on him, Shannon felt that the evening had not been wasted.

"I don't know why I shot—bad temper, or pique, or something. I used to be fairly useful with a gun, but the light wasn't as good as it might have been."

"Who is it in there?" insisted Audrey. "Who do you think it is —Mr. Malpas?"

"He is one, and there are probably others," said Dick.

"But are they there all the time?"

He nodded.

"Very likely."

"Phew!" Audrey fanned herself with her hand. "I'm not going to make a good detective! I wanted to scream."

"Not so much as I did, Miss Bedford," said Steel. "Can you go out of your way to drop me at Middlesex Hospital? I must have this hand dressed."

They made a detour and dropped Steel to have his injury attended to. Then they crossed Oxford Street, and down dingy cinema-land, which in London is Wardour Street.

"You ought to have brought a policeman with you. Captain Shannon," she said with sudden gravity.

He laughed.

"I don't think we're likely to be molested between here and Scotland Yard."

Half-way along Wardour Street she saw a glow of light strike the roof of the cab through the little peep-hole at the back, and, turning, looked out. A big car was just behind them, and was drawing to the right to pass, at a place where the street narrowed so that there was scarcely room for two vehicles abreast. Almost before she could think, the inevitable happened. The car swerved quickly to the left, pinned the smaller taxicab against the edge of the sidewalk, jacking it up till, with a grind of brakes, the machine was flung to the narrow sidewalk.

Dick's first thought was for the girl; his arm was instantly around her, and, pulling her towards him as the cab shivered its frail windows to fragments, he managed to screen her face. At that second the door was jerked open; somebody put his hand in and felt on the floor. Dick turned in time to see the hand grip the bag, and his fist shot out. The blow caught the man's shoulder, and for a second he loosened his grip on the bag, and then, muttering something, he struck through the doorway. Shannon saw the glimmer of steel, and, wriggling round, partly to escape the thrust and partly to get at his pistol pocket, he kicked out with all his strength, and, by luck, hit home, for he heard a grunt and the knife fell amidst the broken glass. In another instant the assailant was gone.

"Stop that man!" shouted Dick.

He had seen the approaching policeman, but his voice was drowned in the roar of engines. The car swerved to avoid the officer, and, turning into Shaftesbury Avenue, disappeared.

With some difficulty Dick Shannon struggled out of the cab, and helped the girl to her feet. The taxi was a wreck, but the driver had escaped injury to everything but his feelings. "Did you get the number?" asked Shannon.

"No, I didn't," growled the policeman, "but he nearly got me!"

"I got it," said the frightened cabman, "you bet I got it! XG.97435."

Dick chuckled.

"I'll save you the trouble of looking that up. Constable. It's the number of my own car! Our friend has a queer sense of humour."

He made himself known to the officer. "I want a taxicab, but I think I'll go with you in search of it," he said. "I don't wish to be alone with this bag."

"Something valuable in it, sir?" said the constable, respectfully interested.

"About three million pounds," said Shannon.

The constable was politely amused. He invariably smiled at his superiors' jokes, and he smiled now.

"Where is your inspector?"

"He may be here any moment, sir. He usually comes round at about this hour. Here he is, sir, with the sergeant."

He hurried forward to meet his superior, and Shannon did not lag far behind him.

A few words explained the situation, and the policeman, delighted with the prospect of getting released from his tedious beat-walking, accompanied him to the flat.

"Hallo!" Dick looked up at his window. He had left the servant with strict injunctions not to leave the sitting-room until he came back, but the lights were out.

"Come into the passage and hold this bag," he said. "Audrey, you stand behind the officer. My William is not usually a man who disobeys instructions."

There was a light-switch in the hall: he turned it on, and a lamp showed at the head of the stairs. He opened the flat door. The hall was in darkness, and when he pressed the control, no light came. Reaching up, he discovered that the bulb had been removed—and recently, for the brass holder was still warm.

His gun held stiffly before him, he walked across the hall, and tried the door of the sitting-room. It was locked. Stepping back, he lifted his foot and kicked. The door opened with a crash that brought the constable half-way up the stairs.

"Anything wrong, sir?"

"Stay where you are," ordered Dick sharply.

Reaching in, he turned over the switch, and the room flooded with light.

The first object he saw was William. He was lying half on the sofa and half on the floor, and the trickle of blood on the sofa told Shannon all he wanted to know.

The safe was open—he expected that—blown out, and hanging on its hinges. The sugar-bowl, with its precious contents, was gone.

He lifted the man to the sofa, and loosened his collar. He was breathing thickly, and a quick examination of the wound told the Commissioner that the injury was not likely to be a serious one. It told him something more: the attack had been delivered only a few minutes before he arrived.

From the sideboard he took a carafe of water and splashed it on the man's face, and presently William opened his eyes, and stared stupidly around him.

"Did you get him, sir?" he asked eagerly.

"No, my son, I didn't get him. He got you, apparently."

William groaned, and, leaving the man, Dick opened the door which communicated with his bedroom, and gave the apartment a quick search. A window at the back was open; he pulled down, and drew the blinds. And here he found other evidence of an intruder's presence. Two drawers in his dressing-table were open, and the contents turned over. Somebody had pulled away the pillows from his bed, evidently in search of something. He came back to find the chauffeur sufficiently recovered to sit up.

"I'll send you along to the hospital. You'll see Mr. Steel there," he said, with a touch of grim humour.

Going out to the landing, he found the stairway in darkness. Somebody had extinguished the stairway light.

"Who put this light out?" he asked.

"Are you up there, sir?" said the policeman in surprise. "I thought you put it out."

"Come up, and bring the bag. Will you come up, Audrey?"

"The bag, sir? You took the bag."

"What!" shouted Dick.

"When you came down just now, you said, 'Give me the bag, and stay where you are.' sir," said the policeman in tremulous tones.

"Oh, you double-dyed goop!" stormed Dick. "Couldn't you see me?"

"It was in the dark, sir," said the policeman.

"Did you see him, Audrey?" asked Shannon. There was no answer. "Where is the young lady?"

"Down here, sir, near the door."

Dick turned and snapped on the light. The passage was empty except for the policeman.

Flying down the stairs three at a time, he flung open the door and walked into the street. Audrey had disappeared!

The bag had gone—that was bad enough. But Audrey had disappeared—that was the loss that turned Dick Shannon's heart to ice.

Edgar Wallace

A Domiciliary Visit

The cabman was still waiting. He had seen "the gentleman" come out with a bag, and then the lady came out, and that was about all he knew. He admitted he was more interested in a conversation he was holding with a brother taxi-driver on the rank. He didn't know which way they went, or whether they went together. He was quite sure the young lady came out after the gentleman.

"Gentleman be—blowed!" snarled Shannon. His language was almost justifiable. "What did he look like? Was he young or old?"

The cabman did not know. He was facing the wrong way at the time to see properly. But he thought he was an elderly gentleman. He insisted upon the thief being of gentle birth and, pressed, he wasn't sure that he had seen the lady go at all.

Dick went back to his flat with a heart as heavy as lead. "I'm sorry I cursed you. Officer," he said. "It was my own fault. I should have made sure there was nobody in the flat before I attended the chauffeur. Come up. Do you know anything about first-aid? You can look after my man while I telephone."

Within a minute every police station in London knew of the robbery. Motor-cyclists were starting out to warn the patrol men to look for a man with a bag, and—here the description was explicit—for a girl in a mackintosh coat.

Williams was now recovered sufficiently to tell all that he knew, which was not much. He did, however, confirm Shannon's theory that the robbery had occurred only a few minutes before he arrived.

"I was sitting at the table, reading the evening newspaper, when I thought I heard a sound in the bedroom. I listened, but it seemed to me that it was only the flapping of the blinds, and I didn't get up. The last thing I remember was reading an account of an Old Bailey trial."

The back of the building in which his flat was situated looked out upon the flat roof of an annexe built out from Lower Regent Street, and he realized for the first time how simple a matter it was for a burglar to gain admission through the rear of the premises.

"They were pretty quick workers," was all he said, and leaving Williams to be escorted to the hospital, he went on intending to take the taxi on to Scotland Yard.

As he crossed the sidewalk a man touched his hat. It was the plain- clothes officer who patrolled that beat, and Shannon knew him by sight. In a few words he told what had happened and described the girl. The detective shook his head.

"No, sir, I didn't see the lady, and I don't remember anybody carrying a bag. I was standing at the top of Haymarket, outside the Tube station, where thousands of people pass, but I think I should have remembered anybody carrying a grip at this time of night."

"You saw nobody who might be concerned in the robbery—none of 'the boys'?"

The officer hesitated.

"As a matter of fact, I saw one," he confessed; "a man you pointed out to me a few months ago."

"Slick Smith?" asked Dick quickly.

"Yes, sir, that's he—Slick Smith."

"Which way did he come?"

"He came up the Haymarket, and I thought he was in a bit of a hurry. I said good night to him as he passed, but he either didn't see or didn't want to see me. He was wearing a dark blue trench-coat, and had evidently been out in the rain for some time, for it was wet through."

"What time was this?"

"About five minutes ago. He crossed towards the Pavilion, and there I lost sight of him."

Headquarters had no news when Dick arrived. He would have been surprised if they had; and he waited only long enough to consult the Chief on duty before he went in search of Slick Smith.

The American crook was not at home; had not been home since very early in the evening.

"I don't know what time he'll arrive," said the landlord. "In fact, I never hear him come in. He's a very quiet man, one of the best lodgers I've ever had."

The landlord did not protest when Shannon went up to the rooms occupied by Smith, for he was well aware of the character of his tenant, the police having conveyed information to him a very considerable time before. The door was fastened, but the lock was very easily manipulated and Dick went into the room, making a quick but thorough search for any evidence likely to incriminate Smith in the outrage.

If Slick Smith had been a Sabbath school teacher or the leader of a Band of Hope—indeed, anything that was wholly innocuous and pure —his belongings could not have afforded any less evidence of his criminal propensities. Dick was in the midst of his examination when he heard the door downstairs open and a low-voiced conversation. A little later Smith walked in, a smile on his cheery face, a very large cigar in the comer of his mouth and a twinkle in his eye.

"Good evening, Captain," he said cheerily. "If you'd sent me a note, I'd have been at home to meet you. What I like about the English people is their friendliness. Fancy your calling on me!"

Dick shut the door.

"Give me an account of your movements since five o'clock," he said curtly. Smith scratched his chin.

"That is going to be difficult," he said. "The only thing I'm absolutely certain about is that I was in the Haymarket at a quarter to ten. One of your bloodhounds saw me, so it would be absurd to deny that I was there. The rest of the time I have been loafing around. And there's no use my telling you where, Captain Shannon," he said with evident sincerity, "because you know that, if I said I was at Boney's at four fifty-five, why Boney would swear I was sitting right there up against the stove, even if I was a hundred miles away. But if you've any doubt of my bona-fides, Captain, there's an agency in the village called Stormer's, who have had a sleuth on my heels for months. I guess they'll be able to give you a schedule that will satisfy you—unless I slipped him." He chuckled. "I do that sometimes, and it rattles him to death.

I'll tell you what. Captain, let's show hands. You've had a burglary at your flat tonight."

"How do you know that?" asked Dick sternly.

Again Slick Smith laughed.

"I saw a policeman on duty outside the door as I came past ten minutes ago," he said dryly, "and another policeman taking a fellow with a broken head off to hospital. A man hasn't got to be clever to know that there was sump'n doin'. Unless you've gone in for the movie business, and I didn't notice a camera or a battery of Krieg lights around. Do you want me for that burglary?"

"I want you for nothing," said Dick shortly. "You are a known bad character, and you were in the vicinity of the Haymarket at the hour thieves broke into my flat. What's the matter with your face?"

From the moment he came into the room Smith had steadfastly kept one side of his face in the shadow, and now Dick gripped him by the shoulders and turned him round so that the light fell upon that side of his face. From the cheekbone to a point above the left ear was a long, ugly graze that had taken off a portion of the man's hair.

"That is a bullet's track," he said. He touched a slight wound on the man's jaw that was skilfully dressed. "And that is a cut—the cut that broken glass would make. Who has been shooting you up. Smith?"

"I didn't get his name and address," drawled the other. "I was in a hurry."

"Shall I tell you how you were shot, and the position you were in? You were standing behind a window; the bullet struck the glass, grazed your forehead, ricochetted alongside your head, and a splinter of the glass—" He stopped. He saw a tiny, glittering speck on the shoulder of the man's wet trench-coat, and reaching forward, pulled it from the cloth in which it was buried. "That's glass."

They looked at one another, neither speaking. The smile had gone from Slick Smith's face, but the humorous eyes still held a twinkle.

"There's the making of a good detective in you. Shannon," he said. "A violin and a shot of 'coco', a few monographs on cigar-ash, and a scrapbook, and, gee! you'd have a queue waiting outside your house in Baker Street! I was shot at—that's true. And it was through glass —through the glass of a taxi window. I've got a feud with one of those cheap gangsters from Soho. I can give you the number of the taxi I was riding in, if you want to investigate."

He took a card from his pocket and put it on the table. Dick saw the number pencilled on the back. Slick's alibi was well prepared.

Shannon was exasperated by the coolness of the man; his nerves were on edge, and he knew at the bottom of his heart that the loss of a fortune in uncut diamonds concerned him less than the question of the girl's safety.

"You make me feel a fool. I suppose I am," he said... "Smith, will you be candid with me to this extent? My flat has been robbed, and I've lost very valuable property, which belongs to somebody else. But that isn't troubling me so much as"—he hesitated—"as another matter. When I went to the flat I was accompanied by Miss Bedford. I've an idea that you've met her?"

"I saw her once," said Smith.

"Whether you were concerned in the robbery or not doesn't, for the moment, matter a row of pins to me. Will you tell me this: did you see Miss Bedford tonight?"

"Did I see her? I certainly saw her," said Smith with a broad smile, "and I'm hoping to see her again if somebody hasn't run away with her. Doughty Street is a mighty cold and windy place for a young lady to be standing all this time."

"Doughty Street!" gasped Dick. "Where is she?"

"She was outside the door a few minutes back," said Smith.

Audrey's Story

Before the words were out of his mouth, Shannon was flying down the stairs. In the street he saw the figure of a girl walking up and down.

"Audrey!" he cried joyfully, and before he realized what he was doing he had taken her in his arms. "My dear, this is wonderful!" he said, and his voice shook. "You don't know what this minute means to me."

"Didn't Mr. Smith tell you I was waiting?" she asked, gently disengaging

561

herself. "He wouldn't let me come in until he had found whether you were there."

"Then he expected me to be here?" said Dick in surprise.

"He thought so: he said that this would be the first call you'd make."

He hustled her into the house and up to Smith's room, Smith receiving his new visitor with the greatest calmness. And then the girl told her story.

"I was near the door, when I heard you, as I thought, come down the stairs and say something in a whisper to the policeman. It was not until the man dashed past me and opened the door that I realized I was mistaken. Dick, it was Mr. Malpas!"

"Malpas? Are you sure?"

"Positive," she said emphatically. "I couldn't mistake him. He wore a soft felt hat and his coat collar was turned up to his chin, and that awful nose... ! My first thought was to scream. And then my hand, which was in my pocket at the time, touched the silver badge, and I began to realize a detective's responsibilities."

"And you followed him?" said Dick. "You mad woman!"

"He was across the road by the time I had made up my mind, and I flew along after him, keeping him in sight. He walked down Panton Street into Leicester Square and turned up towards Coventry Street, and I kept behind him and at a little distance. At Coventry Street he crossed the road, passed up the little street that runs by the side of the Pavilion Theatre, and, crossing Shaftesbury Avenue, walked quickly up Great Windmill Street. I saw a car waiting by the sidewalk, but didn't realize that it was his until he jumped in and started it moving. And then I did a very foolish thing. I shouted 'Stop!' and ran towards the car. Instead of going off at top speed, as I expected him to, he looked round and kept the machine going at a slow pace, just fast enough to keep ahead of me, and then he suddenly stopped, and I came up to it before I realized what danger I might be in. It was a closed limousine, and I could not see the face of the driver. The street was dark, and there was no light of any kind inside the body of the machine.

"'Is that you, Miss Bedford?' he asked. Although all along I was certain it was he, I was simply struck speechless when I found that my suspicions were correct. 'Come inside; I want to speak to you,' he said. I turned to run, and he was out of the car like a flash. There was nobody in sight, and I was terrified. I don't know how I got away, but I did. Looking round, I saw that I was not being followed, and the car couldn't be seen, of course, because I had turned three or four corners before I lost my breath and could go no farther. Just as I was deciding that I ought to look for a policeman and tell him, Mr. Smith walked into view. I had a fright; I thought it was Malpas. That is all, except that Mr. Smith brought me to your flat, and on the way we met a detective, who told us you had been inquiring about him."

Dick drew a long breath.

"So the mystery of your omniscience is a mystery no longer, Smith. How came you to be in that neighbourhood?"

"I was following the young lady." Not a muscle of Smith's face moved, not an eyelid twitched. "That is what I was doing—following the young lady; though, if I'd known she was one of Stormer's women, maybe I'd not have been so anxious. Quis custodiet custodes ipsos? That's Latin, and it means 'Who shall trail the trailer?' And now I'll guess you are wanting to go. Captain, and I'll not detain you. Nothing is missing as far as I can see, but if you find any of my property in your pocket when you get home, maybe you'll send it me by express delivery."

Dick drove the girl to her hotel, and with the relief which her safety brought came the reaction. Somewhere in London were diamonds to a fabulous value; and that they were in the possession of their unlawful owner did not make the situation any less serious.

A Reconciliation

Audrey woke the next morning, a little bewildered, to discover herself in an apartment as richly appointed as her new lodgings were plain. There was a tap at the sitting-room door; she unlocked it and scurried back to bed as a trim maid came in, wheeling a little wicker trolley on which her breakfast was laid. By the side of the plate was a letter, and, glancing at it, she uttered an exclamation of surprise. It was from Dora, and was addressed to her, not only at the Ritz-Carlton, but gave the number of her suite. Audrey smiled. Good news travels almost as quickly as bad, she thought, and opened the heavily underlined letter, wondering what had led her sister to take this unusual course. The first few lines filled her with amazement.

My dearest child,

I wonder if you are ever going to forgive me for all the horrid things I've done and said to you, and for my terrible and wicked conduct a year ago? The remembrance that you went to prison innocently for an offence which was really Martin's, haunts me. And when I recall my dreadful attack upon you, I can hardly believe that I was sane. I want you to let bygones be bygones, and to come and see me. I've a lot to tell you —one act of mine I can at least undo. Will you be a forgiving angel and telephone me?

Your loving sister, Dorothy.

"Dorothy?" repeated Audrey, frowning.

Yet, despite the conflicting emotions which the letter aroused, on the whole she was glad. The maid had hardly gone before she was at the telephone. Dora's voice answered her.

"Of course I'll come and see you—this afternoon if I can. And you're not to worry about the—the Holloway incident, I can't speak more plainly on the telephone, but you understand?"

"Yes, dear," said the low voice of Dora.

"You haven't asked me what I'm doing here."

"Oh, I know all about that," said Dora's dispirited voice. "You're working for Stormer's, aren't you?"

Audrey gave a gasp of surprise. "How did you know?"

"Somebody told me; but that doesrft matter. You will come, and you do forgive me... ?"

Audrey went to her bath, feeling a lightness of heart that she had not experienced for many a day. Deep down she was fond of her sister, and her enmity had been a real trouble to her. It seemed as if one of the major unhappinesses of life was dissipated. She did not, however, forget her curious mission. While she was dressing she took advantage of the maid's presence to ask about the mysterious Mr. Torrington.

"They say he's a millionaire," said the maid, in that despairing tone in which people who are not millionaires speak of those who are, "but I don't see what pleasure he gets out of his money. He never goes anywhere, never does anything, sits in his room all day, reading and smoking; goes sneaking out at night—not to theatres, as any other decent gentleman would go, but just loafing around the streets. That's not what I call enjoyment. Now, if I had all that money I'd see life! I'd go to the Palais du Danse every night, and to all the good pictures you could see in the afternoons."

"Perhaps he doesn't dance," said Audrey.

"He could learn," said the girl. "A man with that money could learn anything!"

"Is he in his room now?" The girl nodded.

"He was five minutes ago, when I took him in his breakfast. I will say this for him, that he's very polite and his habits are regular. Do you know that he's up at half past five every morning? It is a fact, miss. The night porter has to take him in coffee and rolls at that hour! He says he has been in the habit for years of getting up at half past five, and he can't break himself."

"Has he a secretary?"

The maid shook her head.

"No, he hasn't got a secretary, not even a parrot," she said vaguely.

In the course of the morning Audrey got in touch with Stormer's and made her brief report. It could have been briefer, because she had nothing really to tell. But apparently the Agency was well satisfied that she was on the spot. They seemed easily pleased, she thought.

At three o'clock that afternoon she knocked at the door of the house in Curzon Street, and was admitted by a new maid, and it was characteristic of Dora that the delinquencies of the old one should be the subject-matter of her conversation.

"She got a little too fresh, and she admitted people without telling me they were in the house, after I had given her strict instructions that I was not at home to them." Then, realizing that the conversation was not exactly as she had planned it, she caught the girl by the shoulders and looked lovingly into her face. "You have forgiven me, girlie?"

"Why, of course, dear."

For some reason, Audrey felt awkward and gauche. It was as though there was some tension in the air that she felt without being able to define. Perhaps it was the absence of Martin which disconcerted her. She expected to see him; the reconciliation was incomplete without his presence. And it was strange that Dora made no reference to or apology for his absence.

"Sit down, my dear, and let me have a good look at you. You haven't changed very much since the old days, really you haven't. Nobody would dream that you were a year older than I."

Audrey looked up in amazement.

"A year older?" she said.

"That is why I wanted to see you. You'll have some tea?"

"But I don't understand you, Dora," said the girl, ignoring the invitation. "I am not older than you; I am a year younger."

Dora's slow smile was almost convincing.

"You're a year older, darling," she said. "Dear mother was responsible for the mix-up. For some reason, which I bitterly regret, mother did not like you, and her dislike took a queer expression, as we have reason to know."

"I always understood that I was born on the ist of December, 1904—" began Audrey.

"On the 3rd of February, 1903," smiled Dora. "I have your birth certificate. I wanted to show it to you."

She opened the drawer of the secretaire and from a blue envelope took out the long oblong slip.

"There it is, dear—Audrey Dorothy Bedford. That was mother's first husband. I told you that she never called you by your name."

Audrey was examining the document, bewildered.

"But she told me... she said you were the older—lots of times. And, Dora, I remember you were always in a class higher than I at school. If what you say is true, then my father—?"

"I told you that your father was on the Breakwater, but that isn't so." Dora dropped her eyes. "It was my father," she said brokenly. "He was an American who came to South Africa and met mother when she was a young widow with a child only a few weeks old. They were married three months later."

Audrey dropped down into a chair. "How queer!" she said. "But I am Audrey! And we are both Dorothy? That must be so. But"—she shook her head helplessly—"I can't believe that I'm older than you."

Dora checked her rising anger with a great mental effort, but what she had to say was interrupted by a cry from the girl.

"I can prove I'm the younger!" she said triumphantly. "Mother told me where I was christened—at a chapel in Rosebank, South Africa!"

In the bedroom above the room in which they were talking Martin Elton, his ear to the floor, listened; and grew suddenly haggard. Audrey Torrington must be put away! By what way, in what fashion, he did not care. He waited, listening, and when at last her foot sounded on the stairs he got up and opened the door.

Dora's voice, laughing and care-free, came up to him, and presently the street door closed and he went down to meet his wife.

"Well?" she asked, and then she saw his face and shrank back as if she had been struck.

"Martin... you wouldn't."

He nodded.

A life stood between him and the lavish prosperity which had been his life's dream. He had taken his decision.

Mr. Torrington's Secretary

Mr. Willitt was invariably nervous in the presence of Dan Torrington. He was more so now under the searching scrutiny of the old man's eyes.

"I will allow Stormer to understand many of my peculiar requirements, but when it comes to a question of appointing a secretary, I must be the best judge, Mr. Willitt. Will you tell or cable your principal to that effect?"

Willitt shifted uncomfortably. He was already sitting on the edge of the chair, and any further movement would precipitate him to the floor.

"We have no desire to dictate, or even to suggest, Mr. Torrington," he said awkwardly, "and Mr. Stormer understands that you are quite well able to manage your domestic affairs without assistance. But he particularly wishes this person engaged."

"Let Stormer engage him, then."

Torrington was smoking a cigarette through a long black I holder, his back to the fire, his thin legs outstretched.

"By all means let Mr. Stormer engage him—he has my permission. I, for my part, will offer no suggestion."

"It's not a him, it's a girl," blurted Willitt.

"Then I certainly will not employ her!" retorted the other emphatically. "A girl would get on my nerves. I don't understand them, and I should be one half the time offending her and the other half apologizing." He glanced at the crestfallen face and laughed. "You seem to have set your heart on this. Who is she?"

"She is the young lady who was employed by Malpas."

"Malpas!" said the old man softly. "Is she by any chance the friend of that very engaging young man Captain Shannon?"

"Yes, sir," said the other.

"Oh!" Torrington stroked his chin. "Is it Shannon's wish?" he asked at last.

"Shannon knows nothing about it; it is entirely Mr. Stormer's idea. The truth is—" he began.

"Now we have it," said the other dryly. "I thought that you would pass through that painful process—tell me the truth!"

"She is in our employ, and we want somebody near you in case things go a little wrong."

"And is she one of those capable females who will put them right?" laughed the old man. "I'll oppose you no more. Tell her to see me this afternoon. What is her name?"

"Audrey Bedford."

The words conveyed nothing to Torrington.

"I'll see her at three—?"

"She's in the hotel at this minute; won't you see her now?"

"You brought her, did you?"

"She's staying here," said Willitt. "In fact, Mr. Torrington, she has been instructed by us to devote her attention to you, and she is in course of carrying out those orders."

Torrington chuckled and rubbed his hands. "So that is it!" And then his face grew graver. "Send her along. Miss Bedford? I'm not so sure, if my recollection of the girl is right, that I shan't have all my time occupied in protecting her!"

Willitt slipped out of the room and returned in a few minutes, ushering in the girl, and Dan Torrington took her in from the crown of her little hat to the toes of her dainty feet.

"Anything less like a detective I have never seen." He shook his head.

"And I have never felt," she laughed as she took his hand. "Mr. Willitt says that you want me to be your secretary."

"Mr. Willitt is exaggerating," said Torrington good-humouredly. "The one thing I don't wish is for you to be my secretary, but I'm afraid I shall be forced against my will to ask you to accept that position. Are you a capable secretary?"

"I'm not," she confessed ruefully.

"So much the better." Torrington's smile was infectious. "I don't think I could endure a capable secretary—competence is a most depressing quality to have around one. At any rate, you will not open my letters furtively and photograph their contents. And I'm equally sure I shall be able to leave money around without missing any. All right, Mr. Willitt, I will talk with this lady."

He felt strangely drawn towards the girl; a curious sympathy which he experienced the moment she came into the room made the appointment not only less irksome, but even desirable.

"Your duties are nil," he bantered her. "Your office hours will be when I really require assistance—a moment which will probably never arrive. I remember you now; you were the girl who got into hot water a year ago."

That wretched jewel robbery! Was she never to be allowed to forget that year cut out of her life?

"You have a sister, too, haven't you?"

"Yes, I have a sister."

He bit his lip; the light danced on his spectacles as he stared into the fire. "A bad lot." And then, quickly: "Forgive me if I have hurt you at all."

"I'm not very hurt; but I don't think she is quite as bad as people imagine," said Audrey quietly. "A woman is happiest when she has no history, but—?"

"You're wrong," he interrupted. "There isn't a woman without a history. Character is history and history is character. Certainly she's happier if she hasn't the history which a marriage with Martin Elton would attach to her name. Oh, yes, I know the gentleman remarkably well, though he'll never guess that. You worked for Malpas, you say? A somewhat strange gentleman."

"Very," she said emphatically.

"Do you think they will ever catch him?" he asked after a pause. "You know there is a warrant out for him?"

"I didn't know, but I guessed," she said.

"A nice man, do you think?"

"Mr. Malpas? I think he is a horror!"

A faint smile dawned in the old man's face.

"Oh, you think he is a horror, do you?" he said slowly. "Well, maybe he is. All right. You had a bit of a shock last night?—Of course, you were the girl with Shannon when the diamonds were lost?"

She stared at him in amazement.

"Is it in the newspapers?" she asked, and he chuckled again.

"No; it is in my private newspaper! You saw them, eh? Heaps and heaps of them, beautiful little yellow stones—they belong to me!"

She was speechless with astonishment. He made his claim in an ordinary tone of voice, as he might have said, "That book is mine," or "This is my room."

Three million pounds' worth of uncut stones! It was hardly believable that this man, who made so calm a statement, could accept their loss so philosophically.

"Yes, they're mine, or were," he said. "You'll find the seal of the Hallam & Coold mine on every one of them. Mention that fact to Shannon the next time you see him, though I should imagine he knows."

"He never told me."

"There's a whole lot Shannon doesn't tell you that he knows, and one day somebody is going to get a shock," he said.

Suddenly his eyes dropped to her feet, and so long did he stare down at her shoes that she shifted her feet uncomfortably. And when he spoke he said an astounding thing.

"In wet weather it hurts a little, doesn't it?"

"Yes, a little," she was surprised into saying, and then she gasped! "Hurts… ? What do you mean… how did you know?"

He was laughing as she had never seen a man laugh. There were tears in his eyes when he finished. He saw her flushed face, and was penitent.

"Forgive me! I am distressing you. You see, I am an inquisitive man, and I made inquiries about you from the prison officials—the doctor told me a lot!"

And then, abruptly, he turned the talk into more conventional channels and nodded towards his writing-table.

"There are a heap of letters there; just answer them."

"Will you tell me what to say?"

He shook his head.

"There is no necessity. To people who write for money you can say 'No'. To people who want to see me, you can say I'm in Paris; and to newspapers who write asking for an interview you can say I died last night and my end was peaceful."

He put his hand in his pocket and took out a crumpled envelope.

"Here's one that requires a special answer," he said, but did not give her the letter.

"Just write: 'There's a boat leaving for South America on Wednesday next. I will stake you to the extent of £500 and your passage. If you value your life you will accept my offer.'"

She wrote the words rapidly in longhand.

"To whom shall I send this?"

"To Mr. William Stanford, 552 Portman Square," said the old man, looking abstractedly at the ceiling.

What Bunny Saw

There were certain peculiar features about Mr. Torrington's suite at the Ritz-Carlton, features which the girl did not notice until she was alone that afternoon in the sitting-room, Torrington having gone out. All the doors were fitted with bolts, and, opening a window to watch a fire that had broken out on the upper floor of some premises almost opposite, she was amazed when the doors were flung open and three men came in at a run.

One, she knew, was a Stormer agent; the other two were strangers.

"Sorry to startle you, miss," said the agent, "We ought to have warned you not to open the windows."

"What happened?" she asked. "What did I do?"

"I'll tell you later," said the man, pulling the sash carefully and snapping back the fastening.

When the other two had gone: "You touched an alarm. No, you can't see it, because you didn't really set it going until you moved the catch. There is no need to open the windows—this room has a special system of ventilation."

"A burglar alarm?" she gasped. "I never guessed I was doing anything so foolish."

"There's one on every window; there's one on every door at night. I'll show you something."

Even the most stern and inflexible of private detectives becomes indiscreet in the presence of a pretty girl. He took her into Mr. Torrington's bedroom, a plainly furnished apartment, remarkable for the few articles of furniture it contained. There was a double bed with two sets of pillows.

"He sleeps that side, and fortunately he's a very quiet sleeper. If by chance he put his head on that pillow—" He pointed to the other and lifted it gingerly. Running from one corner was a thread-like wire, which disappeared under the bed. "Any pressure on the pillow would bring the night men."

"But Mr. Willitt didn't tell me there were more watchers than me," she said, a little chagrined, and then laughed as she realized what little value her own assistance would be to Torrington in a moment of peril. "Is there really any danger to him?" she asked.

"Well," said the man vaguely, "you never know."

She had time that afternoon to write a hurried letter to Dora, whom she had left in a somewhat electrical atmosphere. It was all rather absurd, after what had passed, to quarrel over a question of age. Her mother was so eccentric that it was quite possible that she had taken this peculiar course of pretending that the younger was the elder. At any rate, it was not worth while quarrelling about, and she sat down and wrote to her sister:

Dear Dora,

I think we were both rather foolish. I am Dorothy or anything you like, and you are my younger sister! Already I have taken that maternal interest in you which comes so natural to the head of the family I I will see you again very soon.

She signed it "Dorothy".

Dora had the letter by the evening post. She was at dinner, and passed it across to her husband without comment.

"She has more intelligence than you, my friend," said Martin, reading and putting it down. "It was lunacy to try to rush matters. You should have let the idea soak in, or else given her a chance to get acquainted with you before you sprang it on her."

"Anyway, I'm not going through with it," she said briefly. "If it came to a show-down, there's the birth registered at Rosebank. It would only take the cost of a cable to prove that Audrey was telling the truth."

He fixed his speculative gaze upon her, and, irritated by his scrutiny, she got up abruptly from the table.

"Don't go," he said. "Shall I show you my profit and loss account for this year? You'll have a fit when I do. Here's a letter that will interest you."

He took it from his pocket and threw it down within reach of her hand.

"From the bank?" She opened it quickly, and her face fell. "But I didn't know you were that much overdrawn, Bunny," she said. "I thought you owned stock."

"I do. The bank has got it against the overdraft, and the stock has depreciated considerably of late. We're in a pretty tight corner. I admit I've been in worse, but then, I wasn't so soft as I am now—better fitted for the rough-and-tumble of starting again. Now, I've got a little set in my habits, and I don't intend going rough, anyway. That letter means nothing, except that she's humouring you. Audrey has got to go away."

"Where?" she asked breathlessly.

"I don't know yet. We'll get her somewhere abroad until you fix things."

"But if she disappeared, and I made my claim, they'd know at once there was something wrong. You don't think Shannon's a fool, do you?"

"Shannon!" he said contemptuously. "I'm not worrying about him. I'm thinking of Slick Smith and what it's going to cost me."

"I shouldn't worry very much about him."

"You wouldn't, eh? No, I guess you wouldn't. I do. It is not only in connection with Audrey and all he knows and guesses that I'm thinking of him. You remember the night I went gunning for Lacy Marshalt? I guess you do! There are very few walls I can't climb, and I got up to the roof of Malpas's house, which is next door, just before the fuss started down below."

"You mean the murder of Marshalt?"

He nodded. "I was there just a few minutes before, and Shannon spoke the truth when he said the police-station clock saved my neck. At the far end of the roof, on Marshalt's section, there was a detective on guard. He didn't see me, and he didn't see the man who came hand-over-hand up the rope, opened the skylight in Malpas's and dropped in. I did. I saw trouble coming, and I got away quick."

"You saw the man go through the skylight? Then you saw the murderer!" she gasped.

"I saw more than that," he nodded. "When he got down below into the little store-room under the skylight, he lit a candle and took out of his pocket a half wig, a false nose and a chin. When he'd fixed them—why, his own mother wouldn't have recognized him for anybody but Malpas."

"Malpas!" she gasped. "Who was it?"

"Slick Smith," was the answer.

Moving an Idol

Sergeant Steel came to Shannon's office in response to a call, and found him in the midst of reading a very long cablegram. From the Western Union headline, which he recognized, he gathered it was from America, and expected his Chief to make some reference to its contents. But apparently it had nothing to do with the case, for Dick turned the sheets upside down and addressed himself to the business for which he had sent for Steel.

"Take a plain-clothes officer with you and admit yourself to 551 Portman Square. You will probably find the controls are off. I want you to wait and watch the removal of the Malpas god. As soon as it is gone, close the house and report."

"Are you moving the idol?" asked the other in surprise.

Dick nodded.

"I've arranged with the Builders' Traction Company to have a lorry and twenty men before the house at half past three. See that they get in, watch the loading, and escort the idol to Scotland Yard. I've told the transport company to cover it up, or we should have half London following the trolley under the impression that we're giving an exhibition. I've arranged for its reception at the Yard. When we've got it there, two of our engineers will make a very thorough examination, and I think this will throw a light upon Malpas and his methods, and—Steel!"

The sergeant turned back.

"I had a talk with one of Marshalt's servants today. She came with a whole lot of useless stuff about things that mean nothing, but she let out one interesting fact. Marshalt was really scared of the man next door. I've been thinking that all that talk and appointment of Stormer's men to watch out was sheer bunk. But it was true. One day this woman had to go into Marshalt's study to take some coal, and she just got into the room when three knocks came from the other side of the wall. You remember I told you that Miss Bedford heard the same signal. Marshalt and Tonger were together, and the effect on Marshalt was to reduce him to jelly. That's what the woman said, but I'm allowing a generous margin for exaggeration. I don't know whether you've any cut-and-dried theory, but remember that Marshalt and Tonger were in the room together when the knocks came. And Marshalt was scared sick."

Steel considered this new point.

"I don't see how that adds to our knowledge, sir," he said, and Dick Shannon showed his teeth in a smile.

"It adds a lot to mine. It tells me who was the two-faced villain who was on the other side! Now get along."

Half an hour later Sergeant Steel, accompanied by one plain-clothes officer, walked up the steps of 551, fitted his key in the tiny lock and admitted himself and his companion. The light was burning in the hall, and in the big room above apparently nothing had changed except that somebody had drawn the curtain over the idol.

"Pull back those window curtains," said Steel. "Let's have a little real light in this place."

So saying, he switched off the lamps. In daylight Malpas's room was even more funereal than it was under the glare of the electric.

"I don't know why the Chief wants us to watch the removal," grumbled Steel.

"Our people have been squealing about this job," said the other, "and they will be glad Captain Shannon has decided to cut out the guard for good."

Steel looked at his watch.

"The contractor's men will be here in half an hour, and then we'll see what this old idol looks like in the Black Museum."

"Are they moving it? Is that the idea, Sergeant?"

"That is the idea," said Steel, idly turning the pages of a book he had been reading when he had been in occupation.

The officer strolled up to the statue and examined it curiously.

"It will take some moving," he said. "It looks to be cast in one piece, and it must weigh a ton. I wonder the floor supports it."

"The floor doesn't; the wall is built out underneath. Captain Shannon had a hole knocked into it to see if there was any hidden mechanism there, but there wasn't."

"Who are doing the moving?"

"The Builders' Traction Company," said Steel. "Did you wedge open the door downstairs?" he asked, with a pretence of carelessness. The place was on his nerves. Half an hour passed, and there was no sign of the contractor. He took up the telephone and immediately missed the familiar buzz of the receiver and tapped the hook.

"The 'phone is dead. Has anybody ordered it to be cut off, I wonder?"

He glanced nervously at the door, and, obeying an impulse, walked across and planted a chair so that it was impossible that it should close. The light was fading in the sky; he put on the lamps again, to find that they did not work.

"I think we'll go," said Steel hastily, "but don't touch that chair!"

He himself vaulted over it and went down the stairs quicker than he had moved since he had been a boy. The wedge at the door still held. As he stood there he heard the upper door shut.

"What was the hurry?" asked the plain-clothes man, coming out after him.

"You've been never on duty here, have you?"

"No. Not that I should mind. Our people made a fuss about it, but it looks an easy job to me."

"It would," snapped Steel, "And it would look an easy job to anybody who doesn't understand it. Go round to the store in Orchard Street and 'phone the traction company: ask them how long they'll be."

He himself paced up and down the pavement, keeping one eye upon the open door, his uninjured hand on the butt of the gun that he carried in his pocket.

His walk took him a few yards beyond the open door on either side, and he was turning when he saw a yellow hand come round behind the door and grip the wedge—the hand of a man, a flesh-and-blood man, and Steel was afraid of no man in the world.

Whipping out his gun, he leapt the steps, and, as he did so, the wedge was withdrawn and the door began to close. It was within an inch of coming to rest when Steel flung himself against the dark panelling, and for a second it held. And then somebody inside added his weight to the springs, and the door closed. Steel stood, panting and exhausted, leaning against the black panels and then, looking round, saw his assistant coming back at a run.

"I got on to the traction people; they say that the order was countermanded this afternoon by Captain Shannon himself."

"I'll bet it was," said Steel bitterly. He looked up at the blank windows. "When we get back to the Captain we'll learn that he gave no such order. That was a good idea of mine about the chair... go along and 'phone him—no, I'd better do that."

He got through to Shannon immediately, and the Commissioner listened in silence. "No—I gave no order. Let the matter stand for tonight, Steel. Tomorrow I will open the house and you'll see things happen. Go, watch the back and see what happens."

He rang off and tapped on the hook until he got the ex change again.

"Give me Electric Supply Corporation," he said, and when at long last he had reached the official he wanted: "This is Captain Shannon of headquarters. As from tomorrow afternoon at four o'clock I want all electric current to be cut off from 551 Portman Square. Precisely at that moment—can you fix it without entering the house? Good!"

In the meantime, the disgruntled Steel and his man made their way to the mews behind that side of Portman Square on which the Malpas house was cited. They were half a dozen yards from the entrance when a well-dressed man walked out, swinging a polished malacca cane.

"Slick Smith!" gasped Steel. "And he is wearing yellow gloves!"

The Flat Burglar

Mr. Slick Smith had developed the social craze for making afternoon calls. This new weakness of his broke into his hours of sleep, for it meant rising at an unusual hour—he was sometimes up as early as noon.

He was known by the police to be an expert hotel and flat thief, but in truth Mr. Smith had attainments beyond these sordid limits. Unconscious of the sensation which his yellow gloves had excited, Slick Smith strolled westward until he came to the busy Edgware Road, and, turning northward, he strolled at his leisure into Maida Vale. In that excellent thoroughfare there are many blocks of residential apartments, some of the highest grade, rented at a price which only a wealthy stockbroker could hear without swooning. There were others where professional men who worked for their living could afford to live, but these latter, for the moment, had no interest for Slick Smith.

It was along the broad carriage drive of Greville Mansions that he walked when he left the sidewalk. This imposing block was occupied by families so wealthy that they could afford, for the great part of the year, to live somewhere else. In other words, a flat in Greville Mansions was the accompaniment of a country house, and thirty per cent of the flats were as a rule untenanted all the year round.

There were two entrances, behind each of which was the brass grille of an elevator, attended by a smart man in livery. Into one of these sedate halls, with its redwood panelling, its neat janitor's office and perfectly carpeted floor. Slick turned. He beamed upon the janitor.

"I wanted to see Mr. Hill," he said affably.

"Mr. Hill is out of town, sir. Did you come about a flat?"

"Ya-as," drawled Slick. "Lady Kilfern's flat is to rent, I understand?"

"To let, sir, you mean. Yes, it is to be let furnished. Have you come from the agents?"

The yellow glove went inside the well-fitting coat, and there came forth, between two fingers, a blue slip of paper, which the janitor read.

"That is all right, sir. This is an order to view Lady Kilfern's flat. Will you come with me?"

He took him up to the second floor, unlocked a magnificent door and led the way into her ladyship's apartments. Slick did no more than glance over the sheeted furniture, and then shook his head sadly.

"I'm afraid that this is the front of the block. It is? I understood it was at the back. I am a bad sleeper, and the noise of the traffic disturbs me."

"There's nothing to let at the back, sir."

"Whose flat is that?"

They stood on the landing, and he indicated a door behind the lift cage. The janitor told him the name of the tenant—a lawyer—whilst Slick strolled leisurely down the passage to the big window that looked out on to the back.

"This would suit me admirably," he said. "A fire escape, too. I'm rather nervous of fires."

He leaned out of the window and took a survey of the courtyard below. He saw more than this; he noted that there were patent locks on the door of No. 9, and that a man of nerve, holding to the edge of the fire- escape landing, could just reach the window of what was apparently No. 9's hall.

"I should like to see one of these back flats, but I suppose that is impossible?" he said sadly.

"Yes, sir; I have a pass-key in case of fire or accident, but I am strictly forbidden to use it."

"A pass-key?" Mr. Smith was charmingly puzzled. "What is a pass- key?"

Displaying the satisfaction with which the man of limited intelligence explains something which is novel to others and familiar to himself: "This is a pass-key," he said, and produced it from his waistcoat pocket with some labour.

Slick took it in his hand and examined it with interest.

"How extraordinary!" he said. "It looks like like any other key. What system does it work on?" He looked the man straight in the eye.

"That's beyond me, sir," said the janitor gravely, even reverently.

He put back the key in his pocket, and at that moment the lift bell rang.

"Excuse me, sir," he began, but Smith caught his arm.

"Can you come back again and see me? I'd like to get your opinion about this front of the house flat," he said anxiously.

"I'll be back in a minute, sir."

When he returned, having deposited a carload of people on an upper floor. Smith was standing where he had left him, a thoughtful figure.

"As I was saying, sir, these pass-keys—" The janitor put his hand in his pocket, and a startled expression appeared on his face. "I've lost it!" he gasped. "Did you see me put it back?"

"I'm sure you did. Why, there it is!"

He pointed to the carpet at the man's feet.

"I wouldn't have lost that for a fortune," said the relieved janitor, and again the interruption of the bell called him to the nether regions. "You ought to go up and see the roof, sir. There's a fine view. I'll take you up."

"I prefer to walk," said Slick Smith. He waited till the lift was out of sight, and his preference for walking took him in three strides to the door. He pushed it gently and it opened, as he expected it would, for he had unlocked the door, fastened back the catch and pulled it close again, all in the time of the janitor's first absence. Now he let the safety catch drop, and went swiftly from room to room.

The place was handsomely furnished, and evidently the plutocratic lawyer had some artistic taste, for the pictures which hung in his small dining-room included two veritable old masters. But Slick Smith was not worrying about pictures. He was after valuables of a more portable character, and in five minutes he had made a most scientific exploration of the best bedroom's contents, and all that he regarded as worth taking he took, slipping the articles into the capacious pocket of his tail-coat. This finished, he had another look round.

He was particularly interested in the kitchen and the contents of the larder, feeling the bread to discover its newness, smelling the butter, examining an opened tin of preserved milk that stood on the kitchen table; and at last, as though he were satisfied that there was nothing worth eating, he crept up the passage, and listened at the door. The whine of the elevator came to his ears, and, stooping, he lifted the flap of the letterbox and caught a glimpse of it passing upwards. Instantly he was out, had closed the door, and was waiting in the hall when the janitor came down.

"Oh, here you are, sir. I wondered where you'd got to."

"I have decided to take her ladyship's flat," said Smith, "but I presume that you do not attend to that side of the business?"

"No, sir, I don't," admitted the man. "And thank you, sir."

He took the munificent tip which Smith slipped into his hand, and the yellow-gloved man walked out, and, some distance along Maida Vale, hailed a taxicab, and gave the driver an address in Soho.

Getting rid of the cab, he passed down a side street, and Stopped outside a little jeweller's shop. Glancing left and right fo make sure that he had not been followed, he dived into the dark interior, and a little man in a skull-cap shuffled behind the curtain.

"What is this worth?" He passed a ring across to the jeweller.

"If I gave you five I'd be robbing myself."

"If you offered me five I'd be murdering you," said Smith good-humouredly.

And then the door opened and a square-shouldered man walked in.

"Hallo, Smith! How's trade?" Smith looked at the Scotland Yard man with a smile. "Doing a little buying and selling?" said the officer pleasantly.

"I gather that you've been tailing me up?"

"How could you think of such a thing?" said the other, shocked. "Let me have a look at that ring."

"I didn't buy it, I didn't buy it!" protested the little jeweller. "He offered it to me, and I told him to take it away!"

"Where did you get this, Smith?"

"It was a present from my Aunt Rachel," said Mr. Smith humorously. "In fact, it is my own ring, and Captain Shannon will be very pleased to identify the same."

"Shannon would?" said the other, nonplussed.

"Sure he would," said Slick, "Come along and see him. But I'll save you trouble; look on the inside, will you?"

The detective carried the ring out into the daylight, and read the inscription: "To Slick from Auntie."

"Well, I'm—?"

"I dare say if you're not, you will be—and I wasn't trying to sell it. I was merely—the fact is, dear lad," said Smith, with engaging candour, "I spotted you when I got out of the cab, and I felt that I ought to bring a little brightness into your dull and drab life. If you'd known your job, you'd have detained the cab to find where I was picked up. But, alas! you don't. Do you want me to go to Shannon?"

The detective jerked his head sternly.

"One of these days—" he threatened.

"A good title for a song: I wonder you don't write it," said Slick, and walked all the way back to Bloomsbury, whistling.

Until there came to him a sense of his folly. If that smart detective had arrested him and searched him... Slick Smith went cold at the thought.

The Lever

A man engaged in the peculiar work which was Mr. Martin Elton's speciality, necessarily accumulates, in the course of the years, quite a large number of documents which must be kept in a safe place, where they cannot attract the attention of the curious. For such things cannot be destroyed without risk or exposed without danger.

Martin relied very much upon the pigeon-holes of his brain for data, and in this respect he was well equipped, for he had one of those extraordinary memories that never forget the smallest detail, and in turning over the pressing problems that awaited treatment, and in searching his mind in all directions for the necessary assistance arid the inducements he could offer to obtain that help, he recalled a four-page memorandum, written in the neat handwriting of Big Bill Stanford.

Stanford was something of a paper strategist. In the old days it was his delight to work out to the last button the "combinations" of every contemplated coup. Most of these had been destroyed, but there was one which had struck Martin at the time as being so ably compiled, that he had kept it, partly as a curio and partly with an eye to the future. Papers such as these, with other intimate matters, were kept at the safe deposit. That afternoon, Martin paid a visit to the vaults, and spent half an hour examining and destroying much that was no longer of value. When he came out, he had in his breast pocket those four single sheets of note-paper which might very well prove to be a powerful lever when it came to influencing Bill Stanford to his way of thinking.

Reaching home, he sent for a district messenger, and dispatched him with a note to Stanford, and half an hour later his telephone bell rang. He gathered from the quality of Stanford's voice that the man was annoyed.

"See here, Martin. I can't run about like a pet dog every time you send for me. What do you want?"

"I wish to see you. It is really important." Stanford growled something, then: "You'd better come here tonight, and see me."

"I'd better do nothing of the kind," said Martin. "You take your instructions from me, Stanford, as usual, whether you're Marshalt's nominee or not. I want you here before five."

"What's the idea?" Stanford's voice was sharp and suspicious. "I told you I was not free for anything."

"Come and tell me that," said Elton, with a touch of his old impatience. "Don't say it over the wire, with half the busies in London listening in. You don't suppose I would send for you if it wasn't urgent, do you?"

There was a long silence at the other end of the wire, and then Stanford spoke in a milder tone.

"All right, I'll come. But don't think that you've got me so that I'm obliged to take orders from you, Elton. You've got to get this right—"

Martin Elton cut him off at that point. He knew his man too well to allow him to get started on a telephone argument.

A few minutes after five, Stanford came, and he came in a cold temper. Martin was lying on the settee, a favourite posture of his, and looked up from a book as the man flung into the room.

"What in hell do you mean by sending for me as if I were a coolie, Elton? You've got a nerve—?"

"Shut the door," said Martin. "You're a bit of a loudspeaker, my friend; if you want to tell your sorrows to Curzon Street, I'll lend you a soap-box."

"Do you think I've nothing to do but run about after you?"

The man was white with anger; he had that quality peculiar to criminals, and not entirely absent from more law-abiding people, an immense vanity, which was easily hurt when his own dignity was threatened. Martin waved him down.

"There is no sense in quarrelling," he said. "This is serious; otherwise, I shouldn't have sent for you."

He got up, took a cigar from the cabinet and lit it. He offered the cabinet to the other, and Stanford sulkily accepted. Then he dropped his bombshell.

"Audrey Bedford has gone to Stormer's, and that child is a fast worker."

"Audrey? You mean your wife's sister?"

Martin nodded.

"Gone to Stormer's? I should worry! Those people mean nothing to me —or to you, either. And if you've brought me from Portman Square, neglecting my duties, to tell me this, you're wasting my time!"

"I tell you she's a fast worker," said Elton slowly, "and she's a keen worker too, Stanford. You're not forgetting, are you, that she did twelve months in Holloway for carrying stuff you had stolen—?"

"Don't say 'you', say 'we'," said Stanford angrily.

"We won't split hairs," agreed Martin. "She did the time. How do you think she's feeling about it—sore, eh? I guess you'd feel sore if you did twelve revolutions of the moon in prison for a crime you didn't commit?"

Stanford was eyeing him suspiciously. "Well, what about it?" he asked, when the other paused. "I suppose she does feel sore, but she's got a new job now and doing fine. Why do you think Stormer's took her?"

"I'll tell you—because she's been to them and split all she knows about the robbery, and they've set her on to collect evidence. Don't forget that Stormer's act for almost every embassy in London."

William Stanford laughed contemptuously. "Well, she can collect all the evidence that is collectable as far as I'm concerned," he said. "And she can start a museum, and then I shouldn't care. Is that all?"

"Not quite." said Martin. "Do you remember you wrote out a little plan of campaign for that Queen of Finland job? Do you remember how you scheduled every possibility, even drawing a little plan of the place in the park where the holdup should be, with detailed instructions as to how the getaway was to be made?"

"I remember," said Stanford after thinking; "but it was destroyed."

"It wasn't destroyed," said Martin coolly. "It was such a perfect piece of work that I very foolishly kept it. Audrey was here two days ago —she came while Dora and I were out, and went up into Dora's room to put her hair straight. Dora keeps the key of my safe deposit in her bureau."

Stanford was looking hard at him. "Well?" he said.

"Today I went to the deposit to get out some money that I had there. I found the money, but all my papers are gone."

Stanford went white. "You mean that my little plan went with the rest?"

Martin nodded very slowly. "That is what I mean," he said. "Now don't get up in the air," as he saw the blood come up to the man's face, and the impotent rage gleam in his eyes. "I know I was a fool to keep it; it should have been destroyed at once, especially since, if I remember rightly, you used names. I'm as much in this as you are, and in as much danger—more, because she's got something on Dora and me that she hasn't got on you."

Stanford was rubbing his hands together, a nervous trick of his.

"You've let me down, you swine!" he said in a fury "Keeping a thing like that!"

"Who wrote the names on the paper? If they weren't there, you could snap your fingers at them," interrupted Martin. "The real fault was yours, I'm not going to pretend that I'm not to blame, but if there's a trial, and a jury say that paper is sufficient evidence against you, Stanford, it will be your own cleverness responsible for the conviction."

Stanford shrugged his shoulders. Behind his apparent strength and his bluster he was something of a weakling, as Martin well knew.

"What do you want me to do?" he asked, and for half an hour they discussed ways and means.

Audrey Goes to Dinner

There would be no need for her attendance that night. Mr. Torrington was very emphatic on the point, though there was a kind tempering to his sternness to which the girl instantly responded.

"So if you have any theatre engagements or dinner-parties, or if you've got some plain sewing to do, you'll have all the time you want."

"Are you going out—?" she began, and was instantly apologetic. "I ought not to have asked you that, and I really didn't ask in my role of amateur detective, but out of..." Here she floundered, seeking without success words to convey her meaning.

"Out of sheer friendliness?" he suggested, and she nodded. "I guessed that. No, my child, I'm staying at home tonight." He looked at the clock on the mantelpiece. "After dinner I have an important interview."

He opened the door for her, and she went out, liking him. She was glad to have this time absolutely her own, for Dora had asked her to come to an early dinner. She was going out, she said, and was not dressing up, so would Audrey come as she was?

The girl had not seen or heard from Dick Shannon that day, and she searched the newspapers in vain for any reference to the diamond steal. When Torrington had spoken about the matter on the previous day, she thought the news was public property; but apparently he had some source of information which was not available to the press, for she found that no newspaper gave so much as a paragraph to the happening. She wished she could see Dick—if only for a few minutes, though there was nothing in particular she wished to say to him. But he hadn't 'phoned or called —she was glad of the distraction which Dora's dinner-party offered.

It was her sister who opened the door to her when she arrived.

"Come in, my dear," she said, kissing her. "I've had another domestic upset. My cook left this afternoon, and my new maid is out for the day; I hadn't the heart to keep her—she was visiting her sick mother. So you'll have to forgive all the deficiencies of dinner—happily, the fastidious Martin has gone to his club."

"I thought you were both going out?" said Audrey in surprise.

"So we are," smiled Dora, "and Martin is coming back to collect me. He had to meet a man, and I suggested that he should dine at the club, and return afterwards."

The table was laid for two, a picture of a table, for Dora, whatever her faults, was an excellent housewife. So perfect was the little dinner that followed, that Audrey might have suspected that the cook, before her departure from the scene, had prepared the meal—which was the truth; for that angry lady had only left half an hour before Audrey arrived, and this was brought about by a baseless accusation of dishonesty, well calculated by Dora to wound the thickest-skinned domestic servant. She had hated parting with the woman, even temporarily, though she knew that an abject apology in the morning would bring her back, and Dora thought it no shame to grovel to a good cook.

Half-way through the dinner: "We're going to have one small bottle of wine to celebrate the family reunion," said Dora gaily.

Getting up from the table, she took a bottle from a silvery bucket, and deftly nipped the wire of the cork. Audrey laughed.

"I haven't tasted wine since—" She remembered the night she had dined with Marshalt, and hurriedly dismissed that unpleasant recollection.

"I don't think you've ever tasted wine like this," Dora prattled on. "Martin has many faults, but he is a wonderful connoisseur. There aren't four dozen of this champagne in England, and when I told him that we were using a bottle tonight, he writhed!"

The cork came out with a pop, and she filled the glass till its creamy head overflowed the side.

"Here's to our next merry meeting," said Dora, and raised her glass.

Audrey laughed softly, and sipped.

"Drink!" said Dora. "That isn't the way to drink a toast."

Audrey raised her glass with great solemnity and did not put it down till it was empty.

"Oh!" she said, and gasped. "I suppose it is very beautiful, but I haven't an educated taste. I thought it was rather bitter—like quinine."

Half an hour after, Dora's new maid unexpectedly appeared.

"I thought you were going to the theatre?" said Dora sharply.

"I have a headache, madam," said the maid. "I'm very sorry, but the ticket you gave me will be wasted."

"Come in," said Dora.

"Perhaps you would like me to wait at table, to save you and Miss Bedford—"

"I've finished dinner," said Dora, "and Miss Bedford has just gone. I wonder you didn't meet her."

Mr. Torrington Surprises

The visitor who called at the Ritz-Carlton was expected and no sooner did he give his name than the clerk called a page.

"Take this gentleman to Mr. Torrington's suite," he said, and Martin followed the boy to the elevator.

Daniel Torrington, in slippers and dressing-gown, shot a keen, inquiring glance at the man as he came in, and without any great show of cordiality motioned him to be seated.

"I have an idea I've met you before, Mr. Torrington," said Martin.

"I'm as certain that we haven't met, though I know you very well by repute," said Torrington. "Take your coat off, Mr. Elton. I had your request for a private interview, and there were many reasons why this should be granted. You are, I believe, the brother-in-law of my secretary?"

Martin inclined his head gravely.

"I have that misfortune," he said.

"Misfortune?" The old man's eyebrows went up. "Ah, I see what you mean! You're thinking of her criminal past?"

He did not sneer, but there was an under-current of sarcasm in his tone, which Martin, sensitive to such things, detected immediately.

"That must be a great sorrow to you and your wife. This unfortunate girl was concerned in a jewel robbery, was she not? I'm not sure whether she was the miscreant who held up the Queen of Finland in Green Park, or whether she planned the theft."

"She was caught with the jewels in her possession," said Martin.

The interview was going to be much more difficult than he had imagined.

"She was caught with the jewels in her possession?" repeated the other. "Well, now, isn't that too bad! Of course, I knew all that before I engaged the young lady, though I presume you came here with the object of protecting me from her machinations?"

Again Martin felt that cold chill of disappointment. The old man was laughing at him, despite his set face and his air of courteous concern.

"No, I didn't come with that object. I came on a very much more intimate matter," he said soberly, "and one which touches you nearly. You will forgive me if I refer to something which must be very painful to you?"

Torrington nodded. The eyes behind the powerful glasses were fixed immovably on Martin's face; his whole attitude was antagonistic. Martin felt it more keenly at that moment than he had before.

"Mr. Torrington, many years ago you went to prison in South Africa for illicit diamond buying."

Torrington nodded.

"Yes, there was a frame-up, organized by the greatest scoundrel in the diamond fields, one Lacy Marshalt, who is now, happily, deceased. I was certainly the victim on that occasion, and, as you say, I went to prison."

"You had a young wife"—Martin hesitated—"and a child, a little girl, Dorothy?"

Again Torrington nodded.

"Your wife was greatly shocked by your arrest, and never afterwards forgave you for the shame, as she thought, you ad brought upon her. And soon after you were taken to the Breakwater she left South Africa, and since then I think it is true that you did not hear from her?"

"Once." The word came like the snap of a whip. "Once, my friend, she wrote—yes, once!"

"She came to England with her baby and an elder daughter, changed her name to Bedford, and lived on a small income."

"Annuity," interrupted Torrington.

Whatever emotions he experienced, he did not betray by so much as a twitch of muscle.

"An annuity which I purchased for her before my arrest. So far you are right. Go on."

Martin drew a long breath. Every word was an effort in this atmosphere. He felt like a man striving to pick a hole in a granite wall.

"Your late wife was rather eccentric. For some reason, best known to herself, she brought up Dorothy"—he emphasized the word—"to believe that she was the daughter of her first husband, and the other girl was taught that she was the elder. I don't pretend to explain the mind of the woman—" began Martin.

"Don't," said Torrington. "Well, all these things may or may not be true. What then?"

Martin Elton took the plunge.

"You are under the impression, sir, that your daughter Dorothy died. That is not true. She lives; she is in England now, and is my wife."

Daniel Torrington was looking at him; his eyes seemed to pierce their way into the secret places of the visitor's very soul.

"Is that the story you have to tell me," said Torrington at last, "that my little Dorothy is still alive and is your wife?"

"That is the story, Mr. Torrington."

"Ah!" The old man rubbed his chin. "Is that so?"

591

A long and painful silence followed.

"Do you know the story of my arrest—the circumstances? I see that you do not—I will tell you."

He looked up at the ceiling, licked his lips and seemed to be reconstructing the scene in his mind.

"I was sitting on the stoep of my house at Wynberg—I always came down to the Peninsula for the summer—and I remember I was nursing my baby. You know what a stoep is, I suppose? It is a broad, raised porch that runs the length of the house. I saw Marshalt coming round the shrubbery, and wondered what brought him, until I saw the two detectives who were following. He was scared of me, scared sick! As I rose and put the child down in her cradle, he pulled a gun and fired. He said I shot first, but that is a lie. I wouldn't have shot at all, but the bullet struck the cradle, and I heard the child scream. It was then I drew on him, and he would have been a dead man but for the agony of mind I was in about the child. As it was, I missed him, and his second shot smashed my leg. Did you know that?"

Martin shook his head.

"You never heard about the shot that hit the cradle, eh?"

"No, sir; that is news to me."

"I thought it would be; The child wasn't badly hurt; the bullet just nicked her little toe and broke the bone—I wonder your wife never told you," he drawled.

Martin was silent.

"My little Dorothy isn't dead—I've known that for a very long time. I've been looking for her, and, thanks to my friend Stormer, I have found her!"

"She knows?" said Martin, his face ghastly.

Torrington shook his head.

"No, she doesn't know; I didn't want her to know. I wanted to keep that from her until my work is complete. And I've pretended to everybody about me, except one man, that she is a stranger to me. Ask the innocent Mr. Willitt, who almost begged me on his knees to make her my secretary." His cold eyes did not leave Martin's face.

"Your wife is my daughter, eh? Ask her to come here and show me her left foot. You can fake birth certificates, Elton—that makes you jump, my friend—but you can't fake little toes!"

He rang the bell, and, to the man who came: "Show this gentleman out," he said, "and when Miss Bedford returns, will you ask her to come straight to me?"

Martin went home like a man in a dream, and Dora read disaster in his pallid face. She drew him into the drawing-room and closed the door.

"What is the matter with you, Martin? Did you see him?"

He nodded.

"He knows," he said huskily.

"Knows—?"

"He knows Audrey is his daughter—that is all. He has known it all the time. He's had Stormer looking for her. He was going to tell her tonight, I suppose you know what this means to you and me?"

He sat with his face buried in his hands.

"It ought to mean a fortune to us," she said, and he looked up quickly.

"You wanted to do this, and I agreed against my will. It was my idea to tell the old man that she was his daughter. It was you who said you'd rather die than see her with all that money. Where is that fortune coming?"

She nodded slowly.

"He'll pay to get her back, if—"

"If what?"

"If she is still alive," said Dora Elton. "And if nothing... else has happened."

A Lady Calls on Mr. Smith

The landlord of Mr. Slick Smith was a tolerant, easy-going man. He knew that his tenant lived on the shady side of life, but that neither heightened nor lowered Slick Smith in his estimation. To him, his lodger was a man who paid his bill regularly, was invariably courteous, gave no trouble, and was grateful for any little services which the landlord, a highly respectable lawyer's clerk, could render to him.

He had had what he called a heart-to-heart talk with Smith as soon as he discovered his nefarious calling, and that conversation might be summarized into a sentence, "You may do what you like, but you must not bring me or my house into disrepute."

Visitors he looked coldly upon, for visitors savoured of conspiracy; and, to do him justice. Slick Smith seldom offended in this respect.

The landlord heard a knock that night. It was eleven o'clock—that hour which separates, in some intangible fashion, the sheep who go to bed before and the goats who frolic after. The landlord himself went to the door and found a young and prepossessing woman—a stranger to him, and, as far as he knew, a complete stranger to his lodger.

"Mr. Smith?" he said dubiously. "No, I don't think he's in, miss. Can I give him a message?"

"It's very important; I must see him," said the girl in almost peremptory tones.

The landlord hesitated. Visitors of any kind he objected to, but lady visitors at eleven o'clock at night offended him beyond measure. Nevertheless, thinking there might be some good excuse for her presence —that she might, for example, be a sister or a messenger from his sick mother, or something equally proper—he went upstairs and knocked at the door, receiving no answer. Turning the handle, he walked in. The room was untenanted, and he went back with a message that was consonant with his principles.

"Mr. Smith isn't in, miss," he said, closed the door upon her, and went back to his pipe and his law book.

After a while he thought he heard somebody walking down the stairs, opened the door and peered out. It was Mr. Smith.

"I didn't hear you come in."

"I haven't been in long," said Smith in his usual genial tone.

"Are you going out?"

"I heard a knock and thought it was for me."

"There was a lady came to see you—" began the landlord.

"I expect it is she," said Smith.

His landlord felt it the moment to assert his authority.

"If you'll excuse me, Mr. Smith, I don't like visitors at this hour of the night, and, of course, you'll not ask the lady in?"

"If I do, perhaps I can borrow your parlour," said Smith. "I think this is rather an important business message. In fact, it is from my friend Captain Shannon, the Sherlock Holmes of Scotland Yard."

The landlord knew that Captain Shannon was eminently respectable, and granted the necessary permission, even going so far as to put on all the lights in the parlour.

"Come in," said Smith. "You're from Captain Shannon?"

"Yes," was the reply—all of which the landlord heard, as it was intended he should hear, and was satisfied.

He heard the low murmur of their voices in the drawing-room for a quarter of an hour, and then the girl went out, and Smith sought him.

"It is rather more important than I imagined," he said gravely. "Captain Shannon is in a serious difficulty, and has called me in— we frequently help the police out of their difficulties."

This was news to the landlord, but he was satisfied, being a simple man who knew nothing but law, and lawyers are notoriously childlike.

Slick changed from the evening dress he had been wearing when he had returned, into a lounge suit, put on a fleecy overcoat, and, taking from a drawer one of the many implements of his craft, joined the girl, who was waiting for him at the corner of the street, and walked with her as far as Southampton Row.

Glancing over his shoulder as he walked down the Row, he saw the inevitable Stormer man following him. When he called a cab, his shadow followed his example. Smith didn't trouble to look; he knew. At the Marble Arch: "Where to, sir?" asked the cabman.

"Greville Mansions, Maida Vale," said Slick.

He came to that aristocratic block with the air of a proprietor, as he was well entitled to do, for he was the temporary tenant of a handsome suite on the second floor, and uniformed porters would, for an indefinite period, touch their hats to him.

The night liftman took him up, exchanging commonplaces about the weather, and bade him good night, leaving him, as he believed, to the enjoyment of that dreamless sleep which is the right of all men wealthy enough to rent a ladyship's flat at twenty guineas a week.

*

That same evening Sergeant Steel and his superior were two of the council of three that met at Dick's flat. The third was the inspector in charge from Marylebone Lane, and the subject of discussion was 551 and its artistic treasure.

"I am still undecided about moving the idol," said Shannon, "but the orders to the electric light company stand. I've had one of their engineers to see me, and he says they can cut off the supply from the conduit outside the house. Which means that the power that has helped Malpas and his friends will no longer be available."

"I take it you'll have the place opened before the supply is cut off? Otherwise, it may lead to endless difficulties," said the inspector.

Dick agreed.

"I'm satisfied that we shall paralyse the activity of Mr. Ghost, though it is also possible that, when the current is cut, we shall imprison our friend in some secret hiding-place and leave future generations to unearth the mystery."

"In that case," said Steel, "we shall never see Slick Smith again."

Shannon laughed.

"You think Smith is the king pippin of the crowd?"

"I'm certain of it," said the other emphatically. "Hasn't it struck you as remarkable. Captain Shannon, that Smith has invariably been around when we've seen these demonstrations? This afternoon I saw him walking out of the mews, immediately following the appearance of a yellow-gloved hand at the door. And he was wearing yellow gloves!"

"So do fifty thousand other people wear yellow gloves," said Dick. "It is the fashion amongst the smartly dressed men of London. You can keep Smith in mind, though I'm not satisfied that your view is the correct one."

"There's something wrong with him, anyway," insisted Steel. "I mean something out of the ordinary. He is wanted badly on the other side —I've never seen him without he had a Stormer man on his trail, and Stormer's don't take all that trouble unless they think they have a good kill ahead."

Dick smiled as he thought of the latest recruit to the Stormer corps.

The meeting broke up at half past ten, having decided upon the plan of operations for the following day; and at a quarter to eleven Steel made his round of the many and curious clubs that had sprung up in London since the war. There were dance clubs and supper clubs; some in gilded saloons; not a few in furtive cellars, converted at great expense into halls of gaiety by the engagement of the inevitable syncopated orchestra and a loose system of membership. He noted the normal irregularities, and checked them for future action. His tour finished, he strolled home. The clock was booming the quarter to twelve as he came into Upper Gloucester Place, where his lodgings were, and his hand was in his pocket, feeling for the key, when he saw a man walking quickly towards him on the opposite side of the road. There was nothing unusual about a quick walker at this hour of the night, nor even remarkable in the fact that he carried a bag; for Marylebone Station is within a stone's throw, and arrivals by the late trains often passed through Upper Gloucester Place on their way to their homes.

He didn't recognize the man as he came into the focus of a street lamp, but the bag certainly seemed of familiar shape. For a moment he debated with himself, and then, though every cell of his body called loudly for sleep, he turned back and pursued the bag.

There was practical reason for his act. In his then nervous state, if he had omitted to make a closer inspection and satisfy himself that his eyes had deceived him, he would have lain awake for hours, cursing his laziness. The chase was a little absurd, for one bag is very much like another, and, seen across the width of a street on a dark night, and by the unsatisfactory street light, the resemblance is even more complete. But he was determined to see that bag, and quickened his pace, as he had need to do, for the man ahead of him was walking rapidly, though the grip was so heavy that from time to time he changed his hand.

His way led down Harley Street, but he kept on, and then, at this stage of his annoyance. Steel began to run. He was within a dozen yards of his quarry when the man turned, and, seeing his pursuer, followed his example and ran swiftly, turning into a side street and diving into one of those narrow mews which abound in these parts. Bag or no bag, the fugitive had a reason for his flight, and Steel's policeman instinct aroused, he sprinted. There was no policeman in sight, and the runner with the bag evidently knew the beat so well that he could avoid the unpleasantness of meeting a representative of the law; for he doubled round again. This time he was not so fortunate; there was an officer on point duty at the corner of the street, and the quarry checked, hesitated a moment, and then, as Steel went up to him, put down his bag, and, dodging under the detective's arm, flew like the wind.

In that brief space Steel recognized him; it was Slick Smith! Should he go after him? He decided that the bag was his proper objective. At this moment the policeman, who had seen the flying man, came up. "Go after that man and get him," said Steel, and turned his attention to the bag.

At the sight of it his heart leapt...

Dick was undressing when his subordinate dashed in, his eyes blazing with excitement, and the big leather grip in his hand.

"Look at this!" he said, and Jerked it open. Dick looked in dumbfounded amazement.

"The diamonds!" he said in a whisper.

"Slick Smith had 'em!" cried the detective breathlessly. "I spotted him going down Upper Gloucester Place with the bag, and followed him, though I didn't know it was he. And then he bolted, and when I came up with him he dropped the bag."

"Slick Smith? Where was he coming from?"

"From the direction of Park Road," said Steel rapidly. "I thought I should drop dead when I opened the bag and saw what was in it."

Dick ran his fingers through the stones.

limb.

"I don't know where I've been," he said wearily. "How long is it since I disappeared?"

When they told him he groaned.

"I've been two days in a cellar under the warehouse. If I hadn't found a scrap of paper that had fallen down from the street, I'd have been dead. When is Captain Shannon coming back?"

"He is searching the warehouse now," said the local sergeant.

Dick's inspection of the warehouse added very little to his knowledge. He found the main door unlocked, but no sign of his assailant. There were several underground apartments where the man might have been kept prisoner. He found one which communicated with the street, and it was here that he discovered something even more important. At the foot of the flight of stone steps leading down to the basement he saw a green-labelled carton, and picked it up. It was the cardboard case which had contained ammunition for an automatic pistol, and was obviously that which was missing from the box in Marshalt's store-room when he had made his cursory inspection. He handed it to Steel without a word.

"Malpas is here somewhere," whispered the detective, and looked round nervously.

"I think not," said Shannon quietly. "Our friend only takes one shot a night." He glanced up at the ladder-like stairs leading to the upper part of the warehouse.

"I hardly think it is worth while searching upstairs. I'll ask the sergeant to do so tomorrow morning."

The man who stood by a gap which had once been a window in the upper part of the building heard this decision with relief. It saved him from the risk which would follow a jump in the dark.

He gave Dick Shannon a very good start before he felt his way downstairs, and, peeping cautiously forth to see whether an officer had been left on duty (a disconcerting habit of the police), he went up to the edge of the staging, peered down, and, with some reluctance, lowered himself into the boat and pushed into the cavernous dark. His hand touched the cold water, and he shivered.

"War is certainly hell!" said Slick Smith.

Marshalt's Story

By the time Shannon reached the police station Marshalt was sufficiently recovered to talk of his experiences.

"Frankly I can give you very little information, Captain Shannon," he said, "except about the beginning of this adventure. As you have probably discovered, I was lured into Malpas's flat by a note, which asked me"—he hesitated—"to meet a lady there—a lady in whom we are both interested. I admit that it was the worst kind of folly for me not to have suspected a trap. The man hated me—a fact which is, I think, known to you. But I was curious to see him; I'd heard so much about this mysterious Mr. Malpas."

"When did the note reach you?"

"About half an hour before I went out. I was dining at Rector's with some friends of mine and, as a matter of fact, I was just leaving the house when Tonger brought the note—as Tonger will tell you—?"

"I'm afraid Tonger is beyond telling us anything," said Dick quietly, and Lacy Marshalt stared at him.

"Dead?" he said in an awe-stricken whisper. "Good God! When did he die?"

"He was found dead within half an hour of the attack on you."

The news seemed to strike the man speechless, but after a while he went on:

"I don't know whether it was a premonition, or whether it was a remembrance of the warnings I had received, but before going out I went up to my room, took off my shirt and put on an old bullet-proof singlet that I wore when I was in the Balkans a few years ago, looking for concessions. It was very uncomfortable, but, as it proved, this precaution saved my life. I went out without any overcoat intending to walk back to my house, and knocked at the door of 551, which was immediately opened."

"You heard no voice?" asked Dick.

Marshalt shook his head.

"No, the door just opened. I expected to see a servant there, but, to my surprise, there was nobody visible, but I heard somebody from up the stairs say 'Come up'. Naturally I followed the instructions. I walked into a big room, heavily draped with velvet, but empty. Then it was I began to feel a little suspicious, and was walking out of the room when, to my amazement, the door closed in my face. The next moment I heard somebody laugh, and, looking round, I saw a man, who was obviously disguised, standing at the far end of the room. 'I've got you now!' he said.

"He had a revolver in his hand, one of the old-fashioned kind. Realizing the impossibility of getting out of the room, I ran towards him. I hadn't taken two steps before I was tripped up by a wire, and rose only to be caught again. I thought he was bluffing, and my object was to get to him and take the gun away from him. I was only a few paces from him when he fired, and that is all I remember, until I woke up in dreadful pain, and I guessed—look!"

He pulled open his shirt and showed a pink discoloration, the size of a man's hand, on the left of his chest.

"Where were you when you recovered consciousness?"

"I remember very little clearly after that," said Marshalt, frankly. "I must have been awake often, and once I remember the old man jabbed a needle into my arm. It was the stab of the needle that woke me then, I think. I tried to rise and grapple with him, but I was as weak as a child. From time to time I have come to my senses, but always in a different place, until I woke one evening in that dreadful cellar, handcuffed and helpless. Malpas was looking down at me. He did not tell me who he was, and although I racked my brains I couldn't recognize him. But apparently I had done him some bad injury in South Africa. He told me that that night was my last on earth. It was when he had gone that I found the paper and fortunately there was a stub of pencil in my pocket. I waited my opportunity. It was a terrible business getting to my feet, but eventually I succeeded and was able to push up the note to a young man who peered down; he seemed so startled at the sight of a man in evening dress—and what an evening dress!—that he nearly bolted."

"You've no recollection of being taken back to Portman Square?"

Lacy shook his head. "None whatever. Now tell me about poor Tonger. How terrible! Who killed him? Do you think it was Malpas?"

"Tell me one thing, Mr. Marshalt: is there any kind of passage or doorway between your house and Malpas's? I will admit that I have made a very careful examination without discovering any."

Marshalt shook his head.

"If there is, Malpas must have made it, but I doubt it." He frowned. "Now you mention the fact, I remember that I made a complaint once about a knocking noise that I heard. Both I and Tonger have heard those knocks from time to time. What he was doing I can't tell you. By the way, did Stanford get to my house? It occurred to me in my few waking moments that some time ago I named this man to take charge of the house in case anything happened to me."

"Why did you do that?" asked Dick.

"It happened years ago, when I knew Stanford and was more friendly with him than I am now. In fact, to be candid, before I knew that he wasn't straight and honest. It was at a time when there was a scare —you remember, a gang kidnapped a Greek millionaire, and held him to ransom? So Stanford is at the house?" He pulled a wry face. "Probably it is all right," he said, "and, if I remember, the stipend would insure me against—well, I won't do him that injustice," he added, "but really, he is not the type of man I would have chosen."

He offered Dick his hand. "I can't be sufficiently grateful to you for all you've done for me. Captain Shannon. You've saved my life. If you'd been even five minutes later...." He shivered.

Dick did not reply at once, and when he spoke he made no reference to the service he had given to the millionaire.

"Will you tell me this, Mr. Marshalt?" he said. "Though you say you did not recognize Malpas, you must have had some idea as to who it was, some lingering suspicion?"

Marshalt hesitated. "I have," he said. "My own impression—you will think it is fantastic—Malpas is a woman!"

What Audrey Saw

Audrey Bedford had a dream, and it was a particularly unpleasant one. She dreamt she was lying on a narrow ledge like the top of a T, the lower stalk of which was a high tower. And as she lay, her head racked with a distracting pain, the tower swayed backward and forward, and she with it. Every now and again the board upon which she lay tipped up gently, and she screamed in her sleep and clutched tightly to the edge, expecting to be precipitated into the black void below.

The reality was a headache; that was her conscious obsession. It was an ache that began behind her eyes, shot to her temples, and thence, by a million fiery routes, to the back of her head. She groaned as she turned over and buried her face in the crook of her arm. She had never had such a headache. She reached out for the bell by the side of her bed, and in a confused way went over the remedies she would use, beginning and ending with a cup of tea. She wanted that drink very, very badly; her tongue was parched, her mouth bone-dry, and she had a horrible taste. She turned over again, groaned and sat up.

It was quite dark, and she was not lying on a bed at all; she was on a mattress and there was a blanket over her, and when she reached out she touched the floor. Unsteadily she rose to her feet, leaning against the wall to prevent herself from falling, for her head was going round and round. Then she began to feel for the door, found it after a while and pulled it open. It was dark outside. At the end of what seemed to be a long tunnel she saw a little glimmer of light and staggered towards it. One-half of her brain told her she was walking down a short, unfurnished corridor, and that the light she saw was a naked lamp hanging by a wire from the ceiling.

She saw a wash-bowl in a little room leading off, and went towards it gratefully. When she turned the faucet, the water was brown and discoloured, but presently it ran clean, and, using her hands as a cup, she drank greedily.

She washed her face; a towel was hanging from a peg —it almost looked as if it had been placed there specially for her benefit, for there was no furniture in the apartment save the mattress and blankets.

She let the bath-tap run; the sound of the running water was very companionable. Then, sitting down on the projecting window ledge, she tried to get back to the beginning of this experience. The last thing she remembered was talking to Mr. Torrington. No, it was later than that; she was in her room, putting on her hat to go out. Step by step she traced her conscious movements, and came, with a start of horror, to the dinner table of Dora Elton, and the wine that creamed and bubbled and tasted so vilely. Dora!

Frantically she searched the recesses of her memory to carry her beyond that last remembered period, but in vain. She was at Dora's house. She remembered now that the woman had once told her that the upper story of the Curzon Street establishment had never been furnished.

She was still stupid from the effect of the drug; but only now did she understand why it was so dark. Every window was covered with a thick shutter, the shutters being held in place by a steel bar, hammered tight into a socket. Using all her strength, she tried to lift one after the other, but though she made a complete circuit of the room, she found none that would yield.

The door was locked; she looked through a keyhole, but could see nothing. And then her exertions, on top of the drug, produced the inevitable result. She felt her knees give way, and had just sufficient presence of mind to lower herself to the ground before she again lost consciousness. She woke feeling cold and stiff, but the headache had almost gone, and she retraced her steps to where the water was.

She managed to find a light in the room where she had been when she first woke. This proved a bare apartment except for the mattress on the floor and a broken chair. By dint of tugging she managed to get a stout rail loose: it was her only weapon, and would be of little service if she attempted to use it in her present weak state. But it was something; it lent her a little more confidence. By degrees she managed to pull the remainder of the chair to pieces, until she got a stout leg and a portion of the back, and with this she attacked the bars of the shutters, but without result.

Hungry and weary, she lay down on the bed, pulled the blanket over her, and fell asleep almost immediately. When she woke, it seemed warmer, and her hunger had subsided to a numb, gnawing pain. She sat on the bed, trying to think. And then she heard the sound of a voice. A man was speaking. Was it Martin? No, it was too deep for him. She crept to the door and listened; and as she did so she heard a stealthy footstep on the stair just outside the door.

Who was it? Her heart beat tumultuously. The voice from below came again, and, hearing it, she almost swooned.

It was Lacy Marshalt! She put her hand to her mouth to arrest the scream. Lacy Marshalt, and he was talking. "Yes, it was somewhere here..."

She was going mad—she must be. Mad already! Somewhere below was Lacy Marshalt, and Lacy Marshalt was dead!

And then as she stood, frozen with horror, the footstep sounded again inside, and, crouching down, she looked through. A faint light illuminated the staircase, and she saw the figure of a man, but his face was turned away.

"It was somewhere here," said Marshalt's faint voice again. The man on the landing was listening as intently as she. While she looked, he turned his head. She saw the long nose, the pointed chin and the high, bumpy forehead. Malpas! When she looked again, he was gone.

Malpas and Marshalt! What did it mean? Her limbs were trembling; she had to use the wall as a support as she crawled back to her room. She was not in Curzon Street at all: she was in the hands of the devil-man! The horror of it seized her, and for a second her reason rocked. And then somebody rapped softly on the passage door.

She held her breath and waited, her eyes fixed on the place where the terror would appear.

The Man on the Landing

The tapping was resumed after an interval. Audrey kept quiet, scarcely daring to flicker an eyelash. Did he know she was there? The thought occurred to her at that moment that Dora and her husband must be in the secret of this awful house.

Again came that dreadful tapping, and then silence. She waited for half an hour before she dared move. There was no noise; the house was as still as the grave; no sound of voice or footstep came up to her as she listened at the door, and she went back to where she had been, only to start up again at the sound of a key turning in the lock. From where she sat she could only see the wall of the passage. Something rattled, and then the door closed again.

Was he waiting in the passage for her? Her heart fluttered at the thought, and then the absurdity of the idea occurred to her. Why should he wait in the passage? Nevertheless, she had to summon all her courage to look out, and when she did she could have cried for joy, for on the floor was a tray, holding a hot coffee-pot, rolls, bread and butter, and thick slices of cold meat. She carried the tray into her room, and ate cautiously. How hungry she was she only began to realize now; and it was not until most of the viands had disappeared, and she had drunk her third cup of coffee, that she stopped to regret that she had not looked round the corner when the man was still in the passage.

But perhaps it was Dora. No appeal could be made there, she thought. Neither did her hope lie with Martin, if hope there was.

And now she could think clearly and logically. Why had they done this? What was gained to Dora or her husband by this senseless act? That Dora hated her she knew; she would go a long way to hurt her, she was just as sure. But Dora would hurt nobody unless she profited herself, and what profit there was in shutting her up in Malpas's house she couldn't understand. But she was in Malpas's house; that made her serious again.

She turned on all the switches she could find; the light, like the running water, gave her a sense of company. When, would the next meal come? she wondered. Should she make an attempt to see the man or woman who brought it? Several times she made a journey to the door to listen, but the stillness was unbroken.

It was on her seventh visit to the door that the scarcely audible sound of somebody descending the stairs reached her. She knelt on the floor, her eyes on the rather large keyhole, and presently she was rewarded. Something dark passed before the door and stopped on the broad landing. She saw him clearly now, or as plainly as the dim light permitted. He wore a long coat that reached to his heels; his head was covered with a black slouch hat. For a moment he stood there in a listening attitude, then he put out his hand, and a part of the wall opened—a door, scarcely more than six inches square, so well camouflaged by the design of the paper that covered the wall that Dick Shannon had passed it a dozen times without detecting its presence.

She looked, fascinated, as his hand went into the opening. She saw a flash of blue flame, and the lights in the passage went out. Then he turned. He was coming towards the door. She told herself he would pass and go upstairs again, but, even as she looked, she saw the end of the key coming into the hole, and, turning, she ran, screaming, down the passage and slammed the door of her room tight, and stood with her back against it...

The outer lock clicked open.

Dora Will Not Tell

Dick Shannon returned to his flat at four o'clock in the morning, having escorted Lacy Marshalt back to his house, and witnessed the embarrassment of Mr. Stanford at the sudden apparition.

He found two men in his sitting-room, one a sleepy-eyed but dogged William, the other...

"Why, Mr. Torrington, you're the last person in the world I expected to see!"

The man was changed, his tone of light banter had gone. Dick recognized this the moment he spoke. "I want to see you pretty badly. My daughter has disappeared."

"Your—?"

"My daughter—Audrey. You didn't know that she was my girl? I can't go into the story now, but Audrey Bedford is Audrey Torrington, the child of my second wife."

Dick was looking at him through a haze.

"I'm dumbfounded," he said. "Audrey... she has disappeared, you say? But she has been staying at your hotel!"

"She went out last night and didn't come back. I let her go out because I had arranged to meet Martin Elton, who had something to tell me —something which I knew and something which I guessed."

Briefly he narrated all that bad passed at the interview with Martin.

"Unfortunately for him I knew all the facts and guessed what he was driving at before he'd finished; and I left orders that Audrey should be told I wanted to see her when she returned. At eleven o'clock she had not come in; at midnight, when I sent to inquire, thinking she might have gone to a dance, she was still out. Knowing that young girls nowadays keep up until all hours, I wasn't alarmed, till one o'clock came and then two. Then I communicated with headquarters; they told me you were out and that you would be notified as soon as you returned. I couldn't wait any longer, so I came here."

"Where did she go?" asked Dick.

Mr. Torrington shook his head.

"I don't know. She merely said she was going out; she told nobody where. I haven't, of course, searched her room—I didn't want to take that course until I was sure."

"We'll search it now," said Dick, and drove him back to the hotel.

The night porter who opened the door to them had no news. "The young lady hasn't come back yet, sir," he reported. He took them up in the elevator to her room, and opened the door for them. The bed had not been slept in; her night-dress had been laid across the turned-down sheet; a glass of milk stood on the side-table. Dick saw a well-worn writing-case by its side, and this he opened, examining the letters quickly. There was none which gave him the slightest hint of her destination until he saw, in the microscopic

612

waste-paper basket with which hotels supply their guests, the torn-up fragments of a letter. Tipping the basket on to the table, he began to put the pieces together.

"This is from Mrs. Elton; it was written today." Presently he had it complete. It was a note telling her to come early, and there was a significant P.S.: 'Please burn this letter. I hate to think that my letters are lying around, especially in a hotel, where everybody sees them.'

"I will see Elton. You needn't come, Mr. Torrington," said Dick quietly.

The old man demurred, but presently saw the wisdom of this course, and left Dick to go alone.

The Elton house was in darkness, but he had not to wait long before he saw a light appear in the passage. It was Martin Elton; he was in his dressing-gown, and might have just come out of bed, but for the tell-tale evidence of cigar-ash on the front of the gown.

"Hallo, Shannon! Come in. You're rather an early caller," he said, as he c losed the door.

"Is your wife up?"

"I don't know—I'll see. Do you want her?"

"I want you both," said Dick.

When a police officer speaks in the tone that Dick Shannon employed, there is very little ultimate profit in argument.

Dora came down in a neglige within a few minutes of his arrival.

"Do you wish to see me, Captain Shannon?"

"I want Dorothy Audrey Torrington," he said.

"I don't—" she began.

"You don't know what I mean, of course. Now listen, Mrs. Elton. Your sister came here to dinner at your invitation. You sent her a letter which you asked her to burn, but which she did not burn, but tore up. She arrived at this house somewhere about six o'clock." And then, as a thought struck him, "Let me see your maid."

"My dear Captain Shannon, what use can the maid be? I will tell you all I know. I don't want the servants brought into this," said Dora tartly.

"Go and bring her down."

Martin went upstairs to the top floor of the house, knocked at the door, and was almost staggered when the door opened immediately and the maid came out, fully dressed, and wearing an overcoat.

"What the—?" he began, and she laughed.

"What do you want, Mr. Elton?"

"Captain Shannon wishes to speak to you," said Martin, recovering from his surprise. "He is inquiring about madam's sister. You know, she dined here tonight, and you'd better tell Shannon that you were here all the time, and you remember her going."

She made no reply.

"Here is the girl," he said, as he brought the servant into the room, and Dora glared at her. "Why are you dressed like that?" she asked angrily.

"Because I always dress like this when I'm going out," said the girl.

She was a red-faced, healthy-looking young woman, somewhat stocky of build.

"Now, my girl," said Shannon, "Miss Audrey Torrington—or as you know her, Miss Bedford—was dining here tonight, I believe?"

"I believe she was, sir. I wasn't in the house when she arrived, and I didn't see her go. Mrs. Elton sent me out to the theatre, and dismissed the cook an hour before Miss Bedford arrived, so that there were only three people in the house—Mr. and Mrs. Elton and Miss Bedford."

"I was not here at all," said Martin, in a rage, "I was at my club!"

"You were in the house, upstairs," said the girl calmly. "I didn't see Miss Bedford go, because I was at the other end of the street, talking to one of our men. I saw a cab drive away, and by the time I got to the house I think Miss Bedford really had gone."

"One of your men? What do you mean?" asked Dick. She made no answer, but produced from her pocket a small, five-pointed silver star.

"I'm one of Stormer's people," she said, and seeing the dismay in Dora's face, "So was your previous servant, Mrs. Elton. I have been waiting for you. I expected you would come." She was talking to Dick Shannon. "The only thing I can tell you is that Miss Bedford is not in this house; I've searched it from garret to cellar."

Martin Elton's face was ghastly; it was his wife who fought to the last.

"How very romantic!" she sneered. "A woman detective! You were a pretty bad housemaid."

The girl interrupted her,

"I cleared the table"—she was still talking to Shannon —"and I put what remained in Miss Bedford's glass into this." She brought out a tiny medicine phial from her pocket; there was just sufficient wine to cover the bottom. "And this I found in Mrs. Elton's jewel-box later in the evening."

Dora made a snatch at the little blue bottle she held, but the girl was too quick for her. Pushing her aside without an effort, she placed it in Dick's hand.

"I think you'll find it is butyl chloride. There is no label; that was washed off. But it smells like butyl."

Shannon's face was hard and set; his eyes fixed Elton's with a snaky glitter.

"You've heard what this lady said, Elton. Where is Audrey?"

"You want to know?" Martin answered him, "Well, I can tell you, but you've got to pay—no, not money I mean. I want twenty-four hours for Dora and me to get out of the country. Let me have that, and I'll tell you where she is. And you'd better pay the price, Shannon," he said meaningly. "She is in greater danger than you'll ever guess. Will you promise?"

"I'll promise you nothing," said Shannon. "Not to save Audrey's life would I let you loose! Where is she?"

"Find out!" cried Dora defiantly. "If this woman 'busy' knows so much, maybe she'll tell you some more."

Dick said nothing further. From his hip pocket he drew a steel bracelet and snapped it on Martin's wrist, and he made no attempt to escape, though, as the steel touched his flesh, his face went suddenly old. Perhaps the ghosts of his dead boyhood had arisen; the calm of cloistered walks; the green of playing-fields; the tradition up to which he once strove to live.

"You'll not handcuff me!" screamed Dora, as he gripped her arm. "You shan't! You shan't!" But the woman from Stormer's slipped behind her and caught both her arms. In another second she was linked by a more material bond than that which bound her to the man by her side.

Stanford

Dick took them to the station and ordered their detention. He could not charge either until he was certain. As he was coming down the steps he asked the girl from Stormer's a question he had forgotten to put to her.

"Has he had any visitors lately?"

"Yes—Stanford. They had a row about something. I couldn't quite gather what it was—something about a plan. But I couldn't hear very well, Mrs. Elton was standing so near the door that I dared not listen."

"Do you think Stanford is in this?"

She shook her head.

"It is difficult to say. I've an idea that they were bad friends. I heard Elton shouting over the 'phone to Stanford, and by his replies I gather that there was a row of some kind."

"I saw Stanford tonight," said Dick Shannon thoughtfully, "and he certainly did not seem to have anything on his conscience." He held out his hand. "I do not approve of private detectives," he said, with a faint smile, "but I'm beginning to become reconciled to Stormer's!"

He thought at first that he would return to the hotel to tell Torrington what had happened, but instead he briefly explained over the 'phone, and, promising to call later, he went on to Portman Square. If any spot in London had earned his undying hatred, that agglomeration of stately houses certainly had. He knocked and rang, and knocked again. It was ten minutes before he made anybody hear, and then it was Stanford himself who opened the door. At the sight of the detective an uneasy look came to his face. Dick could have sworn that he was trembling.

"Where is Miss Bedford?" asked the detective without preliminary. "And consider well before you reply, Stanford. I've just taken Elton and his wife and put them inside, and there's a hell of a cosy cell on the same row that

Edgar Wallace

you'd just fit!"

The man stared at him stupidly; he seemed at a loss to find words to reply.

"I don't know what you mean about Audrey Bedford," he said at last. "How should I know? I've been here all evening; you saw me here yourself. She wouldn't come to this house, anyway." And then, as though divining that Shannon had no exact information, he went on more boldly: "What has Martin Elton to do with me? I quarrelled with him—you ought to know that. I had a row with him about some stuff of mine that he lost."

A voice came from the top of the stairs. "Who is that?"

"It is Shannon," growled the man, and Marshalt came downstairs, fastening his dressing-gown.

"Did you want to see me. Shannon?"

"I called to see Stanford. Audrey Bedford disappeared last night, after dining with her sister at Curzon Street. There is evidence that she was drugged and taken away in a cab somewhere. There is every reason to believe that this man knows all about it."

"I know nothing," said Stanford doggedly.

"Come up to my room," interrupted Marshalt. The three went up to the study, and Marshalt put on the lights.

"Now, let me hear this."

"You've heard all you're likely to hear, Marshalt," said Stanford roughly. "This 'busy' has nothing on me. I have got a clean record, and he can't bluff me into confessing up to something I didn't do."

"If it comes to a question of pulling in, I've got you!" said Dick. "Two nights ago we found certain things in the interior of an idol in Malpas's house—more uncut diamonds than I've ever seen before. Before we could remove them, something happened. The diamonds disappeared. Five minutes later the lights went out again; somebody had blundered, and we found them all in a big brown grip, that has since been recovered."

Marshalt's face was a study. "Diamonds... in an idol!" He turned slowly to Stanford. "What do you know about that, Stanford?"

"Nothing!" snapped the man.

"Maybe you know nothing about the bag they were packed in—a new bag, bought from Waller's, of Regent Street the same afternoon—bought by you!" Dick's accusing finger pointed at the man. "Waller identified you tonight. We've had him on the 'phone at his house at Eitham. He remembers selling the bag; it was soiled inside, and he sold it cheaply. And the man he sold it to was you!"

Stanford did not reply. He stood, one arm resting on the marble mantelpiece, looking down into the big empty grate.

"Did you hear what Captain Shannon said?" Marshalt asked sharply.

"I heard. I've nothing to say."

"Where is Audrey Bedford?"

"I've nothing to say," said Stanford. "You can pull me in if you want. And as for the bag, why, you're in dreamland! I've never bought a bag in my life. I steal all my grips!"

"Do you know Slick Smith?"

"I've seen him," said the other sulkily. Then, in a sudden rage: "If you want to take me, I'll go. If you're bluffing, I'll call your bluff!"

Dick shook his head.

"I'll not take you now. I'm going to have that bag question thoroughly threshed out tomorrow. You can be where I can get you, and if I find that you're concerned in this abduction, you will be too sick to be sorry!"

Short a distance as it was, Dick Shannon fell asleep between Portman Square and the Ritz-Carlton, and had to be wakened by the cabman.

"You're all in," said Torrington, whence saw the detective, and then anxiously: "Do you think those people really know? They are not lying?"

"You mean the Eltons? Yes, they know."

Torrington paced his sitting-room.

"Could I see them?" he asked.

Dick hesitated.

"They are under arrest, of course?"

"Technically, they're detained. I've not charged them yet," said Shannon. "There is no reason why you shouldn't see them."

He did not ask Audrey's father why he wished to interview the Eltons. He knew, and yet did not want to know. The information he had failed to secure by threats Torrington would obtain with money.

"Can you get them out? I know I'm asking something that you hate to do, and I know. Shannon, that there is nobody in the world to whom Audrey's safety means more than it does to you."

The struggle in Dick Shannon's mind was short. "Come with me," he said, and they returned to the police station.

To the station sergeant: "You can release those people I've detained," he said. "If I want them I know where to find them."

He left the station premises before Elton and his wife had appeared, and walked wearily up the stairs to his flat as the clock was striking five.

The faithful William was waiting. "Get the alarm clock and set it for nine. You needn't bother to get up," said Dick.

He kicked off his shoes and his collar, and putting the clock on a chair within a few inches of his head, he lay down on his bed fully dressed and was asleep in a second.

At nine o'clock he woke to the sound of a musical earthquake, and went, half asleep, to his shower, and even the icy-cold water did not have its usual effect, for he nodded as he stood. He might have gone to sleep on his feet if William, peeping in at the door, had not brought him to his senses.

"You'd get a better shower, sir, if you took your clothes off," said William respectfully.

Dick woke with a start, to find himself clad and saturated. He had a hasty breakfast between telephone calls. Torrington had not returned to his hotel, and the watchers in Doughty Street had seen no sign of Slick Smith; which fact did not bother Dick. If only they would leave Slick Smith alone...

He had rung the bell for William to clear away, when Torrington appeared.

"I tried every inducement with them," he said, sitting down wearily, "and the man is willing to help me. But the woman!"

"She dominates him, eh? Do you think they know?"

"They know all right," said old Torrington drearily. "Her hatred is terrible to see. It is as though all the loathing which her mother developed for me had been inherited and passed on to poor Audrey. I offered them money—I offered them what was tantamount to safety," he added frankly, "though I knew you wouldn't approve of this. I said I'd give them enough to live luxuriously for the rest of their lives, and put an aeroplane at their disposal this morning to carry them to France. But nothing I said could shake her. The man is at the end of his tether, but Dora seems to grow in strength as her position grows in danger. Stanford knows."

"Have you seen him? What makes you say he knows?"

"Elton let it out by accident. Just the first syllable of the name, but I am sure he is in it."

"I'll see him again," said Dick. "I have to go again this morning. I am taking Lacy Marshalt into Malpas's house to see what I can get from him first-hand."

"You wouldn't like me to come?" asked the old man anxiously.

"I'd like you to sleep," said Dick, putting his hand on Torrington's shoulder, "I can stand this a little better than you."

Torrington shook his head.

"I couldn't sleep. Old people require less than others. Do you mind if I wait here? I can't bear to go back to the hotel."

Dick's cab had scarcely disappeared round the corner when there stepped from the shelter of an all-night druggist's almost opposite the man who had been an interested spectator of his departure.

"Atta!" said Slick Smith. He, too, would have given a thousand dollars for ten hours' sleep.

By the Back Way

Slick Smith had to exercise unusual caution. He knew that every plain-clothes officer in London was on the look-out for him, and he was not the type on whom a false beard sat with any dignity.

The weather was in his favour; the rain continued and continued and still continued. Mr. Smith inwardly blessed the inclement elements; they gave him an excuse to walk under the very noses of men who were watching for him. He pulled down the brim of his soft felt hat, turned up the collar to his eyes, and crossed the road.

Taxicabs are scarce on rainy days, for what the drivers call the "amateur riders" dig up their pennies and indulge in orgies of locomotion of which they would not dream on other occasions. But luck was with him; he found a fast brand of taxi disengaged.

"Pick up that long yellow car. You'll overhaul it in the traffic of Regent Street. Keep it in sight," he said, and was, in fact, on Dick's trail before he was clear of the block which accumulates even in the early hours of the morning on Oxford Circus.

As the crook suspected, Shannon was making for Marshalt's house. When he was sure on this subject he varied his directions, and was dropped within fifty yards of the square, at a point beyond observation. The mews at this hour of the morning was filled with noise, for the chauffeurs were tuning up in their garages, and one or two trollies, less delicately constituted, were being prepared for the day's work in the open.

All the men were sufficiently engaged in their own business to be incurious, and nobody noticed the stocky man who strolled aimlessly along the wall separating the courtyard at the back of the square; nor did anybody see him dive through the door that brought him to the back of Malpas's house. And if they had, so many strange men had loafed about the mews these days that they would have marked him down as a detective, and taken no further notice, for interest in the Portman Square murder had almost evaporated.

Dick, neither knowing that he was being followed nor caring if he had known, was shown in by one of the maids, and immediately taken up to the study, where Mr. Marshalt sat alone, gloom on his face, which was not dispelled by the announcement of his visitor.

"I want to see Stanford, Mr. Marshalt, but in the meantime I'd like you to accompany me to this house of mystery and tell me just what happened to you."

The man got up with some reluctance.

"I hate the place," he said testily, "but it is due to you that you should know just what happened. Can you get in?"

"I have a key, if the controls are off."

He explained the system under which the doors were opened and closed.

"I guessed that, of course, when I went there," nodded Marshalt. "In fact, I've had the system offered to me, but rejected it. It would be very awkward if the current failed."

"The current will fail this afternoon," said Shannon. "I'm arranging to have it cut off at the main. Will you come now, or would you rather wait until you've had your breakfast? I'm in no hurry."

"I'll come now," said Marshalt, rising.

He went down with the detective, put on his mackintosh, and they left for the house together. The key turned in the lock of Malpas's front door and it opened. Dick saw a wedge of wood lying in the hall, and kicked its thin edge under the open door, Marshalt watching interestedly.

"You would like me to tell you just what happened on the night I was shot? I came in here," he said, "and, as you know, there was nobody to receive me."

He led the way up the stairs, talking all the time. On the landing he stopped.

"I was somewhere about here when the voice bade me come in. I think I said I was at the bottom of the stairs—no, I am more correct in saying that I was somewhere here."

They went into the long room and Dick pulled open they curtains.

"Now, will you describe to me where Malpas stood when he fired? Place yourself in that position, Mr. Marshalt."

Lacy walked to the end of the room until his back was to the hidden statue.

"He was here," he said, "and I was where you are standing."

"The whole thing is perfectly clear to me." Dick was speaking very deliberately. "I think I had the solution a week ago—it's—"

Bang! The door had closed.

"What was that?" asked Lacy, startled.

Shannon didn't turn a hair. He was inured to these happenings.

"Looks as though the door's closed on us."

He strolled across and tried to pull it open, but without success. Then: "Where is Stanford?"

"He's in my house somewhere," said Marshalt slowly. "Who did that?"

"That is what I am going to find out—today," said Shannon, "and you will help me. And there goes the door!"

It was opening slowly.

"That's queer," muttered Marshalt.

He walked quickly from the room and looked over the banisters.

"That is very queer! But you told me about an idol—where is that?"

Dick went back with him into the room and pulled aside the curtains, and started back with a cry. The idol was there—and something else. Lying limp across the black marble pedestal, his head hanging down on one side, his feet on the other, was Big Bill Stanford!

The Last Victim

Dick jumped forward and made a quick examination.

"He's not dead," he said, "but he soon will be unless we get help. Will you run back to your house and 'phone the Middlesex to send an ambulance? This telephone isn't working," he said, as he saw Lacy looking at the instrument on the table.

After he had gone. Shannon made a quick examination of Stanford's injuries. There were three bullet wounds, one through the shoulder, one that had its entrance under the heart, a third that had ripped the neck. The man was unconscious, and might or might not be in extremis. Shannon examined the pedestal: it was thick with blood, and he had hardly finished his inspection and stanched the flow that was coming from the shoulder wound, when the shrill bell of the ambulance sounded in the street below, and in a few moments, the white-coated attendants were lifting the unconscious figure to the stretcher.

"How did it happen?" asked Marshalt with a perplexed frown. "I left him in my store-room—the place where I keep odd things. The truth is, I'd had a few sharp words with him. I'm not satisfied that he knew nothing about

Audrey Bedford, and I told him so, and he answered me to the effect that he was leaving the house. I'm perfectly satisfied that he was killed there after you and I came out. It is terrible, terrible! What is this man Malpas? He must be a fiend incarnate!"

"You are safe in saying he's that," said Dick. He looked thoughtfully at the door. "I'm so tired of searching this house after these kind of happenings that I don't think I'll trouble again. Stanford wore no collar and tie. Did you notice that?"

"Yes; I thought that was strange. When I saw him he wore both."

"Just show me where he was," said Dick, and they came out together and into the house next door.

The first thing he saw, hanging on a peg in the store-room, was a collar and tie.

Shannon saw one of the two remaining maids. Stanford had been seen that morning; the girl who had let Dick in said that she had seen him in the store-room from five minutes to a quarter of an hour before the detective's arrival, and that was the total extent of the information he was able to get. The man had occupied Marshalt's room until the owner of the house had returned, and he had shifted his things up to the suite which had been occupied by Tonger in his lifetime.

The Commissioner had seen these apartments before, and he found nothing now that helped him in any way. Stanford's meagre baggage contained only a few articles of clothing, a. Continental time-table and a few toilet necessities.

Dick came down again, bitterly disappointed, for there was nothing in his hand that brought him any nearer to the mystery of Audrey Bedford's disappearance.

He had sent Steel to the bedside of the wounded man, with instructions that he was to remain there until he was relieved, and check any statement the wounded man made, either in his delirium or upon recovering consciousness, a contingency for which the hospital authorities were not prepared. As soon as he had made his report, he drove to the Middlesex, and was admitted into the private-ward to which Stanford had been taken. Steel was standing beside the bed, looking down at the unconscious man.

"He knows where that girl is," said the sergeant.

"Has he talked?" asked Dick quickly.

"Only in his sleep; when they were giving him an anaesthetic before probing down after the bullet, he cried out, 'I won't tell you where she is!'"

"That's not much; he probably thought he was speaking to me. There's nothing to be gained here."

He stood indecisively on the steps of the Middlesex Hospital, with the sense of being a beaten man, wondering which way he should turn next. He could not believe that she was in Lacy's house—it was impossible that she should be taken to the house of mystery, every room of which was open to search. So he argued, and precisely at that minute Audrey Bedford was running, screaming, down the passage, and behind her the sinister figure of Mr. Malpas.

The Pivot Wall

For a long time after Dick Shannon's departure Lacy Marshalt sat at his desk, his head in his hands. Presently he leaned back and pushed a bell. One of the maids answered after a long delay. "Who else is in the house?" he asked sharply.

"Milly, sir."

"Tell her to come here."

From his pocket he took a crumpled handful of notes and Treasury Bills, selected a few and smoothed them out. By the time the girls returned there were two little heaps before them.

"There is your salary for a month in lieu of notice. I am shutting up the house and going abroad."

"When do you want us to go, sir?" asked one of the girls in surprise.

"I want you to go at once. I intend leaving in half an hour."

He himself watched from the head of the stairs whilst their boxes were being removed, and at last saw their cab pass out of sight. Then he walked down, put the chains on the door, double-locked and bolted it, and returned at his leisure to the study. His face was set in a smile from which all humour had vanished. He was thinking of the man who had tried to rob him once, and would have betrayed him, the man who, with a belated return to decency, had refused to speak until...

For half an hour he gave himself up to his thoughts. Lacy Marshalt was something of a dreamer. The tinkle of the doorbell, followed by a thunderous knock, aroused him. He walked to the window and peeped out. On the doorstep were Elton and his wife. And Torrington—yes, he recognized Torrington, though he had not seen him in years. An inspector of police and four men, who were obviously detectives.

He took his letter-case from his pocket, extracted a flat handle and a bodkin, and fitted the one into the other. Then he walked to the mantelpiece and thrust the bodkin deep amidst the wood foliage that framed the fire-place. He turned his wrist, and, without a sound, mantelpiece and fire-place swung round on a central pivot. He had the profile of the huge idol to the right, and fire-place in section to the left. Then, opening the bottom drawer of his desk, he lifted a false bottom and took out a little box, and for a second busied himself. A half-wig, a long, pendulous nose, a pointed chin, so perfectly coloured to his face that even an expert would not know where nature began and art commenced—he fixed them with deft fingers.

Then he turned the bodkin again and the mantelpiece swung back to its place. The knocking on the door was continuous, and presently he heard the smash of glass. He had taken the key out, and that would not help them, he thought.

Stepping inside the semi-circular fender, he pushed the bodkin; home and turned again, this time to the left.

As the hearth and wall swung round he put down his foot to ease the little shock which came when the fire-place came to rest. Once a clumsy Tonger had let it stop with such a jerk that a hot coal had been flung out into the Malpas room. Again the bodkin came into use, and, standing aside, he saw the fire-place turn back to its proper position. He unfitted the steel blade with curious deliberation, replaced it in his pocket and then went up the stairs, very slowly.

Audrey Bedford was there. Reluctantly, painfully, Stanford had told him. And now all that began this tragedy which had overtaken him, and had robbed him not only of the fortune he had accumulated, but promised to rob him of life itself, was to end as it began—with Audrey Bedford!

He paused at every landing to anticipate his grim final triumph over the hounds of the law, who were baying at his door, eager to seize him and to drag him to that dreadful dock, where the red-robed, white-haired man gave judgment of death. Lacy's smile was fixed: it had become frozen on his face. All his plannings... his strivings, his clever manoeuvres.

And then he remembered something that struck away the smile. Why had the door controls operated whilst he was with Dick Shannon? Was there a reason for that? He shrugged. The climate—a score and one things might affect an electric connection...

Now he was outside the door and bent his head, listening. He heard a light footstep in the passage and smiled again. Half the fierce joy that came to his heart was in the anticipation of the terror his appearance would strike when her fearful eyes met his.

He opened the little cupboard in the stairs and turned a switch, and knew that at that moment the lights had gone out in the empty room through which he would soon be passing in search of his prey. He needed no light, not even the trick lamp he had carried to illuminate his face to terrify all who saw him. The darkness belonged to him, and to her.

He turned the key. As he did so he heard her light steps fly along the passage, heard her babble something, and the slam of a door. In another second he was inside; the key was pushed into the lock and turned. He was alone with her. Audrey Bedford was beyond the help of God or man.

His sensitive hands touched the wall. Slowly he crept along until he reached the first door and opened it. He could hear no sound of breathing, but he must be sure. Round the walls he went, across the centre, his arms outstretched, and again reached the passage. A second room—this was where she had been. He felt the bed with his foot, but heard no sound, and again made a circuit of the room. He stopped at the opening of the third room and listened. She was there! He sensed the presence, heard somebody breathing.

"Come here, my little dear. You can't get away from me this time! We have an appointment; it has been a long time delayed, but you must keep it today!"

He heard the sound of feet on the floor, and somebody slipped past him; but he was too quick, and again stood in the entrance.

"Your lover is downstairs, my beloved—the dunderheaded Shannon and his confederacy! And your father! You didn't know you had a father, but he's there. He'll see you... later. You and I are going out together. That's a good end for the man he hates, but he'll find no joy in it."

Suddenly he lunged forward and caught an arm. It was not the arm he expected. As he stood a strange and terrifying green light showed level with his breast. He was looking into his own face—nose, chin, head!

Another Malpas—fearful, monstrous—had him by the arms.

"God! What is it?" he screamed, and tried to get himself free.

"I want you," said the hollow voice. With a yell Lacy Marshalt struck at the hideous figure and, turning, ran. As he did so the lights came on, and looking back he saw a replica of himself! Malpas! But he was Malpas! "Damn you!" he sobbed, and pulled his gun. The automatic spat once, twice.

"Save yourself a whole lot of trouble, my friend," said his double. "Your cartridges are blank—I changed them nearly a day ago!"

With a howl of fury Lacy flung the pistol at him. The man ducked, and the next minute had Marshalt by the throat.

And somewhere in the dark background stood Audrey, her hands clasped in an agony of fear, yet in her heart a new-born life.

The Double

Dick had joined the group at the door, and now the knocking had ceased. A requisitioning jemmy had been forced between the lock, and the lock was creaking loose as the last blows were being hammered home.

"She is here—you're sure?"

Martin nodded.

"Stanford took her away last night. He said he would get her into Malpas's house."

Shannon had already tried the front door of 551, but the controls were on.

"Do you know what has happened to Stanford?"

"I've just learnt," said Elton in a low voice.

At that moment the lock broke and they poured into the hall. Dick led the way upstairs. The study was empty, and this time he went straight to the fire-place and began looking for the aperture which he knew existed there somewhere. The way in that must be through the fire-place and nowhere else.

Presently he found the hole, fitted poor Tonger's homemade bodkin, and the triangular sides gripped on the sensitive mechanism. As he turned the handle, the fire-place swung, and those who stood behind him had a clear view past the-statue of Malpas's room.

"Don't touch that handle," he warned them, and ran across the gap, stopping only at the table to switch over the controls.

He was dashing through the open door when he heard the two shots fired. Dick stopped, his face as white as death. Only for a moment did he pause, and then went on. Fast as he ran it seemed to him that his feet were leaden.

As he reached the door it was flung open. Two men came out—two men so identically alike that he stared from one to the other.

"Here's your bird. Captain Shannon," said the shorter of the two, and flung the handcuffed prisoner into the hands of the waiting detectives. Then, with one sweep, he removed wig, nose, and chin. "I think you know me?"'

"I know you very well," said Dick. "You are Slick Stormer—or, as you prefer to be known to the London police, Slick Smith!"

"Got me first time—but when did you recognize me?"

Dick smiled.

"A clever detective like you ought to know," he said.

Dick saw somebody else in the passage, a timorous somebody who kept as far away as possible. In another minute he had raced down the corridor and had caught her in his arms.

Slick took a quick glance and closed the door.

"Maybe you'd like to see your daughter, and she'll be glad to see you, but she knows this fellow better than you, I guess," he said, and Torrington nodded...

What Slick Said

"I've never been quite sure whether you took me at my own valuation, or whether you were one of these reserved Englishmen who believe nothing very much, and only then to oblige a lady," said Slick Smith, a magnificent host, sitting at the head of a dinner-table that night.

"I came into this case nineteen months ago, when I had a letter from Mr. Torrington giving me all the facts he possessed, and asking me whether I could trace his wife and verify the story of his daughter's death. Incidentally, he told me a great deal about Mr. Lacy Marshalt that interested me both as a detective and a human being.

"I've got some experience of the unpopularity of private detective services, especially in England, where they are regarded as a joke, and a joke in bad taste at that. And I knew that, if I was going to do any good in this business, it was vitally necessary that I should pass into the underworld with the necessary credentials. I therefore communicated with Captain Shannon, in my capacity as Stormer, telling him that a notorious American crook was expected to arrive in England almost any minute, and favoured him with a very vivid description of what this hideous scoundrel looked like. I got the usual warm-hearted 'Your communication shall receive our attention' from headquarters, but I happen to know that the moment Slick landed he was picked up, trailed to London, warned, cautioned —in fact, all the things happened to him that usually happen to the imported article.

"Fortunately, very few people in London know me. I've always made it a rule, since I established my agency in London, to come into no case personally, and only three or four of my best staff would be able to identify me on oath. But those three or four are mighty useful, for they not only can identify me, but they can't identify me, and that is valuable!

"Another important advantage was that, as Slick Smith, I could always have one of my men with me without attracting the suspicion of the criminal classes. You remember I was invariably trailed by one of Stormer's men—he'd have lost his job if he hadn't!

"My other job was to discover the whereabouts of a very large number of diamonds which had been stolen from Mr. Torrington's mine in the past few years, and which both his police and the South African force were certain had been brought to England. And I was able to unearth a very considerable traffic. In South Africa, as you know. Captain Shannon, it is a penal offence to be found in possession of a diamond, unless you can account for it to the satisfaction of a magistrate—I'm talking about uncut diamonds now. For years Lacy Marshalt has been such a trafficker. He was engaged that way when he was acting as detective for the Streams Mining Corporation, and when he framed up a charge that sent Mr. Torrington to the Breakwater. He's been that way ever since. But the trading of diamonds in South Africa is a dangerous game, both for the seller and the buyer; and he hit upon the idea of coming to London, establishing himself in a big house, and arranging a regular courier service to bring the stones over. But obviously he couldn't do this as Marshalt, because, sooner or later, somebody was going to squeal. And the day the squeal went up to heaven. Lacy Marshalt, who in the meantime had scraped into the South African Parliament, and had been scraped out again when the electors came to their senses, would go down to the dark hulks where the bad men go.

"He bought the two houses in Portman Square at a time of great depression in house property, and they were bought in different names. 551 was purchased through a bank. Engaging a good Continental firm to fix the electrical fittings, he left the principal, and to my mind the cleverest, piece of mechanism to the last.

"Lacy Marshalt is an engineer. He is one of those people you read about every day, who might, had he chosen an honest path, have made a fortune; not that they ever would, but judges have those illusions.

"The control was too fiddling a job and too much like hard work for Lacy.

631

The fire-place and statue were a labour of love. The statue he bought in Durban: I traced it nearly a year ago, and knew all about its mechanical thorax. But the pivot opening was entirely his own. He lived alone in his house—Tonger at that time was still in South Africa, acting as his agent—for four months before the work was completed, and then he brought his man home. And just before he came, Malpas appeared in the London directory. Malpas, the buyer of diamonds who could never be caught!

"Tonger is the real tragedy of this story. He married rather late in life a youngish woman who died and left him with a daughter, of whom he thought the world; and it was real bad luck for Tonger to have her come into contact with Lacy Marshalt. You'd think that Tonger, being his friend and helper, would make a difference. No, sir! Nothing ever made a difference to Lacy, and when the inevitable happened, and Tonger wanted to know certain things. Lacy seized on the arrest of Torrington as a heaven- sent opportunity for shifting the blame, persuaded the girl to name Torrington as her lover, and got her away to America, where he allowed her a reasonable sum a week, threatening that, unless she did as he wished, which was to write to her father regularly and tell him how happy she was, he would stop the allowance and ruin Tonger, who as she believed held some responsible position in Marshalt's office.

"New York is no worse a place for a woman than any other big city: that is my experience," said Slick thoughtfully. "I guess the same old devil perches on the top of the London Monument as sits im the fifty- fourth floor of the Woolworth building. The girl went her own way—drank a lot, got into debt, but dared not tell Lacy. Then one day, in a panic, she jumped the boat and came to London. I think you saw her that day you had your first interview with friend Malpas?"

Audrey nodded.

"She was the woman who knocked at Marshalt's door."

"Yuh! Poor Tonger must have nearly died when he saw her. At any rate, as I have reconstructed the matter, he took her in, hurried her up to his apartments and kept her there for days, probably trying his best to induce her to tell him the truth—he may already have guessed it. Then one day Lacy found out she was in the house, and knew that, once Tonger got on his track, he was doomed.

"He decided to act then and there. Tonger was sent to Paris with a letter that meant nothing—I've seen it. It was to a man who did business for Marshalt. Whilst he was away Marshalt got the girl out of the room, and probably told her to go to the park and wait for him. Consider this"—Slick raised his finger to emphasize the point—"Tonger's daughter was a dipsomaniac. She was drunk when she was first seen in London, and we've got evidence from the servants that, the week before he died, Tonger had an extraordinary amount of whisky in his room —he who hitherto had never taken drink. It was she who soaked —not Tonger.

"When Marshalt found that she had this craving, it was easy to give her a flask with enough cyanide to kill a regiment, and tell her to go into the park, well knowing that, sooner or later, she would drink from that flask and never move further. But he tried to do too much. He intended that night seeing Miss Bedford—Torrington. He wanted to see her pretty badly, so badly that he wouldn't put off the engagement. Then Tonger came back.

"There was no need for Marshalt to explain the disappearance of the woman, as he knew nothing about her: she might have gone out by herself. You may be sure that she went out by the back way—the way a certain lady used to come in when she paid her surreptitious visits to Lacy. It wasn't likely that Tonger would learn that very evening that his daughter was dead, and yet that is exactly what did happen! Tonger made his discovery at the very moment Marshalt was waiting in Malpas's room for the arrival of Audrey Bedford.

"What Marshalt intended, I don't know. I guess he would have produced the letter making an appointment in that apartment, but that is mere speculation—we shall never know. At any rate, he did not meet Miss Torrington. Maddened by his discovery, Tonger, who knew the secret of the mantelpiece and had fashioned a key to it, opened it, passed into Malpas's room and confronted his treacherous employer. He was, I think, armed with an old-fashioned pistol, and Marshalt spoke the truth there. He fired twice, and Lacy went down. The bullet-proof shirt he wore—not because he had been in the Balkans, but because he was scared to death that some day Torrington would come on the scene—saved his life. While Tonger, half demented, was searching the desk, Marshalt recovered, staggered back to his own room and shot Tonger in his tracks.

"The controls of Malpas's house are fixed in many places. There is a switch on the stairs, there is a set of switches below, one on the desk and another in Lacy's study.

"What happened immediately afterwards is also a matter of speculation, unless Marshalt spills it. He was going to make his escape when he heard the servant scream, and probably saw Captain Shannon run down the area steps. That was his opportunity; he slipped out. If you remember, the door was open."

Dick nodded.

"Now, Marshalt had already prepared a hiding-place for himself. In the character of a lawyer or something of the sort, he had a gorgeous flat in Greville Mansions, where he was called 'Mr. Crewe'. I happen to know, because I have occupied an adjoining suite to some purpose. He got there that night, nursed his bruise—he had a slight wound, too—and then came back to get the diamonds. I know, because I've seen him."

"Who was the man whose face I saw through the skylight on the night of the murder?" asked Shannon.

"Me," said Slick Stormer calmly.

"But your men on duty on the roof said—"

Slick laughed.—"Why do you think they were on the roof? They were my alibis and protectors! The last time you were questioning one of them I was crouched behind a chimney-pot not a yard away from you. Of course they hadn't seen me! They'd have lost a good job if they had! I was always around that roof. Climbing is my speciality, though I'm not such a good climber as Martin Elton, who didn't have a rope lowered to him as I did.

"Marshalt's job was to scare everybody out of the house. He hated like poison that police guard, because he wanted to get at the diamonds that were in the idol's tummy, and naturally he could only do that by getting rid of the police. Wearing his evening dress and a made-up face, he appeared—as himself! The poet says that we can rise on stepping- stones of our dead selves to better things. Tennyson, was it, or maybe Browning? It's good enough for Longfellow. That is how Marshalt figured it out—that he could rise on that stepping-stone to handle all these good and sparkling gems. He got desperate after the hiding-place was discovered, and with the help of Stanford, who had to be taken into the secret, he cleared the idol under your eyes. But Stanford was a bungler, and unused to the mechanism, and after the diamonds had been put in the bag he started monkeying with the mechanism to see how it worked, switched out all the lights, and incidentally brought the statue round into the room. He must have had the bag in his hand at the time, and put it down in a fright on the pedestal, and naturally, when the statue turned again, it took it back."

"What was it burnt my hand?" asked Steel.

"The fire-place! When you reached out, the thing had revolved, and you'd put your hand on the hot bars of the grate from which the coal had only recently been removed. You recall. Captain Shannon, that there was generally a smell of hot iron in the room when these demonstrations occurred.

"After you'd got away with that, he followed you. Stanford went down to the Haymarket and did his little burglary—I saw him come out, as a matter of fact, but I thought it was unnecessary to tell you—whilst Marshalt followed you in his car and engineered an accident. The honour and glory of recovering the bag goes to Stanford, who was still in the flat when you found your man knocked out.

"The money retrieved, Marshalt's first thought was to get the bag away. He took it to his flat in Greville Mansions: this I know, for I found it there when I broke in to look for Miss Torrington. I didn't find her, but I saw the bag, and only gave it up when I saw I could turn it over to good hands without being arrested myself.

"Now, Marshalt is a suspicious man. He found that the bag was gone, and naturally he suspected his confederate. The shooting of Stanford, you'll find, occurred just before you arrived this morning—I understand he was artistically draped round the pedestal. That nearly completes the story. Again we must guess what happened between Stanford and Marshalt. The probability is that Marshalt only found then that the young lady was concealed on the premises, and, knowing that the game was up and the fortune was lost, he went to have his revenge on the daughter of the man he best hated. Unfortunately for him, I have made a practice for a long time of being in that house when the people that came in from the Cape brought their diamonds. I was there once in broad daylight, tapping the walls, and Marshalt heard me—Miss Torrington heard me, too—I wanted to know all about that pivot door. I have twice impersonated the mysterious Mr. Malpas and got away with it. It was a hobby of mine to be Mr. Malpas whenever I broke in, for I knew that a day would come when he and I would meet face to face, and I was hoping that he suffered from a weak heart. I scared one young lady all right," he said, and Audrey could smile at the recollection.

"I screamed, didn't I?" she said ruefully. "I didn't hear you calling my name for a long time."

"I scream myself sometimes," said Smith, "or want to!

"There is only one thing left to tell you, and you know that already. Shannon. You knew it before you got that summons to Fould's Wharf. Once he recovered the diamonds, it was up to Marshalt to make a dramatic reappearance. It was very nearly too dramatic, let me tell you! He got into the water under the pier, locked the handcuffs himself, and with the key of the cuffs in one hand and a gun in the other, waited for you to turn up, as he knew you would, within a specified time. But you were delayed five minutes on the road, and in that five minutes a tragic thing happened: by accident he dropped the key of the handcuffs in the water, and couldn't release himself! If you hadn't got there when you did, he'd have drowned. When you came, it was easy. He had his gun in his hand —if you'd kept your light on him you would have seen it, but he asked you to take the light off, and immediately you shut down your lamp he fired two shots at you, dropped the pistol in the water—I've since recovered it—and the rest you followed. If he had killed you —there was the proof of his innocence—he couldn't have done it.

"And now, Miss Torrington, I'll thank you for that badge."

She gave a gasp of surprise, felt in her bag and produced the silver star.

"Thank you," said Slick gracefully; "and I hope you're not offended. I never allow anybody to keep a star after they've passed out of my employ, and gone into the establishment of a rival."

His eyes met Dick's, and they were laughing. "That is a joke," he said. "You won't see it because you're English! But do you mind if I indulge in one private laugh? Ha! ha!"

The Worst Man in the World

Table of Contents

Although these experiences are told in story form, they represent the personal narrative of one who served many terms of penal servitude, and were related to the author, who met with this remarkable convict a few days after his last release from prison.

The First Crime

First published in The Premier Magazine, London, July 11, 1922

WHEN I left Dartmoor prison some seven years ago, the Deputy saw me in the governor's pokey little office hung around with the art exhibits of former convicts.

"Smith," he said, "I suppose there is no use my saying that I hope I shall never see you here again?"

"No, sir," said I. "I should hate to disappoint you, and the chances are that I shall be back in a year or two. I used to under-rate the intelligence of Scotland Yard, but my views have undergone a change."

The Deputy laughed.

"I think you're the worst man in the world," he said, "because you commit crimes deliberately, and it seems to me that you have as deliberately chosen your career; I have never known another prisoner who has cold-bloodedly set himself to go wrong as you have. And yet you were a gentleman, you have education and natural gifts, and you can't go straight."

"I can go straight, sir, but I don't," said I.

We walked up the sloping hill to the big steel gates, and I stepped out into the space before the guard-room.

"I was reading up your record yesterday," he said. "You have been in prison six times. You have been flogged and punished in other ways, and yet none of these things have a deterrent effect upon you. I am afraid that one of these days you'll toe the chalk line."

"That I shall never do," said I, for if he had but known, the only thing I ever saw in prison which filled me with fear was that little T drawn in chalk on the trap of the scaffold where a condemned man puts his feet.

And sitting in my little bungalow on the Sussex shore, with a somewhat adventurous life behind me, and no further desire or need for going on the dodge, I think it is unlikely that I shall ever be hanged. For murder is a cheap and cowardly business, and I do not think it is in me to commit so beastly a crime, even if I had not helped strip a few men who had been "hanged by the neck until they were dead."

Executions have always put the wind up me, and I've never known anybody who was so callous that they were not affected. I have seen a hangman reeling along the exercise ground drunk with the horror of his job, and I have looked one famous young killer of men in the eyes—one of the Billingtons had hanged twenty-one men before his twenty-first birthday!—and read the gloomy terror of his soul.

And I have known a warder who went white in twenty-four hours. There was a man hanged in a northern gaol, and the fellow was a brute. He tried to kill one of the warders in charge, the man I am speaking about, and spent the last three days of his life in a straight-jacket.

And as the procession formed up, and he came out of his cell, he turned to the warder and said:

"I hate you! I'll hate you after I'm dead!"

And when the drop fell, and the man was undoubtedly past all knowledge of life, he seemed to shake his upturned face—masked as it was with the linen "cap"—at the horrified warder as he gazed down.

And now let me begin the somewhat uninteresting preamble to the story of my life.

For the past three months I have been wallowing in criminal apologia. In other words, I have been reading the very many volumes which have been constructed by eminent criminals who were sufficiently in the public eye at the time of their conviction to justify enterprising editors in securing their reminiscences.

They are unconsciously humorous, these recollections, for they are apparently written by white-souled creatures, who committed no crime, and who were quite innocent of the charges brought against them. Not a small portion of these volumes, varying in size and importance from library editions to paper-backed, ill-printed sixpenny brochures, is devoted to an indignant refutation of the charges which brought them into penal servitude. They "never done it"—it was always the other fellow.

The writers contribute nothing to the world's knowledge of the criminal classes, and precious little to our faith in humanity. Their books and recollections are hypocritical twaddle, sometimes amusing, more often sickening, and in more cases than one these wretched autobiographies are employed as a peg upon which to hang charges against the unhappy officials who do their best, and their honest best, to administer the law.

In four cases out of five the autobiographies are written up by professional writers who introduce their own elegant language somewhat incongruously.

The remarkable thing about these recollections of mine is that they are recollections of an admitted criminal, and a man who takes pride in the fact that he was never adequately punished for his breaches of the law, and who recalls with a complacent satisfaction that, despite the punishment which he has undergone, he has missed that which, if every man had his due, would have been his in addition.

Since most of the volumes of reminiscences start with a genealogical-tree, and an exposition of the respectability of the writer's forbears, I will be so far conventional as to say that my father was a very excellent man. He was, in fact, a peer of the realm, which seems a somewhat melodramatic and unconvincing claim, but it is one which must be made because it is the truth. My brother was and my nephew is the present holder of the title, and it is a queer fact that had my nephew died in France—as he nearly did—I should have been "my lord." Happily he lives and has, I hope, many years of vigorous life before him,

I was educated at a famous school, which it will serve no useful purpose to mention, and at a military school, whence I was gazetted to the first cavalry regiment which left these shores for South Africa after the outbreak of war. I do not purpose giving you the story of my adventures in South Africa, but it is sufficient to say that I made a fool of myself over a woman in Cape Town, had a row with the senior major of my regiment, and another row with yet another superior, and was out of the Army before the war had comfortably settled down.

I came home, and was received by my male parent at Southampton. We had lunch, and he was as nice as the circumstances allowed. He explained to me that he was not a very rich man, but I was the first of the family who had ever disgraced his name. He thanked his Maker that my mother was dead, and said most of the things that a man with a limited vocabulary and a dearth of original ideas would say under the circumstances. He wound up with a suggestion that I should go back to South Africa, join the South African Light Horse as a trooper, and extinguish myself in a blaze of glory.

I thought it was a good idea, and it was certainly advice which I should have passed on to somebody else, but so far as I was concerned it did not raise so much as a thrill. I told him so.

The upshot was that he gave me £500 and told me to go to hell. Those were his exact words.

I suppose that I should say here that I have been through many brands of hell since that beautiful morning in June, 1901. But if I said that I should be a hypocrite, too, for hell is only the unendurable and the unimaginable, and my worst experiences have deserved neither of these descriptions.

I left Southampton by the night boat for Havre, and gravitated to Paris. I had been there three days when I got into a row at one of the night-places. The row ended in my arrest and my being fined, and I was instructed to leave Paris as soon as possible.

I left France by way of Monte Carlo and the Riviera and I was back again in England on September 13th, 1901, arriving in London with exactly four shillings and tuppence-halfpenny, a five-franc piece, and no immediate prospects of making a decent living with a minimum of hard labour.

It was here, at Charing Cross railway station at half-past eleven o'clock at night, that I resolved to be a criminal. I reached this decision calmly and deliberately. After all, I come from a long line of criminals. The founder of my house was a robber who stole land, the reviver of our ancestral glories was a woman who was a very close friend indeed of one of the Stuart princes.

It is true that very few men resolve upon a career which involves a total disregard for the law. Men drift into crime as, with more happy results, other men drift into other professions. It is largely a matter of early training and environment. What are known as the "criminal classes" are people whose natural and instinctive predatory impulses are unchecked by discipline. Every babe is born into the world a conscienceless thief, and is taught by nurses and mother, by schoolmaster and father, and, finally, by an appreciation of the law's true majesty that of all the goods in the world only a very few are his, and even those must be consumed or employed in accordance with the ritual of behaviour.

The idea which is behind all the Prisoners' Aid Societies and the like, that crime is the phenomenon of good people becoming suddenly bad people, and the further absurd belief that these suddenly bad people can be turned back into good people is as fallacious as would be the suggestion that a snub nose can be converted into a Roman nose on the impulse of a moment.

This digression is by-the-way. I was in London. I was broke. I had no desire to "work," because work implied a fixity of habit and a certain drab sameness of existence. I declare to-day that I regard prison life as infinitely more satisfying to the romantic soul than the most comfortable of Government jobs. In prison a man of culture and imagination cannot stagnate nor be content with his lot. If it is only the ambition to be a free man he at least is the possessor of aspirations. Moreover, he dreams, and that is very blessed.

I drove to an hotel in the City, and was shown to a dull and gloomy room, uglier than any of those bright and cheery apartments in which delinquency is stored for recuperation and renewal. And I remember I sat until the day broke puzzling out how best I could begin.

Has this ever struck you—that for hundreds of years architects, tailors, builders of all kinds, iron-masters and the like, have devoted their best energies to the frustrating of thieves! The dominant note of civilisation is suspicion. Billions of money have been spent not only to induce mankind to the paths of virtue but to take jolly good care that it did not stray. The first essential of all houses is that none shall be able to enter except authorised persons. The steel-makers produce bars for the windows and locks for the doors. The tailor contrives cunning pockets which cannot be picked. Corporations have been formed to keep the loose cash of the community in safe keeping—it seems that the first essential of manufacture shall be security against the thief.

All night long I planned and thought, and always I came up against locks, bolts, and bars.

I had—and have still—a sister; she is a woman of the low intelligence which is peculiar to her class. A hard, mercenary, ungentle woman, she married a worthy mate in a long-faced prig who collected china and wrote wearisome articles in the dull reviews. They had a house in Portman Square, at which I have dined just as often as I had to. It was a house very near to one at which King Edward was a frequent visitor. John X., my brother-in-law, had, I knew, one peculiarity. He always kept a reserve fund of a thousand pounds in the house. I cannot exactly remember what was the reason he offered for this eccentricity, but I have a vague idea—and this, I admit,

I may have unconsciously invented—that he once found himself without money after banking hours on a Saturday when an emergency arose calling for his immediate departure for the Continent.

I lay down on my bed at five o'clock in the morning with my object well defined. My plan, however, was more or less nebulous. I made a survey of the house the following afternoon. It backed on to a mews, and there was a door communicating with a small yard, a door which apparently was used by tradesmen. Usually, even in big London houses, tradesmen go to the front, descending a flight of steps to the area-kitchen entrance.

Whilst I was examining the front of the house a victoria drove up, and my sister and brother-in-law descended. They went into the house, and immediately afterwards another carriage pulled up, and this time a man got out assisted by a footman. He had something the matter with his leg, and had to be assisted up the steps by the footman, who came down to meet him. Evidently he was some friend of John's. I came nearer to the door the better to see, for as the footman took the visitor along the hall he left the door wide open. Here was a chance, and on the impulse of the moment I took it. I walked casually up the steps and through the open door. I was well-dressed, and I looked a gentleman, and I could always find an excuse for entering the wrong house if the servant spotted me. But he didn't. The lame man's arm was round his neck, obstructing his view, and his back was towards me as he helped the man into what I knew was John's library.

I passed the open door of this room and ran quickly up the carpeted stairs. My real danger was that I might meet one of the servants, or John and Millicent, but there was nobody in sight. The first floor consisted of a drawing-room and Millicent's sitting-room. At the back was the housekeeper's room, and another apartment where the family sometimes breakfasted.

On the next floor were the principal bed- and dressing-rooms, a sort of study where John burned the midnight current over his review articles, and a sort of conservatory built out on a balcony at the back of the house. I heard voices above, and recognised one as Millicent's. The other was evidently a maid. Millicent is a representative of that old nobility which expresses its patrician qualities by making the lives of servants a burden. I turned into the side passage, which I knew led to the housekeeper's room. It was any odds against old Mrs. Fenny—which is not her name—being in her room when Millicent was rampaging around.

And here my luck was with me. The door was locked from the outside, but the key was in the lock. The room was not only empty, but on the one table of the room were a number of lists and three bunches of keys. The door of the wardrobe was open, and there was not a single article of clothing in the room. I guessed at once that Millicent was without a housekeeper. The poor old lady had probably been fired (I learnt afterwards that the housekeeper I had known had been dead for three years, and that it was the second of her successors, a young and attractive woman, who had been turned out, for reasons which I need not give).

The wardrobe was a big, old-fashioned affair which might, in a moment of emergency, become a useful hiding-place, but I guessed that the room itself would be all the hiding-place I wanted. I opened the door cautiously, took out the key and locked the door from the inside. Then I went to the window and had a good look round. The window faced the mews, and outside was a flat, lead-covered roof about ten feet square. I didn't know, nor do I know now, what room it covered, but it seemed a fairly easy way out of the house if I were pressed, or if somebody tried to enter the room. But nobody did. I sat in that infernal bedroom from three o'clock in the afternoon until eight o'clock at night and I was famished. There was not even a glass of water. I had taken off my shoes and had put them in my two pockets, and most of the time I spent sitting near the door on a chair, listening.

The only clue I had as to the family movements was when I heard John say, evidently answering some inquiry which had been fired down the stairs by Millicent:

"Balfour says he will look in, but that will rather crowd the box."

Which was very good news. For it told me they were going to a theatre. It was nine o'clock when I ventured forth. Happily my sister is an economical soul, and insisted upon all unnecessary lights being extinguished even when she was in the house. The hall below was dimly illuminated, and there was only one light on each landing, and those fairly dim. There was no sound or movement when I walked up the stairs. The servants would be in the kitchen, I thought, though I was mistaken. I had reached the upper landing when I heard a door close at the end of a passage corresponding to that which led to the housekeeper's room on the floor below. I opened the first door handy, and slipped in. The room was in darkness, but I saw that I was in Millicent's bedroom. Owing to the carpet on the landing and stairs I heard nothing more. After ten minutes' waiting I went out again into the passage and made for John's bedroom and study. The bedroom was easily entered, but the door leading to his study was locked. I went again to the passage and listened. Presently from down below came the slam of a door. If that meant that the person I had heard had gone below to the servants hall I could take a risk. I put on the lights and explored the room, and found the key in a drawer of John's dressing-table. A few seconds later I was in the study. I had been in this room before once in my life, and I knew that John kept his reserve in an oaken cupboard.

If I give an account of my first crime in detail it is because every incident of that exciting night is stamped on my memory. But I will spare the reader of these notes a description of the horrible hour and a half I spent over that infernal cupboard. If John had had a safe like a rational being I should have given up my attempt at once. As it was I went to work, and hot work it was. The cupboard was set in the wall. It was an old-fashioned affair, but an expert burglar with a kit of tools would have had the door open in five minutes. After some consideration I hit upon this method. There was a coal-fire laid in the study, and this I kindled. It was half-an hour before I could heat the poker sufficiently, but when I did I began to bore a hole through the door. It was another hour before the hole was big enough to put my hand through, and by that time the room was thick with smoke and reeking of scorched wood. My danger was that the smell of the burning would reach the hall, and I was a bit rattled at the thought.

At the end of what seemed hours—I had my watch open on a chair beside me—I got my hand in and found the tin box where the money was kept. The box was too big to pull through the hole, and if it had been locked John would have saved his money, and his reputation would not have been imperilled. But it was not locked. It was filled with paper, and I dragged out handfuls of letters before I came to the nice, crepe-silky feeling banknotes. There were sixty-three notes for a hundred pounds, and I slipped them into my pocket. The letters I glanced at. They were from a lady, and really I was tempted to put them under Millicent's pillow. John I knew as a prig. I never suspected him of being such a smug hypocrite. I only half read one letter, and chucked the rest on to the fire. I washed my hands and dried them in John's bedroom, and then, pulling on my shoes, I opened the door and stepped out into the passage—face to face with a servant girl!

She saw me and gave a yell, then flew down the stairs screaming at the top of her voice.

I only hesitated a moment, then ran down after her. I had not reached the first landing when I heard a man's voice immediately below, and, turning, ran up the stairs. The top floor was the fourth, and consisted of servant's attics. I ran into one, shut and locked the door behind me, for my pursuer was at my heels. As to one thing I was determined. I would not reveal my relationship with John or Millicent even to them. Not because I wanted to save the family name or any nonsense of that kind, but because I knew that

John would prosecute and I did not want the additional publicity. An ordinary burglar would get a few lines in the papers and pass out of the public mind, a "lordly burglar"—I can imagine the headlines!—would be a marked man.

The servant's room was an attic. Outside the open window, as I had seen, was a parapet. I got through the window and ran along the stone coping, which extended for the width of three houses. Then I dropped about eight feet to the flat roof of another house, crossed the roof to where the top rungs of a fire-escape showed even in the darkness, and went down until I found myself on a narrow balcony. There was a big window, which was open a little at the top, and I lifted the bottom sash without any difficulty and stepped in. The room was dark, but I had hardly put my foot upon the floor when it was brilliantly illuminated.

I was in a beautiful bedroom, and, unfortunately, it was occupied.

Sitting up in bed, staring at me with a white face, was the most beautiful girl I had ever seen.

"What do you want?" she gasped.

"I'm a detective," I said. "I'm after a burglar who has got into your house."

I didn't wait for any further explanation. I was through the door and down the stairs in a few seconds. Fortunately for me, I met not a soul. The front door was chained and locked, but I got it open and was in the street in time to see two policeman going up the steps of John's house.

The Snake Woman

First published in The Premier Magazine, London, July 25, 1922

I ALWAYS think and speak of her as the Snake Woman, although there was little about her that was snake-like. Reading this, as she may, she will think my description an uncomplimentary one; but you shall judge if it is just.

The most amazing thing about the Snake Woman is this: that only two years ago an American of German or Scandinavian descent committed exactly the crime which the Snake Woman planned!

Edgar Wallace

I met her after my third—or, it may be, my fourth—job.

One of the first crimes I committed required all the nerve and resourcefulness of an experienced criminal, and had I known the difficulties which would beset me, I certainly would have tried some easier method of acquiring wealth.

It was nothing less picturesque than a Hatton Garden robbery, which involved the breaking into an office and the opening of a steel safe. I got into the office easily enough, for I had made friends with one of the clerks, whom I met at a music-hall—I had no idea of robbing his employer until he told me where he was working—and, by pretending to be interested in the methods which are employed to prevent burglaries, I succeeded in getting from him minute particulars of how Mr. Bernstein—that was not the name of the eminent dealer in precious stones—guarded his treasures.

The result was a haul of ninety-six diamonds, half of which were uncut, which I afterwards sold in Amsterdam much below their value; but this haul had its drawbacks. The young clerk told the police all about the well-dressed stranger who had made the inquiries, and gave so faithful a description of me that, even though I shaved off my moustache and adopted a pair of spectacles and a studious look, I had an uneasy feeling that every policeman whom I passed was looking at me suspiciously.

The consequence was that when I was eventually arrested—taken red-handed breaking into a jeweller's shop through the skylight—why do jewellers always have skylights?—the youth came up and recognised me, and my first introduction to one of his Majesty's judges resulted in my being sent to penal servitude for five years. Five years for a first conviction was rather thick, but, of course, it was no more than I deserved. Happily, I had cached about five hundred pounds at a suburban branch of a well-known bank, and had been sufficiently shrewd not to take a cheque-book or passbook from the banker; so that when the police searched my belongings there was nothing to indicate that I was a man of wealth and position.

I shall never forget my first introduction to Wormwood Scrubs, and I must confess that I was agreeably surprised at the cleanliness and the rough comfort of prison life. An ordinary prisoner, in spite of what the cinema pictures tell you, does not wear knee-breeches and grey stockings, with broad arrows stuck all over him. He wears a stout, brown pair of trousers, a waistcoat and a coat of the same material, a blue and white shirt, and a queer little hat. Even when he is transferred—I am talking of the present time—to Dartmoor he does not acquire grey stockings.

I was doing hard work, but not too hard. The food was coarse, but wholesome, and I really didn't feel as depressed as I might have done, realising that I should be out again in three and a half years if I behaved myself.

In three months' time I was put on a train at Paddington with six or seven other unfortunate gentlemen, and despatched to Dartmoor. We were chained together, and I do not think that my most intimate friend would have recognised the unshaven young man who stood at the head of the chained gang as the some-time officer of a crack cavalry corps.

It was a long and tedious journey before we reached Princetown, but at Dartmoor one felt, for some extraordinary reason, tremendously at home. The moment I left Princetown Station I realised that I was amongst friends. People did not stare at us; they regarded us as part of the natural scenery, I suppose.

In Dartmoor I was placed in B Ward. I remember marching up from the station, passing under that grim arch with its grimmer jest carved in its granite face, and halting before the great steel grille that led into the prison proper, whilst the head warder checked us over before he turned the big key in the gun-metal lock and the gate swung open to admit us to what has been picturesquely described as a living hell, but which, in reality, is not half as bad as it is painted. I admit, of course, that it is bitterly cold in the winter; but Dartmoor was one of the first prisons to adopt central heating, and though it is old and smelly, and should be pulled down and replaced by modern buildings, it is one of the most comfortable prisons I have ever been in. Its cells are large, light, and airy, the food is good, and the discipline, though strict, is not oppressive.

The second impression was the depth of the recesses in which the cell doors stood, and the narrowness of those yellow doors. They do not appear very formidable, those doors, with their little ventilators; you feel that with a good kick you could break them in. I have often wondered how they got the Tichborne claimant through those narrow entrances. (I have seen the lasts of his boots in the cobbler's shop scores of times, and it is one of the things they pull out to show visitors.)

As I have said before, I have read most of the memoirs of distinguished prisoners, but from none of these do I receive an exact impression of Dartmoor. Most of the writers, being "innocent," are obsessed with their grievances, and they seem surprised that the warders and officials of the prison did not share their illusions.

The Snake Woman came into my life a few months before I had completed my sentence.

As my term of imprisonment was nearly at an end, and as, moreover, I had got into the star class by my good conduct—and it is the easiest thing in the world to be well conducted in gaol—I was allowed a certain liberty of action. I had only worked for a few weeks in the field, and I had not been in the quarry at all.

One afternoon I was sent to paint a barn situated about a quarter of a mile from the gaol, and although, officially, I was under the care of a warder, I was in point of fact my own master. I carried the paint-pot up the road, and was turning into the field where the barn was situated, when I heard the sound of a horse's galloping feet behind me, and looked over my shoulder.

It was a woman, and she was riding astride, which was rather unusual in those days. I turned my head to the front, and heard the horse approach closer and closer. Presently it fell into a walk, and just as my hand was on the gate the rider came abreast.

"Man," said a low voice.

I looked back. It was a pretty face I saw, hard, but pretty. My memory is of level eyebrows and two big dark eyes that seemed to search my soul.

"You will get into trouble," I said in as low a voice as hers, "if you are seen speaking with a convict."

"When will you be released from gaol?" she asked, to my surprise.

"In May, the fourteenth to be exact," I answered.

"What is your name?" she asked hastily. "Where can I find you? I have a job for you that may give you enough money to start you in life."

Her question knocked me out, and I was very anxious to end the interview, if for no other reason than that I did not want to be seen speaking to a member of the public, an indiscretion on my part which would cost me many marks and a cancellation of my remission of sentence.

"Write to John Smith, c.o. Aylesbury, Newsagent, Castle Street, Pimlico," I said, giving her the name and address which I had used for my erratic correspondence.

She repeated the words in a low voice, and then, touching the horse with her heels, she moved off. Only just in time, for that minute a warder came round the corner of the road.

"Did you speak to that lady?" he asked.

"Yes, sir," I replied. "She asked me which was the Tavistock Road, and I told her that she must not speak to a prisoner."

"She spoke to you first, did she?" he asked suspiciously, and looked as though he would have liked to have called the lady back, to be certain that I had not annoyed her, though Heaven knows, very few prisoners who are allowed out of gaol are ever guilty of such impertinence.

At any rate, the lady was now cantering, and was too far off to be called back, and the "screw" seemed satisfied, for he told me to go to my job.

About two hours afterwards, when he came to collect me, to march me back to the working party, he said:

"That lady is staying in Princetown at the Duchess Hotel; it is queer that she didn't know the way to Tavistock."

"That is what I thought, sir," said I; and there the matter ended.

Immediately on my release from prison I made for London. I confess that, although I had given this strange woman an occasional thought, I had not taken any very serious notice of her remarkable introduction to me, deciding in my mind that, moved to pity by what she thought my unfortunate circumstances, she had impulsively decided to give me a hand to lead a better life.

I never expected to hear from her, and I was amazed when I made my call that same evening at the little shop in Pimlico where my letters were addressed, to find one written in a strange but feminine hand, addressed to Mr. Smith, and not only marked "Private," but heavily sealed.

My curiosity was immediately aroused, and at the first opportunity I tore open the flap and extracted a heavy and expensive sheet of notepaper which bore no address or signature. It ran:

"When you receive this, please put an advertisement in the agony column of 'The Times,' saying 'Will meet you at nine o'clock to-night near the Magazine, Hyde Park.' I shall be wearing a black costume and a veil."

The spirit of adventure is never stronger in a man than on the day he is released from prison. The theory that prison crushes a man's spirit is all bunkum. I needed no second telling. And by great good luck, I was in time to get an advertisement in "The Times" that night, and it appeared the following morning.

At nine o'clock, just as it was getting dark, I made my way to that part of Hyde Park where the Powder Magazine is situated. A slight drizzle of rain was falling, and the pathways and seats were deserted. I had not been there three minutes before I saw a woman in a long black raincoat coming toward me, and as she neared me I saw that she was veiled. She had half passed me when she turned.

"Oh, it is you," she said. Her voice was low and musical, and I know it at once. "I should not have recognised you now that you are shaven," she said.

I fell in by her side as she crossed the road and made for one of the paths which stretch across the Park.

"What were you in prison for?"

"Burglary," said I.

I heard her utter an exclamation, and I had a curious sense that she was pleased to hear of my crime. A few seconds later she set any doubt I might have on that subject at rest.

"I am glad," she avid. "Have you been in prison before?"

"No," I confessed.

"And I suppose now you are going to lead an honest and upright life?"

I detected the irony in her tone. It amounted almost to a sneer.

"I am sorry to disappoint you," said I, "but I have no such intention. I shall make an heroic effort to keep out of prison, because Dartmoor, with all its advantages, is a little dull."

She said nothing, and we paced slowly in silence across that desolate stretch of grassland, as the rain pattered down in a hesitating way as though the clouds had not yet decided whether they would let their volumes loose upon the earth, or carry them to a land which was in greater need of humidity than ours.

"There are two chairs under that tree, I think," she said, stepping over the border, and walking across the grass. "We can talk there; there is nobody about to-night, thank goodness."

I put a chair for her, and sat by her side.

"Now, Mr. Smith—I suppose 'Smith' is not your name, but that doesn't matter—I am going to tell you what I want you to do. I want you to commit a burglary."

I gaped at her.

"You're not serious?" I asked.

"I was never more serious in my life," she said earnestly. "Though it isn't exactly a burglary that I want you to commit. My husband, who is many years older than myself, is constantly making fun of me because of my dread of burglars. He says that nobody would ever dare to break into our house in Langdon Square, and my object in seeing you is to induce you to convince him he is wrong."

I was puzzled, and showed it.

"I don't quite see why you should take all this trouble," said I. "You mean, of course, you want a fake burglary?"

She nodded.

"I have taken the trouble, Mr. Smith," she said quietly, "because it is very important to me that my husband should not leave me alone so frequently, knowing, as he does, my terror of burglars."

"You are not exactly showing your terror of burglars at this precise moment," said I, with a smile. "Now, tell me, where do I come in in this matter?"

"You mean, how much will I pay you?" she asked quickly.

"No, no! I am not so mercenary as that. Am I to appear in the dead of night in your husband's bedroom?"

"I will pay you five hundred pounds," she said. "Let us settle that matter now. I will arrange for you to enter the house by the kitchen door, which I will leave ajar. You will make your way up to the first floor and hide yourself in the drawing-room, behind the screen which I will have placed for you. I shall be dining with my husband at the time, and shall bring him up to the room. When I cough twice, you are to come from your place of concealment and cry 'Hands up!'"

"Oh!" said I cautiously. "Am I to be armed?"

"Of course you are to be armed!" she said impatiently. "I want you to look like a burglar. You ought to wear a mask and have a revolver. Here it is."

She put her hand in the fold of her dress and took out a neat little Browning,

"It is loaded," she went on, but the safety-catch is down."

"And then what happens?" I asked curiously.

I guessed rather than saw the grimace she made. Evidently there was no love lost between herself and her elderly husband.

"I expect he will faint," she said drily, "and you will make your escape. I will arrange that all the servants, except the parlour-maid and the cook, are out of the house, and you will have no difficulty in making your way to safety. You are not afraid, are you?" she asked sarcastically.

"Not at all, madam," said I. "But it seems to me to be an extraordinary job.

Do I get paid—"

"You get paid on the night," she said. "Behind the screen, on a little table, I will leave a pocket-book containing the money. You will put it in your pocket, and there will be an end to the adventure. Will you do it?"

I hesitated. It seemed a strange commission, and, candidly, I did not like it, the reason for my dislike being the necessity for carrying a loaded pistol into a dwelling-house, for the punishment meted out to the armed burglar is infinitely more drastic than to the burglar who is unarmed. Still, five hundred pounds was five hundred pounds, and it was not my business to question the lady's good taste or wifely affection.

"I'll do it," I said.

I have called her "a snake woman," and it was at that very moment that I got that snaky impression. It was not the undulation of her fine figure as she rose to her feet, nor her stealthy movement as she crossed to the path by my side, nor yet the hint of those fascinating eyes of hers which I had seen when she raised her veil. All I know is that a thrill ran down my spine, and it was some time before I could shake off the unpleasant feeling which her presence created.

She left me in the middle of the path, after giving her final directions, and I followed her at a distance, until I saw her enter a car near the bridge and drive away.

My first business was to find out who lived at No. 609, Langdon Square. I found it was Mr. and Lady Mary Krain. Krain was a City man, and his name was well-known to me. During the war he was, I believe, under suspicion, because of his German origin, but apparently he was sufficiently a patriot to escape any more unpleasant consequences.

Wednesday night was the time arranged, and at twenty minutes past nine I walked down the area steps of No. 609 and pushed at the kitchen door. It was open, and I entered, closing the door softly behind me. I was in a long passage which ran parallel with the kitchen, and terminated in a flight of stairs leading up into the hall. Her ladyship had laid her plans very carefully. Neither the cook nor the parlour maid nor any other servant was in sight, and a very dim light burnt in the hall, and I went up the stairs and into the drawing-room, which was illuminated by one electric globe.

It was a handsome drawing-room, furnished in that costly fashion which only the vulgarly rich can bring themselves to perpetrate. There was the screen. I stepped behind, and found a tiny table on which was a pocket-book. I opened the book, took out five hundred-pound notes, replaced them, and put the book in my pocket. Then I fixed my mask, and was preparing to wait, when it struck me that it would not be a bad idea if I made a reconnaissance of the room in case my way of retreat was barred.

There were three long French, windows opening on to a balcony, and if the worst came to the worst, there was an easy escape into the street. And then I was walking back to my place of concealment, after listening at the door, when on a round mahogany table, I saw what appeared to be a square of silk as though it were flung there by a careless hand. I put my hand on it, and felt something hard beneath. It was a Browning pistol! And it was loaded. I stood there for a minute, trying to piece together the scheme at the back of the lady's mind, and then I began to see daylight. Quickly I slipped down the magazine, emptied the cartridges into my hand and put them into my pocket; then I carefully drew back the bolt and extracted the one remaining cartridge which was in the chamber. This done, I replaced the pistol where it had been, under the square of green silk.

I had hardly done so when I heard voices on the stairs, and stepped noiselessly back to my place behind the screen. The door was opened, there was a flood of light, and I heard a man's complaining voice asking why any light at all had been left on in the drawing-room.

Between the frames of the screen I had a glimpse of a stout, bald man with a grey-black moustache. He was in evening-dress, and in his shirt sparkled a diamond of immense value. Behind him was the Snake Woman, and now I felt that my description of her was justified. She wore a tight-fitting dress of velvet, innocent of any embroidery and cut low before and behind. The only jewel she displayed was an emerald brooch pinned across her breast; her black hair fall in two waves, framing a white and aesthetic face that emphasised the darkness of those glowing eyes of hers.

"There's another thing," said Mr. Krain, as though he were continuing a conversation; "I will not have that man Thurgood here. I have told you about this before, Mary. I will not have it! The man makes love to you, the servants are talking, and although I take no notice of servants, I am not going to be made a laughing-stock. If you want a young man to love you, wait till I'm dead." He chuckled. "That'll be a good twenty years yet, my dear, and you won't be so attractive then."

"How dare you!" Her voice was vibrant with passion. "To insult me before—"

"Before whom?" asked Mr. Krain contemptuously; and then in a more kindly voice, he went on, "Drop him, Mary; he's a waster. No good can come out of it."

"Indeed!" she said coldly; and I saw her move to the table and her hand creep under the silk. "Let me be the beat judge of that."

She coughed twice.

"Have you got a cold?" asked Krain, peering round at her through his spectacles.

It was at that moment I made my dramatic appearance. My mask on my face, a pistol in my hand, I must have been a terrifying object.

"Hands up!" I said.

He spun round, his face pallid.

"What—what!" he stammered, and then I saw the thing which I expected. The Snake Woman took deliberate aim at him, and pressed the trigger. There was a click, and she stared aghast.

Krain was looking at me. He had not seen what she had done.

"I have taken the liberty of unloading your pistol, Lady Mary," said I, as I made for the door. "Don't move! My pistol is loaded, and I shall have no hesitation in sending you where you intended sending me. If you make a noise, I'll tell the truth. Do you understand that?"

I slipped through the door, closed it behind me, and in a few seconds was in the street. At the corner stood a policeman, and I bade him a cheery

Edgar Wallace

good-night as I strode past, both my hands in my overcoat pockets, one gripping a black mask, the other a ten-shotted pistol.

The Snake Woman was clever, but not as clever as she might have been. She intended killing her husband, and then shooting me. She had brought me there for the purpose. Her story would have been that she was surprised by a burglar, a man with a criminal record who had recently come out of Dartmoor, and that the burglar had shot her husband, and that she, in turn, had shot the burglar in self-defence. Who would doubt the word of Lady Mary against an ex-convict? It was a pretty plan. I remembered it some three years later, when I strolled into the Divorce Court and heard the undefended petition of Mr. Krain.

On the Cornish Express

First published in The Premier Magazine, London, August 4, 1922

THE average warder is neither brutal nor tyrannous; he is a very human individual, poorly paid, and in consequence recruited from the same class as you recruit your army. Often he is an old soldier, with all an old soldier's dislike for hard work. He lives all the time in fear of the "half-sheet"—in other words, the complaint that brings him before the governor, and when you realise that a complaint of any prisoner must be investigated, and if there is the slightest ground for such complaint the warder gets a telling-off, you can understand that a warder's life is a dog's life.

I would personally sooner be a thief, because a thief is sometimes out of prison, and at the worst, if I am captured, and sent to a long term of penal servitude, I can only be reduced to the same sordid surroundings, the same wretched atmosphere, as the honest warder endures.

I am not going to attempt, in this short biography, to engage in the heart-breaking task of prison reform, My own opinion is that prisoners, particularly short-term prisoners, are treated a jolly sight too well; but what did always amuse me was the star prisoner. Men are placed in a certain class, and because they are so promoted there is a prevalent idea that they are less liable to the contamination of their companions. It is rather like putting a

659

man in a special kind of jacket and turning him loose amongst small-pox patients, telling him that because he is wearing a blue coat he will not be infected!

Are crimes hatched in prison? I suppose they are. Men in the solitude of their cells think out new schemes of getting easy money, and usually take some prison friend into their confidence. A prison friendship is very much like ship-board friendship: it is very violent whilst you are in prison, but it peters out the moment you are free. The average lag is a criminal and nothing will reform him; he is a man of low mentality, and very often on the border line of imbecility. You have only to see the faces of the men who are constantly and continually in prison to realise that crime is a disease with them, and invariably the criminal is created by hereditary influences. His father and mother have bequeathed to him a weakness of resistance, an inability to reason logically, and the basis of all crimes, with rare exceptions, of which I am an exponent, is the inability to prevision the effects which follow causes.

Thirty per cent. of habitual criminals should be in lunatic asylums, which really means that they should be placed in a lethal chamber and destroyed. They do not really constitute a menace to society, because they are so foolish, so stupid in their methods, and so readily captured, that their return to prison is inevitable. Their vanity is beyond belief. Nothing delights the habitual lag more than to have a photograph of his wife and children on his shelf, and these he displays with every evidence of pride to the few people who visit him in a humane spirit.

One has heard a great deal about the romance of crime, and I dare say in some respects the criminal is a romantic individual. But a great deal of the romance is sheer imagination, Men like Dick Turpin have been exalted by imaginative novelists into the character of something chivalrous and splendid. Dick Turpin was a butcher boy, a horse thief, and a coarse, illiterate boor. The glamour of his ride to York on "bonny Black Bess" is chiefly remarkable for the fact that he never did ride to York, but to Lincoln, where he engaged in horse thieving.

Edgar Wallace

Crippen was a much more intriguing figure than any of those ancient "heroes" of crime,

Yet I will not deny that in my experience, even apart from the serious case of the Snake woman, I have been the witness of more than one incident which could, without any stretch of imagination, be described as romantic.

When I was in Gloucester Gaol, after my meeting with the snake woman, my first conviction, I met a man named Towner, a well, set-up, good-looking fellow of twenty-six; he had been arrested in Gloucester itself on a charge of defrauding the Post Office, and was serving a sentence of nine months' hard labour. He and I were together in the tailor's shop. I was serving six months for theft committed on the Cornish express, and our sentences expired together.

The romance really began with my steal. There was a lawyer who had come up from Plymouth to sell some properties. I got to know of this through a "nose" who made a profitable business by supplying information to criminals, and I followed him for three days before I stepped into the same carriage that was carrying him back to Plymouth. My objective was a black leather bag which he carried with him, and which he put beside him on the seat of the carriage.

His name, and of course I am giving a fictitious one, was Boglant, and he was a type of family lawyer—a sour, scowling, miserable-looking man—whom it was a real pleasure to rob.

At the end of the train was a carriage which was to be slipped at Swindon for Gloucester and Cheltenham, and my job was to get the bag in reasonable time before we reached Swindon, make my way to the Gloucester coach before it was disconnected, and escape as well as I could. With this object I had brought, inside a large brown kit-bag, an exact replica of the lawyer's black bag, and my job was to ring the changes.

I put my brown bag on the seat and strolled along the corridor on a tour of inspection. I had made a very careful study in preparation for this job, and what I was looking for was the electric wire which connects the dynamo beneath the carriage with the lighting apparatus, and the switch wire which runs the length of the train and has its termination in the guard's van. It is the business of the guard to turn on the lights before any long tunnel is reached, and I had chosen a tunnel to the west of Didcot for my purpose.

I had no difficulty In discovering the switch wire, and when we were about a quarter of an hour from the tunnel I took some wire-cutters from my pocket, cut the strand, and made my way carelessly back to the compartment, where the lawyer was sitting hunched up reading a newspaper.

I opened my own bag, pretending to study its contents, but in reality gripping the replica of the lawyer's bag which it contained, and no sooner had we plunged into the darkness of the tunnel than, slipping it out with one hand, and taking the lawyer's bag with the other, I made a quick exchange. It was not a long tunnel, and we soon again emerged to the light, where he found me sitting opposite to him. I saw him glance at the bag by his side, and a little frown gather on his face, and for a moment I thought he had detected the exchange. But no, he was apparently satisfied, which was a testimonial for me, for I had spent a very long time in making the dummy bag as exactly like his as it was possible.

"They ought to turn these lights on in the tunnels," he complained, and I warmly agreed.

Presently I asked:

"Does this train stop at Gloucester?"

And he looked over his paper.

"No," he said, "this is a through train to Plymouth. Exeter is the first stop. The Gloucester portion is in the rear; the carriages slip at Swindon."

In mock alarm, I gathered up my bag containing its precious contents, and hustled off into the rear of the train, and was only just in time, for the guard and an attendant had already detached the covered alleyway between the coaches. The carriage slowed at Swindon, and getting out on to the platform, I saw the other portion disappearing in the distance. A quarter of an hour later, having been attached to a local train, we pulled out, and I lost no time in making an examination of the bag contained in mine. It was locked, and I was glad to know that I had guessed its weight fairly accurately when I had loaded up the bag which I had passed to the lawyer with old books and papers.

Two slashes of my knife revealed its contents. To my dismay, there was no money, with the exception of about eighty pounds contained in an envelope, and marked punctiliously, as a lawyer would mark it, "Cash Sale No. 4, Motorcar."

He had been selling the effects of an estate which he was administering, and I presumed that No, 4 Motor car was part, of the property. The rest of its contents were bundles of documents, and I turned them disconsolately over, cursing my bad luck. I expected the old man to have taken all the proceeds of his sale in cash, and all I had got was a beggarly eighty pounds.

There was one thin envelope sealed and marked in pencil, "Fetter Lane Safe Deposit." In ink was written "Elsie Doran, will of Bertram Doran." What attracted my attention to this was the fact that it was half torn across. That struck me as strange, for the tear was a new one. The first thing I did was to take the bag and all its papers, and waiting until we crossed a stream, threw them through the open window into the water. The money I put, into my pocket, and as I did so I saw that I had omitted to throw out the "Elsie Doran" envelope.

Just at that moment the train began stopping at what I knew was a wayside station where we were not due to stop. Running into the corridor, I looked out of the window, and my heart for a moment sunk. There were three policemen in uniform standing on the platform. I dashed back to the carriage, took the envelope, and threw it out of the window, watching to see where it fell. The wind carried it down the steep embankment to a clump of bushes, and I had hardly seen its fate before the carriage door opened and an inspector of police came in.

"This is the man," he said.

To cut a long story short, the lawyer had discovered his loss almost as soon as the carriage was slipped, and had telegraphed information to the police. I was taken to a little village lock-up and searched, but beyond the money nothing was found upon me. I say beyond the money, but that was quite sufficient to secure my conviction, for Boglant had taken the numbers of the notes in his pocket-book.

I expected at least that I should be sent to the assizes, but to my delight I was dealt with summarily, and given six months' hard labour.

I shall never forget the lawyer's look of disgust when he heard sentence passed.

When I was in the cell awaiting my transfer to the gaol the gaoler brought the old man along, and we had an interview through the broad, square peep-hole.

"Now look here, Smith," he said, "I bear you no malice, but if you will tell me what you did with the papers you took out of my bag, I will give you ten pounds."

"I chucked them in the river," I said, "with the bag. They seemed a very uninteresting lot of documents."

"I dare say they did," he snarled. "Did you throw all of them into the river?"

"Every one," said I promptly.

As a matter of fact, I had forgotten the "Elsie Doran" envelope, or honestly I should have told him, for I had no particular reason for keeping back that information.

He asked me one or two further questions, and left. I might say, in passing, that in spite of the fact that I gave him all the information in my power, he conveniently forgot the ten pounds he had promised me.

This man I met in Gloucester Gaol was, as I say, a fairly decent fellow, with a good education and a considerable sense of decency. We agreed to meet in London after our releases, but, as a matter of fact, we were discharged on the same day, and travelled to London together.

He told me a great deal about the underworld which I never knew. There was a meeting place at Finsbury, a sort of Bohemian dance club which afforded people on the crook an opportunity of forgathering. I must confess that I was agreeably surprised when I saw the club, which occupied two floors. It was well conducted, nicely but not extravagantly furnished, and I was told that it was a model of what clubs should be. The men who ran and

Edgar Wallace

frequented the place could not afford to have any kind of scandal, and so it was more possible to get drink out of hours at any of the fashionable West-End clubs than at this thieves' kitchen.

Membership was not confined to one sex, and when I turned up to meet my friend I found him sitting at a little table taking tea with a pretty girl. I was surprised to find a girl of her appearance in such a resort. She was evidently a lady. You will judge of my surprise when Towner said:

"This is a friend of mine, Elsie; we came out of 'stir' together."

She looked at me with a cold, appraising glance, and nodded.

"If Gloucester is any worse than Holloway, I congratulate you," she said quietly.

"Holloway?" I said, startled. "You don't mean Holloway Prison? You haven't been there?"

She nodded and smiled, but it was one of those smiles which have no real humour in it, and I thought I detected a hint of pain and shame behind the brave show she made.

When we left the place Towner told me her history. She had come to London as a governess, and when she rejected the attentions of the father of the children whom she was teaching, a charge was faked against her, and she was sent to prison for three months on her first offence. Perhaps it is unfair to say that the charge was faked. A valuable diamond brooch had been found missing, and she was accused and arrested. I have every reason to believe that the woman who lost the brooch, the wife of this man who had persecuted her, found it, and rather than admit that she was in the wrong, and lay herself open to an action for false imprisonment, she secreted the brooch in the girl's room. At any rate, I am convinced that this was a genuine miscarriage of justice.

In prison she met other women, and after vainly attempting to secure work she drifted into a criminal gang.

"She hates the life," said Towner; "and I have done my best to keep her straight. If I could get a bit of money together, I would ask her to marry me, and take her to Canada."

"Why don't you marry her to start with?" said I.

He shook his head.

"Not as I am situated," he said seriously. "It wouldn't be fair—what chance would she have as the wife of a crook?"

"What was she in prison for last?" I asked curiously.

"For getting a situation with forged references," said Towner. "She wants to go straight, that I'll swear, but what can she do? And yet her father was a rich man. He left all his property to a cousin. Apparently he had a quarrel with her mother just after he made the will, and before the child was born. When he died this will was produced, and every penny has gone to a swine of a lawyer."

Suddenly I remembered.

"Elsie! What is her other name?" I

"Doran," he said; and I gasped.

"What was the lawyer's name?"

"A young fellow named Boglant."

"A young man?" I asked.

"Yes; his father is a lawyer, too. Old Boglant is one of the hardest nuts in Plymouth."

"Elsie Doran," I repeated; and then I told him the story of the lawyer's bag and the envelope I had found half torn across.

"Are you sure?" he asked quickly. "Did you say that it was the will of Bertram Doran?"

"That was written in pencil across the top, and it had been torn."

"It is the will that her father made after the other," said Towner excitedly. "She always felt there was one. We must see her at once."

He called a taxi and we drove to a quiet street in Holloway, where Elsie Doran occupied two rooms. She was surprised to see us, and no more surprised than the landlady, who had some doubt about admitting us, until I explained that I was Elsie Doran's lawyer, and must see her at once.

She listened in silence while we told the story.

"I am sure that is it," she said; "but what is the good?"

"I'm going to make a search of the railway embankment. I know the exact spot where the paper was thrown," said I.

"Six months ago?" She shook her head. "I don't think you will find it, Mr. Smith; and if you do, it will hardly have survived the rains and storms of the past six months."

"Four months and a half, to be exact," said I. "There is a chance, because the place I threw it was not part of the station premises, and the cleaners would not go to the trouble of tidying the bushes at the bottom of the embankment."

Towner and I left the next morning by train, and we reached the wayside station soon after one o'clock.

The station-master recognised me immediately, and greeted me with a broad grin. I told him that I had lost a pocket-book when I had been arrested, and was anxious to find it; and he was sympathetic, as all law-abiding people are sympathetic to criminals when they think that they are getting the better of the law. He was quite certain that I had thrown fabulous sums of money from the railway carriage window before I was arrested, and volunteered to help. I think he was surprised when I accepted the offer of his assistance.

We trudged along the embankment, and came at last to the spot where I had thrown the envelope. I explained to the station-master that it was a paper and not money, and he shook his head.

"I don't think you'll find it," he said; "we had a flood here two months ago. All those fields"—he pointed—"were under water, and the floods came half-way up the embankment."

Mentally I agreed with him, but we began to search, although I was certain that we were foredoomed to failure. The bushes were covered with verdure, and there was not a trace of any kind of paper to be seen; but, nevertheless, I did not lose heart, and in the middle of my search I remembered that I had located the exact spot where the envelope finally rested, because it stood in a direct line with a large elm tree in the middle of a near-by field.

We spent two hours in the search, and I was giving it up, when suddenly the station-master said:

"There's a paper up there," and pointed up to a tree which overshadowed the bushes.

We found the will wedged between two twigs, absolutely dry, and not so much as discoloured.

Afterwards the station-master recalled the fact that the night I was arrested there was a heavy wind storm, and probably the envelope had blown to its resting-place, the only spot where it could be sheltered from the torrential rains which had followed.

With trembling fingers, Towner opened the flap and took out the document, and, looking at him, I saw his face was white.

"This is it," he said; "made by her father three months before his death, and actually witnessed by Boglant!"

The will left most of his property to his daughter; there were a few legacies to servants, a hundred pounds to Boglant, and certain provisions as to the disposal of his estate. The sum involved was a considerable one, something like sixty thousand pounds.

We reached Plymouth that night, and found the office of Boglant & Boglant was closed. Hiring a taxi, we drove out to his big house on the Torquay road, and I went in to interview him, leaving Towner outside.

He recognised me instantly, but to the fat-faced young man who sat with him at dinner I was, of course, a perfect stranger.

"Well, you scoundrel," said Boglant, "what do you want? If I had known you were 'Mr. Smith' I would have had you kicked out."

"Smith!" said young Boglant apoplectically. "Is this the blackguard that stole your bag, father?"

"I am the blackguard," said I gently.

"What do you want?"

"I want the name of a good lawyer to represent Elsie Doran," said I, "and probably you can recommend me one, as you know them all in these parts."

The old man's face went grey.

"What do you mean?" he said.

"I mean that amongst the documents that were not destroyed was the will of the late Bertram Doran, which left the whole of his property to his daughter, and which you kept, carefully stowed away in the Fetter Lane Safe Deposit, until you decided to draw it out and destroy it. You began by tearing it, and then decided that you would wait until you got back to Plymouth and burn it, that, being a safer method."

He collapsed into his chair.

"There is no other will," he said hollowly.

"There is another will which you have witnessed," said I gently.

"I suppose you have come to blackmail me," he growled, after a pause.

"If you gave me the wealth of the Indies that will would have to be proved," said I. "You are going to restore every penny you stole from this girl, and you will give me a thousand pounds for keeping my mouth shut. Otherwise, you and I will be meeting in B. Ward."

I can only add that he made restitution, and that he paid me my thousand. It is the only money I have ever made by blackmail, and it was very sweet to spend.

The Master Criminal

First published in The Premier Magazine, *London, August 22, 1922*

IS there a real master criminal? I doubt it. John Flay was the nearest I have ever met, and it is strange that even in Dartmoor I had never met him, though I helped flog one of his agents and incidentally heard the first mention of his name.

I had not been in Dartmoor long before I was removed to the punishment cells, not as a victim, but as an official, if an orderly can be called an official. Until the second year of my confinement the punishment prisoners were merely insolent or lazy convicts, and in consequence were introduced to the plank bed and carpet slippers. On two occasions we had men who had run amok in the fields, who were brought into the punishment hall, struggling more like wild beasts than men, and thrown into the padded cell. One of these, however, was a genuine lunatic; the second was a brute who had tried to kill a warder, and for him there could be only one punishment. Day after day he went before the Visiting Justices, and I learnt that he had been sentenced to fifteen lashes with the cat-o'-nine-tails. But the sentence had to go to the Home Office for confirmation. It was a fortnight later before my warder ordered me to get out the triangle.

One cell in the punishment hall is used as an irons store; the walls are covered with handcuffs and leg-irons, and in the centre of the cell stands a steel triangle, which, with the assistance of another convict, I got out and fastened to the floor. At eleven o'clock the next morning the prisoner was brought out, his hands manacled, and attached to a chain running from a pulley at the top of the triangle. His legs were fastened to two of the steel uprights, and a warder turned a wrench which drew his hands high above his head.

I had never seen a man flogged before, and it was a pretty ghastly experience. I subsequently confirmed, as I then suspected, that the real punishment of flogging is that moment of time before the fall of the whip. The cat-o'-nine-tails in itself consists of a handle about eighteen inches long, covered with blue felt; it is a tremendously thick handle, and wants a man with a very big hand to encompass it. Suspended from this are nine cords, the tip of each being bound about by yellow silk. The warder who administers the flogging stands at a distance from his victim, generally a little to the left, and extends the arm holding the cat until the hanging thongs are within about six inches of the man's left shoulder. The doctor says "One," and the flogger brings the whip round his head so that the lash follows roughly the figure eight before it falls. It is this horrible whistling sound which, to my mind, is the devilish part of the punishment.

In flogging you are not allowed to hit above or below the shoulder-blades, and an expert warder—I believe they receive five shillings for each flogging—will not deviate by so much as an inch from the line where the lash originally falls. Many people are under the impression that flogging eventually kills a man because the whip falls across his kidneys. That, however, is a great mistake. The whip is not allowed to fall below the line I indicate; if it does, the doctor will stop the flogging.

The prisoner took his punishment without a word, and when it was finished I placed a big piece of lint, which I held in preparation, across the shoulders, fastened it so that it could not slip off, and the man was taken back to his cell,

"John Flay ought to have had this!" was only comment; and that was the first and only time Flay's name was mentioned.

I had hitherto doubted the existence of the master criminal, for it seemed to me that the man fared best who "worked lonely."

I say, without boasting, that I probably made more money by illicit processes than any other criminal in the business. I have literally made thousands and spent thousands. If I had been one of those saving criminals one reads about, but never meets, I should probably be the wealthiest man that ever went in or out of a gaol. As it was, I was poor but happy, for life is very sweet to a philosophical convict.

I once got into contact with a doctor, a man of good birth, who had been engaging in some swindling practice into which I was dragged at the last moment. When the jury had retired and we were waiting in the room below, he told me that if he got a term of penal servitude he intended finishing everything with a dose of cyanide potassium which he carried loose in his waistcoat pocket, and which the warders had overlooked in their search. I knew it was pretty certain that he was going to get from three to five years, just as I was as certain that I should get off with about three months, because the part I had played was an insignificant one, and as we were tried at the Hereford Assizes, where my record was not known, I did not doubt that the judge would take a very merciful view of my offence.

Before we went up to the dock I took the chief warder aside.

"That fellow has a dose of cyanide of potassium in his pocket," I said, "and he is liable to commit suicide unless you take some steps to deal with him."

I told him where the poison was concealed, and, cursing me heartily, he was searched, and the drug taken away from him.

Ah I expected, he got three years, and, as I had hoped, my sentence was twelve months in the second division. We were placed in adjoining cells, and bitterly he cursed me for a traitor and a blackguard because I had betrayed him. I waited till his wrath had burnt itself out, and then I said:

"My friend, you have only one period of life to live, and it is stupid to curtail what may be a most enjoyable experience. You will be out of prison in two and a half years, with all the world to rove in, and all the opportunities for making good before you. It is better to be a living thief than a dead bishop."

He served the first part of his sentence in the name prison an myself, and before he was taken off to Dartmoor, or Portland—I am not sure which—he found an opportunity for thanking me.

Suicide in the consequence of a diseased vanity. The thought of what people are saying about him drives a weak man mad, and he prefers the oblivion of death to the consciousness of their disapproval. I have never had any sympathy with suicides. Suicide, to my mind, is the most objectionable form that conceit can take. Much more do I sympathise with the attitude of an old lag I met in Dartmoor who had shot a policeman and did not expect to be released from prison until he was sixty-four.

"I shall be in the prime of life," he said to me one day, when we were shovelling coke in the big yard, "and I am going to have a good time. I haven't decided whether I shall go to Brighton or Margate to live."

I was able to give him a tip as to how to get an honest living, and when I came out of gaol, by a curious coincidence, I came upon him, and saw that he had carried out my suggestion. He had a piano organ, on the front of which was painted, in legible letters, the words I had suggested, and which he had evidently committed to memory. They ran:

"I am an ex-convict, and have spent twenty-five years in prison. This is the only honest way of making a living which does not bore me stiff."

He told me he was taking between five and six pounds a day in silver and copper. The British public love frankness, and they have, thank Heaven, a sense of humour. He told me that the police never dared to move him on for fear of exciting the indignation of the populace, and that when they did shift him from any pitch, a perfect hail of silver coins came from his sympathetic audience.

It was more than an ordinary coincidence, this meeting with William Billington, for whilst I was talking to him there came upon the scene the most remarkable man I have met in my criminal career.

A great deal has been written about John Flay, arid I suppose he will go down to history as one of those legendary heroes of the underworld about whom romantic writers wax enthusiastic. In appearance he looked like one of those American professional men whom one meets at the holiday resorts on the Continent. A tall, clean-shaven man, with gold-rimmed spectacles and a broad brimmed black hat, he was always dressed neatly and unobtrusively, and not once during my knowledge of him did I ever see him wear an article of jewellery. He contented himself with a nickel watch that you can buy for five shillings, which was attached to a brown leather guard, and yet, in spite of his lack of ostentation, there was a time when John Flay was worth nearly half a million pounds.

Beyond the incident to which I have referred, I had never heard of him, which was remarkable, remembering that I had spoken to some of the best-known criminals in England, but it was evident, from the respectful manner in which old William greeted him, that he was a person of some importance. At first I thought he was the chief constable, and when he had gone, I asked William:

"Who is your classy friend?"

William looked uncomfortable.

"Oh, that's Mr. Flay," he said awkwardly; and I could get no other information out of him.

I saw Flay again that evening in the lounge of the hotel where I was staying. He came across to me. He was smoking a long and particularly fragrant cigar.

"So you're a book, are you?" he said, without any preamble. "William tells me that he met you in the Home of Rest. I am John Flay."

"I have never heard of you," I said coolly. "What is your particular line of authority—police or prisons?"

"Neither," he said, and offered me a cigar. "You're called Smith, and I suppose that is not your name. You were a gentleman, too."

"I am still," said I, biting off the end of the cigar, and lighting it.

He looked at me for a long time scrutinisingly, and then he said:

"The worst of you fellows is that you have no organisation at the back of you. You take all sorts of chances that you need not take, and at the critical moment, when you want a friend, he is not there to lend a helping hand. You'd be an invaluable man—in an organisation."

"What kind of organization?" I asked flippantly. "Are you a member of one of those gangs one reads about in the magazines?"

He took no notice of my jest, but continued to eye me keenly.

"You wouldn't take all the profit, but then you'd take some of it, and be sure of getting it without trouble." He leant across the table and lowered his voice. "Suppose you were at Boulogne next Monday week with a diplomatic passport, which means that your baggage wouldn't be searched, and somebody coming off the mail-train handed you a bag and you took it aboard, and brought it to an address I will give you in London, would that be worth two hundred?"

I returned his gaze now, for I knew that he was talking business.

"What will be in the bag?" I asked.

"That will be nothing to do with you! You could be, for the first time in your life, absolutely innocent. But I will put your mind at rest. There would be a million francs in the bag, and I am only offering you two hundred because about ten people have to get their share, and then the notes have to be changed. Would you like to do the job?"

I nodded.

"What about the diplomatic passport? That's rather a difficult one to get."

"Don't worry; the passport will be in your hands before you leave London. Maundy and Spear are the two detectives on duty on the boat. Do you know them?"

I shook my head.

"Do they know you? That's a little more important."

"No," I said. "I don't imagine so."

"I shouldn't have asked you," said Flay thoughtfully, "only the man whom I had intended to bring the bag across doesn't quite look the part. You can carry clothes, and you look rather like a young Foreign Office official."

I laughed.

"Aren't you afraid of my double crossing you?" I asked; and his saturnine features creased in a smile.

"No, I don't think so," he said quietly. "I never make mistakes in choosing my man."

Little more than a week later found me on the platform at Boulogne, and my presence was explained to the officials by the beautifully forged diplomatic passport which had brought me ashore. It lent likelihood to the proceedings that I was to meet the Orient express, and that the man from whom I had to take the bag was travelling in the Constantinople coach. There is nothing remarkable in the meeting of this train by diplomatic officials. In fact, I believe it is done twice or three times a week.

The train came in, and a stout, bearded Frenchman stepped lightly down and looked at me quickly.

"M'sieur Smith?" he said.

I nodded, and he placed in my hand a big leather portfolio. I took it from him, and, with a nod to the Customs officials, I passed through the office on to the wharf. I had already secured my embarkation ticket, and in a few minutes I was sitting at ease in the handsome little cabin of the Invicta.

At Folkestone I was again saved the bother of a Customs' examination, and the coupé which had been reserved for me on the Pullman was very inviting and warm after a somewhat rough crossing.

At Victoria a handsome motor-car was waiting for me; it had been pointed out to me before I left London, and I jumped in, to find it was already occupied by a man, who spoke no word until we were clear of the station.

"Here is your money," he said, and handed me two crisp notes.

"And here is your bag," I smiled. "It was an easy job. I'd live honestly if I had a commission like that every week."

He dropped me at the corner of Whitehall, and neither of us mentioned the name of Flay. I had hardly stepped upon the pavement, and the car moved off, before a hand touched me on the shoulder, and I turned to see the jovial face of Inspector Stelling, of Scotland Yard.

"Hallo, Smith!" he said. "Getting into society?"

"Yes," I replied.

"Nice car that," said Stelling, looking after the retreating limousine.

"Not a bad car. It belongs to a friend of mine who is trying to reform me," said I.

"Is John Flay trying to reform you?" said Stelling, in mock surprise. "Where have you come from?"

I was silent.

He evidently knew the car, and I wondered why so astute a man as John Flay should be identified with such a handsome machine. My wonder was set at rest by his next words.

"That's the car Flay uses," he said. "It is supposed to be the property of his doctor, who is as big a crook as he is. Where have you come from, Smith?"

"From Victoria Station," I said. "I have been down to Brighton."

"You came up on the Continental," he said very patiently. "I saw you and followed you here."

And then, looking past him, I saw that there was a car drawn up a dozen yards away from where I had been set down, and evidently he had followed us in this.

"Bless my life, Stelling," said I blandly, "we poor, innocent crooks can keep no secrets from you. Yes, I went down to meet a friend at Folkestone, but he didn't turn up."

"You had a bag when you came out of the Pullman—a sort of portfolio. Where is it now?" said Stelling. "And I am sure you will excuse my curiosity when I tell you that the National Bank of France has been robbed of ten million francs."

"Good effort!" I said. "But I am no bank robber, Stelling, and so far as having a bag, I can only assure you that your eyes have deceived you. I carried no bag or portfolio, or anything that would look like a bag or a portfolio. Oh, yes," I said, as though I had suddenly remembered. "I carried the bag of a lady when she was alighting from the Pullman, and gave it to her when she got into her taxi."

It was a shot at random, but I knew that the station platform was so crowded that he could not have been able to observe my every movement.

"I guess you're lying," he said. "But it doesn't matter very much. I know where to find you when I want you."

"May our meeting be long deferred," said I, and left him, feeling just a little uncomfortable.

I found means of getting into touch with John Flay that night. He had given me a telephone number where I could call him, and I told him briefly and guardedly what had happened.

"That's all right," he said. "I saw Stelling following us."

"Were you in the car?" I asked.

"I was driving," was the laconic reply. "Don't worry. Good-night!"

About a week after that I was working on a scheme I had invented, having as its object the removing of a petrol millionaire's superfluous cash. It was a very ingenious scheme, and it has been one of my regrets that I never carried it into execution. What really arrested me in my career was a meeting with Inspector Stelling at a certain bar near Piccadilly Circus. It was, I thought, an accidental meeting, but the truth was, as I learnt, that he had had me under observation for a week, and this fact alone was sufficient to postpone my great attack upon the oil-King.

"I am going to tell it to you straight, Smith, for I feel that I can trust you," he said. "I want Flay very badly, and if you can give me any kind of help to rope him in, you will not regret it."

I told him then and there, and with perfect sincerity, that I knew nothing more about Flay than that I had done one job for him.

"I won't ask you to tell me what the job was," he said shortly, "because I know. You were the man who brought across the stolen notes from

Boulogne. They were handed to you by a man named Lefèvre, who was arrested the next day. I am not going to go into the matter at all. Flay may have been the organiser—he certainly was the receiver; but it is the business of the French police to track him down if they can." Then he told me what I had half suspected, namely, that John Flay was the genius who organised more clever burglaries than any other man in England. He not only organised them, but he financed burglars who wanted a kit, he paid for their defences when they were arrested, and generally acted as a service bureau to the underworld. In return, he got the lion's share of most of the crimes. He handled the jewellery and the stolen stuff, and marketed them in some mysterious way which the inspector had not been able to discover.

Flay I did not see again for nearly three months. I had no need of him, and apparently he had no particular use for me. I was down to my last sovereign when I got information about a house at Highgate which was reputedly kept by an aged miser, Mr. Wellinghall. My informant got his information from an old woman who acted as a sort of daily housekeeper. She had never seen her employer; he was eccentric and apparently a little mad, and had all his food sent up to him on a little hand-lift from the kitchen, and never under any circumstances appeared in public. He dusted and swept his own room, and was apparently a man of wealth and substance, for he always paid in cash, and nobody had ever seen a cheque of his. That meant he had a lot of money on the premises, and since I have a rooted objection to people who hoard their fortune, I determined to give Mr. Wellinghall a look up.

It was a big, rambling house, neglected and dirty in appearance, but an easy house to burgle, I should think. The night I chose for my preliminary visit I was again checked by Stelling, who overtook me as I was walking across the path.

"Have you seen Flay lately?"

"No," I replied.

"Now, come across. Smith," he began coaxingly. "You know he was in that picture steal."

I remembered having read in the morning that somebody had taken two pictures from one of the Midland art galleries, and that they were worth some twenty thousand pounds, but beyond noting the fact and wondering in what manner these huge pictures could have been taken away without attracting the notice of the police, I had not given the matter much thought.

"I know you weren't in it," Stelling went on, "because my people have been watching you; but Flay is in it. I swear."

"I ask you to believe me, Stelling," I said, "that, as a lover of art, I strongly disapprove of picture stealing. I know nothing more about Flay than what I have already told you, and that if I did know, I should not squeal. Happily, I don't."

This seemed to satisfy Stelling. We had a drink together, and we parted.

I waited until it was dark before I went to Highgate on my second visit, and arriving there, I made a thorough reconnaissance of the house.

The house stood in a rank garden, and the back window, which I forced, gave me no trouble at all. I found myself in an empty room, littered with packing-cases and pieces of old furniture and the like, and made my way carefully into the passage and up the stairs.

At last I came to the small room which had been described to me, and which I knew lay next to the secret apartments of the miser. I carried no weapon, but a jemmy and the usual tools, in the use of which I had become almost an expert. The door was locked. No gleam of light showed under, and with the utmost care I inserted my skeleton key, and, after three attempts, succeeded in turning the lock. The room, as I expected, was in darkness. There was light in another room leading from this, which, when I put my lamp over it, proved to be a dilapidated drawing-room.

Stealthily I moved across the carpeted floor toward the light, and my hand was on the knob, when there was a blinding flash of light. All the lamps in the drawing-room had been suddenly put on; I heard the click of the switch, and I spun round to meet the level barrel of a revolver. But it was not the pistol, and it was not the sight of the two big canvases propped against the wall at one end of the room, that took my breath away. It was the unexpected apparition of Mr. Flay. He was as astonished as I.

Suddenly he put down the pistol, and laughed silently.

"Well, I'm hanged!" he said. "What are you doing here?"

Without waiting for me to reply, he went on:

"I suppose you've heard of the old miser who lived in this house. Well, my boy, I am the old miser who sleeps all day and mustn't be disturbed on any account."

"I haven't heard that story," said I. "I hope you will accept my apologies, Mr. Flay, for intruding upon your privacy."

He was still laughing silently to himself. "We must get a bottle of wine on this; it is the funniest thing that has happened to me for years," he said. "Yes, this is my Aladdin's cave, and you are the only man who knows of its existence."

He went to his bin, a black, square box near the fireplace, and took out a gold-topped bottle, opened it deftly, and filled two glasses which he took from the cupboard.

"Here's better luck in your next enterprise," he said; and at that moment the door opened, and in walked Stelling.

And behind Stelling I could see the stairway was crowded with "splits."

"It's a cop," said Flay philosophically. "This gentleman is not in this," he said, pointing to me. "He's a visitor."

"I dare say," said Stelling sarcastically, "and now he is going on a visit to Portland."

They gave John Flay seven years, and to me they gave twelve months, and I was innocent of everything—except burglary!

The House of Doom

First published in The Premier Magazine, *London, September 5, 1922*

I SHOULD very much like to meet the man who said, "Never interfere between husband and wife," and take him by the hand. He is probably dead.

One of the first things I did when I came out of prison was to look round for a nice genteel way of swindling the public. Perhaps it is not exactly right to say I looked round when I came out. I had been looking round mentally all the time I had been in prison, and I hit upon an ideal plan, which I proceeded to put into execution.

In prison I met a man named Manson, who was doing time for frauds on bookmakers, and he gave me an idea that enabled me to live twelve months without breaking the law. I might say that my intention was to give the law as bad a jolt as possible, but, as things turned out, it was not necessary. On my release from prison I met a friend who was a member of a well-known smart night club, and he took me to lunch there.

It was the day before the Derby was run, and the club had a sweepstake, in which he took ten tickets, one of which he gave to me for luck. By the oddest chance I drew the winner, and received the magnificent sum of £450. I had now sufficient capital to carry out the scheme I had formed in prison.

I took a furnished flat in Jermyn Street, and securing a directory from a Turf society, I personally wrote to three hundred bookmakers throughout the kingdom, giving them the name of my bank, and requesting that a credit account be opened. It was a long and tedious business; it took me three days to write the letters. Of the three hundred, two hundred wrote back, telling me that an account had been opened in my favour, giving me a credit limit from £10 to £50. I started betting on the Monday and, nearly every bet I made cost me £3 for telegraph fees alone. My intention was to take a race, which had about eight runners and, reducing the eight to about four that had any chance, to telegraph fifty bookmakers one horse, another fifty the second horse, and so on. In this way I should be certain to find the winner, and I need not bother with the losers.

At the end of the week, when the cheques and the bills came in, I should have a sure profit, and the men who had won could whistle for their money,

But on the very first day an extraordinary thing happened. The butler, who I also think was the proprietor of the block of flats in which I was staying, told me that he had a tip for the four o'clock race from his nephew, who was head lad In one of the Wiltshire training stables, and I departed from my original plan and wired this horse to two hundred and seven bookmakers. It won at eight to one, and as the least I had had on was £2, the profit on my day's working was an enormous one. It gave me, in fact, nearly seven thousand pounds profit, and eliminated the necessity for running crook,

On the Thursday, thinking that I might have some difficulty with the bookmakers if I had only backed one horse, and that a winner, I decided to send them all a horse which I had picked out for no particular reason, except that none of the newspapers had picked it, and therefore it was likely to lose. To my amazement, it won at a hundred to eight.

My week's betting—I backed two losers on Friday—produced me a profit of ten thousand, three hundred pounds. There was really no reason in the world why I should ever steal again, I have always contended that we people of good birth are the only people who have acquired the art of spending money; but, encouraged by my success, I prepared to operate the bookmaker robbing plan on a more elaborate scale.

There was a small printing business in a South Eastern suburb for sale, and for a few hundreds I purchased it, leaving its conduct to an old man who had been in the employ of the firm for years. I chose this particular business because it had rather a high-sounding name. There had been three partners—Witherby, Dixshalt and Green. At the cost of another hundred pounds, I turned this office into a limited liability company, took an office in the city, and furnished it. "Witherby, Dixshalt and Green, Ltd.," looked good upon acetate notepaper, so did my name as managing director, the list of my agents in Cape Town, Sydney, New York, Bombay and Calcutta, and a further list in which I described the firm as printers and publishers, stationers, printers' agents, etc.

For the first time in my career I used my own name, but this time I tackled one of the London bookmakers, and asked for credit on a more extensive scale. Unfortunately, I also wrote to a big paper maker, in my capacity as managing director, and ordered an immense quantity of paper, purposely putting the figure per pound much lower than the market price, which I had taken the trouble to ascertain. I did this with the intention of establishing my stability, believing the firm would write back, regretting that they could not fulfil the order at the price. Unfortunately, the particular paper I had asked for—and I had chosen the quality and character at random—had been overstocked in their warehouse, and, to my horror, they confirmed the order and informed me that supplies would be made the following week. They also enclosed an invoice for eighteen hundred pounds. I thought I would be able to get out of this by writing cancelling the order. I was too interested in the re-opening of my betting career to bother about paper.

I am not exaggerating when I say that at the end of the week I was over thirty thousand pounds in credit; but before these bills could be paid, I was arrested on the charge of running a dud firm, my record was brought up against me, and I was also identified as the associate of a man who had committed a number of frauds upon bookmakers.

I found that the paper makers had put through an enquiry as to my stability long before I had cancelled the order, and had placed the matter in the hands of the police, when they discovered that my highly sounding company was only a tiny little printing office.

Anyway, the "busy fellows" were after me like a pack of hounds, and I was sent down for ten years—a very serious sentence. And I might have been back at this moment in Dartmoor, but for the fact that a flaw was discovered in the indictment, and, before the Court of Criminal Appeal, my conviction was quashed.

My first step on my release was to claim the money the bookmakers owed me. They could produce no proof that I intended defrauding them, and on the threat of taking the matter before Tattersall's Committee, I managed to collect a very considerable sum of money, the major portion of which was now in my possession. And I left England for Wiesbaden in double quick time.

From Wiesbaden I went on to Marienbad, and it was whilst I was in Marienbad that I met Kiltin and his wife. The man was a swindler of some kind; I have never been quite certain what his game was, but he had made a large sum of money and was engaged in "doing it in." A hopeless vulgarian, a man whose brutal and foul tongue knew no restraint when he was angered, he had the strength of an ox and no little skill as a fighter.

I believe he had originally ornamented an East End boxing ring, and had graduated to crime by those methods with which the public is so familiar.

His wife was a slim, pretty girl, socially his superior, I should imagine, passionately devoted to this great brute, and in some terror of him.

The man, however, had passed his boxing days, was undertrained and overfed, but still a dangerous animal to tackle, and I should never have dreamt of touching him, but for the fact that my bedroom was next to Kiltin's, and I was awakened at three o'clock in the morning by the sound of a woman's sobs, and the unmistakable noise of blows being administered by a heavy hand.

In Germany it is not unusual for men to beat their wives, but it is a practice to which I have never grown accustomed, and I was out of bed and in the passage knocking at their door before I realised what I was doing. The man opened the door and scowled at me.

"What do you want?" he asked.

I had met him the previous day, and he recognised me.

"Is anything wrong?" I demanded; and then I saw over his shoulder the huddled figure on the floor; her cheek was blood-stained, he had cut her mouth with his huge fist, and one of her eyes was red and swollen.

Kiltin had been drinking, I think, and I afterwards learned that this was the second time there had been such an occurrence, and that he had been threatened with expulsion from the hotel by the management If it happened again.

"You don't mean you have been hitting that girl, do you?" I asked.

His answer was a blow aimed wildly at me, which, if it had reached home, would have done me no good at all. But now I was as fit as possible. Penal servitude is a fine training for a man with a taste for athletics, and I dodged the blow and landed him two on the point before he realised what was happening. And then the woman, struggling to her feet, came at me like a fury. She scratched and bit and screamed, and before I knew what had happened, the corridor was full of people. I was glad to get back to my room.

In the morning the Kiltins received notice to go, and their luggage was brought down to the hall as soon as it was packed. I saw the man and he saw me. Coming over to where I sat, he glowered down at me, his hands in his pockets.

"The first time I ever meet you, my friend, I'll fix you," he said.

"It will be a pleasant change alter wife-beating," sad I. "You used to be in the Ring, I'm told—you should make a champion."

He was apoplectic with rage, and I was prepared for him to hit at me there and then, but apparently he thought better of it, and left me, muttering under his breath.

When I got back to London, I put through a few inquiries, and discovered, as I had thought, that the man was a known bad character. He had been in prison four or five times, mostly for offences against the person, assault, unlawful wounding, etc. Consideration for safety induced me to move West. I took a little house at Torquay, and had quite a pleasant time living on my ill-gotten gains.

Unhappily for me, the Kiltins came to Torquay, too, and, by an odd coincidence, took a furnished house in the same road as I was living. I met Mrs. Kiltin on the beach road, and she scowled at me as though I were her worst enemy instead of being, as I had intended, her best friend.

There was living in Torquay at the time a Colonel Mansil, who had a wonderful collection of emeralds. Some infernal person told me about this collection, and naturally my mind was occupied with the colonel and his property when it should have been engaged in securing a lead to a better life,

The long and short of it was that I broke into the colonel's handsome house in Babbacombe, or, rather, St. Mary Church, was returning at four o'clock in the morning with about two hundred pounds' worth of stones in my pocket—the bulk of the collection was in a safe—when, passing the Kiltins' house, which I had to, I saw Mrs. Kiltin standing on the doorstep in her nightgown, and bearing the marks of a recent thrashing.

I hesitated. What could I do? Any interference on my part must inevitably have the effect of making her hate me worse than she did. And yet my heart bled to see that frail figure standing on a chilly morning shivering before the closed door of her house.

"Can I be of any assistance?" I asked.

She turned her bruised face to me.

"Go away," she said hoarsely—"go away, or he will kill you, too."

She was so vehement that I hesitated no longer, and went on my way to my house.

I was arrested that afternoon. On whose information? On the information of Mrs. Kiltin, who had seen me returning, and had learnt that I had suffered a term of penal servitude for a similar offence. It was she, who, when she was reconciled to her husband that morning, and when she had heard that a burglar had broken in and stolen the emeralds, had gone straight to the police and told them all she knew.

As I say, never come between husband and wife.

I served my imprisonment in Exeter Gaol—I got the surprisingly light sentence of nine months' hard—and I carried with me to my confinement the memory of that brutal face of Kiltin, and the eager, venomous eyes of his wife as they sat side by side in the court and heard the evidence.

I hadn't been in gaol a month before Kiltin had the audacity to apply, on some pretext or another, for permission to see over the gaol, and secured a Home Office order, What excuse he gave, heaven knows, because the Home Office is very chary of granting these permissions, but there he was, strutting beside the chief warder, when I came out of my cell one afternoon to do a little window-cleaning on behalf of the State. His grin of triumph, however, produced no emotion in my placid bosom. I am impervious to scorn, and men of Kiltin's calibre are quite incapable of annoying me.

The warder was opening a cell door in order to show him what they looked like, and I had to pass him. As I got abreast of him he said, under his breath:

"Nice place this, eh?"

"You'll see it for yourself one of these days," I said in the same tone; but little did I dream that my prophecy would come true.

About four months later, when I was within a few weeks of release, I learnt that the condemned cell was occupied by a man who had been convicted of wife murder. His name I was not told. As a matter of fact, I had few opportunities for gossiping, for I held a responsible position—I was assisting the schoolmaster to bring order into the chaotic minds of the criminal Yokels of Devonshire.

A pending execution makes very little difference to the routine of the prison; you might imagine that there was nobody within those high red walls to whom every minute passed all too rapidly. The day before the execution I and the other privileged prisoner were marched out into the yard, through the little glasshouse where our photographs had been taken when we arrived, to the coach-house, which was about a dozen paces away. It is an ugly, rectangular little building, with a roof like an inverted V, and built into a tiny hillock; it is the dampest place in the prison. The prison van rests on two wooden runners which are laid across an open pit. We had to draw out the van and tidy up. The brick-lined pit is about eight feet deep, and I found that the two traps do not fall away directly from the entrance of the pit, but work on a fulcrum bar principle—I think that is the right term.

I noticed that there was an inch of water at the bottom of the pit, and then recalled the fact that it was in this little shed that Lee, of Babbacombe, suffered his great ordeal. It will be remembered that the trap would not fall, and the reason is apparent even to-day. The shed is so damp that, given a heavy fall of rain, such as had occurred the night before his execution, the wet trap would swell, and whilst it was true that they sawed away a portion of the trap, it was equally true that, in their agitation, the warders sawed at the wrong place! The walls, even when I saw them, were running with water, and the little lever at the left of the trap as you enter the shed, was thick with rust.

Set into the trap are two rings, and on one of the flaps I noticed a chalk mark like a letter "T". It was very faint, and I asked the warder, who was a genial sort of soul, what it meant. He then explained the procedure of execution. When a man is to be executed, the governor of the gaol notifies Pentonville, which is the headquarters of the prison system, and Pentonville sends down a rope, a linen "cap"—which is a small piece of coarse linen with elastic loops to go over the ears—and a piece of chalk, the chalk being intended to mark the place where the condemned man's feet will stand.

We cleared all the gear, cleaned the lever, and pulled up the trap which the warder tested. Brr! I shall never forget the thud and clang of that falling platform. In one corner of the shed is a further trap-door leading to a flight of stone stairs into the pit. It is down these stairs that the doctor passes to examine the body after the drop has fallen.

There was no sign of a rope, of course, but from wall to wall ran two beams, between which were three stout steel rods to which the rope is affixed.

I confess that I slept very well that night. I am told that prisoners are restless on the eve of an execution, but that did not apply to me. The man had committed a brutal murder, and I am a strong believer in the death penalty even for people who do not commit murders. For example, I think if the Government had any intelligence they would have hanged me, for I was a more dangerous criminal than any of the poor fools who fill the cells of Britain's prisons.

The night before, the prisoners who were in cells on that side of the ward which overlooked the execution-shed were moved to the opposite side, and we were kept locked in till five minutes past eight the next morning, I heard the bell toll, and in my imagination I heard the thunder of the falling trap, but it did not thrill me. Wilde, when he was in Reading gaol, suffered agonies in that moment and imagined more than the truth.

"The hangman with his gardener gloves,
Slips through the padded door,
And binds one with three leathern thongs,
That the throat may thirst no more."

At nine o'clock I and a man named Thayle were marched up to the shed. The door was locked and the chief warder was waiting outside. He unlocked the door and we went in, and I had my first glimpse of a judicial death.

When the cloth that hid the man's features was removed, I looked down upon the face of Kiltin!

Edgar Wallace

The Last Crime

First published in The Premier Magazine, London, September 19, 1922

THE last time I came out of prison with the deputy's words ringing in my ears, "I think you are the worst man in the world," was a remarkable day for me.

I can't say that I was very much impressed by the deputy's moral sayings. Advice and admonition are more or less superfluous to a man of intelligence, who knows when he is doing wrong, who knows what must be the inevitable end if he continues in his wrong-doing, and who certainly has no need of another's point of view to urge him to the obvious course.

As I told the gentleman who wished to commit suicide, life is very sweet, and life does not necessarily mean freedom. It means the enjoyment of one's faculties. And they can be as well enjoyed by a philosopher in gaol as they can in a Hyde Park Lane Flat.

Throughout my career of crime I had been under the mistaken impression that my real identity was unknown to my aristocratic friends and relations. I never dreamt that my brother-in-law, so respectable a man, should advertise the fact that he was related to a felon. Nor did I dream that my dear sister, that cold, heartless, and ambitious woman, would make the delinquencies of her brother a subject for tea-table conversation.

And yet that is precisely what had happened I found.

On the evening of my day of release I went to a theatre. I recovered my clothes from the place where I had stored them, and transferred some of the money I had on deposit at my bank, and it was a considerable sum, to my current account.

I dined well and wisely, and strolled across to the Hay market to see a certain play which I had heard about from an artistic-minded convict. Nobody, of course, knew me, and to the average member of the audience, I had the appearance of a youngish middle-aged man who had probably been abroad. My face was tanned with the glorious sun of Devon, I was fighting fit and in the best condition, and as nature has endowed me with my share of good looks, I flatter myself that I put up a presentable appearance.

After the show was over I got my coat from the cloak-room and strolled into the vestibule, intending to walk to my hotel. Suddenly I heard a sweet voice say:

"Excuse me!" and I turned to meet a glorious pair of blue eyes and one of the prettiest faces it has been my lot to look upon. "How do you do, Captain Penman?" (I have camouflaged my name, naturally.)

Nobody had called me "Penman" for years, and I could not for the life of me place her, although her face was familiar.

"You don't know me, although we've met."

A smile trembled at the corner of her beautiful mouth, as though she were quietly amused.

"I am afraid I am very rude indeed, for I do not recall you," said I. "The fact is, I have been abroad."

She shook her head at me.

"Captain Penman, that isn't true," she said, lowering her voice. "Will you see me home?"

Nothing pleased me better, and I called a cab arid followed her into it.

She lived in St. John Street, Adelphi, and had a comfortable flat with two eminently respectable servants, who were waiting up for her when she arrived.

"I am going to have coffee, will you take a cup with me?" she asked. "And please take off your coat, Captain Penman."

She slipped her cloak from her dazzling white shoulders, and again looked at me quizzically.

"I know you are terribly puzzled as to where we met," she said. "The truth is that our first meeting was more unconventional than our second. I was in bed when I saw you last."

"In bed?" I gasped.

She nodded, still smiling.

"I think it was your first crime, Captain Penman, although perhaps your brother-in-law will not agree with me. And you escaped over the roofs of the houses in Portman Square, and you came into a room occupied—"

"Good lord, I remember!" I said. "You were the lady whose sleep I so brutally interrupted?"

She nodded.

My mind went back all those years, and I tried to recall the face that I had seen on that night. I remembered it was beautiful, but somehow I could not recall a definite vision.

"You are probably wondering why I am not in Portman Square now," she said quietly, "My father died penniless, but fortunately I had had a training at an art school, and I wrote a little. I am now a magazine illustrator. Yes, your brother-in-law told us all about it," she went on, after the coffee had come in and the servants had disappeared. "And your sister made no secret of the fact that she had been burgled by a man who held the Distinguished Service Order. What have you been doing? You have been in prison, I know."

"Several times," I admitted. "In fact, I am now one of the consistently regular patrons of Princetown's principal hotel."

She looked at me steadily, gravely, but not disapprovingly, I was glad to note.

"I have wanted to meet you for a long time," she said. "And once, when I was on a sketching tour across Dartmoor, I stayed for two whole days in Princetown, hoping to see you marched out with the other men."

"You should have called in and seen me at home," said I; and she laughed at my irony.

"What are you going to do now?" she asked.

"I haven't quite decided upon the type of crime, but it will be something exhilarating, you may be sure," I said.

"Do you like it—this life?" she asked, and I shrugged.

"Of course you don't like it, but I mean it isn't altogether abominable to you?"

"Not at all," said I. "It is very amusing in many ways. In some ways it is a bore."

"Did you ever meet in your travels a man named Price Wold?"

I shook my head.

"Is he one of us?" I asked, and a half smile came and faded upon her lips.

"He is not a convicted scoundrel," she said, and apologised hurriedly. "I mean he is a scoundrel but he has never been convicted. I wondered if you had ever heard of him. He was a soldier years ago. I am going to marry him," she added simply.

I could only stare at her.

"Marry an 'unconvicted scoundrel'?" said I. "You are taking rather a risk, aren't you?"

She nodded.

"Mother doesn't like it. She lives in the country with my aunt, and, poor soul, she doesn't know the reason I am getting married is to save her dear feelings. I don't know why I am telling you all this," she said with a nervous little laugh. "It was sheer caprice that made me approach you. I was hoping you were feeling a little sad yourself so that we could commiserate with one another."

"Why are you marrying this man?" I asked quietly. It seemed almost, as if f had known her for twenty years, we had fallen so quickly into the confidential strain.

"Because I must," she said. "Captain Penman, I suppose you are so well acquainted with the follies of the world that you won't be very shocked if I tell you that I had a love affair with my music master. In a sense it was quite innocent, though it might not have been but for the fact that my father found out in time. I had written him a number of letters; he was not a gentleman in the best sense of the word, though he was very fascinating to me.

"When I look back on that time I wonder if it was me at all," she said thoughtfully. "The letters I wrote to him were—well, they were foolish, I never think of them without shuddering. I was only a child at the time, and in many ways an ignorant child. I learnt afterwards, when the affair was broken off, that the man had boasted of our close acquaintanceship. As a matter of fact, it was through his indiscretion that my father got to know, I was terribly cut up at the time, but I thought the whole thing was over and done with and the memory of Carlo had passed from my mind, when I learnt, about three years ago, that the letters were in the possession of Price Wold, whom I had met at my father's dinners, and whom I had regarded as a very amiable middle-aged man, rather fat and talkative."

"I see," I said slowly, "Then your marriage is the price of the letters?"

She nodded,

"It sounds like a chapter from a 'shocker,' doesn't it?" she said unsmilingly. "But that is the truth. He has told me in so many words that unless I consent to marry him he is going to make my mother acquainted with the contents of the letters. That would kill her. She is so sensitive to scandal that my father never told her a word about the affair."

"Do you like him?" I asked.

"Who, Price Wold? I loathe him, I hate him!"

Her voice was vibrant with suppressed passion.

"I don't mind his being so much older than I, but there is something repulsive about the man. And he is a criminal, Captain Penman, a real criminal, greater than any you have met in your travels. I am perfectly sure that he has been living on blackmail for years. When I saw you in the vestibule, I wondered for a second if you knew him or if you had any influence with him. I know that you are quite famous amongst the people of the underworld. Ah! You did not like to hear that. It is the first time you have shown any sign of discomfort!"

"I am not exactly proud of being a little hero amongst the crooks of London," said I with some asperity, of which I was rather ashamed afterwards. "No, I do not know Mr. Wold, but if it will serve you in any way I will get acquainted with him. Where does he live?"

"At Babbington Chambers," she said, but shook her head again. "I don't think it would serve any useful purpose—meeting him, I mean. But it has been a great relief," she smiled, "to lay my burden on you and to pour my woes into a sympathetic ear. You are really not going to commit any further crimes, are you, Captain Penman?" she asked earnestly. "I shall hate it, knowing you. I am sure I couldn't sleep if I thought of you, now that I have met you, lying in a cell at Dartmoor or working with those horrid men in the fields."

I was silent. She had introduced into my life a novel embarrassment.

"Let us hope for the best," I said piously.

"But there is no sense in my hoping unless you are hoping, too," she said, "and now I am going to turn you out, for I have to get up at half-past five in the morning to finish a sketch. I always work best in early morning."

I had said good-bye to her, when I saw a long cord coiled upon the window ledge. I should not have spoken about it, but she followed the direction of my eyes.

"That is my milk cord," she said, "and it is appropriate that you should see it, after I have been boasting of my early hours. The milkman comes at six o'clock, whistles, and I let down the cord. It saves me a journey downstairs at an hour when I am not usually fully clad."

I don't know whether it was the cord, and the train of thought which that set in motion, or whether I had already begun to think things out subconsciously, but I left Beryl Manton with my plan of operation almost complete. The clock of St. Clement's Dane was chiming midnight when I came into the Strand, and, calling a taxi, I told him to drive me to the end of Knightsbridge, where Babbington Chambers was situated. I did not know, and had never heard of Wold, but I knew Babbington Chambers, an abiding place of the vulgarly rich and perhaps the most expensive flats in London.

The only man on duty at this time of night was the lift attendant, and as the lift was going up when I entered the swing doors, it was all to the good. Fortunately for me, my plan for getting upstairs unobserved failed, for the lift was an open one, and the attendant, an old soldier, checked its ascent.

"Are you looking for any number, sir?"

"Yes, I want Mr. Wold," I said.

I should eventually have had to go to the attendant and ask him, for I found that only one or two flats had name plates.

"His is number sixteen on the third floor. I'll take you up, sir."

"Thank you," I said.

"He's got a party to-night," said the attendant as the lift shot up. "I suppose you're going to it, sir?"

"That is my intention," said I.

I pressed the bell of No. 16, and a manservant opened the door. He seemed to take it for granted that I was one of the expected guests, for he took off my coat and hung up my hat.

"What name shall I give?"

"Captain Penman," said I, using my own name for the first time for many years.

The drawing-room into which I was shown was crowded with people. They were mostly girls of the chorus-girl type and the kind of young man one meets at night clubs, and everybody seemed more or less—well, I will say jovial. I hesitate to describe any woman as being under the influence of drink.

I knew my man the moment my eyes lit upon him. He was broad and gross of build, tall, red-faced, and black-haired, and he came towards me with a look of doubt on his face.

"How do you do, Wold?" I said. "You don't remember me? I am Eric Penman."

"Glad to meet you," he said; "but I don't quite place you."

"You invited me to come to your party a week ago," said I.

I thought it was likely that a man of that kind might, in his cups, issue invitations indiscriminately.

"Oh, did I?" he said, relieved. "I suppose when I met you at the Porters. I was so well bottled that night that I don't know whether I invited people or not."

With this he waved a general introduction to the company, and I became engulfed in a crowd of bright-eyed girls and half-drunken men, who were all trying to talk at once. In a second my arm was grabbed by a girl with bobbed hair and a heavily made-up face.

"Do you know Saucy?"

"Saucy?" said I, thinking she was referring to some girl who was present.

"Saucy Wold," she said. "Of course you know him!" with a little hiccough. "This is his last bachelor party; he is going to be married, he has just told us."

I will not attempt to describe the three hours of discomfort I spent in the heated atmosphere of Price Wold's drawing-room. Long before the company made a move, I slipped out of the room, watching a favourable opportunity when the servant had gone to his pantry to find more champagne, and, making my way along the heavy piled carpet of the corridor, I came at last to what I decided must be his bedroom. I shut the door and put on the lights, making a rapid search. In one corner of the room stood an old-fashioned secretaire. I pulled down the flap and opened the drawers, not daring to hope that Beryl's letters would be left so exposed.

The only thing I found was a loaded revolver, which I slipped into my pocket.

I began to search for secret drawers, but without success. And then I made a careful examination of the walls for some secret hiding-place, and found it behind an engraving—a small circular combination safe let into the wall. To attempt to open this without the code word was a waste of time. What I did find in one of the drawers was a dozen pairs of Indies' black silk stockings. This, in a way, was an unexpected windfall, for a silk stocking was the very thing I wanted. I did not stop to consider what those stockings were doing in a bachelor's bureau, but I had my own theory.

With a pair of nail scissors I found in the dressing-room I snipped the stockings in two and cut two eye-holes. This done, I fitted the broad end of the stockings over my head—it made an excellent mask. Then I looked about for a place of concealment, and found it in a long clothes cupboard at the further end of the room. All being ready, I switched out the lights, slipped off the mask, and returned to the hall, and, finding my hat and coat, removed it to the cupboard in Wold's room. Then I took up my stand in the cupboard and waited.

The dawn was breaking when Wold came into the room. I heard the mumble of his voice as he gave some instructions to his servant, and then the snick of the key as he locked the door.

I had a very considerable while to wait, for he took his time about disrobing. At last I heard the click of the lights going out, and the creak of his heavy body on the bed.

I had previously got into my black evening overcoat, and now, pulling the mask over my face and settling my top-hat upon my head, I opened the door gently and stepped out into the darkened room. There was no sound save his heavy breathing, and I listened at the door to discover if the manservant was still about. Apparently he had gone to bed, too.

When I had assured myself of this, I turned on all the lights, and Wold sat up in bed, his mouth wide open, glaring at the strange figure which had appeared at the foot of his bed.

"If you make a sound," I said, "I'll kill you. I may have to kill you as it is, but I don't wish to do so unnecessarily."

"Who are you?" he gasped.

"Don't raise your voice above a whisper."

"Anyway, you've come to the wrong place," he said, breathing quickly. "I have no money in the house."

"What is in the safe behind the picture?" I asked, and I saw him start.

"Nothing," he said. "No money, only a few private papers."

"What is the code word?"

"I'll see you to blazes before I tell you," he exploded; but as I raised the revolver he shrank back.

"What is the code word?"

I saw his lips trembling, and I knew he was in a devil of a fright.

"Tank," he said huskily. "You'll find no money there I tell you."

Covering him with one hand, I pushed aside the picture and swung the dial. The thick door opened, and putting in my hand, I pulled out three bundles of letters. One glance told me that they were in different handwritings, but I had no time to sort them out, and dropped four parcels into my pocket—the fourth I took for luck.

"What are you doing?" he shrieked, his wrath getting the better of his fear, as he sprang out of bed.

Before he could open his mouth, I struck him, and he fell on to the floor with a groan.

"Shut up," I hissed, "you blackmailing toad!"

At that he looked up.

"And so you've been sent to get the letters. Who sent you—Dolly?"

"I haven't the pleasure of Dolly's acquaintance."

"Then it was Beryl."

"And Beryl," said I, "is as much a mystery to me."

"Then it must be Constance," he said. "By gad, I'll have you for this, my friend."

"Don't call me your friend, unless you want me to flog you," said I sternly; and backing away from him, unlocked the door, took out the key and inserted it in the outside of the lock. "If you make any trouble, I shall come back for you," said I. "I shall stand three minutes outside this door, and your first shout will be your last."

I stepped out of the door, locked it, and was out of the front door and half-way down the stairs before I realised that I was still wearing my mask. I stopped only to pull this off, then strolled boldly into the streets.

It was quite light now. So light that the position for me was a dangerous one. I had to pass Hyde Park Corner, where three policemen, a coffee-stall keeper, half a dozen taxi-men saw nothing unusual in the appearance of a man in evening-dress on his way home, but would instantly recognise me once a hue and cry was raised.

I did not take a cab from the stand, but waited until a "crawler" overtook me; then I jumped in and told him to drive me to the Hotel Cecil. I stopped him short in the Strand, and went by a back way to my own hotel. Going to my room, I changed out of my dress clothes into a lounge suit, and, to the porter's astonishment, I left the hotel an hour after I had gone in, for I had spent some time burning the two packages of letters which I did not want.

Who Constance was, and who was Dolly, I have never discovered. There is little doubt that Price Wold earned a comfortable competence by blackmailing girls whose letters fell into his hands. It so happened that Beryl had no money to give, which, in a way, was worse for her.

At a quarter to six I was in John Street, Adelphi, under Beryl's window. I whistled, and heard the window sash rise, and presently there came down the cord I had seen on the window ledge. To this I affixed the bundle of letters, tying them tightly, and gave the cord a jerk.

I watched the dangling bundle until it disappeared into the room. Presently Beryl's head came out and her eyes met mine. She said nothing, nor did I. But her little hand went to her red lips, and she threw me a kiss. I was very well rewarded.

And now I am no longer the Worst Man in the World from one woman's point of view. She sits knitting on the verandah which overlooks the green-grey seas. Sometimes I see her turn her head in my direction. Price Wold did not prosecute. He left the country the next day, himself fearing prosecution.

Beryl sometimes expresses her scepticism as to whether I have reformed.

"You know, this must cost an awful lot of money," she said yesterday, fingering the pearl necklace about her white throat, "and I am perfectly certain the money you have in the bank ought to be in somebody else's bank, dear."

"That may be, dear," said I, "but the pearl necklace is your very own. It is a wedding present, bought specially for you, with tainted money, I admit, but it was not my tainted money."

"What do you mean?" she asked, open-eyed.

"I found it in Wold's safe," I said. "There was a little card inside: 'To Beryl on her wedding day.' I thought I had better bring it along, for already I was harbouring matrimonial designs."

The Super Pack Ebook Series

If you enjoyed this Super Pack you may wish to find the other books in this series. We endeavor to provide you with a quality product. But since many of these stories have been scanned typos do occasionally creep in. If you spot one please share it with us at positronicpress@yahoo.com so that we can fix it. We occasionally add additional stories to some of our Super Packs so make sure that you download fresh copies of your Super Packs from time to time to get the latest edition.

Science Fiction Super Pack #1: ISBN 978-1-63384-240-3
Science Fiction Super Pack #2: ISBN 978-1-51540-477-4
Science Fiction Super Pack #3: (Forthcoming)
Fantasy Super Pack #1: ISBN 978-1-63384-282-3
Fantasy Super Pack #2: ISBN 9781-51543-932-5
Conan the Barbarian Super Pack: ISBN 978-1-63384-292-2
Lord Dunsany Super Pack: ISBN 978-1-63384-725-5
Philip K. Dick Super Pack: ISBN 978-1-63384-799-6
The Pirate Super Pack # 1: ISBN 978-1-51540-193-3
The Pirate Super Pack # 2: ISBN 978-1-51540-196-4
Harry Harrison Super Pack: ISBN 978-1-51540-217-6
Andre Norton Super Pack: ISBN 978-1-51540-262-6
Marion Zimmer Bradley Super Pack: ISBN 978-1-51540-287-9
Frederik Pohl Super Pack: ISBN 978-1-51540-289-3
King Arthur Super Pack: ISBN 978-1-51540-306-7
Alan E. Nourse Super Pack: ISBN 978-1-51540-393-7
Space Science Fiction Super Pack: ISBN 978-1-51540-440-8
Wonder Stories Super Pack: ISBN 978-1-51540-454-5
Galaxy Science Fiction Super Pack #1:ISBN 978-1-51540-524-5
Galaxy Science Fiction Super Pack #2: 978-1-5154-0577-1
Science Fiction Novel Super Pack #1: ISBN 978-1-51540-363-0
Science Fiction Novel Super Pack #2: (Forthcoming)
Dragon Super Pack: ISBN 978-1-5154-1124-6
Weird Tales Super Pack #1: ISBN 978-1-5154-0548-1
Weird Tales Super Pack #2: 978-1-5154-1107-9
Poul Anderson Super Pack: ISBN 978-1-5154-0609-9

Edgar Wallace

Fantastic Universe Super Pack #1: ISBN 978-1-5154-0981-6
Fantastic Universe Super Pack #2: ISBN 978-1-5154-0654-9
Fantastic Universe Super Pack #3: ISBN 978-1-5154-0655-6
Imagination Super Pack: ISBN 978-1-5154-1089-8
Planet Stories Super Pack: ISBN 978-1-5154-1125-3
Worlds of If Super Pack #1: ISBN 978-1-5154-1148-2
Worlds of If Super Pack #2: ISBN 978-1-5154-1182-6
Worlds of If Super Pack #3: ISBN 978-1-5154-1234-2
Argosy All-Story Weekly Super Pack: ISBN (Forthcoming)
Fritz Leiber Super Pack #1: ISBN 978-1-5154-1847-4
Fritz Leiber Super Pack #2: ISBN (Forthcoming)
Vampire Super Pack: ISBN 978-1-5154-3954-7
Max Brand Western Super-Pack: ISBN 978-1-6338-4841-2
Charles Boardman Hawes Super Pack: ISBN (Forthcoming)
The Edgar Wallace Super Pack ISBN: (Forthcoming)

Ingram Content Group UK Ltd.
Milton Keynes UK
UKHW011837230523
422246UK00004B/30